CROWN
OF
VENGEANCE

CROWN OF VENGEANCE

BOOK ONE

of The Dragon Prophecy

MERCEDES LACKEY
and JAMES MALLORY

 A Tom Doherty Associates Book NEW YORK

CROWN OF VENGEANCE

Copyright © 2012 by Mercedes Lackey and James Mallory

Map by Jon Lansberg

Design by Susan Walsh

A Tor Book
Published by Tom Doherty Associates, LLC
175 Fifth Avenue
New York, NY 10010

www.tor-forge.com

Tor® is a registered trademark of Tom Doherty Associates, LLC.

Library of Congress Cataloging-in-Publication Data

Lackey, Mercedes.
    Crown of vengeance / Mercedes Lackey and James Mallory. — 1st ed.
        p. cm.
    "A Tom Doherty Associates book."
    ISBN 978-0-7653-2438-2 (hardcover)
    ISBN 978-1-4299-9286-2 (e-book)
 I. Mallory, James.   II. Title.
    PS3562.A246C76 2012
    813'.54—dc23

                                                            2012024534

First Edition: November 2012

Printed in the United States of America

0 9 8 7 6 5 4 3 2 1

To all of those who have accompanied me on this journey: my dear coauthor, Mercedes Lackey; our mutual agent, Russ Galen; our skilled and long-suffering editor, Melissa Singer (without whom this book could not have been what it has become); my dear Dennis, always the ready gadfly; and of course, my beloved Diogenes, faithful friend and companion, this volume is respectfully dedicated. And to Rafal Gibek and Terry McGarry, princes among copyeditors, my deepest thanks for your yeoman labors on my behalf.

–JAMES MALLORY

ACKNOWLEDGMENTS

Many thanks to our tireless, unbelievably good copyeditors, Terry and Rafal. Authors rant when copyeditors are bad and never say a peep when they are outstanding.

Well, we're changing that. Thank you, Terry McGarry and Rafal Gibek. Without you this book literally would not have been possible.

CONTENTS

CROWN
OF
VENGEANCE

POWER AND PAIN

The Endarkened cannot make, they can only mar.

— Thurion Pathfinder, *The Scroll of Darkness*

Before Time itself came to be, *He Who Is* had been: changeless, eternal, perfect. And all was Darkness, and *He Who Is* ruled over all there was.

Then came the Light, dancing through the perfection of the Dark, separating it into Dark and not-Dark. Making it a finite, a bounded thing. Where there had been silence, and Void, and infinity, there came music, and not Void, and Time . . .

A world.

At first, *He Who Is* did nothing, for it was only by the creation of that which was not *he*, not *his*, that *He Who Is* was able to perceive Himself, and He was spellbound by the discovery of His own beauty.

But the Light was not perfection. The Light was change, a change as infinite as the changelessness of *He Who Is*. Time was swift to One Who had only known timelessness, and by the time *He Who Is* became aware of the danger, it was too late to avert it.

But it could yet be repaired. And so *He Who Is* turned the Light's weaving against it, for by its very nature, the Light implied the Dark. All things in its World possessed opposites, for no thing could be named if it did not possess an antithesis. Fire and water, time and eternity, leaf and star . . .

Life and death.

The first life raised up by the Light was green: leaf and branch, bud and seed, flower and fruit to sweep over the face of the land. It changed the harsh stone, beautifying it with a thousand living shapes. It flourished for a time, until *He Who Is* conjured plague and blight and rot that swept across the land, devouring the green life down to bare rock, making the land stark and sterile once more. But plague and blight and rot were merely tools, and they did not slay all. The green life was reborn, and with it came red life: beasts of earth and air and water. Red life took on a thousand shapes and filled the land, until there was no corner of it that did not hold red life and green.

And once more *He Who Is* woke from the contemplation of His perfection and rose up out of the deep darkness. He kindled the forests to flame, slaughtered the schools and flocks and herds, set red life to feed upon itself just as it fed upon green life, set green life to poison red. Hunger fed upon hunger until green ocean and green earth were red, and all the work of the Light was undone.

But in the destruction of the red life, the Light realized *He Who Is* meant to take the world from them, the beautiful world of shape and form and time and boundary they had created. Light could not destroy the Darkness without destroying itself, but it could bring life to flourish again where destruction had walked.

And to this life, it would give weapons.

Once again, life was reborn from death. The new life was neither green nor red. It was as silver as the Light itself. Rot did not extinguish it nor did death destroy it. It was as changeable as *He Who Is* was changeless. It grew and changed and spread to all the places red life and green life had been, and then it spread farther still. Light itself coursed through the veins of silver life, and Light fell in love with silver life. Light left the high vault of heaven and scattered itself across the land, and silver life traveled to the places of the Light to rejoice in it.

But *He Who Is* vowed He would win in the end. This time, He did not strike at once. This time He bound His war into time, to let His tools learn from the enemy He would ultimately destroy. To all the things of the Light, *He Who Is* held up a dark mirror. For the Bright World, a World Without Sun. For life and love, death and pain. For trust, treachery. For kindness, power.

For skill . . . magic.

He Who Is created thirteen instruments as eternal and changeless as He Himself, instruments whose sole purpose was the destruction of the Light and all the Light had made. And when His Endarkened had completed their task, the world would once more be what it had been before the Light had come. Changeless. Eternal.

Perfect.

<hr />

Virulan was First among the Thirteen, king of the Endarkened. He had always been king. He always would be—how not? His subjects were loyal to him, and to *He Who Is*, who had planted the Tree of Night, who had set the Shadow Throne in the Heart of Darkness, who had placed the Crown of Pain upon Virulan's brow.

Who had set him his task.

At first, it had seemed that to accomplish the task they had been set would be a simple matter, for they could not die, and the Brightworlders could. And so Virulan and the Twelve took to the sky each night, slaughtering without cease until the terrible bright light by which the Brightworlders marked time came again.

And time passed, and Virulan soon saw that this was not enough. The Brightworlders were too many. Slay a hundred, and a thousand sprung up in their place. Again and again, the Endarkened had scoured a place of life, only to return and find it fecund once more. No spells that Virulan and his Twelve could cast were terrible enough to do the bidding of *He Who Is*.

If he had been capable of it, Virulan would have despaired.

But he was not, and so he sought counsel.

He Who Is had granted them the boon of eternity, but all gifts must be paid for. The Endarkened did not sleep, just as they did not age, but an

Endarkened who did not regularly seek a period of silence and contemplation would enter eternity in truth—not death, for they could not die, but the inability to perceive Time.

Such an Endarkened would be useless to *He Who Is* and it would be his fate to be forever sealed away in a chamber in the Deep Earth. Virulan had no desire to lose the favor of *He Who Is*. Virulan carefully marked the passage of time by the shifts and changes in the Deep Earth and retired to his secret chamber regularly.

This time, he had a greater goal than his own survival.

"Dread and beloved Lord of Darkness and Endings, hear Your loyal and devoted acolyte . . ."

The realm of time and matter was no fit habitation for the Lord of All Things, and so Virulan sought Him in His own place. Virulan knew himself to be a created thing, a tool, and like any tool, fitted for the needs of his task. To destroy the realm of time and matter, Virulan himself was a thing of time and matter. But not entirely. That part of Virulan that sought audience with his dread master was neither.

It was a realm beautiful beyond description: lightless and empty and sterile. Virulan's spirit rose to that place, and waited.

WHAT DO YOU WANT OF ME?

Each syllable thrilled through Virulan's entire being, bringing such ecstasy that he nearly forgot his purpose. To speak words in answer would be to profane this holy emptiness. Virulan opened his thoughts to *He Who Is*, knowing He saw all.

THIS IS NOT A TASK BEYOND YOUR SKILL. I HAVE GIVEN YOU TOOLS.

Before Virulan could shape a question, he had been thrust back into the world of time and form. But he was not in his bedchamber. He was in a place in the World Without Sun whose existence he had never suspected.

The Black Chamber.

It lay at the center of a vein of black glass a thousand miles thick. Virulan could feel the vastness of stone above him, and his heart swelled with pride: the Brightworlders boasted of their vast lands, but the World Without Sun was a thousand times greater.

To any senses but his own, the chamber would have been unremittingly black. Virulan saw a thousand shades of darkness, hues that no other race had words for. The darkness showed him a chamber carved of the living rock. Every inch of the walls and ceiling was covered with deeply incised symbols.

Master their meaning and Virulan would take within himself the faintest echo of the power of *He Who Is*. Virulan's birthright was to command sorcery—and here was the grimoire from which he must learn

But that knowledge came at a price.

In the center of the chamber there was a long hollow spike of obsidian that stood heart-high. This was the Obsidian Blade, the instrument of sacrifice that made its victim one with the symbols upon the walls. For any other, what Virulan now contemplated would be nothing more than a gateway to the most agonizing death of all—but Virulan was first among the Endarkened, first shaped by the hand of *He Who Is*. He spread his great scarlet wings and thrust himself into the air. For an instant, his golden horns brushed the vaulting ceiling of the chamber.

Then he fell.

The Obsidian Blade pierced his body.

The chamber rang like a crystal bell with his agonized screams; the glyphs upon the walls bloomed into dark fire, searing their meaning into his skin. He hung there, writhing, impaled, until his screams dwindled to sobs of agony, until his consciousness fled into a nothingness deeper than anything he had ever known.

But when he rose up an eternity later, the sorcery that was his birthright thrilled through his veins with every beat of his heart. Virulan went from the Black Chamber to the foot of the Tree of Night and summoned his Endarkened to him. There he opened their heritage to them, a sorcery fueled by death, a sorcery great enough to give them the victory they craved.

And once again, the Endarkened swept forth from Obsidian Mountain.

The slaughter they wreaked now was a thousandfold greater than before. They glutted themselves upon blood and pain and gorged upon the flesh of their victims. The land around Obsidian Mountain became a wasteland where nothing lived, and each night they ranged farther.

And it was still not enough.

❊

"What must I do?" Virulan cried. His scream echoed back from the stony vault that was the roof of the world and brought no answer. Save one.

"You must use the tools *He Who Is* has given us, my king."

Uralesse was first among the Twelve, as Virulan was first among them all. Only he would dare to approach Virulan when Virulan walked in the Garden of Night. When he saw his king's gaze upon him, Uralesse groveled low to the ground, his great ribbed wings wound tightly about his body in submission, his horned brow pressed against the stone.

"Do you say I do not?" Virulan growled. His fangs ached to rend Uralesse's flesh, even though the words he had spoken were words Virulan had long held in his own mind. He had taught his knowledge of sorcery to his people—but only a fool would give up every advantage, and so Virulan had not taught them all he had learned.

"I say only that the first among us is surely greater than any of us," Uralesse said, unmoving.

"You are wise, my brother. Rise, and walk with me."

Uralesse rose gracefully to his feet and allowed his wings to open fractionally. For a time they walked together in silence.

"The Bright World continues to live," Virulan said at last.

"Yes," Uralesse agreed, his wings drooping in sorrow. "Each pure thing we make becomes tainted once more. It is as if life replenishes itself as water inexhaustibly fills a spring."

"I shall learn the Bright World's secret," Virulan said. "And I will make of it talons for their throats."

"Let it be so, my king," Uralesse said.

⊰⊱

Now Virulan worked the greatest sorcery he had ever imagined. He returned to the Black Chamber and there he studied the runes and the glyphs until he was certain his spell would succeed. Then he sent his Endarkened into the Bright World once more, but this time not to slay. This time, he ordered them to bring its creatures to him alive.

It was a reaping that would long endure in the stories the Brightworlders told one another. The chambers of the World Without Sun became filled with life: weeping and lamenting, profaning the beauty of the Endarkened realm by its very existence. Night after night, the Endarkened flew, and harvested, until the World Without Sun could hold no more.

In a space above the Black Chamber, Virulan had made a place. Its only entrance was through an opening in its ceiling, and it contained only one object: a gigantic mirror of black obsidian. As his subjects had hunted, so had Virulan prepared the mirror. And when it was ready, he ordered all the captives slaughtered at once.

The Endarkened had learned to love the pain of their victims, learned to cherish each scream and tear. Torture was their highest art, but today, Virulan did not call for art, but for blood. And he received it. The halls of the World Without Sun were awash in blood, a red and stinking tide that flowed through halls and down staircases, rushing ever deeper into the Deep Earth until it came to the place where the Obsidian Mirror waited. Hot fresh blood poured through the opening in the ceiling and filled the room to the brink.

And the Mirror drank in the life, the power, the blood, until all the blood was gone, and only the Mirror itself remained.

Then Virulan and his brothers feasted. And when the feast was done, Virulan went to stand before the Mirror.

"Show me what I wish to see," he commanded, and the Mirror did. It showed him the Bright World as the Brightworlders saw it. It showed him their lives and their fates. For a very long time, Virulan watched, and learned. He left the Mirror only to seek the silence and stillness that preserved his existence; at each Rising he returned to the visions of the Mirror once more. A thousand Risings came and went before he had learned what he must know.

And then he left the Obsidian Mirror, and went to the Heart of Darkness, and seated himself upon the Shadow Throne, and summoned Uralesse.

"I have learned what I wished to know," he said without preamble when Uralesse groveled before him. "And I would hear your counsel."

"Tell me how I may serve you, my king," Uralesse answered.

"The Brightworlders cannot be slain," Virulan said flatly.

Uralesse raised his head in shock, his pupilless yellow eyes going wide. "*He Who Is* has said it must be," he protested.

"And so I have summoned you, for you will hear the Brightworlders' secret and understand. *He Who Is* made us to destroy all the Light has made. He has not set us to destroy the Light itself, for that is a task He reserves for His own, once ours is done. But ours will never be done, my brother. *He Who Is* has given us great sorcery—but the Light has given life the ability to multiply itself, increasing faster than thought. Once you spoke of an ever-filling spring and I thought it merely clever poetry. But it is not. And we are few!"

His last words were a howl of anguish.

"Then we must be more than we are," Uralesse said strongly. He dared to sit back on his heels at the foot of the Shadow Throne, but did not rise. "You who are the wellspring of all sorcery, who have dared to gaze upon the naked ugliness of our foe—you know their secret! We will take it and use it against them!"

For a long time, Virulan gazed at his counselor in silence. "Let it be so," he said at last. "Summon our brothers."

⟊⟊

When all the Endarkened were gathered together, it was a communion of such beauty that Virulan nearly wept to behold it.

Rugashag—Shurzul—Khambaug—Bashahk—Dhasgah—Gholak—
Lashagan—Marbuglor—Arzhugdu—Nagreloth—Orbushnu—Uralesse—
each was more glorious than the next. And each one of them was
dedicated to only two things.

The destruction of all life.

And becoming the supreme power in the World Without Sun.

Virulan did not condemn such ambition: he shared it. Soft emotions of
trust, love, and loyalty were suitable only to soft things, like the Brightworlders. But that hardly meant he intended to give up his supremacy—or
have it taken from him. He had made his preparations for this moment
carefully and in secret, weaving a skein of spells as delicate as the ones to
create the Obsidian Mirror had been forceful. He was the last to enter the
Heart of Darkness, and when he did, his brethren knelt to him in a great
rustle of wings. Virulan seated himself upon the Shadow Throne and
gazed upon them for a long time in silence before he spoke.

This is the last time I shall look upon you in the way you were made.
The thought did not bring regret, but excitement. It was the first step
upon the road that would end in the triumph of the Endarkened.

"*He Who Is* has given me many good things, and I have shared them
all with you," King Virulan said. "He has asked only one thing of us in
exchange for all the pleasures He has allowed us. And now, at last, I shall
make it possible for us to serve Him fully."

He did not wait for the questioning rustle of wings to subside, but
struck at once. Spellfire leaped from the walls, the ceiling, the very floor
of the chamber, wrapping the bodies before him in a scarlet cocoon. His
brethren—his comrades—fought magnificently, but they were powerless
against a sorcery that fed upon the very magic in their bones. And when
the sorcery had run its course, his brethren were changed.

All but one.

"I would not have you lack a true companion, my king," Uralesse said,
entering the chamber again. "And so, I took care to place myself outside
the compass of your spell—though only in anticipation of your own fore-
sight." He bowed deeply. "If you were to be lost, my king, who would father

the great race of Endarkened you will send into battle? And so, for the sake of peace in our realm, I thought the matter best settled at once."

All about him, his once-brothers ran their hands over transformed flesh: deep bosoms and graceful hips, new beauty cloaking the ancient power of their birthright. Female, as the Brightworlders were female. From their bodies he would call a horde, a legion, a race of Endarkened. Thousand upon thousand, enough to darken the sky with their wings.

Enough to destroy all who walked beneath the sun and the moon.

It had been no part of Virulan's plan to spare any of them the transformation. Just as he was first among the Endarkened, greatest in power, so it was only right that his seed should sow the death of all life.

Uralesse had tricked him, first anticipating his intention, then escaping his spell. It indicated a cleverness that Virulan did not trust . . . but which might prove useful in the war to come.

And if it did not, there were other spells, and sealed chambers within the Deep Earth.

"Foolish Uralesse," Virulan said grandly. "You have exerted yourself for no reason. My spell was never intended to fall upon you. It is as you said: my intention was always to spare you, for the very reasons you suggest."

Uralesse bowed low, but his golden eyes held a mocking light. "And now, my king? What shall we—your loyal and most submissive subjects—do now?"

Uralesse rose to his feet and spread his wings. Still on . . . her . . . knees before his throne, Rugashag gazed up at him, her savage beauty a display of fury and confusion. He stretched out one taloned hand and raised her to her feet.

"We shall wait, Uralesse my brother," King Virulan said. "We shall wait."

CHAPTER ONE

THE FALL OF FARCARINON

Even as we reckon time, our history is long—so long its beginnings have been worn away by the passage of time. Long before Man came to be, we were. It could be said that our history begins with the Endarkened, for that terrible conflict scoured away all that we had been before it, leaving us one purpose:

Survival.

—*Peldalathiriel Caerthalien, Of the Reign of Great Queen Vieliessar*

Perchelion used to tell me the Hunt rode through every storm. When I grew old enough to question I said I did not believe her. I remember how she slapped me, and said I would never become a knight of my father's meisne, for to doubt the Starry Hunt meant I would never wield a sword. I remember I laughed, and said there were not enough storms in all the year for them to do that . . .

Ladyholder Nataranweiya forced her mind to focus on such ancient trifles, for to allow it liberty would mean she thought of things it would not be good to think on now. Her child-swollen body shuddered harder than the cold should merit, even as the horse's body shook with weariness.

Lightning stitched the woods to sudden brightness, and in its light she could see Falthiel, his face turned toward her, shouting something. She could not make out the words over the howl of the wind and the thunder of the horses' hooves. Dioniron had given their mounts enough of the battle cordial to poison them: they would run until they died.

They would have to. Caerthalien's dogs were a candlemark—no

more—behind them now, and Nataranweiya knew they outnumbered the scant handful of her surviving protectors.

Suddenly her mount put a foot wrong, slipping and staggering through mud and autumn leaves for a handful of terrifying moments before finding its balance and running on. The near-fall jarred her agonizingly, but Nataranweiya did not cry out. She would not shame her Bondmate, even though all her broken soul yearned for was to follow him into the death he had found. Serenthon Farcarinon would have made her queen over all the Hundred Houses. If only Serenthon had never known of Amrethion's Curse. If only he had not taken it into his heart, as if it were a lover's message meant for him alone.

As reasonable to wish he had never known of the sun, or the sky, or the trees.

Why was our Bond not enough for you? Why must you reach for more?

"Near, my lady!" Beleval shouted, his voice loud enough to cut through the roar of the storm. *Near to the Sanctuary of the Star.*

Near to safety. Near to revenge.

Pain gripped her, this wave coming sooner than the last, and when it passed she tasted the blood from where she'd bitten her lip. She had been upon the birthing couch when the traitors had come. That the child had delayed even from nightfall to nightfall was more grace than she had hoped for; the unborn babe would not grant her yet more clemency. She must be delivered soon or this nightmare ride would have been for nothing.

Only within the Sanctuary of the Star could she be safe.

The bright call of a warhorn sheared through the noise of their flight and jarred her back to full consciousness. Any daughter of the Hundred Houses learned early the strategies and treacheries an enemy might use to gain what it wished. She knew their pursuers had no need to signal an intended attack. It was an attempt to startle the prey into rash action, so they might be easily taken.

The horn called again, closer.

Suddenly Nataranweiya found herself alone. Moments later the full fury of the storm struck her; so much water was flung at her by the wind that she coughed and choked on it. The shock was so great that in her exhaustion it took her precious heartbeats to understand what had happened. *Beleval and Dioniron have turned back.*

The three of them had been in the lead. If Beleval and Dioniron had turned back to throw themselves against their pursuers, the others had as well.

Farewell, farewell, friends, companions, cousins! We shall meet again in Tildorangelor, beneath the trees. . . .

She would have wept, save that her tears had all been shed long before. Now the sky must do her mourning. She could not open her eyes against the wind to search for the lights ahead, but they must be there. They must.

Her mount's gait was even more jarring now. It had run the sun down out of the sky, its drug-maddened gallop as unchanging as the beat of drums. Even in her exhausted, pain-racked state, Nataranweiya knew the instant that rhythm changed. The horse slowed from a gallop to a jarring trot, forced itself to a gallop again, staggered to a stiff-legged exhausted canter and held there. Nataranweiya could hear the desperate whistling sound it made as it fought for air, for *life*—

The animal lost its fight between one step and the next. She felt its muscles go slack, even as the hot blood of its death sprayed her, she was already kicking her feet free of the stirrups and releasing her cold-cramped grip on its reins. She must throw herself from the saddle or be trapped beneath its body when she fell. Who had first taught her that? She no longer remembered; nor was she the bright slender girl who had learned that lesson any longer. She screamed at another wave of pain that rose just as she flung herself free. *Hurry, you must hurry, they will hear, they will follow. . . .* Then all thoughts were driven from her mind until it passed.

She crawled from beside the horse's body as soon as she could. With shaking fingers she ripped the jeweled clasp of her fine fur cloak open, shedding its sodden weight in the mud.

Hurry. To your feet, witless girl, you must run now. . . .

She crawled.

Three times she was forced to halt by the agonizing pressure on her abdomen. She barely knew when she reached the Sanctuary gates. They stood eternally open in both warning and promise that no conflict might enter here. She clawed herself to her feet along one pillar.

Beyond the gate. Inside. You are not safe until you are within. Not safe. Not safe . . .

⊰⊱

For six centuries Maeredhiel had served the Sanctuary of the Star. Let the children come and go in their season, let a new Astromancer be chosen each time the ever-living Vilya bore its fruit; what was that to her? Maeredhiel had made for herself a place and a peace that none would take from her. Did not Lightborn need to eat and sleep? Did not the workrooms and stillrooms run more smoothly when there was a proper supply of herbs and fruits to hand for decoction and enchanting?

And did not young Candidates tear their tunics and outgrow their sandals, here just as within the walls of the Keep in which she had been born?

The time was late, and tomorrow as always would be a day of much work, yet Maeredhiel found she could not sleep. She had already checked the storerooms and the sleeping rooms for possible storm damage, and even visited the high tower where Celelioniel spent so many nights. The Astromancer had not gone there tonight, for clouds had obscured her beloved stars, but still Maeredhiel was uneasy. Tonight's storm was fierce and unseasonable.

Fool! she berated herself. *Are you yourself an Astromancer, to know the stories the stars whisper? What troubles you is indigestion and age, nothing more.*

She hesitated in the antechamber of the Shrine, adjusting her hooded shawl. It was always as bright as summer noon here, for the walls and ceiling shone with Silverlight renewed again and again since the day

Mosirinde Peacemaker had first set this place apart. The stone floor was inlaid with a silver wheel whose arms pointed the true directions, and the ceiling was inlaid with the star pictures that edged the Hunt-road. It was both promise and warning, as was the depiction of the Silver Hooves themselves upon the great bronze doors at the far end of the chamber. Beyond those doors stood the Shrine of the Star itself.

As if her musings had summoned Them, the antechamber was filled with a sudden blast of cold.

No one would come to the Sanctuary in this storm merely to bid us good greeting, Maeredhiel thought in alarm. She clapped her hands to summon the servants—the simple cantrip she wore on a string about her neck ensured her summons would be heard in their bedchambers—and hurried to open the inner door. Gusts of wet wind skirled around her and she turned her head away.

"... please ..." The word was the faintest of whispers.

How did you come here? Maeredhiel wondered, gazing down at the bundle of muddy rags barely discernible as a living body. She stepped over the body to pull the outer doors back into place, peering out as she did, but if any followed, they were as dark as the storm.

"Mistress, what—?" It was Elithreth, one of the Candidates in his Service Year.

"What else but someone seeking Sanctuary?" Maeredhiel answered. "A woman, and with child," she finished smoothly. "So use care."

With Elithreth's help, Maeredhiel lifted the supplicant to her feet and helped her inside. Many came to the Sanctuary of the Star seeking that which only it could supply. Normally such a one would place a hand upon the bronze doors of the Shrine and make their formal petition before being sent to hospital or resting chamber. Maeredhiel did not think this one had that much strength left in her body—if she and Elithreth had not supported her, she would have collapsed. Every footstep she took left pools of muddy, bloody water upon the stone floor, but in the stronger light of the antechamber, Maeredhiel saw the glitter of silver, moonsilver, and gems.

Noble—and with child—and hurt—and alone. None of these things boded well for the peace of the Sanctuary. "Your name and your House, Lady?" Maeredhiel asked, her voice low and urgent. Celelioniel would wish to know these things—and at once.

The traveler struggled to answer, turning her face toward Maeredhiel—Maeredhiel saw blood-bitten lips, bruises, abrasions—but any reply she might have made was cut off by a gasp of pain.

Best to place her in a retiring room until I can call Mistress Healer's lazy servants to bring a litter. "Come, Elithreth, we will—" she began.

But her words were cut short by the arrival of the Astromancer herself.

"Is it she? Is it now? Oh, this creature has come in an evil time!" Celelioniel Astromancer cried. She looked like a creature demented, with her shorn hair in disorder and her thin woolen robe kilted up past her knees. Her feet were bare and earth-smeared. *She has come from the Shrine,* Maeredhiel realized with a pang of unease.

"I know not who she is, Lady," Maeredhiel said. "But surely this poor creature cannot be anyone's great enemy?" She struggled with the visitor's full weight now, for at Celelioniel's cry, Elithreth had released his hold on her and backed away.

"'*When stars and clouds together point the way—And of a hundred deer one doe can no longer counted be*'! It is the Prophecy, Maeredhiel! It comes true—now—for has not Caerthalien a sennight hence led the breaking of Farcarinon? Here—*here!*—lies the Doom of the Hundred Houses!"

Maeredhiel turned away so that Celelioniel would not see her face. When Celelioniel had begun her research, she had known no more of Amrethion's Curse or the Child of Prophecy than any Sanctuary-trained Lightborn might know. Maeredhiel would never know what steps had led Celelioniel to *The Song of Amrethion,* and what hints gleaned from ancient histories had led her to decide she alone could unriddle Amrethion's Curse. But whatever she had found there had terrified her. Maeredhiel had watched the obsession—the madness—grow from the day Celelioniel had become Astromancer, nearly a century ago.

I pray the Vilya fruits soon, she thought sorrowfully. *And my lady goes far from this place that has done her such harm.*

"Lady, no harm may enter here," Maeredhiel said soothingly. "Only let me bring this one to Mistress Healer Nithrithuin before her babe is brought to harm, and—"

"It is the babe I fear!" Celelioniel wailed. "Does not *The Song of Amrethion Aradruiniel* speak of the birth of a babe who will cast down the High Houses? A babe whose birth will herald the beginning of great Darkness?"

Suddenly Celelioniel darted forward and seized the woman's chin, gazing into her eyes for a moment before springing back and wailing as if she were but a babe herself.

"Sanctuary . . . I claim . . . I must . . ." the Lady whispered. The Astromancer's touch seemed to drain the last strength from the supplicant; rather than drop her, Maeredhiel knelt with her upon the stone floor. As she did, her heart sank further: nestled in the hollow of her throat was a pendant, a Vilya blossom of moonsilver. Somewhere, this woman's Bondmate awaited her. The Soulbond was the greatest joy any *alfaljodthi* could know, and the greatest sorrow as well, for once the Bond was made, to slay one half of it was to slay the other. Two lives might end this night—if not three.

"Your name, Lady, and how you came here," she asked again, though she thought the Lady might be past hearing. "You lie before the Shrine itself. None will carry you away."

Maeredhiel had nearly made up her mind to send Elithreth for Mistress Healer without waiting for Celelioniel's order, for the Sanctuary Healer would be willing to overrule the Astromancer if Celelioniel's hysterics continued. But Celelioniel's wailings had roused others.

"What disturbance is this?" Hamphuliadiel Lightbrother had obviously been roused from his rest, for his Green Robe bore signs of having been hastily donned and he had bound it with a simple acolyte's cord. "I should have been summoned before you opened our doors!" Hamphuliadiel added.

"You are not Astromancer yet, bold one," Maeredhiel muttered, lowering her eyes lest he should read her words in them. She was saved from whatever reply Hamphuliadiel might have made by the arrival of yet more strangers.

Outer and inner doors slammed open as one and three *komen* in Caerthalien green and gold stalked into the antechamber. "There she is!" the foremost barked out. "Farcarinon's bitch in whelp!" She reached up and unlatched her helm. "Has she claimed Sanctuary?" she added, the mocking tone in her voice making it clear what she thought the answer would be.

"She has," Maeredhiel answered, her voice bold and loud over the howl of the wind. "Ladyholder Nataranweiya of Farcarinon has set her hand upon the door of the Shrine and set her words aloft for the Silver Hooves to hear!" She could not say why she spoke so, save the long-burning anger in her heart against those who would dice with the lives of innocent folk.

The knight drew back with an angry curse, placing her hand upon her sword.

"Yet if it is her own will to leave . . ." Hamphuliadiel began.

"We turn none away who seeks Sanctuary," Maeredhiel said sharply. "Nor do we permit weapons within it," she added, glaring at the swords the Caerthalien knights still bore. "Elithreth, you must lead our guests to the stables, so they may put up their horses, then see them lodged in our guesthouse."

"Yes, Mistress Maeredhiel," Elithreth answered, sounding relieved to be given a task that would take him from the Astromancer's presence. "My lords *komentai'a*, will you accompany me? And say, perhaps, if there are others abroad who need shelter this night?"

"I thank you, young one," the nameless knight answered. She could do nothing else, for no one would dare to profane the peace of the Sanctuary of the Star—nor rouse the anger of its Mages. "Yet I say I will remain to see what is done here. Nimboroth, take you my sword and blades."

"It shall be done, *Komen* Harthelin," Nimboroth answered.

"And shut those damned doors!" Harthelin added.

At least someone gives ear to orders this night, Maeredhiel thought sourly, as a loud banging and the sudden absence of wind told her Harthelin's order had been followed.

By now the antechamber was filled with the curious and the concerned. "I would see Ladyholder Nataranweiya beneath the hands of the Healers," Maeredhiel said again, raising her voice.

"Name her Lady-Abeyant, of your courtesy, for her traitor-lord is dead," Harthelin said with a mocking smile.

"Perhaps . . ." Celelioniel said, as if speaking to herself, ". . . perhaps we can yet outrun our fates."

At last Mistress Healer Nithrithuin arrived. She knelt beside Nataranweiya and laid quick hands upon her. "Why lies she upon cold stone?" she demanded, glaring at Celelioniel. "Is it more of your addled prophecy, witless one? Go!" she demanded of the nearest Lightborn. "Summon a litter from the hospital—and bearers."

"I should be honored to bear Serenthon's sow wherever she must go," *Komen* Harthelin said.

"I know not what cause you have against this lady, but I say to you, you may not bring your quarrel here," Nithrithuin said sternly.

"I?" Harthelin answered. "I hold no quarrels but that of my lord, and it is his word—the word of Caerthalien—that Farcarinon shall be cast down and ended."

Two of the hospital servants appeared, carrying a litter between them, and swiftly and efficiently transferred Lady Nataranweiya to it. Nataranweiya would not release her death grip upon Maeredhiel's hand, so when the servants lifted the litter to carry it away, Maeredhiel had no choice but to accompany them.

⚬⚬⚬

The Sanctuary hospital was a quiet place. It trained the Lightborn who would become Healers throughout the Fortunate Lands, and was the last resort of those whose hurts could not be mended by their own Lightborn. This realm was Mistress Healer's jealously guarded domain, over which she ruled as absolutely as the Astromancer ruled the Sanctuary itself.

Here Nataranweiya was laid upon a bed in one of the small chambers used for the healing of Banespells. A stool was brought for Maeredhiel, as each time she tried to pull free of Nataranweiya's grip, the lady's agitation because so great that Mistress Healer told her to remain.

What came next should have been done in decent privacy, but the hallway outside the room was crowded with Lightborn and gawking servants, and *Komen* Harthelin had not withdrawn when Nataranweiya was set upon the bed, but leaned against the wall, her arms folded across her chest.

Servants entered with braziers and such other things as might be required for the ease and comfort of a patient. A touch of Nithrithuin's hand unmade each seam of her patient's garments, and their jeweled fastenings rang upon the floor as Nithrithuin pulled them away. Those ragged clothes had been sodden with blood, so the chamber now stank of it.

"My daughter . . . my daughter . . ." Lady Nataranweiya moaned until her words were cut off by a new spasm of pain. She thrashed weakly upon the mattress.

"Not even the Silver Hooves can hurry a birthing babe," Maeredhiel said for Harthelin's benefit. She possessed no understanding of the birthing mysteries, but no daughter of the Hundred Houses grew to adulthood without knowing how much blood a body could hold—and how much blood one could lose before they must ride with the Starry Hunt.

"No!" Celelioniel said, forcing her way through the press of servants and dropping to her knees beside Maeredhiel. "She must not be hurried! Delay—you must delay the birth until dawn. Then we will all be safe!"

Maeredhiel made to get to her feet. If Celelioniel's madness had fixed upon this inconvenient Lady and her even-more-inconvenient babe, Maeredhiel wished to be elsewhere. But Lady-Abeyant Nataranweiya still would not release her, and though a week-old kitten could have broken that grasp, it was enough to hold Maeredhiel where she sat.

"Where is the birthing-woman?" Celelioniel demanded, sounding frantic now. "Where is Thelfelient Lightbrother?"

"At Farcarinon," *Komen* Harthelin said, the mockery in her voice enough to make Maeredhiel set her jaw. "He was called to attend the birth of the heir. So I am told."

"Surely in all the Sanctuary *one* Healer skilled in midwifery remains?" Maeredhiel snapped, her patience—never great—coming to an end.

Harthelin laughed in triumph. "No Healer can stay the lady of Farcarinon from the journey she must make. Indeed, she fails because my lord of Caerthalien has succeeded for all of us, and Serenthon has gone to the Vale of Celenthodiel before her!"

"Silence, armored whelp!" Nithrithuin Lightsister rapped out. "You attend here by our courtesy, nothing more."

Maeredhiel felt a spasm of relief at the intercession of Mistress Healer, for no one would willingly cross one whose services they might someday need. But when Nithrithuin Lightsister laid her hand upon Lady Abeyant Nataranweiya's forehead, she drew back sharply, shaking her head.

"I am no Great Power, to Heal death," she said. "It is as this sword-wielding bully says—the Lady tarries but for the sake of the babe. Then she will follow her Bonded upon the road to the Vale of Celenthodiel."

And the babe will soon follow, Maeredhiel thought grimly. *For if Serenthon and Nataranweiya are dead, any who wishes to become Farcarinon's War Prince must see their child slain as well.*

"The child's name," Celelioniel said urgently. "I must know it! The Prophecy—"

Nithrithuin shook her head sadly, but took Nataranweiya's hand in hers. "The lady your daughter," she said softly. "How shall she be named?"

"Vielle—Vieliessar . . ." Lady Nataranweiya whispered. "Her name— Her name must be—"

"An odd name for Farcarinon's heir," Harthelin said. "To name for the Light what would have cast all of us into darkness."

"You know not what you speak of!" Celelioniel cried. "Therefore be silent!" Once more Maeredhiel felt the thrill of power ghost over her skin, and Harthelin did not speak again.

B oth will die," Maeredhiel whispered.

She did not know how long she had been here, for the healing chambers were windowless. She knew only that Nataranweiya's struggles grew weaker and that she could not push the babe from her body. Celelioniel's near-constant fretting and pacing had driven away nearly all who had come to watch the birth. Again and again the Astromancer would vanish upon some mysterious errand, always to return with more impossible demands: Nithrithuin must hasten the birth. Nithrithuin must delay it.

"Perhaps you would like her to simply slit the woman's throat and simplify matters?" Maeredhiel snapped at last, goaded beyond endurance.

"Not her throat," Nithrithuin Lightsister said softly as she approached the bed once more. Maeredhiel saw the gleam of a knife in her hand and realized that Mistress Healer was taking pains to conceal the weapon from Celelioniel. "The mother is lost, but the babe may yet be saved." Before Maeredhiel could shape a question, Nithrithuin had lifted the blanket from Nataranweiya's unmoving, sweat-drenched body. She set the point of the blade against the stretched flesh of the Lady's swollen belly . . .

. . . and slashed with one quick motion.

Celelioniel's cry of anguish blended with Nataranweiya's even as Nithrithuin reached into the wound with ruthless hands and lifted the blood-slimed form of the infant into the light and air. Another moment, and the infant's angry squalls filled the chamber.

"Your daughter lives," Maeredhiel said. But too late. Farcarinon's lady would hear no more.

"Fool! Witless meddler! A curse upon you and all your House! Let Penenjil's fortunes be tied forever to Farcarinon's!" Celelioniel's voice soared and cracked with rage—no, Maeredhiel realized uneasily, not rage.

Fear.

"Let it be so, Lightborn," Nithrithuin said, bowing her head in acceptance.

At the far wall, nearly forgotten, *Komen* Harthelin stirred at last. Her laughter, when it came, startled all of them.

A week later, Celelioniel sent Vieliessar away into fosterage.

Years would pass before she returned.

❦

The Wheel of the Year turned upon its great Festivals. In Flower Moon was the Kite Festival, when young girls flew their kites against each other, and afterward braided their hair in the style of maidens. In Rain Moon the tribute caravans went to the Sanctuary of the Star, and those who had been Called at Midwinter made their journey with them. In Sword Moon the princes rode to war, and those who had flown their kite or leapt the fire the year before rode with them, as squire and page and arming page. In Thunder Moon the people of the Great Keeps waited eagerly for news of victory or defeat, for the ransoms and penalties levied would affect the fortunes of all. In Fire Moon was the Festival in which boys wishing to become men dared the flames, and blazes were kindled on every hill. Harvest Moon marked the end of War Season, and at Harvest Court fates and fortunes were set: this one to the Swordmaster for training, that one to apprentice to the Warlord, those youths and maidens who had distinguished themselves in War Season to be granted the spurs and sword of a maiden knight. Rade and Woods and Hearth were for Landbond and Farmfolk to bring the harvest and prepare for winter; in Frost Moon the first snows fell. Snow Moon followed, and with it the Midwinter Festival.

Each year at Midwinter, the Lightborn Called to the Light in all the youths and maidens of their lord's domain, to see which of them were most truly Pelashia's Children, and the children the Lightborn chose went to serve at the Sanctuary of the Star. Cold and Ice and Storm were the moonturns in which the land slept, and the *komen* hunted and feasted and fought one another in the Challenge Circle in their lord's great hall. And then Rain Moon came again, and the year truly began.

The Great Wheel was kept differently in Farmhold and village and border keep than it was in the Great Keep, but Varuthir knew nothing of those ways. Rade Moon had come twelve times since she had taken her first breath, and she knew no world but the Great Keep of Caerthalien. As far back as she could remember Varuthir had been told by everyone she should be grateful she had a place at Caerthalien now that her mother and father were dead. In truth, she thought little about her own Line: she was of Caerthalien, and this year at Harvest Court she could make her petition to Lord Bolecthindial to train in arms. Knights didn't care if they were fosterlings and neither did anyone else. Knights fought for the House they were born into (unless they were captured and had to pledge allegiance to another House) and if they fought well, they could gain rich rewards and even pledge *komentai'a* to one of the princes of the House, to serve him or her always and ride to war as part of their meisne. They might even be granted estates where they might have dozens of servants, and meisnes of their own, and nobody but the head of the Line Direct could tell them what to do. They sat at the tables at the front of the Great Hall and everyone looked up to them. They had *adventures*.

She'd paid no attention to the preparations to send the tithe-wagons and the Candidates to Sanctuary, for it didn't concern her. Ivrulion Light-Prince hadn't even *looked* at her at Midwinter.

That was before the day Mistress Nindorogond held her back after the day's lessons were finished.

All the castel children were schooled to read and write and do sums, for whether one had been born a servant or a lord, such knowledge was useful. Later, those who would become *komen* and commanders of a taille or a grand-taille would learn maps, geography, and history along with horsemanship and swordcraft, but for now, all learned together, whether their place was castel servant, treaty hostage, or future knight. *Perhaps I will not need to petition Lord Bolecthindial,* she thought. *Per-*

haps *Mistress Nindorogond means to tell me now I am to train as* komen.

Mistress Nindorogond waited until the schoolroom was empty and silent. Varuthir waited with her, standing silently before the great table piled with scrolls and wax tablets and ciphering frames. When the last to leave had closed the door behind her, Mistress Nindorogond looked up.

"You have been an apt pupil, Varuthir," she said at last. "I am pleased that you will be given this opportunity. All know that the Sanctuary is a place of great learning as well as great Magery."

"I do not understand, Mistress. What has the Sanctuary of the Star to do with me?"

"You know that Storm Moon is nearly fled. Caerthalien sends its tithe early this year. In a fortnight the wagons go. And you go with them."

"To the Sanctuary?" Varuthir said in horror. "But I—But *why*, Nindorogond?" she'd stammered in shock. "Prince Ivrulion—"

"This is not a matter that concerns him," Nindorogond said sharply. "This has been a thing settled since the day you were born. It is for the best."

"But I—" Varuthir said again. "But they'll *see* I have no Light in me! How long do I have to stay there? Do you mean I . . ."

Her words stumbled to a halt as she stared at Nindorogond's face, for in the set of her lips, Varuthir could read her answer. *Forever.* Never to follow the Way of the Sword, to be a great knight, to earn War Prince Bolecthindial's regard . . .

"You cannot mean I have to stay there forever!" she'd cried in protest. "I want to be a knight! I want to fight for Caerthalien!" Caerthalien would need her. The Long Peace that had followed the Breaking of Farcarinon had been all she had ever known, but for the last two summers, there'd been raids along the borders as the High Houses gauged one another's strength. War would come again soon.

"It is for the best," Nindorogond repeated, and Varuthir had run from the schoolroom before Mistress Nindorogond could see her tears.

⊰⊱

When the first shock of Nindorogond's announcement passed, Varuthir went to everyone she knew among the lesser nobles of the Court trying to find some explanation, some way to undo this terrible fate. Everyone who would answer her said the same thing. *It is for the best. It is a matter settled long since.*

She would go to the Sanctuary. But she would never leave it.

She thought of simply running away—but where would she go? She couldn't just walk up to a manor or a farmstead and ask them to take her in: as soon as they discovered she was promised to the Sanctuary, she'd be sent there, for to stint the Sanctuary was to risk the wrath of the Silver Hooves. There were parts of the Fortunate Lands claimed by no House, wild lands that had become the lairs of outlaws and bandits, and she thought of making those her destination. They at least would not send her to the Sanctuary!

But to reach the Wild Lands she'd need a cloak, and good boots, and to steal a horse from the stables—and not just the horse itself, but its saddle and bridle. She had a cloak, gloves, and boots, for in the days that followed the settling of her fate, gifts had come to her from Caerthalien's Ladyholder—green leather boots with silver heels, the leather stamped in gold with patterns of twining vines; a matching green cloak of the best wool, lined with white fox fur; and fur-lined riding gauntlets to match both boots and cloak. But from the candlemark Nindorogond had told her she was to go to the Sanctuary, Varuthir had always been watched. Four times in the last fortnight she'd nerved herself to slip away to the stables, and four times she'd been stopped, or turned back, or noticed.

And now she'd run out of time.

A sennight ago the Called who were to go to the Sanctuary had arrived at Caerthalien. The preparations for departure had been going on since yesterday's dawn. They would leave today.

The morning dawned grey and rainy, as if it were late autumn instead of early spring. It was too early for the leaves to have returned to the trees, and the flagstones of the outer courtyard were still covered with straw each night so ice would not form on them by morning.

She had not slept the night before, and had dressed as soon as it was light enough to see. When Mistress Tiradil tapped at the door to summon her, she simply walked out into the hallway, leaving the door open behind her.

"It is for the best, Varuthir," Mistress Tiradil said quietly. "Someday you will understand that."

I shall never see this room, this place, these people again, Varuthir thought to herself, and silently set her jaw against her tears of anger and grief.

The time of the morning meal at Caerthalien was a good candlemark away, and the Great Hall was empty except for those who would be riding out today and the servers bringing out pitchers and trays and baskets for the meal to come. Berthon and Athrothir—two of the other Called—were already there, eating bread and cheese, drinking mulled cider, and chattering happily about what was to come. They were Farmfolk, and in the ordinary way might never have expected to see the Great Keep in their lives. But if they gained the Green Robe, they would live in luxury for the rest of their lives. They would live in a Great House even if they did not become Mages, for those who completed their Service Year at the Shrine without becoming Lightborn were eagerly sought after as servants.

Varuthir walked toward them, feeling as if her feet were shod in lead and not in leather. Berthon offered her a tankard of cider, but she had no appetite, and mutely shook her head. A few minutes later Thurion, the last of this year's Candidates, rushed in. With his arrival, the *komen* who were to accompany them began getting to their feet.

Varuthir hung back until the last minute, wishing desperately that some reprieve would come. She dawdled long after the *komen* and the Candidates had gone out to the courtyard, pretending she'd gained a sudden appetite.

Perhaps she could simply hide somewhere. They would not delay the caravan's departure just to look for her. Perhaps they would not think it worthwhile to commit a taille—or more—to escort her after it. Perhaps she would have another year at Caerthalien. Anything might happen in a year.

As she was edging her way toward the door that led back into the Keep there was a flurry among the servants, and Ladyholder Glorthiachiel strode into the Great Hall, her personal Lightborn beside her.

Glorthiachiel of Caerthalien was a commanding presence, her husband's equal in all things. For centuries she had ruled over the Caerthalien lands, and would rule for many more. The first time Varuthir had heard Ladyholder Glorthiachiel and Lord Bolecthindial Caerthalien called "Hawk" and "Hound" she'd been struck breathless by the presumption, but the rude nicknames suited them, for Ladyholder Glorthiachiel was as beautiful and dangerous as any of the falcons in the castel mews, and her husband was as relentless and tenacious as any hunting hound.

To Varuthir's amazement, Ladyholder Glorthiachiel beckoned her over. Varuthir's heart leapt with hope at this unexpected summons. It had all been a mistake! She wasn't meant to go to the Sanctuary at all, and Carangil Lightbrother had discovered the error and told his mistress, and now Ladyholder Glorthiachiel had come to give the order that would mean she didn't have to leave.

But Glorthiachiel's first words dashed that hope. "So today you leave us, child," she said, and Varuthir nodded mutely.

Ladyholder Glorthiachiel smiled, as if this were a day for great celebration. "In ten years and two, all the time you have lived beneath my roof, it has never come to my ears that you spoke of your parents, and I find that a curious thing."

"I know they are dead," Varuthir said in a low voice. "I had hoped—"

Ladyholder Glorthiachiel's smile widened and her eyes gleamed predatorily. "Indeed they are. You are too young to know the history of the Hundred Houses, so what I tell you now will mean little. But you will remember it. Oh, yes. You will remember it all the days of your life. You, who will toil as a servant, were born to be War Prince of Farcarinon! It was Caerthalien that erased Farcarinon as if it had never been. You are Vieliessar Farcarinon—the last of Farcarinon—and you are *nothing!*"

In all the days of her life, Varuthir had tasted scorn and indifference aplenty, but never had she been hated as she saw Ladyholder Glorthiachiel hate her now. For a moment it was incomprehensible—what could she have done to merit this?

I have done nothing. It is my Line—my House . . .

She had heard the tale of the Breaking of Farcarinon all her life. She had never known it told the tale of her parents' murder. And never had the story been sung of the last survivor of Farcarinon. But if Ladyholder Glorthiachiel spoke true, she was not Varuthir of Caerthalion. She was Vieliessar of Farcarinon—no, more: she was *Vieliessar Farcarinon.*

And Caerthalien . . .

"Murderess!" Vieliessar hissed in rage. She took a quick step forward, scrabbling for the knife upon her belt. She would slay the enemy of her House, and in her own death buy honor and a place at the Starry Huntsman's right hand.

But Carangil Lightbrother was quicker than she. He raised his hand and Vieliessar felt a sudden icy tingling everywhere on her skin. Suddenly she was unable to move, to cry out, to demand *vengeance.*

"Today my vengeance is complete—Vieliessar Farcarinon!" Ladyholder Glorthiachiel said mockingly. "I would not have you leave us without knowing all I have taken from you. Fare you well, Farcarinon. And live a long, *long* time."

I shall see you drown in your own blood! Vieliessar thought in fury. But it did not matter how hard she fought the *geasa* that had been placed upon her: the frenzied anger she felt did not transmute itself to action. Instead her body made a formal deferential bow, her feet turned her away, and her body walked from the Great Hall to the courtyard. Her hands plucked her gloves from the sash of her tunic and pulled them on, and her hands lifted the hood of her stormcloak to cover her hair. Without her will, her hands laced its drawstrings tight against the rain and the chill. Her body walked sedately to the bay palfrey that would carry her to debasement and imprisonment; her hands grasped the cantle, her foot set itself into the stirrup.

No matter how hard she tried, she could not make a sound.

❧❧

It would take the caravan a fortnight to travel from Caerthalien to the Sanctuary of the Star. Traditionally the Candidates' processionals were exempt from attack, though this tacit truce was something that held only among the Hundred Houses—outlaws and Broken Spurs might see nothing more sacred than a rich prize for the taking. For that reason, tribute caravans traveled with an armed escort in addition to the servants and drovers. Berthon, Thurion, and Athrothir laughed and chattered, excited by the journey and delighted with everything they saw.

The night's mist still hung heavy over the fields and meadows as the gates of Caerthalien rattled open. The winches creaked as the heavy bronze portcullises were raised over the inner and outer gates; heavy chains rattled over pulleys and then the outer doors—massive slabs of bronze-bound oak—swung outward as their counterweights were released.

At last Runacarendalur of Caerthalien could spur his mount through the inner gate, through a long narrow tunnel, and through the outer gate. He took a deep breath as Gwaenor began to prance, the warhorse's joy at reaching the open air plain to see. Both horse and rider relished the chance to be out and doing, and as Gwaenor danced, Runacarendalur laughed aloud.

"Is it not a beautiful morning, Helecanth?" he asked.

"Any morning is beautiful when one is not yet dead," the chief of Runacarendalur's personal guard grumbled.

"And so it will be a beautiful evening, too," Runacarendalur said teasingly. "For you cannot think anyone will offer insult to a Sanctuary party—still less when a full double-taille of Caerthalien's finest ride with it?"

"I think one stone can end a life—if it is the right stone at the right time," Helecanth answered dourly. "And you are not such a fool as to think yourself safe even within the shadow of your father's walls," she added, frowning at him. Instead of a battle standard, for this journey Helecanth carried the long white pennion that would tell all who saw it this was a Candidates' Escort bound for the Sanctuary of the Star. The pennion itself was sodden with rain, and hung down limply, its silk growing more transparent the wetter it got.

"Let us go more than a bowshot from Caerthalien before you begin fretting at every shadow," Runacarendalur protested, laughing. It might be Helecanth's duty to worry—for she was charged with his safety—but the countryside had been quiet for longer than he liked to remember—for so many years together that the time had been named the Long Peace.

Some suggested the Hundred Houses waited to see if the Starry Hunt meant to strike them down for the Erasure of Farcarinon, for the doing was against the Code of Battle. Serenthon Farcarinon had done only what any of them might do when he had schemed to make himself High King. Some said they waited for the Curse of Amrethion to fall upon them. In fact (as Runacarendalur knew) there was a far simpler explanation: the war against Farcarinon had been costly. Thousands of blooded warriors and trained warhorses had been lost, tracts of land laid waste— and the wrangling over who should gain Farcarinon's lands had nearly bred a second war.

Serenthon was a fool. We have lived since the time of Amrethion and Pelashia without a High King, Runacarendalur thought. *Yet I will say this for Farcarinon: the battles against it were glorious.*

"Helecanth," he said abruptly. "Do you think the Hundred Houses need a High King to govern them?"

"I say that if you do not rein in, we will reach the Sanctuary a sennight before the wagons do," his Mistress-at-Arms said.

Runacarendalur glanced over his shoulder as he checked Gwaenor. The wagons were far behind them. His taille—which knew its business was not to indulge their commander's fancies where his father could see—rode sedately at the head of the column, their bright cloaks and lacquered armor the brightest spot of color in the grey overcast day. Just behind the knights rode the Sanctuary Candidates—two Farmfolk more used to mules than palfreys, a Landbond who had probably never seen a horse before a sennight gone, and . . .

Better if she'd been slain before she was a day old, Runacarendalur thought grimly. *Better even that the Lightborn had fostered her within the Sanctuary so she knew no other life.* But the Sanctuary of the Star had no provision for the care of a child. Her fate had been set from the moment she first drew breath: to return to the Sanctuary of the Star in her twelfth year, never again to set foot outside it lest she find her death.

At least she does not know her true parentage, he thought. Perhaps the Lightborn would be kind and she never would.

⊰✦⊱

I am Vieliessar of Farcarinon! Caerthalien killed my parents! I will have vengeance on them—on all of them! Only the spell held her silent. Losing her hope for her future and what she'd thought was her House was a doubly bitter blow: she'd dreamed ever since she was a child of becoming *komen* to Caerthalien. But the Magecraft that held her imprisoned and silent granted Vieliessar one unlooked-for boon.

It forced her to think.

Ladyholder Glorthiachiel did not have to tell me the truth.

If Ladyholder Glorthiachiel had told her of her parentage and then said that Caerthalien had wished to show mercy to a helpless child, Vieliessar would have been grateful and devoted. Instead Ladyholder Glorthiachiel had sent her into exile bearing the knowledge that she—a child—was held their enemy.

Why?

She had no answers.

⊰✦⊱

In the last fortnight, his world had grown wide. Thurion had never been farther from home than the fields his family worked for Menenel Farmholder, and if the Light had not awakened in him, he would have lived and died without ever going more than a mile from the hut in which he had been born.

There were not enough Lightborn in all Caerthalien's domain to visit every crofthold and farmstead each Midwinter, so it was the custom for all the children of a certain age to be sent to the nearest manor house to be overlooked. His father had not wished to risk the loss of Thurion's labor, even though—should it come to pass that Thurion Landbond became Thurion Lightbrother—Lord Bolecthindial would make a great award to his family. At ten, at eleven, at twelve his father had said he was too young to make the sennight's journey there and back, for Brightwater Manor lay far distant from Goldentrees Farm.

But in the spring following his twelfth year, the Light had awakened in Thurion without being Called. He had been able to hear the speech of beast and growing thing as plainly as he heard the words of his family and kin. His father had beaten him uncounted times for tale-telling, yet Thurion could not keep from speaking of what he knew.

That winter, for the first time in Thurion's memory, Menenel Farmholder hosted Dilvalos Lightsister beneath his roof and made a great feast for all who toiled upon his lands. Dilvalos Lightsister had looked into Thurion's heart and said, *"This one shall go to the Sanctuary in the spring,"* and her words were such a telling as not even one of the great lords could set aside.

It was barely Storm Moon when Thurion was summoned to Menenel Farmholder's house to hear that he must journey to Caerthalien. He hoped to say farewell to his family, but Menenel insisted he must start for *Komen* Radanir's manor house at once. The journey would have been more speedy if he had not gone at a wagon's pace, but Thurion had never ridden a horse.

Komen Radanir's husband had tsked over Thurion's smock and leg-wrappings and knitted shawl of oiled wool, and said such garments would not do for Caerthalien's Great Keep. He'd given Thurion a tunic, trousers, and the first boots he had ever worn, then said it would be a long cold ride to Caerthalien and given him a fine wool cape as well. Thurion was ashamed to say he had never ridden a horse, but somehow

Komen Radanir had known. She said Thurion must learn, and quickly, but there had only been time for a lesson or two before they set off for Caerthalien.

And oh!—he'd thought *Komen* Radanir's fine manor house was wondrous enough, but Caerthalien's Great Keep was more magnificent still. In the castel there was magic everywhere, and the bed he slept in was soft as down and covered with many soft blankets in more colors than he had thought possible. More wonderful even than that was the food. He ate until he was full to bursting, and there was yet more food—so much food that full bowls and platters were returned to the kitchen from every table. He had asked, the first evening, if this were some great feast day, and the others had laughed . . .

But Thurion didn't care. A scant sennight was barely time enough for him to list Caerthalien's wonders. And not once was he called upon to do any work at all. It was as if he had fallen into an endless holiday.

A few days after his arrival, Berthon and Athrothir joined him at the keep. Berthon was the son of a knight, Athrothir the son of a castellan—one who held the manor house of a knight when he or she rode off to fight. They teased Thurion greatly about his wide eyes, for Berthon had visited the castel many times with his father and Athrothir had lived all his life in a rich manor house. Yet despite their teasing, Thurion thought they might well become friends, for—as *Komen* Radanir had explained to him—they would be a full turn of the seasons at the Sanctuary of the Star, tendering their service to the Lightborn. Then, if those of the Sanctuary, who would look more deeply into their hearts than had those who had Called the Light at Midwinter, felt them worthy, they would begin their training as Lightborn.

A whole year at the Sanctuary! And honor to his family, and to Menenel Farmholder, and to *Komen* Radanir. So Thurion simply laughed when Athrothir and Berthon spoke mournfully of the privations those in their Service Year endured, and told them he would be sure to give them advice on how to bear up beneath them.

They were not the only ones making the journey to the Sanctuary of the Star this springtide. There was Varuthir. Berthon, who knew all the gossip, said she was a fosterling of House Caerthalien who had lived all her life here. Thurion was far too shy to speak to her; she seemed as distant and unreachable—and as beautiful—as the winter stars.

Perhaps—if I become Lightborn—she will look kindly upon me. Perhaps, if she is not betrothed already . . .

In the castel, as on the farms which made up the estates which made up the domain of Caerthalien, betrothals came early, for what better way to seal a contract or to plan for the future? One might set aside a betrothal in the name of greater fortune, or if those promised to it disliked the idea enough to win their parents' agreement. But the most certain way to break a promise, a handfasting, or even marriage itself, was a Bonding. Not even a Lord of the Line Direct could stand against the magic that bound Bondmates together for the rest of their lives. Such unions were deeply blessed, but the sorcery that tied soul and soul together created a binding so deep and true that one heart could not continue to beat if the other was stilled. Thurion well recalled the day when Henion (Bonded, as all knew, to Aglahir) had been plowing the field with a new team and had fallen and been trampled by the young, skittish beasts. Though Thurion had only been a child, he remembered how Aglahir had run screaming from the main house to the field and found Henion, though the fields were far and only the Bond had given her knowing. Henion had not survived to see the next day's dawn, and Aglahir had been dead by the following nightfall.

So though the first time he saw Varuthir Thurion thought he had seen his heart's twin, his destined Bondmate, he was grateful to realize he had not. This did not keep him from adoring her in silence and secret.

When at last the great day came for their departure, there were wonders enough to distract Thurion from the contemplation of his love. Not only were they to travel with a company of knights—a thing he had known already—but Caerthalien's heir, Prince Runacar, was to escort them. The prince was a glorious figure in Caerthalien livery, with armor enameled just the shade of his surcoat and a great black destrier who pawed the flagstones and snorted steam from his nostrils. Thurion was just as glad to be riding the gentle mare Filioniel Horsemaster had chosen for him, for he had grown fond of her, and he could *tell* she liked him as well.

On the journey to Caerthalien he and *Komen* Radanir had stopped each night at a farmstead or manor, but on the journey to the Sanctuary of the Star they would sleep in pavilions, just as the knights did when they went off to war. On the road, the four Candidates were much in one another's company and Thurion fell even more deeply into love with Varuthir, though she spoke few words to anyone and seemed to wear grief like a heavy weight.

⊰⊱

Ten days' travel saw the convoy deep in the Unclaimed Lands that bordered the forests surrounding the Sanctuary. Runacarendalur had escorted four previous groups of Candidates to the Sanctuary of the Star: even in the depths of war, Candidates from every House made the journey, for nowhere else could those with the Light receive training, and without the Lightborn there would be no one to Heal the sick and the injured. To make the fields bear fruitfully, to enchant stone and wood and cloth to endure, to do all the thousand tasks that required Magery. For that reason, even when House and warring House met upon the road to the Sanctuary gates, they nearly always passed one another in peace.

And in the gap between "nearly" and "always" fell reason enough for Caerthalien to send Runacarendalur forth a full moonturn early. He would gladly have brought an escort of a hundred, but to do so would be to reveal the thing Caerthalien needed to hide—that Farcarinon's last daughter traveled with them.

She was too tempting a prize.

⊰⊱

Knowing it was only a fantasy, Vieliessar spent the days of her journey hoping for some reprieve from the future she saw before her.

There'd been a hundred chances on the journey to run. But the problem remained: where would she go, and how would she gain vengeance on Caerthalien?

Again and again she'd come to the very edge of wishing Ladyholder Glorthiachiel had never told her who she was—but to wish that would be to deny her father, her mother, her House. And she could not. House and kin were sacred. Vengeance was sacred. She would have learned that same lesson in Aramenthiali. In Vondaimieriel. In Sarmiorion.

In Farcarinon.

Even if she managed to escape to another House and persuade its lord to grant her knightly training, the outcome would be much the same as if she remained in the Sanctuary of the Star: if and when she fought, she would fight for the House to which she had pledged her fealty. Not for Farcarinon. Farcarinon would still be unavenged.

No. She must watch, and wait, and plan. No matter how much she loathed the thought, her best—her only—chance to be avenged on her parents' murderers was to continue to the Sanctuary of the Star.

Four more days of travel would see them at the Sanctuary, and the last of them would be spent in the Flower Forest that surrounded the Sanctuary of the Star. Thurion had stretched his eyes at the thought of a Flower Forest so large it would take a whole day to ride through it, and the prince had laughed and said Caerthalien's eastern reaches held Flower Forests greater than that.

Thurion had looked to Varuthir to see if she thought this as great a wonder as he, yet she seemed not to have heard Prince Runacarendalur's words. She stared off into the distance and her face was still with grief.

He knew she walked the bounds of the camp each night until the spell-lamps were covered and all composed themselves for sleep. In the first days he had been too tired to do anything but seek his bed after the meal, but when that exhaustion had passed, he'd often spent those candle-marks in games or in hearing story-songs of great deeds, for even though

Helecanth was very grand, she said she was happy to have the telling of them to fresh ears. But Varuthir had never joined them. It did not seem good to him that something so joyous as this journey should make one so beautiful so sad, and so, this night, he left Athrothir and Berthon to their amusements and sought her out.

Thurion had become accustomed to the sounds of the camp at night—the faint grunts of tethered horses, the grinding sound of grain being chewed, the long sighs of the oxen, the jingle of bridle and clink of stirrup as the sentries rode the bounds. Tonight there was a new scent upon the wind, for one might smell the blooms of a Flower Forest even from so far away. He soon found Varuthir, a dim figure in the darkness, only the silver embroidery on her cloak gleaming in the light from the pavilions.

"You should be happy," Thurion blurted out when he reached her. It was not what he'd meant to say. He had intended to say he cared for her, and worried about her, and had seen her sadness. He might even have asked if she missed her friends from the castel, for he felt certain she'd had many.

"I?" she asked, turning. The distant glow of the lanterns fell full upon her face, framed in the white fur of her cloak's hood, and she twined one long ebony braid between her fingers. "I was not born to be happy," she said in a low voice.

"I don't know why," Thurion answered, his tongue stumbling over the words. "To be Called to the Sanctuary of the Star—I always hoped to be summoned there, even if it is only for a year, as it might be, you know, and . . . Berthon will be made a knight, if he is not found to be Lightborn, but such as I—to become one with the Light is a great honor—" At last he managed to stop talking, cursing his clumsy tongue, for he had meant to offer comfort, and instead he saw Varuthir's eyes glitter now with tears.

"It is an honor I never sought, nor is it one I shall gain," she said flatly.

"Have you Seen this?" he blurted. "The dreams that come—if you have Light—they do not matter unless—until—"

But she held up her hand to stop him. "The dreams I held were not of this. I thank you, Thurion, for your kindness," she added after a pause. "You do not know me, and so it does you honor."

It was plainly a dismissal, but he could not bring himself to leave. "Do you—do you think—when we are at the Sanctuary—" he began, but she shook her head and he fell silent.

"You do not know me," she repeated. "But you will. And then you will . . . Then you will have your answers." Still she did not send him away, so Thurion stood with her in silence until *Komen* Helecanth summoned them both to their beds. He wondered at the words she had spoken, and it was not long before he could place knowing upon them.

CHAPTER TWO

CHILD OF THE PROPHECY

Listen, child, and I will tell you a tale that is both true and real. Long ago, in the morning of the world, when there was nothing but Jer-a-kalaliel itself, nine stars looked down from the sky and saw the beautiful land we live in. And they were so enchanted by its beauty that they fell from the heavens. And each place one fell to the ground was more beautiful than the next, and because each was so beautiful, great Flower Forests grew up where each of the nine stars fell down. And the Flower Forests contained every tree and plant that grows, and some that remain only in Tilinaparanwira the Lost, which grows behind the East Wind.

—Ancient Nursery Tale

The Sanctuary of the Star was not just one building, though only one building was the Sanctuary itself. That building was like a great keep in miniature—three stories of grey Mage-forged stone with a doorway that led directly to the Outer Sanctuary. Within that building, all were bound by the Peace of the Sanctuary, which obliged even those who had declared blood feud to pass one another by without raising a hand in violence.

The Caerthalien party was met on the road by Othring Lightbrother, saying Caerthalien's was the first caravan to come this season. He greeted all four Candidates individually, but Thurion thought his gaze lingered longest upon Varuthir. Thurion thought they might stop to wash off the dirt of the road before entering the Sanctuary, but as soon as they'd dismounted, Prince Runacarendalur unbuckled his swordbelt and handed his weapon to *Komen* Helecanth.

"Come," he said. "The sooner I have delivered you to the care of the Mistress of Servants, the sooner you may settle into your new lives."

At his words, Varuthir started, then stared at Prince Runacarendalur with hot eyes before turning away.

The four Candidates followed Prince Runacarendalur and Othring Lightbrother through the main doors of the Sanctuary. Thurion had heard many storysongs of this place, yet somehow it was unlike every one of them. It was not as grand as the telling in *The Rade of Bringaer*, for the stone was not as white as new milk, nor was it vaster than all the Great Keeps in Jer-a-kalaliel together. But to see the great bronze doors, with this piece and that bright-shining from the touch of uncounted hands, and to know that beyond it one might see stone struck by the Silver Hooves of the Starry Hunt's own destriers . . . that made Thurion's heart beat fast and the breath catch in his throat. It was a long moment before he had eyes for the woman who awaited them.

She did not wear the green robe, but she wore the Sanctuary's badge upon her tabard. She was not young, for her braids were streaked with grey, and yet there was such dignity and power about her that for a moment Thurion was certain he gazed upon the Astromancer herself.

"I am Mistress Maeredhiel," she said crisply. "Candidates, I greet you in the name of the Sanctuary of the Star. Until the day you are Called to the Light—if you are—you are my responsibility. In your Service Year you will take your orders from me. Now, who is it the Sanctuary of the Star has the honor to welcome this day?"

It was a wonder in a day of wonders that Mistress Maeredhiel had, until her last sentence, ignored Prince Runacarendalur as if he were any servant boy. Now he spoke, his speech as deferential as if he spoke to Lord Bolecthindial himself. "Caerthalien entrusts to the Sanctuary of the Star Candidates Berthon, Athrothir, Thurion, and—"

"I am Vieliessar Farcarinon, War Prince of Farcarinon!" Varuthir said, stepping forward. "I come as a prisoner, not a Candidate! Though Caerthalien slew my parents, Farcarinon yet lives!"

⊷⧓⊶

There was a moment of electric silence, and Runacarendalur cursed himself for eleven kinds of fool—and then cursed his mother for good measure, as he was certain this was of Ladyholder Glorthiachiel's weaving. Who else could have—or would have—told the girl her true name?

"That's as may be, girl," Mistress Maeredhiel said briskly, "but here we care nothing for the quarrels of the Hundred Houses—nor will you, if you have wit."

Vieliessar opened her mouth as if to protest, then closed it again, glowering wordlessly. Berthon and Athrothir were backing away from her, their expressions as shocked as if she had named herself Beastling. Thurion alone clearly had no idea what her declaration meant, for he simply gazed at her, his expression puzzled.

"Prince Runacarendalur, the Sanctuary of the Star thanks you for your service," Mistress Maeredhiel said, as if there had been no interruption. "Will you visit the Shrine while you are here?"

Runacarendalur took a hasty step backward, and cursed inwardly at the gleam of amusement he saw in Maeredhiel's eyes. He knew the day would come when he must stand within the Shrine and be judged by the Silver Hooves, as his father had been before him—but Pelashia grant that day still lay far in the future!

After a moment, he recovered himself enough to bow. "Alas that my duties do not permit it," he said ironically. "But I will commend your great diligence to my father, when next I see him."

"Caerthalien has always done us every courtesy," Maeredhiel answered blandly. "Come along, you four. If you are waiting to be presented to Hamphuliadiel Astromancer, you will stand here forever. He is far too busy to waste his time on children."

⊷⧓⊶

The outer doors of the sanctuary closed behind Runacarendalur, and Mistress Maeredhiel began walking away. "*Farcarinon?*" Athrothir said, staring at Vieliessar in stunned amazement. "But—Serenthon—"

"Your interest in the history of the Hundred Houses does you credit, young Athrothir," Mistress Maeredhiel said repressively, stopping and looking back at them. "And I say again—for what I am certain is not the last time—until the day you leave us, neither rank nor House concerns you. Now come."

Thurion walked forward at once; after a moment Berthon and Athrothir followed. With nowhere else to go, Vieliessar trailed after them. She wasn't sure whether to be pleased to see Athrothir put in his place so sharply, or irritated that her announcement had not carried more weight. The only thing she was certain of was that it had come as no surprise to Prince Runacarendalur. *May the Silver Hooves spurn you at your death, faithless betrayer!*

"You will be called to serve during your first year in all the ways you—or *some* of you—have been served in the past," Maeredhiel said as she led them along the corridor. "Those who have been in service before you will assist you in learning your tasks. The Sanctuary has few ordinary servants, not enough to do all that is required. Your labor will be needed."

"What will we have to do?" Berthon asked, a little timidly.

Maeredhiel fixed him with a skeptical eye. "What *can* you do, young Berthon?" she asked. "No matter. You will learn. We have hosted all manner of Candidates in our time, from Landbonds to heirs to the Line." She glanced toward Vieliessar.

Two corridors led away from the Antechamber of the Shrine; they had turned along the *tuathal* one. As they walked, Mistress Maeredhiel named each chamber they passed and gave its function. The chambers on the ground floor *tuathal* side were used only during the day, for study, practice, or meditation.

"This side passage leads to the stairs down to the Library," Maeredhiel said, gesturing. "Perhaps someday you will see what lies within it." She led them up the great stone staircase to the second floor.

There was a long hallway at the top of the stair, and Maeredhiel again turned left. The walls were lined with small plain doors, set so closely together that Vieliessar knew the rooms behind them must be nearly as small as the winter blanket closets at Caerthalien. Every door was closed. "These rooms are for those who have begun their training in the mysteries of the Sanctuary, as well as for those Lightborn who return to us for a time, as many do."

At the end of the hallway was another staircase leading to the top floor of the Sanctuary. As Maeredhiel began to ascend, she continued her lecture. "Because you come so early, there are none here to place you with, so to save myself work, you lads will share a room. Do not expect such consideration for long. You will later share rooms with those of every House and fighting will be punished severely."

Athrothir opened his mouth and closed it, Berthon looked as if he'd only just realized where he was, and Thurion looked as if he was hearing only what he'd expected to.

"It matters not what clothing or jewels you have brought with you. It will all be sent back with your escort. While you are here, you will wear the livery of the Sanctuary, as I do. Should you be Twice-Called to the Light, you will wear the green tabard of a Postulant. While you are here, you will wear no jewelry, no scent, no ornaments in your hair— nor may you dress your hair high upon your head or wear more than four braids. You will rise at the candlemark appointed to rising and you will seek your bed upon the candlemark appointed to sleeping. You may not walk outside the Sanctuary without permission, nor may you enter the Sanctuary garden without permission, nor may you cross the bounds of the Sanctuary lands at any time. If you do not wish to eat what is served to you, you may hunger. If you do not wish to perform the tasks set for you, you will be sent from the Sanctuary and your House will be notified of your disgrace when the next Candidates arrive."

As Maeredhiel spoke, Vieliessar saw Berthon and Athrothir exchange looks of horror, for even Farmholders might expect—on feast days—to go in fine clothing and perfume, with colored cords and combs for their hair.

She'd had few enough of those things at Caerthalien. What disturbed her more was that now she would never have them—because she would never leave the Sanctuary of the Star.

The rooms on the top floor were each meant to hold six Candidates. All the doors were open, so as they passed they could see that the beds were stacked in pairs, with the upper bed held off the floor by elongated legs. Each room was barely large enough for three beds and a warming brazier. The mattresses were bare, and thin, and at the sight of them, Athrothir and Berthon once again exchanged looks of dismay.

At the end of the hallway, Mistress Maeredhiel stopped in front of a room that looked much like any other, save for the piles of cloth—blankets and bedlinens, along with tunics and trews in the grey of a Sanctuary servant—that lay upon the lower bed closest to the door.

"Change your clothing and stand before your door when you are done. Bring what you now wear with you. Vieliessar, come with me."

She thought to rebel, but again the question stopped her: if she ran, where would she go? And so, silently, she followed Maeredhiel back along the hall to a room with only one pile of cloth upon the bed. She walked inside and Maeredhiel followed, closing the door behind them.

"I don't belong here," Vieliessar said as she unlaced her stormcloak. Catching Maeredhiel's faintly scornful look, she added: "I mean, I don't belong here. Aren't there rooms where the— Where those who will remain here forever stay?" she finished reluctantly.

Maeredhiel studied her for a long moment in silence. "It would please me immensely to know why you think you belong in one."

"A moonturn past, Mistress Nindorogond said I was to go to the Sanctuary and bide there forever. Upon the day of my going, Glorthiachiel of Caerthalien gave me my true name."

"Scratch Caerthalien and touch pitch," Mistress Maeredhiel said in disgust. "I had wished to choose my own time to tell you of your heritage.

All you will be thinking of now is vengeance upon the destroyers of your line—and if I know that blood-maddened shrew my brother's greatson married, she'll have been sure to tell to tell you it was House Caerthalien that crushed House Farcarinon beneath its bootheel."

"You are Caerthalien!" Vieliessar spat. "Why—"

"I am Mistress Maeredhiel of the Sanctuary of the Star!" Maeredhiel answered hotly. "Caerthalien is nothing to me—nor can it be to you. Look you, girl. You were sent as a Candidate, and so a Candidate you shall be. If the Light comes to you, you will become Lightborn, and that is a problem for another day. Think long and hard, Vieliessar Farcarinon, before showing the Light even if you possess it, for a Mage may be called from the Sanctuary where a servant cannot be, and you must never leave here. Do you understand why?"

"Because I am *Farcarinon*," Vieliessar said bitterly.

"Indeed you are," Maeredhiel said. "Vieliessar Farcarinon, the last of the Line, and do you set one foot beyond the bounds of the Sanctuary, your life is forfeit. I was here the night Lady Nataranweiya came to us. Lord Serenthon was dead, and the lady his Bondmate was dying, yet she won through to Sanctuary so that she might give you life. If you possess one-tenth her bravery, there is greatness in you."

Vieliessar stared in shock, for Maeredhiel spoke of her unknown mother—and her House—with something almost akin to approval. "Do you—? Are you—?" she stammered, her anger forgotten.

"It was I who saw you named, and Celelioniel Astromancer—she who left us these four years past—who set the Peacebond upon you as you drew your first breaths. And know now if you did not before—the Peacebond is why you lived, but it ran only until you should return to us."

"Then I need never have come here at all," Vieliessar said bitterly. "I might have had my freedom, knowing no prince could strike me down and risk the Peacebond's vengeance."

"That is not so. Did Celelioniel Astromancer try to set the Peacebond on you without some term to it, the Hundred would have forced her to lift it," Maeredhiel answered. "Failing that, they might have imprisoned you—or forced you into some marriage to lay claim to all that Farcarinon once held—or worse."

Vieliessar turned away, dropping her cloak and her gloves to the bed.

"You will hear me," Maeredhiel said, and her voice rang with such iron authority that Vieliessar looked up in surprise.

"None knows better than I how Caerthalien breaks hearts and lives, child. Six hundred years gone, my brother slew Aradrothiach of Cirandeiron, who would have been my Bondmate. War Prince Palierlaniel Caerthalien did not like the thought of a Caerthalien daughter going to Cirandeiron—and so she summoned Aradrothiach to the betrothal feast, and my brother slew him."

"But you aren't dead!" Vieliessar blurted, and Maeredhiel smiled sardonically.

"I knew Aradrothiach for my destined Bondmate, but our Bond was not yet made. Haramarthien could slay my beloved without risk to me— and so he did. But that night I fled to the Sanctuary of the Star, and here I have remained. And I say to you, Vieliessar Farcarinon: patience is the true sword of vengeance. If you can keep Caerthalien uneasy in its bed for century upon century, knowing you are alive and well, it will be a vengeance well crafted."

"That is not vengeance enough for me!" Vieliessar protested hotly.

"Ah, well, Celelioniel swore you were the Child of the Prophecy," Maeredhiel said mildly. "Undoubtedly you will think of something better. Now, dress yourself, for we have spent too long in idle chatter."

Before Vieliessar could ask the dozen questions Maeredhiel had put into her mind, the Mistress of Servants swept from the room and closed the door behind her.

Child of the Prophecy, Vieliessar thought dazedly. *What Prophecy? Why should Celelioniel Astromancer have set a Peacebond upon me if the Hundred Houses chose to erase Farcarinon?*

Sighing, she leaned over to pull off her boots. She did not know what she should do now—but the one thing she had gained from Maeredhiel's words was the knowledge the Sanctuary meant *time*.

She would wait.

And plan.

The dormitory wing echoed emptily at first, for the day before the first caravan train arrived, the Candidates now finishing their Service Year had been sent to sleep in a vast windowless chamber in the other wing of the third floor. The new Candidates saw them only in passing, for it was the Sanctuary servants themselves who oversaw the training of those entering their Service Year.

Spring meant not only the arrival of the Candidates, but of great lords coming to make luck-sacrifices at the Shrine for fortune in the coming War Season, and Lightborn returning to the Sanctuary for counsel. Rare was the day when no tribute caravan arrived—and then two, three, five each day. Each, when it departed, carried away with it those who had ended their Service Year without being called to the Light as well as those newly come to the Green Robe.

In the first days, Vieliessar found herself too weary each night to even think of escape, for each day began before sunrise with the sound of Mage-conjured bells. Those who were to serve at table or in the kitchens hurried through their washing and dressing and hastened off to begin their tasks while their fellows savored a few moments of leisure before being summoned to the first meal by more bells. When the meal was done, the Postulants went to their lessons, the Lightborn to their still-mysterious tasks, and the Candidates to their work. Few of the Candidates were accustomed to their labors, for few of them had been Called from families in service to a Great Keep or manor house. Mistress Hamonglachele, in whose keeping lay the Sanctuary guesthouse and the duty of hospitality to visitors, had claimed many of them for her work, while Pandorgrad Mastergardener, who managed the gardens, claimed more.

Waking and sleeping, the days of the Candidates were governed by the sound of magical bells that chimed sourcelessly in empty air: bells to wake them, bells to send them to their meals, bells to send them to their scant candlemarks of leisure and from there to their beds. Each third fortnight their sleeping rooms were changed, and that was all to the good:

if you misliked your bedchamber companions, six sennights would see you with different ones. The prohibition against naming their Houses was heeded by almost no one, but at least Vieliessar was not the only one to refuse to name her House. She felt daring enough in claiming her name.

Spring became high summer, then dwindled away into autumn. Vieliessar's body hardened to her new work and her mind grew quick to find the best and easiest way to accomplish each task she was set. Though she began to find leisure in the evening, she kept from the Common Room, where Candidates and Postulants alike gathered for games of *xaique* and *gan* and *narshir*. She wanted no friends among those who had slain her family—for the destruction of Farcarinon had not been Caerthalien's alone, but the work of many Houses—nor did she wish to befriend those she would some day be called upon to serve. No, she would use her free time to plan her future—her *true* future, not the one Caerthalien meant her to have.

But somehow her plans of escape and vengeance grew no further.

Winter stalked the bounds of the Sanctuary like a great white wolf. Each day was much like the next—no feast day celebrating a House's triumph nor Festival to mark the turn of the year was celebrated here. And then, it was spring and the first new Candidates were soon to arrive to begin their Service Year.

Now it was Vieliessar and her fellow-Candidates who were sent to the Long Chamber. They would sleep there until their final fates were revealed, as the caravans of their Houses arrived, and the new Candidates would occupy the familiar dormitory rooms. There was excitement and confusion when they arrived, as for the first time in a full Wheel of the Seasons they were free to choose where they might sleep, and among whom. And each contemplated the future to be so soon revealed with both excitement and dread. None of them knew—even now—who would stay and who would go, and while the shared year of toil had forged many strong friendships, the next time many of them met might be when the battle lines of their House's armies clashed.

This is why we were told not to name our Houses, so those of us who go on to become komentai'a *might be spared the knowledge they had slain those who once were friends,* Vieliessar thought, surprising herself. None of them had understood that until it was too late.

And each night the Long Chamber held fewer tenants than the night before. Some departed with the caravans. Some donned the green tabard of a Postulant. There seemed to be no metric for knowing who would go or who would stay.

Baramrin and Eradrin and Feinel had shown no hint of the Light in all the moonturns they'd been Candidates—or nothing more than any other had, since all save Vieliessar had been sent here by the word of the Lightborn—yet now they were Called.

But they never tested us! They never asked! Vieliessar thought, half indignant, half disturbed. *They never even taught us anything. . . .*

But in looking back on the matter-of-fact spellcraft she'd seen in the last fourteen moonturns—Silverlight and Silversight, Healing, Calling Fire with a snap of the fingers, speaking with beasts and awakening the soil with a touch, Vieliessar realized that wasn't true. They'd all learned without realizing they were being taught: When and how the Magery was used. The cost of using it. The things it could do.

Perhaps the teaching itself is the test.

Vieliessar knew that true understanding of what it meant to be one of the Lightborn could only come if one were Called. The Postulants had all been willing—even eager—to talk with the Candidates about what they learned, but much of it was like one who was blind attempting to understand what sight was.

It's like flying, some said. *Like running before the wind and knowing every current in the ocean beneath you,* said others. *Like dancing. Like riding a fast horse.*

Like a hundred other things that only one of the Lightborn could understand.

It was a full moonturn before the last of the Candidate caravans came and went. This year Hallorad was the last: a Less House so far to the east that beyond its eastern border lay nothing but leagues of windswept grassland and Graythunder Glairyrill itself. Hallorad left no new Candidates, but bore away Inadan, Thadaniach, Gaen, and Dirthir—the last four who'd shared the now-echoing Long Chamber with Vieliessar.

Her Service Year was over, and she had not been Called.

In the refectory everyone ate together, the servants at one end of the chamber and Hamphuliadiel Astromancer at the other. The meals were plain, simple, and unvarying: tea and boiled grain for breakfast; tea and vegetable soup at midday; tea, bread and cheese, and soup at eventide. Though there might be as many as a hundred of them in the Sanctuary at one time, the Candidates were not the largest group at any meal. The Postulants outnumbered them by half again, for one might be a Postulant for ten years, or twenty, before taking the Green Robe. Each year ten or fifteen—rarely more—increased their numbers. Each year a handful of the Postulants dared the Shrine and departed the Sanctuary.

Caerthalien had arrived on the same day as Oronviel and Aramenthiali, so she did not know which of the dozen Candidates that had arrived that day were Caerthalien's. Berthon and Athrothir had left with the party, but that evening, when she had come to the refectory, she saw Thurion wearing the green tabard of a Postulant, seated among those others who had been Twice Culled. He'd smiled when he'd seen her, and Vieliessar had been surprised at the happiness she felt at the sight of him in Postulant's garb. It was not that they were friends, since she had kept herself apart during the past year. But in an odd way she could not put a name to, Thurion's Postulancy was a triumph in which she could share.

This night, for the first time since she'd come to the Sanctuary, she had no true place: not servant, not Candidate, not Postulant. Having been given no other direction, she seated herself once more among the Candidates. At least she was neither the oldest nor the youngest among them: she'd turned thirteen last Rade Moon, and the youngest this year were barely ten; twin girls who had come on the same day Berthon and Athrothir had left. The eldest of the new Candidates was Iardalaith. He was sixteen, and though Vieliessar did not know quite when he'd arrived, she had heard that he had already been in training to become a knight when he was sent here.

What shall become of me now? she thought forlornly. With the departure of the last of the failed Candidates, she was certain that she would at last be sent to the Sanctuary's servants' quarters to begin her imprisonment in truth. *Weeping over spilled tea does not bring fresh,* she thought. It was one of Maeredhiel's favorite sayings, deployed whenever she thought one of them was spending too much time in self-recrimination and not enough in fixing the problem.

When the meal was over, Vieliessar stood uncertainly beside the table. Those Candidates—*this year's Candidates,* she mentally amended—who didn't have evening tasks were already shuffling out of the refectory, drooping with a weariness she well remembered. She'd nearly made up her mind to return to the Long Chamber—perhaps she was to have it all to herself for the Wheel to come—when Maeredhiel strode over to her.

"If you like the refectory so well you linger here, I'm sure a task may be found for you in the kitchens. If not, then come," the Mistress of Servants said briskly, before turning away.

Vieliessar followed, confused, as Maeredhiel led her toward the Postulants' sleeping rooms. Was Maeredhiel taking her back to the Candidates' dormitory?

But as they passed along the corridor, Maeredhiel stopped and slid a door into the wall, revealing the spare—but private—sleeping cell of a Postulant: bed, chest, standing brazier, and low wooden stool. The shutters across the window were closed and barred, but the room was still chill. The basket of possessions that Vieliessar had carried to the Long Chamber sennights earlier was set upon the bed.

Vieliessar stood in the doorway, not knowing what was expected of her, as Maeredhiel crossed the room to stand in front of the brazier. The Mistress of Servants stared at it fixedly—and suddenly Vieliessar heard the crackle of kindling charcoal and smelled burning.

"You said you were no Mage!" she hissed accusingly.

"I said I had not enough Light in me to become one, but Fire is the first and easiest spell," Maeredhiel answered calmly. "Come in and close the door. I do not wish to heat the entire Sanctuary, and there is not enough charcoal here to do so, in any event."

More lost than before, Vieliessar did as she was told.

"You wonder why you have been given the quarters of a Postulant, when you have not been Twice-Called. True enough, you have not. But when Hertherilian was Astromancer here—do not cudgel your brain, girl, that was five hundred years gone, and no one ever remembers the names anyway—it was a thing not unknown for a Candidate to do two and three and four years of service as we awaited their kindling. I cannot bring to mind just now whose demands caused us to shorten the time, but what one House has, all must have; they are like quarreling weanlings with vast armies. It matters not. What matters is that there is precedent for delaying the decision about you. Yet I should prefer you away from the new Candidates, lest you give up all our secrets before they have a chance to discover them." The faint smile upon Maeredhiel's lips mocked her own words.

"You mean I . . . ?" Vieliessar wasn't sure whether to be relieved or horrified. A year ago she'd been certain she did not wish to become Lightborn. Now she realized she wasn't certain of anything at all.

"Impossible though it seems, you may yet be Called to the Light," Maeredhiel said dryly. "So you will sleep here rather than among the servants. Fear not that you will have candlemarks of idleness to bore you, for you will work harder now than you have before. There are many tasks of delicacy that we servants do not entrust to the Candidates, for I will tell you this plainly: each one of you made more work than you accomplished."

"We worked hard!" Vieliessar protested, stung by Maeredhiel's unfairness. *Most of us.*

"And so you did, child. But one in a hundred Candidates comes to us with servant's training. Some are the offspring of craftworkers or Farmholders, but most of you are Landbond, who barely know what it is to live within walls. It takes decade upon decade to train up a skilled servant."

"The Candidates were older once," Vieliessar said suddenly. She didn't know where the thought sprang from, but even the unflappable Maeredhiel looked surprised.

"Indeed they were, though that was much before my time," Maere-dhiel answered grudgingly. "The Archives say that once the Lightborn did not Call the Light, just watched and waited until the Light appeared of its own. But it is of no matter. The world is always changing, and has been since Celephriandullias-Tildorangelor fell." She stepped away from the brazier and took a step toward the door. "In the morning I shall see to it that you are properly dressed and then we will begin."

"Wait!" Vieliessar said, for Maeredhiel was obviously about to leave. "You said upon the day I arrived that I was the Child of the Prophecy. What prophecy? Why—"

"Now you see what ignorance pride breeds, for you might have had your answers long ago, had you been willing to listen," Maeredhiel said. "I am no Lightborn nor patient teacher, so do not seek them from me. I will tell you this: your answers are here, but you will not like them overmuch."

⊰⊱

The Mistress of Servants had spoken nothing other than the truth when she said Vieliessar would have much to learn, and though Vieliessar tried many times to get Maeredhiel to speak further of the Prophecy, she always received the same answer: if she had been willing to listen, she could have had answers moonturns ago. Before Flower had become Sword, she had stopped asking: Mistress Maeredhiel had spoken no less than the truth that night, for she had much to teach and was de-termined Vieliessar should learn.

To her surprise, she did not find the servant's garb she now wore to be a shameful burden, simply because no one seemed to care whether she went garbed in servant's grey or Lightborn green or Farcarinon vert and argent. The new Postulants—even Thurion—were far too busy to notice her. The Lightborn cared for little and saw less beyond their own work. The new Candidates barely saw anything beyond the ends of their noses, as she knew from experience.

Vieliessar saw more of Maeredhiel's truth as she came to understand that the tasks the Candidates performed were not even a tenth of the labor needed to keep the Sanctuary running smoothly. Worse, it seemed that each task bred a thousand more, all of which must be performed to exacting standards. Maeredhiel had said it took decades to train up a skilled Sanctuary servant. Vieliessar soon decided the Mistress of Servants had been optimistic: two decades, or six, or a dozen would not be time enough to learn all she must know to be a servant of the Sanctuary of the Star.

In her Service Year, the Candidates' work was confined to the kitchens, the laundry, the stables, and the guesthouse. Now Vieliessar's duties lay in all the places she had once been forbidden to enter. She began to learn the mysteries of the work rooms where medicines and spices and perfumes were compounded, to clean the delicate equipment after use, to restore each object to its proper place, to note which supplies were running low and must be restocked. She learned what materials each of the meditation rooms required and how to tell if they were running low. She learned which rooms she might enter when they were vacant, and which she must never enter at all. She learned to assist Hervilafimir Lightsister and Nithrithuin Lightsister in the hospital, to pack a travel-bag that contained all one of the Lightborn might need to set a spell or to increase a spell's effectiveness. She learned to serve tea with self-effacing silence and the beginnings of effortless grace when the princes and great ladies of the Fortunate Lands came to the Sanctuary on business.

She learned to navigate the maze of secret halls and stairs that were the Sanctuary's hidden face. By their means, a Sanctuary servant might vanish from sight on the ground floor of one wing and reappear on the top floor of the opposite wing without having been seen anywhere between.

And she learned that no matter what Hamphuliadiel Astromancer might eat in the refectory, in his private rooms he gorged on rich delicacies and often required a cordial afterward in order to settle his stomach.

Nor did her days become her own with the second bell rung at the end of the evening meal, for Maeredhiel ordered that the time between dinner and bed must be spent in the Servants' Hall. The servants welcomed her as one of their own and Vieliessar discovered, to her surprise, that they were as proud of their service as any Warlord Prince of their domain. At first she sat stiff and silent until Maeredhiel released her to her sleeping chamber, but as spring and summer slipped away, she began to find among the servants the friends she had not made among the Candidates of her Service Year.

It had taken her a long time to learn to sleep comfortably in the small austere room that was now hers—not because it lacked the luxuries she'd once taken for granted, perfumes and soft blankets and softer mattress—but because it was hers alone. In all her life, up until the moment Maeredhiel had walked out of the chamber, Vieliessar had never had a room entirely to herself. She grew to treasure those candlemarks when she didn't have to be what someone expected to see, and could simply *be*.

And though it wounded her pride sharply, Vieliessar admitted—if only within her heart—that her plans for revenge were better enacted by a woman than by a child. She would remain here for another year, or two, while Caerthalien forgot the very fact that she had ever existed.

"—and now it is Frost Moon, and it is one, two, three, four, five, six sennights to the middle of Snow Moon, and there will be dancing, and sweetcakes, and riddles—" Melwen singsonged, moving her round counter along the *narshir* board. She was one of the youngest of the Sanctuary servants—so Maeredhiel said—but Melwen could not number her years even if asked; she did not seek anything greater of her life than that each year should be like the last.

Vieliessar stifled a sigh. In six sennights it would be Midwinter, and she knew no one at the Sanctuary celebrated the festival days that marked the turns of the Great Wheel. Last year she had been too angry to care, but this year all she could think of was what she would miss. At Caerthalien, Midwinter meant a whole sennight of feasts, each more elaborate than the last, and the Lightborn seeking the Light in those old enough. As was Harvest Court, Midwinter was a sennight in which no feuds could be started or vengeance taken, and everyone in the castel mingled freely, as if they were equals, for it was the custom for the high-born to put off their finery and wear the simple clothes of servants, and for the servants to put off the livery badges which indicated to which household they belonged.

"—and fortunes, and farings, and songs," Maeredhiel said, finishing the sentence without looking up from the tablet upon which she was fig-uring accounts, for what was in their stores must last through the winter, and Hamphuliadiel Astromancer must know what tithe-goods to ask of the Hundred Houses in the spring. "But you must remember, Melwen—Vieliessar has not yet been with us for a full turn of the year."

"You've never seen Midwinter, Vielle?" Melwen asked, sounding horrified. "We celebrate it every year, because we give thanks for the Light that kindles and will bring us new Candidates in Storm and Rain and Flower!"

"And we give thanks for the chance to bring something out of the kitchens that is not the everlasting soup and porridge," Mistress Morgae-nel commented dryly. "If I did not get the chance to bake pies and roast venison once a year, I think I would go mad!"

Vieliessar had been surprised to discover that many of the Sanctuary servants were wed. Mistress Morgaenel and Master Duirilthel were re-sponsible for the kitchens, for overseeing the kitchen servants (a domes-tic meisne second in size only to Mastergardener Pandorgrad's own, but augmented by many of the Candidates) and for feeding the hundreds of souls who resided at the Sanctuary of the Star. The two of them bickered constantly over which was Master (or Mistress) Cook and which one was Master (or Mistress) of the whole of the Kitchens, and Vieliessar had lis-tened to them for an entire season before realizing the argument had been going on for centuries before her birth and would never be resolved until the two went before Queen Pelashia in the Vale of Celenthodiel to demand a judgment.

It had never occurred to her that Morgaenel Mistress Cook (or Mis-tress Kitchen, depending on who told the tale) would grow as tired of creating their bland fare as they did of eating it.

"And each Midwinter we pretend we do not see the Postulants sneak away to Rosemoss Farm, though some of them have done it for years," Hamonglachele added merrily. It was Mistress 'Chele's business to see that the guesthouse was kept in proper order, and she laughingly decried the shortcomings of all those who occupied it.

"As you know full well, for you encourage them to sneak into my store-houses for sweets and gifts—and allow them to hide them beneath your roof once they have," Duirilthel pointed out.

"Whose storehouses, dearest heart?" Morgaenel asked with mock sweetness. "I am the Mistress of Kitchens, so they are my stores, I say."

"And again I am heartbroken to tell you, sweetest love, that skilled as you are in your craft, you are Mistress Cook, merely," Duirilthel responded.

The familiar bickering began again, and Vieliessar reached for the dice cup and turned back to her game. But now she thought of the coming Midwinter with curiosity and wonder instead of despair.

⬥⧉⬥

Soon enough Pandorgrad covered the spell-lantern, just as he did every night to signal the end of the evening. The Servants' Hall was lit with Silverlight, but unless one were Lightborn, one could not simply kindle and snuff it at one's convenience, so rather than living day and night amid the spell's ghostly blue radiance, it was best to have it in a form one could shroud.

At that wordless signal, Vieliessar got to her feet. The others would seek their beds here in the servants' quarters, save for Radanding and his two ostlers, who slept at the stables. Only she must traverse the passages and staircases to her Postulant's cell on the second floor, the thing that marked her as belonging neither to one place or the other.

As she did nearly every night, Maeredhiel accompanied Vieliessar as she left the Servants' Hall. Vieliessar had long since learned that Maeredhiel slept little, and spent most candlemarks after lantern-darkening checking to see that all in her domain was as she would wish it. Usually they parted at the foot of the first staircase, but tonight, when they reached the antechamber to the Shrine, Maeredhiel stopped.

"A word with you, girl."

Vieliessar turned back, searching Maeredhiel's face for some sign of the other's wishes.

"The Candidates—as you have cause to know—are kept close. But in six sennights, we shall all pretend that those we serve—Postulants and Lightborn both—do not slip away after dark to revel at Rosemoss Farm, just as they have done each Midwinter since the Sanctuary stones were laid. It would be a simple thing for you to join them. I say to you: you are Lady Nataranweiya's child and War Prince Serenthon's heir. Do not think it is a thing unknown."

Maeredhiel spoke of them as if they still lived, as if Farcarinon was more than a name and a wilderness. "I am heir to nothing," Vieliessar answered, surprised by the grief she felt.

"Think that if you must. Do you think Athrothir and Berthon kept what they knew to themselves? Outside these walls, your life is anyone's to take. "

"What loss could that be to anyone but me?" Vieliessar demanded.

Maeredhiel smiled tightly. "Why, if Celelioniel did not hold it precious, she would never have saved it. Sleep well, Child of the Prophecy."

Maeredhiel turned and walked away. Vieliessar could have followed her, clutched at her sleeve, demanded answers. *Why do you call me that again and again? What does it mean? What do you mean?*

But she knew she would lose her dignity, not her ignorance. Maeredhiel would not give answers unless she chose.

And she does not choose! She merely seeks to torment me with hints and riddles!

⚏

At the Sanctuary, they did not celebrate Midwinter for an entire sennight, but Fourth Night was when the Light was Called, and on that night, there was a feast laid out in the Servants' Hall of delicacies that never had—and never would—grace the tables in the refectory. Roast pork, venison, and chicken; meat pies of mutton and dove; glazed fruits, spiced fruits, fruit pies and honey-cakes; cordials and a dozen kinds of cider and spiced creamy *xocalatl* (part of Domain Amrolion's tribute) hot enough in every sense to scorch the mouth.

Even those who spent little time in the Servants' Hall in the ordinary way of things were here tonight: all of Pandorgrad Mastergardener's people, all the kitchen staff, and every one of the ostlers and farriers and horse-tenders who inhabited Radanding Stablemaster's domain. The tables and chairs had been removed to make room for a long trestle table filled with food and drink and the Servants' Hall was noisy and crowded, filled with talk and laughter and the honest yellow light of candles and oil lanterns. Vieliessar ate until she was full to bursting, only to discover there was more to come.

A cheer went up as Morgaenel and Duirilthel entered with a tray so large it took both of them to carry it. Upon that tray was something large and round and white.

"The luck! The luck of the year!" Several of those present raised their cups in a toast.

"What is it?" Vieliessar asked in confusion, for the sweet-course had been upon the table for half the night.

"Ah, I had forgotten you would not know the custom," Maeredhiel said. "It is not kept in the castels, for it would not serve for any but the War Prince to receive the luck."

"What luck?" Vieliessar demanded, but Maeredhiel was already leading her to where a space had been cleared upon one of the tables for the cake.

"Who is the youngest here?" Duirilthel asked, waving a cutting knife. "Is it Celeth? Lelras? Nidos? No! I think it must be Vielle!" He swept her a flourishing bow and presented her with the knife.

"You must cut the cake now, and be sure everyone gets a piece," Maeredhiel said. "And save yourself one as well."

The cake was heavy, filled with fruits and honey and cased in a thick sugar icing, but at last everyone had been served and all that remained upon the tray was crumbs.

"I told you to save yourself some," Maeredhiel said, holding out a napkin-wrapped piece. Vieliessar could smell the spices as she lifted it to her lips. The morsel was only a bite or two, for the cake, though large, had needed to serve many—and Vielle popped it into her mouth unthinkingly. A moment later her teeth closed upon something hard. She made a noise of dismay and spat whatever it was into her hand.

On her palm rested a tiny silver disk with a rearing Unicorn stamped upon it.

"I told you the one who received the silver luck-charm in their portion would gain fortune in the coming year," Maeredhiel said. "And see? It is you."

Much fortune Farcarinon has gotten from the Unicorn thus far, Vieliessar thought sourly. *For it was the Unicorn Throne that destroyed us.*

But it was a pretty thing nonetheless, so she tucked it into the pocket of her skirt. Perhaps later she could find a way to braid it into her hair.

The rich food made her sleepy, and it was not very long before she took her leave, for tomorrow would again be a day of labor. But despite everything, the secret Festival seemed to promise that her strange new life need not be one of everlasting penance. As she walked to her sleeping chamber, she wondered how many of the doors around her concealed empty beds whose inhabitants kept revel at Rosemoss Farm.

Less than a mile from where I stand, and it might be at the far side of the Arzhana . . . But tonight, even thoughts of her demi-imprisonment failed to dampen her optimistic mood.

She opened the door to her sleeping chamber. It was winter-cold, especially in contrast to the warm hall she'd just left, and she shivered as she crossed to the brazier. She kept a small bowl of embers on her windowsill, for true fire was something not much used in the Sanctuary and she had little patience with flint and steel. But tonight, the embers husbanded from the previous night's coals had gone out.

The brazier full of unkindled charcoals seemed to mock her, and she unconsciously stretched her fingers out toward it in the gesture she had seen so many times from one of the Lightborn. Fire, Maeredhiel had often said, was the first and simplest spell . . .

What am I doing? Vieliessar withdrew her hand as quickly as if she'd been burned and turned to collect flint and steel. After a frustrating series of attempts, she managed to strike sparks to the bed of tinder beneath the coals, and the flames licked upward. Once warmth began to radiate through the room, she changed for bed.

As she sat brushing out and rebraiding her hair, she realized that it was nearly two years since she had come to the Sanctuary of the Star. She could no longer remember the last time she had seriously plotted to escape. She had learned more than she'd thought in her time here, and everything she learned told her that escape, while not impossible, was futile. Caerthalien warred with Aramethali, Aramethali with Cirandeiron, Cirandeiron with Telthorelandor . . . and all with Farcarinon. Fall into the hands of any of the Hundred Houses and she would become a pawn-prisoner at best, a corpse at worst.

It was a bitter knowing. She had not yet given up hope of revenge upon Caerthalien, but the day she might achieve it was farther away than ever.

⟢⟁⟣

Snow Moon gave way to Cold Moon and the Sanctuary returned to its normal rhythm. Cold became Ice, and everyone—even the Postulants—became unsettled with the anticipation of Rain Moon. The Candidates because the end of their Service Year would bring with it the knowledge of who was to stay and who was to go. The Postulants, for much the same reason, for soon those who were to leave the Sanctuary this year would be sent to keep Vigil in the Shrine. It was the time of year, Melwen said, when common sense was as rare as Unicorns, and anything might happen.

Soon enough, Vieliessar discovered Melwen had spoken no more than the truth, for she spent an entire morning cleaning up a disaster in one of the stillrooms. She had not been told what had happened, but every jar and beaker had shattered, and the resulting slurry of salts and oils and herbs stank vilely. She brought sand to soak up the mess on the floor, and swept it up. She was careful not to let any of it touch her, but by the time Godrahir Lightsister, Mistress Stillroom, came by to check on her progress, the stench had given Vieliessar such a headache that the Lightsister took one look at her and told her to stop working and go into the garden for air. She went without thinking, even though she had not set foot outside the Sanctuary itself in nearly two full turns of the Wheel.

The gate to the Sanctuary garden was a homely wooden thing. Beside its door, a peg board held cloaks that any might use—for none of those living here owned such an item. A tray below was piled with wooden clogs, to be placed over the Sanctuary's usual footgear: heavy wool socks soled with leather. Vieliessar took a cloak, slipped on a pair of clogs, and opened the door. As soon as she stepped away from the shelter of the wall, the wind began pulling at the cloak, forcing her to hold on to it. The air held the raw smells of earth and stone and Vieliessar shivered with the cold, though the sharp clear air eased her sick headache.

It was strange to be in the open air after so long a time indoors. She walked the path into the garden as cautiously as if she crossed a bridge made of swordblades. Maeredhiel had been careful to explain that the gardens were not truly protected by the Peace of the Sanctuary, and so if someone wished to ride all the way to the Sanctuary of the Star to slay the last of Farcarinon, they might do so in the garden without incurring more than the annoyance of the Lightborn. Vieliessar thought it unlikely that the Night Brotherhood—if that secret guild of assassins were anything more than a nursery tale used to frighten willful children—would seek her out, and if trouble came, she was no more than a few hundred steps from one of the many doors leading to refuge.

Once I dreamed of becoming a great warrior and riding all across the land with sword and bow. I promised myself Flower Forests to explore, stags to course, great hawks to fly at my leisure. Now my world is no wider than these garden walls.

The garden itself covered five hectares of land and was surrounded by a low stone wall. Within it stood trees usually found only in a Flower Forest, husbanded here by Magery: the namarii that gave its wood to Sanctuary spells, the uluskukad whose ghostly radiance lit the gardens at night, and in the center of the garden, an ancient Vilya, in full flower despite the season. The Vilya's fruiting governed the reigns of the Astromancers, for the ever-flowering Vilya fruited only once a century, and across the land, foresters kept watch over the Vilya in their care and vyed to be first to bring word of its fruiting to their lord

At the center of the garden Vieliessar stopped and turned in a slow circle, filling her eyes with all she saw. Beyond the wall lay the fields of Rosemoss Farm. In a fortnight or so, spring plowing would begin there, but for now, all there was to see was the greyed stubble of last year's harvesting. Beyond the fields stood Arevethmonion Flower Forest. All the way to the edge of the Flower Forest everything was grey and dun-gold. Only the forest itself was green, as Flower Forests always were.

To the left of the Sanctuary's main gate was the guesthouse and stables. They might as well be in the Vale of Celenthodiel for all that Vieliessar would ever go there. The low stone wall was the boundary of her world. And so it would be until the end of her days, unless she fled into a life where death was her constant companion.

A year ago she'd raged against her confinement. This year she'd thought herself growing content with something that would—somehow, someday—end. Now she knew that contentment for a false calm—for to be locked away galled her spirit as much as if she wore a red-hot crown of barbed iron. The Silver Hooves punished cowardice. Queen Pelashia turned her face from those forsworn. Vieliessar had sworn to avenge Farcarinon, and she could not yet say if she was a coward or an oathbreaker, but she feared she was. How could she do what she had sworn? And how could she face the long centuries ahead of her if she let the name of Farcarinon vanish into the shadows?

"I thought I'd be the only one out here on a day like this."

She repressed a cry of alarm at the sound of the voice behind her, for she knew it. She turned as Thurion emerged from the stand of namarii.

Like her, he wore a borrowed cloak and clogs. His hair—uncut for two turnings of the Wheel—curled against his neck and around his ears. It would not be cut again until he dared the Shrine.

"Godrahir Lightsister sent me to walk in the garden," she said briefly.

"Then I shall be glad of the company," Thurion said easily, coming toward her. "Rondithiel Lightbrother told me he could as easily teach a pig the mysteries of the Light as me, and sent me to take exercise.

"You are solemn," Thurion added, as if he heard what she did not say.

"For what cause should I be joyful?" Vieliessar snapped, anger suddenly winning out over prudence. "I whose birth holds me prisoner within these walls!"

Thurion gazed at her as if he was seeing her for the first time, and she wished she could call back her rash words. "Do you find it such a hardship?" he asked softly.

"You will leave here someday and go back to your home," she said. "I—"

To her surprise, Thurion laughed bitterly. "My home! Do you not know what I am?"

"A Postulant," she answered, puzzled. "Someday to be Lightborn."

"I am Landbond, son of Landbonds," he said. "When I return to Caerthalien, I will not go home. It is not the will of Bolecthindial Caerthalien that the Light should shine upon the Landbond. I will go wherever he says I must go, to serve who he says I must serve. Rondithiel Lightbrother tells me my person is sovereign and my life is my own. And he lies. The family I dare not claim and may never again see is held hostage for my obedience."

"I . . . I had not thought," she said slowly. She knew there was always resentment of the Landbonds among the Candidates, for they must be taught to read and write when they came to the Sanctuary, and so their service was less than that of those who already possessed those skills.

"Prisoner, hostage, I care not if you are Farcarinon, or Caerthalien, or the Child of the Prophecy. My family does not even own the roof above our heads. A third of what we harvest each year goes to pay Menenel

Farmholder for our shelter and our seed grain. All we have ever asked is that the great lords do not ride across our fields and spoil our work—and if they do, or even fight across them, there is nothing we can say without punishment. Do you think the quarrels of the Hundred Houses matter to me? How has your life been harder than mine?" Thurion demanded.

Vieliessar gazed at Thurion as if he was something she had never seen before. Landbonds served the Farmfolk and the Farmfolk served the Lords *Komen*: all knew that. She'd known Thurion was Landbond, but she had never thought about what that *meant*.

"Don't you wish to be Lightborn?" she asked at last. Thurion smiled.

"I could never be happy as anything else," he answered with quiet sincerity. "It is . . . It is as if I had lived all my life in a small dark room, hearing voices beyond the locked door. And then one day the door was opened, and I walked out into . . . this," he said, gesturing at the garden around them. "You must think I am very foolish," he finished, smiling gently.

"No," she answered. "You talk about things I don't understand, but that's different. Last year—when the Postulants would talk to us about the Light, do you remember?—none of us could understand what they wished to tell us of. And now you can."

Thurion smiled at her again and this time his smile was radiant. She realized, with an unsettled pang of discovery, that Thurion saw . . . Not Varuthir, whose name and existence had been a lie. Not Farcarinon's powerless heir, despised for merely existing. But Vieliessar. Just . . . Vieliessar.

"I cannot change your birth, or mine," he said quietly. "Nor can I set aside the fate placed upon you when you first drew breath. But you are wrong if you think this—" He swept a hand outward, indicating the garden, and the wind blew his cloak back off his shoulders with a snap. "—is the only world. Come with me, Vielle, and I'll show you."

It was the first time he'd called her by the eke-name that Melwen and the other Sanctuary servants sometimes used. It was the way a given name might be shortened by a lover, a child, a parent. Would Nataranweiya have used it, if she and Serenthon had lived and Farcarinon yet stood? Even to wonder was a painful thing.

"Come," Thurion said again. "I will show you a world wider than all the Fortunate Lands."

She followed him back inside the Sanctuary, grateful to pass out of the chill. Thurion led her to a passageway as narrow as any of the hidden ways within the walls, and suddenly Vieliessar could hear Maeredhiel's voice, clear in the ears of memory: *This side passage leads down to the stairs to the Library. Perhaps someday you will see what lies within it.*

The staircase was as narrow as the passage, and it went down a long way—two floors, or perhaps three. Niches in the stone walls held lanterns that glowed with Silverlight.

"Anyone—anyone who is not in their Service Year—may come here," Thurion said. He paused, as if he were listening to his words. "I mean . . . anyone of the Sanctuary. Even the servants. Lightborn from Graythunder Glairyrill to Great Ocean return here to study."

Vieliessar let his remark pass without comment. She knew Thurion hadn't meant to remind her that she was nothing more than one of the Sanctuary servants. To be a servant at the Sanctuary of the Star was to be placed above warlords and princes—so Morgaenel Mistress Kitchen-Cook always said.

At the bottom of the staircase was a latticework door, gleaming golden in the dimness. It was ornate enough, Vieliessar decided, but hardly very grand. In Bolecthindial's castel the outer doors to the Great Hall were as high as three tall men, their opening wide enough that three *komen* in full war panoply could ride through them side by side. The images on their Mage-forged door panels told the story of Caerthalien's great triumphs, and though they were cast of solid bronze, they were so perfectly balanced that the youngest servant could open and close them with a touch. This was merely an ancient door of cracked, painted wood, no larger than the door to her sleeping cell.

"This is the Library of Arevethmonion," Thurion said. His voice was hushed, but his tone was as proud as if he were its master and ruler.

"It is named for the Flower Forest?" Vieliessar asked.

"Or she is named for this," Thurion said, and tugged open the door to the Library.

When Vieliessar followed Thurion through the doorway, her nose was suddenly filled with the sweet scents of vellum and leather. Silver-light filled the chamber with a moon-pale radiance brighter than any full moon. The door was small, but the space beyond was as high as the stair had been long, and larger from back to front and side to side than Bolecthindial's Great Hall—larger, perhaps, than the Sanctuary itself. Every wall she could see was filled with square storage niches, and each niche was filled with scrolls. A gallery halfway up the wall seemed to go all the way around the room, to give access to the niches higher on the walls.

Nor was this place unoccupied.

I had wondered where the Lightborn and the Postulants vanished to all the day, and now I know. . . .

The center of the chamber was filled with long tables—and because she had spent candlemark upon candlemark tending to the Sanctuary's furnishings, she wondered who cared for all of this, for no one in the Servants' Hall had mentioned the library as part of their duties. Several of the tables were covered with stacked scrolls, opened scrolls, and even maps, over which green-robed Lightborn and grey-robed Postulants bent in study.

"I . . . didn't know . . ." she whispered.

"This is only the main room," Thurion said, turning back and coming to her side. "The others—"

"So many scrolls," Vieliessar interrupted. "It would be a life's work to read them all!"

"Praise to Sword and to Star we Postulants do not have to," Thurion answered, his voice low and amused. "It is a great enough task merely to learn the catalogue which tells us where they are."

He stepped away from the doorway again, and this time Vieliessar followed him.

※

Any text brought to the Sanctuary and deemed by Cirthoriach Light-sister to be of worth or interest is shelved here. There are poems, storysongs, travelers' accounts . . . even histories that the Hundred Houses would not wish preserved, for the tales they hold are not, I am told, the tales sung at feast days," Thurion said dryly, as the two of them walked along the right-hand wall.

Vieliessar's eyes were stretched wide at all she saw—and even more at what she imagined. A hundred of these scroll niches would have held every scroll in Caerthalien's library. And there were hundreds, and hundreds, and hundreds more. All filled.

"There is a workroom beyond this to repair damaged scrolls," Thurion said. "The spell of Keeping ensures nothing decays or fades, but it won't prevent damage, or staining—or keep the Lightborn from making notes on the edges of the text," Thurion said, the laughter in his eyes inviting Vieliessar to share the joke. "There is a chamber beyond the workroom which holds texts on spellcraft, locked away lest we be tempted to take a short road to our understanding of the Light. It would not work, in any case—and would certainly do great harm."

"I don't understand," Vieliessar said. "If they are but scrolls . . . How can one be hurt reading a scroll?"

Thurion came to a stop, frowning with the effort of trying to explain. "It is . . . as if you or I were given all the articles of knighthood—sword and spear, armor and shield, spurs and destrier—and sent into battle against one who had earned them all through years of honest training. We would die."

"I would not go into battle unless I were sure I could win," Vieliessar said firmly.

"But you would think you could," Thurion said. "Because of the—"

"I would not," she retorted. "You make it sound as if the Postulants are fools. If a thing is a task beyond one's strength, one should not attempt it."

Thurion made a helpless gesture. "To . . ." He shook his head. "It is a temptation."

"Those who are so easily tempted are better off without Magery," Vieliessar said decisively. "But—are you not here to learn spells?" she added.

"There are no spells when one becomes one with the Light," Thurion said.

Vieliessar nearly stamped her foot in exasperation. Not a handful of moments before, Thurion had spoke of a spell set to preserve the scrolls. "There are either spells or there are not," she said tartly. "You said—"

"There are. There aren't. It's . . . one must learn to *listen* first."

"To what?" Vieliessar demanded, and Thurion simply looked frustrated.

"To the world," he said.

His words made no sense, though she'd become used to the idea that nothing the Postulants said when they talked about the Light ever did. "How long does it take to learn this . . . listening?" she asked instead.

"All your life," Thurion answered. His face softened, and it was as if he gazed upon something beautiful she knew she would never see.

She did not know how long they spent wandering through this other Arevethmonion, as Thurion showed her its treasures with the joy and pride of a War Prince showing his Great Keep to his bride. He plucked scrolls from their niches, saying she must read this one or that. For the first time since she had come to the Sanctuary, her duties and obligations—even the injuries done to her Line—were forgotten. There was a set of scrolls containing a history of the Hundred Houses, one which was a copy of only the *major* songs of *The Song of Amrethion*, a scroll on games (*xaique* and *gan* and *narshir*), and the three scrolls of *Halbaureth's Journey*, which Thurion said was about Halbaureth of Alilianne—as House Ullilion was once called—who had traveled farther east from the shores of Great Ocean than anyone had ventured since, crossing Graythunder Glairyrill itself. "If you never leave these walls, still, you will travel farther in Halbaureth's company than anyone of the Hundred Houses can ever boast of," Thurion said.

She was only recalled to herself when her arms were so filled with leather-cased scrolls that she had to devote most of her attention to keeping them from spilling out of her grasp and onto the floor. *When shall I have time to read all these?* she thought in bemusement.

⊲⊟⊳

That evening Vieliessar went to her chamber immediately after evening meal and read long into the night. She'd chosen the *History of the Hundred Houses,* and knew already it would be more than the work of a sennight or even a moonturn to understand it all. It was true that each history was simple enough: founding and lands and alliances made, the names of the heads of the Line Direct, summaries of battles fought and children born. But each account contradicted the next, and the one she knew best—the History of Caerthalien—held both more and less than she'd expected it to. It was only the knowledge that morning would come and be filled with tasks that caused her to hood her spell-lantern and prepare herself reluctantly for sleep.

But sleep was long in coming. *It is like a child's wooden puzzle,* she thought. *Only with tales of past times. Which is true? Any of them?* She wondered if there was enough time in all the world to list the contradictions between the stories and to seek a pattern.

In the middle of the night she awoke sharply, as if summoned to battle. Words she had set aside in her shock at Thurion's anger—then forgot entirely at the wonders he showed her—echoed through her mind.

"Prisoner, hostage, I care not if you are Farcarinon, or Caerthalien, or the Child of the Prophecy."

Thurion had the answers Maeredhiel had said were here.

CHAPTER THREE

THE SONG OF AMRETHION

When stars and clouds together point the way
And of a hundred deer one doe can no longer counted be
When peace is bought with maiden mother's blood
And those so long denied assert their ancient claim
When scholar turns to sword, and warrior to peace
And two ford rivers swelled with mortal gore
When two are one, then one may speak for all
And in that candlemark claim what never has been lost.

—*The Song of Amrethion Aradruiniel*

Vieliessar had avoided the Common Room in her Service Year out of anger and false pride, and in the year that followed both out of uncertainty as to her place and by Maeredhiel's design. Tonight she dared it, for there was no other way to find Thurion to question him.

She hesitated long in the refectory after the evening meal was done, for to enter the Common Room, filled as it would be by Postulants and Candidates, would be to expose herself to . . . what?

She wasn't sure. She was half a servant and half a Candidate, and the War Prince of no House, and that was a thing that unsettled her thoughts every time she considered it, for in all the Fortunate Lands, to be born was to know one's entire future. Only the Light could change that, though not entirely. For all their power, the Green Robes still served.

But whatever you are, you are no coward, she told herself fiercely. Ignoring the questioning looks of the Candidates clearing the tables, she shook out her skirts and walked to the Common Room.

Hearing laughter and talk as she approached the doorway, she nearly turned aside to seek the silence and solitude of her rooms. But then she heard Thurion's voice, and pride and stubbornness drove her across the threshold. She spied Thurion at a table with many whom she recognized: some of them had shared her Service Year, but most had not.

Namritila and Borinuel were of her Service Year; Borinuel had come from Calwas with Anginach and both had become Postulants. Borinuel had once said Anginach's strategy for success was to make sure everyone else failed; all Vieliessar knew of Anginach was that he'd spent his Service Year seeing how much he could shirk his duties before he drew Maeredhiel's wrath. Mathingaland had been a Candidate in the year before hers; he liked to talk a great deal, making long speeches as if he instructed children, but his careful marshaling of facts and details others skipped over enabled Vieliessar to follow the conversation, no matter the topic. Arahir came from so far to the east that her House spent its time battling the Beastlings instead of the rest of the Hundred Houses. She wore a gryphon feather around her neck, for she had killed one years before she had come to the Sanctuary, and had been allowed to keep that trophy despite jewels and ornaments being banished. Brithuniel fretted constantly about the coming day when she must cut her long braids to take the Green Robe. Monrhedel was one of the few whose House she knew—he was more interested in history than in magic, but returning to Jirvaleg as one of the Lightborn would allow him to ask War Prince Edheluin to free his parents from their forced oaths of fealty so they could return to House Onegring's lands and the children they had left behind there.

"Vielle!" Thurion's face and voice held nothing but honest pleasure in seeing her. "Come! Sit! We are arguing—as usual—but it is no great matter."

Hesitantly she crossed the room and took the seat she provided for her.

"Oh, who counts deer anyway?" Namritila said crossly, clearly continuing the previous conversation.

"Amrethion Aradruiniel, clearly," Borinuel answered. "Or he wishes us to."

"That is a thing not yet established," Mathingaland said, clearly as unwilling as the others to set aside the argument. "*When stars and clouds together point the way, And of a hundred deer one doe can no longer counted be'*—"

"Clear as a murky river," Arahir interrupted in disgust. She seemed to notice Vieliessar for the first time. "But this must bore you," she said.

"Perhaps it would—had I the least notion of what you were discussing," Vieliessar said dryly.

She would not ask Thurion about the Child of the Prophecy in front of the others, and to take him aside would only draw more attention to her presence. But as it developed, she had no need to.

"You are fortunate not to be a Postulant," Thurion said, a faint note of self-mockery in his protest. "They keep us reading from morning to night, and we must memorize it all. It is from *The Song of Amrethion Aradruiniel*. You must know it."

She nodded slowly. Parts of it had been performed at the great feasts held in Caerthalien. "It's long," she said.

"Longer than you know," Thurion said ruefully. "Some say Amrethion Aradruiniel wrote the *Song* himself, having foreknowledge of his doom, others say it was written by members of his court in the first days of their exile. Still others say it's not one *Song*, but many, all stitched together into an uneasy patchwork. Everyone knows *The Song of Amrethion's Rade* and *The Song of Pelashia's Gift*, but there are scrolls and scrolls of it here, and the last part, after *The Song of the Doom of Celephriandullias-Tildorangelor*, is just a long jumble of meaningless poetry. It's supposed to be a prophecy that someday there will be a new High King upon the Unicorn Throne, and there's a Child of the Prophecy whose birth will herald the fall of the High Houses."

So Maeredhiel named me. Vieliessar was torn between relief and disappointment: naming her "Child of the Prophecy" seemed to be nothing more than an obscure joke of Maeredhiel's, especially if the Child of the Prophecy was supposed to destroy *all* the High Houses. (Her own ambition was no more grand than the slaughter of all the Caerthalien Line Direct.) But surely Celelioniel Astromancer had believed it. She had set Peacebond upon Vieliessar at the moment of her birth because of that belief. But Vieliessar had been at the Sanctuary long enough to hear somewhat of its previous Astromancer. Celelioniel had drifted into madness in the last decades of her reign.

"It seems unlikely," she said.

"I know," Thurion said quietly. "Most of my teachers think the last part of Amrethion's Song is nonsense, or some code we have lost the key to. But we have to memorize it anyway. I never thought I would be tired of scrolls and of reading—but that was before I spent so many candlemarks in the Library."

"But come! Share our pain," Namritila said. "You are High House raised, you will have heard parts of *The Song of Amrethion Aradruiniel* all your life! Yet what are we to make of—oh, go on, Thurion, your voice is better than mine. Give her the verse about the Throne!"

Thurion smiled and nodded. "Here's one I warrant you haven't heard, Vielle:

> *"For twice upon five hundred lives, the Throne of Shame shall sleep*
> *   unknown*
> *And Celephriandullias-Tildorangelor a haunt of shadows lie*
> *The Happy Lands shall ring to blood and battle through the wheel of*
> *   years*
> *While all who husband hidden secrets die . . ."*

"But Celephriandullias-Tildorangelor is a nursery song!" Vieliessar said in protest. "You know it, I'm sure: 'The city of Celephriandullias-Tildorangelor was as bright as jewels. White were its walls and sun-gold-gleaming were its roofs, and its ruler was Amrethion Aradruiniel, and his meisne was a hundred knights. The first was Prince Cirandeiron, who rode a white horse and had armor of gleaming silver. His destrier's armor was silver, too, and there were diamonds set in his shoes. The second was Queen Telthorelandor, who rode a golden horse and had armor of brightest gold. Her destrier's armor was golden, too, and he was shod in cairngorms and purest gold. The third'—"

"Yes, yes, yes—it goes on forever!" Arahir protested laughingly. "A hundred knights for the Hundred Houses, each more beautiful than the last. I wish we studied that instead of Amrethion's Song—I'm sure it makes as much sense!"

⊰⊱

But alone in her rooms at the end of the evening, Vieliessar was unable to dismiss the *hradan* Maeredhiel had laid upon her so easily. There must be more to her words—to Celelioniel's belief—than an esoteric joke, and Vieliessar became determined to discover what it was. But it was far more difficult than she hoped. To find a copy of the text was easy enough. But *The Song of Amrethion Aradruiniel* filled twenty close-written scrolls, and there were tenfold more written *about* it. After that night, the nine of them would often gather in the Common Room at the end of the day. Vieliessar had been doubtful of her welcome at first—she was no Postulant, to understand their talk of magic—but Thurion's friends seemed as interested in her tales of keeping the stillroom ready for use as she was in their tales of using it, and she was never made to feel less than they by the things they found to talk of.

Not all the Postulants were so welcoming. Many, seeing her in the Common Room in the grey tunic and skirts of a servant, spoke ostentatiously of their studies in magic. Vieliessar quickly realized Thurion's circle was made up of those who did not care.

"'Stars and clouds point the way . . .'" Thurion mused one evening, turning his teacup around between his palms and frowning down at it as if the fragrant amber liquid were a scrying pool. "I am not sure what that phrase can mean. That the stars show the time, and the season, and even hold Foretellings for those skilled to read them is something everyone knows. And of course omens may be taken from the sky and the weather—providing the weather has not been caused by a Mage bringing rain or warmth out of season!" he added, smiling.

"I still say it is a copyist's error, and that it should read: 'when stars *or* clouds point the way,'" Mathingaland said determinedly.

"But then they wouldn't be pointing *together*," Thurion argued. "And without those syllables, the stanza doesn't scan," he added.

"It's madness to look for sense in *Amrethion's Curse*," Namritila said. "I do not think it is a part of the Song in the first place. It must be a satire, like *Manurion's Ride*, or, or, or *The Wedding of Inglodoth!*" she finished triumphantly.

"If it were a satire, 'Tila, we would surely know that much, even if we had lost the meaning. It takes the same form as all the prophecies set into *The Book of Celenthodiel*. It just doesn't make any sense! Consider: 'When scholar turns to sword, and warrior to peace,'" Arahir said. "Everyone knows that *komentai* become scholars, not the other way around. And does a warrior turning to peace speak of the *komentai'a* or of something else? Even scholars will fight when they or their House are in danger, anyway, so how can one say they *ever* turn to peace?"

"Of course, the opening section should be: 'When scholar turns *from* sword, and warrior to peace,'" Mathingaland announced firmly. "The rest of the line is a riddle for philosophers, not for Mages. If any of us could answer those questions, then we could solve Aradruiniel's Prophecy, lift the Curse, and restore the Unicorn Throne."

Arguing about the meaning of songs or poems was a time-honored way to pass an evening, and the young Postulants were entirely willing to make *The Song of Amrethion Aradruiniel* their text, even without the excuse of explaining it to Vieliessar. Unfortunately, none of their arguments had yet produced any answers. They had argued the opening lines since Midwinter, and would probably still be arguing them come Midsummer.

But soon it was Storm Moon, and Vieliessar was no longer able to spend pleasant evenings with Thurion's friends, for this was the servants' busiest time. The Sanctuary did not run on the same calendar as a Great Keep did: there, the inventories of blankets and linens were taken twice a year, when winter things were changed for summer. Here, the inventory was done once a year, just before the Candidate Caravans arrived. And so she set the matter of Amrethion's Song aside, for she doubted Thurion and his friends could spin truth from riddles where generations before them had not. To them it was a pleasant pastime, a game of scholarship. And almost—almost!—she agreed, and yet . . .

Celelioniel had believed—so deeply she had set her will against the War Princes of the Hundred Houses to preserve Vieliessar's life.

And Vieliessar did not know why.

Yet.

⚓

The first Candidates did not arrive until Flower, then made up for their delay with a vengeance. This meant long days for everyone— and overcrowding, chaos, and tents pitched across the fields of Rosemoss Farm as if the Sanctuary were under siege. It would have been child's play for Vieliessar to vanish into the crowds of people coming and going, and for the first time in many moonturns she revisited her dreams of escape. But she had been fourteen last Rade: old enough to know no Free Company would follow one still a child. In Arevethmonion she had seen texts on battle, on strategy, on arms. She could not train herself in the skills of a knight, but she could learn about them against the day she could order knights against Caerthalien.

I shall go next spring. Next spring.

She did not have many free moments to consider her plight, for in addition to an influx of new Candidates, this was the season when those princes from beyond the Mystrals made their luck-sacrifices to petition for good fortune in the coming War Season. Only the High Houses in the West might dally and make their visitations in Sword itself—and so from Storm to Sword, the stones of the Shrine ran red with blood.

For those sennights, Vieliessar's dreams were so unsettled that it was as if she did not sleep at all. So whether she tossed and turned, or simply read the candlemarks of night away from her store of Arevethmonion's scrolls, the result was the same.

And her work suffered for it.

I said namanar incense, not berroles!" Priagor Lightsister snapped. With a furious gesture, she struck the *shin'zuruf* box from Vieliessar's hands. The translucent bone-clay—more delicate and beautiful than the finest glass—shattered into a thousand shards as it struck the floor, and the meditation chamber was filled with the musky scent of powdered berroles resin.

"I am sorry, Lightsister, I thought—"

"Witless drudge!" Priagor snapped. "Do not think! Bring namanar to Kalyes-chamber at once!" With an angry toss of her head, the Lightsister swept from the room.

She asked for berroles, not namanar, Vieliessar thought mutinously. Berroles was the usual incense for meditation: namanar was powerful, its fumes bringing visions of distant times and places. *Or did I just assume?* she wondered, as she hurried in the direction of Maeredhiel's workroom, for the namanar was kept under lock and key. It hardly mattered. The truth was what a Lightborn said it was.

Here in the Sanctuary only, she consoled herself. *In the Great Hall, truth is beneath the tongues of the princes.*

"I must have namanar incense," Vieliessar said, breathless with haste. "Priagor Lightsister commands."

The wall behind Maeredhiel's worktable contained hundreds of keys hanging on hooks: some, long untouched and black with age, hanging near the ceiling; others, bright with frequent handling, within easier reach.

Vieliessar had never seen a key before she had come to the Sanctuary—in Caerthalien's Great Keep, doors were barred, or spell-sealed by Mages— but (as Maeredhiel had noted tartly) one could neither expect the many poisons used in the stillroom to lock themselves in, nor would the Light- born wish to be dragged from their studies a hundred times a day to lock or unlock a door or cabinet.

"T't," Maeredhiel said. "That one holds herself as if Ullilion were one of the High Houses, instead of Cirandeiron's hound. Where is the box—or am I simply to give her the whole jar?"

"I—" Vieliessar said, and stopped, overcome by humiliation. She should have gone first to the store room to get an incense-box before com- ing to collect the namanar.

"You are not usually so careless," Maeredhiel observed. "Must I send you to Mistress Healer?"

Vieliessar shook her head, unwilling to admit to sennights of wake- fulness and broken sleep.

"T't," Maeredhiel said again, and took a small silver incense box from a drawer before reaching unerringly to the wall behind her to pluck down a silver key. Only Maeredhiel knew what key fit which lock—if she went to walk in Celenthodiel tomorrow, someone would need to spend days casting Knowing to recover her lost knowledge. She got to her feet and opened a cabinet that contained rows of featureless stone jars. Grunting a little with the effort, she carried one to her worktable and removed the lid. The acrid scent of powdered namanar-wood filled the room, and despite herself, Vieliessar wrinkled her nose. With a swift efficient gesture, Maeredhiel dipped the silver box into the jar, tapped it once against the lip to shake free the excess, then closed the box and set it on the table.

As she was about to hand it to Vieliessar, she stopped. "You have been asking the Postulants to unriddle the Prophecy for you," she said. Vielies- sar couldn't tell from her tone whether it was an accusation or not. "Come back when you have finished doing Ullilion's bidding," she said, and Vieliessar nodded.

⊰⧉⊱

Vieliessar hurried back the way she'd come. There was nothing—not even a painted symbol—to distinguish Kalyes-chamber from Lovine-chamber, but learning the name of every room within the Sanctuary of the Star had been a task of her Service Year. She tapped lightly, then opened the door. Priagor Lightsister was already seated upon one of the floor cushions, and Vieliessar could see the heat-shimmer from the coals in the firebowl upon the low table before her. She regarded Vieliessar with narrow-eyed irritation as she set the silver box on the table.

"And see you clean up the mess you made," Priagor said.

Vieliessar said nothing. The Sanctuary's servants were supposed to be invisible, merely an extension of the will of the Lightborn. Priagor Lightsister turned away, and Vieliessar slipped noiselessly from the room. She allowed herself a moment of wry amusement as she sought the service cupboard where the cleaning supplies were kept. At least she had been raised in a Great Keep and seen many Lightborn before her Service Year: the Landbonds knew of the Lightborn mainly from storysongs, and were shocked to find they could be petty, or cruel, or greedy, or unreasonable. But in many ways, the Lightborn were no different than anyone else.

She quickly repaired the damage in Lovine-chamber, sweeping up the broken box and the spilled incense, then carefully wiping the floor with a wet cloth to make sure she'd removed every crumb and shard. She left the door open when she exited, to signify the chamber was not ready for use, and hurried back to Maeredhiel's workroom.

Maeredhediel was just closing the locked case again when Vieliessar entered the workroom. She opened her mouth to speak but Maeredhiel held up a hand for silence. Vieliessar waited, caught between impatience and apprehension, as Maeredhiel organized the scrolls on her worktable to her satisfaction. Then she looked up and said, "It is not a good thing for you to link yourself in the mind of any with Amrethion's Prophecy, lest you remind some of that which has never been well hidden."

"Surely what Celelioniel Astromancer did is no secret?" Vieliessar demanded.

"Perhaps not. Perhaps her madness excuses all, and the Hundred account the Peacebond as an ailing woman's fancy. Yet I do not think she was mad. And I knew her better than some."

"But—" Vieliessar stopped, and chose her next words with care. "It is said no one can unriddle Amrethion's Prophecy. Yet Celelioniel believed it was I whom Amrethion named."

"You have been somewhat in the company of the Postulants, and seen that learning becomes, for many among the Lightborn, as the Way of the Sword to the *komentai'a*."

Vieliessar nodded slowly.

"Celelioniel wished to know of the beginning of things, and sought her answers in the most ancient songs. Though her House is in the Grand Windsward, and the journey to the Shrine of the Star a thing not quickly compassed, she came many times to consult this scroll or that. It was small wonder that when the Vilya fruited at last, and her peers said she should rule the Sanctuary, she was filled with joy, for it meant a century of study, far from the demands of Moruilaith Enerchelimier."

Maeredhiel paused, looking as if she was not certain she wished to say what she meant to say next.

"In the first year of Celelioniel's reign, Serenthon Farcarinon came to the Shrine. Woods Moon was late in the year for such a journey, but he was new-Bonded, and any *alfaljodthi* might seek a Foretelling then. I know not what happened within the Shrine, but after he went away again, Celelioniel's interest fixed upon *The Song of Amrethion*, and that interest soon became obsession. I think she may even have petitioned the Silver Hooves for understanding of it, but for many turns of the Wheel only those much in her company knew of her studies, and who is that save the servants of the Sanctuary? But a score of years gone, she began to speak of Amrethion's Curse as if it were something of which she had full knowing, and of the Child of the Prophecy as a *hradan* to come in her lifetime."

Vieliessar stood transfixed, hardly daring to breathe, for Maeredhiel had never spoken so openly.

"From the moment Farcarinon's allies turned upon Lord Serenthon, Celelioniel was like a soul demented. She swore that Serenthon's allies meant to make Farcarinon the 'doe' of Amrethion's Prophecy—and when Nataranweiya came to us that night, she would have done anything to avert your birth."

"And yet I live," Vieliessar said, when Maeredhiel fell silent.

"I know not why," Maeredhiel said bluntly. "Perhaps she feared to go against the will of Amrethion Aradruiniel. Perhaps she thought to keep you safe beneath her hand, and avert the evil day."

"Perhaps she realized she had been wrong all along," Vieliessar said boldly.

"Perhaps," Maeredhiel said heavily. "I know not. But I know this: Amrethion named the Child of the Prophecy the Doom of the Hundred Houses. It would be an ill thing for the War Princes to see you as that doom."

<hr />

For days Vieliessar brooded over Maeredhiel's words, and found no sense in them. For a while she avoided the Common Room entirely, until Thurion sought her out and said her friends missed her company. She did not wish to admit she missed them as well, but she allowed Thurion to coax her into returning. But when she did, she took care to feign disinterest in *The Song of Amrethion Aradruinel*.

She was not sure why.

From Sword to Frost life at the Sanctuary of the Star returned to its accustomed pace. Still caught between, Vieliessar spent her days in service and her nights in study, reading through the holdings of Arevethmonion. This year, word came of battles fought between the War Princes, and injured came to the Sanctuary.

The Long Peace was over at last.

⧓

Vieliessar twirled and swayed as she made her way to her sleeping cell, clutching the small silver Unicorn token in her hand—once again, she had taken the luck-token in the Midwinter cake. Around her ankles, her grey skirts furled and unfurled as she moved. She remembered the Midwinter dances at Caerthalien, intricate and elaborate. This year she had stayed at the feast until the very end, drinking all the pledges to health and luck that concluded it. Her head reeled with hot spiced ale, and she thought she would have danced—were there anyone here to dance with.

The doors to the Postulants' cells were tightly closed—they were either soundly sleeping or still drinking in the year at Rosemoss Farm—and it was with relief that Vieliessar reached her own room without meeting anyone. Now to bed, and pray that she did not wake in the morning with ale-sickness.

When she opened her door, her euphoric mood vanished, and she groaned in dismay. The inner shutters were open—the latch was unreliable, and often slipped—and she hadn't closed the storm shutters. Her sleeping chamber had been open to the winter air for candlemarks and was ice-cold.

Shivering, she went to the window and closed both inner and outer shutters. The dish of live coals had been blown from the windowsill and lay dead on the stone floor. It hardly mattered; coals took candlemarks to burn down to greatest heat; even if she lit them with her flint and steel, she would spend a long, cold night.

Ah, if only . . . She reached out toward the copper brazier, shivering, imagining welcome heat against the palm of her hand. In the next moment, the tinder kindled into flame with a bright flare and blue flames danced over the surface of the coals themselves. A wave of heat rose from the bowl, making the air shimmer. Vieliessar sprang backward as if she'd been burned. She stared at the thing which could not be.

The coals still glowed.

Fire is the first spell and the easiest. All the Postulants say so. Anginach Called it while he was still a Candidate. . . .

Though the room was warming quickly, Vieliessar felt an inward chill. She was Lightborn.

And all she could think of was Maeredhiel's warning. *"Think long and hard, Vieliessar of Farcarinon, before showing the Light even if you possess it, for a Mage may be called from the Sanctuary where a servant cannot be."*

She knew, Vieliessar thought. *She knew even then this day would come. Maeredhiel said Celelioniel wished to keep the "Child of the Prophecy" under her hand—the Sanctuary's hand. Because I am such a danger to the Hundred Houses. If only that were true!*

If she became Vieliessar Lightsister, she would have a greater power at her command than the dragons of the earth . . . and never be able to use it to claim her vengeance. Had Farcarinon yet stood, Vieliessar Lightsister could not have ruled over it. But Farcarinon had been erased, and her life would be forfeit should she leave the Sanctuary. *"A Mage may be called from the Sanctuary . . ."*

If Maeredhiel had known this day would come, she had given Vieliessar counsel on how she must meet it as well.

Tell no one.

Snow Moon became Cold Moon, then Ice, and Vieliessar began to dimly comprehend the world through which the Lightborn moved. Suddenly the currents of magic were as visible—or at least as *perceptible*—as the ripples on the surface of a lake. There were a thousand things she could compare it to, and none of them was the Light's true likeness. Vieliessar had listened uncomprehendingly to Thurion describe the process of spellsetting many times, but now it made sense: as a fish moved through water, the *alfaljodthi* moved through power. The Lightborn could see what others could not: the webs and currents of that power. And seeing it, could draw upon it, shape it, *transform* it.

For almost a full turn of the Wheel she fought to step back into the skin of one Lightless. It was a battle she was doomed to lose, for the Light Within demanded to be used, just as limbs and senses did.

And yet, if she wished to keep her secret, she could ask for neither help nor training.

But that did not mean she could not practice. Knowing what to do was simple: the Postulants all spoke freely of the training exercises. She must learn to trust the Light above her physical senses. And Calling Fire was simple enough.

But once a Postulant mastered Fire and Inward Sight, Silverlight was the next spell. It was a thing she dared not attempt within her sleeping chamber.

The meditation and practice chambers were heavily Warded against the mishaps of Candidates learning to wield the Light. One of her tasks was to clean and prepare the chambers for use. No one would notice if she spent a few more minutes on the task than it actually took. All she needed to do was wait until that duty fell to her once more in the natural way of things.

And a few days later, it did.

She hurried through her midday meal, for Cindil-chamber would be needed in the first candlemark after midday. Vieliessar had once thought the chambers unpleasantly stark. Now she could see the colors of the Wards which made the stone walls a tapestry of shifting opal and turned the polished wooden floor into a mosaic of amber and gold. Her servant's tasks occupied only a few minutes—to bring fresh incense of the proper kind, to fill the water jug, to make certain the chamber was clean and orderly—and then she was free to work undisturbed.

"You breathe the power in, then you imagine how you wish it to go. But it isn't really like that, because in a way you're actually remembering something you never saw. Oh, I can't explain it, Vielle—I can just do it!" Thurion's frustrated words echoed through her memory.

All that was required for Fire was to scoop up a scrap of the power that surrounded everyone and concentrate it for the instant needed to kindle something into flame. It was not so with the thousand other spells the Lightborn could command. Each one had a name, a shape, a presence, as if it were something one might hold in one's hand, like a *xaique* piece—and for each Lightborn, there was one spell that was theirs above all others to command: their Keystone Gift. That Gift shaped their training and their studies: a Keystone Gift was the strongest talent a Lightborn possessed, from which they might weave a new spell to add to the Sanctuary's store of Light. Spells could not be written down, nor could the knowing of them be spoken into the ear. The shapes of the Greater Spells could only be passed mind to mind, so that any Lightborn who wove and crafted a new spell must come to the Sanctuary to pass it to as many other Lightborn as possible. It was against Mosirinde's Covenant to keep a knowing restricted to the Lightborn of one's own House. Spellcraft must pass among the Lightborn as freely as wind across the land.

Lesser spells were bound into the stones of the practice chambers, so that the Postulants might See them and take them for their own. Vieliessar knew as well as any Postulant the order in which the spells must be learned, for there was a Teaching Song about it: *Fire and Sight and Silverlight, Find and Fetch and Send and Shield, Weather and Ward, Keep and Heal . . .*

She'd seen Silverlight cast all her life. She closed her eyes and held out her hands . . .

And Silverlight rushed into her mind as if she had opened a floodgate. Suddenly there was brightness behind her closed eyes, as if she held the moon between her open hands. With a startled cry, Vieliessar flung it away, only to see the spell-symbol in her mind become another equally familiar shape as the power did her bidding. She opened her eyes, and saw—in horror—that the bowl of the brazier was now shining with an all-too-familiar light.

No! Don't!

In vain, she tried to douse the glow. All she managed to do was make the metal glow even more brightly. Sadimerial Lightsister would soon arrive; Vieliessar's breath came hot and hard with fear. The Lightsister would see Silverlight cast on the brazier. . . .

Darkness! I want it to be dark! Vieliessar thought in blind panic. *Unmade! Untouched! As if I never—*

She felt *something* shift inside her mind, but before she could turn her inward eye to see it, a wave of cold sickness washed over her. She staggered backward, her hands covered with a sticky dust.

The brazier had gone dark.

But it had also turned to grey stone and was crumbling away.

If she had not been so terrified of discovery, horror and disbelief would have held Vieliessar frozen. What had been, moments before, a bright copper bowl on a bronze tripod was now . . . rock. Ore.

Unmade.

She was on her hands and knees, trying to scoop the pieces into her skirt, when she felt the now-familiar tingle of the presence of one of the Lightborn. She looked behind her apprehensively. For a long moment she held Sadimerial Lightsister's gaze.

"The work will go faster if you use a broom, girl," Sadimerial said at last. "And have a new brazier brought from storage. I had not known Filgoroth wished to challenge me again so soon."

Vieliessar fled, holding a skirt full of dust.

⊰≍⊱

Who Filgoroth was, and why he would challenge Sadimerial, and how, Vieliessar never found out. All she knew was that no one accused her of being Lightborn. She swore she would never again do anything so unsafe, but a few sennights later she was in Oiloisse-chamber. Oiloisse was utterly empty, for some practice had gone awry and its furniture had not yet been replaced. This time the Silverlight came easily—a moon-pale globe she could hold in her hands. She could feel the spellshape in her mind try to twist from simple conjuration to be-spelling an object, but there was nothing within the bounds of the Wards for it to fix on.

She still did not know how to unmake what she had made, but forcing it against the Wards worked well enough.

And time passed.

⚜

Each year, the hot breathless days of Thunder Moon brought a pause in the Sanctuary's unceasing labor, for the days were hot, and many in the Sanctuary—save those Candidates who had incurred Maeredhiel's special displeasure—came to the gardens take a candlemark or more of ease when the sun had passed its fiercest. Behind her, Vieliessar could hear the shouts and laughter of a group of Postulants playing a counting game, the soft distant sounds of someone practicing upon the harp. The song of a flute wound through its soft sweet notes—hesitant, unpracticed, but holding the promise of mastery to come.

The chirring of insects, the soft hot breeze, the smooth warmth of the Vilya's bark beneath her hands, all lulled her. *Was I ever so young as these new Postulants?* she wondered in bemusement. They had all thought themselves on the verge of adulthood when they came to the Sanctuary, but it had been a very long time since she had been a Postulant. To number those years Vieliessar must think hard, and count Midwinters upon her fingers.

She ducked back against the trunk of the great Vilya that dominated the garden as two of the Postulants ran past her, shrieking excitedly in their play. They reached the low wall and scrambled over it, racing along one of the narrow paths between the fields of standing grain in the field beyond. *Landbonds,* she thought to herself, seeing cropped hair and faces narrow with a lifetime of starvation. *At least they return to a better life than that, Twice-Called or not.* One trained at the Sanctuary could be sure of a place in a Great House, for the Lightborn preferred Sanctuary-trained servants. One thought blended inevitably into the next: *Soon Thurion will go. It is already past time.*

It was not that after a dozen short years of study Thurion could know all the Light held . . .

. . . but that the knowing came from the Light itself, not from Lightborn teachings.

I could be happy here blended, in a seamless instant, with: *I am happy here.* Vieliessar no longer wondered at her good fortune in remaining hidden from discovery. She had wished for nothing else, desperately, for moonturns. A wish, a desire, *need*, was the beginning of a spell. She could spend the rest of her life learning all the Light had to teach.

She got to her feet, shook her long skirts free of grass, and walked slowly across the garden. The low stone wall at its edge marked the boundary between the Sanctuary gardens and Rosemoss Farm, and its smooth grey stone was hot against her hands. Beyond the farm and its fields lay Arevethmonion. She could feel the radiant beat of its life against her skin like a second kind of sunlight. She would never walk beneath the Flower Forest's canopy save as a fugitive or a prisoner. The thought had brought her reflexive rage and sorrow since the first day she had come here, but she could not remember the last time she had looked upon Arevethmonion and thought of herself as a captive: the wall beneath her hands marked the outermost possible bounds of her world, but at last the thought gave her no pain. Nothing endured forever, and what must be, must be.

Suddenly she heard a thin wail of distress from the direction of the young Postulants. One was standing. The other was huddled at his feet. As she watched, he tried to pull himself upright.

The front of his grey tunic was dark with blood.

She did not stop to think. She vaulted the wall and went running toward them. When she reached the pair, she knelt down beside the wounded Postulant.

"Go—Rian?—and fetch Mistress Healer Hervilafimir from the healing chambers—or any you find there! *Go!*"

Rian fled toward the Sanctuary as if the Starry Hunt Itself pursued him.

"Here, let me see," Vieliessar said, trying to pull the child's hands away from the wound. To truly Heal required Light, but for small wounds and sickness there were many things one could do to ease suffering, even without the Light, and Nithrithuin Lightsister had begun to teach Vieliessar these minor mysteries.

Bright blood welled from between the Postulant's fingers and he whimpered in fear.

"What is your name, child?" Vieliessar asked.

"Garwen," he said. "Of—" He gasped, and the blood ran more strongly. *"It hurts!"*

As if that cry were a summons, Vieliessar felt the power rise up in her, forming its spellshape in her mind. She could see the dark flaw in the brightness Garwen showed to her inward eyes. A sharp stone. A careless fall. Before she could stop herself—before she could *think*—the Healing broke free. Blue fire leaped from her hands, and she could See it pour into the dark wrongness. Garwen's breathing eased.

Behind her, Vieliessar heard running footsteps.

"What has happened?" Hervilafimir Lightsister cried.

"She Healed me," Garwen said, his voice giddy with relief. "The Lightsister Healed me!"

⊰⧉⊱

Hamphuliadiel Astromancer possessed an Audience Chamber where he could receive the petitioners and supplicants who came to the Sanctuary. Though it was said to be so opulent as to stun any of the War Princes to wordlessness, no one who had actually seen inside had ever spoken of what they saw, and its vestibule was as stark and unadorned as any other chamber in the Sanctuary, save for the elaborately carved wooden door that led into the chamber itself.

Vieliessar had been waiting here for a long time.

She had fled—from the field, from the garden, to the only place she could think of to go: Mistress Maeredhiel's workroom. Only then had she realized she was covered in Garwen's blood. Maeredhiel had taken one look at her stricken expression and sharply ordered her to wash and change. Vieliessar tried to explain what had happened, but Maeredhiel refused to listen.

She had barely finished scrubbing the blood from her hands when a wide-eyed Postulant appeared, sliding back her door without tapping to announce that Hamphuliadiel Astromancer wished Vieliessar to attend him at once. She'd assumed she would be brought before him immediately, but her wait stretched. The delay gave her time to reflect, and her thoughts weren't happy ones. Just as no Candidate had ever returned to the Sanctuary after the end of their Service Year bearing newly awakened Light, no Postulant had ever refused training—much less hidden what they were. What was the penalty? Would she be sent from the Sanctuary?

He cannot do that. He knows it will mean my death.

A year ago, or two years, or five, she would have bargained with the world, tossing out hopes as one might toss dice from a cup: dreams of allies found, of victory achieved, of safety, fortune, safe concealment as she worked toward her vengeance. She knew now these were no more than the fantasies of a heartsick child.

It was two candlemarks past the time for the end of the evening meal when the door to the Audience Chamber finally opened.

"You may present yourself to the Astromancer now," Galathorntha-dan Lightbrother said.

Vieliessar followed Galathornthadan through the door, telling herself she must not gawk lest she rouse Hamphuliadiel's anger further, but she could not stop herself. The chamber was the size of the Refectory, and more opulent than any she had seen within Caerthalien's Great Keep. Its floors and walls shimmered with Warding, and her feet passed over carpets that would ransom a Lord *Komen,* laid over flooring that was an intricate pattern of inlaid woods and precious stones. Nor were the walls any plainer: beneath the opal coruscations of the Wards she could see that they were painted, hung with tapestries, and lined with treasures the Hundred Houses had brought to the Sanctuary to curry favor with the Lightborn down through the centuries.

At the far end of the chamber, Hamphuliadiel sat. Vieliessar stopped abruptly, so quickly that Galathornthadan walked six paces on before noticing.

He enthrones himself as if he would be High King!

She stared at the Astromancer, struggling to conceal her shock. Hamphuliadiel's chair was wide enough for any two men to sit upon, and its back extended several handspans above his head. Perhaps it was wood, or perhaps ivory, but it was hard to say, so thickly was it encrusted with gems and gold. Such a seat might have been cold and unpleasant, but Hamphuliadiel had surrounded himself with green silk cushions filling the empty spaces. The green of his robes merged into the green of the cushions.

Galathornthadan stopped, frowning at her, and Vieliessar started walking again. But she was no longer afraid.

She was angry.

⊰⬧⊱

Hamphuliadiel regarded the child standing before him, her aura flaring and flickering with anger and half-shielded power, and hated Celelioniel for her foolish superstitions even more than he had before. Her mad belief in ancient fables had led her to see prophecies in nonsense-rhymes, and that delusion had kept Farcarinon's get alive.

And now it meant Hamphuliadiel was faced with a choice no Astromancer before him had ever needed to make.

Even the lowliest Landbond knew that power must be paid for in power. The small and simple spells that so impressed the common herd could be cast with no more power than that which lived within one's own skin. The Greater Spells required more. There was power in blood, in pain, in death—but to tap those sources brought madness and an eternal soul-hunger. There was power in soil and water and plant and tree— but to take from these was to render them lifeless and sterile. Only the Flower Forests held power enough to fuel the spells of the Light. And so, a thousand generations past, Mosirinde had founded the Sanctuary of the Star and forged her Covenant: to take only from the Flower Forests.

But the Lightborn were as corruptible as the great lords themselves, and so one secret was held by each Astromancer and passed only to the next: it was neither power and ability, nor Light Within, that made

Candidate into Postulant. It was the choosing of the Astromancer, who gazed upon the spirits and futures of all who entered the Sanctuary and passed a covert judgment which could not be appealed. This was why the Light was so rarely discovered among the great nobles; their arrogance made them difficult to control. It was a simple matter to lay the most gossamer of *geasa* upon each departing Lightborn, so that they would simply . . . not see Light where it was . . . inconvenient.

And so he had done, as Celelioniel had done before him, as every Astromancer had done for reign upon reign.

And now the child who was War Prince of Farcarinon by blood and birth stood before him. He had never thought to gaze so upon the future of the last scion of Farcarinon . . . until today, when news had come of her Healing. And then he had discovered he could not. There was no clear line through the years to come that said: *this shall be and that will not.*

He wished to blame mad Celelioniel, or even the vexed mooncalf herself—but he sensed no spellcraft. Whatever clouded the girl's future owed nothing to Magery.

Amrethion's Prophecy exists only in a madwoman's ravings! he told himself angrily. *Who is to say there are not many whose future is cloaked? Perhaps all War Princes are born so.*

And perhaps the stars did not care that Vieliessar was not truly a War Prince.

None of this *would matter if she had lived out her days as a Lightless drudge!*

But she had not.

Kill her? Train her? There was no third road—he might call Lightborn to Burn the Light from her mind, but that was only a slower death.

"What have you to say for yourself?" he demanded.

He saw her chin come up and her eyes flash.

"I say that I did not ask this. Nor would you now know of it save by mischance." She spoke with the pride of one who knew herself to be War Prince even now, and her words and her voice were a pledge of defiance.

I can kill her where she stands! How dare she take such a tone with me?

In the years of his reign, Hamphuliadiel had received War Princes and Warlords, bearers of the noblest blood in the Fortunate Lands. They had, they thought, flattered him and bribed him into doing their will, never knowing that none of them had caused him to do anything he had not decided upon in advance.

For a moment his rage was so great that the opulent chamber seemed small and far away. *It would not be an act of war. Farcarinon does not exist.* He closed his hands on the arms of his chair so hard that his fingernails turned white from the pressure. He could see Galathornthadan standing behind her, and saw Galathornthadan's eyes go wide with fear at the sight of his anger.

"I only wished to save my own life, Astromancer," Vieliessar added. Her voice was softer now, and her eyes penitently downcast.

"You do not serve the Light by hiding from it, Vieliessar," he said, and felt satisfaction. He sounded as a true Astromancer should sound: paternal, just, fair. They would never whisper in dark corners of his madness or mock him in their Great Halls for his faith in moldering prophecies. The Light was Magery, not mystery. His name would be remembered forever as the Astromancer who lifted the shroud of capriciousness and inscrutability from the Sanctuary of the Star.

"I do not understand how I am to serve it," Vieliessar answered, and now, to Hamphuliadiel's approval, she sounded like a sulky child, not a War Prince. "I serve no House—and my life is forfeit if I leave the Sanctuary."

"Perhaps that will change—should it be your wish and that of the Light," Hamphuliadiel answered. *Yes. That is the answer. I was a fool not to see it at once. Let her become Vieliessar Lightsister. And should she become a danger, I will send her to Caerthalien, or Vondaimieriel, or Sarmiorion, or Aramenthiali. And she will not return. And I shall be blameless.*

"For now, there is much for you to learn."

⋈

Once again Vieliessar's life changed. No longer were her days spent in the meticulous pursuit of invisible perfection. She exchanged the skirt and tunic of a servant for the grey robe and green tabard of a Postulant, and it quickly became clear that she fit into this new life far worse than she had fit into the old. She had already read, for her own pleasure, most of the scrolls the new Postulants were set to learn, and as for Magery . . .

She had long since mastered the score of lesser spells whose practice occupied the days of the youngest Postulants, yet she was lost when she was placed among the eldest ones—those who might dare the Shrine this year or next—for she understood none of the theory upon which the practice of the Light was based.

"It is hopeless!" she burst out. "What does it matter to me whether Mosirinde or Arilcarion or even Timirmar crafted the Covenant? I shall live out my life bounded by Arevethmonion!"

"And yet you will still find the Covenant of great value," Rondithiel Lightbrother said placidly. "For it holds the reason for all we do."

Vieliessar shook her head stubbornly. "In the Healing Tents of a battlefield," she said. "But when shall I ever see such?"

"You think with the short sight of the Lightless," Rondithiel admonished her.

He lifted the teapot from its cradle and poured both their cups full again. Its ingredients were gathered in Arevethmonion and compounded by the Postulants themselves, for the blending of teas was an art closely allied to the blending of potions—and it was best to practice those skills first on compounds that could do no harm. Tea in all its infinite possibility was the only delicacy permitted to those residing at the Sanctuary, but the Candidates and the Postulants were too young to appreciate it, and the servants far too busy to treat tea as an art. The tea which fueled the Sanctuary as much as the Light itself—the tea that Rondithiel poured—was the homely Forest Hearth mixture.

The two of them were seated in Oiloisse-chamber, and Vieliessar thought longingly of the days when her only interest in it had been to sweep the floor. She had spent from Thunder to Rade—her birth moonturn—being told first that she had too much skill and then too little; that her scholarship outpaced that of her new peers and that she knew nothing of any use. At last, Rondithiel had bidden her attend upon him here, and she could do nothing but obey.

Rondithiel Lightbrother had trained many generations of Lightborn, for long ago his War Prince had granted him a boon, and he had chosen to spend the rest of his life at the Sanctuary of the Star, for his great love was teaching. But it was not Magery he taught. Rondithiel taught the understanding of Mosirinde's Covenant.

It was said that Mosirinde Peacemaker had founded the Sanctuary of the Star and served as its first Astromancer. It was she who decreed that an Astromancer might reign from Vilya fruit to Vilya fruit, no longer. It was she who had set down the rules that governed the lives of the Light-born: that the power to wield spells could not be drawn from blood or from earth, but only from the wellsprings of power a Flower Forest com-manded.

"There is more to the Light than you yet know, Vieliessar. The spells that are all the Lightless see are but a fraction of what being Lightborn means. There is the knowing."

"I have spent years in meditation, Lightbrother," Vieliessar said, try-ing to conceal her exasperation.

"And yet you have never worked any of the Greater Spells of the Light," he observed.

She looked at him with puzzlement now. "Such would be dangerous without a guide," she said carefully.

"And I am ready to stand your guide," he said. He set a sphere of bronze on the table. "Transmutation is one of the Greater Spells, but this chamber is well Warded. At worst we will destroy a few pieces of furni-ture."

Vieliessar stared at the bronze ball as if it might explode. She thought back to her first experiments, of her panic at being unable to Banish the Silverlight, of how the brazier had crumbled away to rock . . .

"I do not know the spell," she said hopefully.

"Come, give me your hand. I will show it to you," Rondithiel Light-brother said. He held out his own.

She had the terrifying sense of being trapped and fought down her instinctive panic. She did not know what would happen to someone who refused to learn Magery—but she was certain Hamphuliadiel's wrath would fall heavily upon that one.

She had no choice.

She reached out and set her hand in his.

It was as if she had touched one of the Teaching Stones in the beginners' workrooms: suddenly, bright to her inward sight, there appeared a construct of shape and color and sound and texture and taste. It was all of these things, and none of them. It was the spellshape of Transmutation.

"Now," he said, releasing her hand and gesturing at the sphere.

Every instinct screamed to her that this was a trick, a trap, but no matter how she tried, she couldn't figure out what shape it must take. Everyone knew she had the Light. Rondithiel had taught generations of Lightborn. So she called the spellshape to the front of her mind, and reached out to touch the metal, letting the Magery unfold itself in her mind. Metal to wood . . .

"What are you doing?"

Rondithiel's shout jarred her out of the weaving. She gasped, opening her eyes. He was staring at her with a look of horror on his face. On the table between them, the metal sphere was distorted and discolored—but not transformed.

"I—" Suddenly a great wave of sick dizziness swept over her. She tried to raise her hand to brush her hair from her face, and discovered she could not. A moment later she was sprawled ungracefully across the floor cushions, struggling to breathe.

Rondithiel hurried around the table. He lifted her into his lap and held her teacup to her lips. The liquid was nearly cold, but nothing had ever tasted so sweet.

"Transmutation is a Greater Spell!" he shouted. "You cannot work it without drawing upon Arevethmonion!"

⋇

The Light exacted a price for the weaving of spells. Magery must be paid for; power drove spellcraft. For the little spells, power of the body. For the Greater Spells, the power of the Flower Forests. While she had been hiding her Light, practicing only in secret, Vieliessar had never attempted the Greater Spells for just that reason. To draw upon Arevethmonion was a thing that would surely be noticed—but she had thought its power would come to her at need, just as the power for the lesser spells had.

"After the first time, yes," Rondithiel said, when he had brought her to health again and discovered her error. "But the first time . . . one must be shown the way."

"I wonder that any spells are ever worked in all the Fortunate Lands," she had answered irritably. "For to name all the Flower Forests in the land is the work of days."

"So the Lightless believe," Rondithiel said with grave amusement. "The Lightborn know there is only one. Once you are known to Lady Arevethmonion, you are known to all the Flower Forests that may ever be."

There was more to the matter than that. The spellstones that marked the boundaries of the domains of the Hundred Houses kept the Lightborn's spells from ranging across the whole of the land in search of power. Nor did the power of one Flower Forest within a domain spill into the next at need. There was more for her to learn than she had thought. It was two moonturns of careful instruction before she attempted a Greater Spell again.

But with Rondithiel's aid, she made a beginning.

⋇

I can do this.

Vieliessar stood before the great bronze doors that separated the Sanctuary from the Shrine. She was naked, her only ornament a long knotted cord looped about her wrist.

The first act of each Postulant was to accept a handful of flax seeds. It was their task to plant the seeds, and harvest them, spin flax into thread, and weave thread into cord, and at last, when that was done, to bind the knowing of their spells into that cord.

The last act of each Postulant was to enter the Shrine of the Star, there to keep vigil, and emerge Lightborn. Those who survived departed the Sanctuary at once, speaking to no one.

Those left behind might know that this one or that one of their fellow Postulants had gone to the Shrine, but nothing more.

Some entered the Shrine and never emerged again.

She remembered a Rain Moon, years ago, when Thurion had come to her sleeping chamber to whisper last messages to those he loved, before coming to stand where Vieliessar stood now. He had charged her with duty to his family if he did not come forth again, for by his duty to Caerthalien he meant to secure the freedom of his family, and if he failed, he would not have them think he had forgotten them.

She had not wished to accept that duty, but she had. And when he had gone to the Shrine, she had knelt upon the cold stone beside her bed and pledged her own life to the Silver Hooves, if they must have one that night.

She had risen before dawn to hide in the shadows of the Antechamber. And had seen Thurion walk free.

Will I be as fortunate?

She reached out to touch the bronze of the doors, to trace the shapes of spirit-horses and the powers that rode them among the stars. *In my end is my beginning.* Generations of Postulants had touched them so, and the doors gleamed bright-burnished where they had.

Strange to think that here I was born and here my mother died.

In Rade Moon, Farcarinon had fallen, Nataranweiya had died. If Vieliessar chose, a simple conjuration would show her that night, but such a folding back of years could not show her what she most desired to see: the thoughts that had lain in Celelioniel's heart when she had shaped Vieliessar's fate.

Survive this night, and the Lightborn taught that her person would be inviolable—not even a War Prince dared raise his hand to one of the Lightborn, lest the Sanctuary punish both House and Line. But there was no House waiting to welcome her, and Farcarinon's enemies might yet look upon Vieliessar Lightsister and see Vieliessar Farcarinon. Should someone let her out of life, without clan and kin and Line she would vanish as if she had never been.

Go now, before you lose your nerve.

The doors ghosted open beneath her touch, and Vieliessar stepped over the threshold and into the Shrine of the Star.

The first things to reach her senses were the touch of cold earth beneath her feet and the iron scent of old blood. The next was the beating of raw power against her senses and Wards, as if she basked in some sunlight that did not warm her. Though the Shrine was open to the sky above, it was as dark as a deep cave this night, but Silversight showed her three tall stones beneath an open sky. A fourth flat stone was set into the ground between them; the Shrine itself was nothing more than stone and earth.

Nine Shrines are given to the Trueborn, nine places where the breath of first creation still can be felt upon the skin. Nine where the powers hear us when we call.

She knew what she must do now. It was not teaching, but *knowing*, here in that place where it was eternally the morning of the world. Vieliessar stepped to the center of the triangle of great stones and stretched out her hand. The veils of power resolved themselves to a single starbright blade, cold as moonlight. She closed her fingers around it, feeling hot blood well up from her palm and dissolving the conjured blade as if it were ice in fire.

Blood pooled in her palm as her gaze was drawn to the stones of the Shrine. On their surfaces she could see the patterns of uncountable handprints; some the faintest blue shadow against the stones, some shining as brightly as the moon. She stepped into the center of the triad and pressed her hand against the stone. For an instant she felt its cold grittiness against her palm, then the surface she touched seemed to become as hot and supple as flesh.

Brightness flared up between her fingers.

She heard the sound of a bridle clink.

That homely sound in this uncanny place made her startle in shock. She turned, and only her utter disbelief in what she saw kept her from going to her knees.

"You have come to end us."

Power blazed from the armored rider like heat from a hearth. His armor was of no kind she had ever seen, yet as she tried to fix its details within her mind, she found she could not. Nor could she name its color, nor the color of the horse he sat. To see him was as if she heard the words of a story-singer and her own mind made of them an image crafted to her own desire. The longer she stared, the more visible the host behind him became, so many hundreds of riders that she knew the Shrine could never have contained them all, nor would it have been possible to see each one so clearly if they'd been here in truth. Yet their leader's destrier switched its tail and pawed at the ground as she had seen many horses do. *The Starry Hunt stands before me,* Vieliessar thought, and felt not joy, not terror, not grief—merely a fathomless wonder that They should be and she should see Them.

Then the words the Rider had spoken came sharp in her mind. "I could not," she said, half protest, half judgment.

"Yet you shall. For you are Farcarinon."

Each syllable the Rider spoke resounded through her as if it were the beat of a great war drum. She could feel her heart pounding in her chest as hard as if she'd been running, as slow as if she were in deep meditation. It was three heartbeats before she answered, and she only understood the sense of her words as she heard them, for it seemed as if she merely recited a speech someone else had crafted.

"Farcarinon is gone. There is only I." *Farcarinon will endure until the end of my life—but I am only one—but how shall I end You—but why would I wish to?*

The Rider inclined His head as if He had heard both the words she spoke and the words she had not. It was the grave salute that prince might give to prince, and for the first time, Vieliessar felt fear. No, not fear—*terror*. The weight of the Rider's pronouncement, the Rider's grief, was a palpable thing, making her body tremble with a burden too great for mortal flesh to bear. *Who am I that the power which shapes our lives and our destiny should regard me thus?*

"*You are Farcarinon,*" the Rider said. "*Death in life. Life in death.*" In the Rider's words Vieliessar heard more than simple recognition. There was judgment—and sorrow. "*You will be known when We are forgotten,*" He added, and raised His hand. Salute, benediction, warning . . . she did not know.

In the next moment her sight became uncertain, as if she gazed not into shadow, but into the brightness of the sun itself. Her eyes were filled with light and her ears with a sound as if a whole army roared out its battle cry, and she could not say in that moment if she stood upon the ground or rode through the heavens on a destrier made of moonlight and shod with stars. Someone shouted in a language she did not know and for an instant it seemed she gazed down from a great height at a landscape of darkness, of ice and shadow. Before her hung a balefire, burning star-pale with magic. A *komen* knelt beside it, and with him stood a creature neither Trueborn nor Beastling, with blood welling in the palm of her hand.

"*The Land calls you. The People call you. I call you. He Who Is would return to the world, and so we summon you.*"

"*And will you spill your own blood to save the land?*"

The creature—woman, but nub-eared and red-skinned as no Trueborn could ever be—held out her wounded palm to the Rider, as if her blood held a compulsion even He must obey. Even her blood was strange, for it was red as flowers. . . .

❦

Vieliessar came to herself with the stiff and aching limbs of one who has spent too long motionless in too cold a place. As she raised her head, she could see the sky above was grey with dawn. She clambered to her feet, clutching at one of the standing stones to steady herself before she remembered what she touched.

Dream? Vision? In this moment she could not say whether what she had seen was truth or the expression of her own buried desires. *Does the Hunt always come? Do the Silver Hooves bow down to each of the Lightborn? Is this how all who come to this place are tested and tried?* Had she given the proper answers? Or was she dead even now, a homeless ghost, doomed to vanish like morning frost the moment she stepped from the Shrine?

Vieliessar looked toward the doors of the Shrine and spied a bundle of green cloth, placed there by some Lightborn candlemarks before the beginning of her vigil. She turned back to the Shrine and saw the print of a hand deep-sunk into the ancient altar stone. Slowly she reached out and set her hand into its shape. It fit as if the eternal stone had been as malleable as bread dough and shifted at her touch. She felt the weight of an unimaginable fate bearing her down. For an instant a thousand evasions crowded her mind: to leave the Sanctuary of the Star this very candlemark, to keep moving until she left the bounds of the Fortunate Lands completely; to offer up her name, her House, her *life*, as a sacrifice to unmake this destiny.

She could. But . . .

Serenthon knew his fate. Celelioniel foretold it when he came here.

In that moment of realization it seemed to her she could see him: Serenthon Farcarinon, War Prince, First among the Hundred Houses, bold and beautiful and arrogant. He had known before he began he would fail. He had known his Bondmate would die, that Farcarinon would be unmade, that all who had trusted him would die . . .

That someday his daughter would stand here, to be Sealed to the Light.

If Serenthon-my-father could embrace such a fate for himself and all he loved, then I shall not disgrace him.

She lifted her hand from the imprint in the stone and walked steadily to the doors of the Shrine, tying the knotted flaxen cord about her waist as she went. Custom said she must now return to the domain of her birth and there present herself to the Chief Lightborn of the War Prince's court. But she was Farcarinon, and the officers of her father's court were slain or fled. So she picked up the green robes that lay upon the stone and carried them, still naked, back to her sleeping cell. She took up a knife and cropped her long black hair close to her head, then donned the Green Robe, tightening the silver cord about her waist. Then she sat upon her bed and waited for someone to come and tell her who she must become now.

CHAPTER FOUR

THE VEILED PATH

Then spoke Berendriel, Notariel's Heir: I do not set my foot upon Your stirrup, I do not set my hand upon Your horse. I shall not ride the night wind, nor leave my House, my komen, or my kin.

And the Star-Crowned, Hunt-Lord, Master of the Silver-Shod answered: As you say, so it will be. Your name shall be no longer Berendriel but Mazhnune. You shall battle forever, a hungry ghost, and never will you die and never will you live.

—*Berendriel's Song*

"Fall back! Fall back!"

"Stand!"

Thurion Lightbrother waited at the edge of the battlefield. His mare's thoughts were a background hum in his mind. Sariar was wise in the ways of battle, and knew there was no danger here for her, even though the din of battle made Thurion wish to cover both his ears and hers. It wouldn't help. True Speech brought him the thoughts of the *komen* bell-clear above the screams of the wounded, the battle cries, the thunder of drums, and the clash of metal upon metal.

The wind was sharp with the first stirrings of autumn. On Menenel Farmholder's land the sky would have been bright and clear, for the Lightborn worked their weather magic over the Farmholds to provide fair weather for the last sennights before harvest, keeping the rain from the fields until the year's crop was safely housed in barn and mill. They worked no such Magery over the battlefields. The sky was grey with low clouds, the wind harsh with the promise of rain before sunset. If it *did* rain, the fighting would not stop. Injuries would increase as warriors attacked blindly and destriers slipped on the uncertain ground.

Would it be any different if I and my brethren were not here? If the komentai'a—*if the War Princes—knew injury could bring a lingering death or a lifetime of agony? In the Sanctuary they say we are the essence of the peace of the Fortunate Lands. I sometimes think we bring war, not peace.*

He remembered his first battle, so many years ago now. His teachers at the Sanctuary had told him over and over of the necessity to shield himself, to refuse to hear the minds around him. He hadn't truly understood why until the moment when Caerthalien and Oronviel took the field against Aramenthiali and Ivrithir, he had thought he would go mad—from the noise of sword against shield, from the clamor of mind-voices, from the agony of the wounded and the dying.

He had heard it all, on that first of many battlefields.

He had never learned to deafen himself to the sounds.

Today Caerthalien fought against Ullilion. The combat would have been uneven save for the fact that Ullilion—somehow—had gained wealth enough to summon the best of the Free Companies to its banner: between them, Foxhaven and Glasswall had brought four thousand swords to the field, and Blue Deer had come with another twelve hundred. Now Prince Domcariel of Caerthalien was calling for the Caerthalien *komentai'a* to retreat, while Prince Runacarendalur was demanding they stand. With each engagement they fought, the rift between the brothers widened: Runacarendalur, brilliant and imaginative, leading his *komentai'a* to battle as if to a festival dance; his brother Domcariel, cautious and traditional, slow to adapt to an enemy's change in tactics. Days of fighting the enemy on the battlefield became nights of fighting each other in pavilion and castel. Thurion had seen too much of it. The Lightborn were invisible, like the servants.

He'd imagined his life would be different when the Light was Called in him. Everyone knew the Lightborn were the equals of princes, their spells vital to the wealth and security of their House. All the storysongs said the Green Robe erased kinship and caste, allowing the lowliest Landbond to drink from the same cup as his War Prince at the high table.

Like so many tales, it was both true and not true. The great lords venerated their Lightborn and gave them pride of place in their halls. The Lightborn negotiated treaties and terms of surrender, and moved freely between House and House, carrying messages. Some might counsel their lords and their *alakomentai'a*. But no Lightborn bore weapons in battle, and skill at arms was the measure of worth in the Hundred Houses, so none of them—even Ivrulion Light-Prince—had true power.

Thurion watched as Prince Runacarendalur's meisne surged forward, piercing the Ullilion line and striking for its standard-bearer, for War Prince Dendinirchiel Ullilion had taken the field in person, with Athagor, her consort-prince, beside her as her shieldbearer. To cause Dendinirchiel to yield—or to slay her outright—would bring a swift Caerthalien victory. But in a moment Runacarendalur would be surrounded, for Blue Deer's warriors were riding out from Ullilion's *tuathal* flank, and Prince Domcariel still hesitated. A moment more and Runacarendalur would be lost.

But at the last possible moment, Domcariel spurred his mount in the direction of his brother's battle standard and the knights of his taille followed. True Speech gave Thurion his words, but he would have known what they were even without it: *Caerthalien and the star! Caerthalien!*

Suddenly Thurion saw a familiar flicker of light upon the field—the cast-aside sword of a Caerthalien knight, the signal its owner was leaving the field. He turned to Sariar and swung gracefully into her saddle—the *komen* would need escort to the Healing Tents—but just as he prepared to urge the mare onto the field, another Lightborn galloped past and sent her mount dancing quickly through the battle itself.

Narcheliel. It must be her.

Narcheliel Lightsister took dangerous chances. It was true that any *komen* would not knowingly strike one of the Lightborn. It was also true that it was nearly impossible to separate friend from foe in the heat of battle. He saw her gain the side of the yielding knight, laughing as she did so. It was Celethor, one of Domcariel's taille.

He'd taken his eyes from the larger battle for only a few moments, but that had been time enough for Caerthalien—and Runacarendalur—to gain the victory. There was a great roaring as everyone on the field shouted at once—in joy or in sorrow—and Thurion saw Ullilion's banner fall in surrender. The Caerthalien warhorns sounded: *Victory, victory, victory.* After their call had died away, the Ullilion horns sounded, calling their *komen* back to their lines. The two armies disengaged, then both sides sounded the last call of the day: *Search for the wounded.*

Sighing, Thurion swung down from Sariar's back and led her toward the place in the horselines where the palfreys were kept. To clear the field of those who could not seek Healing under their own power was the task of servants, not Lightborn. There would be work enough for his hands and the Light as soon as the Caerthalien forces returned to camp.

There always was.

The nobles threw themselves into celebration as soon as they returned to camp. The Lightborn did not. Even Ivrulion Light-Prince toiled in the Healing Tents while his father and brothers celebrated. The Lightborn worked as they always did, measuring their labor against the power they drew from the Flower Forests, and ending their night's toil when to continue would be to take too much. But even those who could not be Healed immediately must be tended, lest their injuries grow worse.

Many Lightborn chose to leave such tasks to servants, but Thurion liked to know what Healings he would be called upon to do later, so even after no more Healing could be done that day, he worked beside the servants as they washed limbs, bandaged wounds, and dosed the injured with cordials that would take away pain, reduce fever, or give dreamless sleep. Caerthalien had gained the victory near noonday, but it was long past sunset when Thurion left the Healing Tents.

The night was windless but the air was chill, and he shivered. *Let this be the last battle Caerthalien will fight until spring.* Thurion could not hope it would be the last battle Caerthalien would ever fight, for the Hundred circled around one another like dogs around a piece of meat. *Perhaps someday I shall not have to watch it as it happens,* he thought tiredly. But that day was centuries distant: only those Lightborn far advanced in years—or so favored they need not contend with the rigors of a battlefield encampment—did not ride with the army in War Season.

Thurion shivered again. The warm cloak he'd worn to watch the battle had been taken by his bodyservant when he gone to the Healing Tents, and Denerarth had undoubtedly returned the cloak to Thurion's tent, as he always did. Thurion might have stepped back into the warmth of the Healing Tent he'd just left and sent one of the other camp servants for it, but he could never bring himself to order others around as if by right. He took a moment to gain his bearings, then began to walk toward the Lightborn tents. The pavilions of the camp were pitched in the same places every time—had been, Thurion suspected, since the days of High King Amrethion Aradruiniel.

But no. In the days of High King Amrethion there was no battle or strife. How I wish I had lived in those days. It would be pleasant never to have to hear the cries of the injured, see the damage hooves and weapons could do. *At least Vielle is spared this.* His path led him past the great pavilion where the victory feast was going on. Within it, he could hear, as he'd expected, Runacarendalur's voice raised in anger, Domcariel trying to shout him down, and Ivrulion saying just the wrong thing at the wrong moment—by intent, Thurion knew for a fact. Beneath their voices, like the deep resonant counterpoint of a complex work of music, he could hear Lord Bolecthindial rebuking his warrior sons. Thurion determinedly focused on his own thoughts, refusing to hear the words, both said and unsaid. It would do him little good to know his masters that intimately.

He would think of Vielle instead. She had power such as Thurion could barely imagine. Power to have every spell she learned burn as strong in her as if it were her Keystone Gift. He wondered if she had kept the knowledge of how far she could surpass them from her teachers until the day she dared the Shrine.

He'd left the Sanctuary while she was still a Postulant, but time had once again made them friends. He had needed that time to recover from the shock and disappointment of discovering she'd wanted to hide herself from embracing the greatest joy he could imagine. In the end, he had understood—she'd been content as a Sanctuary servant, and to become Lightborn made her life uncertain and potentially dangerous.

So she had complained of her teachers in her letters, and the Lightborn had gossiped in his hearing, and from those things Thurion had pieced together the truth. *As powerful as Pelashia Celenthodiel, mother of all magic. And none of those in the Sanctuary knew. I'm not sure Vielle truly knows, even now. Light grant she has no cause to find out, for if she does, it will be because disaster has befallen her.*

The extent of her power would only be tested if she were to leave the Sanctuary of the Star, for outside its shelter she would need to call upon all her Lightborn arts to preserve her life.

"Master Thurion! You should have sent for me!"

Thurion blinked, realizing he'd reached his own pavilion.

"I've told you how many times not to call me that?" he asked, with no hope his wish would be heeded any more on this occassion than it'd been the last thousand times.

"As many times as I've ignored you, Master Thurion," Denerarth answered. "As you would know full well had the cold not addled your wits. But I suppose if you are too cloudwitted to send a servant for me—and for your cloak—you cannot be expected to remember such things. Come! Inside before you freeze quite to death! And I suppose you have not eaten since this morning?"

Thurion's tent was a pavilion only by courtesy, for it was so small that there was only room for him and Denerarth, but compared to the hut Thurion had grown up in, it was both spacious and private. Silverlight made the interior as bright as day, and a brazier lent it welcome heat. He sniffed, catching the scents of both Summerbark tea and pear cider on the warm air.

"You know I have not," he answered, sitting down on a stool to pull off his boots. "I was working. But I hope you have."

"Oh indeed. Fine feeding from the prince's own victory table," Denerarth said. "Where *you* should have been."

"I told you, I was busy," Thurion answered mildly. Denerarth made an exasperated noise and paused to drape Thurion's warmed cloak about his shoulders before pouring a mug of steaming cider and placing it in his hand.

"And will be just as busy come the morrow," Denerarth said.

"If the Flower Forest is restored. If we are not to move the camp. If—"

"As you know full well, we'll be here another fortnight, while Ullilion ransoms its knights and settles the surrender provisions. And as you know that, why try to Heal everyone now? There's plenty of time before we break camp."

"Yes, yes, yes—plenty of time. But why should they suffer longer than they must?" It was an argument they had each time—and would probably have until one or the other of them died. Thurion supposed he was lucky to have a servant who was neither overawed by him nor who refused to serve a Landbond's son.

"If they're suffering, Master Thurion, then Night's Daughter is not the anodyne she is rumored to be. Now drink. I've warmed your bed for you, and there's cheese and meat pie if you've any appetite."

Thurion smiled faintly. He never had any appetite after a day in the Healing Tents. *At least* she *is spared this,* he thought vaguely.

Perhaps—in another year or two—he might petition Lord Bolecthindial to allow him to return to the Sanctuary for a time.

If Caerthalien did not receive any great challenges.

If its eternal wars and intrigues went well enough to grant House Caerthalien a season or two of quiet.

If.

⊰≍⊱

As Vieliessar settled once more into the life of the Sanctuary, she found it had become yet again a different place, for now she joined a company that had no match anywhere in all the Fortunate Lands: those Lightborn who made the Sanctuary of the Star their home.

At first, her mind was filled with what she had seen within the Shrine. She spent candlemarks in the Great Library scouring the books of prophecy and legend for some explanation. *The Jade Mirror* spoke of the interpretation of dreams or visions. *The Book of Veils* recounted those methods that could be used to evoke a foretelling or even a prophecy. *The Fire Alphabet* listed fulfilled prophecies that were the fruit of more than one foretelling. None of them held any hint of what the Huntsman had spoken of, so she turned again to *The Song of Amrethion*, only to find it as cryptic as before.

Slowly the urgency of her vision faded. It began to seen like a story-song she had once heard, a matter which had little to do with the life she lived. She had wondered, before she dared the Shrine, if taking the Green Robe would mean a life of idleness, but no. There were tasks to perform such as she might have found beneath the roof of any noble house: spells must be set, woven into clothing or horse harness or any of a dozen homely objects; cordials must be compounded and en-Lightened, food preserved.

When all who had known her as a fellow Postulant were gone, there would be teaching and guiding for her to do, but for now, her hands were deft in Healing, her mind quick and clever at Warding; she could conjure impenetrable invisibility about herself, Call forth storms and lightning, tame the fiercest creatures of forest and plain and Summon them to her hand, and those things were enough for her.

There were times the acceptance of her fate troubled her: to die forsworn was a terrible thing, unless one could pass the unkept vow on to another, but who could she lay such an impossible task upon? Who would take it up? Was it right to compass the weaving of Caerthalien's utter destruction at all?

She no longer knew. The vengeance her child-self had yearned for had

been in her power for many years. Even before she had taken the Green
Robe she could have stepped from Arevethmonion to Rimroheth and
gone to Caerthalien Great Keep. There she could have Unmade Caerthalien's stones into mist and shadow, struck Bolecthindial and all his
Line dead with Mage-conjured lightning. . . .

And she had not, for even then, each year she had passed taught her
more of the Light. She had learned at last to see it in the way Thurion had
spoken of so long ago—and to see the world as a vast machine, a flour
mill or cistern pump made up of lives and years, meant for no other purpose than to hold and reveal the Light. Set against that, the death of
Caerthalien seemed a small and useless thing. It would not raise Farcarinon from the dust, nor check a single prince's greed and ambition.

Perhaps, she thought, *Maeredhiel was right, when she told me my
greatest vengeance would be simply to live.*

And so the years spun onward, first at a stately measured pace, then
faster—so it seemed—as Vieliessar gained greater years of her own. Each
springtide was a new surprise, each summer a wonder, each autumn a
glory and a sadness, each gem-bright winter a new mystery.

She was content.

⊰⊱

"Come! Vieliessar, you must come! Now! A Healing is needed!"
For a moment Vieliessar was dazed with sleep. She had only
reached her bed a few candlemarks ago, for someone had been needed to
bespell Rosemoss Farm to ensure good harvest, and no one else knew
the delicate spells as well as she. Hearing Hervilafimir's voice did nothing to ease her confusion, for Hervilafimir had been called back to Nantirworiel years before, leaving the healing rooms in charge of Lightbrother
Thelifent. But none of the Lightborn left the Sanctuary forever, and Hervilafimir had recently returned, for Healing was her great love.

And in this time, it was needed more than ever before, for the Hundred Houses fought one another from Sword to Harvest, and the Beastlings pressed hard upon their borders, searching for any sign of weakness.

"I am awake, 'Fimir," Vieliessar sighed, sitting up in her bed and running her hands through her short-clipped hair. She snapped her fingers and the room blinked into brightness. It was still at least a candlemark till dawn. Hervilafimir's grey tabard, worn to protect her green robes from the blood and dirt of the healing chambers, was spattered with blood and muck. She looked tired and frightened.

"Please, Vielle. I know you are weary, but if you do not come, Amlunan will die, and I know not what Lord Manderechiel will do!"

"I am coming now," Vieliessar protested, getting to her feet and reaching for her robe. "How is it that Ladyholder Dormorothon could not aid him?" she asked, her voice only slightly muffled by the robe she was pulling over her head. Ladyholder Dormorothon of Aramenthiali was also Dormorothon Lightsister, and Vieliessar could not believe that Aramenthiali's Lady would not Heal Aramenthiali's Warlord.

"She has tried!" Hervilafimir said. "He took his wound in Sword, and she labored over him sennight upon sennight before bringing him to us!"

"Then why is he not yet dead?" Vieliessar grumbled, slipping her feet into her leather-soled stockings. It was Fire Moon now, which meant eight sennights at least since Amlunan had taken his injury. She Called a basin of water to her and splashed her face, then Sent it away again and took a deep breath. "No, tell me as we go. He is in the healing chambers, is he not?"

"These four candlemarks," Hervilafimir answered, as they walked from the sleeping room. "I would not have called upon you, but I cannot break the spell."

"Spell?" Vieliessar said sharply. To bespell the Warlord of a House for baneful purposes was treason if done by that House's Lightborn, and warcraft if done by another House. Either was impossible to imagine.

"Dormorothon has said it was no Lightborn, but one of the Beastlings who did this."

"She is here?" Vieliessar demanded, her mind racing. Aramenthiali lay east of Caerthalien; half a dozen domains and the Sanctuary itself lay between them and the Western Shore. Where had Amlunan taken such hurt?

"She is," Hervilfimir said grimly. "Nor will she leave his side—she and all her entourage."

Their conversation had taken them down the staircase and along the corridor that led to the healing chambers. Vieliessar's steps slowed. She could see the echoes of the Banespell clinging to the walls and the floor like filth.

'Fimir knew it was a Banespell—she would have Warded the treatment chamber . . .

But it was as if there were no Shields at all. Vieliessar's spellsight showed foulness like liquid shadow pooling upon the floor, bedewing the walls, wafting through the air like an evil fog. Banespells drew power from their victims and could even claim the lives of those around the afflicted.

It is the great mercy of Sword and Star that there are few patients here today, Vieliessar thought, for the whole of the healing chambers would need cleansing once Amlunan had been Healed.

Or had died.

The Banespell eddied around those standing sentry in the hall.

Ladyholder Dormorothon's hair was as short as any other Lightborn's, but she wore a veil of glittering silver gauze that masked its length. She wore the green-and-silver of the Sanctuary, but the cut and fabric of her garments was as elaborate as any Lady of a High House might wear, and her ears, neck, wrists, and fingers were heavy with jewels. Behind her stood two *komen* with surcoats of Aramenthiali blue and gold over their armor, and beside them, two youngsters who had not yet reached their second decade. One wore the heavy padded leather that proclaimed her an arming page, the other the soft and fashionable silks that marked him as Dormorothon's personal page.

"You may not loiter here," Vieliessar said sharply. "Lightsister, you know this well. If you will not go to the guesthouse yourself, then send your people there at once."

For a moment it seemed as if Dormorothon would argue, but then she raised her hand. "Geleborn, take the others to Mistress Hamongla-chele. I will remain to attend Amlunan," she added, staring challengingly at Vieliessar.

"You will go with them, for if your power was great enough to aid Amlunan you would not be here at all," Vieliessar said sharply. She did not wait to see if Dormorothon obeyed.

Vieliessar strengthened her Shields, then sent Power to the door of the chamber in which Amlunan waited. Energy crackled over and through the Banespell, but did not dispel it. She had not thought it would. She slid the door aside.

The healing chamber was large, for it was as much a place of teaching as it was a place of healing. Disease and injury could befall both Light-born and Lightless alike, and in cases where Healing need not be done, the proper spells could still lift pain from the sufferer. To the Lightless, it seemed all that was needed was a touch or a gesture—and so Vieliessar had believed herself until the day she had first come under Hervilafimir's tutelage. In truth, the Lightborn must first see the patient whole and un-marred, and next, eliminate the discord between their self as it was, and as it had been and would be. If only the flesh required aid, that was a simple enough matter. If spirit or mind had been harmed—or if the suf ferer were bespelled—the task was more complex.

The Lightless believed that sometimes a Healing failed. The truth, as all Lightborn knew, was that if the Healer survived, the Healing had not failed. But there were times a Healer must choose—their own life, or the life of their patient.

I shall not choose, Vieliessar told herself grimly.

Amlunan should have been in the vigor of his middle years, his body filled with the strength and grace of a life spent upon the battlefield. The warrior who lay upon the bed was gaunt with illness, his body prema-turely withered and frail. His long black hair was dull and lifeless, his cheeks sunken with pain. The stench of bane and wound-fever assaulted Vieliessar's senses. The new, white bandages that Hervilafimir must have placed upon his wound were already stained with wound-poison and his ivory skin had a grey undertone. Yet his dark eyes were bright and aware. Were he not strong, he would have died sennights ago.

"Lightsister," he said, his voice a croaking whisper. "Have you come to summon the Silver Hooves to bear me away?"

"I come to cast out the hurt you have taken," Vieliessar said crisply. "Naught else." Walking the few steps to his bedside made her skin crawl even through her shields. It was as if she was immersed in a chill river of slime.

"My Lady has tried. Your own Healing Mistress as well. Who are you to set your power above theirs?"

"One whom Hervilafimir thinks shall prevail," she answered. She knelt beside his bed and reached for his hand.

"I would know your name," Amlunan insisted, struggling to raise himself to a sitting position and failing in his weakness.

"And I would know how you came to take this hurt," Vieliessar answered. Amlunan had been Warlord of Aramenthiali in Serenthon's day; she would not conjure old enmities to complicate her task. Her fingers closed around his hand. It was cold and clammy, and she could feel the tremors of pain that passed through him.

"As any might," Amlunan whispered, closing his eyes. "Aramenthiali sent aid to Cirandeiron. They suspected Daroldan of betrayal, though Daroldan was bound to peace by treaty. In the forest of Avribalzar did Aramenthiali absolve Daroldan." He paused, struggling for breath. "A she-beast did this. She struck me with a spear. Slain by Guiomar Light-brother, she slew him in turn. At first, I knew not of her deceitfulness." Even that short speech had exhausted him. He turned his head away, gasping for breath.

Vieliessar had questioned Amlunan to summon to the surface of his mind his memories of that day. His words were of less import than his thoughts. As if she had been there, Vieliessar saw the dimness of the forest, the furred form of the Beastling shamaness as she reared up out of concealment to strike. The Beastlings were clever, and their sorcerers doubly so—she could see, now, how the Banespell had defeated both Hervilafimir and Dormorothon. Amlunan's wound was in his thigh, but the spear had not needed to pierce his flesh to do him harm. It had been crafted to transform the energy of Healing to feed shields that would make Healing impossible, while continuing to work its evil behind them.

My power is greater than theirs.

Once she had dreamed of becoming a Knight. She had already survived more and fiercer battles than any save the greatest of *komentai'a* could boast of. It was not for her skill at Healing that Hervilafimir had called her, but for her power.

It was time now to ride to battle once more.

She closed her eyes.

Merely to break through the Banespell's defenses to read Amlunan's true self was a terrible fight. She was forced to drop her own shields to See him clearly, and from that moment, the Banespell fed upon them both.

She had expected that. It was how she would win.

She felt the Banespell's coldness slide into the marrow of her bones and knew her life to be measured now in heartbeats. Felt the malevolent shield its mistress had crafted for it wrap itself about her, sealing her away from all aid her brethren might render.

Sealing her within its compass with the one she sought to Heal.

Sometimes these spell-battles returned to her in dreams, clothing themselves in words and homely form. Sometimes she knew herself clad in armor of green and silver, wielding a sword that burned like starlight, mounted upon a destrier as white as the moon, fighting alone against a vast and ever-hungry horde of Beastlings until sword, armor, destrier—all—were stained with monstrous ichor.

Now she held the image of Amlunan strong within her mind, demanding of the Light that what she saw must become the world's truth. Because she desired it. Because she willed it. Because the world itself must bow to the will of the Lightborn.

If the Lightborn was strong enough.

She felt Arevethmonion's life beat brightly against her skin. Hers to command. Hers to wield. If she chose, she could drain it to dust, until nothing remained of it but sterile sand. She could drain the life from every leaf and stalk and tree and flower, then reach out and take the lives which filled the Sanctuary of the Star. Take the beasts of the fields, the birds of the air, the fishes of river, lake, and the vast ocean itself.

All could be hers, if she chose.

But not today. Even the vile sorcery of the Beastling shamaness was not great enough to outmatch Arevethmonion's might, wielded by one who did not count the cost. Brightness beyond sun, beyond fire, beyond the matchless blaze of Silverlight filled her senses.

In that moment, it seemed the Light had voice, a living consciousness like her own. *This is what I give, if you are strong enough to take it . . .*

And her Healing was done.

She blinked dazedly at the walls of the Healing chamber. She felt suddenly alone, as if a dearly loved one had left her, for spellcraft was not without cost. Like a magnificent destrier, its power was the Lightborn's to call and command, but to control its power was wearying as riding a high-couraged stallion and bending the beast to one's will. Every Healer was taught to keep back enough power from the green life upon which it fed to heal one's own hurts. This time, she had not been able to.

For long moments Vieliessar stared, exhausted, at nothing. Amlunan's breathing had evened into true and restful sleep. She knew she should rouse herself and bring the news to Hervilafimir, but she could not find the strength. She came to herself at last as gentle hands lifted her to her feet.

"The jewel of Aramenthiali lives," she heard Maeredhiel say. "As does nine-blessed Arevethmonion, despite your efforts. Now sleep."

⟞⟼

By the time Vieliessar could rise from her bed once more, Aramenthiali had departed the Sanctuary, but it had left behind it unexpected treasure.

"All I know is what I have said," Hamonglachele said. "*Komen* and great lords may speak before us as if we are nothing more than chests and tapestries, but they would surely notice if a tapestry were to question them!"

Vieliessar laughed, and shoved her counter across the *gan* board with one fingertip. Even as a Postulant, she had never entirely abandoned the Servants' Hall, for it seemed uncivil to her to abandon old companions merely because of a change in fortune. Though she now wore Lightborn green, the servants still welcomed her as one of their own—and in truth, who else might she call friend? Candidates stayed for a scant wheel of seasons; Postulants for a decade or two. She could number upon her fingers the Lightborn who tenanted the Sanctuary for even half an Astromancer's reign—and she did not call Hamphuliadiel or his court of sycophants 'friend'.

"Did a tapestry hear that the Child of the Prophecy had risen in Haldil, I think even it would cry out," Vieliessar said dryly.

"'Aramenthiali helps to hold the West without thought for its own advantage because in the East, the Four Score behave as unruly children,'" Hamonglachele quoted mockingly. "Think you such a marvel can be true?"

"If Malbeth of Haldil is Child of the Prophecy, anything is possible," Vieliessar said. "And I have you surrounded, Mistress 'Chele."

Hamonglachele looked down at the board and laughed. "The student surpasses the master!" she cried. "I have nothing left to teach you."

Vieliessar smiled, then scooped her counters off the board, for it was nearly time to dim the lamps. She tidied away the *gan* set and thanked Hamonglachele for the game, then walked from the Servants' Wing back to her chamber.

It was a place less stark than her Postulant chamber had been. Her clothing belonged to her now, rather than being from a common store, and she possessed a fine carved chest that held winter and summer robes and underrobes. A shelf hung upon her wall, deep enough to hold scrolls borrowed from the library plus cherrybark canisters of her special tea blendings and a flat book where she recorded her experiments and recipes. Beneath it was a table at which she might sit to read or write, and a cushion on which to kneel. Though her bed was no softer than her Candidate's bed had been, its frame was carved and polished and her blankets were of new wool.

She did not set the walls alight as she entered, but went to the window and folded back the shutters. Fire Moon was waning. Soon it would be Harvest—and what of Haldil then?

She was certain 'Chele knew as well as any here that Celelioniel had named her—and not Malbeth of Haldil—Child of the Prophecy. But to the Sanctuary servants, the title was empty words, a riddle meant only for scholars.

Or, as Haldil clearly had decided . . . a pretext.

There were a Hundred Houses divided into Great and Less, but any child of a great court knew there were more divisions than two. There were the Great Houses whose position was unquestioned—Caerthalien, Aramenthiali, Cirandeiron—which had held their places since Amrethion High King ruled. There were Less Houses which would never aspire to greater rank—Hallorad, Penenjil, Kerethant. And there were Less Houses which swore themselves High—but when one spoke of the "Four Score," one spoke of the Less Houses of whose status there was no dispute. Those were the Houses held in clientage by this High House or that. In exchange for its protection, a High House demanded a yearly tithe, the right to call upon its client's levy knights in time of war . . .

. . . and the renunciation of the Less House War Prince's claim to the Unicorn Throne.

But Haldil did not look so high as to make itself High King's House. Haldil was a House of the Grand Windsward; in claiming Malbeth as the fulfillment of Amrethion's Prophecy, War Prince Gonceivis had declared "The time of High House and Low" was ended.

Which meant Haldil—and those who followed Haldil—renounced their clientage to their overlords in the West.

The tale had been played out a thousand thousand times in the histories she had read. The Hundred Houses fought among themselves. They would fight until the end of the world over who was to be High King. They had fought for thousands of years.

Haldith knows it does not hold the Child of the Prophecy. Enerchelimier has only to ask Celelioniel Lightsister to bear witness to that—should Enerchelimier wish to avow itself loyal. That she named me is—I think—no secret.

Haldil's gambit was a clever pretext, nothing more.

And the Twelve will fling themselves upon the pretext like a hawk upon a lure, and never ask the question they should ask.

Why do the Four Score rebel against their accustomed masters? Why now?

Such speculation was only another game for her—like *xaique*, like *gan*, like *narshir*. She was Lightborn, of no House. The strivings of the Hundred could not affect her.

So she thought.

⊰※⊱

Beru, I cannot find the *Jade Mirror* scroll," Vieliessar complained. Beruthiel Lightsister, Arevethmonion's Mistress, laughed quietly. She had succeeded Cirthoriach Lightsister as mistress of Arevethmonion in the usual way: beginning in her Postulant days with a taste for scholarship and a fascination with the Great Library's mysteries, she had returned many times through the centuries to assist the then-mistress of Arevethmonion in her tasks, before gaining a boon of her War Prince that permitted her a longer stay. The Astromancer served from fruiting to fruiting: the Mistress—or Master—of Scrolls served until age or disinterest made them lay aside their duty.

"How sad it is to see one once so promising in scholarship set that promise aside!" Beruthiel teased. "*The Jade Mirror* has been archived. No one thought it of any significance, and there is little enough space for scrolls as it is."

"But . . . I cannot find *The Book of Days*, either. And I was certain there was more than one copy. Or *The Fire Alphabet*. Or *The Book of Veils*. And I was looking at them, well . . . not so long ago."

"What do you wish to know?" Beruthiel asked, her smile fading. "I have but little skill in walking the Veiled Path—but if something troubles you, there is no reason you should not go to the Shrine and bespeak the Silver Hooves yourself, you know."

"It isn't the future I wish to see, but the past," Vieliessar said. "I suppose I must go into the storage archives, then."

"It is . . . you must seek the Astromancer's permission," Beruthiel said, sounding embarrassed. "Those books are in the Locked Cases, and . . . I know you are no Postulant, but the Astromancer has given orders that all the books of spells and prophecy are not to be released except upon his word."

A word Vieliessar knew she was not likely to receive, now or ever.

"It was a few moonturns after you took the Green Robe, I think," Beruthiel added.

"So long as that?" Vieliessar forced herself to smile, as if her heart was untroubled. "It was but a fancy, Beru. Do not distress yourself."

The news of Haldil's rebellion had sparked her curiosity—for *The Song of Amrethion Aradruiniel* seemed an odd and esoteric pretext for rebellion. She would have set the notion aside, save for a chance remark Rondithiel Lightbrother had made.

Hamphuliadiel Astromancer's house was Haldil.

There was no proscription against knowing the Houses of the Lightborn. In fact it was often a matter of vital importance, for the swiftest messages went forth by spellbird or Farspeaking, and such communication lay solely within the hands of the Lightborn, who would render no aid to a House not their own. If Gonceivis Haldil had taken his cause for war from some meddling of Hamphuliadiel, perhaps the reasons lay within the scrolls that spoke of the Prophecy.

But what she found was more troubling to her than any news of distant rebellion, or thinking the Astromancer of the Sanctuary of the Star chose to make the Hundred into counters on a *xaique* board.

There was no longer a full copy of *The Song of Amrethion* anywhere on the shelves—the last scroll in every available copy, the scroll containing the Prophecy-or-Curse, had been altered so it no longer contained it. The commentaries on the Song were either missing entirely, or the vellum had been cut and re-glued so the chapters analyzing the Song were gone. And as she'd just discovered, it was not just the Song. *The Jade Mirror* was an important text, how could Beruthiel, could anyone, say it was of no importance? *The Book of Days, The Book of Veils, The Fire Alphabet* . . . every book recording prophecies was either missing entirely or locked away as if it contained dangerous spellcraft.

All those texts should be here, so the Postulants could learn from them.

Those lacunae led her to investigate the Histories, but there were disturbing gaps there too. The scrolls detailing the lives of the Astromancers were gone. She could find their names, from Mosirinde Peacemaker down to Hamphuliadiel—but no texts of their lives more recent than Timirmar Astromancer's, and there had been thirty Astromancers since Timirmar's reign. Where were the lists of decisions made, of Postulants who became Lightborn in each reign, the lists of spells cast, Healings performed, Foretellings and interpretations made?

A library of magic without magic is a poor library indeed, Vieliessar thought sourly. *If I make known those things Hamphuliadiel has done, I will have no allies to help me make all as it was. Nor will his fears of me be allayed. Yet he fears me already . . .*

And Hamphuliadiel had always found fault with her even when both law and custom were on her side.

He has often mocked Celelioniel's obsession with Amrethion's Prophecy. But I think he must believe in it, or why would he take such pains to render it impossible to prove? It cannot merely be for Haldil's benefit. No War Prince truly seeks his causes in ancient lore. He has done this to us—to the Lightborn.

To me.

Celelioniel had named Vieliessar Child of the Prophecy, the one whose birth would—so Amrethion had written—herald the coming of the Darkness and bring an end to the Hundred Houses. Celelioniel had chosen Hamphuliadiel to carry on her work. It was why she had supported his bid to become Astromancer. But once he had, Hamphuliadiel had betrayed her. Clearly he meant to dismiss all thought in anyone's mind that the Prophecy might be true. He'd already removed every scroll that would help the Lightborn decide for themselves.

If the question arose.

When it arose.

Foretelling was not Vieliessar's spell to call. She did not know what the future held, and in truth, she had never wanted to, for what she had learned in her vigil within the Shrine had frightened her more than she had ever wished to admit. Now she wished she had tried harder to master it. At least then she would know when the Darkness her birth had foretold would come.

Perhaps it is I who am the Darkness. Why else would Hamphuliadiel hate me so?

⬦⬥⬦

Those words came back to Vieliessar many times the following winter. It was the hardest winter she had ever spent.

She spent it outside the Sanctuary.

They had learned of the Windsward Rebellion in Fire, and it had taken her through Rade to discover what Hamphiliadiel had done to the Great Library. Through all that winter she had stayed quiet and meek, but then Flower came, and a new year of Postulants were chosen.

There were only six Lightborn residents at the Sanctuary these days, a fraction of the number there'd once been, and Hervilafimir's and Beruthiel's duties occupied so much of their time that they could not be spared to shepherd new Postulants into the knowledge of the Light. Vieliessar's practice of spellcraft had never been either elegant or conventional enough to satisfy her fellow Lightborn—Rondithiel thought it must be because of all the time she had practiced in secret; Pamaneith

Lightbrother thought it was because she had come to the Light so late. But even if no one wished her to teach the Light itself, Vieliessar knew as much about its theory and history as any here.

And more than some.

She began innocently enough. But moonturn followed moonturn, and she turned from teaching the Candidates what they could still find upon the shelves of Arevethmonion to teaching them of those scrolls which now existed nowhere but in her memories. She could not bear for these Postulants to go forth into the world crippled and half educated.

She hadn't thought what she did would be discovered at all; Hamphuliadiel paid little attention to the Postulants and no one else would think what she was teaching was at all unusual. But one morning, a sennight after she'd begun, she'd barely settled herself in her seat in the Refectory, thinking of little more than the Postulants she would see today, when Momioniarch Lightsister came to stand behind her chair.

"Hamphuliadiel Astromancer summons you to attend him at the Shrine, Lightsister," she said.

Puzzled, Vieliessar nodded. "I come," she answered. She got to her feet and waved away the young Candidate who was serving breakfast.

When she reached the antechamber of the Shrine, Hamphuliadiel stood in its center. Everyone was at the morning meal, even the servants; there was no one to see. Behind him, as if he were a great prince and they his *komentai'a*, stood Galathornthadan and Sunalanthaid. *Two more from Haldil*, she noted automatically, for of the four Lightborn who seemed to attend upon Hamphuliadiel as if it were their only task, only Orchalianiel was not from Haldil—and Orchalianiel was from Bethros, to which Hamphuliadiel also had ties.

"Lord Astromancer," Vieliessar said, still confused. She shivered. The outer doors of the vestibule were open, as they were each day, and the air here was cold.

"I have done all I could to save you, Vieliessar, for it is in my mind that to lose one of the Lightborn for any cause would be a terrible loss.

My patience is infinite, but my wisdom is not. All I can do is present you for judgment to an authority greater than my own."

"Who judges me?" Vieliessar demanded. "For what crime? I have not trans—" *I have not transgressed against the Covenant.*

"I will not debate with you," Hamphuliadiel said sharply, raising his hand.

Suddenly Vieliessar felt the touch of a spell settle over her skin—and with that touch she was once more a child standing before Ladyholder Glorthiachiel in Caerthalien's Great Hall. This spell stopped her words, but not her volition. She took a step toward Hamphuliadiel, barely forcing herself to stop before she struck him.

"Your spirit is too cunning," Hamphuliadiel continued, as if she had fallen silent of her own accord. "It leads you into folly. And so I say this—as Arevethmonion has revealed your corruption, let Arevethmonion judge if you are worthy to dwell among us. I lay upon you this charge: go from the Sanctuary of the Star to dwell in Arevethmonion. If she will shelter you, return to us in Rain, healed and welcome."

Her horror and rage were enough to sweep away the spell of Silence as if it were never cast. "Rain is four moonturns from now," she said hoarsely. Who had told Hamphuliadiel—*what* had they told him? Why was it so important to him to banish the study of prophecy from the Sanctuary of the Star?

"I will fetch my cloak and boots and go," she said quickly, before he could bespell her to silence again. Once she was out of his sight, she could Cloak herself and reach the Servants' Hall by the secret passageways. She could leave a message for Rondithiel or Pamaneith—Maeredhiel would see it was delivered . . .

"You will go as you are," Hamphuliadiel answered.

Momioniarch Lightsister stepped into the vestibule and opened the inner door. The freezing wind of Snow Moon swept into the antechamber: Winter High Queen with her *komentai* of snow and sleet and ice. Suddenly the floor seemed colder and Vieliessar's Green Robe thinner than they had moments before.

She'd miscalculated badly. Underestimated her opponent, underestimated the need for caution. And now there was nothing she could do but obey the "judgment" that was in truth a coward's method of execution. Stay and kill him—she could—and she did not know what would happen next, only that she would have shattered the holiest custom of the Sanctuary.

Maeredhiel will see I am gone. No matter what tale Hamphuliadiel tells, she will see through it. I pray the Silver Hooves she does. Of all who were present on the night of my birth, she is the only one I dare trust.

"I will see you in Rain Moon, Lord Astromancer," Vieliessar answered, her voice hard.

She turned her back and strode from the Sanctuary.

⊰⊱

It had been cold inside the Sanctuary. Outside, it was freezing. The trees and hedges of Rosemoss Farm were bare and leafless in winter's cold. Her breath was a white cloud, and her skin burned. Before she'd gone a dozen steps toward the outer gateposts, her leather-soled socks were wet through, for it had snowed last night and no one had yet swept the path this morning. Still, she did not stop or hesitate, for she was certain Hamphuliadiel or one of his lackeys watched to see what she would do.

As she passed through the outer gates of the Sanctuary of the Star, she could not keep from shuddering. Outside the Sanctuary. Outside its bounds. Prey for any hunter willing to defy ancient custom.

A Lightsister is no man's prey. The Covenant did not say she could not defend herself—merely that she could not use the Light for the benefit of her House—or any other—in *war. And I am Vieliessar of Lost Farcarinon—I have no House!*

One step. Another. She called up her shields. They formed a barrier against the implacable wind, just as they would deflect arrow or swordblade, but they gave no heat. Arevethmonion was green, lush with eternal springtide . . . and more than half a mile away.

By the time she gained its shelter, her body ached with cold, though as she stepped beneath the trees, her skin tingled with the power all around her. It was not magic. Not precisely. It was that stuff of which Magery was woven, as thread was turned to cloth upon a loom. Light within called to Light without, and so the Flower Forests heeded the call of the Lightborn, feeding their spells, making them possible. She stepped from the road into the shelter of the trees. Only then, concealed from any who might watch, did she permit herself to slow, to stop, to hug herself against the cold and the fear. It was warmer here in the Flower Forest . . . but not as warm as it was in the Sanctuary.

Witless girl! You have sent Postulants to Arevethmonion year upon year to gather the ingredients for cordials, for incense, to gain vision and prophecy! You taught them that the Flower Forest holds food, shelter, and medicine, just as Hervilafimir taught you. Well, now you may see this storehouse and citadel and larder for yourself.

Warmth and shelter were her first needs. To Call an object from wherever it was to one's hand was a simple skill, providing that one knew precisely what one wished to call and where it lay. But when she tried to Call one of the heavy winter cloaks from its hanging-peg beside the garden door, then her wooden sandals from her sleeping cell, she could summon neither.

The Wards around the Sanctuary were strong—but they had always been set to keep the untutored spells of the Postulants from getting out, not to keep one of the Lightborn from reaching in. Undoubtedly Hamphuliadiel had changed that. To break them was not beyond the power she might call if she wished—but to shatter the Wards might be to shatter the walls as well. And it would be an act of violence against the one place in all the Fortunate Lands where violence was forbidden. She would find another way.

She walked for candlemarks, moving deeper into the heart of the forest, warming herself with movement. Arevethmonion was hushed and watchful around her—she had gone deeper into the Flower Forest than anyone had in her knowledge or memory. Craftworkers might enter a Flower Forest to bring away felltimber, hunters might pursue game beneath its branches, but only Lightborn had ventured into Arevethmonion since the Sanctuary of the Star had been founded, and they stayed mostly at the forest's edge.

At last she reached a clearing, a space opened up by the death of trees so ancient that the width of their fallen trunks towered above her head. *Here*, she thought. She must have shelter, a place to sleep. She would make them here. She could cause the forest earth to flow and re-form as a potter shaped clay. She formed the shape of her intention in her mind and raised a hand to begin.

And stopped.

She could feel Arevethmonion's heartbeat, the Flower Forest's soft breath. Unfair—*wrong*—to impose her will upon Lady Arevethmonion simply because she could. She waited, holding the shape of her intention, her need, bright upon the surface of her mind, reaching out with Lightborn senses for Arevethmonion's response. Her years of training had taught her that the Light required patience: she was prepared to wait as long as she must before beginning. She closed her eyes.

Her mind wandered from this fancy to that, as it would when she spent too long in meditation. Vieliessar thought of the hare eluding the fox with speed and disguise, the vixen hiding from the hawk and the wolf in deep, warm burrows. She thought of mice and bears sleeping the winter away, of all the inhabitants of any forest who preserved their lives by guile and who survived the winter in safe shelter.

When she opened her eyes again, the clearing looked very different. She stepped away from the place she had meant to put her sleeping place. *Not there. Here.* She touched the trunk of the fallen tree. Time and animals had stripped away its bark; insects burrowed into its wood, seeking food, shelter, sanctuary. In a century or two it would be gone—rot and weather would have returned it to the forest, to feed its successors. Meanwhile it would give her not only heat and shelter but concealment.

When the earth had transformed beneath her Magecraft, there was a deep burrow beneath the trunk of one of the fallen trees, one that could barely be seen from outside. She had made a chimney within the tree itself—a small matter to visualize a channel through the dead heart-wood, with its opening near the tree's distant crown—and there was felltimber in plenty.

Almost she conjured a spring to appear where none had been, before she remembered to listen for Lady Arevethmonion's voice. When she had, she walked a short distance to where a tiny stream flowed among the trees, its current brisk with winter snow. She drank her fill and returned to her burrow. She set a spellshield before the door before she kindled her fire, and soon smoke was drawing sweetly through her chimney.

She curled up against the back wall to think. Survival was her first need. The plan she must implement when she returned to the Sanctuary was the second.

The shelter she had built was vital to both, she realized. No matter his fine words, Hamphuliadiel meant her to die here. In a sennight, a fortnight, a moonturn he would send someone to Arevethmonion to find her body. It did not matter whether he sent friend or foe; he would undoubtedly look into the mind of whomever he sent to see what they had seen. Or—if he possessed more resources than she imagined—he would send a warrior who would slay her if she was found alive.

It might be nothing more than her panic and imagination which painted this future, but she must behave as if it were real. She had studied enough history of the Hundred Houses to know their tangled tales of alliance, betrayal, murder, and assassination. Even one of the Light-born could be slain if someone wished it ardently enough. And anything that had happened once could happen again.

If anyone sought her, she must not be found.

⊰≣⊱

Learning Lady Arevethmonion's rhythms occupied her through Snow Moon and into Ice. The Flower Forests were timeless places, and it would be a simple matter to tarry here for a year, a decade, a century, without awareness of the passage of time. The eternal springtide of the

Flower Forest gave her fruit, mushrooms, tender roots, even honey . . . a far more lavish table than in the Sanctuary's Refectory. She wove blankets of grass, shaped sandals of felltimber, dug river clay to line her fire pit and conjured Fire to bake it hard.

She listened—always—to the voice of the Flower Forest.

It was as if she spent her days in a waking dream, her mind growing closer to the vast green mind of the Flower Forest—of *all* Flower Forests, for whether a league or a thousand leagues apart they were all one. Magery had taught her how fragile the world was, how only her own conscience could protect it—now Arevethmonion showed her she did not have to find that strength alone.

Listen, and I will tell you a story, a true story . . .

It was the phrase with which the talesingers and songsmiths began their performances, giving the promise of truth. Lady Arevethmonion made the same appeal, the same promise.

Listen.

Ice became Storm. Vieliessar stood in the shadow of one of the great trees, barely a step from the road to the Sanctuary, watching unseen as hounds and hunters sought her. Six were mounted, and of that number, two wore the armor of knights. Their cloaks and surcoats were featureless white—as were the saddlecloths and trappings of their mounts—just as if they were arming pages, unannointed by battle. But they were far too old for that, and her inward sight showed her that their armor, shields, and weapons all glowed with the deep blue fire of spellcraft.

With the knights rode four huntsmen armed with bows and spears, and beside them, afoot among the animals of the pack, walked the Master of Hounds and his apprentice. The hounds were as diverse as the hunters: tall swift *hikuliasa*, noble sight hounds as swift as an arrow's flight; merry and tireless teckle hounds, able to track prey over stone and water candlemark after candlemark; fierce thick-muscled boarhounds able to course the most savage prey—even several of the earth-dogs legendary for their willingness to suffer any injury in pursuit of their chosen prey.

Knowing that she had been right in her most mistrustful fantasy did not make Vieliessar happy. It only showed her how much Hamphuli-adiel—or someone—feared her.

But if she was feared, she was also loved. The Light ensured there was no scent for the teckles to follow, and the Light gave her the power to render herself unseen, but it was the skill she had learned from Lady Arevethmonion that allowed Vieliessar to follow the hunters on noiseless feet, leaving no track upon the forest floor.

They spent three days searching Arevethmonion for her, and did not even find the places she slept.

Thoughts of war, declared and secret, had occupied Vieliessar's mind even before the arrival of the hunters. Her thoughts—and her dreams—were troubled, and she apologized often to Lady Arevethmonion, for her tangled emotions were mirrored in the slow mind of the Flower Forest, troubling its serenity. But she could not—dared not—leave the riddle unexamined.

Serenthon Farcarinon had declared war, fought, and died. Celelioniel had proclaimed Vieliessar Child of the Prophecy, and Vieliessar believed Celelioniel had pledged her to war with that naming before she had drawn ten breaths.

But against whom?

She reviewed all she'd ever learned of the Curse. Once—in the reign of Amrethion and Pelashia, millennia ago—the Fortunate Lands had been at peace. All Trueborn had done fealty to High King Amrethion and Great Queen Pelashia, and of that time little record remained, for what tales were there to tell of a happy, peaceful land? Then the queen had died, and the king had gone mad, and no one had been crowned High King after him, for his children and hers were all gone.

There were a thousand tales of how Pelashia had died, of Amrethion's fate, of their children. It didn't matter which one was true. From that day to this, the Hundred Houses had been at war with one another, each vying to make its prince High King, while Amrethion's Song moldered in scholars' libraries. Somewhere, sometime, the destined Child would be born, and that Child would destroy the Hundred Houses. ("*You have come to end us,"* whispered the voice of the Starry Huntsman in her memory.) The Child of the Prophecy would claim that which had been lost; innocuous enough, but the Prophecy also spoke of a Darkness which prepared itself for war in unknown lands.

Who?

She considered a hundred enemies and dismissed them all. "Darkness" couldn't be the Beastlings, since the lands they infested were hardly unknown. "What was lost"—and waiting to be reclaimed—was obviously the Unicorn Throne and the High Kingship. And each of the War Princes had been trying to do exactly that since the fall of Celephriandullias-Tildorangelor.

But who would bring the end of the Hundred Houses, and who would sit upon the Unicorn Throne? The same person? And how was the Child of the Prophecy to accomplish this? Even if she broke the Covenant, she could only turn the Fortunate Lands into a lifeless desert. If Vieliessar pledged herself to their destruction, the Hundred would defend themselves in every way they could. Even if she only struck down the Houses of the Great Alliance that had ended Farcarinon—Caerthalien, Aramenthiali, Cirandeiron, Telthorelandor—the Lightborn would band together to destroy her.

Either the Prophecy is true in every detail or it is not true at all, Vieliessar thought in exasperation. Celelioniel had believed in the Prophecy and preserved Vieliessar's life. Whether Hamphuliadiel believed in the Prophecy or thought it meaningless nonsense, he should not be trying to *kill her.*

It made no sense.

And Hamphuliadiel had put the explanations far beyond her reach.

FEAR AND BETRAYAL

Under King Virulan's rule, the World Without Sun . . . flourished.

Time had mantled Obsidian Mountain in a sheath of lifeless ice. In the frozen land over which it brooded, day and night were of equal length, each occupying half a Brightworld year. Here the Endarkened, their bodies obedient to King Virulan's sorcery, produced offspring, and their numbers grew.

And with it, their curiosity.

That which lived could be shaped. The Endarkened could not truly share their magic—and had no wish to, in any event—but they could share much of their essential nature.

The first creatures of their making were the Lesser Endarkened.

They were less than half the height of the Endarkened, though few of them could stand fully erect. Wingless, tailless—or with short stubby tails—hooved instead of footed, their brows and spines barbed and ridged, their skin as black as the Shadow Throne, rough and scaled.

Nor were they nearly as clever as their tall and beautiful cousins.

The Endarkened delighted in these new creations. They were lazy and sly and treacherous, but they were incapable of posing a threat to their creators. The Lesser Endarkened performed that toil for which the Endarkened had little taste: enlarging the caverns and passages of the World Without Sun; tending the vast farms of strange pale fungus, the soft writhing worms and tunneling insects for whom the kiss of the sun was fatal, the lakes of glowing blind fish. The numbers of the Endarkened had increased to the point where the power of the Deep Earth alone was not enough to sustain them. Eating had become, not an occasional amusement, but a necessity.

As much of a necessity as pain.

The children of *He Who Is* were bound by the laws of time and matter, and even His vast power could not create—in that realm—a sorcery that did not require payment. Their power came from the pain and fear of their victims and from the anguish and despair of their victims' deaths. Each spell they cast was paid for in the blood and suffering of others.

The Endarkened wouldn't have it any other way.

The Endarkened never left witnesses to any of their hunts, nor any sign a hunt had occurred, by King Virulan's decree. He did not intend his people's prey to suspect the existence of their hunters until the day his preparations were complete, and his legions rose up out of the earth to begin their slaughter.

But his people must have slaves, and food, and entertainment, and so they ranged across the world.

Hunting.

To the ranks of their shambling, bestial courtiers, they added slaves from every realm in the Bright World: Centaurs, Minotaurs, Gryphons, Bearwards, Hippogriffs, Aesalions, Elves, and more. Each provided special delights to the Endarkened. It was their greatest delight to capture any of the Winged Ones, to drag them beneath the earth, to rip the wings from their bodies. The Winged Ones never lasted, but their suffering was beautiful to their enslavers.

Those creatures of deep forest were nearly as fragile. Bearwards pined for the cool green life that was taken from them. Fauns died quickly of grief. Pixies and fairies, trapped away from their fields of flowers, starved slowly, their bodies glowing beautifully in their death agonies.

Centaurs and Minotaurs lasted much longer, prized by the Endarkened as much for their strength as for the torture they could withstand.

But the greatest prize in any Endarkened slave hunt was the Elves.

The Elvenkind were hard to take without suspicion. The creatures called themselves *alfaljodthi*—Children of Stars—and their shape was a mockery of Endarkened beauty. Their skin was grub-pale. Their long pointed ears only made more obvious the lack of beautiful golden horns. Their mouths were filled with stubby pointed teeth, their toes and fingers were blunt and soft. They had neither wings nor tails.

But they were durable—as much as any Brightworlder was—and they suffered beautifully.

The first Elves the Endarkened took as slaves cried out to Aradhwain the Mare, and wept for their herds, and the vast openness of the Gold-engrass. Time passed in the Bright World, and the new Elven captives lamented for their beautiful palaces among The Teeth of the Moon, and cried out to Manafaeren Law Lord to deliver them. Time passed, and they cried out to Amrethion and Pelashia, to the Sword-Giver and the Bride of Battles, to the Starry Hunt.

None of their Brightworld powers saved them.

And Virulan had been confident none of them ever would.

⚜

"What is your name, little Elfling?" Rugashag purred. The Royal Consort's eyes glowed gold with anticipation; her scarlet skin was flushed brilliant with lust. All around her, King Virulan's favored court-iers murmured in anticipation of the treat about to be presented.

The captive's face was contorted with terror—for Rugashag had been careful to bring him to the Heart of Darkness by a way that made him fully aware of the horrors of his fate—but there was no other mark on him. Rugashag had found him in the western reaches of the Golden-grass, and followed him carefully for a long time to be certain he could be taken in secret. The Elfling had been so concerned with hiding from his race's many enemies that he had not noticed one more hunter.

Fool, Virulan thought.

Rugashag had brought him directly to the Heart of Darkness, know-

ing King Virulan took special pleasure in watching new captives' realization of their fate. He knew that she hoped by these shows of submission
to lull him to the point she could destroy him. He cherished each spark
of her futile rebellion, just as he had from the beginning. One day—if he
grew bored enough—he would end it.

"What *are* you?" the Elfling whispered, his voice shaking with beautiful terror.

"We are death and pain and darkness. We are your masters," Virulan
said, smiling hideously. "Kneel."

Virulan rose to his feet, his nostrils flaring as he inhaled sharply. He
had grown used to the stink of soil and sun upon the flesh of new slaves
over the centuries. But this was . . . different.

Irritating.

"No!" the Elfling shouted. He flung himself away from Rugashag, the
tatters of his green robes swirling about his limbs. "I will never serve you!
Never!"

Rugashag laughed mockingly, spreading her wings and baring her
fangs.

The stink Virulan had sensed grew stronger. He took a step forward.

"The simplest spell . . ." the Elfling whispered. Tears glittered in his
eyes.

And then his body erupted in flame.

The Endarkened sprang back in surprise, though mere flame had no
power to harm them. The captive began to scream in agony, and the sweetness of the sound held Virulan transfixed for a fatal moment. By the time
he doused the flame with a spell, the captive was dead.

"I swear to you, my king, I would never—" Rugashag babbled, throwing herself to the floor in terror. No one else in the chamber dared to move
so much as a wing.

"*Magic,*" Uralesse hissed. "The maggot-things have *magic.*"

"Yessss . . ." King Virulan said broodingly. "It is weak, compared to
ours. But you did not know that when you brought me this Elven Mage,
did you, my dear Rugashag?"

"I swear to you— My king— I swear—" she babbled, scrabbling backward, her mouth hanging open in horror.

"Indeed you do," Virulan said. "Let us see what else you will swear—with the proper inducement."

He gestured languidly, and two of the Lesser Endarkened came to bear his consort away.

His *former* consort.

CHAPTER FIVE

THE WAY OF THE SWORD

A commander is often faced with two bad choices and no good ones. One gains the victory by concealing that truth from the enemy.

—Arilcarion War-Maker, *Of the Sword Road*

For days Vieliessar's dreams had been troubled, filled with the clash of swords, the screams of the dying, images of a vast battlefield upon which thousands fought. When she drifted from sleep to waking, it took her long moments to realize that the sounds had followed her into wakefulness.

No battle should come here! she thought, scrambling through the narrow tunnel of her sleeping-place into the clearing. But that was custom, not law. Only the Sanctuary itself was sacrosanct. She kilted up the skirts of her green robe and ran toward the sound. She must see.

When she reached the edge of the Forest and looked out over the winter-bare fields of Rosemoss Farm, she saw that the fields were as yet unplowed and the snow that lay on them was patchy and thin. Empty. The sky was clouded, the air was heavy and wet, and she could smell woodsmoke. Somewhere a dog barked.

There is no battle, she told herself in exasperation. *I have mistaken dreams for Farseeing, nothing more.*

She was about to turn back into the trees when she saw a bright flash in the distance: pale sunlight on armor. She heard shouting and the mellow, demanding call of warhorns. A moment later she felt the faint trembling of the ground as it resounded to the beat of hooves. Destriers. Many of them.

The first of the riders thundered into view. She saw the white-and-silver of Penenjil—the grey stallions marking their riders as the feared Silver Swords of Penenjil, never defeated in battle—the tawny and gold of Enerchelimier, the tawny and marron of Calwas.

But the Silver Swords of Penenjil never ride to battle outside Penenjil's lands—and Calwas has never made alliance with Enerchelimier in all the history of the Hundred Houses!

She barely had time to form her thought before their pursuers became visible. Purple and gold: Haldil, its House colors almost indistinguishable from the tawny and marron of Calwas. Deep blue and green: Bethros, barely distinguishable at this distance from Hallorad's green on green. She knew the colors and blazons of all the Hundred—and she knew Haldil and Bethros to be enemies as often as allies.

There were perhaps a dozen who fled, and twice that number pursuing. When they reached the open field, the fleeing *komen* wheeled their destriers and stood to battle.

Vieliessar had read hundreds of songs of great battles but had never seen one. As if she were a songsmith, she marked how the bright blood slicked the silver blades, how droplets seemed to trail in the air after a blow. She heard the hard dull sound, like an axe upon wood, as a sword struck through armor into flesh, the high, ringing bell sound when it struck shield or blade instead. She saw destriers, mortally wounded, unhorse enemy knights and batter them to death upon the frozen ground, then fall, screaming in rage and pain as they disemboweled themselves in their frantic attempts to stand. Steam curled skyward from open wounds, as if the battlefield was afire. Blood pooled upon the earth and the thick metal scent of it filled the air.

Against all expectation, more wearing the colors of Bethros and Haldil fell than those they sought to slay, for the knights of Penenjil, Enerchelimier, and Calwas fought as if they were demented, drunk on the very blood they spilled. Vieliessar saw a knight of Calwas fling himself from his destrier's saddle as it fell, grab the tack of a riderless mount caparisoned in Penenjil colors, and drag himself to its back.

This is what you were born for, she thought, even as she flinched at the screams of the wounded. This implacable conviction was a terrible, aching weight in her chest, the sight before her both horrible and exciting. Once she had dreamed of fighting upon such a battlefield. Then she had been trained to care for its survivors. *There will be no survivors today,* she thought. This was no formal combat, where the injured could throw down their swords and ride back to their own lines if they could not fight on. The knights upon the field before her would fight until they died.

And this—even this—might be some trick to lure me out of hiding, she thought furiously, *for the time I have left with Lady Arevethmonion grows short, and Humphuliadiel must be more subtle when I am in the sight of all.*

As if her thoughts had the power to command reality, the Calwas knight she had marked turned his Penenjil mount from the field. The blood-maddened destrier reared and fought, desperate to rejoin the battle though it was bleeding from a dozen wounds. At last its rider prevailed, and the grey warhorse flung itself from the field.

Directly toward Vieliessar's hiding place.

She stood her ground. Half in disbelief, half with the desperate need to Heal at least one of the injured. The grey's rider had dropped his sword as he fought for control of his mount, and his armor was so slicked with blood that the bright metal looked as if it had been enameled.

Arevethmonion would be safety. Arevethmonion would hide him.

But when he was no more than a bowshot's distance from where she stood, she heard a sound like the crack of an ice-laden tree limb. The destrier went down as if it had struck a tripwire, crashing to the earth so hard that it lay stunned for a moment, and Vieliessar could see the ruin of its shattered foreleg. Once more the knight managed to jump clear as the animal floundered desperately, trying to rise. He staggered to his feet, hesitated, then turned back to the destrier. He flung himself upon its neck, pinning it to the earth as he slashed its windpipe, and the great beast at last lay still.

But that stroke of mercy seemed to have taken all the knight's strength. He tried to get to his feet, staggered, fell full-length against the frozen earth, and began to crawl.

Vieliessar was running toward him before she thought. "Down," she gasped, falling to her knees beside him. "Be still. I will Heal you and they will not see us." Concealment was a simple spell. She cast it without thought.

Every Healer in the Sanctuary knew how to remove the complex armor of the *komen,* for an injury could not be Healed if it was still transfixed by the metal that had caused it. Beneath the blood-sodden surcoat she could sense the spearhead that had slipped beneath the armored chestplate. Her hands slipped in blood as she worked the intricate fastenings to allow her to lift his helmet free.

His hair was shorn close to his head.

She knew him. Anginach. Anginach Lightbrother of Calwas had been a Candidate in her Service Year. He'd Called Fire one night in the Common Room—terrifying all of them, including himself. He'd become a Postulant, taken the Green Robe, and returned home years before.

How had he come to be here, in armor, bearing a sword?

"Vielle—Vieliessar. P—praise the Silver Hooves . . ." He reached toward her, wincing as fresh blood forced itself between the plates of his armor, but he was too weak to complete the gesture.

"Be still," she repeated. She could not take the time to feel her shock at seeing him in armor—she could already sense him dying.

"Healer . . . too," he gasped. He coughed, spattering her with his blood. "Lost— The proof— Ah, Farcarinon, forgive— Forgive—"

"You have never harmed me," she said. "Please. You must try!" With all her skill, she willed her energy to him, willing Anginach the seconds she needed to save him. But the deeper she knew his body, the more she realized it was hopeless. She could not Heal him.

No one could.

He had poisoned himself.

His body told her a tale of days and nights of no food and little sleep, of riding madly across a frozen landscape to reach the Sanctuary of the Star. There were cordials one could take to force the flesh to burn its store of future years in a sennight or a moonturn, to give impossible strength and endurance. They were dangerous at one dose, fatal at two or more. All Lightborn knew the recipes. Anginach had used it.

"Lost," he repeated. He fought to say more, to tell her what urgency had sent him to the Sanctuary in disguise when he might have come openly in safety, what had caused Calwas and Penenjil to ally themselves . . .

Why he had begged her forgiveness, for he had never stood her enemy.

It was too late. Anginach drew a deep breath. And did not draw another.

He called me Farcarinon. The words she had left unheard in her desperate fight against time sounded in her mind like the mortal beat of the war drum. *Why? Why? Why?* Her hands at last freed the catches of his armor. She pulled it from his body with reckless haste, throwing each piece as far as she could. Collet, besages, rerebrace, vambraces, breastplate, greaves, pollyns, cuisses . . . *I shall not let them see my Lightbrother in this falsehood!* When he wore nothing more than chain shirt and aketon, he was light enough for her to move.

The battlefield was quiet. She dared to glance back at it. Haldil and Bethros had won, though they had paid a high price. Two knights in purple and blood-spattered gold stood over a kneeling Penenjil Silver Sword with drawn blades. The other two victors were searching among the dead.

The Silver Sword removed her helmet. The Haldil sword swept down. The blow did not sever her head from her neck, but it killed her.

Vieliessar dragged Anginach's body into the trees. *Hide me, Lady Arevethmonion!* she begged. *Hide us!*

The veils of misdirection and invisibility that had shielded her before—half of her making, half the will of Arevethmonion—held fast.

Would the knights mark the absence of one of their foes? Would they search the Flower Forest? What she had seen had been no proper war. Early spring was not War Season. And even if it were, Haldil and Bethros, like Penenjil and Calwas and Enerchelimier, were Houses of the Grand Windsward. Why travel so far from home to do battle?

She dragged Anginach through the forest until she was out of breath. She knew she was leaving a track behind her that a blind *hikuliasa* could follow, but she would not leave him in his shame.

There were no sounds of pursuit.

In a deep clearing beside another pool, she pulled chain and aketon from his body, drew the point of the broken spear from between his ribs. His flesh was inscribed with the tale of his desperate flight: raw flesh and open sores, bruising and broken bones, a gauntness clearly due to starvation. Beneath the aketon, a length of filthy, blood-sodden parchment was pressed to his chest. She carefully lifted the parchment free and set it aside, then used handfuls of water to wash his flesh clean. As she did, she realized that the knotted flaxen cord he should be wearing—that all the Lightborn wore beneath their robes—was missing.

I will not send you to Tildorangelor unknown.

It was the work of a moment to untie her own cord and knot it about his waist. But what now? Those who went to ride upon the night wind— princes, nobles, *komen,* and Lightborn—gave their bodies up to unchanging Fire. Only the Landbond and the cursed went into the earth. She would not summon Fire within Arevethmonion's sacred precincts, nor bury Anginach as if he were Landbond.

In the end, she left him in Arevethmonion's keeping and simply walked away. She did not look back. She never returned to the place where she had left him to his journey.

She took the parchment with her.

She stopped beside the stream near her sleeping place to wash the blood from her hands and clothing. The parchment she had taken from Anginach's body was a length such as might have been used for a scroll. It was torn at one end and glued closed with drying blood. Carefully, she immersed it in the stream, rinsing it clean, then unfolded it gently. The interior surface was covered in tiny, precise writing. Vieliessar's eyes widened. She recognized the hand.

Celelioniel of Enerchelimier.

Celelioniel *Astromancer.*

⇥⇤

I never meant to turn my hand to The Song of Amrethion. *My interest was in Mosirinde's Covenant. Many have said that it was her enchantments which caused the Flower Forests to be. Today we draw upon them to work our Magery, as the Covenant commands us. But Mosirinde taught more of what we must not do than what we must: of the dangers of necromancy and blood magic, of taking so much energy from Life that we leave Death in our wake. How came she, I wondered, to know so intimately the perils that might befall us?"*

As Vieliessar read, it was as if she heard Celelioniel's living voice. Not the ravings of the mad Astromancer whom all now mocked, but the careful researches of the scholar, for like so many of the Lightborn, Celelioniel was first a researcher and historian. Vieliessar decided that she held the preface Celelioniel had written for her annotated copy of *The Song of Amrethion* and assumed that the rest of the scroll was now the spoil of those who had harried Anginach and his escort to their deaths.

Celelioniel must have taken it away with her when she returned to Enerchelimier, Vieliessar realized. *Did she realize Hamphuliadiel meant to betray her when it was too late for her to stop him? Or could she not bear to give it up?*

There was no way to know.

Celelioniel's preface broke off in the middle of a sentence—Anginach must have torn it loose and hidden it when he'd realized they were pursued—but Vieliessar had enough to draw conclusions about the whole. Celelioniel had begun by attempting to fix one moment in time: the birth of the Flower Forests and the inception of the Covenant the Lightborn swore to husband the land. Celelioniel wanted to know how this knowledge had been gained, for no child fears the fire who hasn't been burned. And so she had learned of a Darkness—hungry, implacable, biding its time and gathering its armies until it rode forth from its obsidian halls to slake its unslakable hunger on all that was. An enemy as real and malign as any Beastling army—but an army whose first attack upon the Hundred Houses lay not in the primordial past, but in the future.

Vieliessar would never know what steps had led Celelioniel to *The Song of Amrethion*, and what hints gleaned from ancient histories had made her realize Amrethion's Curse was not gibberish. But by the time Celelioniel Astromancer traced the ancient history of the Darkness back to the beginning of Lightborn Magery, Serenthon's feet were already set upon the road of the High Kingship.

How came this to Anginach's hand? How came he to seek me?

She realized then that it had not been Vieliessar Lightsister whom Anginach sought, nor even Vieliessar Farcarinon.

Anginach had sought the Child of the Prophecy.

Her.

To warn her.

Darkness comes! Vieliessar thought in horror, as Celioniel's words fell into place in her mind. *As Amrethion foretold!*

Farcarinon's fall was the last of Amrethion's forewarnings.

It comes in my lifetime. This is why Celelioniel placed Peacebond upon me so long ago. She feared to hasten its coming by so much as a sennight.

The Hundred Houses must be warned.

But even as that thought came to her, despair thrust it aside. What could she say? Who could she tell? Proofs might be found in the Library of Arevethmonion—if Hamphuliadiel had not locked them all away, perhaps even destroyed the priceless scrolls.

Hamphuliadiel had sought to kill her. He would not do that if he thought the Prophecy was false. He believed, just as Celelioniel had.

He believes, and conceals the books of prophecy so no one can duplicate Celelioniel's work. He seeks to keep the events Amrethion foretold from coming true by killing me. He cannot seek my life openly, lest in doing so he gives others proof that I am indeed what Celelioniel named me: Child of the Prophecy, the Curse and Doom of the Hundred Houses.

She did not wish to claim that destiny. She didn't even know what it *was*.

What am I to do? What?
She could find no answer.

⋇

I *have no right to ask your forgiveness."*
In the heart of Arevethmonion, Vieliessar dreamed.

The chamber was filled with light. It was airy and inviting, the white stone of its walls little more than punctuation for the enormous panes of leaded glass that took the summer sunlight and turned it into a thousand many hued sparks of fire. The one who sat at the delicate table in the center of the pool of sunlight was both familiar and unknown. His long black hair was caught back by a thin band of moonsilver about his brow. Its intricate braids were similar to those worn by the komen, *but instead of being woven into a knot at the base of his neck, the long braids hung free.*

He was writing. The rhythmic measured movement of the pen across the surface of the vellum made the rings he wore cast a changing pattern of bright sparks on the vellum and the surface of the table.

"And it would be unseemly of me to do so. I suppose it would. But I can hope for your understanding. Hatred and fear are heavy chains. I know this. Or I will know it."

The place was one Vieliessar had never seen, yet somehow she knew it. Celephriandullias-Tildorangelor, the Lost City. The royal city, from which Amrethion Aradruiniel had reigned.

He stopped writing and looked up, meeting her gaze. She was startled to see that his eyes were not the black of the eyes of every person she'd ever seen. This one's eyes were the darkest shade of gold.

"Believe this: I would not have set so heavy a task upon you if there had been any other way. I can only hope . . . But that is foolishness. I may tell myself you will prevail. I will never know."

"What . . . ?" Her voice emerged in a rusty croak, as if long unused, and the fact that she had spoken at all held her suddenly paralyzed. She had studied the ways of prophecy and Foretelling for many years. No one

who had left any record had ever been anything more than an invisible watcher, swept along by the logic of the vision.

"I . . . I do not yet know if I shall," she said. She could speak, she could move, and to do those things filled her with an awe not far removed from dread.

"Nor do I," he answered, meeting her gaze as if she stood before him in flesh. "I do not know, spirit of future days, if you are male or female, great prince or humble servant. I know only that the land needs your strength."

"Can you— Will you— What enemy? What—"

He raised a slender hand, and Vieliessar fell silent.

"I cannot answer you, spirit. I do not have the answers you seek. Today my beloved, my queen, my Pelashia, presented me with our firstborn. A son. To secure his safety and that of my kingdom, she has set upon me a great spell, that I may prophesy of things yet to come."

His queen. Pelashia Celenthodiel, who had given Light to the Lightborn. She was gazing upon Amrethion Aradruiniel. The last High King.

"She will die. You will die," Vieliessar blurted. "Your lords will rise up against your children. There has been war from your day to mine."

She saw Amrethion's golden eyes darken with grief. "It is well I shall remember nothing of this when I wake," he said softly. "I could not bear it."

"You must remember!" Vieliessar said urgently. "If it has not yet happened, you can change it. You can save your Queen and your realm—write plainly of the danger so your children will know, and fear, and prepare—"

"It cannot be," he said sadly. "When my beloved came from Tildorangelor to become my bride, she knew even then the doom that lay over our race. To name it plainly would be to summon it before we could defend ourselves against it."

"How can you say that?" Vieliessar demanded. She forgot she dreamed, she forgot she argued with one millennia dead. All that mattered to her in this moment was making him understand. "We aren't ready! You name me Child of the Prophecy, and I have never held a sword! There is no High King, just a hundred jealous princes quarreling among themselves! If the *danger is as terrible as you say, we will not prevail. We will die. If you love us—your people, your children—please! Tell me what comes!"*

"Darkness," Amrethion said. "Darkness. *I have done—I will do—all I can. My queen's power binds the coming ages in chains of prophecy. These words will be a beacon of Magery that gains power with the passing of centuries, spirit, until at last you are summoned forth."*

"You're afraid of it," Vieliessar said, *in a voice that trembled with fury.* "Whatever it is—whatever you say I must face—you're so afraid of it you want to hide behind cryptic poetry and hope—hope!—that I can do what you cannot."

"I do hope," Amrethion answered. "I—we—hope we have made the right choices." *He gazed into her eyes, and there was no hint of apology in his expression.* "If Pelashia named Darkness to me—if I remembered this moment out of time and acted upon my knowledge—the alfaljodthi *would be destroyed. And so she remains silent. And you have long years in which to grow strong. You will understand when you confront Darkness."*

She took a step forward—unwilling to listen to his arguments, un-willing to think they might hold truth—but as she did so, the beautiful room with its strange delicate furniture, its king who had never worn armor nor held a sword, seemed to dwindle in every direction at once. As she fell from dreaming into true sleep, she had the strange sourceless insight that often accompanied dreams. She saw herself for an instant as Amrethion would have seen her: a barbarian coarsened by genera-tions of war, born out of violence and murder and carrying them with her into whatever future she could create.

She thrashed herself into wakefulness, gasping for breath. For a mo-ment she could not remember why grief was a cold and terrible weight in her throat.

Then she remembered her vision of Amrethion, and wept.

What am I to do? What am I to do?

⚜

A fortnight later, the weather turned soft, and spring plowing began at Rosemoss Farm. The first caravan of the season passed through the Flower Forest on the way to the Sanctuary of the Star.

It was time to return.

Her steps were slow with reluctance. She would be returning to live beneath the roof of her enemy, just as she had in childhood—but she had not known Caerthalien was her enemy until the moment she left it. She meant to go before Hamphuliadiel in the rags and dirt of her banishment, for they would give her the semblance of humility and penitence he required. It would be a hard thing to endure, but she had done harder. Perhaps—with enough time—she might win his approval. His help. She could not imagine herself as the agent of the Prophecy, destroying the Fortunate Lands and all who lived within its bounds. She would die first.

As she stepped onto the path that led through Arevethmonion, she heard the jingle of harness in the distance and the earth beneath her feet vibrated to the slow thud of draft oxen's feet. She stopped and waited.

"I greet you in the name of the Sanctuary of the Star, Prince Anarolodh," she said.

It had been a simple matter to cast True Speech to Hear the lead rider's name, and she had not needed it to know his house or rank, for he wore the scarlet and sable of Gerchiliael, with the wheat-sheaf of lesser cadency below the crossed swords of its device.

Anarolodh inclined his head. "Lightsister," he said. "In the name of Dondialoch Gerchiliael, I thank you for the Sanctuary's care of us. Will you ride?" he asked.

"I will walk," she answered, and took her place at his side. He touched his spurs to his palfrey's flanks, and the procession moved slowly forward once again. If Prince Anarolodh found her disheveled condition odd, the thought of it did not trouble the surface of his mind.

Dilvalos Lightsister joined them half a candlemark later. She had not been at the Sanctuary when Vieliessar had been banished, so the Caerthalien Candidates must have been the first along this road this season. She gave Vieliessar a startled look—clearly she knew of the banishment—

but said merely: "There is a great disarray before you, for everyone seems to have set forth the moment the roads were dry. Caerthalien arrived at yesterday's dawn, and before its wagons were half unloaded, Cirandeiron and Telthorelandor came as well. We shall have all the Seven here together, for Mangiralas and Rolumienion are expected today, and Inglethendragir and Ullilion tomorrow."

And Hamphuliadiel will be much occupied with their envoys, for all but Ullilion are High Houses, Vieliessar thought. "It will be much work for Mistress Hamonglachele to care for them all," she answered, keeping her voice low so that Anarolodh did not hear two Lightborn speaking of such homely things.

Dilvalos frowned. "That is—" she began, and stopped, as if she had been lured into speaking of things she must not.

⌁║⌁

Pavilions were spread out all across the fields surrounding the Sanctuary. Vieliessar let Dilvalos lead Prince Anarolodh and the new Candidates into the Sanctuary antechamber, while she went with the wagons into the courtyard as if this were her assigned task. The stableyard was chaotic, for Radanding Stablemaster's staff had been sharply winnowed as Candidates rejoined their Houses or passed on to the Postulancy, and there was another wagon train already here, bearing a banner in the violet and silver of Inglethendragir.

Inglethendragir had risen from Low to High upon Farcarinon's bones.

"Mistress Morgaenel greets—" A boy in the grey livery of the Sanctuary servants came rushing up to the wagons and stopped, his eyes going wide with consternation at his inability to identify the device before him.

"Greets Gerchiliael and bids them welcome," Vieliessar prompted gently. She kept her face smooth, but she was puzzled. Mistress Morgaenel's place was the kitchens, not the guesthouse.

"—and says I am to show you where you may set your pavilions, for the guesthouse is full."

"Are we to wallow in mud as if we were Windsward rabble?" *Komen* Thalien demanded. She was the leader of Prince Anarolodh's Twelve. "Make room—or shall I do it for you?"

"*Komen* Thalien, it is our great sorrow that we have so little space for guests," Vieliessar said quickly. "But Inglethendragir will bear you company." She gestured toward the field, hidden now by the buildings of the outer courtyard. Her Green Robe might be stained and tattered, but it still marked her as Lightborn: at last *Komen* Thalien nodded.

"Very well, brat. I will look at your mudhole."

The boy hurried off and *Komen* Thalien followed. Now Radanding Stablemaster approached, with two of his assistants in tow. He was as shocked to see Vieliessar as Dilvalos Lightsister had been—but his gaze held something more than mere surprise.

Grief.

And warning.

"You are needed in the guesthouse, Lightsister," he said brusquely, before turning to walk quickly down the line of wagons to see what must be unloaded.

If Hamphuliadiel did not know already that she was here, he would within a quartermark, and to tarry would only give him new fuel for his discontent.

But only a fool disregarded a warning given by a friend.

❦

The guesthouse was an odd building—a manor house wing with no manor attached. It was long and narrow, set behind the stables and across a broad courtyard paved with smooth river stones. Its ground floor held a bathhouse, a refectory, the workroom of Mistress Guesthouse, and a storage room for those things used in the guesthouse alone—blankets and linens, perfumes for the bath, and wines and strong cordials. On its second floor lay the sleeping chambers. Depending upon the demands of its guests, it could accommodate up to sixteen visitors, but the interior walls were designed to fold back to create larger rooms, and if Caerthalien and Cirandeiron were both in occupancy, their princes would both insist on great state. Battle might be forbidden upon the Sanctuary grounds, but there were other ways of challenging a rival than with a swordblade.

In all her years at the Sanctuary, Vieliessar had never crossed the courtyard to the guesthouse, for it lay beyond the bounds where her life was sacrosanct. Now she hurried past the refectory, where loud talk and laughter proclaimed the guests at their morning meal, and closeted herself quickly in Hamonglachele's workroom, sliding the door closed behind her.

It had much the look of Maeredhiel's workroom in the Sanctuary—the same litter of scrolls and wax tablets upon the broad table, the same low stool. On the wall behind the worktable, instead of a collection of keys, stood a slateboard upon which was painted the plan of the sleeping chambers. Within each square was a cryptic notation in chalk, saying who occupied each one. Above the worktable itself hung a suspended grid of sixteen silver bells, each engraved with the design of the flower for which each guesthouse chamber was named.

Vieliessar seated herself upon the stool, wondering how long she would have to wait and more conscious than ever of her unkempt appearance. Her feet were bare, and they and her hands were callused with moonturns of hard work. Her hair was longer than it should be, and her robe, though clean, was ragged and stained.

She had barely finished her catalogue of the chamber and her person when the door slid back. Vieliessar tensed, but it was Morgaenel who entered. She slid the door quickly shut behind her, and latched it.

"Praise Pelashia! You're alive!" Morgaenel gasped. "The winter was so hard!"

"I came as Radanding meant I should, but I know not why. 'Ilthel, why are you here? Where is 'Chele?"

"She is now Mistress of Servants," Morgaenel said softly. "Maeredhiel has gone to the Vale of Celenthodiel. It was the lung-fever. She took ill just after Midwinter. Hamphuliadiel even sent Momioniarch Lightsister to attend her. No one thought it was serious—even Momioniarch said it might be repaired better by rest than by a Healing. When 'Chele went to look in on her one morning . . . it was too late for Healing."

"May she find happiness in the Vale of Celenthodiel," Vieliessar said quietly. If the spirit truly survived as more than a hungry ghost, Vieliessar prayed Maeredhiel and Aradrothiach would find each other and at last complete their Bond.

This was Hamphuliadiel's work. Vieliessar knew it beyond doubt. He'd worked to erase all trace of Celelioniel's scholarship from the land . . . but there had been one who had been Celelioniel's confidante. Who had been present upon the night of Vieliessar's birth.

Maeredhiel.

If she had thought— If she had known what Hamphuliadiel would do—

"I suppose she did not think it was more than a cough that could be banished with time and rest," Vieliessar answered steadily.

"I am sure you are right," Morgaenel answered. "What else could it have been?"

⊰⊱

Go. Go now before you lose your courage.

It was deep night on the day she had returned to the Shrine.

She had not gone before Hamphuliadiel.

She had thought his enmity was a thing that fell upon her alone, a thing that might be reasoned with. Now she knew it was not. Maeredhiel had died of it. Anyone might be next.

Of a surety, Hamphuliadiel's next attempt upon her would be something more certain than a winter's banishment. She'd already placed her friends in danger enough by giving them the secret of her return to hold. *I shall never again offer up hostages to a madman's will,* she vowed grimly.

She wore a heavy cloak, boots, and the grey tunic and trousers of a Candidate. Over her shoulder was slung a leather bag holding knife, waterskin, bread, and cheese, gifts of Morgaenel. It had been a risk to involve her even that much, but Vieliessar had little choice. She could Shield herself in the guesthouse workroom and so escape discovery, but to move about the Sanctuary would guarantee exposure. Even if Hamphuliadiel discovered she had returned and departed again, it would probably not occur to him to question the Sanctuary servants.

And even if he did . . .

Vieliessar was Lightborn. Servants did not question orders the Lightborn gave. Indeed, Morgaenel had asked no questions.

Go now, Vieliessar told herself.

She eased open the door of the workroom. The guesthouse was dark and silent. She crossed the floor on silent feet and eased open the outer door. Across the courtyard, the Sanctuary of the Star was dark and quiet. The only light came from the lanterns hung upon its gate.

She closed the door behind her and walked into Arevethmonion.

She did not look back.

⊰❦⊱

He had not expected to end his days in a forest cottage on Caerthallen land. If—by the grace of the Silver Hooves—he had lived into old age, Gunedwaen had expected a place of honor at his lord's table, quiet days spent imparting the lore of his long life to the children who would grow to become *komen*—the strong defense of his noble house.

Of Farcarinon.

The shutter rattled. It was autumn, and old bones and old injuries ached in the cold. Striker raised her head, gazing about the room for a moment before returning to sleep. The *hikuliasa* was good company, though Gunedwaen had never decided what purpose had lain in Bolecthindial's mind when he had presented the animal as a gift. Perhaps to mock Gunedwaen's own state, for the beast had been lamed and half wild.

Each winter Gunedwaen thought of letting his fire die, of walking out into the snow and laying his bones down for the last time. Freezing was said to be a gentle death, far more so than the deaths he had dealt. And each year he told himself: *Next year. Not this year. Next year.* Perhaps it was curiosity that kept him living. Perhaps it was the wish to fight one last battle. The Silver Hooves would not take him if he died peacefully, and he had no taste for wandering as a homeless ghost till the stars grew dark.

The shutter rattled again,

"You should show yourself," Gunedwaen said calmly. "If you have come to kill me, I must say you are some years too late."

"You cannot have known I was here," a voice said.

"Had I not learned the skill to see the unseen, I would have perished long since," Gunedwaen answered. He had not been truly certain of her presence until she spoke. Striker raised her head from her paws again, gazing curiously in the direction of the voice. She seemed puzzled. "I would have you show yourself, stranger."

"Are you truly so eager to die?" the voice asked.

"Are you truly so dangerous?" Gunedwaen answered.

There was a moment of silence, then: "Once I would have said I wished no harm to any. I would know who your fealty is pledged to, old man."

"What Landbond pledges to any lord but the next harvest?" Gunedwaen answered mockingly.

There was a snort of contempt from behind him. Striker made a soft sound in her throat.

"I have known Landbonds in plenty, old man. You are not one."

"You are well traveled for one of the Night Brotherhood. If not well informed," Gunedwaen observed.

"Well informed enough to know I have never seen one of the Children of Night, nor have you. I come to ask your House and your fealty. I already know your name."

"If you know my name, you know all there is to know," Gunedwaen answered. With laborious care, he shifted in his seat enough so he could turn his head to see the doorway.

He saw no one there.

Suddenly there was a ripple in the air, and where there had been nothingness stood a figure in a grey cloak, its deep hood doing as much to conceal her face as her spell had done. Striker got to her feet, uttering a low bark of warning. The woman pushed back the hood of her cloak and Gunedwaen saw what he'd expected to see: the shorn hair of one of the Lightborn.

"I do not know who you claim as your lord, for all that you live as Caerthalien's supplicant," the Lightborn said stubbornly.

"A dead house and a failed cause," Gunedwaen said, sighing. "Come, Lightsister, tell me your purpose here." He turned back to gaze into the fire. Her footsteps were soft as she crossed the room to the wood-pile, chose a length of wood, and added it to the coals.

"I seek one named Gunedwaen, once Swordmaster to War Prince Serenthon Farcarinon. I have need of him."

The rekindled fire cast its amber light on her face. He had never seen her before. But he knew her.

"Lady Nataranweiya's child lived," he said slowly.

"Yes," the woman answered. "Nataranweiya fled to the Sanctuary of the Star. There I was born. There I returned."

"Then return there again and live still," Gunedwaen said. "Farcarinon is gone, its children scattered to the seven winds. You cannot claim your father's house from its ashes."

"It took me long to find you," she said, deflecting his words. "I have come to learn all you can teach me of knighthood and war."

Deep in the embers of what he once was, Gunedwaen felt a stirring of old instincts. He remembered the terrible day when Serenthon had received word of Caerthalien's betrayal. Gunedwaen had begged him to sue for terms, knowing Farcarinon could not stand alone against a High House alliance, and for a moment he had seen Serenthon hesitate, about to agree. Then he had looked upon his lady, already great with child, and his face had grown cold and resolute. He shook his head, and spoke the words that sealed their fates.

"I shall not surrender all that I love to Darkness."

Gunedwaen had followed his liege-lord to the battlefield, and saw him fall, and was struck down in his turn. He would have—should have—died there beside him, but his apprentices had carried him from the field and into hiding. Gunedwaen remembered standing in Caerthalien's great hall, weak from fever, his garments torn and stained with the sennights of illness, injuries, hiding. He remembered the moment Ivrulion Light-Prince had bespelled him so he could never be whole again, how the fever for revenge had burned hotter than the wound-sickness that had cost him his arm and the use of his leg, how in that moment all his hopes of vengeance were shattered.

And he laughed. "My lord, are you disordered in your mind? And even if you are mad, what teaching do you think you can gain from a lame, one-armed man? Abandon your thoughts of revenge, I beg you."

He saw her eyes flash with a prince's temper, saw her set her jaw. "I have not come for revenge," she said, and her voice was hard. "I have come to be made Knight by your hand."

Gunedwaen stared at her in sudden doubt, too taken aback to speak. The *komen* began their training in childhood—Serenthon's daughter was decades past her childhood. Even if he wished to try, he did not possess the resources of a War Prince's castel with which to school her. "Go back to the Sanctuary," he said at last. "Go anywhere. My lord, I cannot aid you."

"You must!" she answered fiercely. "Do you think I wish for this, Gunedwaen Swordmaster? I wish nothing more than to live out my life as a child of the Light. But I may not. And to say to you more than this will bring about your death as surely as if I stabbed you through the heart myself."

"My life is not so glorious that I would regret leaving it," Gunedwaen said. "But I would be nine times a fool to give you that which you ask only because you ask it."

"Then swear to me you are Farcarinon's still," she whispered, and even in the dim firelight he could see tears glitter in her eyes.

"I am Farcarinon's until the stars grow cold," he answered steadily. "I beg your forgiveness, my prince. I was borne from the field against my will. I gave no parole to Caerthalien."

None had been needed, after Ivrulion Light-Prince's working.

Farcarinon—what name she bore he did not know—took a step toward him, so swift that Striker got to her feet. But she merely knelt beside his chair and took his hand in hers. Her fingers were soft, her hands those of one who had never held a sword. "There is no need to ask, Master Gunedwaen. You preserved your life until I came for you. And I beg your forgiveness in turn, for I must have your knowledge and skill. Teach me as you taught my father."

"My lady," he said helplessly, "Farcarinon is *gone*."

She smiled at him, and her smile was brilliant with grief. "So I believed for long years. But I do not seek to raise Farcarinon from its ashes."

"Then . . . what?" he asked. "My lord, if any of Prince Serenthon's *komentai'a* survived, they have pledged fealty elsewhere. Or they are useless, as I am."

"Not useless to me, Master Gunedwaen," she answered. "I call you back to service now."

"And I come," Gunedwaen answered steadily. "But you must tell me what brings you here, for I cannot aid you without that knowledge."

"I will be the death of you," Farcarinon answered softly. "Nor shall I tell you all, and you must content yourself with that. But I shall tell you this: I was born Vieliessar Farcarinon, War Prince of Farcarinon, in the Sanctuary of the Star. Celelioniel Astromancer named me Child of the Prophecy, but I would not hear. I beg you: hear all I would not, for our time grows short. High King Amrethion Aradruiniel spoke a Foretelling on the day he fell from the Unicorn Throne, giving warning of the day the Hundred would face an enemy who did not wish to take their lands and wealth, but their *lives*—all life, to the least blade of grass in the humblest field. It is foretold that this Darkness will strip the flesh from the bones of the world, and none of the War Princes knows—or cares!"

"How came you to know these things?" Gunedwaen asked. *How came you to know Aramenthiali's plan? Is this count you bring us of Caerthalien's knights accurate? You say Oronviel will not fight this day—who has said this where you might hear?* The ghost of what he once was rose up in his question.

The words his liege-lord and prince had spoken already were near to madness, but that madness was compounded by the words she spoke next. She told of Celelioniel Astromancer's quest, of Celelioniel's discovery of the truth and meaning of the ancient Prophecy, of her own place within its web.

Vieliessar stroked Striker's head absently as she knelt beside Gunedwaen's chair. "I might say to you Serenthon-my-father received a Foretelling of Celelioniel of the failure of his ambition, of his death, my mother's death, my birth—but who can know what happened that day save those who were there, and they are all gone to the night winds," she said, her voice quiet. "I could say to you all my words are proven in scrolls hidden away by Hamphuliadiel, in Foretellings given by generations of Astromancers, in histories too dry for any but scholars—but such words will not sway princes and knights." She laughed bitterly. "They don't even persuade scholars, for Hamphuliadiel thinks the evil day can be averted by destroying the warning of it. I know one thing only: the Darkness comes, and it comes soon, and if the Hundred Houses are not united against it, then we shall all perish as if we never were. I must do what my father could not do—and if you will not help me, I shall fail."

Years of patient alliances, gifts and promises, and secret treaties had brought Serenthon close to making himself High King—so close the Hundred Houses had not been content with merely humbling Farcarinon, but had destroyed its castels and keeps, slaughtered its *komen,* and carried its vassals off to live out their lives on alien ground. And now Serenthon's daughter sought him out, saying she must succeed at the task that had broken Farcarinon.

"You might fail even with my aid," Gunedwaen said gently. "I cannot give you all the skills you seek. I cannot give you victory."

"The Hundred will not follow a Green Robe," Vieliessar said flatly. "Give me your swordcraft, Master Gunedwaen, and I will put off that robe for a knight's armor. I can see no other way. But if you will not aid me," Vieliessar said quietly, "I will go."

"'Haste gives a thousand knights to the enemy,'" Gunedwaen answered absently. Whether it was madness or a sanity that transcended sense, he would follow Farcarinon's last prince. "Come, my lord. Build up the fire. It is late and the room grows cold. And we have much to speak of before we begin."

The message had been sent from the Sanctuary of the Star in Flower Moon, but hadn't reached Thurion until the end of Harvest, for he had been in the field with the army. The seneschal at Caerthalien Keep had sent the scroll onward, of course, but scrollcase had been left behind to save weight and space in the dispatch rider's bags.

Thurion had thought nothing of it at the time—messages came from the Sanctuary to its former students now and then. In the scroll Momioniarch Lightsister had asked if Caerthalien would permit him to return to the Sanctuary to teach for a year. Thurion had not needed to consult Lord Bolecthindial to know the answer to that: he had sent his regrets by spellbird and forgotten the matter completely until the day he returned, at long last, to his rooms in Caerthalien Keep to find the Sanctuary's green-and-silver scrollcase sitting atop a chest.

He'd picked it up absently, thinking that he could not return it to the Sanctuary until the Candidates went in the spring. When he touched the scrollcase, the Sanctuary's true message was revealed, unrolling in his mind in Hamphuliadiel's voice.

"*To Thurion Lightbrother, greetings. I send you this message in secret not to set you at odds with Caerthalien, but in warning—*" Thurion dropped the scrollcase in surprise. He could not imagine why the Astromancer would send him a message at all, much less by secret means. The case hit the floor and rolled under his bed, and it took him several minutes to retrieve it. Then he knelt on the floor, clutching the silver-stamped leather case tightly as the voice echoed through his mind.

Vieliessar had left—*fled*—the Sanctuary of the Star sometime in the spring. *"I believe she means to break the Covenant in order to take revenge in Farcarinon's name against Caerthalien and the other houses of the Grand Alliance . . ."* Warning was being sent to the senior Lightborn of those Houses—Caerthalien, Aramenthiali, Cirandeiron, and Telthorelandor—which had been crucial to Farcarinon's fall. *"I do not charge any of you with silence. You may tell whom you choose what I have conveyed to you, yet know that I believe it would not be well to make the matter of a disobedient Lightborn too public a matter, lest it seem to involve the Sanctuary of the Star in matters from which it has always stood apart. That Vieliessar is Farcarinon is unfortunate, for reasons you well understand . . ."*

The information was stunning, but not so stunning that Thurion's mind did not race on ahead of it. *"Senior" Lightborn. That can mean oldest, or of highest rank. Perhaps Carangil Lightbrother, as Ladyholder Glorthiachiel uses him to spy on everyone here. Ivrulion Light-Prince must have received this news, whether from Carangil or from the Sanctuary—and some time ago, for I know he has returned here several times since Flower.* Thurion did his best to still his questions, for the message was still unspooling in his mind, and once it had run its course, he suspected the spell would unravel and vanish.

"I am a humble servant of the Light which shines for all whether of High House or Low, and I uphold the justice of the great lords of the Fortunate Lands. I have hunted the rebel Vieliessar from the moment I discovered her gone. My search has been fruitless, and so I send to you, Thurion of Caerthalien, as once—perhaps unwisely—you held yourself her friend. If she comes to you, I charge you by the Light we both serve to take her prisoner by any means you can, and be aware that any tale she tells you is merely trickery and lies that serve her insane desire. Be a strong defender of your noble house, Thurion of Caerthalien, and repay the love and care your Prince has always had for you . . ."

The voice stopped, and Thurion felt a tingle beneath his fingertips as the message-spell unmade itself.

Hamphuliadiel, you are indeed a fool, he thought in annoyance. *It will*

be a great day for the Lightborn when your reign as Astromancer is over.
Words Thurion had never thought to think, but how could Hamphuliadiel—
how could *anyone* who had been at the Sanctuary during Thurion's
training—believe lies could deceive him? He did not need to set a spell of
Heart-Seeing on someone to know the truth: all he had to do was listen to
their thoughts. . . .

The Astromancer's message was a lie. How could Hamphuliadiel
know what Vielle meant to do? Unless she'd told him—and Thurion
could not believe that. He could believe that she had vanished from the
Sanctuary and that they had not found her, but anything beyond those
two facts could be nothing other than conjecture. He rose slowly to his
feet, still clutching the now-inert scrollcase, and tried to decide what to
do next. Go to Ivrulion and tell him he'd received a spell-message from
the Sanctuary? Wait for Ivrulion to speak first? He felt a clutch of angry
fear at being forced to decide how deep his loyalty to Caerthalien ran,
and suddenly words he'd once said to Vielle crowded into memory, the
words as sharp and clear as if they, too, were a spell-message.

*"Prisoner, hostage, I care not if you are Farcarinon, or Caerthalien, or
the Child of the Prophecy. My family does not even own the roof above our
heads. A third of what we harvest each year goes to pay Menenel Farmholder for our shelter and our seed grain. All we have ever asked is that the
great lords do not ride across our fields and spoil our work—and if they do,
or even fight across them, there is nothing we can say without punishment.
Do you think the quarrels of the Hundred Houses matter to me? How has
your life been harder than mine?"*

He heard the hall door creak as it swung inward and turned toward
the sound. He was so convinced it would be Denerarth—returned from
the tasks attendant upon settling the two of them back into their usual
quarters—that he stared at the figure in the doorway for a long moment
in utter silence.

Ivrulion Light-Prince tapped the scrollcase he held gently on the doorframe. "It seems that we have both been favored by a message from the
Astromancer," he said, nodding toward the scrollcase in Thurion's hand.

"It only just reached me, Lord Ivrulion," Thurion said. "I suppose they both said much the same thing."

"Why not tell me what yours says, and we shall see?" Ivrulion replied pleasantly. The pleasantry was a fraud: Thurion had long known Ivrulion to be as coldly ambitious as his father.

"Vieliessar of— Of *nowhere*, I suppose, Lord Ivrulion," he answered, stumbling slightly over the words, for to name someone without being able to name their House was nearly unthinkable. "Vieliessar Lightsister left the Sanctuary of the Star in the spring. Hamphuliadiel does not know where she is. At least, he didn't when he sent to me."

"Did you not find it curious he would send to you? Oh, but I forget— you and she were friends at the Sanctuary."

"We were in the same Service Year." Thurion chose his words carefully; he knew Ivrulion had forgotten nothing. "I suppose we were friends as much as anyone is there." He shrugged. "She was not Chosen when I was, as you know. Later, of course, the Light kindled in her. She took the Green Robe, but I had left long before. Hamphuliadiel thinks she may come here—and charges me to take her prisoner if she does."

"*When* she does?" Ivrulion said, his tone making it clear it was a question.

"My lord, I do not know." Thurion's gaze was clear and untroubled as he met Ivrulion's eyes. His True Speech was far stronger than anyone else's in the castel; the stronger the Gift, the less that same Gift could be used against one. Ivrulion could not hear his thoughts. "The Astromancer believes she left the Sanctuary in order to exact revenge. I suppose he is correct. He has known her far longer than I." He'd told Vieliessar once that each House was like any other. He would not betray Caerthalien to an enemy, but he would not take its causes as his own.

After a moment Ivrulion stepped away from the doorframe and smiled faintly. "I think if she meant to come for vengeance, she would have done it moonturns ago, don't you? Perhaps she became disordered in her wits and simply fled the Sanctuary, but it will do no harm to search for her, and it might even be amusing. I am sure you will wish to accompany me."

"Of course," Thurion answered automatically, and Ivrulion's smile widened slightly.

"Then I will leave you to become reacquainted with a dry roof and your own bed. I shall see you on the morrow."

※

That following day was the first of many Thurion spent in Ivrulion's company. It was uncomfortable, for Thurion knew the War Prince's son still held him in suspicion. *Better that,* Thurion thought, *than that he seek me as an ally.* Thurion had never boasted of the strength of his Keystone Gift, though he knew full well that Ivrulion was aware of it. It was why Thurion ate at the High Table, why Lord Bolecthindial called upon him more often than any others to stand beside him at Court and set a spell of Heart-Seeing upon those whom Lord Bolecthindial deemed to be less than forthcoming.

Alone together, Thurion and Ivrulion visited all the Flower Forests within a day's ride—Rimroheth, Angoratorei, Alqualanya, Valmenandlae, Rolliondale—for the Flower Forests resonated to the Light, and if Vieliessar had entered Caerthalien and used Magery here, some trace should be left. Ivrulion's conversation always seemed idle, but it returned, again and again, to Vieliessar. Thurion had the sense that much of what he said in answer Ivrulion already knew, and while Thurion was careful to tell all of what he knew, he was equally carefull to tell little of what he guessed. Ivrulion spoke of Vieliessar's childhood in the Great Keep and of his hope that she would come to Caerthalien so he could extend to her his personal assurance of protection.

"—of course there must never be any children, but that is a simple Binding to craft, and were she wed to my Huthiel, her position would be assured. And she would be most welcome here, for I have heard that her Healing skill is great. Indeed, Warlord Amlunan boasted of it when we met Aramenthiali upon the field this summer—he would not have lived without her art."

"The Light has indeed blessed her," Thurion answered, taking care to speak as if he believed Ivrulion's words to be true.

At first they rode out every day, but soon days and even sennights passed before Ivrulion proposed another expedition, for they found neither presence nor trace of Vieliessar, no matter now closely they searched the Flower Forests. No further message came from Hamphuliadiel, and at last Ivrulion, bored, pronounced himself satisfied that Vieliessar had never come to Caerthalien. Thurion did not know whether he was satisfied of Vielle's absence or Thurion's loyalty: all he knew for certain was that when he begged permission from Lord Bolecthindial to visit Sweethallow Farm and his family, it was granted as easily as it had always been.

Wherever you have gone, Vielle, I hope you are safe and happy there. And free.

❈

Her footsteps crunched through the crust of new-fallen snow as she ran. The winter air was a sharp knife in her throat; her breath smoked on the chill air. *This is the domain that should have been mine. And if it were—oh, Silver Hooves defend!—for how long should I have been able to hold it against the Darkness?*

She ran on. One league out. One league back. She ran this course every day, at Gunedwaen's command.

The journey to Farcarinon had taken them from Rade to Woods. She could have brought Gunedwaen and Striker through a Mage Door and stepped from Rimroheth to Eldanwarasse in a heartbeat—and the power she would have woven to make her door would have been as palpable to every Green Robe as if she stood beside each one and shouted aloud. Instead she had Called a horse to carry Gunedwaen and Striker. They'd all been surprised when the animal who answered was a lively young mare. Gunedwaen had promptly named her Trouble, but under Vieliessar's spells of control she'd been biddable enough. And—like Vieliessar—Trouble had gone where Gunedwaen commanded her.

First to the place where Farcarinon's Keep had once stood, a wasteland of scattered stone, and then to Eldanwarasse Flower Forest. Farcarninon's domain had become Wild Lands, Gunedwaen said, and were occupied by outlaws and sellswords, but those would avoid the Flower Forests. To feed them and keep them, Vieliessar had scavenged among the ruins of burnt-out steadings for things abandoned or overlooked when their people had been stolen, and the home she made for them was comfortable enough.

During the day she toiled at Gunedwaen's direction: chopping wood, setting snares, and toughening a body which had been accustomed to the soft living of the Sanctuary of the Star. Each night, Vieliessar would sit with Gunedwaen over *gan* or *xaique,* absorbing his lessons on strategy, on the disposition of troops, of acceptable losses, and of tactics. She had read of wars and battles in Arevethmonion's scrolls—now she heard tales of war from one who had fought them.

Gunedwaen did not speak of treaty or alliance or of the thousand matters War Prince and Warlord and Lightborn emissary might settle among them before a House's meisne rode out beneath its banners. He spoke of the sights, sounds, and smells of war—of failing to hear an enemy's approach for the frenzied screaming of disemboweled horses, of fighting for candlemarks when hunger and thirst were two more enemies, of the heavy heat of armor, of battlefields turned to mud by the blood spilled upon them. He spoke of *komen* crushed beneath the bodies of their mounts or trampled by careless hooves as they lay helpless on the field, of slow death when Healers could not reach them, of drowning in a shallow stream, imprisoned by their armor and exhaustion. He spoke of battles fought beneath the terrible sun of high summer and through the bitter cold of late autumn, of being captured, powerless to ransom one's freedom—and being offered a choice between lifelong immurement in some dungeon or ending one's own life with a swift dagger.

He spoke of the ugliness and futility of war, for by war the Houses of the Hundred might rise or fall in power for a season or a hundred seasons, but in the end, they gained nothing but the chance to go on fighting. He spoke of war as the sport of princes and lords, *xaique* played with living counters.

Each night she fell exhausted to her sleeping mat, but Vieliessar's nights were as full as her days, for Gunedwaen was not her only teacher.

❧

L*ady Indinathiel! Githonel and Kamirbanath have returned from Tildorangelor!"*

She raised a hand to her hair. Her head felt strangely bare without its dressing of veil and jewels, but she had no time for such fripperies these days. "What have they found?" she asked sharply.

"Nothing." Zenderian's face was a study in anger. The emotion sat strangely upon his gilded and begemmed face, the backdrop of elaborate costume and mannered gesture. Zenderian, of all the Court, kept himself as if Amrethion Aradruiniel had not betrayed them all. "Arwath and Calebre still elude us."

"Once Pelashia Celenthodiel's spawn are dead, we will be safe." She spoke with confidence, but she did not hold such faith and belief within her heart. Once the queen had died, it had been moonturns before Indinathiel had realized the king was no longer fit to rule; moonturns more before she had been able to convince the other courtiers he was not tainted but mad. By then it was too late to call the Council together to choose a legitimate successor and force Amrethion to abdicate, to gain the warrants necessary to purge the kingdom of the defiled.

Indinathiel did not know whose hand had finally struck Amrethion down in secrecy and darkness, only that it was not hers. It did not matter. The rot ran deep. Pelashia's children had fled the moment their true heritage was known, but their sons and daughters had formed an alliance and sworn that one of them would be Amrethion's successor.

Not while I breathe, *Indinathiel thought grimly. She had loved her mad, foolish liege—she would not see the kingdom he had made given over to rabble and monsters. . . .*

Vieliessar's dreams were not of the future. Since the day she had walked from the Sanctuary of the Star for the last time, she had dreamed of the death of Amrethion Aradruiniel . . .

And of the of war that had followed.

Amrethion had prophesied her birth and sealed her fate. But any Lightborn knew a prophecy wasn't a spell. Prophecy did not compel. Prophecy predicted, telling a true tale of things that had not yet happened. But Amrethion's Prophecy had not contained a place for her, as she had once thought. It had contained a shape into which she must be fitted by a force as monstrous and uncaring as winter's cold or forge's heat. From the moment she had claimed the mantle of Child of the Prophecy, she'd felt the terrible appetite of fate devouring all that had been Vieliessar and leaving behind the tool that would serve its need.

And so the lost and forgotten nobles of Amrethion's Court quarreled beneath her skin, showing her a thousand ways to fall short of the goal she must reach. Success or failure on the battlefield was the least of them. In her dreams, Vieliessar learned a thousand ways to fail. A thousand things she must not do. The consequence of every action, based on a dozen—a hundred—possible deeds of her allies, her enemies, and those who did not wish to choose a side.

Zenderian had lost the whole of his army crossing the Mystrals when the weather had turned and he had not. Githonel had burned the standing crops to force the enemy to capitulate, and when the tide of battle had turned, his own forces had faced starvation. Kamirbanath had believed the enemy general would honor a truce. Melicano had taken useless hostages. Indinathiel lost a third of her forces when an amnesty extended by an alliance of Western lords caused them to desert. Nelpanar had refused to bring her cavalry to Tengolin's aid because of an ancient feud between them, and so the day was lost.

The vast and terrible wisdom that spilled through Vieliessar's dreams and into her waking candlemarks was a yoke for her neck, a weight upon her shoulders. Ignorance of the enemy. Ignorance of events. Failure to make alliances. Failure to keep them. Plague, assassination, blockade, privation—each was a weapon that had broken in those long-dead courtiers' hands. Knowing so many things she would otherwise have learned at the cost of defeats and deaths should have brought comfort. It only showed her that knowledge could not give security or victory. She could face a score of possibilities, knowing she must choose one, and see nothing but defeat at the end of every road.

Parmanaya had been tricked into leading her army through forests unclaimed by either side. Parmanaya and her army vanished without a trace.

Merrindale had two choices once his supply train was burned—stand and fight against a force four times the size of his own, or retreat across the High Hills without food or equipment.

Noremallin's army mutinied. He could execute the ringleaders—and never trust their successors. He could meet their demands—and see his army in the hands of the enemy. He could slip away in the night with a handful of trusted advisors—and leave his army leaderless and vulnerable. He could flee to the enemy's battle lines with information that would destroy his army—and be branded a traitor by all he loved.

Great Queen Pelashia Celenthodiel had died, slain in the forest of Tildorangelor, and High King Amrethion—her beloved, her Bondmate—had died of heartbreak. This was the history that everyone knew, the history Vieliessar had been taught all her life. But in her dreams there was no Bond, no quick and romantic death: Amrethion had survived, had gone mad and cruel: his own nobles had slain him before turning to fight among themselves.

The war begun with the death of Amrethion's queen continued to this day.

Vieliessar did not want to believe it. She could fight to steel her sleeping mind against them, but the moment she dropped her defenses, the dreams returned. And so her nights were filled with the clash of sword upon sword, of the thunder of cavalry at the charge. With the screams of the dying, the shouts of the victors, and a mystery she could not comprehend. Why had the children of Amrethion and Pelashia been forced to flee? Why did those whose lives she spied upon in her sleep believe Pelashia's children were tainted, unclean?

She did not need to ask who they were. That much she knew. The dishonorable, the tainted, the unworthy lords whom Indinathiel and so many others fought through her dreams . . .

. . . were her ancestors.

⊰⊱

Her time was running out.

It was past time for Gunedwaen to begin her knightly training, but that would not be possible without a Healing. She'd long known Farcarinon's Swordmaster followed her only out of old loyalty, not because he believed she could unite the Hundred Houses. That didn't trouble her, since she could see no way to do it herself. But Gunedwaen did not even believe she could break Ivrulion Light-Prince's binding. He would not let her try because he thought she would fail—just as he thought she would fail to bring the Hundred Houses to heel.

But I will not fail.

She knew this as she knew her own name, yet the knowledge gave her no comfort. Her spells had never worked as she'd been told they should—or worse, worked when they should not have. She had learned to dissemble, to pretend she saw the Light as her teachers did, to pretend she grew slowly into the power to Heal those for whom all hope had been lost. Most of all, she had learned to pretend that Healing was her sole strong Gift, for the Sanctuary prized its Healers and there was always work for them within its walls.

But since she had fled the Sanctuary, she had become truly aware of the power she wielded. Healing, True Speech, Overshadow . . . each Gift she tested was as strong as the next, stronger than anything she'd read of in the records.

They said that Thurion would become one of the great ones. My power is greater still.

She wanted to believe all this was because the Light had not been Called in her, but instead had come in its own time. Even before the dreams had come to challenge what she knew of history, she had wanted to believe any of the Lightborn could do all that she could, if they only had the years she'd been given in which to listen for the Light Within.

For one moment, sharp and painful, Vieliessar wished she was back in the Sanctuary, sitting in the Common Room surrounded by her friends and fellow scholars. She could have taken her questions to them. Only she'd never told any of them the truth when she had the chance. And if she had a second chance, she still would not. Maeredhiel had laid upon her the weight of a destiny she could neither embrace nor escape, making her a creature from a storysong: Child of the Prophecy, a hero for whom her House had died, and who must somehow save the whole world. She'd hidden from it for as long as she could, hoping to find allies, hoping to be proven wrong, hoping the weight of war and death she carried by simply being Serenthon's heir could be set aside . . .

Her thoughts so occupied her that her attention was only summoned back to the here-and-now as her boots crunched through a crust of half-rotted snow. She blinked, looking around herself. She had reached the edge of Eldanwarasse without noticing. The young trees of its outermost edge lay several yards behind her, and even so, the air around her was soft with promise, warm enough to melt the drifts of winter.

It was spring outside Eldanwarasse as well as in.

There was no more time.

⊰⊱

"You've become amazingly fleet of foot if you are back so soon," Gunedwaen said without turning away from the hearth.

"You have always told me a warrior must have two strong arms and two sound legs to wield a blade—or teach the wielding of it," Vieliessar answered.

"So I have," Gunedwaen answered evenly. He spoke to the flames, not to her.

"And so it is time for you to become my teacher in all things," she said. "My lord prince—"

The words were humble. The tone was not. Gunedwaen reached out toward the stick that helped him walk and Vieliessar knocked it away. She was done with arguing.

She closed her eyes. To her inward sight, Gunedwaen's body was caged within a web of Magery: kin to the spells that preserved fruit and grain and meat in timeless suspension until they were needed. If she had not spent so many years as a Sanctuary Healer, she would not have known where to begin, but every spell, every enchantment, had a beginning, no matter how well hidden.

"Stop! Damn you, foolish child, I said—" Gunedwaen roared in pain as she began to attack the Binding; Vieliessar had always known that to lift it would cause as much pain as setting it had.

Striker lifted her head at Gunedwaen's shout, then pushed herself to her feet, growling in fear before starting to bark. Gunedwaen struggled to his feet, only to fall in the next moment, cursing Vieliessar between ragged breaths. Striker backed away until the corner of the hut stopped her, whining as Gunedwaen scrabbled upon the floor, flailing helplessly. His hand found the walking-stick and he tried to use it to stand. When he could not, he struck at her with it. The blow was weak, with no strength behind it. His speech became a breathless gabble of argument and entreaty: what she meant to do could not be done; he would be useless to her even if she could break the Binding; his life was hers to take but he begged she would be swift and merciful.

And then there were no words, only screams.

Once, long ago, she would have ceased working out of belief that such a spell could not be broken. Out of pity. Out of mercy. She had wrapped herself in the lie that she could feel these things from the moment Glorthiachiel had spoken her true name, had clutched it to her through all her years at the Sanctuary. She'd wished to be like the others—like Celelioniel, like Maeredhiel, like Thurion—for to admit the truth would be to accept a freedom that was terrifying.

This was the truth she had spent so long running from: there was no pity in her, no mercy.

And no fear.

Distantly she was aware that the screaming had stopped, but it was of little importance. She had worked her way into the heart of the spell. She could trace each elaborate web of power, its interlacing, its intention, until it was as if she had set the spell herself. Thus far she had done no more than a Healing Mage of skill and power could do, though in all the Fortunate Lands there were less than a hundred who could do as she had done, and none of them would have been willing to try. What she did next was a thing none of those others could have done: she Unbound the weaving, thread by thread, line by line, layer by layer, until it was gone.

And then she did a thing no Lightborn had ever thought of doing.

She reached into Gunedwaen's body with her magic. Once it had been whole, and deep within it, the body remembered its true shape, as a seed knew the shape of the plant it would someday become. From that seedling-self she drew the pattern she must follow; from Eldanwarasse she drew the power to knit up withered muscle, to summon bone and skin and flesh from nothingness, as if she forced a tree from seed to wide-branched tree in candlemarks instead of years. The power she Called to her need roared through her limbs and her senses like the storm whose winds the Starry Hunt rode, until its intoxication filled her body and mind. She knew she could not merely Heal Gunedwaen, but roll back the centuries he carried, until all the skill of his long life was held within the body of a warrior in his prime. She could build herself an army of such knights, bind their wills to her as if they were extensions of her own limbs. With such an army at her command, she could be unstoppable.

But at what cost?

Gasping with the effort, she released Eldanwarasse's power. The loss of it made her cry out in protest, and almost—almost—she reached for it again, to hold it close, to grant herself such ascendancy that she would need to do nothing more than stretch out her hand and say: *my will be done,* and all the Hundred Houses would bow, would kneel. . . .

No! I will not!

But without it, she felt small and cold.

Reluctantly, she opened her eyes. The fire on the hearth had burned down to ash and ember, and the only illumination was the glow of Silverlight from the spell-lanterns, for morning had become evening as she had worked. Her body was stiff with long stillness and her muscles protested as she moved.

She walked to the woodpile, laid sticks and logs on the hearth-grid, then kindled them with a thought. Gunedwaen was unconscious, gripped by the exhaustion that followed any Healing. There was blood on his face, though she had Healed the injuries he'd done to himself in his agony.

When Vieliessar had first left the Sanctuary of the Star she would not have been able to lift him to his feet, but the moonturns of training had served her well. On their journey to Eldanwarasse she had aided him to mount his horse many times, but now his body felt oddly unbalanced, the new presence of the once-missing limb making him seem like a stranger. When she laid him on his bed, she undressed him, as much from a need to see her handiwork as for his comfort.

His arm had been cut away a handspan below the shoulder by the farmers who had sheltered him after the downfall of Farcarinon. The stump had been seared—such Lightless mock-Healings were commonplace among those who only saw one of the Green Robes at their lord's whim—but there was no mark anywhere now to show that had ever happened. Joint and tendon, muscle and sinew, all reborn. She traced her fingers lightly over the skin. The ugly knotted scar in his thigh was gone as well. The limb, withered from years of disuse, was whole again.

She felt nothing. Not triumph, not fear. It was merely a thing which must be done so that she could become what she must be.

CHAPTER SIX

LEAF AND SWORD, FLOWER AND SHIELD

In Bethros, they sing songs of Princess Ringwil's stainless honor, who said: "Where you exile Einartha, so send me, for my love is as great as my loyalty."

But the song they sing in Haldil is The Song of Ringwil, *for it was Ringwil who betrayed Bethros, and by this pretense sought sanctuary in Haldil thereafter. There is no Song of Einartha, who called Ringwil to the Challenge Circle when she discovered the truth, and whom Ringwil spared to toil as a kitchen-servant until the end of her days.*

—*A* History of the Hundred Houses

"Again."

Gunedwaen waited implacably, the elaborate braid only the Lords *Komen* had the right to wear a cool weight against his neck. He watched Vieliessar wipe the sweat from her brow with the back of her hand and attempt to stifle a sigh as she turned to retrieve her mock weapon from the grass—some distance away—where it had landed.

He held his wooden practice sword as if it were the deadly weapon he had once proudly borne. The strangeness of having two good hands to grasp its hilt, two good legs to carry him forward in this deadly dance, was nearly forgotten. He was once more who he had once been: Sword-master to House Farcarinon.

"A duel can be decided in moments. A battle lasts from dawn to dusk. If you tire after a candlemark, or two, or four, you will die."

"I am not tired." She lifted the wooden weapon and turned to face him, though still standing outside the practice circle he'd marked in the soft earth.

"Losing your weapon is another way to die," he said, raising his own. He saw her mouth thin—not anger, but determination—and she paced quickly toward him, weapon at the ready as she stepped across the boundary of the circle. When the two blades clashed, it was a almost a surprise not to hear the ring of steel on steel.

Mornings were for drill, the same drills every *komen*-to-be practiced from their tenth, twelfth, fourteenth year. Endurance, speed, awareness of the sword's position, its range, the guards and counters and strikes.

Afternoons were for turning those drills into practice against a living opponent.

Vieliessar circled him, searching for an opening. Gunedwaen gave her none. Each time he felt her settle into a pattern he would attack, striking at her sword, her body. Some of the attacks got through. Fewer than yesterday. Fewer than a sennight ago.

Pride had carried him through the long cold years of being a pensioner of Caerthalien, and pride demanded—on the day she placed the wooden sword in the hand she had given him—he be all he had once been.

He had hoped—still—to teach her that determination was not enough. Desire could not replace the years of training she should have had. And so, that first day, he had attacked with all his skill. The practice swords were strong enough to break bones—she had crafted them from ahata— and he did not pull his strikes. Each time their swords clashed he'd disarmed her. The practice had gone on until her hands were too bruised and weary to clasp her sword's hilt, until exhausted muscles would not obey her command.

She'd offered no word of complaint.

On the second day, she managed to retain her sword during one engagement in ten.

By the fifth day, Gunedwaen searched his heart: was he giving her false confidence in her skills? Was he allowing her success she did not deserve? He redoubled his efforts to overwhelm her.

It worked—for a time.

She was better than she ought to be. Better than she *could* be. She wasn't his equal, but the skill she now possessed should have taken her years, not sennights, to achieve.

But wars are not fought afoot by knights with wooden swords.

He knew her hope of uniting the Hundred Houses was madness. It did not matter. What mattered was that she had come to him to be made a knight. And he could not do it. The training of a knight began afoot, it was true, but it continued on the back of a palfrey, translating the patterns already graven in muscle and nerve to fighting from the saddle. Last of all, with a destrier, learning to ride a weapon as well as wield one.

He could not give her the armor that would fit her like a second skin, the destrier who would be her companion and salvation on the field. But it was good to hold a sword again, even if it was merely a wooden one.

Just as it was good to teach his prince that she was not—yet—his equal.

He did not manage to disarm her again. But he could tire her, forcing her to attack while he merely defended, attacking in return only when she let her attention lapse. They fought on until she was staggering with exhaustion. But he was equally weary, and if he struck her unconscious, she might die before she woke. So he stepped back, across the edge of the circle, raising his sword in salute to signal the end of the bout. For a moment he thought she might follow and press the attack, for her gaze was fixed and distant and she swayed on her feet. But a moment later he saw her chest heave, a stuttering interruption to her ragged panting, and she stepped back as well, lowering the tip of her sword to the earth to keep her steady.

"A good day's work. I am looking forward to a good hot bath," Gunedwaen said mildly.

There had been one thing Gunedwaen had insisted on before he'd begun to teach Vieliessar swordcraft, and it was not for self-indulgence's sake. A body bruised from a long day of practice must be given a chance to relax instead of stiffening. Stiff muscles tore and sprains and bruises then led to further injuries. He'd thought of nothing more esoteric than a deep tub, for Lightborn magic could easily heat water.

Instead, she had made a hot spring within the Flower Forest.

The surface steamed pleasantly, for even within Eldanwarasse the evening air was cool. He sighed in content as he stepped into the water and settled himself. Vieliessar sat opposite him, sighing as she raked splayed fingers through her hair. It was nearly chin-length by now, still much too short, but far longer than he'd ever seen a Lightborn wear it.

"You will weary of teaching me long before I have gained the skill I must have," she said with a sigh.

"You are a promising pupil," he answered neutrally. He hesitated over what he must say next, but she was not only his student, but his liege: he owed her truth. "And I have said before: I cannot give you all that you must have."

"How not?" she asked, as if his answer might have changed in the past sennights.

"Lord Vieliessar, with my time and your patience, I can make you the equal of any knight afoot. But a knight does not fight afoot. And I cannot give you—"

"Sword, or armor, or warhorse." She sighed deeply. "So you have said. And I have listened."

"Surely there is . . . some other who might aid you in your hope?" Gunedwaen asked cautiously. It was the first time he had. Before he'd begun to train her, he'd thought her purpose to be unattainable. Now he thought her success merely doubtful.

"Some other of my father's meisne—who yet live?" she asked, her voice wavering between scorn and weariness. "Think you that I do not know where each of them bides? All have sworn fealty to new lords, Master Gunedwaen. To Farcarinon's honor and theirs, there were not many who survived to do so. No quarter was offered on Farcarinon's last battlefield, and those *komen* who survived the day were slain if they would not swear. Filioniel was Farcarinon's Horsemaster—he toils now for Caer-thalien. Farcarinon's Warlord has taken service with Oronviel, for Caer-thalien was ever generous with its leavings. Gwaenabros Lightsister cannot aid me—in truth, she may stand now my enemy, by Hamphuliadiel's grace. To which of these should I present myself, saying I mean to cast down the lord to whom they have pledged?"

Gunedwaen said nothing. He'd known Farcarinon's last day had gone badly, but never—even in legend—had one of the Hundred Houses been *erased*. If he had not been sick and crippled when he was brought to Caerthalien's Great Hall, he, too, would have been given the choice between pledging fealty to Caerthalien and swift execution. But it had amused Bolecthindial to have a Binding set upon him and to force him to live as his supplicant, and so Gunedwaen had not been sworn.

Vieliessar shook her head wearily, and poured water from her cupped hands over her face and neck. "They will not follow a Green Robe," she repeated stubbornly.

Nor will the Hundred follow a lone knight, no matter how brilliant her armor and sharp her sword. He did not speak the words. She knew that truth as well as he did.

⊰⊱

Rain became Flower became Sword.

The tasks Gunedwaen set Vieliessar became more demanding, her training nearly brutal, and nothing she did seemed to please him. Where they had once shared the simple chores of their little homestead equally, now every one of them fell to her: wood gathering and water fetching, hunting game and cleaning and cooking what she caught. She rose even earlier than before. Her morning runs stretched for many leagues and she ran now with a pack of stones upon her back. Nor did she run alone, for as often as not Gunedwaen paced her on horseback—forcing her to a faster pace, chivvying her onto uneven ground, even striking at her with his practice sword as she ran. In the practice circle his attacks had become unremittingly savage, targeting elbow, knee, shoulder, every vulnerable point. Their bouts began when she was tired and ended when she was staggering with exhaustion. The only task he had not assigned to her was the crafting of the shields he now wore in their practice—a *komen*'s shields for forearm and shoulder. He had burned them from ahata-wood and bound them to his arm with strips of buckskin, and no matter how hard Vieliessar tried, it was a rare day when she could land a blow anywhere but upon the ahata's unyielding surface.

She wore no shields.

On any occasion Gunedwaen did not have a weapon in his hand— and many when he did—he would badger her with questions.

She commanded the center of the army. She had ridden to the attack. The enemy's center line collapsed instead of engaging, and reserve forces her scouts had not seen swept in from both sides. What did she do?

She commanded a reserve force. She could see the main force was outmatched, but she had not received the command to engage. What did she do?

She commanded the deosil wing of the army. The enemy charged, attacking the tuathal wing instead of the center. She gave the order to support the tuathal commander, and just as she did, a force twice the size of her own attacked her from behind. What did she do?

"I order my force to take to the air and fly out of danger, of course, which is as likely as my being attacked from behind!" she snapped. "Gunedwaen, this cannot happen! I would have seen them—they could not get behind our lines, or—"

"It is all these *texts* you have read which convince you of this," Gunedwaen said crossly. "Very well. Undoubtedly it is as you say." He set down his bowl and got to his feet, walking from the hut. Striker heaved herself to her feet with a long-suffering sigh and followed him.

Vieliessar set down her nearly untouched supper and pushed the heels of her hands wearily against her eyes. Everything ached, and she was no closer to unifying the Hundred than she'd been half a year ago.

And no closer, so it seemed, to becoming a knight.

The minutes passed, and Gunedwaen did not return.

She got to her feet.

When she stepped outside into the night, Gunedwaen was saddling Trouble.

"Where are you going?" she asked. "It's the middle of the night."

"It is barely two candlemarks past sunset," Gunedwaen corrected. He tightened the girth, and swung into the saddle. "And *I* am going nowhere. *We* are going somewhere."

"Where?" Vieliessar asked doubtfully.

"Come along and see," Gunedwaen answered. He clicked his tongue at Trouble and the mare moved off.

⁂

The broken stones of Farcarinon Keep were ghostly in the moonlight. It was the full moon of Sword, its light so bright there was no need to conjure a globe of Silverlight to show them their way. Gunedwaen had said nothing about their destination, and Vieliessar had not asked. The only time they had spoken was when she stopped him so he could take Striker up on Trouble, for the old *hikuliasa* had begun to lag behind.

She'd only been here once before in body. In mind, she'd been here a thousand times since the day she'd learned her true name. Promising vengeance. Demanding answers. Mourning the life she could have lived.

She had renounced her vengeance and received her answers, and her mourning time was done.

The watchtowers and the outer wall were nothing more than shattered stones scattered across what had been the meadows and orchards of the keep, and the keep itself, from ramparts to deepest cellars, had been forced to collapse in upon itself, until all that remained was a low hill of stone that time and the seasons had covered with grass and flowers. A small portion of the inner curtain wall remained standing, the only thing to say that once a proud fortress had stood upon this spot.

The road that led to the castel gates was bright in the moonlight; the earth, hard-hammered over the centuries, giving way only grudgingly to the encroachment of the meadow. Trouble's hooves, noiseless on the soft summer earth, clopped faintly as Gunedwaen guided her onto the road. The ditches that had once lined it had fallen inward years before, leaving only shallow depressions in the grass.

As they crossed the boundary where the outer wall had once stood, Striker raised her head from where she lay across Gunedwaen's knees and gave a soft, interrogative bark. An instant later, Vieliessar heard the clink of a bridle and realized there was someone here. She forced herself to pretend she'd heard nothing. Gunedwaen must know someone awaited him—awaited them.

She steeled herself against betrayal. *Just as well to see it come now, if that is what comes, for if I cannot bind my House's last vassal to me, what hope do I have of binding princes?*

A moment later, a stranger rode out of the shadow.

His grey gelding's coat had been rubbed with powdered charcoal to make it dull and dark, but there was no disguising the quality of the animal, the kind which only a great lord—or a great lord's favorite—might ride. Neither horse nor rider displayed the badge of any House; the rider wore a dark hooded cloak, but Vieliessar could see the unmistakable angled shape of a scabbarded sword beneath the cloak, and her ears brought her the faint sweet jingling of chain mail.

Gunedwaen reined in and waited. Vieliessar stood, silent and watchful, at his knee.

The stranger stopped, pushed back the hood of his cloak. The silver of his mail-shirt gleamed at his throat, and now she could see that the cloak's clasp was enameled. A red otter on a white field. Oronviel.

Farcarinon's Warlord has taken service with Oronviel, for Caerthalien was ever generous with its leavings . . .

"Rithdeliel is a friend," Gunedwaen said quietly. He shifted Striker in his arms, and Vieliessar took her and set her on the ground. The *hikuliasa* wandered over to the grey gelding, who lowered his head to sniff at her, unimpressed.

"An ally—perhaps," Rithdeliel corrected.

"Ally, then," Gunedwaen conceded. "It has been far too long."

"Not as long as I expected, since I thought you dead," Rithdeliel said. "Your message was a surprise."

"As was your answer. I had not thought you saved any of Gwaenabros's Finding charms."

"You will admit it came in useful. I assume this is the girl? Have you proof she is who she claims to be?"

She stepped into the space between the two horses.

"I am Vieliessar Farcarinon, daughter of Serenthon War Prince and Nataranweiya, his Bondmate and Lady," she said. "Declare yourself, knight of Oronviel."

She saw him smile. "Rithdeliel, Warlord of Oronviel, begs leave to declare himself to you, Vieliessar Lightsister."

She turned her back on him without answering. A bright flash of memory showed her Ladyholder Glorthiachiel doing just this to show her displeasure to one of Caerthalien's court. She had not thought of her childhood in longer than she could remember, and for a moment the memory actually made her want to smile.

"Why should I trust him?" she asked Gunedwaen, her tone just short of a demand. "Who has broken his pledged word once will break it twice."

"Rithdeliel was once Warlord to House Farcarinon," Gunedwaen answered.

She gestured impatiently, brushing away his words. "So much I knew even before I came to you," she answered pitilessly. "And I knew him forsworn of his allegiance to Farcarinon. If he is indeed forsworn by pledging to Oronviel."

"'He' is here," Rithdeliel said. "And were you a true knight I would challenge you for such accusations. Do you think I forswore Farcarinon lightly?"

"I think it is a marvel and a wonder you survived to do so," she answered, turning back to face him.

"Caerthalien did not wish to see too many of its own executed, no matter where their lawful oaths had since been given," Rithdeliel answered. "Or do you not know the whole of this tale? I shall tell it to you. I was chief among the knights in Lord Ethradan's house—unfortunately for us both, for Serenthon Farcarinon had already set himself to walk the road that would slay him, and for this cause he played suitor to Caerthalien. There he met my Lady, and knew her for his Bondmate. And so Lord Ethradan of Caerthalien, Nataranweiya's father, gave her as her dowry as many of his household as he could spare, myself among them, trusting our loyalty and care would keep her alive."

"It did not," Vieliessar observed.

She saw sharp-cut lines appear around Rithdeliel's mouth as he clenched his jaw tight upon his anger. When he spoke again, his words were as cold and stinging as spitting snow.

"I was taken from the battlefield in chains that last day," he said, his words soft and precise. "You live because of what I and my army did upon that field. We held the Alliance there until Lady Nataranweiya could flee Farcarinon Keep, though we were outmatched a hundred to one. To this battle War Prince Serenthon had summoned everyone who had ever borne a blade, or who might do so soon, and they were slain in their hundreds: aged greatmothers and children who had not yet leaped the fire or flown their kites. They are no more than names written on the wind, for no kin survived to place their names upon the Tablet of Memory. We in our hundreds stood against the Alliance in its thousands. Of the flower of Farcarinon, not one in a thousand survived the day. Those of us who did paid dearly, for we languished in chains until the day you returned to the Sanctuary of the Star, and many who had walked from the field did not live to walk beneath the sun again. When I was brought forth from the darkness at last, it was to hear Oronviel would ransom me from Caerthalien, if I would pledge fealty to War Prince Thoromarth. I had seen Serenthon fall, and I knew all of Farcarinon dead with him, for if the House had survived, Bolecthindial would not have sold my name as if I were a Landbond in the field. Farcarinon was dead," he repeated heavily. "And so I pledged to War Prince Thoromarth, and I have served him faithfully since that day. I came here for Gunedwaen's asking, and for my love for Serenthon, but I do not know that I wish to give up either freedom or life to the impatient tantrums of a child."

"I have learned patience from the cradle," Vieliessar answered, her words following his, beat upon beat, as if they clashed with naked blades. "And I am no child—you of all should know this, who so auspiciously marked the day of my birth. Know this as well: I would gladly have ended my days within the Sanctuary of the Star, save that the Hundred Houses face an enemy they are too blind and selfish to see. To prepare them against the day of its coming I must become a knight. And I shall, Rithdeliel of Oronviel. Do not doubt me."

"You speak of the Prophecy. *The Song of Amrethion*," Rithdeliel said accusingly, and Vieliessar could only stare at him in astonishment. "Oh, come, Lightsister," he added, his tone turning sharper. "Serenthon Farcarinon knew of it. He too said it spoke of an enemy to come, and that his kingship would unite the Hundred Houses against it. And so the Hundred killed him."

Again her answer was swift. "They killed him for fear of a collar about their throats, and for the promises he made to gain and keep his allies. I will not bribe as if I am weak; I will not flatter as if I must beg victory to favor me. I will triumph or I will die—and on the day I am crowned, there will be no High House or Low, nor will there be noble and Landbond. There will be one land and one people, and they will be mine."

For a long moment they stared at each other in silence.

"It has been too long since I have risked my life for something worth the risk," Rithdeliel said at last. He nodded slowly, as if sealing an unspoken bargain. "Very well. Say what you would have of me."

⊰᙭⊱

The ring and hiss of steel was loud in the practice ring, where two knights mounted on destriers backed and circled for advantage. The rich smell of ripening hay filled the still air and motes of dust pounded from the straw underfoot turned the air to gold. The sun beat down on the combatants, turning the layers of metal and padding they wore into instruments of torture. Fire Moon was the hottest moonturn of the year, as if summer expended all her heat in one last profligacy before the cool of autumn and the long slow slide into winter.

One combatant rode a muscular roan, the shields of his pearl-enameled armor enameled in the red-and-white of Oronviel. The other, mounted on a bay mare, wore the bare-metal armor and bare shields of a maiden knight. Neither spared a hand to the reins, for destriers were trained from foalhood to answer to the weight and pressure of an armored rider, to move as an extension of the knight on their back, to kill if asked.

Both destriers knew that today was not a day for killing. Neither animal had taken the field in years, too old to bear up under the rigors of a full campaign and long days of war. They spent their peaceful retirement training future knights in the deadly equestrian dance of horse and rider.

Rithdeliel gave his mount the signal to back out of range. Were this a battle—and were he mounted on Varagil—he would signal Varagil to spin and kick. Such a blow from a hoof could shatter bone, even through armor. Since this was not true battle, he brought his mount instead around to his opponent's off side, so that she would have to strike across herself to defend or attack. If she turned in the saddle to strike a better blow—a common beginner's mistake—she would be off-balance, unable to properly signal her mount and vulnerable to being either dragged or shoved from the saddle. He was looking forward to a swift conclusion to the mock-combat—this was his opponent's first fight from the back of a destrier—but as he urged his stallion forward again, his opponent's mare spun, slamming her rump against his stallion's neck. Reflexively, the animal beneath him sprang sideways—only a moment of distraction, but time enough for his opponent to go on the attack once more.

Rithdeliel backed the stallion quickly out of range and raised his sword, indicating the match was over. To continue would be to risk injury, even with peacebonded blades, for a fall or unintended kick could be as fatal here as on the field.

For a moment his adversary sat frozen, as if she wished to continue the attack. Then she saluted in turn.

"A good beginning," Rithdeliel said. He patted the stallion's shoulder and the roan stretched his neck and shook his head, as if shaking off the glamour of battle.

"What more is there?" Vieliessar's voice was sharp.

"Come. Let us return the horses to the stable and get ourselves out of this armor," Rithdeliel said, not answering.

◈

He swung down from the stallion's back in the stableyard, moving lithely in the many-jointed flexible armor, and tossed the reins to one of the ostlers. When he turned to help Vieliessar down, he saw that she had vaulted from the saddle as lightly as he, and for a moment, Rithdeliel felt the same unease he'd felt the first time he'd watched her spar on foot against Gunedwaen. *Three moonturns is not time enough to make a knight, or even three years. And Gunedwaen swears she had not even held a practice sword until last Hearth Moon. She is unnatural. . . .*

Her back was to him; she had drawn off one heavy gauntlet to scratch her mare behind the hinge of her jaw. "I am who I need to be," she answered as if he'd spoken.

He was uneasy enough that he might have questioned her further, but Varagil had sensed his presence, and a loud, demanding neigh now came from within the stable. "I am summoned," he said briefly, walking quickly away.

A few moments later, Vieliessar joined Rithdeliel at Varagil's loose-box. She'd removed her helmet; her sweat-sodden hair, still too short to braid properly, was plastered flat against her skull.

"Raemeros is a gallant steed, and she has taught me well," Vieliessar said, watching him with Varagil. "But she cannot serve me in battle."

"She'll do well enough to get you killed," Rithdeliel said brusquely. "Even if you believe that by some fortune you can declare against the High Houses and gain anything but your death."

"Ah, but I will not do it alone," she said, grave laughter in her voice. "There is Gunedwaen."

Y ou cannot just *ask* for the Unicorn Throne," Rithdeliel said.

The three of them were in Rithdeliel's own rooms rather than Candlebrook Manor's Great Hall. A half-played game of *xaique* was set out on a nearby board; a tea service waited on the sideboard, the pot already filled with its infusion and awaiting hot water. He lived in the clutter of one who lived surrounded by servants but who had no wife and family to nag him to tidiness: half-read scrolls, half-mended bits of tack, and delicate, broken pieces of armor littered every surface except the dining table.

"So you and Gunedwaen have said before," Vieliessar pointed out. "And I shall not merely ask. One army takes another, just as in *xaique*. If I defeat the War Prince of a House and gain his domain, I gain his army as well. With each War Prince I defeat, my cause grows stronger."

"This plan only works if you *have* an army to begin with, and I do not see one," Gunedwaen said.

"You might once have persuaded the Free Companies to back your cause—if you promised them lands and estates and the settlement of old grievances," Rithdeliel added. "But now . . ."

Vieliessar's flight from the Sanctuary over a year earlier had borne bitter fruit. Goaded by Hamphuliadiel Astromancer's claim that she sought vengeance on the Old Alliance, and fearing that she would seek to bring the Free Companies under her banner, Caerthalien and Aramenthiali—of all unlikely allies—had joined Ullilion and Cirandeiron to scour Farcarinon of those who made it their refuge. The Harrowing of Farcarinon had begun at the end of Sword—a few bare sennights after she and Gunedwaen had come to Oronviel—and stretched through Thunder into Fire.

The power of the Free Companies had been broken decisively. Of the hundreds of mercenary companies that had once sold their services to the highest payer, only Foxhallow and Glasshaven remained—surviving because these two, the largest Free Companies, possessed granted lands far to the east of Farcarinon.

"Their combined force would not have been sufficient to take even Oronviel," Vieliessar pointed out reasonably. "The Free Companies do not have Lightborn to Heal their warriors; Oronviel could put every knight they'd wounded back into the field the following day, and so stand against them forever—and if they acted outside the Code in order to win, Oronviel could declare them Outlaw. We have seen this War Season how outlaws are dealt with."

Those who had escaped the Harrowing were now outlaws in truth. No War Prince would offer them a place. The shattered remnants of the Free Companies had turned to banditry to survive.

Rithdeliel glanced toward Gunedwaen. The old Swordmaster's eyes held an expression that was half exasperation, half resignation. He knew as well as Rithdeliel did that a lone knight had no hope of conquering the Hundred Houses and making them crown her king. And both of them knew it was impossible to persuade Vieliessar of that. All she would say was that she *must* unite the Hundred Houses, therefore she *would* unite the Hundred Houses.

"Mercenaries, or the army of a single House—both approaches are too conservative," Vieliessar added, twisting the stem of her winecup between her hands. She glanced from Gunedwaen to Rithdeliel. "Would you trust any of the War Princes to honor their pledged word?"

Gunedwaen's answer was a bark of derisive laughter. "Your life is the answer to that, my prince!"

Vieliessar nodded. "Just so. No matter what they say—what guarantees, what pledges, what hostages they give—any of the War Princes will break their sworn oath. Do you not see what that implies?"

There was a moment of silence. "To me, it implies I would sign no treaty with them if my life depended on their keeping of it. But I am sure this is not what you mean us to understand," Rithdeliel said with ponderous sarcasm.

There was a brief flash of laughter in Vieliessar's eyes, though her face remained composed. "But you are right, good master Rithdeliel. No treaty with any of the Hundred has worth. So from declaration to victory, my campaign can run only one War Season."

Gunedwaen threw up his hands in exasperation. "It is not enough for you to say you will make the Hundred declare you High King—now you will defeat them all in one summer!" At his feet, Striker raised her head inquisitively, then lowered it again, seeing nothing interesting was happening.

"As you say," Vieliessar said mildly, raising her cup to drink. She refused to speak further of her plans that evening, and the talk turned to gossip of the coming Harvest Court.

Four great feasts turned the wheel of the year: the Kite Festival of Flower Moon, the Fire Festival of Fire Moon, the Midwinter Feast of Snow Moon, and Harvest Court.

Unlike the other festivals, its time was not fixed: Harvest Court fell upon the first full moon after the Fire Festival, whether that lay in the moonturn of Harvest or not. Loremasters said it was the oldest of the festivals; storysingers spoke of a time before the building of Celephriandullias-Tildorangelor by the first High King, when the folk had not lived beneath roofs of stone, but roamed the land following the great horse herds, a time when the harvest the name spoke of was not grain, but souls—for it was their claim that Harvest Court had once marked the half of the year in which the Starry Hunt had ridden over the land, taking whom it would as its prey.

At Harvest Court, by ancient custom, any might approach the War Prince to receive justice, no matter how humble their degree.

⚜

The gates of Oronviel Keep stood open. Across the outer courtyard—a space designed to box in attackers so they could be slain from above—the massive doors of the Great Hall stood open as well. Trestle tables were set out beneath the fruit-heavy trees of the castel orchard as well as in the Great Hall, for at Harvest Court, War Prince Thoromarth held a great feast for all who wished to attend. There would be horse races and foot races; prizes given for the most elaborately decorated loaf of bread, the most enticing new tea blend, the most beautiful weaving, the best new song and poem and tale—even for the most elaborate illusion cast by Oronviel's Lightborn. The feasting and games would begin at dawn the morning after the full moon and continue until sunset on the seventh day afterward, and in between the contests and the celebrations, War Prince Thoromarth would hear the petitions of any who came before him. Even an outlaw or a traitor knight could come to Harvest Court and be heard, for all the Houses of the Fortunate Lands declared peace and truce for the whole of the festival.

The day was summer-warm, and the high windows in the Great Hall had been flung open to let the last of summer into the keep. From the makeshift race course laid out between the orchard and the craftworkers' village—a space more often used to muster Oronviel's troops for battle—came the sound of cheering and hornsong. Horses raced in the morning when it was cooler; in the afternoon, once the prizes for the winning horses had been given, there would be footraces.

Within the Great Hall, Oronviel's great lords, and any others who wished to see, were gathered to hear their master give justice. Rithdeliel watched impassively as yet another petitioner stepped forward. He'd considered and discarded the idea of bringing Vieliessar and Gunedwaen to Harvest Court to beg sanctuary. It was true that Harvest Court was the time when banishings and outlawing could be set aside and pardoned, but Gunedwaen had been Caerthalien's prisoner and Vieliessar fell under the Sanctuary's dominion. And Thoromarth of Oronviel was no fool.

The clatter of sabatons against the stone of the outer courtyard roused him to instant alertness.

The figure who appeared in the doorway wore armor enameled in silver, as if to mock the unadorned plate of the unfledged knight. Her tabard and cloak were pure white, as if she came to Harvest Court to seek knighthood, but silver spurs gleamed on her feet and she wore swordbelt and scabbard. The empty scabbard was the only concession she made to the fact that she was entering the presence of a War Prince, for her helm was locked into place, rendering her anonymous.

"Rithdeliel—who comes?" Thoromarth asked.

"I do not know, Lord Thoromarth," Rithdeliel answered, forcing his voice to show none of the anger he felt. He was not forsworn—in truth, he did not *know*.

All around the hall, watchers flurried like a cote of doves and whispered urgently to each other. But no one tried to impede the silver knight's progress as she walked slowly and deliberately the full length of the hall.

"I give you good greeting, stranger knight," Thoromarth said, as she stopped before him. "Remove your helm so I may look upon your face, and say what justice you would have of Oronviel."

"I would have Oronviel's lands, her knights, and all who lie in your hand. By the most ancient law of the princes who rule, I challenge you to single combat without quarter, and when I win your nobles will yield Oronviel to me and your heir will swear fealty."

"You are mad!" Thoromarth hissed.

"Your pardon, my lord prince," Eiron Lightbrother, Chief of Oronviel's Lightborn, said quietly, leaning over to speak softly in Thoromarth's ear. "This is law, made in the time of Mosirinde Peacemaker, and all the princes bound themselves to obey. At Harvest Court, such a challenge can be made. It must be accepted."

Rithdeliel knew that what Eiron said was far from impossible: the Hundred Houses had bound themselves to many rulings in Mosirinde's time. None could be set aside without the agreement of all the Houses together, something unlikely to be forthcoming.

"Withdraw your petition, stranger knight, and you may leave my hall unharmed," Thoromarth said when Eiron stepped back.

"I do not withdraw it," the silver knight said. "I demand of you combat for all you hold. This is the second time of asking."

There was a long moment of charged silence, then Thoromarth laughed. "You shall have your battle—" he said.

"Father!" Princess Mialvialla had half risen from her seat.

"Silence!" Thoromarth snapped. "I say, you may have your battle, stranger knight. But I know the old law as well as you. My champion will meet you, not I. By the law you so imprudently invoke, mine is the right to choose the time and place. On the last day of the Festival, on the assembly field at midday. Present yourself then or hold yourself foresworn, and a coward."

The silver knight bowed. "I shall be there, Thoromarth Oronviel."

She turned and strode from the hall. Neirenmeirith Lightsister separated herself from the onlookers and followed.

"An amusing end to a tedious morning," Thoromarth said brusquely, getting to his feet. "Come. We may be in time for the last of the racing."

⊰⊱

On the day appointed, five days after Thoromarth's morning court had been so rudely interrupted, the nobles of Oronviel gathered on the assembly field.

The craftworkers had enclosed the space Eiron Lightbrother had indicated with strong wooden panels painted in the red-and-white of Oronviel, leaving two gaps in the panels wide enough to ride a horse through. The barrier would keep onlookers away from the two combatants. A raised platform had also been constructed; a framework above it hung with pavilion-weight silk to shelter those below from the midday sun. Lord Thoromarth and his favorites would have an excellent view of the battle.

How could she do such a thing as this? The question repeated endlessly in Rithdeliel's mind as he waited just outside the arena. It was a betrayal that hurt more keenly than being sold to Oronviel so many years ago. He had trusted her. He had loved her for Nataranweiya's sake. She held Gunedwaen's life in her hands. *And this is what she does with it!*

His edginess communicated itself to his mount; Varagil sidled and tossed his head nervously.

"Be easy, old friend. It will be over soon," Rithdeliel said, patting the burly grey's neck. He was Thoromarth's champion, as the Warlord always was. If he had been free to do so, he would have ridden to Candle-brook and laid her in chains, Lightborn or no, but even if Thoromarth were willing to excuse him from his Harvest Court duties, he would certainly have Rithdeliel followed, and then all would come out regardless.

Perhaps she will not come, he thought, glancing toward the sky. *If she has told Gunedwaen of her plans— If he found them out by some other means—*

Then he heard the roar of the onlookers and knew he was not to be spared. He spurred Varagil forward.

She walked into the arena as calmly as she had walked into Harvest Court. The only change was that she now carried weapons: broadsword and dagger. The dagger was not to fight with; it was carried by the *komen* to cut themselves free of harness or even their own armor on the field. Rithdeliel was grateful she had not come mounted, for Thoromarth would instantly recognize any animal she rode. He supposed it wouldn't make a great deal of difference once her identity was discovered.

Rithdeliel was sworn to Oronviel. He would not foreswear himself. For oath and for honor, he would have to kill her.

She stood facing the dais on which Thoromarth sat. "I have come at the day and candlemark appointed, Thoromarth of Oronviel, to fulfill my promise to you. Here, in the third time of asking, I challenge you in the person of your champion, for all you hold within your hands!"

Rithdeliel saw Thoromarth smile. "Speak to me of that again, stranger knight, when my champion lies dead by your hand," Oronviel's War Prince called. "Begin!"

Any reply she might have made was drowned in the cheering of the crowd.

Rithdeliel spurred Varagil forward. There was not enough room for him to reach a full gallop, but there was certainly enough room to maneuver. Rithdeliel's blade was poised. He had every advantage: height, speed, and a trained destrier. His first blow should shear through her armor between cullet and helm. Varagil would do the rest.

I will make this quick, for your lady mother's sake.

At the last moment, just before he reached striking range, Varagil shied.

There was laughter from the dais as Varagil crabbed sideways and back. Rithdeliel dug his spurs into the stallion's flanks, forcing him to settle. He trotted the destrier around the circumference of the ring to settle him further: this was a strange situation, and Varagil had always been high-strung. As Varagil moved in a wide circle around Vieliessar, she turned so she was always facing her enemy. Rithdeliel pressed his heels into the stallion's sides and shifted his weight forward. Varagil answered the command easily, cantering forward. Once again Rithdeliel raised his sword to deliver the fatal blow.

Once again Varagil plunged sideways, carrying Rithdeliel out of reach.

Exasperated, he snatched at the reins and hauled back savagely. Varagil reared, shaking his head, kicking out harmlessly with his fore hooves as he staggered a few steps backward.

This cannot be Magery! Eiron stands beside Lord Thoromarth—he would sense it! This time Rithdeliel kept a tight hand on the rein, hauling the destrier's head down as he spurred him forward.

The outcome was the same.

"Are we to sit here all day watching you show off, Lord Rithdeliel?" Princess Mialvialla called down.

Without answering, Rithdeliel turned Varagil back toward the opening in the barrier. He swung down from the saddle, leaving the reins hanging: Varagil would be quiet enough if no stranger approached him.

When he walked back into the arena, Vieliessar waited for him in silence: the Lightsister who wished to become a knight, who had struck the spark to kindle the tinder of his resentment of Farcarinon's destruction. Rithdeliel had believed in Amrethion's Prophecy because Nataranweiya had, and had always believed that when the day and the enemy came—if they did—the Hundred Houses would band together to face it.

And now it did not matter. When the day came, if it came, he would not see it.

War was the art, the duty, and the recreation of every child of the Hundred Houses. Their artificers forged unbreakable swords, crafted armor as pliant as heavy silk. A knight who wore it could run in it—as long as his strength held out—could even dance in it.

Today's dance would be brief.

He expected to strike the first blow. Not to wait for the enemy to strike was the hardest lesson to teach to the young trainees. Whatever advantage you gained from learning how the enemy fought was negated by the fact that you'd taken the first hit.

Vieliessar did not wait. As he was still walking toward her, she sprang forward. She did not bring her blade down from above as if she were chopping wood—an attack which would have given Rithdeliel precious seconds of warning—but swept it up from below as he was still registering the movement.

He caught the blow on his shield. The force of the impact jarred down his spine. He turned the parry into an attack, aiming a midline strike at her ribs, where dozens of narrow plates gave the armor flexibility at the cost of strength. *Anywhere your body flexes is where you should attack your opponent.* The lecture he had delivered to thousands of children of Caerthalien, Farcarinon, and Oronviel played through his mind as his blade rang and slid over hers—parry, disengage—and each of them sprang back. Fighting mounted, the blade's length was an advantage. On foot, it meant they could not close with one another.

The next exchanges came punishingly fast, blade meeting blade, meeting armor, the blows ringing out like the hammer of the smith at the forge. A part of his mind registered the noise of the crowd ebbing away to silence. They had expected a swift butchery. He was Rithdeliel of Oronviel, Warlord to Thoromarth Oronviel. Bruised vanity made him redouble the speed and fury of his attacks.

He would not think of what he had learned in these scant minutes in the arena. He was a master of war, his skills honed for centuries, honed by a thousand battles.

She was his match.

There are things I have not taught you yet!

He turned to catch her blade, not on the face of his lower shield, but behind it, trapping it between the lip of the shield and his metal gauntlet. Such a maneuver was risky: the sword would shear through the bolts holding the shield in place if they took the full force of the blow. This move was nothing one would use in battle, but a duelist's maneuver. A trick for entertaining one's comrades. *I remember Serenthon, bright as a new blade, conceding his defeat at Nataranweiya's hands. . . .*

Rithdeliel had spent his life assembling miracles. Only one time had he failed. Now he caught Vieliessar's blade, let it slip behind his shield to catch and hold, let it slide past him as he swept forward. He flung his sword into the air, and the moment it left his free hand, he struck her on the side of her helm with all the power in his clenched fist, then seized his weapon as it fell.

She staggered backward, stunned, and her fouled blade grated free. He moved forward to press his advantage as she lowered her guard—

Her sword whipped up. If she'd tried any conventional attack, Rithdeliel's strike would have slammed home, but she set the point of her blade against his chestplate and *shoved*. There was a moment's ear-hurting squeal as the sword's point skated harmlessly over the surface of his armor as he staggered back. Then she was on the attack once more, her blade moving so fast—a dozen attacks, a dozen feints, a dozen counters— that it was impossible to see and assess each one. Instinct—the bone-bred knowledge of every strike that could be delivered by an armored warrior—let Rithdeliel meet each attack. But his advantage was gone now—if it had ever truly existed. She was forcing him inexorably backward across the soft loose earth of the arena. He tried to shift her, to turn her, without success. She directed her attacks to his sword-hand, so he must meet them with his blade rather than prepare a counter.

She was magnificent. He wanted to shout to the watching crowd that this, *this* was how Farcarinon offered battle.

He wanted to tell her to disengage, to flee while she could save herself, for Thoromarth had sworn no binding oath to spare her life.

Rithdeliel must kill her. He no longer thought it would be easy.

He dropped his blade and grabbed her sword between his metal-banded palms, keeping his hands flat, for to clasp the blade as one clasped a swordhilt was to lose fingers. He twisted the weapon as he pulled her toward him; she released her grip abruptly and Rithdeliel staggered back a half-step as she dived for his abandoned blade. It took him only a heartbeat to get his hands around the hilt of the sword he held. By then Vieliessar was on the attack again.

In just these few moments the engagement had changed from an execution to a battle. Now it became a contest of endurance and strength. The time for flamboyant attacks and risky counters was over. She struck with the flat of her blade, not from any desire to spare him, but because the flat would deliver more force without bouncing away. Even now she did not attempt any of the conventional strikes—she struck at hip, at thigh, at shin until his body ached and his legs became treacherous. Each time he attacked, she moved inside his guard, robbing his blows of their power.

But her success could not last forever. With his last strength, Rithdeliel sprang backward and aimed a lethal, two-handed swing at her shoulder. She could not get her blade up to counter in time—she spun, turning her back to him for a vital moment in order to catch the blow on her shoulder-shield. Off balance when the blow landed, she was knocked from her feet and fell to the earth.

He stepped forward as she rolled to her back. She would not be able to rise before he delivered the killing blow.

She didn't try to escape. Instead, she swept her blade sideways and struck him between greave and sabaton with all the force she could. It was a blow that could not be struck on the field, for in war, knights did not fight afoot. And so the join between leg and foot was but lightly armored, meant to be defended by the sheltering metal of the stirrup.

Here, on the field below Oronviel Great Keep, it was a crippling blow. White-hot pain in his shattered ankle made him check his strike. Vieliessar drew her knees up to her chest and kicked out powerfully, knocking him away. The damaged ankle would not bear his weight and Rithdeliel went sprawling.

Up, you fool—get up!

On her feet by then, Vieliessar stamped on his wrist with all her weight, then kicked his sword away. She dropped to her knees beside him.

"Yield!" she demanded, her voice low and urgent.

He shook his head mutely. He was Oronviel's champion. He could not yield.

She dragged him to his knees, kneeling on his calves in a grinding squeal of metal against metal and wrenching his helm from his head. The sun was bright. It did not seem to have moved at all in the time their battle had taken. Her fingers clenched in his hair as she pulled his head back. He felt the whisper of her dagger at his throat.

"I have defeated your champion, Thoromarth of Oronviel! Yield to me your lands!" she shouted.

There was a moment of frozen silence; then Thoromarth laughed.

"Go ahead and slit his throat if you like! You have not won until I say you have!" he called back.

Rithdeliel braced himself to die, his only regret being he would not see how this ended. Then he felt the edge of the dagger leave his throat. A moment later he saw it glitter in mid-air. She had thrown the weapon at Thoromarth.

There was a flare of bright violet light as Eiron Lightbrother swept up his hand to Shield his lord. Rithdeliel had seen Mage Shield cast many times in skirmishes with the Beastlings; it was permitted when the enemy was not *komen*.

When it struck the Shield, the dagger should have dropped away as if it had been flung against stone.

It did not.

The blade hung in the air as if it were caught in a spider's web. Around it, Eiron's spell flared as bright as flame, but though the dagger was caught in his spell, it was not *held*. Dazzling amethyst fire spread outward from the dagger until the whole shape of the shield could be seen, surrounding Lord Thoromarth and trapping him in his seat. The dagger slowly slid forward.

"I have won," Vieliessar repeated implacably.

"Kill her!" Thoromarth shouted.

Rithdeliel could see the faces of all who sat within the viewing box. They could not decide whether to flee—and have to face Thoromarth's anger when this was over—or stay where they were lest they become the next target. Princess Mialvialla rose to her feet and flung her own dagger. It veered sharply, turning in the air like a bird in flight, and buried itself in the soft earth. *Magery. She uses Magery in battle* . . . Rithdeliel thought numbly. Princess Mialvialla gave a harsh cry of fury, looking around for other weapons.

The dagger inched closer.

"Who are you?" Thoromarth demanded, seeing no one would— *could*—carry out his order. If Thoromarth's voice held fear, Eiron Lightbrother looked as if he gazed upon his own death.

The silver helm hit the ground a few feet away from where Rithdeliel knelt.

"I am Vieliessar Farcarinon, and I have come to claim your lands, your armies, and your fealty—or this day I will take your life and the lives of all who will not pledge to me!"

Thoromarth was invisible now behind the wall of violet flame, and the dagger embedded in the spell could no longer be seen.

Suddenly the world went dim and wine-colored as a second Mage Shield surrounded Rithdeliel and Vieliessar. It flared and dazzled brightly—he did not know why, for he could see no missile, no weapon, yet it was obvious that the Lightborn standing in the crowd must have attempted to obey their lord. The metal taste of terror filled his mouth at the thought of two Lightborn battling. What spells, what horrors, would they unleash?

"Abomination!" Eiron shouted. "You betray the Covenant!"

"I do not do battle by the Light, Eiron Lightbrother!" Vieliessar cried out. "But I will have what I have won! Your life or your pledge, Thorom-arth Oronviel!"

She will have to kill him, Rithdeliel thought in sudden cold fear. He could not imagine what would happen then. How many would she have to kill today? *Mialvialla will not give up her inheritance—*

The Mage Shield that protected the two of them crackled and flared again. And held fast.

"I yield! I yield!" Thoromarth shouted suddenly. "*I yield!* You have won my domain in fair challenge!"

The unnatural, spell-driven light vanished.

"Come, then, and swear to me before the sight of all," Vieliessar demanded.

As Eiron helped the once-lord of Oronviel to his feet, Rithdeliel could see the blood that welled from the wound in Lord Thoromarth's throat.

❦

*I*t is a good beginning. It is not the whole.*

It was nearly midnight before Vieliessar was able to dismiss Tho-romarth's servants—hers now—from her bedchamber, and with them, the last of the Court who wished to know the answer to just one question, or two, or three.

One remained behind.

"I would have honesty of you," Vieliessar said to Thoromarth. True Speech could tell her the tenor of his mind, but only if he thought of what she wished to know, and Lord Thoromarth was not an introspective man.

"I have given you honesty since I gave you my oath," Thoromarth answered.

"I slew your lady wife, your heir, and three more of your children," Vieliessar said bluntly. "Your own Chief Lightborn would not accept me as Prince. Yet you seem content to follow where once you led."

"Am I a lackwit?" Thoromarth demanded sharply. He sighed deeply, recognizing this was not a true answer. "And my loyalty is a chain about your throat, for Eiron will not be alone in thinking I am bespelled to surrender my domain. Yet I have pledged to serve Oronviel above all things until Amrethion Aradruiniel returns, and to this oath I am faithful."

"Today you might have taken your death, and known Princess Mialvialla would have demanded I prove my challenge against her in turn."

"I have always believed that the Silver Hooves shape our fates," Thoromarth said heavily. "Warriors die in battle gladly, knowing we will ride the night wind forever. I should have trusted Them, and taken the challenge you made. But I did not. In my heart I thought I could sacrifice Rithdeliel, who served me as faithfully as he served Farcarinon. If he died, I would then have you slain. If he lived, you would be dead, and I would still rule. And Oronviel would have peace."

"An odd desire for a War Prince," Vieliessar said.

"What do I gain from war? You will know as well as I that Caerthalien and Aramenthiali have nibbled at my borders for centuries, allying themselves with any who would aid them. As did I. As will you. And why? Because it is all we know. Let Caerthalien's lands—or Aramenthiali's—stretch from the shore of Great Ocean to the Grand Windsward, and what changes? Nothing. We fight for glory and for sport, and any who does not wish to do so must buy peace in the blood of his own children. My Nanduil, who should have been heir after me, lies hostage in Caerthalien. Aramenthiali sent me Daustifalal to wed, and by that marriage I secured the east for a season. Perhaps it was my hope that, in pledging to serve you, I could make your rule an easier thing. And there would still be peace."

She reached out and covered his hand with her own. "I swear this to you, Thoromarth of Oronviel. Though I pledge Oronviel to war, I do not go to war for glory or for sport. When I have gained victory, I promise you peace from Great Sea Ocean to Graythunder Glairyrill."

"How can anyone make such a vow?" Thoromarth said slowly.

Vieliessar smiled faintly. "Follow me and see."

Three days later, Vieliessar left Lord Gunedwaen to hold Oronviel

Keep and rode out at the head of fifty of her new-sworn knights. She wore neither the red otter of Oronviel, crowned and garlanded as befit its War Prince, nor Farcarinon's silver wolf. Except for the quality of the destrier she rode—an animal truly fit for a prince—she was as anonymous as any of her knights. Sorodiarn pranced playfully as Vieliessar led her knights down the road that led from the keep. She sat the mare's back as easily as if she had been born it. So many of the things she did now came to her with ease, as if she remembered something she'd once known well, rather than as new skills she had to learn.

She would never permit anyone to know how much it frightened her.

<hr />

"We cannot permit this!" Ladyholder Glorthiachiel spoke as if her wish could make a thing reality.

"My lady, I am certain that—" Carangil Lightbrother stopped, as if even he could not say what he was certain of.

"Well, don't just stare at me, you cloudwit!" Ladyholder Glorthiachiel turned away in frustration, seeking fresh prey. "We must invade Oronviel!"

"Now?" Runacarendalur strode into the chamber, his hair still disheveled from his interrupted morning's ride. "May I remind you, my lady mother, that it is Rade Moon, not Sword? And if you mean my lord father to invade one of our treaty vassals out of season, I think you might have summoned me to your council."

Ladyholder Glorthiachiel's dressing chamber was crowded: not only was Carangil Lightbrother, her personal Mage, present, but several of Runacarendalur's brothers and sisters. Only War Prince Bolecthindial Caerthalien—of those who might reasonably be thought to have an interest in any war of Caerthalien's—was absent.

Runacarendalur tossed his rain-spattered cloak over the nearest chair and leaned back against the wall. Ivrulion was wearing his blandest expression—one Runacarendalur had mistrusted from infancy—and Gimragiel was (as usual) falling over himself to match or even exceed their mother's fury.

"How can you treat this as if it is some jest?" the Ladyholder demanded. "This treacherous viper— This outlaw, oathbreaker, this— Who knows what she will do? One of the Lightborn setting herself up as War Prince!"

"It's impossible." Princess Angiothiel spoke with as much conviction as her mother had.

"Yet it seems to have happened," Runacarendalur pointed out. "And apparently old Thoromarth is still alive. I'm sure he'll convince her to honor his treaties."

"We should crush them," Prince Gimragiel announced.

Runacarendalur sighed. "Yes, Ragi, of course we should," he said patiently. "As soon as they *do* something. Our treaty with Oronviel does not require her to consult with us over changes to her ruling house."

"She is *Farcarinon*," Ladyholder Glorthiachiel hissed.

Farcarinon is gone. Runacarendalur didn't bother to say so, nor did he say it was likely that Vieliessar, having been raised at Caerthalien until her twelfth year, might be more trustworthy than Thoromarth. It would only prolong the argument.

The news of the change in Oronviel's fortunes had reached Caerthalien two days before. War Prince Atholfol Ivrithir had sent an envoy. Lord Bolecthindial had received her privately, then summoned Runacarendalur so she could repeat her message. Runacar shouldn't be surprised that Ladyholder Glorthiachiel knew the messenger's news: half the Court probably did by now. The tale was like something crafted by a story-singer: at Harvest Court, an unknown knight had challenged Thoromarth for his lands. She had defeated Thoromarth's Warlord and champion and revealed herself to be Vieliessar Lightsister.

And that, Runacarendalur thought, *is where matters become complicated.* For Vieliessar Lightsister's life was forfeit outside the bounds of the Sanctuary of the Star. More, after she had fled the Sanctuary, the Astromancer had ordered all the Lightborn of the land to seek her. Well and good, and no problem for any but the Lightborn.

But when Vieliessar Lightsister became War Prince Vieliessar Oronviel . . .

What then?

For a Green Robe to set aside Magery was as much a storysinger's tale as War Princes being challenged for their lands. "'Rulion," Runcarendalur said suddenly, cutting into the conversations going on around him, "has anyone ever *stopped* being a Green Robe?"

Ivrulion regarded him with faint suspicion. "It is not something you *stop*," he said pedantically. "Yet—yes, there have been Lightborn who set aside their Magery. You will recall the story of Ternas of Celebros."

"No," Runacarendalur said simply, and Ivrulion grimaced.

"Ternas Lightbrother was one of the sons of War Prince Farathir Celebros. All others in the Line Direct were killed, save the greatson of Farathir's heir, Prince Methestel. Ternas became Methestel's guardian; when Methestel Heir-Prince was slain on his wedding day, Ternas renounced his Light to became War Prince. It was a very long time ago."

"What has that to do with anything?" Ladyholder Glorthiachiel demanded.

"It is precedent," Runacarendalur said. "If Vieliessar wishes to cease to be Lightborn, there is no proscription."

"Words, words, *words*!" Ladyholder Glorthiachiel snapped impatiently. "I suppose you will say next that there is no proscription against her conquering Caerthalien!"

"None—save the same reason Thoromarth never has. Oronviel cannot muster an army of sufficient size. I suppose they might have done it before this spring, if Thoromarth had been willing to empty his treasury, but we have made that impossible."

"At the cost of raids and banditry," Gimragiel said sullenly.

"I shall be certain to tell Father he must consult you before planning his next campaign," Runacarendalur purred. "I am certain your strategies are equal to your generalship."

Gimragiel shouted in fury and clutched his belt knife. Ciliphirilir jumped to her feet and shrieked as if she were the one being threatened. Angiothiel's *hikuliasa* bounced toward her, barking happily. Ivrulion stepped between Runacarendalur and Gimragiel. "This solves nothing, brothers," he said reprovingly.

"It brings us back to the question at hand," Runacarendalur said, walking over to retrieve his cloak. "If Vieliessar chooses to become War Prince—as she might have done if her father had not been a fool—what must Caerthalien do? And not only is that a matter for Lord Bolecthindial to decide, but I remind you all: no one goes to war in winter. Especially in a winter where we shall be much harried by outlaws."

The Harrowing of Farcarinon had already begun to bear its bitter fruit, and Runacarendalur could only hope the outlaws would soon retreat to their winter camps to give Caerthalien time to prepare its defense.

"So we are to wait for the spring, to give Serenthon's whelp time to craft her revenge!" Ladyholder Glorthiachiel said.

"If she sought vengeance, Mother, she would have taken it the moment she took the Green Robe," Runacarendalur pointed out.

"You sound as if you are her defender!" Princess Angiothiel said with an angry giggle.

"Never that." Runacarendalur turned toward his sister and gave her a mocking bow. "I am merely realistic. And if we are to fight Oronviel come War Season, be sure I shall win our victory." He turned, bowing this time to Ladyholder Glorthiachiel. "But that decision has not yet been reached."

⬥⬦⬥

Do you think she merely wishes to rule Oronviel?"

Ivrulion caught up to him before he reached the staircase. Runacarendalur had suspected he would. It was unkind to say Ivrulion spied on his brothers and sisters—and their mother—but it was probably no more than the truth. He and his children were outside the succession unless all the other possible heirs to Caerthalien died first—and that was some two hundred of the Lords *Komen*. And yet . . . Ivrulion had been raised as heir-prince until the day he had been sent to the Sanctuary.

There were times Runacarendalur wondered if Ivrulion thought it a fair trade.

"Possibly," Runacarendalur said. Ladyholder Glorthiachiel's voice could still be heard, faintly, in the distance. "Think, brother. Vieliessar did not go to the Sanctuary because the Light had been Called in her. She went to break the Peacebond Celelioniel Astromancer had laid upon her at birth. Because she was Farcarinon. Father had no choice in that. If he wed her to Huthiel—or any other of the Line—we would have had everyone from Aramenthiali to Daroldan at our throats."

"Yet the Light came to her," Ivrulion said.

"Something no one could have predicted—did you? Did Carangil? Did Seragindill? But even the Green Robe could not win freedom for her. I think her captivity weighed heavy enough that she chose the only path to freedom there was."

"A domain on our border," Ivrulion pointed out.

"A domain holding as many from Farcarinon as ours, or Aramenthiali, or Cirandeiron, or Telthorelandor. No doubt some of Serenthon's vassals remembered old loyalties and helped her to possess Oronviel." Runacarendalur shrugged. "Oronviel shares no border with Farcarinon, at least. Tell Father to send some envoy to her, to see if she means to abide by Thoromarth's treaty with us. If not—" He shrugged again. "War."

"War indeed," Ivrulion said, with a thin, cold smile. "Enjoy the day, brother." He bowed slightly, then turned and strode away.

I believe I shall, brother. I believe I shall pay a call on Domcariel, and ask him why he was not invited to Mother's improvised council of war. Of course, I wasn't invited either—but I believe the knowledge that she held one will come as a great surprise to Dom. And he can be reliably predicted to run to Father with the news. . . .

To win in the Challenge Circle was a skill entirely different from commanding an army, and if War Prince Vieliessar did not lead her own army—at least for a campaign or two—she would not hold Oronviel by next Harvest. The idea of going to war against such an innocent was appealing. Far less appealing was the specter of war within Caerthalien. Ladyholder Glorthiachiel had led armies, and her hatred of Serenthon Farcarinon had not diminished with his death. Such hatred had been known to ripen into warfare, and her first opponent must be Bolecthindial. A House, so weakened, would be easy prey for its enemies. Better Lord Bolecthindial know at once how his lady's temper lay, and if he chose to do what best pleased her, then they would be at one, and Caerthalien the stronger for it.

Cheered by the pleasant prospect of the coming War Season, Runacarendalur went in search of Prince Domcariel.

CHAPTER SEVEN

THE HIGH KING'S ARMY

The queen came riding and sang the song of freedom,
The queen came riding and truth was on her tongue.
The High cried out against it, but truth was on her tongue.
Truth forever. Landbond free.

—Tunonil Landbond, *The Song of Freedom*

Before she had left on her strange autumnal Progress, Vieliessar had spoken to all those Lightborn who remained at Oronviel, telling them they were free to go or to stay, and that she would place no restriction upon their use of the Light so long as they remained faithful to Mosirinde's Covenant.

Many had gone—if not out of Oronviel, then at least back to their families—and some of the castel nobles had complained bitterly, for there were so few Lightborn remaining that their spells were occupied on necessary tasks, not in finding a lost glove or keeping bathwater hot. Finding no ally in their new War Prince, some had summoned their own Lightborn from their estates, only to discover that the War Prince's decree had gone before them, and those Lightborn who had not left their lands could not be spared.

Others had accepted the new rules with good humor, for if Vieliessar lightened the yoke of custom that weighted the necks of the commons, she lightened it for her nobles as well. No longer did her lords need to fear their horses, jewels, servants, or estates would be seized because their prince or one of her favorites desired it. No longer did they fear to be punished—or banished—for rumor or lies.

And most unbelievable of all, any who wished were free to depart Oronviel, taking with them all their possessions and any of their people who went with them freely. Generations of war, ransoms, and treaty marriages had left many of the noble families scattered across two or three domains, or five, and among such families, blood ties warred with fealty oaths.

It was slow work to spread her new truths across the land, but all who left Oronviel, noble or servile, spoke of them. The Lightborn spoke to their fellows in other domains, and the crofters who lived along the borders had closer ties with the next steading, whether it lay in Caerthalien, Aramenthiali, or Ivrithir, than they did with their distant lieges. The word of all they would gain when Vieliessar Oronviel became High King passed through Oronviel and then across her borders.

Prince Vieliessar means to be High King. She will be a friend to all who fight for her, and when she is High King, she will hold no grudge against those who did not.

When Vieliessar is High King there will be a Code of Peace. One justice for all, be they highborn or low, not rewards for some and punishments for others.

When Vieliessar is High King, domain will not war with domain, for all domains will be one.

When Vieliessar is High King, the Lightborn will not be taken from their families and hoarded as a glutton hoards grain. They will go where they will and do as they wish. Nor will any children be forced to the Sanctuary against their will.

When Vieliessar is High King, lords will not steal from vassals, from craftworkers, from Landbonds—

When Vieliessar is High King, any with skill may become a knight, or a weaver, or a smith—

When Vieliessar is High King, any may own a horse, or a hound, or a sword—

When Vieliessar is High King . . .

The other War Princes counted the taille of Oronviel's knights and thought it the whole of her army.

Her army was the whole of the people of Oronviel.

※

"Here is where we begin." Vieliessar rubbed the drawing-chalk between her fingers. Rithdeliel's workroom in Oronviel Great Keep was a vast space. One wall was covered with tallyboards listing manor-knights and the number of knights-at-arms they could muster. The center of the room held three enormous tables. One could be covered in sand so that the deployment of forces could be tried before orders were passed to the Lords *Komen*. The other two held maps. She glanced at the men and women around the map table. Rithdeliel, Gunedwaen, Thoromarth. Princess Nothrediel, Thoromarth's daughter, who was the new Cadet Warlord; Aradreleg Lightsister, who was the new Chief Lightborn; Hanniach, knight-captain of the castel knights.

Gazing down at the map before her, Vieliessar thought of the first time she had entered the Great Library of Arevethmonion. The path she had begun that day had led here. She traced her finger along Oronviel's marked border. "How much of the border is disputed?"

Rithdeliel laughed. "All of it, Lord Vieliessar. It is the nature of borders."

"And how far can we go across this . . . disputed border before we are noticed?"

Gunedwaen cleared his throat. "That depends on why we go."

"To secure the land. Here is what is in my mind. My knights will ride through Oronviel as if on progress, each troop under its accustomed captain, and Lightborn will ride with them. They will come, if I do not ask them to prison themselves in the Great Keep once more, if I tell them I send them to Farmhold, croft, and steading to do what seems good to them. My knights will seek out every smallholding, and there the Lightborn will hear of taxes and tithes. They will go also to the Landbonds and hear their words, and such spellcraft as is needed, they will perform. They will discover the habitations of bandits and outlaws. My *komen* will take such creatures prisoner and bring them to me for judgment."

She paused. Gunedwaen looked worried. Hanniach looked doubtful. Rithdeliel looked as if he was storing up objections. "In addition to these tasks, they will find for me every youth or maiden who seeks knightly arms, no matter their degree. These, too, they will bring to me here, so they may be instructed. These tasks they will perform throughout Oronviel." She set the chalk to the map, redrawing Oronviel's borders with a few swift strokes, and in moments she had doubled its size. "These are the borders of our domain. All within it shall know they may look to Oronviel for safety."

"That is an . . . audacious . . . undertaking, my prince," Hanniach said, dubiously.

"It can't be done," Princess Nothredlel said flatly.

"It can," Vieliessar answered.

"To take territory without warfare . . . it is an interesting idea," Rithdeliel said, measuring his words carefully. "And yet, it is in my mind that such small forces as you propose to dispatch on this 'progress' will be easy prey for a larger force. If you must ransom every knight in your domain not once, but a dozen times during War Season, Oronviel will be impoverished by Harvest."

"But I do not mean them to ride during summer," Vieliessar said reasonably. "I mean them to begin now."

"Ride to war in winter?" Rithdeliel said, aghast.

Gunedwaen laughed. "You are not thinking to win a war with the loyalty of Landbond and smallholder, are you?" he scoffed.

Vieliessar did not answer directly. "Aradreleg, where were you born?" she asked.

"On Willowleaf Farm," she answered, sounding puzzled. "My father is overseer there."

"Who rides to war without Lightborn, Gunedwaen?" Vieliessar asked next.

"Idiots," Gunedwaen said. "But—"

"We win wars *now* with the loyalty of Landbond and smallholder," Vieliessar said. "We send their children to the Sanctuary, and then we take them to war. High House or Low, we gather the Lightborn of our domains to us and hold them close."

"But—" Rithdeliel said, and stopped.

"We do it because it is our right," Vieliessar finished for him. "And because we can win no battle without Lightborn to Heal our wounds, light our pavilions, gentle our horses, keep our food from spoiling, and a hundred other tasks. You say that Farmholder and Landbond care not who holds the land they work. I say: give them cause to care, and they will. Return their children to them, provide them with the safety and comfort that Magery affords, and they will give us a land at peace."

"Until someone comes over the border to put an end to it," Thoromarth said.

"Until then," Vieliessar agreed, nodding. "But no army fights in winter, as you say. Let us use this winter to secure Oronviel."

"By raiding beyond our borders," Rithdeliel said, touching his finger to the chalk marks on the map.

"All borders are disputed," Vieliessar reminded him. "Come Sword Moon, our neighbors will find their lands less than they once thought."

⊰✦⊱

"What has this mad plan of yours to do with . . . ?" Gunedwaen asked after Vieliessar had dismissed the others to begin turning her ideas into reality.

"Everything," she said. "I will build an army. I will push Oronviel's borders as far as I may before anyone objects or even notices. If I hold the farms and make them safe, I hold the loyalty of the Lightborn who come from them. Next I shall take Ivrithir and Araphant: both are clients of Caerthalien, as Oronviel is. Ivrithir is small, and Araphant has a dotard for a War Prince."

"Caerthalien and Aramenthiali will ally," Gunedwaen said, speaking slowly and carefully, as if presenting information she lacked. "Oronviel cannot defeat such an alliance on the field."

"Are you certain?" Vieliessar asked. "Wait and see."

⊰✦⊱

When she had been a Candidate, a Servant, a Postulant, and even Lightborn at the Sanctuary of the Star, Vieliessar had read voraciously—for pleasure, for knowledge, for an escape from the grey stone walls which were all she had ever expected to know. Her studies served her in good stead now, for Arevethmonion's holdings were unmatched—and, for most of her time, uncensored. She had eagerly devoured accounts written by the Lightborn who had stood near for every princely council—tales not edited to flatter or excuse, for no lord would ever read them.

When Vieliessar had come upon mention of Farcarinon in such accounts, she had read them closely, for none of Farcarinon had survived to write their own versions. It did not matter that Farcarinon's Lightborn had survived her fall: they had taken oaths to other Houses. But from Arevethmonion's scrolls, she had pieced together the tale no one was alive to tell.

Serenthon Farcarinon's ambitious weaving had begun even as War Prince Hiathuint, his father, lay upon his deathbed. Nearly a full score of decades had passed before its true shape could be discerned, a gossamer net of alliance, promise, and dream that tangled all the Houses of the West, great and less, in its strands.

Farcarinon's first and staunchest ally had been Caerthalien. Aramenthiali and Telthorelandor stood apart, Cirandeiron bent this way and that like a young tree in a storm, first yielding to Serenthon's wooing, next recollecting her ancient dignity.

When Caerthalien betrayed Farcarinon and allied with Aramenthiali and Telthorelandor—and Cirandeiron rushed to join them—many of Farcarinon's allies fled. Others held fast until battle was inevitable, then sued for terms of surrender. Still others had stood fast until the day of the battle itself. Ivrithir had stood with Farcarinon until the morning of the battle, and no one could now say whether that was because Atholfol Ivrithir had been loyal until the last hope was gone, or merely wished to time his betrayal to the moment it would do Farcarinon the greatest harm. Nor did Vieliessar care. She had learned the lesson her father had not lived to learn. By the time her army took the field, she would have rendered it impossible for them to betray her.

⊰⊱

The forest grew, thick and old, all across the border. It would have been impossible to tell where one domain ended and the next began save for the marker stone in the clearing, bespelled with Silverlight so that it glowed softly in the twilight gloom beneath the trees. As Vieliessar approached it, she saw a lone rider moving through the trees to meet her.

So far all goes in accordance with my desire. . . .

Atholfol Ivrithir was more than two-thirds through his allotted span of years, and he had held Ivrithir for most of that time, for a War Prince's heir often came to rule early in life. His youngest child, Heir-Princess Caragond, could expect to burn her father's bones and take his sword no more than three centuries hence—and far less, were Atholfol unlucky.

"Well met, Oronviel," he said, swinging down from the back of his destrier. "I confess, I did not think you would come."

"Neither did my household," she answered, vaulting from Sorodiarn's back. "Or, rather, they wished I would not."

Atholfol smiled thinly. "Yet here we both are. You wish me to void the treaty I have sworn with Caerthalien in order to ally with Oronviel as I once did with Farcarinon. I ask you this: where is Ivrithir's advantage in doing so?"

"If you wish an end to pointless war, your advantage is great. I shall be High King whether you aid me or no, yet I ask your help."

"What help can I give?" Atholfol answered mockingly, spreading his hands wide in a gesture of harmlessness. "Ivrithir is small and poor—the indemnities I have paid to Caerthalien since the day Farcarinon fell have seen to that."

"I do not have the patience for this," Vieliessar answered, her voice edged. "You are inclined to this alliance, or you would not be here. What I want from Ivrithir is your army—all of it. Supplies, mounts, your

Lightborn, your pledge to support Oronviel in all things, passage across your borders for my people, and all those brigands taken in your lands to be turned over to Oronviel for my justice."

There was a moment of silence. "Perhaps I should name you my heir and vow my lands to you at once?" Atholfol asked. "I still see no advantage to Ivrithir in any of this."

"You will no longer have to tithe Caerthalien a tenth-part of your harvests and your cattle," Vieliessar said in a voice of mock-innocence, and Atholfol laughed.

"Hardly sufficient! When your father came wooing me, he promised me greater lands, a share of the wealth of those Houses we cast down, and a place upon his council."

"And I will not," Vieliessar answered. "For it was such bargains that destroyed him. I promise you three things, Atholfol Ivrithir: an end to the ceaseless warfare between House and House, a justice that runs the same for all, whether of High House or Low—and that you will not have to face my army in battle."

"Every child looks to the future with such jeweled hopes, Lord Vieliessar. My Caragond is just the same. She swears that when she is War Prince, she will not be taken in clientage by Caerthalien, that she will take back the lands we have been forced to cede, that she will not give up her children as hostages. I said much the same, when I was her age. Such pretty dreams wither at the first touch of a swordblade."

"And the time I dreamt the dreams of a child is long past, Lord Atholfol. We have lived a score of generations in exile, at war among ourselves, for the inability to agree on who should have the Unicorn Throne after Amrethion and Pelashia. In the west, the Beastlings seek to drive us into the sea. The south is bordered by impassable desert, the north, by mountains so high and cold that nothing can live there. The eastern lands are more embattled than the west, settled only because the alternative was extinction." She stopped, studying him in silence for a long moment. "They speak of you as one who rejoices in war for the sport it offers. I ask you: where is the sport in the slaughter of helpless innocents? You took no new wife after Ninianael's death. Will you see Caragond also face the day when she must sue Caerthalien, or Aramenthiali, or Cirandeiron, to receive her consort's bones for burning?"

"When that day comes—if it does—I shall be dead long since," Atholfol said harshly. "This is a strange wooing, Lord Vieliessar, accompanied as it is by neither gifts nor threats."

"I do offer you a gift. I offer truth," Vieliessar answered.

This time Atholfol roared with laughter, until he had to clutch at the cantle of his destrier's saddle to steady himself. The animal craned its head around to regard him, ears flicking with curiosity.

"By the Hunt!" he said, when he had gained control of his mirth. "I had forgotten you were raised a Green Robe! I cannot eat truth or ride it—what use is it to me?"

Vieliessar had watched the display in silence, knowing it was at least partly an act for her benefit. "Truth is a weapon, Lord Atholfol. I offer you more truth—as a gift. The Free Companies were hunted out of Farcarinon. Such scraps as remain have turned to brigandage. Those outlaws who would once have joined Free Companies and been kept to discipline now have no place to offer their services save to bandits. Nor can Ivrithir, or Oronviel, or any other Less House hire the services of that which does not exist. But that is not the truth I offer—it is a poor thing, and you must know it yourself. What I offer is this: consider the alliance that made it possible.

"A century and more ago Farcarinon was erased and no retribution followed. My present ambitions are known. The Twelve will move to erase Oronviel next. Suppose they succeeded—though I say to you they will not. You know as well as I that no dog's appetite is slaked by one meal. The High Houses would learn that they might expand their lands at the expense of those who cannot stand against them. Not this year. Not even while you yet live. But the day would come when Ivrithir, too, was erased, or forced to flee eastward to the Grand Windsward in hopes of establishing a domain there with what scraps it had retained in its flight."

"You will not terrify me with fearful nursery tales, Lord Vieliessar," Atholfol scoffed.

"How should I, when I have said you will not live to see the day? But once there were a Hundred Houses, and each War Prince possessed an equal claim to the Unicorn Throne. That is why we fight, you know," she added kindly. "Then the Grand Alliance did the unthinkable and now there are only Ninety-and-Nine. With Oronviel's erasure there would be Ninety-and-Eight. Do you think it would not occur to the High Houses that by eliminating the Less Houses they can claim wealth, armies, and land—and eliminate rivals for the High Kingship?"

Plainly Atholfol did not like what he heard, but he was too stubborn to admit it. "Less Houses have risen up before—what care I if fifty Lines are erased, if Ivrithir is not? You ask for an alliance and offer nothing but dreams and promises. Think you I do not know Oronviel's muster to the last maiden knight? You do not have sufficient forces to take Ivrithir in the field, let alone a Great House."

Vieliessar smiled. "Do you think you know the full force I can summon to my call? I tell you this as a further gift, since you must be wooed as if you are a blushing child. I will take all who will swear fealty to me—the raiders who harry your borders, the craftworkers who flee your harsh justice, the Landbonds you tithe into starvation. I shall forge them into a weapon. And I shall take up that weapon, and win."

"Oronviel cannot stand against the Twelve," Atholfol said flatly.

"You speak of the Twelve in alliance and call *me* a dreamer of storysinger's dreams?" Vieliessar mocked. "Caerthalien will come to slay me and all who swore to me. They will bring with them Princess Nanduil of Oronviel, who has been hostage at their court since before she cut her first teeth, and her they will make War Prince. That is their plan, at least. It will not work."

"Why not?" Atholfol asked. He seemed torn between curiosity and disbelief.

"You have not agreed to an alliance," Vieliessar answered.

"You offer a storysinger's tale of peace and justice, but conjure

Celephriandullias-Tildorangelor as you will, what you truly offer is death."

"Is it?" Vieliessar asked. "Perhaps it seems so to you. Tell me, Lord Atholfol, what does an army need in order to fight?"

"Knights, horses, supply trains, Lightborn—" Atholfol began.

Vieliessar silenced him with a gesture. "No. They need to believe they can win. And to want the victory.

"When you ride to battle, your Landbonds pray you will not fight across their fields. Your craftworkers pray you will not demand the impossible and punish them when they cannot achieve it. Your *komentai'a* pray they will find favor in your eyes when the time comes for their ransom to be paid. Your Lightborn pray their shields will hold, and their strength will be great enough to Heal the bodies you ruin for a season's entertainment." She gazed at him for a long moment; the only sound was the wind rustling through the branches above them. "When I ride to battle, it will not be for sport. And no soul I hold within my hand shall be left to the mercy of my enemies."

"You mean to arm your Landbonds," Atholfol said slowly. "They will not fight for you. And even if they would, the Code of Battle—"

"—is a toy. I set my toys aside long ago. I will arm my Landbonds, and my Landholders, and my craftworkers. They will fight for me. All in the Fortunate Lands whom you in your wastrel lives have cast aside will fight for me, for I will offer them justice."

"An army of rabble and outlaws," Atholfol said, but he sounded uncertain for the first time. "They will never prevail against trained knights."

"Come against us and see. Though if you join us, you will probably get a better view," she added, as if the thought had just occurred to her.

"I . . . believe I shall," Atholfol said slowly. "If only to see that haughty pup Runacarendalur's face when he realizes he is to take the field against hayforks and blacksmith's hammers." He let out a deep breath, as if he had been holding it for much longer than they'd stood here. "Very well. Alliance. Safe passage across my borders; my army to call. I am not certain I can promise the brigands, though. My *komentai'a* are used to executing them as they find them."

"No matter," Vieliessar answered lightly. "Send your knights to me and I will instruct them properly. And so that your lands do not lie undefended, I shall send my army to you, to keep your borders and bring me your outlaws."

"You truly mean to do this," Atholfol said, as if only now realizing it.

"I do," Vieliessar answered.

"Very well. We have no Lightborn here, but once they were not needed for the swearing of oaths." He drew the dagger from his belt and pulled off his heavy leather hunting gloves. Holding the blade steady, he scored a long even gash across the palm of his hand, then held the blade out to her.

The kiss of the steel against her skin was first cold, then burning. She held out her hand, and he clasped it.

"Vieliessar Oronviel, I renounce my claim upon the Unicorn Throne and swear that while I yet draw breath I shall do all that lies within my power to deliver it into your hand," Atholfol said.

"Atholfol Ivrithir, I take your oath, and for this pledge of loyalty I swear I will not allow you to lie unransomed in the halls of my enemies, nor languish a prisoner in their dungeons, nor permit your body to be dishonored in death."

They stood a moment longer, hands clasped, then Atholfol let go and stepped back. "I suppose I should go and tell Bedreithir Warlord she will not be spending the winter beneath the comfort of her own roof. You may expect the first of my levies within the sennight."

"I shall leave them escort at Torchwood," she answered. "You are welcome to come yourself, of course," she added, knowing the offer would not be accepted.

"I think it will be more entertaining to keep Bolecthindial in suspense some while longer. I believe he wishes to try Lady Dendinirchiel's patience next summer, and does not wish Lord Manderechiel to take overmuch notice when he moves his army across Farcarinon to reach Ullilion, for he bid me raid against Aramenthiali when War Season comes. But I am certain there will be many reasons I cannot."

"Or it may be that you will do more than raid against Aramenthiali once a few more moonturns have passed," Vieliessar answered, gravely pleased. "I give you good fortune, Ivrithir."

"And to you the same, Oronviel. And may the Starry Hunt watch over us both," Atholfol answered. He turned away then, leading his destrier back into Ivrithir. Vieliessar watched after him for a few moments before mounting Sorodiarn and riding back to where she had left Aradreleg.

⊰⊱

Before Rade Moon was ended, Sunalanthaid Lightbrother came from the Sanctuary of the Star to demand that Oronviel surrender Vieliessar Lightsister to its justice. He was already out of temper when he reached the castel, for he had been met—before he was many miles past the border—by a troop of Oronviel knights. Despite Rithdeliel's pessimism—and Lady Nothrediel's declarations that the thing could not be done—the majority of Oronviel's knights were happy to have an easing of winter's long sennights of boredom. Hunting was their main pastime in winter, and they quickly found there was good sport to be had in hunting outlaws.

With Lightborn traveling with every troop of knights—just as Vieliessar had promised—Vieliessar could be certain of immediate information from every corner of Oronviel. She was aware of Sunalanthaid's coming a full sennight before he arrived, and used that time to prepare to receive him. For the first time in her life she wore the elaborate finery of a noble lady: the layers of underskirts of stiffened silk, the gilded slippers, the heavy jeweled belt riding low upon her hips, the rings—including the signet of Oronviel—and the heavy bracelets. Her hair, once shorn and worn unadorned to show her status as a Mage, was still too short to braid properly, so she wore it swept back from her temples. A pair of heavy carven combs held it in place; the combs were sewn to a long length of soft, heavy silk that flowed over her shoulders and coiled about her throat.

Not one thread of any of her garments was green.

She chose to receive Sunalanthaid in her private rooms instead of the Great Hall. To do so would emphasize her status as War Prince: Hamphuliadiel had sent Sunalanthaid because he wished to display his authority over her. She had refused requests from Thoromarth, Gunedwaen, and Rithdeliel to be present: she would not receive Sunalanthaid as if he were an emissary from another House. Only Aradreleg Lightsister was present—more proof that Vieliessar feared nothing from the Sanctuary.

She had dressed her private chamber as carefully as she had dressed her body: it held her chair of rank and no other place to sit. The sideboard held wine instead of a tea brazier, and the tapestries upon the walls depicted great feats of Oronviel's past. Beside her chair stood a table littered with scrolls and parchments—nothing Sunalanthaid could not be allowed to see, and all underscoring the truth she wished him to bear witness to: she was not Vieliessar Lightsister, but War Prince Vieliessar Oronviel.

"Lightbrother," she said, as one of her castel guard opened the door to usher in her guest, "I trust you had a safe journey?" She stroked Striker's long head; it was a tiny clemency from a future grown tangled and dark that the companion of Gunedwaen's long exile had survived to enjoy a pampered old age. She watched as confusion played across Sunalanthaid's face: he wished to argue with her—with the very *fact* of her—but could not decide how to begin.

It is a pity Hamphuliadiel did not send a messenger with more cleverness. Perhaps he could not find someone who was both clever and loyal.

"I am here to command your return to the Sanctuary of the Star," Sunalanthaid said at last.

"No," Vieliessar answered. "May I offer you a night's rest beneath my roof before you begin your return journey? Or will you wish to leave at once?"

Sunalanthaid gaped at her for a moment. Those with power—even the reflected power of the Astromancer's lackey—became accustomed to agreement and obedience where they had earned neither. "You can't say that!" he finally managed to sputter.

"Within the walls of my own keep, I can say what I wish," she answered. "I am War Prince of Oronviel by right of challenge."

"You are not," Sunalanthaid said, sounding plaintive. He turned toward Aradreleg. "She is a fugitive from the Sanctuary. Hamphuliadiel demands her return. At once!"

"Then let the Astromancer send his vast armies to take her," Aradreleg said, glancing toward Vieliessar for consent before she spoke. "But first, let him say why he seeks to claim a prince of the Hundred Houses."

"She has broken the Covenant. Her Light is forfeit," Sunalanthaid said at last.

"Bring your witnesses to that charge, Sunalanthaid of Haldil, as I will answer them," Vieliessar replied. Naming his House instead of using his title was rudeness, but she meant it to serve as a reminder she was no longer the Sanctuary's servant—in any fashion. "Farcarinon was taken from me before my birth, and everyone thought I would be content to be so disparaged. But Oronviel is now mine, and I will rule over it as did Ternas Lightbrother over House Celebros in the days of Timirmar Astromancer."

For a moment, she thought Sunalanthaid might ask her if she was telling the truth. Then his mouth firmed into a hard line. "You face serious accusations, Lightborn," he repeated.

Vieliessar leaned forward in her chair. "Say this to Hamphuliadiel: I know both law and custom better than he. Say also that if I had taken Oronviel by unnatural means, my Lightborn would have voided my domain, and they have not."

"Eiron—" Sunalanthaid began.

"Would not pledge fealty to me," Vieliessar interrupted. "For that cause I banished him and a handful of others. You have come here in error, Sunalanthaid Lightbrother. I am Vieliessar Lightsister no longer.

Take that word to Hamphuliadiel Astromancer when you go—and while you are my guest, do not give me cause to seek recompense from Haldil for your actions. Now leave me. I grow tired of explaining to you what you should have learned in your Postulancy."

Watching Sunalanthaid's openmouthed confusion, she knew for truth what she had only suspected: he had come to Oronviel believing Hamphuliadiel's demands would be met with ready capitulation from the nobles and Lightborn of Oronviel. Perhaps he had thought to find Thoromarth ruling on her behalf, or to find her a prisoner, or to find Oronviel in open rebellion against her rule.

He had not.

"I will— I will—"

"You are tired from your journey. I would not have you set forth in such a state. Aradreleg Lightsister will conduct you to the rooms I have prepared for you."

Aradreleg stepped toward him, and Sunalanthaid hesitantly turned to accompany her. Vieliessar could feel his confusion clearly—she would not seek to know more, not while Sunalanthaid hoped to discover her using spells to rule—and she might have pitied him, were he not so blatantly her enemy.

"Yet there is one thing I must require of you first." Both Lightborn stopped at the sound of Vieliessar's voice. "I am War Prince of Oronviel. You will give me the courtesy of my rank, or your stay here will be exceedingly brief."

For a moment she thought he would refuse. But the Sanctuary was far away, and Vieliessar looked nothing like the self-effacing Lightsister who had endured Hamphuliadiel's rebukes and punishments for so very long.

"My lord— My lady— Lord Vieliessar—" Sunalanthaid stammered. "I— Yes."

Vieliessar raised a hand in dismissal. She took up a scroll from the table beside her, pretending to study it until she heard the door close behind them.

⊰∺⊱

Rallying the people to her with the truth—a *kind* of truth, anyway, for she did not expect peace immediately upon her accession to the Unicorn Throne—was only one part of her strategy. Another was to rule over the land as if it were already hers.

The Great Keeps of the War Princes stood in the center of the lands they claimed. It was only sensible: such a placement would put their greatest stronghold far from their disputed borders. Even if the changing fortunes of a House had moved its borders so its keep lay nearer to one border or another, the farther one went from the Great Keep, the less settled was the land and the smaller the farms. More of the land lay under great Flower Forests or simple woodlands, until on the borders of the domain one reached the watchtowers and border keeps. These were large and heavily fortified, held by great lords who were nearly princes themselves. They kept vast meisnes of *komen,* and when the enemy rode across a domain's border, it was the lords of the border keeps who first rode out against them.

But the border lords did not ride out against anything but a troop of enemy knights. It was considered dishonorable to ride to battle in disguise, and so they would go in bright silks and gleaming armor. Their passage could be seen for a great distance.

The raiders who preyed upon the outlying farms had neither bright silks nor gleaming armor, and well knew the value of concealment.

From Rade to Frost, Vieliessar met with the lords of all of her border keeps. To all of them she gave new orders: to ride to the aid of the border farmsteads when they were attacked. Many of her border lords were indignant at these commands, for they considered the border steadings to be there for little reason other than to provide sport for raiding parties from either side of the border. Vieliessar had removed some lords from their appointments and made it clear to all who remained that there would be no raiding, no brigandage, no "sport" in Oronviel.

When the border lords saw that her army patrolled as well—and saw what diversion there was in hunting brigands—Oronviel became a place of peace, not of raids and night terrors, until the pennion of Oronviel, with its red otter on a white field, brought the Farmfolk of Araphant, Ivrithir, and Laeldor—and Caerthalien and Aramenthiali as well— running to their dooryards to greet the patrols; to offer cider, bread, or honeycomb; to ask for aid.

Rithdeliel had sworn her plan would never work. Vieliessar had known it would. The *komen* might be proud and arrogant, but they were not immune to the experience of being greeted by the countryfolk with unfeigned pleasure and honest warmth, rather than with cold suspicion and grudging cooperation.

By Frost Moon, the land Oronviel controlled was twice again what it had been in Harvest, for once her treaty was made with Ivrithir, Vieliessar's knights rode its bounds just as they had ridden hers. Ivrithir's knights were no more immune to the astonishing experience of being welcomed by the Farmfolk than their brothers and sisters of Oronviel had been, and word of the alliance had run ahead of them, so the people of the borders greeted the pennion bearing Ivrithir's tawny bear with as much enthusiasm as they'd greeted the red otter.

⌖

Hearth Moon became Frost Moon, and each day that did not bring word of armies marching toward Oronviel's borders seemed to Vieliessar like a reprieve. There was much to do to in order to turn the impossible to the improbable. Candlemark by candlemark she lived with the temptation to change her course to one that wouldn't seem so much like madness. There was still time to compose a document explaining how she had discovered the meaning behind *The Song of Amrethion*— she still had the scrap of the scroll Celelioniel had written—to ask openly for the help of the Hundred Houses against the Darkness.

No one would believe her. No matter what she did, her fellow War Princes would seek for the hidden motive, the trap, the betrayal. And even if they did not, they would still squabble over who should be War

King over the combined army of the Hundred Houses just as they now battled over who was to be High King.

There is no time for that. They will not listen to argument. Only to armies.

I must have Mangiralas. Not for its destriers, but for its palfreys. If I can build an infantry, I must still get it to the battlefield. And Daroldan— not their neutrality this time, but War Prince Damulothir's promise to support Oronviel. I will need him to demand aid of Caerthalien so she does not take the field against me before I am ready.

Mangiralas, Daroldan, Caerthalien, Ivrithir, Oronviel . . . a thousand threads from which she must weave her future.

Everyone's future.

And so, with a thousand bad choices and no good ones before her, Vieliessar sent messengers to those Houses which had once supported her father's bid to make himself High King, offering their War Princes safe passage and a Midwinter Truce if they would send representatives to Oronviel. Oronviel's Midwinter Feast would be—must be— extraordinary, for Vieliessar must both display her power and take the next step toward what would inevitably seem as a revival of Serenthon's royal ambitions. Worst of all, she could not count on any of the alliances she made this Snow Moon—if any—to stand one moment past the time Hamphuliadiel Astromancer made it known that she believed herself to be the Child of the Prophecy. If the War Princes hated the thought of a High King, they hated the thought of a mystical madwoman even more.

Celelioniel Astromancer had done Vieliessar no favors by her obsession with Amrethion's Curse.

⚜

Though Midwinter was still sennights away, preparations for it were already under way. A feasting-hall crafted entirely of ice was taking form upon the meadow beyond Oronviel Castel. The kitchens were busy day and night. As each dish was finished, the last touches applied by Oronviel's Master of Kitchens, it was cloaked in a Preservation Spell by a waiting Lightborn so that a sennight or a fortnight hence it could be brought to the feasting table as fresh and savory as if it had just been cooked. Unused chambers within the castel were aired and refurbished, temporary stables and paddocks erected, provision made for a full sennight of lavish spectacle.

It was a bit like going to war, Vieliessar thought. And in truth, this was the opening movement of her campaign, for Oronviel would keep Midwinter as if Vieliessar were already High King. In counterpoint to the lavish feasting of the nobles, she would feast the commons as well—and not upon the leavings of the great feasts, but upon bread and mutton and beer, given without stint.

Nor would her Lightborn Call the Light only upon the Fourth Night of the Festival, but upon all seven, turning away none who sought them out and taking none who refused them.

These things were new and strange enough that her ears had grown weary of hearing Gunedwaen, or Rithdeliel, or Thoromarth tell her why they must not be, and now she added one thing more: for the whole of the Festival, all within Oronviel, no matter their degree, had full right of woodland and lesser forest. They might gather what they chose, cut standing trees, and take game.

And take no hurt of it.

When I am High King, none shall starve and shiver in fear through the winter moonturns to enrich those who have no care for them.

But she was not High King yet.

⬦

Today she faced *Komen* Bethaerian in the circle. As with all the Great Keeps, a Challenge Circle had been set into the stone of the Great Hall when it was built: a ring of white granite set into the smooth, dark, Mage-forged slate. Here the knights of the War Prince's household demonstrated their skill and settled quarrels. Here, too, a disgraced knight might regain lost honor and earn a place with the Starry Hunt by facing all challengers until death's blood rinsed reputation clean once more.

Her own reputation among her knights was neither bad or good, but Vieliessar had not led them into battle for season after season. She must convince any who watched that she had set aside her Magery along with her Green Robe. And so Vieliessar met all who wished to do battle within the Great Hall's circle, calling it sport to liven the dull days of winter.

Bethaerian was the commander of Vieliessar's personal guard. It had taken Bethaerian sennights to challenge her, though she had watched the bouts from the beginning. She had put that time to good use, studying Vieliessar's skills. Though Oronviel's War Prince had disarmed Bethaerian quickly, when she slammed her shoulder against Bethaerian's chestpiece to thrust her from the circle and end the bout, Bethaerian stepped into the blow, pulling Vieliessar against her, front to back. Neither of them could launch a further attack in that position, but Bethaerian had not lost.

"I yield," Vieliessar said, laughter bubbling up beneath her words.

Bethaerian released her, stepping across the boundary of the Challenge Circle. Only when Vieliessar was pulling off her helm did she see Aradreleg awaiting her.

"My prince," the Lightsister said, "a Lightborn envoy comes from Caerthalien."

"Is he escorted?" she asked. Her people were smart and loyal, but no one in the Fortunate Lands—save, perhaps, the War Princes themselves—would go against the wishes of a Green Robe. If Ivrulion Light-Prince had refused escort . . .

"Indeed," Aradreleg said, putting Vieliessar's worry to rest. "Peryn Lightsister sends to say *Komen* Berlaindist brings the Lightbrother with all haste."

It wasn't customary for a Lightborn traveling as envoy of a War Prince to give his name, only his House, so neither Peryn nor Berlaindist would know it. "'All haste' is . . . ?" Vieliessar prompted.

"A sennight, *Komen* Berlaindist promises, no more."

"Then there is barely sufficient time to prepare to receive him,"

Vieliessar answered. She had invited Caerthalien to attend her Winter Court, of course, but an envoy arriving a fortnight before the start of the Festival could mean only one thing: Caerthalien meant her to pledge fealty. Word of her ambition would already have reached Bolecthindial. The emissary from Caerthalien must be its attempt to overturn her plans.

They will send Ivrulion, of course. Who else? And Lightborn or no, he will speak among my guests with princely authority. . . .

But when Caerthalien's Lightborn envoy walked into Oronviel's Great Hall at last, it wasn't Ivrulion.

"Thurion!" Vieliessar exclaimed, struggling to keep all the welcome she felt out of her voice.

"War Prince Vieliessar," he answered, his voice steady. "War Prince Bolecthindial sends me to you, for Caerthalien has always stood friend to Oronviel."

"Oronviel thanks Caerthalien for her gentle care of her neighbor. We rejoice in your visit to us and hope you will find all you seek."

"I am certain I shall," Thurion answered, bowing.

"I pray your visit will allow you to partake of our hospitality this Midwinter, as well." She did not ask if he was Caerthalien's envoy to her Midwinter Court, for that would reveal too much. This meeting was a formality, a show enacted for those watching. Later they would have the chance to speak privately.

Caerthalien sends me to discover if you mean to keep to your own borders and honor the treaties Lord Bolecthindial held of War Prince Thoromarth," Thurion said, the words bursting from his lips in a rush almost before the door had closed behind him. "Of course I'll tell him whatever you like, but—that was Lord Gunedwaen of Farcarinon at table tonight, wasn't it?"

The evening meal had been a long and lavish one, but it would be only prudent for any new lord of a small and embattled domain to wish to impress the emissaries of her large and powerful neighbors. Thurion had been seated upon her left hand, in the place of honor.

That he would see what he had seen was inevitable. But only one who still counted himself her friend would have broached the subject so openly.

Vieliessar waved him to a seat as she finished skimming the scroll she held—Gunedwaen's sennightly analysis of the information he'd gleaned from her knights as well as from a number of Oronviel folk who had gone secretly where they would not have been welcomed openly.

Thurion flung himself into a low chair, kicking the hem of his robes out of the way with the negligent ease of long practice. "It was, wasn't it? *The* Gunedwaen?"

"Does it matter?" Vieliessar asked, setting the report aside. There was nothing new there. The War Princes were obviously waiting for Midwinter before declaring for or against Oronviel. At least openly.

Thurion sat upright so abruptly that Striker raised her elegant head. "Of *course* it matters! Vielle! He lost his arm years—decades ago! No Healer has *ever*—" He stopped abruptly, gazing at her with disbelief. "You knew. You knew what you'd done when you Healed him."

She met his gaze squarely. *This,* her instincts said. *This is more important than anything else we will say to one another about my plans and the lies he will tell his Caerthalien masters.* "I knew I could do it before I began," she answered simply. "It was hard, and painful, but it was not impossible."

"It should have been," Thurion answered quietly. His words were not a rebuke. They were uttered in tones of one who looked upon the impossible. "I know of no Healer who could have done it."

"You know what *hradan* Celelioniel laid upon me at my birth," Vieliessar answered.

" 'Death against Darkness, blood expunge blood, burn the stars and save a brand from the burning,' " Thurion quoted. It was the beginning of the passage about the destruction of the Hundred Houses. "Is that what you mean to do?"

"I don't know," she answered. "All I know is that I am the Child of the Prophecy, the Doom of the Hundred Houses. It took me so long to admit it that I do not know if there is enough time left."

Thurion drew a deep, shaking breath, summoning calm, summoning reason. "You think you have deciphered Amrethion's Prophecy," he said, but once again Vieliessar shook her head.

"Celelioniel Astromancer deciphered it. It was why I was allowed to live. 'When stars and clouds together point the way / And of a hundred deer one doe can no longer counted be'—Farcarinon's destruction. Thurion, it does not *matter* whether I am the only one it could be, or simply the one Celelioniel chose. What matters is the *rest* of the Prophecy."

Thurion studied her face. "The Prophecy foretells a time when the Hundred Houses are ended by the prophesied child who becomes High King. It says a Darkness is gathering armies against that day and talks of a false promise coming true and two becoming one. If Celelioniel Astromancer decided *you* were the Child of the Prophecy, she must have believed that the false promise that becomes true means you will become High King, as Serenthon War Prince tried to. But . . . Vielle . . . How *can* you?"

"You are Green Robe and scholar, and once you were friend to me, when I had none. I would tell you a story that is no story. Will you hear?"

"Yes," he answered heavily. "I will hear."

❧

Almost he could imagine himself back at the Sanctuary of the Star on some lazy afternoon when there was nothing better to do than to try to unravel the mysteries of their long and unfathomable history. Vieliessar spoke not of herself, but of Celelioniel's quest to discover the beginnings of the Lightborn, of how they had learned to wield their power.

"In the Sanctuary we are taught that each thing implies its opposite," Vieliessar said. "It is the foundation of our spellcraft. Heal or harm. Make fertile or blight. And not only in our Magery: we see in the world around us that each thing possesses its opposite. Creatures who fly and creatures who burrow, grass eaters and flesh eaters, and for this cause we have always been taught that the Beastlings are the shadow of all we are—but Celelioniel did not believe that could be so. If the Beastlings possessed a Darkness as great as our Light, surely they would have used it to make a desert of all the Fortunate Lands."

"Not if they want to live here," Thurion commented dryly, and Vieliessar made a rude snort of amusement.

"Perhaps. But surely they would make *some* desert. And they would feed their spellcraft upon blood. And we would have learned that those things are wrong from their example. We have learned those things are wrong, but not from the Beastlings. From who, then?"

"Everyone knows the Lightborn—*some* Lightborn—break the Covenant," Thurion said hesitantly.

"And why is there a Covenant?" she asked implacably.

For a moment Thurion was a Postulant still. "Because—it must have been a long time ago—some Lightborn did those things, and . . ." He stopped, because Vieliessar was shaking her head.

"Each thing there is implies—creates—its opposite," she reminded him.

"Theory is no validation of prophecy," Thurion answered, almost sputtering.

"No," Vieliessar agreed. "And Celelioniel did not begin with the Prophecy, but with an attempt to discover how we learned to do as we do. It was Mosirinde Peacemaker who first taught the Covenant—and she also who founded the Sanctuary of the Star."

"But—" Thurion said.

"But no one knows why, or how the Light came to us before the founding of the Sanctuary," Vieliessar agreed. "I will ask you to simply take as true that Celelioniel searched for that answer for years, that *The Song of Amrethion* was the end of her quest and not the beginning, that she discovered that what seems like nonsense to our eyes is instead a simple list of events that will come to pass before . . ." She stopped, and when she went on, her voice held sudden urgency. "Thurion, do you believe that evil can be done in the service of good?"

"Of course not," he answered promptly. "By its very nature, evil destroys and taints all it touches, so anything it touches cannot be good."

Vieliessar bowed her head, and Thurion didn't think he'd given her the answer she hoped to hear. But it was what they had both been taught in the Sanctuary.

"Imagine all the good things in the world. Everything you can. Everything that has given you joy, or a moment's pleasure, or made you happy," she said.

"The Light," Thurion answered softly. The look on Vieliessar's face frightened him, though he could not say why.

"Now imagine that all these good things have an opposite. Not the petty cruelty of the Hundred Houses—for the War Princes may be as kind and generous as they are cruel and petty—but *an* opposite. A being. A race that can only be named *Darkness*."

"You cannot know this!" Thurion exclaimed.

"High King Amrethion warned of them—every Astromancer, every great Seer from Mosirinde Peacemaker to Celchoniel has seen them. Hamphuliadiel has swept all the books of prophecy from Arevethmonion— did you know?—so no other can discover that Celelioniel spoke true."

"It is only a *theory*, Vielle," Thurion said desperately.

"Yes," she answered. "A theory. But suppose it is not. The Prophecy says this Darkness comes, not to conquer us, but to *destroy* us. If I am the Child of the Prophecy, it will come in my lifetime. If the Hundred Houses do not act as one when that day comes, our defeat is certain. So tell me, my oldest friend, what would you have me do?"

There was only one true answer he could give: *If the Prophecy is true, you must do everything you can, no matter what it is, to make the Fortunate Lands ready for the day we must fight as one.*

He could not bear to give her those words.

"All right," he said into the silence. "Let us suppose the Prophecy is as you say."

"You do not believe," she said harshly.

"I want to," he answered helplessly, knowing only as he spoke that the words were true. "But I cannot imagine . . . How can you hope to unite the Hundred and make the War Princes swear fealty to you? Serenthon—"

"Serenthon of Farcarinon intrigued to make himself High King with vows and promises, yet his strongest ally turned against him. Caerthalien was able to turn his allies against him and unify his enemies—because they feared what their lives would hold were he to rule," she answered unyieldingly. "I know his errors. I would not repeat them. But I ask again, Thurion: what must I do?"

His life had trained him to love the Light. His years in the Sanctuary of the Star had trained him to think. "You must fight," he answered, hanging his head. "If we die in battle, the Hunt will claim us for its own, so . . . Vielle, you are the most powerful Mage I have ever seen. Could you—if you were to break the Covenant—"

"—call down lightning from the sky to slay all their armies in an instant?" She gnawed at her lower lip, as if choosing her next words with care. "That thought was in my mind. But I might render the Fortunate Lands a desert without destroying the Darkness. Or the Lightborn might slay me as I fought. Or I might succeed—" She broke off. "One chance in three of victory is not such a match as I would wager upon. If we are to face a great army, we will face it *with* a great army."

"But you have no *proof*!" Thurion cried. "*You cannot make the Hundred bend the knee without giving them proof!*"

"No," Vieliessar agreed. Her voice was hard. "Nor would I offer it if I had—they would only fight among themselves over who was to lead the army, just as they have fought all these centuries over which of them is to be Amrethion's successor. And so I will not ask anyone to believe in anything but me. The War Princes will swear to me, and to each other, and we shall face the Darkness an army of princes. All of us, Thurion. *All*."

"Did you . . . ?" Thurion said. His voice trembled, and he could not finish the sentence. *Did you use Magery to defeat Rithdeliel and gain Oronviel?*

"I will do what I must, Thurion." There was no triumph in her voice.

Tears glittered in Thurion's eyes. He wiped them away before they fell, not caring if she saw. "Vielle ... Is it worth ... *surviving* ... if we cast aside everything that makes us what we are?"

"Once Amrethion and Pelashia reigned over a land without death, without war—without Landbond and craftworker sold as if they were cattle when the luck of battle did not favor their masters. We have already cast aside what we were. I would see us live to regain it," she answered softly.

"I ... I must ... " With great effort, Thurion collected himself. "I suppose I have always known. Who you were. *What* you were. What you would become. I have thought, you know, since the news came to us of Oronviel. About you. The Sanctuary never finds Light in the Lines Direct, you know. I think something must have happened that forced Caerthalien to send Prince Ivrulion to the Sanctuary. Perhaps all of you—"

"I am no different than you, Thurion," she said, but he went on as if she hadn't spoken.

"—perhaps all of you have great power. Perhaps the Sanctuary fears the return of Lightborn like Mosirinde Peacemaker. They should. Have you ever thought about how miraculous Lady Nataranweiya's escape from Farcarinon was? She could have died a thousand times on the journey. She did not. She could have miscarried of you, lost you to cold, a fall from her horse, a dozen things. She did not. She gained the Sanctuary. You were born alive. Celelioniel knew all you say you know, yet she feared your birth as if it were the summoning of the Darkness, not our defense against it. And still she set her Master Spell upon you so you could grow up safely beneath the rooftree of your House's greatest enemy.

"You might have died there. Babies do. Children do. A kick from a horse, a fall from a wall, and all Ladyholder Glorthiachiel would have needed to do was *not* summon a Lightborn to Heal you. But she never got the chance. So you went to the Sanctuary, and there you were no one. Nothing. Powerless. Hamphuliadiel could have slain you and gained favor with any of a dozen Houses. He never did—and then it was too late, for not even the Astromancer may raise his hand against one of the Lightborn without cause. You have walked barefoot among adders every day of your life and never been harmed. Your destiny was always waiting for you. A task set upon your shoulders by Amrethion Aradruiniel himself, ten thousand years ago."

He had not meant to say any of this. It was admission that he believed. But he could not hold back the words.

"I think it has made you . . . more," he said in a whisper. "I do not know why others do not see it. Perhaps you keep them from seeing it, as you kept Hamphuliadiel from seeing you. But they *will* see it. And they will fear you as you fear the Darkness to come.

"I cannot stand against what you have become, Vielle. The time when I might have is long past."

"Do you fear me?" she asked, and in her eyes Thurion saw sorrow, not triumph.

"Yes," he said simply. "And I grieve, for I had a friend whom I loved, and she was but an illusion, a shadow cast by a Great Power."

"I am no Great Power!" Vieliessar protested. "You said yourself—Nataranweiya was my mother—Serenthon was my father—"

"And now you are Child of the Prophecy, not of Farcarinon," Thurion said with gentle finality.

"Will you serve me still?" she asked.

Thurion closed his eyes as if the sound of her voice hurt. "Yes," he answered, opening them again.

She smiled painfully, and in that moment she was so beautiful his heart broke for her. "You will curse my name before we are done," she told him.

"I don't care," he answered steadily. "I will do all that you ask of me." He took another deep breath. "So let us now consider what I am to tell Bolecthindial, and how I am to keep Ivrulion from discovering the truth."

Vieliessar's Midwinter Court was a dazzling affair. Through her Lightborn, by spellbird, she had extended invitations to the princes of all
the Hundred Houses. Only those of the forty Houses of the West could
possibly attend, for the eastward passes were closed by winter, and the
journey from the Western Shore was long and arduous. It did not matter.
Every word spoken within Oronviel's walls on the first night of the Festival would reach the farthest castels of the Grand Windsward before the
seventh.

"I still say you're mad."

"Say I am imaginative, Prince Thoromarth, it sounds better," Vieliessar answered.

"I'll say you're the Mother of Dragons if that's what you want," Thoromarth growled in reply.

First Night. The feast had gone on from sunset to midnight. Two dozen
Lightborn envoys were guests of Oronviel, and if they weren't spies in
truth, their so-called servants certainly were. No one from the High
Houses had attended, but what Ulillion knew, Cirandeiron knew in the
same breath. The Twelve were present, even if they were not here.

"Say I shall be High King, for I mean to be," she said. She walked
through the outer room to the inner as Thoromarth followed. "Wine?"
she asked, gesturing to the sideboard as she seated herself in a chair beneath the window. A spellshield cast a faint shimmer over the opening.

He raised a cup toward her in silent question, nodding at her demur
before filling it for himself. "Giving amnesty to losels and wolfsheads is
one thing—a prince may do as she pleases with her people and I won't
gainsay you. But . . . not sending Candidates to the Shrine? What will
the Astromancer think?" Thoromarth asked.

"I have not made up my mind to it." But soon Oronviel would be set
against the rest of the Hundred Houses, and she had promised her people
she would not take their children from them to be held as hostages. "Forester Lonthorn has been to the Flower Forest. She says the Vilya looks
likely to fruit this spring, so we shall have a new Astromancer." She
gazed down at the surface of the inlaid table beside her. The silver wires

crossing the wood gleamed faintly violet in the spellshield's light. "Thoromarth, why doesn't the Light ever appear in the Lines Direct?"

Thoromarth frowned and glanced back toward the outer room. He was obviously displeased by this change of topic—he had little patience for discussions which seemed to him to be idle speculation—but knew he had no choice but to follow Vieliessar's whims. "It does," he protested. There's you, and . . . Ivrulion Light-Prince of Caerthalien, and . . ." He stopped.

"Let us not forget Ternas of Celebros," Vieliessar said dryly. "But . . . two, from all the Hundred Houses in all the years of the reigns of the last three Astromancers? And I was not expected to have the Light, and Ivrulion's Light was not supposed to be discovered. What we do at the Sanctuary is flawed, Thoromarth."

Thoromarth reached to touch the silver shoeing-nail he wore about his neck. "Hunt defend us, is there *nothing* you do not mean to overturn?" he asked.

"Perhaps I shall like the new Astromancer better than I like Hamphuliadiel," Vieliessar answered obliquely. "We shall see."

"Perhaps you will not live to see him—or her—chosen," Thoromarth grumbled. "Ah well. It is time I sought my bed, to receive the overtures of all those who wish to cast you down and set me once more in your place."

"And I to give these same answers to Gunedwaen and Rithdeliel," Vieliessar answered lightly. "I wish you good rest, such as it will be."

⚉

On the Fourth Night of Midwinter, Lightbrother Thurion of Caerthalien Called the Light in the children of Oronviel Great Keep. It was a graceful nod to Oronviel's clientage to Caerthalien, and if everyone at the Festival already knew that Vieliessar meant to break those ties, the fact that she still played a double game was obscurely reassuring.

It brought back odd memories of her childhood, when she was Varuthir, not Vieliessar. Of watching the castel children walk up to the High

Table in Caerthalien's Great Hall where Ivrulion and other senior Light-born waited to Call the Light. The storysinger sang *The Song of Pelashia's Gift* and each child received a honeycake and a ribbon when the Light-brother was done. Silver for those who would make the journey to the Sanctuary of the Star, gold for those who would not.

Now it was a lifetime later, and she sat in the War Prince's great chair in another Great Hall, and presided over the selection of Candidates who might never see the Sanctuary.

Oddly, with all she said, privately and publicly, and despite the very fact of her existence, the thing that caused the most talk that Midwinter was Vieliessar's treatment of the commons. Night after night, her vassal lords and the Lightborn envoys stood upon the battlements of the keep and looked out over the tables she had erected for the commons' feast.

A waste of good food, they said.

They'll come to expect such tender treatment, and grow lazy.

She cossets them out of weakness.

Sanctuary softness has no place in a War Prince.

But beneath the mockery and disbelief, she sensed . . . fear.

Fear of change.

Fear of ways they did not understand.

Fear of *her*.

And on the morning of the eighth day, those who had kept Festival within Oronviel's walls rode forth, while Vieliessar stood upon the bat-tlements and watched them go. It was hard to watch Thurion ride away, knowing that his pledge to her made all of Caerthalien a danger to him.

But spring was coming.

And War Season.

CHAPTER EIGHT

BATTLE CITY

For twice upon five hundred lives, the Throne of Shame shall sleep
And Celephriandullias-Tildorangelor a haunt of shadows lie
The Happy Lands shall ring to blood and battle through the years
While all who husband hidden secrets die.

Though many seek to gain the crown, no hand shall gain its light
And brother vie with brother for a prize no House can claim
While Darkness breeds in lands unknown, its armies bought with blood
Against the day false promise is made true.

— *The Song of Amrethion Aradruiniel*

The remains of the Free Companies ravaged the countryside as bandits. As she had vowed, Vieliessar hunted them relentlessly. As she had also vowed, she gave each of her prisoners a choice: pledge fealty to her or die in battle.

"I wish to offer you and your people a full pardon."

There was a long moment of disbelieving silence.

"Why?" Nadalforo asked suspiciously.

"So you will swear fealty to me and fight for me," Vieliessar said patiently. "It is better to be my vassal than my enemy. If you or any of your followers have committed offenses in another domain, I do not care. If any offense was committed in mine, I will pardon it. But you must swear to me." She meant to become High King over a realm that held neither High House nor Low, and that was not a thing she could plan to do later, for she did not know how much of "later" there might be. It was a harder path, but she would begin her destruction of the

Hundred Houses with the army that would fight to make her High King.

"But I—I ran off a steading. And Belgund—he broke parole when his lord wouldn't ransom him. And Findron—"

"I don't care," Vieliessar said. "Keep my law. Keep my peace. Fight for me. You'll be fed, clothed, and housed as well as any in my army and treated no differently than any other of my people."

Nadalforo blinked several times, trying to make sense of what obviously sounded to her like madness. "We're mercenaries—or we were. You could—"

"No," Vieliessar said quickly. "I hire no mercenaries. Swear to me. Or leave my lands—and know that the next time we meet I will kill you all."

"But . . . how do you know you can trust me—or any of us?" Nadalforo asked desperately.

"Break your oath to me and see," Vieliessar said. "I do not think you will. Shall we see?"

"I—I—I guess we will," Nadalforo answered.

⬦

Nadalforo—once First Sword of Stonehorse Free Company—was neither the first nor the last to pledge to Vieliessar. Taille by taille, Vieliessar built her army through the sennights of winter. Snow Moon became Cold Moon, Ice Moon, Storm Moon. By Storm, nine moonturns had passed since she had claimed Oronviel and the other War Princes had done little to indicate they feared her. Now the Ninety-and-Nine were preparing for War Season once more—and not with Oronviel. They would discuss her plans with one another beneath truce-flags all summer, and then plot at Midwinter Court to *perhaps* attack her the following year.

"You've told every prince in the land you mean to take the Unicorn Throne. Do you think Caerthalien will hear and do nothing?" Rithdeliel's voice in her memory, crackling with frustration.

Yes, she answered mentally. *I think they will delay and delay until it is too late.*

In another wheel of the seasons, she would be High King, or she would be dead.

⊰⊱

The scent of fresh-cut timber filled her nostrils as Vieliessar rode along the road which led to the keep. The village she had designed to hold—and train—her patchwork army was rising as quickly as grain stalks in summer. The village now occupied both sides of the road—vulnerable and indefensible if an enemy army or even raiders came; a liability in the defense of the keep itself, for it sprawled across the open land that had once surrounded Oronviel Keep, providing concealment for enemies and a hazard to defenders. But if the winter moonturns had brought a trickle of exiles flocking to Oronviel's standard, then Storm brought a flood. Not merely outlaws and Landbonds, now, but craft-workers and Farmholders and Lightborn. Even lesser knights, coming with wives, husbands, children, and all they could bring away from their own domains. They came—every one of them—to fight not for Oronviel, but for Vieliessar.

Vieliessar High King, who promised them justice and an end to war.

She had spent the morning riding the bounds of the Battle City. The whole of it extended through the manor houses and farmsteads nearest the keep; a large area, and one where it was important that she show herself frequently. Those who occupied the city—former mercenaries, former outlaws, the children of Farmholders—would not approach her stewards or *komen* with their grievances, but would bring them straight to her.

The weight of their trust was sometimes the most oppressive thing of all. She longed for a day or two of quiet that she knew she would not get. Her court understood the business of treaties and alliances and pacts, but Serenthon had never asked Farcarinon to host the armies of his allies as if they were his own, nor sent his own knights to serve at the courts of his sometime-enemies. If that had been all she asked of them, it would have been difficult enough—but she also wished them to welcome, and even fight beside, those whom they would have gladly whipped from their halls for the presumption of speaking. As a child and even as a Green Robe, she had thought the War Princes lived lives of leisure and freedom. Now she knew that was only an illusion, a shadow cast by the power each domain lord held in his or her hands. Power could gain one a great many things, but it must be carefully and consciously nurtured.

It is a sharp sword and a heavy fetter, and I have taken up the blade and set the shackles on my own wrists.

She swung down from Sorodiarn's back in the castel stables, fleetingly grateful for the privilege of rank that permitted her to keep her horses close to hand. There was little room within a Great Keep's walls for beasts. Leaving the destrier in the hands of Fierdind Horsemaster, she proceeded to her rooms, cloaking herself in Shadow as she strode from the stable. It was a dangerous indulgence, but she had no desire to be stopped to answer a hundred questions today. She reached her rooms—there were no Guardsmen at her door when she was believed to be elsewhere—and stepped inside.

As the door closed behind her, she felt a sudden surge of the Light. She dropped her hand to her swordhilt, preparing every defense she could. She still dared do nothing that would mark her as Lightborn, even if it meant injury or worse. But the figure who appeared as the Cloakspell vanished was . . .

"Thurion!" she exclaimed.

He was muddy and bedraggled, and—more alarming than that—dressed not in the Green Robes of Magery, but clothes such as any upper servant might wear.

"I cry Sanctuary of Oronviel," he said, in a voice that shook with exhaustion. "Will Prince Vieliessar grant this boon?"

"Of course," she said instantly. "But— What is it? What has happened?"

"Hamphuliadiel . . ." Thurion said. He fell gracelessly into the nearest chair.

"What has Hamphuliadiel done?" she demanded.

"He has said he will not step aside as Astromancer," Thurion said numbly. "He says he will surrender his place only when the Vilya in the Sanctuary's own garden bears fruit—and he would not even have said so much so soon if Ivrulion Light-Prince had not been there to compel him! He swears this is no new ruling, but a return to the earliest practice by which the reigns of the Astromancers were calculated."

"Mosirinde Peacemaker would be surprised to hear it," Vieliessar answered dryly.

She sent for food, made tea, and learned the whole of what Thurion had to tell. Forester Lonthorn was not the only one in the Fortunate Lands who could predict the fruiting of the Vilya. Caerthalien, seeing a new Astromancer was imminent, had sent Ivrulion Light-Prince to the Sanctuary as soon as the roads could be traveled. He had obtained Hamphuliadiel's answer in secret, but he'd Farspoken it to Carangil Lightbrother, and the news had spread from there to most of the castel Lightborn.

And Thurion had risked everything to bring it to her.

"He's lying! There was never such a practice! And I don't think the Vilya in the Sanctuary garden will ever fruit!" Thurion announced, pacing in agitation.

"I'd be very surprised if it did," Vieliessar replied, raising her eyebrows. "What I wonder is why he wants to remain Astromancer. It isn't a position that holds a great deal of power, and if he wants riches and luxury, he can get that at any court."

"No," Thurion said, his voice troubled. "You're wrong, Vielle. There *is* power in the office of Astromancer—if the one who holds it is dishonorable enough to grasp it. You have seen it yourself." He paused expectantly.

"When he charged the Lightborn of all the land to deliver me to his hand?" she asked, for that was what was foremost in Thurion's thoughts. "What I have seen is Hamphuliadiel showing himself a fool."

"No," Thurion said patiently. "It did not work, that is true, for we swear fealty to our lords, not to the Astromancer. But if Hamphuliadiel has century after century to convince all who are trained at the Sanctuary that their first loyalty must be to the Light Itself, and that he knows better than they how they may best serve it—"

Then the Sanctuary of the Star will become the new Hundredth House. . . .

"I would be more troubled by Hamphuliadiel of Haldil's ambitions if I thought he had a chance of achieving them," Vieliessar answered bluntly. "Thurion," she said gently, "if I am High King, I will deal with Hamphuliadiel. If I am not, the Darkness surely will. His ambitions do not matter, save in how we can make use of them."

"And if he moves more quickly than you think?" Thurion demanded. "It is true that those who are sent to the Sanctuary each spring are unimportant in the eyes of the War Princes—save for whom we might become if the Light favors us—but if Hamphuliadiel holds the Candidates hostage, the War Princes must attack or they will seem timid and weak. They cannot attack the Sanctuary, so they will seek another target against which to display their power. And if refusing to give up the Candidates is not enough, Hamphuliadiel can deny access to the Shrine of the Star."

"Arevethmonion is not the only Shrine," Vieliessar said.

"I suppose you think the Hundred Houses will go to Tilinaparanwira the Lost to make their offerings?" Thurion said in exasperation. "Most of them don't even know there *are* Nine Shrines—and don't imagine their Lightborn know any more! Delfierarathadan is too dangerous to seek; Tilinaparanwira is lost; Oiolairwe, Teriqualanweore, and Mirinandwe are beyond the Feinolons—"

"Nomiatemil is in the Mystrals, and I suppose you will go on to say that because there is no guesthouse at Manostar nor pleasant gardens at Earime'kalareinya they will not do either?"

Thurion flung himself into a chair and regarded her with irritation. "I say that since the time of Mosirinde Peacemaker, the sacrifices have been offered at Arevethmonion and the Lightborn have gone there to be trained. If Hamphuliadiel denies access to the Shrine of the Star, the princes will not think that there are seven other places they can go. They will think Hamphuliadiel plots to punish them for not delivering you back into his hands."

"Doesn't he?" Vieliessar said. She pressed the heels of her hands against her eyes, trying to think. In the Sanctuary's library she'd studied war, and in all the centuries the Hundred Houses had fought, Magery had never been a consideration in their plotting. But Thurion was right. Hamphuliadiel had taken the first step toward becoming a prince of the land in his own right. She must assume he would take the next, and the next. And the moment he did, the War Princes would panic.

And *she* would be their target.

"If I can make it seem that Hamphuliadiel's actions—whatever they are—are taken in secret alliance with Oronviel, the War Princes should delay any attack they contemplate," she said slowly. "I know Hamphuliadiel. Even if he means to hold hostages, he cannot let that be known until the last caravan has brought its Candidates and departed. By then, this season's new Lightborn will have left as well. Then he may do as he wishes, and it will be a moonturn or two before anyone notices."

"Yes," Thurion said, nodding. "The War Princes send to make the victory sacrifices when they send the Candidates, and then they go to war. It will not be until Fire or Harvest that they will wish access to the Shrine of the Star again. Now: how will you convince the other Houses that Hamphuliadiel plots with Oronviel?"

"Simple enough," Vieliessar answered. "I shall send Thoromarth immediately to bring away everyone from Oronviel—it will not seem impossible to Hamphuliadiel that I am so unused to ruling that I cannot gather Oronviel's Candidates in a timely fashion. I shall send Ambrant Lightbrother with him to take my word to those of Oronviel who are already in training. The Postulants know a thousand ways to sneak out of the Sanctuary when they are supposed to be in their beds—as you well know—and Hamphuliadiel has no precedent for holding them against their will. Ambrant's Keystone Gift is True Speech; his shields will defeat Hamphuliadiel's attempts to hear his mind, and Thoromarth will swear to any who ask that the Oronviel Candidates come soon, for that is what I will tell him, and beg his pardon for the lie when he returns. And so it will be seen that this year, two Houses of all the Ninety-and-Nine have not sent their Candidates to the Sanctuary: Oronviel and Ivrithir."

"But how will you— *Ivrithir?*" Thurion said, startled.

"War Prince Atholfol has pledged himself to support Farcarinon's claim to the High Kingship," Vieliessar answered. "On my word, he will withhold this year's Candidates. I must see which of his Lightborn I may send to the Sanctuary with Ambrant, for the Ivrithir Candidates will not come away at Oronviel's word."

Thurion sat brooding over her words for a long stretch of silence. "If you do this, it will seem that—whatever Hamphuliadiel does—you knew of it beforehand," he said at last. "But you will lose what new Lightborn you might have gained—" He gestured helplessly. "If the Postulants must come away without daring the Shrine—"

"There are other Shrines," Vieliessar said once again. "For the rest, we shall simply return to the *actual* earliest practices of the Lightborn, when there was no Sanctuary and no single place of learning. Until there is a new Astromancer, Oronviel's Lightborn will train her Lightborn-to-be."

The High King's Lightborn will train her Lightborn-to-be.

⊰⊱

It took her most of a day to persuade Ambrant Lightbrother not merely to do what she wished him to, but to do it with utmost guile. If Thurion had not been there to swear that Hamphuliadiel would refuse to step down as Astromancer, she would undoubtedly still be arguing with him. She wished she could send Aradreleg Lightsister or Peryn Lightsister, or most of all, Harwing Lightbrother, who had found a joyous heart-twin in Gunedwaen, and now served as one of the Swordmaster's most effective spies. But none of them had True Speech as their Keystone Gift: any shields they set about their minds and thoughts, Hamphuliadiel would be able to force.

She spoke with Atholfol in cautious elliptical messages sent by spell-bird. Both Rithdeliel and Gunedwaen believed Farcarinon's old war codes unbroken, and Serenthon had used a different cipher for each of his allies. Atholfol had agreed to withhold this year's Candidates if Oronviel would swear to undertake their training—and to send his sealed writ by messenger to Thoromarth so those of Ivrithir who were to leave the Sanctuary this season would know it was safe to journey with Oronviel's party.

But he would not give her an Ivrithir Lightborn to call his Postulants away.

And perhaps I, too, would be skeptical, had I not such long and intimate knowledge of Hamphuliadiel's mind. Very well. I have warned him, at least.

⧫

She had known since before she left the Sanctuary of the Star that the time she would have to work in would be short, for she had squandered too many precious years seeking to avoid her destiny. Once Thurion fled Caerthalien, she knew she would have to work more quickly still, for the moment his presence in Oronviel was known, Caerthalien had the pretext it needed to attack her out of season. Very soon—in a moonturn, perhaps two—her war would begin, and she would not ride into such a desperately important battle without making a sacrifice to the Starry Hunt and petitioning Them for victory.

She could not go to the Sanctuary of the Star.

But as she had told Thurion, the Sanctuary did not hold the only Shrine.

In the candlemark before dawn, Vieliessar walked from the keep and down the path which led to the oldest part of the craftworkers' village. No dog barked to warn of her passage, no goose bugled a warning. She had a long way to go before the sun rose and she would not take Sorodiarn to this appointment. Her destination was the paddocks beyond the stables. Spring was the season to begin a young horse's training, so it could be exposed to the sounds and smells of battle long before it must stand steady before them. From among the drowsing animals she selected two: a young bay mare, already under saddle, and a pure white colt. She knew Fierdind Horsemaster meant to train Phadullu for her use in case

Sorodiarn was killed, but she needed him now. She mounted the mare bareback and rode away in the darkness; the colt followed tamely.

Mornenamei was the nearest Flower Forest to the castel, and she would need Lord Mornenamei's aid for the morning's work. She reached Mornenamei and vaulted down from the mare's back. The mare could be left here to graze: she would not go far, and if anyone happened upon her, the silver token braided into her mane would mark her as belonging to the castel stables. Vieliessar patted Phadullu on the shoulder and he followed her docilely as she walked into Mornenamei.

A combination of homesickness and longing assaulted her as she felt the Flower Forest's magic enfold her. Her happiness at the Sanctuary of the Star had been dearly bought, but it had been real. She could not imagine there would ever be such happiness for her again.

Ruthlessly she banished those thoughts from her mind. Time enough to mourn her life when she had fulfilled the role Amrethion High King had set forth for her to play. Ten steps, then twenty, then twenty more, then she swung herself up onto Phadullu's back. She nudged him forward at a gentle walk, and before he had gone a dozen paces, the Flower Forest through which he walked was far away from Oronviel.

She could Sense the Shrine the moment she filled her lungs with the air of Earime'kalareinya. She'd chosen it because Manostar was merely a notation in the histories, its location given as "somewhere in Tunimbronor." There were accounts of visits to Earime'kalareinya, for many of the Land-Shrines had continued to receive visitors for some centuries after Mosirinde Peacemaker established the Sanctuary of the Star.

She dismounted again and walked onward. The day was brighter here than in Mornenamei, for she had gone toward the sun. She followed the currents of power until she reached the heart of Earime'kalareinya.

The three stones that marked the Place of Power looked somehow more stark and wild surrounded by the lushness of the Flower Forest than they did in the careful concealment of the Shrine of the Star. *The stones are as weathered as if they stand upon a desolate plain,* she realized a moment later, though this deep within Earime'kalareinya, wind and rain could barely reach them. A flat stone lay on the ground between them, and *someone* was still making offerings here, for the stone was smeared with blood that rain and time had not yet erased.

She stroked Phadullu's silken neck, willing herself to feel the calm and serenity she had learned to summon before setting a great work of Magery, but could not manage it. Her fingers touched the knife on her belt and she hesitated. This was not the simple vigil with which every Lightborn ended training. To call upon Them was to Summon Them— and they might take the summoner as the victory-sacrifice. It was a fearful thing to make petition for victory and risk being taken to ride the star-roads forever.

You made up your mind to do this before you came! she told herself fiercely. She patted Phadullu on the shoulder once more. Obedient to her Magery, the young stallion knelt and she drew her knife.

"Heed me, You Who ride the night winds, who grant triumph in battle and victory in war. I, Vieliessar Farcarinon, Knight and Mage, daughter of Serenthon War Prince and Nataranweiya Ladyholder, come before You here, where the breath of first creation still warms my skin, where You must hear and heed when I call. Take my gift, and give me victory!"

She drew her blade across Phadullu's throat. Hot blood spattered the standing stones, pooled on the rock between them, and soaked into the earth beyond, but the bespelled animal did not move until his body went lax with death. All around her, Vieliessar could Sense the roar of power roused, assaulting her senses as savagely as an autumn storm might batter her body. It seemed to her she must slit her eyes tightly against a raging wind, but she forced them to open and focus. She felt someone watching her. For one terrible moment she thought the Hunt Lord had come after all, and all her sacrifices had been for nothing.

But it was not He.

At the far edge of the clearing, a little way inside the trees, stood a pale shape that seemed to glow with its own inward radiance. *Sending,* she thought first, then, *deer,* since the shape was too small to be a horse and it was undeniably alive.

Then it took a slow step forward and a ray of morning light fell directly on its horn.

A single, sword-straight spike jutting from the center of its forehead, it shone as brightly as if some Lightborn had cast Silverlight upon it—if Silverlight could be whitely radiant and iridescent as a dove's throat at the same time. It was neither horse nor deer. It had a long, slender neck like a deer's, but also a mane—not long and flowing like a destrier's, but roached and bristling like a plowhorse's. Its white coat did not gleam with the glossy slickness of horse or hound, but seemed as if it must be as thick and soft as a cat's.

Komen blazoned their shields with them, noble ladies wove tapestries depicting them, craftworkers adorned a thousand different objects with them, from infants' cradles to shin'zuruf cups to the luck-charms braided into the manes of destriers. The luck-token baked into Midwinter cakes held their image—she had won five of them at the Sanctuary before she had realized it would always come to her and refused to participate any longer. She had sworn to reclaim the throne Amrethion had named for them.

But they are only a legend . . . Vieliessar thought, stunned.

The Unicorn was the most beautiful thing she had ever seen.

She did not know how long she stood motionless, held in place by no spell other than the creature's beauty, but suddenly the Unicorn turned its head, wheeled, and sprang back into the forest.

"No!" Vieliessar shouted. "*Wait!*"

She did not know why she called out as if it would come to her summons. She only knew she could not bear to lose sight of it. And so she ran. As she entered the trees, she saw it vanish in the distance. She ran faster, dodging recklessly between tree trunks, no thought in her mind but to draw near to that shining shape, to reach it, to *touch* it . . .

Even when she could no longer see it among the trees, she ran on in the direction it had fled. When she knew it had gone beyond her reach, she sent out a spell of Summoning—to no avail. It was nearly a candle-mark before she could bear to give up the hunt. The thought she had seen it and would never see it again made her want to weep.

It was real, she insisted to herself. *I saw the sunlight on its horn, its coat—I heard it crash through the brush as it fled. It was a thing alive, and no Seeming sent by the powers nor an evil illusion of Beastling shamans.*

But no matter how hard she tried, she could not fit the sight of it into the world she lived in, the world whose rules she thought she knew.

"The Unicorn is the symbol of the High Kingship."

This was no lesson from her days at the Sanctuary. Scrolls that spoke of the High Kingship had probably been destroyed, since none of the contenders for the throne would wish to provide arguments their ene-mies could use to disparage a rival claim and elevate their own.

No, this was a memory of a time so ancient Vieliessar did not know how to number the years.

Lady Indinathiel gazed out the window at the forests of Tildorangelor, beyond the walls of the city that bore both its own name and that of the for-est: Celephriandullias-Tildorangelor. "We take the Unicorn as the symbol of the High Kingship," she said idly, "for the single horn upon its brow sym-bolizes the High King. There are hundreds of great lords and thousands of knights, but only one to rule over them all. As the horn of the Unicorn is its greatest ornament, so the High King is the greatest jewel of the land. . . ."

The memory-of-a-dream faded. Lady Indinathiel had spoken of the Unicorn as if she were familiar with it as more than a symbol. . . .

I don't understand. Surely the storysingers would have handed down the truth, just as they teach us about all the kinds of Beastling there are in the world, even though—if we are lucky—we will not see most of them.

It was the sort of puzzle she would once have delighted in, following its twists and turns through half-sentences scattered across a thousand different scrolls, questioning other scholars, other students, other lovers of history and truth and knowledge. Now—heartsore at the loss of the beauty she had glimpsed so briefly—Vieliessar told herself it did not matter. The creature was not a danger, nor could a beast of the forest be either enemy or ally. She would take its appearance as an omen from the Silver Hooves that her petition had been heard.

Victory for her cause. Survival for her people.

⬥⬥⬥

L ord Thoromarth's anger was great," Ambrant murmured, his gaze fixed upon the carpet. "He swore you were a most treacherous prince, and that he would cause you to feel the shame you ought to feel for using him in such a deceitful way."

It was Rain Moon before the party Vieliessar had sent to the Sanctuary returned, and within the candlemark of its arrival, Ambrant Lightbrother had come to give her his report. They'd returned six days earlier than expected—unencumbered by Candidates on the outward journey, Thoromarth had simply pushed his company of knights as hard as if they were riding to war. Since the baggage carts that accompanied them were drawn by sturdy draft horses, not the slower and more massive oxen, the entire group had moved at a breakneck speed.

"Indeed?" Vieliessar answered meaninglessly. While she was certain Thoromarth had been furious, he was . . . considerably more direct in his speech than this.

"But Thoromarth of Oronviel is your loyal servant, Lord Vieliessar," Ambrant said grudgingly. "Even before his temper had run its course, he made provision for those whom I placed in his care, and we hastened to return here."

Thoromarth had left the Sanctuary with eighteen from Ivrithir and Oronviel who had finished their Service Year without being Called to the Light, and twelve more who had just taken the Green Robe. When Ambrant rejoined him, he brought forty-three who belonged to Oronviel, from children who had just completed their first year as Postulants to those who were nearly ready to dare the Shrine.

If the company had not been almost entirely Lightborn, the journey would have been far harsher than it was, for Thoromarth had brought provisions for the thirty returning Candidates and new Lightborn he had expected. Instead, he found he must make provision for seventy-three, many of them children. But even the newest Green Robe could Call game to the slaughter, and most had some facility with spells of misdirection and concealment.

"I thank you for your care of your brethren and the care you have taken to discharge my commands," Vieliessar said, indicating the interview was at an end.

But: "My lord?" Ambrant said, and now he seemed—for the first time—troubled and uncertain. She waited politely.

"The Astromancer swears that since the days of Mosirinde Peace-maker it has only been the Vilya in the Sanctuary gardens whose fruit-ing must be taken into account to calculate a reign. And it may be that the Vilya there is of such great age that it fruited in those ancient days, for we speak of them as "ever-living" for good reason. But as I waited to discharge my duty to you, I chanced to walk in the gardens, for I was curious to understand why this tree, of all the Vilya in the Fortunate Lands, should be barren of fruit." Ambrant looked away, gazing out the window of Vieliessar's chamber, looking as though he wished he'd never said anything. "It was bespelled," he blurted out at last, turning back to gaze at her. "I think. I don't— A subtle spell, my lord—had it been a spell of preservation it would have been easily noted. I did not mean to speak of it, for I know that you and the Astromancer are enemies. But I am troubled."

"Ambrant," Vieliessar said, oddly moved by his stammering confession, "I believe you have sensed what is indeed there. I shall tell you why I believe it to be so, and it is a thing I have told few of my people. Yet you have earned my trust."

"I hope I shall always deserve it, Lord Vieliessar," Ambrant said, and what might have been pomposity on any other day came out raw and honest.

"You were at the Sanctuary under Celelioniel Astromancer, were you not?" she asked, and when he nodded, she continued. "Celelioniel left her great work unfinished when the Vilya called her home. She entrusted its completion to Hamphuliadiel, who had been her student for many years. But Hamphuliadiel told Celelioniel what she wished to hear, not what he meant to do. He broke every vow he made to her once he had what he desired."

What she had said was truth, but she would not tell Ambrant the whole. Not yet. It was a heavy weight, and she would place it upon as few as she could. *Hamphuliadiel believes in the Prophecy and for that reason he acts out of fear and arrogance.*

"That— It is an ill thing to hear of the Guardian of the Shrine, but it comforts me," Ambrant answered. "Only let his madness be overthrown."

"It will be," Vieliessar said with grim honesty.

The road to peace would be long and edged with swords, and led as readily to death and failure as it did to the glorious end Oronviel's new War Prince dreamed of. Half her plans were utter madness; the other half, so cunning they chilled the marrow. Thoromarth had known since the day she spared his life that the game she played was deep and secret. He had not known how deep until he rode to the Sanctuary of the Star.

But once he was alone in his own rooms in Oronviel Keep, fed and bathed and wrapped in a chamber robe, his armor taken away to be cleaned, Thoromarth was too restless to sleep. He summoned a servant to bear away the debris of the meal and bring wine, and sat, cup in hand, gazing into the flames dancing upon the coals of the stove.

What did he want? Not now, nor even a moonturn from now, but before he went to ride the night winds? He did not want power—at least, not in the way Bolecthindial or Manderechiel did. His new rooms were spacious enough, he could throw his boots at his servants and be certain his wishes would be followed, and he could go from his morning meal to the stables unhindered to spend a day with his beloved horses. What more could a lord of the Fortunate Lands desire? It had been his duty to rule Oronviel, and so he had, just as it had been his duty to marry Daus-tifalal.

Thoromarth set down his cup, got to his feet, and began to pace. *You've taken an illness from all that time wallowing in the mud. Send for a Lightborn to clear your head. You are going to war, and you will die in battle, and you will ride with the Hunt until the stars grow cold.*

When he turned about at the end of the room, Vieliessar was stand-ing in the doorway.

The overtunic and undertunic and underskirts she wore—each layer slashed and parted to show the contrasting fabric beneath—were as dec-orous and correct as anything his wife or mother might have worn. She was decked with the jewels of her rank and those of a War Prince, heavy rings, bracelets, and linked collar. The veil upon her hair, held in place by a thin band of gold, hung to her waist; the heavy silk swaying with her movements. But somehow no amount of finery could erase his clearest image of her: muddy and bruised and dangerous as a drawn sword, standing before him and demanding he yield everything he was to her.

"My lord," he said, "your message must have gone astray—" He could only imagine he'd been bidden to attend her, and when he had not ap-peared, she'd come looking for him.

"I sent no message," she answered. "May I enter? I wished to see you before you slept. You must be weary. Ambrant looked as if he might col-lapse at any moment."

"It was a hard journey," Thoromarth said curtly, gesturing for her to enter.

"And you do not know—still—what prompted me to such foolish-ness. Did Ambrant tell you of the Astromancer's decision?"

"That he will not step down and that I must ask you for the rest. My lord, the plots of the Hundred Houses are enough—I do not wish to know the intrigues the Green Robes may have."

"And yet you must," Lord Vieliessar answered, seating herself, "for it concerns Oronviel most of all. Sit."

He would have been happier, Thoromarth decided when she had finished the tale, never to know these things at all, though in the end it was as simple a matter as a border war between Ullilion and Caerthalien. The Chief Astromancer intrigued to make himself a power in the land. Lord Vieliessar feared Oronviel would become culpable for his deeds in the eyes of the Hundred Houses. She had taken steps to make it seem she and the Astromancer plotted together, and so avert attack upon Oronviel before she was ready to move.

"I thank you for this word to me," Thoromarth said.

Unexpectedly, she laughed. It was neither bitter nor mocking, but full, and bright, and joyous.

"No you do not, Lord Thoromarth! You wish I had never come to trouble you and fill your head with a thousand unthinkable things you must think about! Now you wonder what I will do next, and hope you do not know. But I have troubled your rest enough. And so I leave you in peace."

She got to her feet in a swish of silk, and before he could rise in deference, was out the door and gone. And suddenly Thoromarth hoped the Silver Hooves would grant him years enough to see Lord Vieliessar upon the Unicorn Throne, for he yearned to hear the squalls and protests of his fellow princes as she made a Code of Peace like the Code of Battle and held every soul in the land to its observance, whether they were of high birth or low

Peace! Your reign brings a thousand gifts, Lord Vieliessar, but peace is not among them.

<hr/>

Lord Bolecthindial unrolled the map Lengiathion Warlord had prepared and spread it flat against the surface of his table. The drawing was so careful and detailed it might almost have been the thing itself, seen as a hawk upon the wing would see it. The map showed Caerthalien and the western lands as far as the Sanctuary. Ullilion's defenses were painted in purple and saffron, Caerthalien's in gold and green, Cirandeiron's in

blue and silver. The ruins of Farcarinon's border keeps were sketched
in a dull grey.

In War Season, Caerthalien rode to war. Other Houses might refrain
from sending challenges with their Midwinter envoys, might spend the
summer moonturns battling the Beastlings—as did Daroldan or the domains of the East—or in hunting outlaws or putting down rebellion among
their own lords, seeking to grow wealthy and strong by avoiding battle.

Not Caerthalien. Caerthalien rode to war. Even last year, when Runacarendalur had led Caerthalien's meisne against the Free Companies,
Bolecthindial and his other sons had taken the field against their enemies. Each successful campaign brought wealth, and sometimes land,
and often surrender-pledges from its defeated enemies. Among the
twelve High Houses, only three had ever rivaled Caerthalien in wealth
and power: Aramenthiali, Cirandeiron, and Farcarinon.

Farcarinon was gone, and this season Lord Bolecthindial meant to
take Ullilion from Cirandeiron. War Prince Dendinirchiel Ullilion held
the southern border of Farcarinon, and Dendinirchiel looked to Cirandeiron. But between Ullilion and Cirandeiron lay the vast wilderness of
Farcarinon. To come to Ullilion's aid, Lord Girelrian would have to cross
the whole of Farcarinon. It would give Caerthalien the advantage.

*And why should it not give us more than that? Farcarinon has lain fal-
low for a century. It is time for the true spoils of victory to be apportioned.*

If Caerthalien could force Ullilion to cede enough territory, Ullilion's
only recourse would be to expand her borders west and claim Farcarinon
land. Censure for the act of claiming a part of Lost Farcarinon would fall
on Dendinirchiel's head, not Bolecthindial's—and each season he could
force Ullilion farther west, claiming always that he seized Ullilion lands,
and not Farcarinon's.

And if the sight of Ullilion's example made High Houses agree it was
a ruinous danger to leave so great an area of land unclaimed, Caerthalien would benefit twice over, for by the agreement the Grand Alliance
had made in Serenthon's time, Caerthalien could claim the third part of
Farcarinon if it were claimed at all.

He turned to the report Elrinonion Swordmaster had prepared for him. Bolecthindial had little patience with sneaking about in the kitchens of his enemies, hoping someone would drop a word of their plans, but as Glorthiachiel was overfond of reminding him, if the enemy came to the field armored and weaponed, one did not bear away the victory by meeting them unarmed.

He prepared to unroll Elrinonion's scroll, then reached for his wine instead. Inevitably it would be more of what he had heard at the beginning of Storm, and at the middle of Storm, and at the beginning of Rain. It was further inevitable that Glorthiachiel knew it already.

The powers that shape our fates mock us. We scoured Farcarinon because it had become a haven of bandits and arrogant mercenaries, thinking we plucked a weapon from the hands of Serenthon's mad daughter. Instead she claims Oronviel—and makes of it a haven for every broken spur and gallowglass in the Fortunate Lands!

Bolecthindial had known since Midwinter that Vieliessar did not intend to simply lie quiet in Oronviel Keep and enjoy the freedom and luxury denied her at the Sanctuary of the Star. In the beginning he'd dismissed her ambitions. He'd laughed when he heard she sent her *komen* galloping to the eight corners of Oronviel in the dead of winter, certain it was a desperate attempt to keep them from rising against her. He'd assumed she would take decades to consolidate her rule, make a marriage alliance, and build up her armies before challenging any of the Hundred.

He'd found matters less amusing when he learned Oronviel and Ivrithir had settled their ancient quarrels. Elrinonion had sent spies into Oronviel and Ivrithir to learn more. From Ivrithir he learned Atholfol meant to support Oronviel's claim to the Unicorn Throne. From Oronviel he learned nothing, because the agents he sent across her borders never reported back.

Bolecthindial drained his cup and reached for the pitcher to refill it. Peacebond or no, he wished they'd drowned Serenthon's brat in her infancy. *Farcarinon never does as it is ordered, and she is Farcarinon to the bone.*

The silence from within Oronviel did not mean Bolecthindial or Elrinonion were in ignorance of her plans. From Great Sea Ocean to the Grand Windsward, the entire realm knew what Vieliessar was doing. The news from Oronviel was nearly enough to make the strange events at the Sanctuary dwindle into irrelevance. After all, it mattered only to the Lightborn who was Astromancer and for how long. . . .

But Ivrulion had sent news this morning through Mardioruin Lightbrother. *At least Mardioruin is discreet,* Bolecthindial thought blackly. *Ivrulion knows better than to send me a message save by a Lightborn personally loyal to him—Carangil Lightbrother runs first to Glorthiachiel with everything, whether it is a scraped knee or the news that we are being invaded. And yet . . . there are things my son will wish no one to know until I have heard them, and so I know I have not yet heard the worst.*

There was a preemptory rap upon his door, and it opened before the servant sitting beside it could ask who was there.

"It is as we thought." Runacarendalur strode into the room, stripping off his gloves. He had come straight from the stables; his spurs and chain mail jingled as he crossed the floor. "The farmsteads upon our eastern border are deserted. Stripped."

"How many?" Bolecthindial asked.

Runacarendalur laughed. "All of them! My troop and I rode the bounds for a sennight and saw no one, save in the border towers. And *they* saw nothing."

He stopped before the desk and glanced at his father for permission before filling a second cup from the pitcher of wine. "They watch, of course. Do not think they shirk their duty to Caerthalien and to you. But they saw no smoke nor fire—nor have I ever hunted border raiders who strip a farm of every blanket and mattress. The Landbonds and their Farmholders are gone into Oronviel. Or should we call it Farcarinon now?"

Bolecthindial glared at him and did not reply.

"What news from the Sanctuary?" Runacarendalur asked with a sigh.

"Ivrulion says he has not been able to persuade Hamphuliadiel to end his term as Astromancer. He returns home at the end of the sennight."

"That much is good to hear, at least," Runacarendalur said.

"Is it?" his father snapped. "Then you will rejoice to learn all of Oronviel's Postulants have vanished from the Sanctuary."

"What?" Runacarendalur said, pausing in the act of drinking. "How? When?"

"Stop hovering." Bolecthindial waved toward a chair, and Runacarendalur threw himself into it. "The message came through Mardioruin Lightbrother. Ivrulion could not say much. But his last letter—" Bolecthindial tapped the rolled scroll that lay on the corner of the table, its seal broken. "—said Hamphuliadiel keeps the Lightborn who have come to ask his mind all very close, offering them feasts and entertainment as if they guested in some great lord's house. Ivrulion said he would make it his purpose to speak with our Postulants there, should he manage to contrive it so the meeting would look like mere chance."

"'Rulion is a Prince of the Line," Runacarendalur pointed out. "Why doesn't he just order Hamphuliadiel to do what he wants?"

"And do what when the Astromancer refuses?" Bolecthindial asked, with heavy irony. "We cannot go to war against the Sanctuary of the Star!"

"I know." Runacarendalur pulled his braid over his shoulder and tugged at it. "Mother wishes to see you. Before you ask, she's seen Elrinonion's latest report."

Bolecthindial glanced toward the still-unopened scroll.

"I know not what Elrinonion says, but Mother says Oronviel is building up a peasant army to slaughter us all in our beds," Runacarendalur added helpfully. "And after what I saw on the border . . . she might be right."

On certain occasions, Lord Bolecthindial took his noon meal in his private rooms attended only by those whom he invited to share it. Today he dined with his wife and children, plus his Warlord and Swordmaster, as was only reasonable on the eve of War Season.

"When you sent your heir to scour Farcarinon clean of outlaws and landless mercenaries, my lord husband, I was certain that would be an end to our problems—not a beginning," Ladyholder Glorthiachiel said with poisonous politeness. "How is it that any traitor knight and hedge bandit can enter Oronviel at will, and we must rely for information on the rumors that unnatural creature chooses to spread? She holds her throne by witchery, you know," Glorthiachiel finished idly.

"Mother!" Thorogalas protested halfheartedly.

"Oh, I don't mean *Magery*," Ladyholder Glorthiachiel said, waving Thorogalas's protests aside. "But there is bad blood in that Line. They are all sly and untrustworthy. Look at what her father did, after all."

"It is nothing more than any of us would have done," Domcariel said, and Runacarendalur glanced at his brother in surprise, for Dom was slow and deliberate off the battlefield as well as on it. "You would be the first to agree, Rune," he added.

"I should be happy to become High King," Runacarendalur said. "I think I would choose a different method, though."

"It cannot possibly work," Gimragiel said. As always, he took their mother's part so thoroughly that he might as well have said nothing and left her to do all the talking. "But think of the disaster to the rest of us when she has lost. If Farcarinon was a refuge of outlaws, Oronviel will be a thousand times worse."

"If I knew *precisely* what was happening in Oronviel, perhaps I would agree," Lord Bolecthindial said, glaring meaningfully at his Swordmaster.

"You cannot know precisely, that is true, Lord Bolecthindial," Elri-nonion said reprovingly. "But it is widely known that no matter what the crime, to go before Oronviel's War Prince and pledge fealty is to be pardoned. As my lord is aware, some insignificant fraction of the Free Companies escaped last year's Harrowing of Farcarinon. They might—perhaps—be assets to an army. But the majority of outlaws are simple thieves who have no training in arms."

"You didn't get Foxhaven and Glasswall, Father," Princess Angiothiel said, biting into a roast dove. "Doesn't Glasswall winter on Sarmiorion land?"

"It doesn't matter if they do," Bolecthindial announced.

"And Foxhaven upon Nantirworiel, though that is even beyond Sarmiorion and the Uradabhur, so it hardly matters." Angiothiel said, stretching out her arm to pluck a candied apricot from the tray in the center of the table. "All I know is if *I* commanded a Free Company and if *I* had seen the rest of the Free Companies slaughtered, I'd consider offering my services to the only War Prince who hadn't been involved."

"Don't be foolish, 'Thia," Thorogalas said. "They will fight for whoever pays them. They're a Free Company."

"And Oronviel's coffers are fat," Runacarendalur pointed out. He glanced at Elrinonion. "Surely Oronviel cannot keep everyone from entering and leaving, Lord Elrinonion?"

"Entering is one matter, Prince Runacarendalur. Leaving is another. And Ivrithir is a third. There I have been able to gain some information, but—as Lord Bolecthindial knows—it does not encourage."

"I cannot believe Atholfol has made common cause with Oronviel!" Ladyholder Glorthiachiel said. "How could he repay our care and kindness with such treachery?"

"Perhaps he thinks his taxes are too high," Angiothiel suggested, and Runacarendalur kicked her under the table.

"There is still time for you to be married into Haldil or Bethros," he told his sister. "I'm sure you would enjoy life in the Grand Windsward."

Angiothiel tossed her head and did not reply.

"I did not summon you here to squabble, nor did I summon you to *discuss* matters," Lord Bolecthindial said. "In two moonturns we ride against Ullilion. The challenges have been sent. The battlefields have been agreed on. To forfeit will mean paying penalties to Ullilion." He paused, regarding Warlord Lengiathion balefully. "Your strategy requires Ivrithir and Oronviel to raid against Cirandeiron so Cirandeiron neither rides to Ullilion's aid nor attacks us while our army is engaged elsewhere. When

I sent that Lightborn to Oronviel last autumn to gauge the girl's temper, you told me you were satisfied."

"My lord, Thurion Lightbrother assured me Oronviel would abide by its traditional agreements," Lengiathion said.

"And yet—oddly enough—Thurion Lightbrother is now nowhere to be found. And Sweethallow—your gift to him upon his return to us— stands empty," Runacarendalur pointed out. He wished 'Rulion were back from the Sanctuary. The news would be fresh, and 'Rulion had always been clever enough to fit together a hundred scattered pieces of information to make a round tale of them.

As the others bickered around the table—save for Lengiathion and Elrinonion, who were being vilified for not doing the impossible— Runacarendalur sat lost in his own thoughts. He wished he'd paid more attention to the girl when she'd lived beneath their roof. He ticked off what he knew of her, hoping the facts would make a story. Took the Green Robe. Fled the Sanctuary and vanished beyond the Astromancer's ability to find her. Defeated Oronviel's Warlord—formerly *Farcarinon's* Warlord—in single combat. Became War Prince, sparing the *former* War Prince. Declared she would become High King. Began seeking alliances, while at the same time making Oronviel a haven for outlaws. Convinced one of Caerthalien's Lightborn to betray them and aid her cause. Talked Atholfol into sending his armies into Oronviel and allowing Oronviel's armies to hold Ivrithir's borders.

There is something more. Something I am missing. I know that, but I do not know what it may be.

"It is obvious to anyone that this plot is Thoromarth's, not Vieliessar's," Gimragiel said sharply, summoning Runacarendalur's attention back to the table. "This foolishness about her defeating Rithdeliel Warlord in combat—we all know that's impossible! She'd been at the Sanctuary all her life—when would she have learned swordplay? It was done so we would spare our treaty hostages. I say we should send their bodies to Oronviel so Thoromarth knows his deception has been uncovered!"

"And what will that gain us?" Runacarendalur asked. "It will not put an end to any of the things Oronviel is doing."

"Does no one find it odd that Thoromarth executed his dear lady Daustifalal the moment that ungrateful Farcarinon brat entered his domain?" Ladyholder Glorthiachiel demanded, her voice high with anger. "And now the Astromancer acts outside of custom—and the Oronviel Lightborn in training at the Sanctuary have vanished! She has beguiled both of them. Anyone may see it."

Everyone knew Lady Daustifalal was of Aramenthiali, Caerthalien's ancient enemy, yet today she was "dear lady Daustifalal" to Mother. *Yet we were quick enough to make common cause with Aramenthiali against Farcarinon,* Runacarendalur reminded himself. Not for the first time, he wondered why his mother hated Vieliessar so much—and if she did, why had she agreed to foster her? There'd been no advantage in it.

"This solves nothing," he said abruptly, setting down his eating knife. "Whether Thoromarth rules in Oronviel or not—whether Vieliessar plots with Hamphuliadiel Astromancer or not—Oronviel cannot go on giving sanctuary to everyone who wishes to flee their rightful overlord. Betroth me to Princess Nunduil and I will take an army to Oronviel in her name."

"So quick to surrender Caerthalien, brother?" Princess Ciliphirilir gibed. She had let her twin carry most of the conversation at the meal, but there was not one thought Princess Angiothiel had that Princess Ciliphirilir didn't share.

"The betrothal can be broken as soon as Thoromarth and Vieliessar are dead and their army of rabble scattered," Runacarendalur snapped. "Or would you rather I broke the Code of Battle instead?"

"Perhaps I may be allowed to rule my own domain for a while longer?" Lord Bolecthindial said acidly. "We all agree Oronviel must be dealt with. But let us not see the threat as greater than it is. Next season is soon enough. It has been the work of years to maneuver Ullilion onto the field without Lady Dendinirchiel squalling to Daroldan before time. I will not waste this chance."

Runacarendalur did his best to curb his irritation. This was how warfare was conducted. It always had been. Ullilion was held in clientage by Cirandeiron, and so could ask her aid, but Cirandeiron's aid came at the price of closer entanglement. Daroldan was another Less House: far enough distant it would not seek to take Ullilion from Cirandeiron, close enough it could ask Ullilion's aid and give aid in return. But for the first time, the ponderous ritual dance that preceded War Season struck him as dangerous. Each War Season since the end of the Long Peace had brought another tiny change in their ancient customs. The Beastlings grew bolder, the Less Houses grew more impatient, the High Houses ruthlessly tightened their grip on their weaker neighbors. The Windsward Rebellion had been the first spark laid to tinder that smoldered still. Another such spark, and the Hundred would kindle into war—and such a war as would not respect treaties or the Code of Battle.

"You need not set aside your plans, Father," Runacarendalur said. "A campaign against Oronviel would be brief, over before you are to meet Ullilion's army. I would not even require the levy tailles—such meisnes as the knights of our own lands hold would be sufficient."

"Three thousand horse against Oronviel?" Domcariel said dubiously. "Oronviel can put twice that into the field."

"With time to call them up, yes," Runacarendalur said. "But Lord Elrinonion says they are with Ivrithir. If we attack swiftly, Oronviel will have to take the field with Ivrithir's horse—if they will follow Thoromarth at all—and perhaps a taille or two of mercenaries who will desert once they learn no quarter is to be offered. The thing can be done—if it is done swiftly."

"Yes. Perhaps," Lord Bolecthindial said slowly, in tones that Runacarendalur knew from bitter experience meant he intended to give the impression of fairness and consideration while not changing his views in the least. "But I think you are making the mistake of measuring your adversaries by your own abilities. The girl is a Green Robe who has not lived outside the Sanctuary since she was a child. Thoromarth is timid and unwilling to take the audacious risks that gain the greatest reward. I need no Swordmaster to gather gossip to tell me these things. The plan they have woven between them tells me all. They will dress up servants and farmers in bright armor and arm them with swords, thinking to mislead us. And when the time comes for battle—as it will—those mist-knights will vanish like mist in the sun, just as 'Lord' Vieliessar's dreams of the Unicorn Throne will vanish. And Caerthalien will remain."

"Caerthalien will remain a *jest* on the tongues of the Hundred Houses!" Ladyholder Glorthiachiel cried. "Husband! Speak all you wish of mist and sun and farmers! Oronviel has become a den of wolves!"

"And if it is, Mother, then any den can be easily cleared in springtide, when the wolves are blind pups," Runacarendalur answered. He turned back to his father. "A moonturn—no more—and I shall bring you Thoromarth's and Vieliessar's heads. I will even drive their rabble-army across the border to prey upon Aramenthiali, if that would please you."

"If you do not do this thing," Ladyholder Glorthiachiel said in a steel-hard voice, "Aramenthiali, Cirandeiron, and Telthorelandor will surely wonder if you have made a secret treaty with Oronviel's so-called War Prince. Holding Oronviel, why should she not assert her claim to Farcarinon as well?"

"*Because she will be dead!*" Bolecthindial roared.

There was a moment of silence.

"You—" he said, glaring balefully at Runacarendalur, "you ride one sennight from today. Tomorrow you are betrothed to Princess Nanduil. She will accompany you to Oronviel. And you, my lady wife," Bolecthindial said, turning to Glorthiachiel, "you will accompany the princess— and the army—so you can have the pleasure of seeing Nataranweiya's brat slain." Bolecthindial returned his attention to Runacarendalur. "I expect you to return with every knight you ride with. I expect my army back a moonturn after it rides, whether you have yet engaged Oronviel or no. And I say this: if this campaign you so ardently desire costs me my victory over Ullilion, you will heartily wish you had died in Oronviel."

Bolecthindial didn't wait for an answer, but pushed himself to his feet. The others—all save Glorthiachiel—rose hastily, standing in silence as the War Prince strode from the room.

The door slammed.

"Dining with Father is always so interesting," Princess Angiothiel said happily.

KNOWLEDGE AND TREACHERY

To discover how the Elfling had managed to escape into death in the heart of the World Without Sun became King Virulan's obsession. He gave Uralesse command of the Dark Guard and sent it forth to hunt—this time not for sport nor for food, but for knowledge.

First Uralesse scoured the Goldengrass, and found it empty from the Winnowing Sea in the east to the shores of Graythunder Glairyrill. West of the Glairyrill, he found those creatures he was accustomed to find: Centaur and Minotaur, Bearward and Faun, Hippogriff and Acsalion and Gryphon. All of these were of the Silver, and to each of them had been given some spark of Light. Many of them had fanned that spark into magic, though no sorcery they possessed was so much as a guttering ember by comparison to that with which *He Who Is* had blessed His most glorious creation. The merest touch of the Endarkened had always been enough to drain their power to nothing.

Uralesse went next to the cities and great castels of the Teeth of the Moon, and found them deserted, crumbling away to dust.

There were no answers there. And so he sought his answers in the only place that remained.

⬥

The Elfling died in silence. Every scream, every whimper, every tear had been taken from him during the moonturns of his agony. Uralesse gazed into the sightless eyes, already clouding in death.

He was no closer to an answer.

He had discovered the silver cord that linked the Elven spellcrafters to the source of their power. He had traced that cord back to its wellspring, summoned Lesser Endarkened to the World Above and drove them with whips and threats into each one. Sometimes the Lesser Endarkened died. Sometimes the Flower Forest died. Uralesse was no closer to the answer King Virulan had demanded of him. That the Elflings wielded any magic at all was nothing more than a mockery of the Endarkened. Once the Elflings had possessed no magic. Then they did.

Some unknown enemy challenged the inevitable victory of the Endarkened.

⊰⊱

"We must attack now, my liege," Uralesse said. "We are many and powerful. Surely victory will be ours."

"Do you say so, dear Uralesse?" King Virulan answered. "Then tell me this: who gave to the Elflings the sorcery that courses through their veins?"

"It is but weak . . ." Uralesse said, daring to protest.

"You do not answer me, my dear brother," Virulan said. He cupped Uralesse's face in his taloned hand caressingly—then clamped his hand tight, his talons shearing through scarlet flesh. Golden ichor welled over his fingers, his claws grated over bone and fang. Uralesse did not dare even to whimper in pain.

Virulan released his grip with a shove that sent Uralesse sprawling to the blood-sanctified floor of the Heart of Darkness.

"Find my answers," Virulan said softly, beginning to lick his fingers clean.

⊰⊱

Uralesse came no more to the Audience Chamber, nor was he to be found anywhere within the World Without Sun, and Virulan came to believe he had chosen exile over confession of failure. Virulan sought him in the Obsidian Mirror and discovered there were now places he could not see. It had been a long time—hundreds of centuries, as the Brightworlders reckoned time—since he had gazed into the Mirror, and now there were places of . . . blankness.

A Brightworlder would have said they were dark, but there was no darkness to those who lived in the World Without Sun. The blankness spread, he discovered, from those places where the Elfling Mages drew their power. Some, Virulan's sorcery permitted him to penetrate, allowing the Obsidian Mirror to show him vague and misty shadows. Others remained blank no matter his efforts.

If Uralesse seeks to hide in such a place, that is nearly punishment enough, Virulan thought. *But he cannot conceal himself in such stinking precincts forever. And when he emerges . . .*

Then Virulan would teach Uralesse the true cost of disappointing his king.

But that was a pleasure he was willing to defer for a time, for there were other matters to concern him. The Endarkened continued to hunt the Elflings for sport, but now, the hunting parties began to report failure where they had once only boasted of success. They had become used to tracking their quarry by the stink of Brightworld sorcery flowing through its veins, for the stench was unmistakable and penetrating. But now, fewer and fewer of the Elvenkind reeked of magic. It was another change in creatures that already changed far too fast for Virulan's taste. He distrusted it.

And at last, Uralesse returned to Shadow Mountain.

Virulan had him dragged to the foot of the Shadow Throne in iron chains heated red-hot by magic. The stink of Uralesse's eternally burning eternally regenerating flesh was sweet incense in his nostrils.

"You left me, my brother," Virulan said, pouting. "You left me for a long time."

"I . . . sought to fulfill your command, my liege, my master, my king," Uralesse answered, gasping with pain. "I have discovered what you seek. I have found that power which granted magic to the Elflings."

Virulan raised his lambent gaze from the sweet spectacle of Uralesse's suffering, frowning in thought. There was no power in the universe as great as the power *He Who Is* had given to the Endarkened . . . but it was not any part of Virulan's plans to provide his subjects with every sharp stick and large stone of the Brightworlders' armory. He inspected the avidly curious expressions of his courtiers' faces for a long moment before coming to a decision.

"Leave us," he commanded.

His court obeyed him reluctantly. Uralesse was not the first of the Endarkened to be erased from existence by their king's wrath, nor even the first of the Thirteen to suffer his fury. But Uralesse was surely the greatest of them to be brought low, and all the Endarkened wished to relish his pain and his punishment.

"Now," Virulan said, when they were alone. "Speak."

"I cannot—" Uralesse began, his words strangled by agony as a gesture from Virulan caused the chains to tighten around him, their heat kindling from red to orange. His skin split from the heat and the pressure; drops of golden ichor welled up to be charred to ash instantly. "I must— The Mirror! *The Mirror!*"

Virulan permitted the chains to loosen, to cool. "What of the Mirror, my beloved?" he purred.

"I must—I must *show* you," Uralesse gasped. "In the Mirror! Then you will see—I have never betrayed you, my liege! My heart beats as yours, my only desire the scouring of the Bright World!"

"Truly?" Virulan said, as if he had been suddenly convinced. He rose to his feet, and as he did, the chains loosened further and fell from Uralesse's body. "Then let us go at once."

And if Uralesse's information disappointed him, there was another chamber, beneath that of the Obsidian Mirror, that would be Uralesse's last sight in the world of Time and Matter.

The Mirror Chamber was just as it had been in the long ago time when Virulan first forged it. Walls, ceiling, and floor were all of mirror-bright obsidian, so that even within its lightless compass, Virulan and Uralesse seemed to walk through an infinite realm, in which they, too, became infinite.

Both brighter and darker than that which contained it was the Obsidian Mirror itself. It seemed to draw into its polished surface even the memory and possibility of light, radiating the breath of the Void as a forge might radiate heat.

"It is . . . beautiful," Uralesse said softly. He, like the rest of the Endarkened, had known of the Mirror—for Virulan made no secret of his greatest weapon—but until this moment, none save their king had been privileged to gaze upon it.

"You have but to think of what you wish to see, and it will appear," Virulan said proudly.

"And so I shall, my master," Uralesse vowed. He knew that to disappoint his liege here would mean his death; there would be no second chance to prove his loyalty. "But first I must tell you why I hid. It was not from you, my king. Never that. But from that which I knew to be my quarry. It took me a year of Bright World time to weave about me such spells as would utterly disguise my true nature."

He saw King Virulan frown. A sorcery such as he had just described was unheard-of among the Endarkened. More to the point, it was unnecessary, for the Endarkened were the greatest sorcerers Above or Below.

"It was needed," he said quickly. "We had never suspected the existence of that which I came to hunt, for it always fled before we sensed it. Had we done so . . . we would have seen the source of Elfling Magery at once."

"Enough of your babble," Virulan growled. "Show me—and then tell me why you did not slay it and bring me its body to prove your claim."

Uralesse bowed his head in quick submission. He turned to the Mirror and concentrated.

The Bright World appeared. The whole sweep of it was held in the curve of the Obsidian Mirror, bounded by high crags to the north, burning desert to the south, trackless water on either side. Patches of numinous blankness dotted the image.

"Some are Wardings," Uralesse said. "Some are strongholds of the Light."

"Do not show me what I have already seen and tell me it is my answer," Virulan said dangerously.

"I do not, my king!" Uralesse protested. "Only, see—here—"

The image changed, the patches of blankness vanishing as Uralesse focused on what he meant to show: a high meadow, where a waterfall spilled from the height into a crystal pool. The meadow was edged by dense forest, whose misty seeming showed it was a wellspring of the Light.

From the edge of the forest, a Unicorn stepped.

The Obsidian Mirror began to whine, as faintly as crystal, at what it was forced to display. A Brightworlder would have called it glorious, beauty incarnate. The two Endarkened did not. Virulan hissed, spreading his wings. Uralesse shuddered. In that instant, he knew his king had seen what he himself had seen: the Unicorn was not merely a creature of the Light. It was Light Incarnate.

With every fiber of his being, Uralesse yearned to debase it.

The Unicorn seemed to realize it was being watched. It threw up its head, and for an instant, gazed directly into the Obsidian Mirror.

And in that moment, the Obsidian Mirror exploded.

CHAPTER NINE

FIRST BLOOD

*The Starry Hunt and the Starry Huntsman do not favor one cause, one
army, over another. Make sacrifices and petitions for victory in their
season, as is right, but know that the Hunt care only for honor and skill.
The Hunt reward the valor of the Lords* Komen *with immortality and
endless battle—but They do not choose the victor.*

—Arilcarion War-Maker, *Of the Sword Road*

Rain became Flower. In a few sennights Sword Moon would mark
the beginning of War Season, when the formal battles arranged
among the War Princes moonturns and even decades before
would be fought. Border raids began as soon as the weather could be
trusted: trials of strength, sport for younger knights, the settling of old
grudges and the foundation for new ones.

The army of Ivrithir rode Oronviel's borders, if not tirelessly, than at
least dutifully and without complaint. By now the whispers Vieliessar
had loosed by Nadalforo and her mercenary comrades had reached every
intended ear: *Come to Oronviel and swear to fight for her War Prince, and
receive amnesty and sanctuary.*

The first who came sought fresh prey and easy victims, thinking they
could slip across the border unnoticed and say to any who asked that
they were Oronviel's sworn knights. They did not reckon with troops of
komen who rode the borders as diligently as foresters might walk their
lords' estates, nor did they expect to be greeted with sword and spear and
bow at every farmstead.

For that was another new thing Vieliessar had done in Oronviel. Nowhere in the Fortunate Lands were Farmholders or their tenants permitted

possession of the sword and spear and bow. The sword was for a knight to
carry to war. The spear and horseman's bow were for knights and lords and
princes to hunt with; the walking bow was for their foresters to clear their
lands of beasts that would spoil their hunts. Farmholders might use the
sling to take hares or birds and to frighten wolves, and use the cudgel and
the stave for defense. To own or to wield a spear or a bow had brought harsh
penalties. To possess a sword had meant death. And so those farmsteads
which could not call upon a nearby manor and its knights for protection
had been easy prey for raiders.

No longer.

She had set forth her proclamation in Woods Moon, knowing a knife
could become a spear easily enough. Skill in bow and sword could not be
granted by decree; it would be enough, she thought, that the weapons
would no longer be forbidden. Gunedwaen had laughed, hearing her
speak her thoughts, and told her she was wrong. Foresters, he said, who
could slay a boar with one arrow loosed from the formidable walking
bow, did not come from thin air, but from Farmhold families. Not only
skill, but bows, were sown wider than she imagined, and as for swords . . .
well, it was well known that any battlefield on which the fallen lay for
more than a night or two would be found mysteriously bare of blades
when the dead were gathered up.

And so all who entered Oronviel seeking to prey upon its folk were
slain or captured, and the prisoners were brought to the Great Keep, and
those who could not swear truly under a Spell of Heart-Seeing that they
meant to pledge fealty to Oronviel were slain, for Vieliessar would loose
no more wolfsheads to plague her people.

Those who swore truly swelled the numbers of those who inhabited
her Battle City. Some had been *komen* in other domains and would fight
for their new liege as they had fought for the old. Those who had not been,
Vieliessar sought to train in a new way: as foot knights.

As *infantry*.

Their weapons would be the walking bow and a heavy pike-spear
such as castel guardsmen carried. They would wear chain instead of

plate, for foot knights could not be asked to bear the weight of a mounted knight's armor through a long day of fighting. Such swords as they carried would be shorter than a mounted knight's sword, to be used when pike and bow failed.

Some called the presence of such lowborn warrior-candidates in Oronviel a burden and a curse. Vieliessar called it a blessing. She could not have taught her knights to become infantry. They would have needed to unlearn too much, and they would have thought fighting on foot to be a foolish and menial task. But she had offered arms to any who asked them—Farmholder, craftworker, or Landbond—and many of the mercenaries who flocked to Oronviel's standard had learned their battle skills not as children, but as men and women grown. Her ex-mercenaries saw the advantage of a dismounted force, and her Commonfolk had nothing to unlearn.

But even if she had wished to, Vieliessar could not spend all her time teaching her army new ways to fight. If her war for the High Kingship was to be won, it would not be won on the battlefield. It would be won because the people of Jer-a-kalaliel joined her freely. She had never planned to win by defeating or allying with the Ninety-and-Nine. She meant to win by drawing everyone else to her standard.

When Vieliessar is High King there will be a Code of Peace. One justice for all, be they highborn or low, and all voices heard.

When Vieliessar is High King, domain will not war with domain, for all domains will be one.

When Vieliessar is High King, the Lightborn will not be taken from their families and hoarded as a glutton hoards grain. They will go where they will and do as they wish. Nor will any children be forced to the Sanctuary against their will.

When Vieliessar is High King, lords will not steal from vassals, from craftworkers, from Landbonds—

When Vieliessar is High King, any with skill may become a knight, or a weaver, or a smith—

When Vieliessar is High King, any may own a horse, or a hound, or a sword—

When Vieliessar is High King . . .

The folk of Oronviel believed her—believed *in* her—because what she did as War Prince of Oronviel was exactly what she promised she would do as High King of the land entire. Her Lightborn were her greatest weapon in that secret war, for at least half of them came from Farmhold or Landbond families:

And if her knights and lords were disappointed by the fact that they could no longer hang poachers as they wished—or beat their tenants for their amusement—they were reconciled by the knowledge that Oronviel would soon be going to war.

⚜

I wonder when my good cousins and fellow princes will notice I have stolen half their lands? Vieliessar mused. It was a whimsical thought, but a serious one as well. She'd cleared her domain and much of the domains it bordered of bandits. Half by patrols, half by recruiting those bandits to serve in her army. She'd sent her Lightborn to tend the people of the border steadings on both sides of her borders. And in truth, even if Harvest were to see the paying out of tithes, many of the folk of the border steadings would not be there to pay: a vast army needed wagons and animals to pull them, servants to cook food and pitch tents and saddle and unsaddle horses. Landbonds had many of the skills her army needed, so she encouraged them to leave their holdings and come to her.

But if her strength and her victory lay in the commons, it did not mean she could neglect either her lords or her knights, for if she won through to peace when she sat upon the Unicorn Throne, she would fulfill the last of Amrethion's promises to his future: *the end of High House and Low.* Equal justice for all meant not merely that there would no longer be great lords and lesser lords. It meant that none could be set above another: she changed little if she simply set those who were now low above those who were now high.

Vieliessar thought idly of how different Oronviel now was from the other domains of the West. In the springtide the War Princes usually went on a progress, traveling with an escort large enough to protect them from treachery or attack. Bolecthindial Caerthalien had taken no less than five hundred of his Household knights when he rode out, but Vieliessar could ride from corner to corner of her own land alone, certain not she would not be attacked. She thought of the story she had so often been told in her childhood: *And the knights of the High King's meisne were all great kings, and each was as sweet-tempered as a sleeping babe, as loyal as a hunting hound, as beautiful as the Vilya in fruit and flower, as strong as the storms of winter, and pledged to care for all they met as ardently as the Silver Eagle tends her hatchling.*

In Oronviel, that nursery tale had come true.

Today, in the company of a mixed troop of Oronviel and Ivrithir knights—her own guard, plus a meisne of Ivrithir *komen* commanded by Lord Farathon of Ivrithir—she rode toward the place where Araphant's borders touched hers. Aramenthiali and Caerthalien used it as a way to enter one another's domains unnoticed. Through the winter, Vieliessar and her knights had used it as a hunting park, clearing it of outlaws.

Oronviel did not share much border with Araphant—a score of leagues, no more—and Vieliessar's border lords had little to do, for Araphant's manors and farms lay in that domain's southern quadrant. Its northern reaches had been left to the stag and the wolf, for Araphant had long been a limp rag chewed by Caerthalien and Aramenthiali, helplessly ceding territory to each. When War Prince Luthilion died, his House might simply vanish, for Luthilion had lived far beyond his allotted years; fate and chance had taken brothers, sisters, children, and greatchildren all before him.

"My lord, someone comes," *Komen* Bethaerian said.

"They ride one of our horses, whether they are ours or not," Vieliessar said, peering at the mounted figure in the distance. "Peace, Betharian," she added, "we are nearly two score."

"If this is no scout for one of your enemies," Farathon of Ivrithir said.

"If an enemy comes in force from Araphant, I will hold myself

surprised," Vieliessar said dryly. "But even if Luthilion rides at Bolecthindial's order, he would head west and come at us over Caerthalien's
border rather than try to bring an army through this forest." On their
own side of the border the trees had been kept thinned by landbond
families driven from their homes and forced to labor. On Araphant's side,
they had grown unchecked for centuries.

"That is so, Lord Vieliessar," Farathon said with a smile, for his
meisne had been riding this stretch of border for the past fortnight and
had spent much of that time in Araphant's forest. "Yet no good word ever
came swiftly."

The horseman had closed the distance to them as they spoke. Neither
horse nor rider was encumbered by a single ounce they did not need to
bear: the animal's saddle was a thin pad of leather, the stirrups mere flattened rings. And the rider, who was little more than a child, wore no armor. He barely checked the horse's mad gallop before he flung himself
from its saddle and ran forward. His mount, freed of direction, cantered
in a wide circle around Vieliessar and her knights, so filled with the
excitement of the run that it hardly noticed its exhaustion.

"The War Prince—*komentai'a*, I must speak with her—my lord of
Greenstone Tower said I would find her near—it is urgent—" the boy
gasped.

"I am here," Vieliessar said, nudging Sorodiarn forward. "Let him
pass," she said, for when she spoke, the boy had started toward her and
Farathon had moved automatically to block him.

"Lord Vieliessar—" the boy began. He was as winded as his mount,
but determined to deliver his message at once. "A meisne—from Araphant—my lord Peramarth did not know their intent until today—
through the wood—"

"How many?" Bethaerian demanded, but the boy only shook his head.

"Why did your lord not use the sun-signal to warn us?" Farathon
demanded, for each of the border towers were equipped with sheets of
silvered glass that could be used to flash simple messages to watchers
many miles distant. At least during bright, clear days.

"Said—not to warn them," the boy gasped.

"You have done well," Vieliessar said, putting warmth into her voice. "Come. You will ride with me. Sorodiarn is a gentle beast and your own steed deserves a rest. We will go to Greenstone Tower and see what there is to see. But first, someone must catch your horse. We are lucky he is tired."

"My lord, you cannot mean to ride toward this peril, after Lord Peramarth has sent to warn you against it?" Bethaerian said. "We must retreat to a place of safety."

"Better to ride to than from," Vieliessar answered. "If knights come through the woods of Araphant, I do not think their number can be a force much larger than our own. Peramarth will be glad of extra swords if it is an attack."

And I shall be glad to be there if it is not, Vieliessar thought. A party of knights crossing from Araphant to Oronviel was so unusual she did not wish to gain information of it second hand, and asking her people to discover whether something unusual was a threat before attacking it was a thing most of them thought was sheer moonstruck madness. *Attack and be safe,* Vieliessar thought. *They do as their greatsires did, and so grudge is heaped upon injury until they breed war.* She knew that asking her people to stop, to talk, to *think* would someday generate a tragedy. *And I can only say that if I meant to rule as all the War Princes have ruled before me, it would be better if I had never ruled at all.*

"Now come," she said to the messenger. "Give me your name and your hand."

<hr />

The distance young Randir had covered in less than a candlemark took the troop of heavy warhorses three to retrace, and when they were near to Greenstone Tower, they were met by a troop of its defenders led by Lord Peramarth himself.

"My lord prince," Peramarth said. When he pushed back the visor of his helm, his entire face was exposed, for the Border Lords might have to fight in any weather. "I did not expect you."

Here so soon or here at all? Vieliessar wondered, for Peramarth's thoughts were a flurry that could not be quickly untangled by True Speech.

"I had thought—" Peramarth began, then broke off. "No matter. Greenstone has stood since the days Araphant was a power in the land, and her walls have never been forced. Permit me to offer you my hospitality until we have repulsed our invaders."

"It seems a strange way to invade anything," Vieliessar commented a few minutes later, from atop Greenstone Tower. It was no taller than the watchtowers in her own keep, but it seemed as if it were, as there was nothing else for miles around and even the tops of the great trees were below them. Standing in this place, she could imagine she stood among the clouds themselves, and by spreading her arms, could join the hawks in the sky.

"I still cannot make the count," Angeleb said, sounding unhappy. He was one of Peramarth's sentries, chosen for his keen vision.

"We saw movement in the forest two days since," Peramarth said, pointing out and down. The area near the border was thick with green-needle trees; Vieliessar had been watching since they'd climbed out onto the roof of the watchtower and had yet to see more than an occasional bright flash. "At first I thought Old Luthilion might have come hunting, though he has not been since before the Long Peace. But see—there?" Peramarth pointed to a gap in the forest cover. "Blight and storm has killed the old trees, and the new ones are not yet grown. They rode across that place just this morning. Two tailles of knights, a Green Robe—and someone with the right to ride beneath the princely standard of Araphant."

Peramarth—she knew—had delayed sending his warning until he was certain the party beneath the trees rode bowshot-straight, and not in the erratic circles of a hunting party. To the Border Lords, giving false warning was as shameful as giving no warning at all.

"Why does he come?" she wondered aloud. "He cannot expect to conquer Oronviel with twenty-four knights and one Lightborn." Gunedwaen had not wasted his efforts spying on Araphant—he had too few people and too many places they needed to be—so she knew nothing more of it than she had learned at the Sanctuary, and that was little indeed.

"Perhaps he comes to offer you a marriage alliance," Bethaerian said dryly. "It would be a brief marriage, at least. Old Luthilion has seen a dozen Astromancers tend the Shrine."

"There is some luck in surviving so long," Vieliessar said, still thinking aloud. "And perhaps wisdom, too. You say he will cross our border, Peramarth?"

"By midday, if they do not stop."

"Then we will greet him and see why he has come."

⧊

Peramarth disliked her plan—a mark of his loyalty, inconvenient though it was—and he liked it even less when Vieliessar said she meant to meet Araphant herself. In the end she prevailed, and sat her destrier before a taille of sixty knights: her own meisne and three tailles from Greenstone.

As the approaching party became visible, Vieliessar could see that tied to Araphant's pennion was a bough of the greenneedle tree, the traditional symbol that the party riding beneath it requested a parley-truce. Beside the knight carrying the princely standard—a leaping green stag upon a sable field—rode another in armor the iridescent green-black of a beetle's wing, and upon his left rode a Lightborn, his hair silvered with great age. When they reached the border stones, they stopped, and the standard-bearer and the Lightborn rode on alone.

The wind blew through Vieliessar's hair, blowing its strands ticklingly over her cheek. She did not wear her helmet; the envoy must be able to know he spoke with the War Prince of Oronviel, not some faceless messenger.

Lord Peramarth's knights were explicitly under her command, and she had given them unambiguous orders. Nonetheless, Vieliessar was proud of their discipline and that of the Ivrithir knights, for she had bidden them all stand still and silent, and not one armored figure moved, even when she rode forward, Bethaerian at her side, to meet the Araphant messengers.

"Oronviel gives you good greeting," she said when she and the two from Araphant had stopped facing one another. "I would know how it is you come to us beneath the branch of truce, for there is no war between us."

"Araphant greets Oronviel," the aged Lightborn answered. His voice was thin, but in it Vieliessar could still hear the echo of the resonance and power it must have held in his youth. "I am Celeharth Lightbrother, Chief Lightborn to War Prince Luthilion Araphant. We ride beneath the branch of truce out of desire to speak with you, Lord Vieliessar Oronviel, honestly and in peace."

"Your lord might have done so many moonturns since," Vieliessar said, nodding in the direction of the green-armored figure who still waited on the far side of the border. She could skim the surface of Celeharth's thoughts easily: he knew Luthilion had come to make an alliance with Oronviel, but what terms he would offer or accept, Celeharth did not know.

He smiled faintly at her mild gibe. "When one reaches my master's years, one does not hasten. Yet he would speak now."

"Events do not always wait upon the desire for reflection. Yet I am eager to hear Araphant's word to me. Say to your lord that I and all with me here accept Araphant's truce, and I offer my own body as surety for his life." She unbuckled her swordbelt and held it out to Bethaerian. Slowly, her thoughts a roil of worry for her liege's safety, Bethaerian took the weapon.

Celeharth inclined his head. "I bring him to your side." He turned and rode back to the Araphant knights. The lone knight-herald holding the pennion of truce sat as motionless as if he were carved from stone.

Vieliessar could feel the tension of the *komen* behind her as if it were a wind she must set herself against. It seemed an eternity before Celeharth Lightborn reached his master's side. His voice did not carry, but his thoughts did.

It is as we hoped, old friend. Oronviel's new War Prince, Vieliessar once-Lightborn, offers us the truce of the body.

Then come, Celeharth. Let us see what we may do to dismay the dogs that bark at our heels.

Slowly the knights of Araphant rode toward their standard-bearer. When they were still a little distance away, Luthilion raised his hand and the knights behind him stopped. Araphant's War Prince removed his helm and unbelted his swordbelt, handing both helm and sword to one of his knights before continuing forward, accompanied only by Celeharth.

If Luthilion's Chief Lightborn was full of years, the War Prince himself was truly ancient. His hair, though still proudly worn in the elaborate braids of a knight, was colorless with age. His face was printed with the lines of all the joys and sorrows he had known in the long centuries of his life, but if his body beneath the bright armor was frail with age, his will was as unyielding as star-forged adamantine.

"I give you good greeting, Oronviel," he said, when his destrier stopped beside his standard-bearer.

"And I you, Araphant," Vieliessar answered.

"I would speak with you regarding matters of interest to us both, yet I would do so in more comfort. It is not seemly for two princes to shout at each other from their destriers as if they were maiden knights hot to win their spurs."

"I listen," Vieliessar answered. Lord Luthilion's speech was slow and measured, couched in the courtly and careful phrasing of centuries past.

"Celeharth tells me you were a great scholar in your time at the Sanctuary. Granting this truth, you will know how many days' travel it is from Araphant's Great Keep to where you find me now. And I am far too old to delight in sleeping on the ground rolled in my cloak. I ask your leave to summon my servants to erect my pavilion, so we may be comfortable together."

"I shall be most grateful for your care," Vieliessar said, doing her best to match the mode in which the War Prince of Araphant spoke. "I ask only to send *Komen* Bethaerian with whom you will, so your meisne and mine know we may be easy together."

"This thought is both wise and cordial," Luthilion answered. He raised a hand and beckoned, and one of his knights urged his destrier forward. Vieliessar heard Farathon draw breath with a hiss, and saw Luthilion's eyes flicker with amusement—*The child prays none of her hot-blooded young swords seeks to protect her, and that is a good sign.* The knight reached for the pennion.

"I commend to you and your *komen'tai'a Komen* Diorthiel, who serves me far more faithfully than I deserve. Diorthiel, here is *Komen* Bethaerian, who will accompany you as you give your word to my servants to bring my pavilion here to me."

Diorthiel looked very much as if he wished to argue. Instead, he simply bowed to Lord Luthilion and rode away with Bethaerian at his side.

Where others might have filled the wait with inconsequential observations on the weather or the hunting, or even with some talk of horses, Luthilion simply sat, as silent and composed as a Lightborn in meditation. So Vieliessar sat quietly as well, wondering with faint curiosity how Luthilion had managed to bring baggage wagons through the dense northern forest. The waiting was broken once by a messenger riding out from Greenstone Tower to ask what was happening—for of course Lord Peramarth was watching all that went on—and being sent back with a curt reply: *War Prince Luthilion and I discuss a treaty under truce-bough.*

When the pavilion arrived, Vieliessar discovered Luthilion had not, after all, found some new way of getting large and unwieldy sumpter wagons through a dense forest. Instead, Luthilion's pavilion was bound to the back of mules. Each mule wore a sturdy saddle with wooden legs atop it—much as if someone had taken a common chair and turned it upside down—and this odd device held heavy packs easily and securely. Vieliessar filed away the information for later use: mules could go where heavy wagons could not, and they moved faster.

The servants worked with quick efficiency. They did not care whether they worked in Araphant, Oronviel, or the Vale of Celenthodiel: servants were invisible, and even in battle were rarely an enemy's target.

"All is ready, Lord Luthilion," Celeharth said at last. Diorthiel stepped to Luthilion's side, managing to give the impression he attended his lord out of courtesy, and not because Lord Luthilion required aid to dismount. Vieliessar allowed Bethaerian to do the same for her, then beckoned to Farathon to join them.

"Come," she said quietly. "If you attend, you may say to Lord Atholfol you know all that took place here today."

Farathon's face went blank with surprise at being so trusted—and perhaps also because she spoke so frankly of mistrust. "Ivrithir is loyal," he answered.

"I trust Lord Atholfol," Vieliessar answered simply. "And was there ever a War Prince who did not wish half his great lords would conveniently die in battle?"

Farathon gave a muffled cough of laughter, and Vieliessar turned away, following Lord Luthilion into the pavilion, seeing that it was much like her own: two rooms, the outer one dominated by a sizable table. There were scrolls in a wooden rack at one side of the table and a tea brazier on the other side; a shin'zuruf pot and cups waited beside the steaming kettle. There were two chairs, precisely equal in ornamentation, set so that neither of the lords would sit with their back to the door. Nearby was another seat: a padded stool without a back. Vieliessar could feel that the pavilion had been bespelled to keep sound from passing its walls.

"My Healer tells me wine is not good for me any longer," Lord Luthilion said, lowering himself heavily into a chair and gesturing toward the brazier. Now that he was afoot, the frailties of age seemed more pronounced.

"Three things the Light cannot Heal: age, death, and fate," Celeharth answered. It had the air of a well-loved and long-familiar argument.

"As you know, Lord Luthilion, I was many years in the Sanctuary,"

Vieliessar replied. "We did not drink wine there." She took the second chair and Celeharth settled himself upon the padded stool. Once they were seated, one of the servants came forward to pour the boiling water into the pot.

"And then you left," Luthilion said, surprising her with his directness. "And next we heard of a challenge in Oronviel, unwisely accepted, and now you say you will be High King."

"Yes," Vieliessar said simply.

"We also hear that you do not promise favors to those who aid you. Nor wealth. That you open Oronviel to outlaws and offer to raise up any Landbonds who come to you to the estate of nobles and great knights."

"I do not promise favors to those who fight for me. Neither do I promise vengeance on those who do not. I offer sanctuary to any who will pledge true fealty to me."

"And the Landbond? Who will till your fields if you fill their heads with dreams of knighthood?" Luthilion demanded, his black eyes sharp. Before she could answer, he raised a hand. "Celeharth, oblige me if you would."

The Lightbrother rose to his feet, and poured tea into three delicate cups. "In my youth," Luthilion said, "a heart for war was measured by the graces of peace. It was not enough to ride well and fight well—one had to dance gracefully, play harp or flute or cithern, compose poetry and copy it out in a fair hand, or craft tea. That art is lost, I fear. Today they rip some weeds from the kitchen garden, boil them into an undrinkable mess, and call it the heritage of Mosirinde Peacemaker."

"They still teach the art at the Sanctuary," Vieliessar said, holding the cup so she could inhale its fragrant steam. "Vilya," she said in surprise, smelling the unmistakable perfume.

Luthilion radiated pleasure, though his face remained impassive. "Had we met some time ago, and in a different way, I believe I might have made a proper knight of you, Oronviel. Yes, there is Vilya in this blend. The fruit, not the flower. I thought it somehow appropriate for our meeting."

"It is a fruiting year everywhere but the Sanctuary gardens," Vieliessar commented dryly.

"Hamphuliadiel cannot expect whatever trick he has used to endure for long," Celeharth said. His eyes flicked to where Vieliessar's knights stood. "Some say he wishes to make the Sanctuary into the Hundredth House, to replace Lost Farcarinon, thinking by that means to avert the Curse of Amrethion Aradruiniel."

"If it were so easy to avert our *hradan*, High King Amrethion would not have needed to prophecy at all," Vieliessar answered. "But I would answer Araphant concerning my Landbonds."

Luthilion waved that away with faint irritation. "I know already you arm them. But what next?"

"I take the High Kingship," Vieliessar answered simply. She did not believe her arguments would sway Lord Luthilion. He was less interested in knowing what she meant to do than in knowing *her*, for she could see in his mind he meant to pledge Araphant to her alliance simply to leave Aramenthiali and Caerthalien a greater thorn in both their paws than Araphant could be otherwise.

She did not have time to hear him say so.

"My lord! A messenger!" Against all proper protocol and courtesy, *Komen* Janondiel burst through the doorway. "We are attacked! Caerthalien attacks!"

⌇

The battle standards carried by the Caerthalien force each flew a narrow red pennion as well the Caerthalien banner, signifying that the army would accept neither surrender nor truce from the enemy. The best thing about going to war in this fashion, Runacarendalur decided, though it was not so much true war as it was the chance to lead a raiding party of truly stunning size, was that he did not have to *wait*. War itself was a thing of temporary truces, of parleys, of days spent doing nothing more exciting than moving the army and the camp to the next battlefield and waiting for the enemy to arrive. There was no need for any of that in this expedition against Oronviel. The only thing he'd had to wait on were the travel wagons of Ladyholder Glorthiachiel and his recent betrothed. It had been a very long time since Mother rode on campaign, and as for Princess Nanduil . . . treaty hostages were not encouraged to develop any useful skills.

Runacarendalur had chosen as his entrance point a place along Oronviel's border where there was no clear sight-line for the watch towers and where the terrain had forced the ancient builders of the border keeps to set the strongholds far apart. Three thousand horse weren't inconspicuous, and Runacarendalur knew his army would be seen, but his strategy relied on the two nearest watchtowers—Hawkwind and Highstone—sending incomplete and useless information to Vieliessar. It also relied on the Border Lords being unwilling to engage a force so much larger than theirs: between them Hawkwind and Highstone could put perhaps three hundred knights into the field, and that only if they had been lately fortified.

As they crossed Caerthalien's eastern border, his advance scouts encountered a taille in Ivrithir colors. Runacar's scouts turned and galloped back toward the army and the Ivrithir knights followed. When Ivrithir saw the main force, the taille turned and fled, but Runacarendalur had organized a vanguard that would be ready to chase down Vieliessar's bands of roving *komen* the moment any were spotted. Fifty against twelve offered little sport, and Runacarendalur did not even get to fight, but there were other compensations. He spread his army into a long line of skirmish—madness against an equal force of enemy horse, efficient when you meant to destroy as much that lay in your path as possible.

The border steadings will entertain my troops and the terrified refugees will spread panic.

But the people of the border steadings weren't terrified. They fought back with bow and spear and sling. It should have been a futile, unequal battle. Unequal it was, but the border farmers had the advantage of surprise and while most of their weapons could not pierce armor, the walking bow could. Runacarendalur lost four knights and a dozen horses in the first clashes.

There were no terrified refugees to spread panic, because there were no survivors.

And worse, the smoke of the burned steadings alerted the Border Towers.

He'd expected no trouble: they were greatly outnumbered, and should have stayed in their keeps and passed warning messages. Instead, the Border Knights sallied forth to ride along his line of march, close enough to tempt the vanguard into giving chase, distant enough they consistently managed to escape without being caught. At night, they harassed his camp—riding through it, pulling down pavilions, setting fire to anything that would burn—so half his army needed to be awake all night to keep watch and guard their horses.

By the fourth day of their advance into Oronviel, the Border Knights had been joined by several of the knight-patrols.

On the fifth day, Oronviel's army arrived.

⚔

It is not possible, Runacarendalur thought. He saw the red-and-white of Oronviel, the tawny-and-black of Ivrithir—and, unwelcome shock, a small cluster of knights in the sable-and-green of Araphant. He estimated the enemy to be three thousand horse. Half of Oronviel's full array. They should not have been able to muster so many on a few days' notice. He'd expected to be a full sennight or more into Oronviel before any part of Oronviel's army could take the field. He'd counted on it, because he'd counted on provisioning his army along the march.

If he'd faced a force of the size he'd originally anticipated, he would have considered simply going around them, forcing them to follow and do battle nearer to the center of the domain. That would allow him the opportunity both to provision his army and to do more damage to Oronviel. But it would not be possible to flank three thousand horse.

At least it's too late to fight today. He glanced at the sky. Nearly midday, so they'd have most of a day to prepare to meet the enemy and scout the terrain over which they would fight. Though this was not a field he would have chosen—it sloped slightly upward, and was littered with debris to trip or lame a destrier whose rider was unwary—it would do well enough. He wheeled his palfrey about and went to give the order to make camp.

⊰⊱

W hy do we stop so early in the day?"
The servants had barely finished setting his pavilion before Ladyholder Glorthiachiel strode into it, glaring at her son. "Is it not enough that we move at such speed one would assume we carried vital messages? Now you propose to sit and do nothing!"

"And how is my betrothed? Sick with joy at this return to her homeland?" Runacarendalur asked.

"Were there anyone else in the Line Direct I could trust upon Oronviel's throne, I would slit her throat rather than listen to another moment of her complaints," Ladyholder Glorthiachiel said. "At least Nataranweiya's brat never whined. Now. Why do we stop?"

"Why, so I may engage Oronviel at dawn," Runacarendalur said, waving vaguely in the direction of the enemy. "Thoromarth has brought, if not Vieliessar's army, then *an* army. You will be pleased to know Oronviel has made alliance with Araphant as well."

"Impossible!" Ladyholder Glorthiachiel snapped.

"Possible," Runacarendalur replied, "and fact. Unless you believe Thoromarth has somehow stolen the War Prince's banner from Old Luthilion and garbed a dozen Oronviel knights in his colors."

Ladyholder Glorthiachiel regarded him through narrowed eyes for a long moment, then gestured peremptorily to a servant to bring her a chair. "Wine," she said, seating herself and shaking out the folds of her voluminous riding skirts. Runacarendalur served her himself; the pavilion was set, but nothing was unpacked yet. He located the chest he sought, took possession of a bottle and two goblets, filled both cups, handed one to Ladyholder Glorthiachiel, and seated himself on a chest.

"How many ride against us?" she asked after she'd tasted her cup and silently let him know the drink was not to her liking.

Runacarendalur hesitated, but any knight in the camp could estimate the size of Oronviel's force as easily as he had, and Ladyholder Glorthiachiel's personal guard would tell her if he did not. "Our forces seem equally matched," he said reluctantly.

"And yet, when you proposed this expedition, you said Oronviel could only bring two thousand—at most—to the field," Ladyholder Glorthiachiel said.

"Obviously Elrinonion Swordmaster should have tried harder to get scouts across Oronviel's border who'd report back," Runacarendalur retorted. "The army is there. We can fight, or we can run away."

"Do not say to me I have given birth to a coward," Ladyholder Glorthiachiel answered haughtily. "Thoromarth is beguiled by that Sanctuary-bred monster. Atholfol's forces will flee the field rather than fight for Oronviel. And Araphant we will deal with in due time."

Runacarendalur inclined his head. "It will of course be just as you say, Mother."

❧

One candlemark passed, then two, as Oronviel's army continued to advance. It moved—as did any army on the march—at a slow and measured pace in order to spare the destriers' strength.

But it did not stop.

Runacarendalur sat his riding palfrey, watching the enemy advance. Only a couple of miles now separated the front of their column from his camp. Two of the banners the knights-pennion carried signified War Princes on the field: Araphant's and Oronviel's. Runacarendalur had never faced Lord Luthilion—Luthilion had last taken the field in Runacarendalur's greatfather's time—but the gleam of his white hair was unmistakable as he rode beside Araphant's standard. Runacarendalur glanced at Ivrithir's banner, but Lord Atholfol was not on the field. *Why do his knights ride here if he does not lead them?* Runacarendalur wondered. He frowned, puzzled, then set the thought aside for now. *And here is Oronviel.* Thoromarth was a familiar sight in pearl-white armor, mounted on his grey stallion. Runacarendalur frowned again. Thoromarth was riding his destrier, not a palfrey. Everyone in the front rank was.

Between Thoromarth and Luthilion, on a bay so pale its coat was nearly golden, rode . . .

Her. That must be Vieliessar.

At first he'd thought the woman might be Thoromarth's standard-bearer, until she leaned sideways in her saddle to touch his shoulder with the easy familiarity of a ruling prince to a favored knight. Thoromarth said something in return and she laughed, gesturing at the army that rode behind them.

I did not expect her to come armored as a knight to this battlefield.

His mother had been sure Vieliessar was merely a mask for Thoromarth's ambition, and even if she were not, it was inconceivable she would ride to war. Yet here she was. She wore silver-enameled armor and the white surcoat with the red otter that marked her as a knight of Oronviel. The bay destrier she rode danced and fretted beneath her hand, yet she controlled him effortlessly.

When the advancing column finally stopped, Runacarendalur was relieved. He watched as it split, then split again, spreading and reforming behind the first line as gracefully as if the whole of the army danced. *They do not wish to be caught unawares while they make camp,* he decided.

Then Thoromarth spoke again and Vieliessar took up her helm and slid it over her head. Runacarendalur could not say why watching her give her helm the small back-and-forth twist to lock it into place made him feel so uneasy. It was something he'd done himself a thousand times. More.

And so has she. Runacarendalur frowned. *Why does she helm if they are to make camp?*

Then—impossibly—he heard the mellow dangerous song of war-horns.

Right flank: wheel. Left flank: hold. Center: advance.

Against all sense and custom, Oronviel was attacking.

Now.

He spurred his palfrey and galloped back to the camp, shouting for the alarm to be sounded, for his knights to arm themselves. Some had heard the enemy warhorns. Most had not. And only a handful were in armor. *This is madness!* Runacarendalur thought in outrage. *The Code of Battle demands challenge be made and answered before the engagement begins! Not a random attack the moment you catch sight of your enemy! This is none of Thoromarth's doing! Vieliessar fights us if she is a hedgerow bandit!*

He reached his tent and flung himself from his saddle. Helecanth's pavilion was pitched beside his own, and she'd come running at the sound of his horse. Runacarendalur noted with despair that his guard captain was as unready to fight as his entire army.

"My lord?" she said.

Runacarendalur opened his mouth to reply, then closed it again as the first of the Caerthalien horns sounded· *To horse, to horse, arm your self, to battle . . .*

"I shall bring Gwaenor," she said, and took off for the horselines at a run.

"My armor!" Runacarendalur shouted as he entered his tent. *If they had reached us before the camp was set it would have been a disaster,* he thought numbly. Only the flanks and the vanguard had been riding in armor, and no one had been riding destriers. *But they meant to attack the moment they saw us.*

Nithiach, his chamber page, came rushing out of the pavilion's inner chamber, a polishing cloth in his hands. Runacarendalur shouted again for his armor and began stripping off his clothes. He struggled with his boots for a moment before sitting down on a chest to yank them off.

His arming page was nowhere to be found. Nithiach would have to serve; there was not time to find Arnarth. As Nithiach returned with Runacarendalur's aketon and padded leather trews, the booming of the war drums overlaid the discordant and clashing sound of the horns.

Lengiathion Warlord always said battles could be won or lost by the speed a knight could arm, and I never believed him. . . .

He struggled into the complex elements of his armor, swearing at Nithiach in his desperate need to be armed, to be *away*. He nearly shouted at Helecanth to leave when she entered, followed by her arming page.

"They advance." She had to shout to be heard over the uproar: horns and drums and knights shouting and the clatter of metal and the screams of overexcited horses. "I have ordered Ladyholder Glorthiachiel's guard to move her wagon back and to keep her and Princess Nanduil inside, even if they must tie them hand and foot and nail the doors of the wagon shut."

"They'd probably rather face Oronviel," Runacarendalur muttered. "Good. How many—?" *How many can we send against them at once?*

"Five hundred," Helecanth said grimly. "Enough to hold them until the rest arm. They will stand—if you are there."

Runacarendalur settled his helm on his head. As he gave it the small twist to lock it into place, the vivid image of Vieliessar doing just the same filled his mind.

<hr />

War was a thing of beauty. Runacarendalur had always believed this. The clash of two lines of knights meeting at full gallop, the moments of bravery and skill that were the fruit of a lifetime of training, the joyful dance of death when two knights fought each other as if no one else existed—He was a prince of Caerthalien, a knight, a warrior: he carried the honor of his House upon his shoulders each time he rode into battle.

But today was different. He'd been given no time to scout the battle-field, to meet with his commanders, to tell each where they must stand and where they must go, to settle the signals that would allow him to deploy hundreds of knights as easily as he flexed the fingers of his hand. Instead, he galloped from camp with barely a sixth of his army and only one thought in his mind: push Oronviel back and buy his *komen* time to take the field. He shouted orders to Helecanth as Gwaenor and Rochonan galloped side by side, and Helecanth put her warhorn to her lips and relayed them to the knights that followed: *Break for the* tuathal *flank. Force it back into the center.*

It was a proven strategy, especially when the enemy could not call up reserves to replace his losses. Since Thoromarth had not been able to position his reserves off the field, effectively he had no reserves—all his force was committed at the same time. The flanking positions were traditionally a fast moving force, meant to sweep an enemy's fighters into the center where they could be hammered by heavy cavalry. If Runacarendalur could force Thoromarth's *tuathal* flank into the body of his main force, he could not only destroy the flanking force but attack the center at a weak point. The main body of the column would have no place to go: if it retreated, the *deosil* wing would be behind it.

It should have worked.

Instead, as soon as Runacarendalur's advance force was fully committed to an attack on the *tuathal* side, the whole of Thoromarth's force spun as if it were a millstone turning on its axis. The *tuathal* flank was not forced against the center: the center swung right as the *tuathal* flank retreated in good order and the *deosil* flank elongated and galloped across what had—seconds before—been the center. In another few moments Runacarendalur's advance force would be trapped between the two flanking forces while the former center line—now an enormously overfull *deosil* flank—continued its inexorable advance on his camp.

It was a stunning innovation in tactics.

Thoromarth could not have done this, Runacarendalur realized, even as his troop spun and struck the wing of Oronviel's army that was coming up behind them. He could no longer see the whole of the battlefield. In moments, it had become a dizzying blur of knights and flashing swords.

And it is but four candlemarks to sunset, and how are you to shape the course of the battle if you are in it?

From the moment he'd proposed this expedition against Oronviel, Runacarendalur had held in his mind the image of how it would go: a raiding party cutting a swathe of destruction across the land from the border towers to the walls of Oronviel's Great Keep. There he would face the force Oronviel placed in the field against him; at the sight of the red pennions flying from Caerthalien's standards, the knights of Ivrithir would flee to their own domain. . . .

That was the dream, and he had not been willing to let go of it. And so he had led his knights into battle as if this were a raiding party. It did not matter that there was no plan of battle to oversee, no order of battle for him to shape and direct, nor that his knights would have been thrown into even greater disorder if he had not led them himself. He had made a disastrous miscalculation—and Caerthalien would pay the price of it.

Father wished me to bring back the army intact. . . .

That was already impossible. But if he could slay Vieliessar, the act would redeem at least a part of his folly. He risked a glance at the larger force surrounding him. Yes. There. The standard of Oronviel. She would be beneath it.

He began to fight his way toward it.

It had taken Vieliessar two days to reach her army, and two days more for her army to reach Caerthalien's force. Lord Luthilion had announced his desire to fight at her side—audacious, for it would show Caerthalien Araphant's disloyalty—and rather than subject the aged War Prince to the long and grueling ride to her western border, she'd told Celeharth to Send to her Lightborn and bring Lord Luthilion west by Mage Door. Then Vieliessar rode west as fast as she could. It was frustrating, for there was a Flower Forest half a day's ride from Greenstone Tower, and she might have walked into it and out into Mornenamei in the same candlemark. But accompanied by her *komen,* she could not—she could not raise the matter of changing what the Lightborn were permitted to do at the same moment Caerthalien was invading in force.

She left Sorodiarn behind at the first change of horses. The journey was not a matter of pleasant rides and soft beds, but of galloping from manor house to manor house, bringing word of the attack and leaving with fresh mounts. Messengers from Thoromarth, from Rithdeliel, from Gunedwaen met her on the road, and so she learned her army already marched to meet Caerthalien. Lord Thoromarth had put them underway the moment word had come to Oronviel Keep.

Gunedwaen led her infantry in Thoromarth's wake, but not to the battlefield. Gunedwaen's place would be a day's ride from Oronviel Keep, for Hawkwind's sentries had not seen a supply train traveling with Caer thalien's army, and if Caerthalien defeated Vieliessar's army—or simply broke through it—the farmsteads of the Manorial Lands would be their target.

Since the moment she became War Prince, Vieliessar had been accustoming her army to the idea that it was more important to win a battle than to adhere to the ceremonial Code of Battle designed to turn war into an eternal game. Once she reached her army, she reinforced that lesson one more time: *The purpose of war is to win so no more battles need to be fought. To win a battle, you must hurt your enemy. Not in some agreed-upon way Healers can put right so his knights can attack you again—but hurt him so he will never want to face you again.*

In this battle, all her teaching, all her hopes, were to be tested. If they lost here, her army would go back to fighting in the ways it knew, and carry with it the seeds of their defeat. But when the enemy was in sight, her *komen* did everything in the way she had taught them. At her order, they attacked at once rather than allowing Caerthalien a night of rest and planning. When Caerthalien took the field with only a fraction of their own numbers, they did not attempt to break off the battle and offer the chance of a negotiated surrender.

And when the enemy's camp was within reach, Vieliessar's *komen* didn't pretend it wasn't because it would be discourteous to spoil the enemy's comfort.

꘎

Gwaenor reared, striking out at the enemy knight with steel-shod forehooves. The enemy knight's destrier tried to escape, but there was nowhere to go in the press of warriors and horses. The armored figure toppled from the saddle. If he made any sound as he died, it was lost in the clangor of battle.

Runacarendalur no longer knew how long he'd been fighting, nor if Caerthalien was winning. He only knew Oronviel's standard was near, that the maddening figure in the blood-spattered silver armor was beneath it, and that he must see her slain if he was ever to know peace again. He roweled Gwaenor's flanks mercilessly, asking the impossible from the great black stallion. Gwaenor snapped and kicked, forcing his way ever closer to Runacarendalur's goal. Runacarendalur tightened the fingers of his free hand around his dagger, his eyes fixed upon Vieliessar. He could not stab her, but he could stab her mount. In the heat of battle destriers rarely noticed injuries, but a fatal blow—something that would bring the golden stallion to his knees—would fling Vieliessar to the ground to be trampled to death. . . .

As if his thoughts were a shout she could hear, Vieliessar turned and stared directly at him. Even with her visor in place, Runacarendalur imagined he could see her eyes.

No.

Some thought of Bonding as a gift, the greatest gift Queen Pelashia had given the children of the Fortunate Lands. Some thought of it as a curse, for it linked two souls together—no matter what heart and mind might wish—so tightly that if one half of a Bonding died, the other would soon follow. Still others, more cynical, thought of it as a myth, either lie or delusion or something crafted of both.

Runacarendalur of Caerthalien looked into the eyes of Vieliessar, born of Farcarinon, now War Prince of Oronviel, and knew the Soulbond of Pelashia Celenthodiel for a curse and no delusion. He felt as if he'd been struck over the heart with a hammer and he knew with a cer-

tainty that transcended thought that Vieliessar was as furious, as horrified, as he was.

*It cannot be set aside, it cannot be undone—one may delay it, knowing
what is to come—refuse it—and live all one's years as a hungry ghost—but
that is all.*

He could not even tell, in this single blinding moment of *oneness*,
which of them was thinking.

He'd been warned, seeing her in the distance as she led her army to
battle. He hadn't recognized the warning.

Bonded.

*Soul*bonded.

Bonded *forever.*

If he'd managed to kill Vieliessar before that horrifying flash of *understanding*, could he have kept this from happening?

The moment was so terrible and all-consuming that Runacarendalur
did something he'd hadn't done since long before he won his spurs: he
forgot he was in the middle of a battle surrounded by armed and armored knights who were using all of their considerable skill to try to *kill
him.* He wasn't sure how long his inattention lasted. All he knew was that
someone was hitting him on the rerebrace that covered his upper arm—
not to injure him, but to gain his attention. He started in surprise, turning in his seat, clutching his sword. He'd dropped his dagger.

Helecanth pointed back toward the camp. She didn't bother to speak;
it would have been impossible to hear her. *Hurry,* she signaled, and
Runacarendalur signed assent.

Haste was a thing easier asked than provided, however. They moved
away from the standards of Oronviel, Ivrithir, and Araphant in whatever
direction offered them space to maneuver. But the farther they got from
the tight cluster of knights, the more they drew the attention of the enemy, and the more often they had to stop to fight their way free. It was
only when Runacarendalur realized he could barely tell Caerthalien's
green and gold from Ivrithir's black and tawny that he realized they'd
fought on past sunset. The false day of twilight would vanish swiftly and

without warning, but Runacarendalur was no longer certain that darkness would bring an end to Oronviel's attack.

He was no longer certain about anything.

His life was in the keeping of one whom everyone from the Astromancer to his mother wanted dead. More than anything, he wanted to ride back to her side. But what he'd do when he got there, Runacarendalur didn't know.

"You have to call the retreat!" Helecanth shouted when they had a moment's breathing space.

"They'll call the night halt soon, and—" Even as he spoke, Runacarendalur realized his words were ridiculous. Was he actually suggesting that an army that attacked in mid-afternoon without stopping to announce the terms of battle would call off the fighting with nightfall simply because it was civilized and customary?

"There's no camp for us to go back to!" Helecanth shouted.

The unbelievable statement shocked Runacarendalur's mind from the last of its daze, and in a few brief sentences, Helecanth explained.

When they'd struck the *tuathal* flank of Oronviel's army, the army had pivoted in place to encircle Runacarendalur's force. By that time, the rest of his knights were aware they were under attack and they took the field even though they had no clear plan of battle to guide them. In its absence, they'd done what seemed to be the most sensible thing: avoiding the center and the heavily reinforced right flank, they rode to attack the left.

"—and Oronviel's *tuathal* wing continued to retreat, pulling our army in after it, until eventually the whole of our force was engaged, and what had been elements of Oronviel's rear guard were facing our camp." Helecanth shrugged. "So they rode down into it."

They cleared the edge of the battle and rode wide to avoid its outliers. In the dusk, neither destrier wished to gallop, and Runacarendalur thought dismally of what would happen if they went lame or broke a leg. But it wasn't until they reached the place where Caerthalien had made camp only a few scant candlemarks before that Runacarendalur realized the full scope of his failure.

No horses. No pavilions. No servants. Nothing, in fact, that he recognized as being the neatly organized camp with its pavilions of bright silk. Even the Lightborn were gone, and—

"Ladyholder Glorthiachiel!" Runacarendalur said in horror. For just one instant, he forgot about being Soulbonded. "They've taken her prisoner!"

"I don't know," Helecanth said, troubled. "I *do* know we need to retreat—if we can. I don't think you were near any of them during the fighting, but— Did you see any knights on the field wearing Oronviel colors, but in brown armor?"

"Mercenaries," Runacarendalur said realizing what she meant. Few sellswords began their lives as *komen* of the Hundred Houses, and those who did were often fortunate to escape their former masters with their lives, let alone with armor, sword, and destrier. Mercenaries did not wear armor in the bright colors of the *komen*. They greased their armor lavishly and then roasted it carefully; the burned-on grease created a weatherproof coating that made them nearly invisible at night. "We knew she was taking them into her army."

"And adopting their tactics," Helecanth said grimly. "Oh, they abide by the Code of Battle if they're paid to. And if they're paid to ignore it, they do that too."

"Sound the retreat," Runacarendalur said. He'd never imagined a simple sentence could hurt so much to say. "We need to find our Lightborn. They'll be able to find Mother."

Now that he stood looking down into the chasm of this disaster, Runacarendalur could see so very clearly all the steps that had led him here. Dismissing the lack of information from within Oronviel as unimportant. Dismissing the alliance between Oronviel and Ivrithir as meaningless. Believing Thoromarth still ruled Oronviel when every action Oronviel took was one Thoromarth would never have considered taking even if he'd managed to think of it. Riding heedlessly to the attack when Oronviel moved to engage, even though that was the final warning of how changed things were in Oronviel since Harvest.

In the distance, Runacarendalur heard another warhorn take up the call to retreat. For a moment it was drowned out by a mocking volley from the enemy: *No quarter—No quarter—No quarter*—echoed across the battlefield like the sound of a scolding jackdaw. He'd thought riding under the red pennion would be a useful convention that would allow him to execute any prisoners he took without breaking with the Code of Battle. But once he'd displayed the red pennion, his enemy was not bound to show mercy any more than he was.

His army would be slaughtered where it fell.

"I must—" Runacarendalur began, about to urge Gwaenor forward.

"You must *not*," Helecanth said urgently, reaching out and placing her hand on his destrier's rein. "We do not know how many we have lost. But if *you* are lost, Prince Runacarendalur, the army will have no leader. And *all* will be lost."

Wise as it was, Helecanth's counsel was bitter to hear.

And now there was nothing to do but wait.

❧❦❧

Every Lightborn studied the Soulbond, for it was a riddle and a mystery: a thing of the Light—of Magery—that appeared among the Lightless. Without warning, without explanation. It behaved as if it were a spell, but unlike a spell, it could not be broken.

She'd known what was happening. Trapped in the midst of the melee, there'd been nothing she could do. She was already Warded against the thoughts of the injured and dying. There were no more powerful Wards she could summon.

It might have been delayed, even averted entirely, for all those who wrote of Soulbonding agreed that for the Bond to form, the two halves of the Bonding must be near each other. The scholars also spoke of desire, but the only desire she'd possessed was to win the battle.

Perhaps that had been all that was needed.

But those were things she thought of much later, when it was not necessary to spend every beat of her heart on surviving—and not merely surviving, but winning in the best way to further her need. The *land's* need.

She'd prepared her commanders carefully on the journey here, from those who commanded a twelve to those who commanded twelve times twelve, so each would know what must be done before they engaged the enemy. She was grateful she'd done so much, for once the battle began it was impossible to know what was going on more than a few feet away. Rithdeliel and Gunedwaen and even Thoromarth had spoken of battles into which a commander could send a messenger to order a meisne to withdraw and could direct the battle as the huntsman directed the hunting pack. But those were not the sort of battles she was fighting.

The orders she had given to Nadalforo as she set her company to ride in the army's fantail had surprised the former mercenary commander but had not shocked her.

"*Loot the camp and take their horses?*" she said, looking pleased. "*Ah, Lord Vieliessar, you're wasted as a War Prince!*"

"*There will be Lightborn and servants in the camp,*" Vieliessar said. "*Harm none of them. Offer them sanctuary. Drive those who will not accept it far from the camp.*"

She did not know, in the press of the fighting, whether Nadalforo had been successful or not. Just as it became too dark to see, she heard the Caerthalien warhorns signaling retreat, and the flurry of mockery from her own knights-herald in reply.

If Caerthalien retreats, it means I have won.

"Disengage!" she shouted into Bethacrian's ear. Bethaerian shoved back her visor and raised her warhorn to her lips. The signal echoed around the field: as it was received, her knights stopped pursuing the enemy.

⚜

There should have been bright, cheerful torches, servants offering cups of mulled wine or tall tankards of ale, cloudy globes of Silverlight shedding their eldritch radiance over the camp and the battlefield.

Instead, there was cold and darkness and the screaming of wounded horses. At least the Oronviel forces were signaling to disengage. He could be grateful for that much.

As more of Caerthalien's knights rode to where the camp should have been—and wasn't—Helecanth switched from sounding the retreat to sounding the call to muster. At last there came the welcome glow of Silverlight through the trees. Runacarendalur let out a long breath of relief. He had not thought his Lightborn would be harmed, but when he had seen what had happened to the camp . . .

The tale the returning servants and Lightborn told was as grim as the battle itself. Knights in Oronviel colors rode down on the camp as soon as the last of the Caerthalien knights had entered the battle. They struck down the guards on the horselines, and as some gathered the livestock together, others ordered all who wished to live to run for their lives. Then they drove the horses and oxen through the camp. The pavilions and their contents were wrecked. The few wagons of supplies—mostly grain for the destriers—were carried off.

"And Ladyholder Glorthiachiel?" Runacarendalur asked, his mouth dry with fear.

"Here."

Her voice was brittle with rage, but Runacarendalur had never heard any sound so welcome. She was riding the destrier of some slain knight, with Carangil Lightbrother leading it.

"I think we can safely consider your betrothal to Oronviel at an end," Ladyholder Glorthiachiel said waspishly. "Your betrothed is gone."

"She ran away?" He'd seen Princess Nanduil only a handful of times—including his betrothal ceremony—and could not imagine . . .

"Had your witless *komentai'a* not ordered my guard to hold us both *prisoner*," Ladyholder Glorthiachiel spat, "I might yet have preserved her for your wedding. But first we *retreated*—" the word was a vile curse in her mouth "—and then they *died*."

"They let you go," he said, light-headed with relief. Oronviel would have taken no prisoners to ransom.

"Yes!" she said. "If you can call it that when I was dragged from my own wagon and set afoot. They carried off the wagon and your annoying bride-to-be. And rather than await the next party of knights, Carangil and I made our way to the wood to await your victory and the return of my wagon. You do not seem to have brought me either."

"Be grateful they spared your life," Runacarendalur answered, relief transmuted to cold fury by fear of what-might-have-been. "Do you see among us here any swordless knights who left the field under parole? We fought without quarter. I do not yet know how many dead there will be."

As the servants returned, he set them to picking through the wreckage of the camp to salvage what they could. There wasn't much. Bedding had been trampled into muck, carpets and furniture were smashed and befouled, provisions were gone. He ordered Carangil Lightbrother to Call back their stolen livestock, only to be told such a use of the Light was not permitted, as it would constitute tactical aid to an army in battle. At least Carangil and the other Lightborn were willing to Call water, since the horses and their riders were thirsty, and fire, since there was no shortage of things to burn.

"Do you think they will attack again tonight?" Helecanth asked, as if she were speaking of a tribe of Beastlings and not the army of one of the Hundred Houses.

"I don't know," Runacarendalur said wearily.

It was full dark now. The battlefield was lit by globes of Silverlight: he could see Oronviel's Lightborn on it, seeing if any survived. It was a small break with custom—the Lightborn did not enter a battlefield even when the day's fighting was over—but it was a break. Another break. He did not have fingers and toes enough to enumerate all the ways Oronviel had outraged the Code of Battle today.

His own camp looked as much like a battlefield as the ground over which they'd fought. Exhausted knights clustered around a hundred small fires, sharing the contents of their wineskins and waterskins. *Four days to our border. No remounts. No shelter. Nothing along our line of march, because we burned it all on our approach.*

And worst of all, he'd lost two-thirds of the army.

There might be a few more survivors found by dawn. Half the servants hadn't come back yet, after all. But as soon as there'd been Silverlight to see by, he and Helecanth had done a rough tally. Eleven hundred of Caerthalien's *komen* had survived.

Far in the distance, Runacarendalur imagined he could make out the constellation of colored lights that was Oronviel's—and Araphant's and Ivrithir's—camp. For a moment he was filled with the wild desire to fling himself upon Gwaenor's back and ride madly toward those bright pavilions. To seek out hers, to put an end to her victory celebration, to put an end to this day.

To put an end to *her.*

⚒

"S top pacing," Thoromarth said. "Anyone would think we hadn't won today."

"A battle—not the war!" Vieliessar answered.

"And at Midwinter I would have said we could not do even that much," Thoromarth answered. "Yet Caerthalien's force lies broken and ours does not. More than that, I have my Nanduil with me again, little though she values that."

Vieliessar had expected Nadalforo to bring her the livestock from the Caerthalien camp. She had not expected to be presented with a weeping and furious princess as well. "I suppose I should be grateful that Nadalforo didn't slay Glorthiachiel of Caerthalien," she said reluctantly, and Rithdeliel laughed, raising his cup in salute.

"Since you wish to avoid open war with Caerthalien for the present, yes," he said. "Though frankly, were I Bolecthindial of Caerthalien, I should not regret her loss overmuch," he added.

Vieliessar looked around her pavilion at her allies and those of her senior commanders who had remained following her victory celebration. Oronviel had won today, and even though they would fight again tomorrow—for she meant to harass Caerthalien across every foot of Oronviel's land—they were entitled to a moment of rejoicing.

"Araphant fought with distinction today," she said. "I thank you for the alliance, Lord Luthilion."

Luthilion waved the compliment aside. "Your tactics were an astonishment to me," he said mildly. "It is true, then, what Celeharth has always told me. There are always new things to be seen in the world. Araphant has little to offer you. But you shall have all that she holds." He bowed without rising; the battle would have exhausted a knight far younger than he, and since Celeharth Lightborn had come from the Healing Tents, he had been attempting to get his Lord to seek his rest.

"You've taken enough blooded livestock to mount these 'foot knights' of yours, at least," Rithdeliel said. "We'll need to wait for dawn to get a true count, but the Healers say Caerthalien's losses were heavy."

"They were." Thurion stood in the doorway, his eyes distant. "Lord Vieliessar, your wounded are tended. Our casualties were light. Many injured, few deaths."

"I would have given odds against that when I saw the red pennion," Thoromarth said.

"I knew when Caerthalien came against us they would seek to slay all they could," Vieliessar said, gesturing to Thurion to enter. "Caerthalien will not rest until the last of Farcarinon is dead." For an instant the years dropped away and she was a child once more, hearing her true name and her fate from Ladyholder Glorthiachiel in Caerthalien's Great Hall.

"If you die, my prince, it is not today," Thoromarth said.

"No, but—" She hesitated, on the verge of blurting out the thing that had happened. She shook her head. "No, I did not die today."

CHAPTER TEN

FIRE AND FLIGHT

"Should" and "would" and "ought" are three great armies who always fight on the enemy side.

— Toncienor of Caerthalien, *The Swordmaster's Book*

"We must go. Now," Helecanth said.

"You're right," Runacarendalur said heavily.

When the first of the Lightborn had returned, he'd ordered word sent to Caerthalien Keep, for little as he wished Lord Bolecthindial to know of his defeat and disgrace, the information was urgent. Once again, he glanced toward the Oronviel camp. Desire warred with desire: if he'd had the least hope he could mount a successful attack, he would have done so. But the destruction of the camp had finished the task the disastrous fight had begun. The knights of Caerthalien had no more heart for battle. *We cannot be all that remain,* Runacarendalur thought, and each time the idea occurred to him, it was as if it were a fresh wound.

"Come, my lord," Helecanth said gently. "We will do this quietly."

Runacarendalur nodded. He led Gwaenor through the shattered camp, pausing at each cluster of knights to pass the order. Gathering them to march could have been done in an instant with the signal horns, but Helecanth was right: the sound would only alert their enemy. And who knew what they would do?

Beyond the far edge of the destruction, Runacarendalur found Ladyholder Glorthiachiel and Carangil Lightbrother. Glorthiachiel was seated on a battered storage chest, a cup in her hand, and someone's fur-lined stormcloak about her shoulders.

Trust Mother to make herself as comfortable as possible.

"Come," Runacarendalur said. "We're leaving."

"So I see," Ladyholder Glorthiachiel said acidly. "Slinking away like curs whipped to kennel."

"If you wish," he answered. "It is not as if Caerthalien has not suffered defeat before. If you wish to stay and explain to Oronviel how that is impossible, of course, I will not compel you to accompany us."

"Would that you'd showed a fraction of such spirit in battle today," Ladyholder Glorthiachiel said. She rose to her feet, handing her cup to Carangil. "My horse," she said.

Carangil led the destrier over and assisted Ladyholder Glorthiachiel to mount. It was undoubtedly just as well, Runacarendalur thought, that Carangil Lightbrother was able to bespell the animal to docility. He didn't doubt his mother's ability to browbeat any living thing into submission, but the need to do so wouldn't sweeten her temper.

Not that anything would at this point.

"You said you would bring back her head," Ladyholder Glorthiachiel said, in an undertone sharp enough to etch steel. "You said the Household knights would be sufficient to rout Oronviel's meisne and a pack of low-born mercenaries."

I did not know I would be facing the daughter of Serenthon Farcarinon, Runacarendalur thought. He walked beside Ladyholder Glorthiachiel's mount, leading Gwaenor. All around them, the remains of Caerthalien's Household knights moved westward, more a disordered throng of refugees rather than an army. Some knights led exhausted destriers. Others rode. There were no horses or wagons for the servants, the Lightborn, or the arming pages. Some of the servants walked beside their masters. Some simply stood and wept as the column slowly formed and began to move—unable to believe any of this was happening, unable to believe they must retrace the distance they had come

At first he thought they would be pursued, for the movement of so many people and horses was not quiet. But to his faint astonishment, no one came. After a while, the column began to move with something resembling organization, for the knights were used to riding to war and their servants were used to following orders. To make sure no one was falling behind—though there was little he could do if they were—Runacarendalur mounted Gwaenor and forced the destrier to trot up and down the slow-moving column of servants and knights.

Gwaenor was irritable and short-tempered, snapping at anyone who was near and lashing out with his heels. It was no more than the other destriers were doing—in their experience, a battle was followed by food and rest—but it made them difficult to control and impossible to ride or lead as a close-packed group. The Lightborn could bespell them—just as Carangil had bespelled Ladyholder Glorthiachiel's mount—but that could be disastrous if they needed to give battle quickly. For now, it was enough that the Lightborn led the column and lit the way, that the remains of the army had formed up into their usual meisnes, that everyone was moving.

He would not think about what must happen when they had to stop: the Lightborn could Call water at need, but the army had no food at all.

"Prince Runacarendalur." A voice at his side jarred Runacarendalur out of his uncomfortable thoughts.

"Nimrosian."

The commander of the Caerthalien Household *komentai'a* smiled effortfully. "We have had better days, have we not, my prince?"

The wry understatement was almost enough to make Runacarendalur laugh. "Far better, old friend."

"Yet this day is not lost, unless you and Ladyholder Glorthiachiel are lost," Nimrosian continued. "Four days to the border—if not more. Yet if you and the lady were to ride on ahead . . ."

"And leave you?" Runacarendalur said, horrified. To abandon one's command on the field was worse than foolishness. It was cowardice.

"We are of little value to Oronviel," Nimrosian said. "Lord Bolecthindial will ransom us, should we surrender. Or avenge us, if our surrender is not accepted. But you and Ladyholder Glorthiachiel would be great prizes. The ransom Oronviel might ask would be ruinous indeed."

"He's right," Helecanth said. "A small party can move fast. And a troop of horse could meet us at the border crossing and even cross the border to bring Ladyholder Glorthiachiel to safety."

"Then you must—" Runacarendalur began.

"You are the only one of sufficient rank to curb the lady's . . . courage," Nimrosian said tactfully. "I beg you, Prince Runacarendalur. For her safety, if not for yours. Go, now. If you are well away by dawn we may be able to convince them you yet ride with us."

He knew they were right, but it was agony to admit it. "I must have another horse. She will not permit Carangil to be left behind."

"I will see to it," Nimrosian said. "Will you inform the lady?"

"Yes," Runacarendalur said, sighing.

"I will remain here," Helecanth said, before Runacarendalur could order her to accompany him. "My armor is known to Thoromarth, and I must bear your standard. Elerosha will ride with you. I will send him to you."

"You must—" For a moment, he could not summon words. "You must send to me, if you are captured. Not to my father."

Even though he could not see it, he heard the smile in her voice as she replied. "I shall expect you to beggar yourself to pay my ransom. Now go."

It seemed only the work of moments for Runacarendalur to reach the front of the column and explain Nimrosian's plan. Ladyholder Glorthiachiel received his speech in an icy silence, giving him the barest nod of assent. Then Elerosha arrived, leading a second destrier. Carangil laid his hands upon its neck and its wild-eyed trembling subsided.

The four riders trotted into the darkness. Soon they had left the slow-moving column behind.

⊰⧓⊱

It was still grey dawn when her chamber-page roused Vieliessar, bringing the word of Oronviel's sentries that Caerthalien's army had stolen away in the night, just as she'd suspected it would. She decided to take five hundred horse to follow the remains of Caerthalien's army and leave two hundred more to guard her supply train. The rest of her people could return to their duties, for no matter how crushing a defeat she had given Caerthalien, this attack might still be a feint to cloak another.

As they rode across the battlefield, flocks of carrion birds startled up from the tangled bodies; in the grey mist of morning she saw the low, slinking shapes of other predators ghost away until they could feed undisturbed once more. Her people would not return to the Great Keep until Oronviel's dead had been removed from the field, but those belonging to Caerthalien would lie here until they rotted.

It was almost impossible to say where the battlefield ended and Caerthalien's camp began. The only difference between the two was that in the camp, the wreckage of bodies was replaced by the wreckage of things: everything a princely army carried to war, shattered and spoiled.

By the time they'd passed both battlefield and camp, the day was bright and the ground was even. Vieliessar's company moved to the trot. They had only gone a few miles when they encountered the first of the Caerthaliens. Their plain dull clothing marked them as lesser servants, those who performed menial work: setting the tents, fetching and carrying. They leaped to their feet at the sound of horses and clustered so closely around Vieliessar's force that the knights were forced to rein their destriers to a halt.

"Vieliessar High King! Vieliessar High King!" First one, then another, spoke the words, until all of them cried her name together as they crowded forward, reaching out to touch her. "Vieliessar High King!"

The destriers began to fret and dance, unhappy at being crowded. Moved—and more than a little frightened by the power of what she had unleashed—she reached out to touch the hands of those who reached out for her. *They look to me for protection now,* she realized. *Not because I am their War Prince but because I will be their King.*

"Let us pass," Bethaerian demanded, her voice tight with tension. "Our supply wagons follow us—you will be fed!"

"Let me pass," Vieliessar said to those nearest to her. "I am not yet High King."

Slowly the crowd moved away, opening a pathway through which the company could ride.

"There is a stream only a little way to the south," Bethaerian said as they rode on. "Do they not hear it?"

"Castel servants," another *komen* answered dismissively. "They have no more wits than sheep."

"Say rather that they are in a strange place, and those lords they looked to for protection have left them," Vieliessar corrected sharply. Gaellas ducked his head, acknowledging the rebuke, but it would take far more than a few small corrections to change the way the *komentai'a* thought.

This was the first group of stragglers they encountered, but not the last. Some sat unmoving at the side of the road, some fled at their approach, some continued walking, but many, seeing her banner, hailed Vieliessar as High King. Whether they wore leather and rough homespun or the silken livery of household servants, the expression on every face was the same.

Hope.

Seeing them and realizing that her promise had been heard and taken to heart even in the stronghold of her enemy, Vieliessar suddenly knew victory was possible. To all who begged for aid, Bethaerian made the same reply as before: their supplies followed.

"They will only steal all they can lay hands on and flee," Bethaerian grumbled as they rode on.

"Back to masters who have abandoned them?" Vieliessar asked. "No. They are my people now."

At midmorning, a cloud of dust hanging above the road before them signaled the passage of Caerthalien's army. "Sound the call to battle."

The enemy forces seemed to scatter in all directions at the first notes of the warhorn, but Vieliessar knew that was merely those afoot moving out of the way of the knights. When they were yet a mile distant, Vieliessar ordered Bethaerian to sound the charge, and they moved from trot, to canter, to gallop. The Caerthalien knights turned in column to face them, and Vieliessar could see Prince Runacarendalur's standard in the first rank.

But he is not here. I can tell it. She could not say how she knew, for it was not possible to see anything clearly in the moment the point of her formation struck their ranks. But she was as certain of it as she was of the count of her own fingers and toes. There was an instant for relief that she did not need to fear for her hated enemy's safety—and anger, for he had abandoned his army and fled, perhaps beyond her reach—and then she was embattled.

She had not let herself think about what had happened on yesterday's battlefield. The storysingers made of Soulbonding a thing that overshadowed both will and common sense, and in the instant she had seen him, she had known both were true, for from the moment the Bond had been formed, she had thought of nothing but killing him. Death would be kinder than a lifetime linked to one who embodied everything she had come to despise—princely arrogance and royal ambition. She remembered Prince Runacarendalur from her childhood: a shining, distant figure who was the embodiment of all she wished to become.

I will not be his consort. I cannot take him as mine—I cannot say to Rithdeliel and Gunedwaen and Thoromarth and all who may come to fight for me: spare Runacarendalur of Caerthalien, for if he should die, I die as well. . . .

She led her company to the left of Caerthalien's center. Gunedwaen had often said a Swordmaster took the greatest hurts from his most unskilled students, simply because they did that which no training could predict. Exhaustion and desperation in the Caerthalien knights lent their attacks the same unpredictability: the blow against which one defended might go high, or low, or strike the knight beside one instead. Worse yet was the moment the back of the Caerthalien column—inspired by some masterful leader—began to swing to *deosil*, for if the column could turn, it might manage to bring forward a large enough force to block her line of retreat and encircle her force.

But the battleground was hemmed in by those who were not lawful targets under the Code of Battle, and knights and destriers collided disastrously with servants and pages who had thought themselves safely on the sidelines of the field. The obvious thing for Caerthalien to do was retreat up the road—the knights might not care about the lives of their servants, but the confusion left them vulnerable to enemy attack. But Vieliessar heard no Caerthalien signal to retreat and regroup, and suddenly she realized that Caerthalien *could not withdraw.* She'd seen no Green Robes in the crowds at the edges of the column and that meant that if any Lightborn had been part of the retreat, they had been leading it, and were now behind the army. Even Lightborn could not outrun blood-maddened warhorses. If the Caerthalien knights broke and fled—if the rearward ranks retreated—the Lightborn would be trampled to death.

She could not afford to care. Could not retreat, hoping Caerthalien would follow, and thus ensure the safety of those who might have been her friends, her comrades, her students. *The purpose of war is to win,* she told herself bleakly, and banished thoughts of the Lightborn from her mind.

Then, as if Caerthalien was a river and a dam had burst, the knights facing Oronviel's swords simply fell away. Vieliessar struck the foe before her hard enough to topple him from the saddle. His destrier reared up, menacing her with its forehooves, but her mount sprang backward with ease, for there was suddenly space through which to maneuver.

She raised her bloodied sword, brandishing it in the direction of the enemy, and spurred Grillet in pursuit. The bay stallion danced along the road, springing into the air to vault fallen bodies, dodging around injured horses. Behind her, Vieliessar heard the call for the chase: *follow, follow, follow.* It was not a battle call, but a hunting call: there was never any need to chase a force of enemy knights on the field. She could hear the thunder of hooves; slowly the front rank of her knights drew level with her. Before them, Caerthalien fled as if it ran with the Starry Hunt Itself. They could not keep to such a bruising pace for long, but it would not matter. Vieliessar galloped her company after them until she judged they had covered several miles, then began to rein Grillet in. It was difficult to do, for he wanted to run, but she managed it at last, sending him onward at a slow trot until the company had reformed behind her.

"We could have run them until their horses were blown!" one of her *komen* objected when they were moving at a slow walk.

"Yes," Vieliessar agreed. "But—did you see? They held their place during the battle for fear of overrunning those behind them: their Lightborn, it must be. And then they ran. So let us go back and find those Lightborn. Once they are in my care, we may harass Caerthalien as we wish."

"That is a good thought, Lord Vieliessar," Bethaerian said, plainly relieved at her reason for abandoning the chase. "Let us seek them out."

When they retraced their steps, they reached a place where the dead had been moved aside, servant and knight piled together, and the road had been filled with the injured. The Lightborn moved among the wounded, offering Healing. Vieliessar counted no more than a dozen of them. A force the size of Caerthalien's would have traveled with fifty Lightborn, perhaps more.

"Who is senior among you?" Vieliessar called, reining in.

By their reaction, the Lightborn had expected her to pass without stopping. There was a quick murmured colloquy between three of them, then one walked forward. "I am Pantaradet Lightsister," she said.

"You are not all the Lightborn that traveled with Runacarendalur's army," Vieliessar said.

Pantaradet shook her head. "We are all who returned to aid the injured," she said simply. "Lord Vieliessar, you were once one of us. Please. We must have food, shelter, a place where these injured may rest. They have done you no harm."

"Summon to you all the Lightborn who rode with Caerthalien," Vieliessar answered. "Give yourselves into my care, and I will care for those you have Healed as well. All may come to me who were in Caerthalien's service."

A look almost of awe broke over Pantaradet's features. "It is true," she said, as if the words were torn from her all unwilling. "I had heard— I did not believe—"

"I shall be High King, Pantaradet Lightsister," Vieliessar said. "And you will be my people. I would have you safe while I make war on those who would make war upon me."

Pantaradet nodded, and for a moment it seemed she might speak further. Whatever she thought of saying, she decided against it. She nodded again instead. "I will summon them, Lord Vieliessar. We are sixty in number."

It was a reasonable count of Lightborn Healers to accompany three thousand knights—especially if one did not intend to have any enemy wounded to Heal. Vieliessar sent Orannet and Janondiel back to her supply wagons to bring supplies for the Healers, then sent two hundred of her *komen* to follow the Caerthalien knights and keep them moving. She waited until the wagons had arrived and the wounded were loaded. Then, at last, she pursued Caerthalien once more.

If only she had been able to take Runacarendalur of Caerthalien prisoner this morning, the day would have held nothing but joy.

After eight interminable days spent fleeing Oronviel, Runacarendalur was filthy and tired, and he *ached*. The four of them had been met at the border by a demi-taille of *komen*—Father's personal guard— and a dozen Lightborn. With fresh mounts, they reached Alqualanya Flower Forest a few candlemarks later, and then Carangil and those Lightborn with Door to Call moved them between Alqualanya and Rimroheth in a heartbeat. It had all been accomplished with such speed that no messenger could have sent word before them, but as Runacarendalur and Ladyholder Glorthiachiel walked from the center of Rimroheth, they found a familiar figure waiting for them.

"'Rulion," Runacarendalur said in surprise. "Am I to be laid in irons? Or do you come to rejoice at our dear mother's return? And mine, of course."

"You look like a Landbond," his brother said flatly. "But I came to warn you, because Light knows your servants won't."

"Warn us?" Ladyholder Glorthiachiel demanded. "Of what?"

"Father . . . entertains," Ivrulion said with heavy irony. "What news Runacarendalur sent of the battle disturbed him. And so we host Cirandeiron, and Aramenthiali, and Telthorelandor."

"What?" Runacarendalur and Ladyholder Glorthiachiel spoke almost in chorus. Runacarendalur could not have been more stunned if his brother had told him Vieliessar had conquered Caerthalien and was awaiting him here.

"Their armies, or . . . ?"

Ladyholder Glorthiachiel glared at him murderously, and Runacarendalur fell silent.

"Their War Princes," Ivrulion said. "And you should be grateful for that, Rune, for the army—what you left of it—is still a fortnight from the border. It is the absence of their provisions, their servants, and our Lightborn that slows them, I suppose, though really, when you consider the matter, a smaller—"

It took a moment for the sense of his brother's words to penetrate. "But the servants— Our Lightborn—" Runacarendalur said, in shock.

"Some of the servants—a few hundred—accompany them. None of our Lightborn."

"Oh, never mind that now! If Cirandeiron, Telthorelandor, and Aramenthiali are within our walls, why are we standing here talking?" Ladyholder Glorthiachiel demanded. "And we will enter by the siege gate, Ivrulion, for I will not permit our adventure in Oronviel to seem as if it were a disaster."

※

For one War Prince to come to another's domain meant either absolute trust between them—which was impossible—or a common goal so important that a temporary amnesty existed until that goal was

met. Runacarendalur did not have to ask why Cirandeiron, Aramenthiali, and Telthorelandor had been sent for: the timing was too exact.

Any thought he'd had—admittedly negligible—of telling anyone that
he had discovered himself to be the destined Bondmate of Vieliessar of
whatever-domain-she-claimed vanished. He suspected that revealing
this would dramatically shorten his life, but loyalty to Caerthalien had
made him at least consider it. But that had been when it would be a thing
known only to Caerthalien. If Father was conspiring with other War
Princes once more . . .

Runacarendalur picked up the winecup on the tray a servant had
brought to his room but set it down again. He'd been summoned to attend Father's gathering as soon as he was washed and dressed. He'd need
a clear head for that—he'd rather walk naked into an ice tiger's den at
Midwinter than deal with any of the Old Alliance. Or their consorts.

He regarded himself in the mirror and thought he looked presentable
enough. No one would think that for more than a sennight he'd been
sleeping under bushes and eating food he wouldn't throw to his hounds.
*I wonder how many Houses will remain of the ancient Hundred once the
dust of battle has settled this time?* he thought.

He gave a last tug to his tunic and walked from his chambers.

⚶

The old records called the chamber directly above the Great Hall the
Audience Chamber, but generations of War Princes had conducted
all their duties in the Great Hall, before the sight of all, or in their private
chambers, before the sight of none. Runacarendalur couldn't remember
the last time the Audience Chamber had actually been used. Just now it
had been dressed as a rather luxurious receiving chamber.

"—stromancer could have picked a more convenient time to enact
this foolishness," Runacarendalur heard as the servant opened the door.
It was Lord Girelrian—War Prince Girelrian of Cirandeiron—who spoke.
She was old enough to be her husband's greatmother, for she had taken

the throne early and ruled alone until the need to secure the Line caused her to make Irindandirion of Cirandeiron her Consort-Prince. Irindandirion was deadly upon the battlefield and fanatical about his clothes and jewels. He kept a dozen catamites and knew better than to involve himself in any matters of rule.

"Oronviel's timing in removing its Postulants from the Sanctuary is interesting," War Prince Ivaloriel Telthorelandor said. "Either Hamphuliadiel plots with Oronviel, or Oronviel wishes us to think he does. Either way, we have sufficient cause to encourage the Astromancer to resign— whether the Vilya has . . . ah . . . fruited, or not."

It was said no one had ever seen Lord Ivaloriel angry, even when the tide of battle turned against him. His detachment on the field was matched only by his even-handedness in ruling his domain; the War Prince of Telthorelandor ruled without favorites or intimates—except Ladyholder Edheleorn, his Bondmate. Runacarendalur barely flinched at the thought of Bonding; the fact that three War Princes were being hosted by a fourth was too shocking.

"Oh, but here is Runacarendalur!" An exquisitely dressed woman, all in green, left her husband's side and swept over to where Runacarendalur stood. She placed a hand upon his chest and gazed up at him meltingly. "Why, you are even more handsome than you were when I saw you last. Soon you will eclipse your father in beauty and I shall be lost."

"Ladyholder Dormorothon," Runacarendalur answered, his voice even. He didn't miss the look of cold venom Lord Manderechiel directed at his lady's back—and at him, for there were two things in the Fortunate Lands the War Prince of Aramenthiali hated above all others: his wife . . . and House Caerthalien.

Dormorothon was Manderechiel's second wife—his first marriage had been a love match, but Lady Ciamokene had died giving birth to Sedreret Heir-Prince, and Manderechiel had chosen to wed Dormorothon, for no Lightborn's children would ever challenge the progeny of his beloved Ciamokene for the right to succeed him. Dormorothon had been plotting even then; she made sure to bind Sedreret to her with ties stronger than blood. And now the tapestry of power patterned by the threads of her weaving was in danger of being disastrously unraveled.

"I see Mother is here before me. Have you yet had time to greet her
properly?" Runacarendalur asked, doing his best to feign obliviousness.
He walked with Dormorothon to where Ladyholder Glorthiachiel stood,
Ivrulion beside her. Ivrulion nodded fractionally as Runacarendalur's
eyes met his: the chamber was Warded against any use of Magery. Ladyholder Dormorothon was not thought to possess the Lightborn Magery
that would permit her to Hear the thoughts of others, but no one wanted
to take any chances.

*It is fortunate that 'Rulion has not also Warded this chamber against
lying, or it would burst into flames and kill us all,* Runacarendalur thought,
as Ladyholder Dormorothon and Ladyholder Glorthiachiel exchanged
remarks about how delighted they were to see each other again, and how
foolish it was for two Great Houses which should naturally be allies and
the closest of friends to ever fight. Runacarendalur avoided glancing toward Ladyholder Dormorothon's husband, for War Prince Manderechiel
and Ladyholder Glorthiachiel had hated each other for centuries, and
Aramenthiali would declare for Oronviel's cause in an instant if Vieliessar would promise him the chance to torture to death every member of
Caerthalien's Line Direct.

If not, of course, for his own overweening ambition.

*Four Great Houses. Four War Princes. And all wish to be High King—
except, perhaps, for Telthorelandor, and there I am simply not sure what
Lord Ivaloriel wants. I don't think anyone is, except perhaps Ladyholder
Edheleorn.*

Ivrulion's presence at the meeting was reasonable enough. As Caerthalien's Chief Lightborn, he was responsible for seeing that none of
Lord Bolecthindial's guests were poisoned or bespelled during their stay.
Runacarendalur, however, was in attendance for no purpose other than
to give a report of the campaign against Oronviel.

"Enough of this," Lord Manderechiel barked. "We take no joy in one another's company. We are here to discover why your heir made such a disastrous botch of a simple raid!"

"If it was so simple, my lord, I am surprised Aramenthiali did not precede Caerthalien to the field," Runacarendalur said. "You also share a border with Oronviel, do you not? But perhaps your spies are better than ours."

There was a moment of silence, then Ladyholder Dormorothon laughed.

"None of us has been able to gain any useful knowledge of matters within Oronviel, Prince Runacarendalur," Lord Ivaloriel said calmly. "I believe we all know much the same things: first Hamphuliadiel Astromancer demands Vieliessar Lightsister be returned to the Sanctuary—so we know she has left it—then we discover she has taken Oronviel from Lord Thoromarth through the exercise of an ancient custom no one has thought to set aside. At Midwinter she declares she will become High King. And now it is Rain, and all we have known for moonturns is rumor."

"One rumor is true," Runacarendalur answered. "The mercenaries who fight for her do so wearing Oronviel colors."

"You said 'they fight for *her*,'" Lord Girelrian said. "We have understood it is Thoromarth who leads the army of Oronviel."

"No," Runacarendalur said, shaking his head. "If that were so . . . I would have won the day. Vieliessar leads them into battle and fights as if she was born in armor."

Damn Father for this. And Mother too. How am I to know what they want me to say if I have not spoken to them privately first? But whatever else Runacarendalur might think of his family, his parents weren't stupid. It must be the truth—or a pretense of truth—he was here to offer. *And it is too much to hope that everyone's spies do not already know what remains of our Household guard, so truth it is. . . .* He recounted the events of that day and night as plainly as possible.

"I do not believe it," Ladyholder Dormorothon said, shaking her head decisively. "I met her while she was still at the Sanctuary—a simple child who knew nothing of the world. A gifted Healer, yes, but hardly a master Warlord."

"Believe what you choose," Runacarendalur said shortly. "If you prefer to think Thoromarth has somehow changed his entire way of waging war in half a year, then perhaps that is more likely."

"We do not need to fight with each other yet," Ladyholder Edheleorn said, implying, with good reason, that they would undoubtedly fight with one another later. "There might be many explanations for Oronviel's new ways."

"Perhaps," Runacarendalur said, fighting to hold to his temper. "Vieliessar may have found some gifted knight whose counsel she follows. Or perhaps one of her mercenaries plans her tactics. We have all made use of them, and we did not do so because they lost battles. But this much is true: she led her army herself and she did not die on the field. If she is not a master Warlord, then she is at least a blooded knight."

"Ah, Bolecthindial, perhaps you should have risked our ire these many years ago and betrothed the girl to your heir," Lord Manderechiel said. "I am sure we would not have asked so very much in reparations for that transgression. And he seems fonder of her than of the Oronviel Princess he has among other things—lost."

"Does your champion accompany you, Lord Manderechiel?" Runacarendalur asked with icy politeness.

"I think we can dispense with this foolishness, Manderechiel," Ladyholder Glorthiachiel said briskly. "We are here to decide what to do in the matter of Oronviel, not to provide Caerthalien with entertainment."

"What to do? To see Vieliessar Farcarinon dead, of course," Lord Manderechiel answered. "What else?"

I know it was a shameful and difficult thing to force you to," Lord Bolecthindial said, candlemarks later, "but it was necessary."

Runacarendalur had been allowed to escape the interrogation soon afterward. Rather than risk encountering the other War Princes or their

Households elsewhere in the castel, he'd gone directly to his rooms, only to find a message summoning him to attend his father later. He'd been even more surprised, when he'd come at the appointed candlemark, to find Lord Bolecthindial alone.

"How could it have been necessary to expose us in our weakness—and me in my folly?" he said irritably.

"I require my former allies to believe Oronviel to be a threat to all of us," Bolecthindial said.

"How can you believe it is not?" Runacarendalur demanded, stunned. "Vieliessar flouts the Code of Battle—she slaughtered most of the Household guard—she—"

"By drawing my old allies close and bleating in terror like a tethered kid, I gain concessions from Telthorelandor and Cirandeiron, and lull Aramenthiali," Bolecthindial answered calmly.

"Do not tell me you sent your knights to be slaughtered for that?" Runacarendalur said hoarsely. *Two-thirds of my army; she slaughtered two-thirds of my army. . . .*

"No," Bolecthindial shook his head. "I believed, as you did, that you would gain the victory. But you did not, and so I must choose another weapon."

"What weapon?" Runacarendalur asked. "How can you believe anything will succeed when your army has failed?"

"It is a weapon I have wielded before," Bolecthindial replied. "Its edge is keen enough to slay any prince."

And he would say nothing more.

❈

Barely a sennight after the defeat of Caerthalien's army, Oronviel marched upon Laeldor. There was little for any of them to do while the army was on the march. Lord Vieliessar had sent Ambrant Lightbrother to War Prince Ablenariel with her challenge the moment she had reached Oronviel Great Keep. He had not rejoined the army along its march, which meant either he was still trying to persuade Lord Ablenariel of the wisdom of surrender or was being detained. Thoromarth had expected Ablenariel to take the field by now, if only in response to the nagging of his Caerthalien-bred wife and the sly proddings of a Chief Lightborn all knew to be inclined toward Aramenthiali. But he had not, and now two more days would see them at Laeldor's Great Keep.

Riding the bounds of the camp each night was the only sign of nervousness Lord Vieliessar betrayed. Thoromarth wasn't sure whether he was glad to see his prince fretting over the future like some ordinary *komen* or worried that her unease was the harbinger of catastrophe. Tonight she had bidden him to ride with her.

"Have you thought of what you will do if you win?" Thoromarth asked.

"*When* I win," Vieliessar corrected.

Thoromarth waved the correction aside irritably. "When you win, if you win. . . . A good commander prepares for failure."

"If I fail, there is nothing to prepare for," Vieliessar said simply. "But I have planned for success."

"I am eager to hear your thoughts," Thoromarth said dourly.

"Should Ablenariel surrender himself and his domain and pledge fealty to me, I will spare his life. Then I shall take the whole of Laeldor's army and add it to Araphant's, and I shall march upon Mangiralas."

"You'd leave Laeldor undefended?" Thoromarth asked.

"If Caerthalien wishes to invest Laeldor, and in doing so spread what remains of its armies thinner still, I shall be pleased to let them do so," she answered. "If Caerthalien and Aramenthiali wish to fight over Laeldor and Araphant, let them. They weaken themselves, and both domains will be mine in the end."

"If you win," Thoromarth said.

"*When* I win," she answered with an edged smile. "If I am forced to fight Laeldor, the end is much the same, save that I execute Ablenariel, and any of his family who will not renounce their claim to the Unicorn Throne in favor of mine. Either way . . ." She hesitated.

"What?" Thoromarth asked.

"Thoromarth, I cannot afford a siege here. I do not have time."

"Shouldn't you say this to Ablenariel? Perhaps it would convince him to surrender."

"I must ask something of you," she said, and sounded so troubled that Thoromarth felt a cold pang of unease strike like an enemy's dagger to his chest.

She did not speak again until she had led the two of them so far from the edge of the camp that they crossed the path of the sentries on watch. "You know Magery is said to be Pelashia's Gift to the *alfaljodthi*," she began slowly.

"My lord, if you wish to speak of Magery, speak to Rithdeliel, or Gunedwaen, or even to your destrier—not to me, I beg you," Thoromarth said hastily. "You know that—"

"I must!" she said, so urgently that Thoromarth reined his palfrey to a stop. "You may not know of the Covenant the Lightborn swear to abide by, which we will keep—which they will keep—even if their liege-lords order them to do something against it. But you know that the Lightborn do not use their arts in war."

"Yes," Thoromarth said, when the silence had stretched long enough he knew she would say nothing more. "This Covenant. They all swear to it."

"No," Vieliessar said. "The Covenant is not the same thing as that promise."

If Thoromarth had felt uneasy before, now he felt dread such has he had only felt the single time he had gone to make sacrifice at the Shrine of the Star. "It must be," he said.

"No," Vieliessar said quietly. "The Covenant is our pledge that we will never draw so much power from the land that it sickens and dies, that we will never draw power from the shedding of blood nor from any breathing thing. In battle, Mosirinde Peacemaker thought, there would be too much temptation. For when victory is sweet, and ardently desired, and so many are slain or come near to death, it would seem a small thing to steal the life of an enemy. Or to let the death of one's own warriors bring one victory. And so we wrap ourselves in custom and let the Lightless think it is a vow."

His father and his teachers, his mother, wife, brothers, and children, had all thought Thoromarth slow-witted. In this moment he wished it were so, so that he would not understand what argument his lord now wove. "Then this Covenant and that promise are the same," he said again, more urgently. *They must be. They have to be.*

"No," Vieliessar said again. "Mosirinde hoped to put an end to war by removing the sharpest blade from the armory of the War Princes. She wished to end the suffering of the Lightborn, for those who drew power from blood went mad. She wrote that they sickened and died, but that before their deaths, they did great harm. And I will not break her Covenant, for I am sworn to it. But I will be High King, Thoromarth. And to gain the Throne, I will use every weapon I have."

The silence stretched between them, as Thoromarth tried to unhear his Lord's words, tried not to understand their meaning. "You have taken my throne from me by trickery and Magecraft," he said at last.

"I used no Magery to best Rithdeliel," she answered steadily. "To defeat Firon Lightbrother's shield afterward, yes. But I had already won Oronviel by right of the sword. You must believe this, if you believe no other thing I say to you. I used only the swordcraft Rithdeliel and Gunedwaen gave to me."

"That is not possible," Thoromarth said slowly. He wished to believe her with all his heart. He'd believed it was so, even when it had seemed impossible, for there had been no alternative. But now she said she had not, would not, set aside her Magery.

"I do not lie," she answered. She smiled, and Thoromarth did not think he had ever seen such an expression of grief. "The High King chose me. He wrote of me in a Song—a prophecy. If my skill in swordcraft owes anything to Magery, it is Amrethion's, not mine."

"Then let the Magery you wield end there!" Thoromarth cried, his voice harsh. "It cannot be— No one can blame—"

"I cannot," Vieliessar answered sadly. "I have not set aside my Light, though I have let you, everyone, believe I have. I will use it on the battle-field—if I must. And I shall ask my Lightborn to use theirs as well."

"They will leave you," Thoromarth said, still grasping for what he knew as truth. "They will not do it."

"Then they will leave," Vieliessar said. "Some will not. Oh, Thorom-arth, how can you think the Lightborn noble beyond desire, beyond temptation, beyond anger? Hamphuliadiel, who was set highest of all of us, grasps after power behind a curtain of lies. Can you think the rest of us are *better* than he is?"

"You must be!" Thoromarth answered. He had never expected to say such words. To her. Of her. "*You* must be! Or is all your talk of justice and truth and peace nothing more than another curtain of lies?"

"What I have promised, I will do," she answered, and in that mo-ment, Thoromarth had the chill conviction that he spoke not to a living woman of flesh, a woman who could sweat and bleed, but to a power as distant and inhuman as the Voice of the Shrine. "I would never have come here if I did not mean to do all I have promised."

"Then why— Why—" To his horror, Thoromarth felt tears prickle behind his eyes. "Why must you tell me what you have?" he asked, his voice a whisper more forceful than a shout.

"If you cannot bear this knowledge, no one can, and I have lost," she said simply. "If I may say to you, my liege-man and companion, my counselor, my friend, that I will use Magery in war, and you will still fol-low me . . . then there is a chance."

He could slay her, Thoromarth thought. Here, his sword against hers, afoot. Or he could take what he knew to her commanders and raise the army up in mutiny against her. He could make such accusations against her as would turn her Lightborn against her. He could say she was mad—that she'd taken his throne by Magery—that she would not be content with gaining the Unicorn Throne, but meant to kill all the War Princes, whether they had sworn to her or not.

He could say everything she'd said since she took Oronviel was a lie.

"Only a chance?" he asked, his voice rough.

"Only that," she answered.

"They will hate you," he said. "They will fear you."

"My enemies, yes," she said. "My friends will see Thoromarth of Oronviel standing beside me and know there is nothing to fear."

And I will, he thought. Realizing that gave him no joy. He had surrendered his throne out of despair and superstition—he saw that now—but all that had followed had come from hope. Hope she could do what she said she would. Hope she *would* do what she said she would.

"Vieliessar," he said, and her naked name in his mouth seemed as if it were the greatest presumption he had ever committed. "Is it—is all this—just for power?"

"No," she said, her voice low and quiet. "It is because Amrethion High King said I must."

"Tell me nothing more," he said, when she would have continued. "I do not wish to know my fate if you should lose."

"I shall not lose," she answered, steadily.

But this night Thoromarth did not join her in her pavilion for talk and merriment.

I need you to do something for me," Vieliessar said.

The candlemark was late; her commanders had departed to their own pavilions. Even her servants, having readied her pavilion for the morning, had gone.

"I know it's not to send challenge to War Prince Ablenariel," Thurion said lightly, "for you sent Ambrant Lightbrother with that. He will barely have finished delivering your message before your army is at Laeldor's walls."

"And when I take Laeldor, I must show the means by which I will take the Unicorn Throne. And that is not by grasping and holding land. What I shall take—and hold—is fealty. The High Houses may do as they like with the land."

"It is like a game of *xaique*," Thurion said. He did not ask if she could do it: for that was a thing no one could know, unless they petitioned the Star-Crowned to draw aside the veil that covered the future.

"Much like a game of *xaique*," she agreed. "If I were playing against a dozen opponents upon a board I could not see. But that is not why I summoned you to this audience."

"Was I summoned?" Thurion asked, glancing ostentatiously around the empty tent. "I thought I came to pay an evening call upon an old friend."

"So you did. And it is from my friend I ask this favor, for it is a thing I would hesitate to demand of a vassal."

"Both friend and vassal, I hope," Thurion said, smiling. "Tell me. What is it you need?"

"Do you recall Malbeth of Haldil?" she asked, rather than answering him directly.

"Yes. Of course." It did not require any feat of memory to recall that name, for Caerthalien had been in the Grand Windsward for the whole of War Season only a few decades past because of Malbeth of Haldil. "War Prince Gonceivis proclaimed Malbeth—his greatson through an elder daughter, if I remember rightly—Child of the Prophecy, and the Less Houses of the Grand Windsward rebelled against the High Houses in the West."

"Yes," Vieliessar said, nodding. "They did not even propose a Candidate for the High Kingship. Rather they claimed that the time High King Amrethion foretold had come, and no longer was there High House and Low. And so I need to send someone to Haldil to say Vieliessar Oronviel shall be High King and fulfill the Prophecy in truth."

Thurion frowned, thinking over what she'd said. "Gonceivis knows *The Song of Amrethion*," he said slowly. "If for no other cause than that Haldil is Hamphuliadiel's House . . . and the Less Houses tried to break with the High by both force of arms and by the sword of custom. Vielle, if you have me say this to him, he will *know* you claim the Unicorn Throne not merely by conquest, but as High King Amrethion Aradruin-iel's prophesied successor."

"Yes. And so it is you who must go, Thurion, for you already know I am Child of the Prophecy. It is the strongest argument I can offer to the Houses of the Grand Windsward, for freedom from the demands of the High Houses is what they desire most of all. And I must make this claim sooner or later," she said, half laughing, half mournful. "And then every fool who once read *The Song of Amrethion Aradruiniel* will comb through it for proof I am mad."

"I could almost wish you were, for the end of High House and Low is not all Amrethion prophesies." Thurion shook his head. "And when Lord Gonceivis asks me of the rest of the Prophecy? Darkness—death—disaster—terrible armies out of the shadows?"

"I leave that in your hands," Vieliessar answered. "Tell him all, or nothing—or lie. If Celelioniel had known what is so terrible Amrethion must send his prophecy down a score of generations to find me—she might simply have told the War Princes what was to come and let that be an end to it. I dare not. I dare not," she repeated, low.

"And if Haldil will not listen?" Thurion asked.

"Then Bethros, or Hallorad, or even Penenjil, for if their Silver Swords do not ride to war outside Penenjil's borders, perhaps they will fight for the Fortunate Lands themselves." She frowned, as a memory struck her. "But that cannot be true. Once, at the edge of Arevethmonion, I saw some of the Silver Swords. They rode with knights of Calwas and Enerchelimier—and Anginach Lightbrother rode with them, in the armor of a knight. He called me Farcarinon and asked my forgiveness. I never knew why, but he carried with him part of a scroll that held Celelioniel's last proofs. He died—they were all cut down by others who followed, and his body was too shattered by battle cordial for me to Heal him. . . ."

"A mystery," Thurion said, as puzzled as she was. "For how should Calwas come to aid Enerchelimier, or cause Penenjil to break ancient custom? But it is settled: if Haldil will not hear me, I will go to Penenjil, and remind the Master of the Silver Swords of that day, for he will know of it. Of that, I am certain."

"You will go?" she said, her voice as light with relief as if she were not a War Prince and he not her sworn vassal.

"At once."

"I will send—" she began, but Thurion shook his head.

"Better if I go alone. You could not send enough knights with me to keep me safe on the Grand Windsward—and I could not keep them safe, either. If I go alone, my spells will guard me and I can use Door to speed me on my journey. I swear to you: I shall go to every court, to every prince of the Grand Windsward, and I shall bring you an army so great that the High Houses will throw down their swords and weep in despair."

"I have known you so many years, and never knew you for a Storysinger," she replied, smiling faintly.

Thurion smiled at the gentle teasing, but only for a moment. "Care for my Denerarth while I am gone. He thinks I can do nothing for myself, and he will worry."

"I shall care for him as if he were my own flesh. And if— And if the day should go against me, I swear to you I will see him safe. And your family as well."

"Then there is nothing for me to fear. I shall bring you your army before the first snows." They were brave words, such as any knight might speak to his heart's lady—if the world were a storysinger's tale. Both of them knew it was not, for Vieliessar's family had been destroyed by fear and ambition and the Light had lifted Thurion from a life of toil and privation to a life of ease and luxury . . . and of knowing his family were held hostage against his lord's displeasure.

But the purpose of stories was to take the ugly, terrifying truths with which one must live and turn them into brave and beautiful ideas one might love. And so Thurion spoke light words of farewell as if his life had become a storysong for a Festival day, and held his fears and worries close until he would be the only one who could see them. And he went to tell Denerarth that he rode alone on a journey but that all would end well.

⁂

Siege was rarely a tactic used by any of the War Princes, for it was costly and difficult and offered little chance for battle. Vieliessar had not intended to besiege Laeldor, for as she had said to Thoromarth three days before: she dared not spend a year, or even a moonturn, in siege. For that reason, she had sent Ambrant Lightbrother to War Prince Ablenariel with a challenge, just as the Code of Battle required. Upon receiving it, Ablenariel Laeldor should have summoned his knights to meet her in battle. Or if he did not want to, he should have sent Ambrant Lightbrother to her with a request for parley.

He had done neither. Vieliessar's army had crossed Laeldor unopposed.

As they went, the commonfolk of Laeldor flocked to her, hailing her as High King and swearing she was their lord. Gunedwaen questioned them, asking what they had seen of the movement of knights and supplies—for however Ablenariel meant to answer her, he would have needed to call up his levy knights—but always the answer was the same: *Nothing We have seen nothing.*

"It is not possible," Gunedwaen said in frustration. "You've had Landbond and Farmholders here from every steading within a hundred miles of our line of march. Landbond see everything—and not one of them has seen knights heading to muster. I'd say Ambrant Lightbrother just didn't deliver your message, except—"

"Except that pompous windbag would never miss the chance to lecture a War Prince while doing his duty," Thoromarth growled.

Vieliessar and her senior commanders sat at table in her pavilion. They had reached the keep itself and had set camp perhaps two miles from its walls. No one knew whether or not they would fight in the morning, but Vieliessar had ordered the feasts and victory sacrifices made just as if they would.

"Say the message wasn't delivered," Rithdeliel said. "Say, oh, his horse threw him and he broke his neck on the way to the keep. Or was eaten by wolves. By now *someone* would have mentioned our presence to Ablenariel, and he would've sent one of his Lightborn to demand we go home."

"So he's just *pretending* he hasn't seen us," Nadalforo said contemptuously. The former mercenary reached out with her dagger to skewer a chunk of meat from the platter in the middle of the table. "Fine for him. But do you think he had time to tell all his nobles his plan before we got here? We've been tromping over manorial lands for the last five days, and the only notice anyone takes of us is to come and try to join the army."

Princess Nothrediel laughed, then quickly covered her mouth with her hand. "Well, it's *true*, Father," she said in answer to Thoromarth's dark look. "It doesn't make any sense! Laeldor can call—" She paused for a moment in thought. "—two score grand-tailles, just as we can. Although really closer to twelve, if you mean knights who can actually fight. They won't all fit in the castel. And it's at least a moonturn and a half before Caerthalien goes to meet Ullilion, so they are all still here."

"And even if Caerthalien has demanded Laeldor's support before time—it is possible, now that the Heir-Prince has lost so many of his father's knights—someone would have seen the companies on the move," Gunedwaen said.

Rithdeliel shook his head, but in bafflement, not disagreement. "Either Ablenariel knows we've challenged him, or he doesn't. Either he has summoned his levy knights, or he hasn't. All we know for certain is we haven't seen them, and nobody else has, either."

"You are too pessimistic, Lord Rithdeliel," Vieliessar said, with grave humor. "We also know where Lord Ablenariel's Great Keep is."

Princess Nothrediel and Commander Nadalforo both laughed.

⬩⧉⬩

The day of the battle—if there was going to be one—dawned clear and cool. The army had taken its final orders from its captains the night before, and in the dim light before dawn its warriors moved into position around the keep. The craftworkers' village was empty when the army reached it, and so were the stables. The craftworkers would have fled to the keep for safety at the army's approach, but the absence of the horses implied a mounted force waiting to strike.

The only problem with that is none of my scouts have seen any indication of such a force, Vieliessar thought in irritation. There were surprises awaiting her today, and she hated that thought. She had done all she could against it: Nadalforo and her First Sword, Faranglis, commanded between them four grand-tailles, all former mercenaries. They did not stand with the main force, but instead rode in a wide circle around it, searching for the secret exit from Laeldor Great Keep and any who might use it.

The rest of the army was gathered before the keep.

From her visions of ancient times, Vieliessar knew that "infantry" had been placed in the first ranks of the army, and had attacked the enemy before the knights charged. But she hadn't had enough time to spend working with either her army or the new infantry to feel confident in such tactics, so she placed them at the far edges of her formation. If the enemy attempted to flank her forces, her infantry could attack. For now she simply wanted them present, both to season them and to let her knights know they would be expected to fight in concert with troops fighting afoot.

War Prince Luthilion led Araphant's Household guard. She had placed his forces on her *tuathal* side to honor him, knowing it was the dearest wish of his heart to die with a sword in his hand. She was certain the Araphant Guard would stand no matter what, for Luthilion was greatly loved and every one of his *komen* would die rather than dishonor him. The knight-levies of Araphant were soft with long absence from the field; she had separated the rest of them into single tailles and scattered them among her troops.

Ivrithir held the *deosil*, led into battle by Caragond Heir-Princess and her brothers and sisters. Vieliessar had left Ivrithir's dispositions up to those who for years had led her knights into battle—or on raids across Oronviel's border—taking only a few tailles to directly support her center. Doing so showed Ivrithir honor, since the *tuathal* side was Araphant's.

Oronviel's knights supported the *tuathal* side and made up the rest of the center. Two of Thoromarth's four surviving children each led a grand-taille, one hundred forty-four knights. Prince Frochoriel of Oronviel had been left to hold Oronviel Keep in her absence and to keep guard over Princess Nanduil, who was still prisoner there—and who had no warcraft in any event.

Bethaerian raised her warhorn to her lips and blew the signal. From Vieliessar's camp, the war drums boomed out their challenge: *come and fight, come and fight, come and fight—*

For many minutes, as the sun climbed higher and the day brightened into color, there was no response, and Vieliessar entertained the mad fantasy that the castel was empty, that Ablenariel and all his people had simply fled, leaving her to cry challenge to the empty stones. Perhaps Rithdeliel had been right and Ambrant Lightbrother had never reached Laeldor. Perhaps he had been summoned back to the Sanctuary to account for his actions in Rain Moon.

Perhaps the Starry Hunt has carried all of them off, and Laeldor will fall to me without a blow struck!

But at last there was movement upon the wall above the gatehouse. Lord Ablenariel had arrived.

The War Prince of Laeldor stood flanked by two warriors in the distinctive round cap-helm and mail shirt of castel guardsmen. He wore armor, but no helm. His Lady, Gemmaire, stood beside him, brilliant in silks and jewels, her long hair blowing in the morning breeze. Bethaerian blew another call on her warhorn, and in obedience, the drums rumbled into silence.

There were custom-hallowed words to speak now. Vieliessar would have ignored them, except that Ablenariel was inside his keep and she wanted him to come out. For one appalled moment she thought she had forgotten them, then she rose to standing in Sorodiarn's stirrups and took a deep breath.

"Ablenariel Laeldor! I, Vieliessar Oronviel, challenge you to lawful battle! Come forth, for your honor and your lands! If you will not set your steel against mine, be known forever as coward!"

Behind her, around her, her knights and warriors erupted in wild cheering. Ablenariel stood silent as the cheering crested and died away, then he leaned over the battlements. "I see no War Prince here! Only a Sanctuary Mage who has forgotten her robes! Go home, little Lightborn! War is not for you!"

"Idiot," Thoromarth muttered, just loud enough for Vieliessar to hear.

"Come forth, Ablenariel Laeldor! This is the second time of asking. Or do you refuse lawful challenge?" she called.

"If you won't come yourself, send your old wet nurse!" Thoromarth bawled. "She's probably a more valiant knight!" He looked toward Vieliessar, his eyes alight with the anticipation of battle. There was laughter from the massed ranks behind them. So far this was sport, as it had always been.

"It has been long since I rode to war," Lord Luthilion said happily. "I thank you for this entertainment, Lord Vieliessar."

"If there is pleasure to be had in it," she said, turning toward him, "the pleasure is—"

Suddenly there was an arrow where no arrow had been, protruding from Lord Luthilion's eye socket and quivering faintly. His hands came up, scrabbling at his face and knocking down the visor of his helm, and then he fell from the back of his destrier. The animal started forward, its nostrils flaring at the scent of blood, then stopped—as it had been trained to—at the absence of weight in its saddle.

There was a ragged cheer from the wall above the castel. At the sound, Vieliessar looked up. Ablenariel and his lady were gone, and one of the castel guard brandished his bow tauntingly.

Sound grew behind her as knowledge of what had happened spread. Cries built to shouts to a roar. She did not know if Ablenariel had given the archer the order to attack. She did not know if Lord Luthilion had been the target or if she had. She did not know whether Ablenariel had left the ramparts because he had been coming to parley or surrender, or trying to flee. None of those things mattered now. She had the sudden sense that this was a moment she could not control any more than she could control the storms of autumn. She might turn it to serve her purpose. Or she might be crushed beneath it. She had taken a thousand steps along this path, and each had been irreversible, but this would be the greatest. She raised her hand. All she felt was terror.

Preservation was a spell every Lightborn knew. It kept food from spoiling, meat from rotting, even ice from melting. But every spell had its opposite.

Rot.

The spell sped from her fingers as the arrow had sped from the bow. There had been a hundred spells laid on every element of the castel's entrance. Vieliessar's spell unmade them all, whether for preservation, for strength, or for endurance. Chains holding the doors of the Great Keep closed rusted away in instants. Bronze gears pitted and shattered. Rope frayed and snapped.

The doors of Laeldor Keep sprang open.

The force of their opening caused them to fall from age-crumbling hinges, caused the great doors to explode into rotted wood and splinters. The outer court was exposed. At its far end, the portcullis that blocked entrance to the Great Hall crashed down, its corroded bronze shattering on impact, leaving the castel defenseless. In that instant, Vieliessar spurred Sorodiarn forward. Behind her, howling for vengeance, came the knights of Araphant.

The outer courtyard was filled with mounted knights. Araphant's knights—Luthilion's personal meisne—closed with them, forcing them back in a tangle of swords and limbs and hooves. Beyond them, the doorway of the Great Hall gaped wide, its doors and bars shattered by decay. Vieliessar's army pushed its way past the knights in the outer courtyard to gain the interior, and within moments, the Great Hall, too, was a battleground.

Vieliessar spared a thought for Ambrant—was he here? a prisoner?—

but she could not stop to search for him and she did not stop to fight. Lord Ablenariel had been on the battlements only moments before: he could not have gone far. But every castel's design was unique, and she did not know where the steps and the passageways were in Laeldor Keep. Abelnariel Laeldor might escape the castel entirely as she searched for him.

No! He will not!

She vaulted from Sorodiarn's back, her steel sabatons ringing and slipping on the stone floor. She yanked off her gauntlet and slapped her bare hand against the wall, summoning the Light as she did. *Knowing.* With the casting of that spell, the whole shape of the castel unfolded behind her eyes, its corridors and secret passages, every mystery the stones held.

She ran.

Behind her she heard shouts. The clangor of metal. Screams. *Was it like this in Farcarinon the night my father's castel fell?* She ran until she found a door that led to the inner courtyard. Across that peaceful, deserted space was a low wall with a door. When Vieliessar struck the door with the pommel of her sword, the rotted wood splintered. She dashed into the mews, which led up to the outer wall. Ablenariel must come down this staircase or know he would be trapped above the gatehouse until he died.

Behind her she heard a soft scrape of metal against stone. She checked and pivoted, bringing up her blade just in time to face attack from two dismounted knights. A vagrant thought slipped through her mind—*I told Thoromarth the truth*—as she closed with them, for nothing would serve her now but the battle skill Gunedwaen and Rithdeliel had taught her, candlemark by painful candlemark. There was not enough space to swing a sword, barely enough to move. She drew her dagger with her left hand as she forced them back. The passageway was narrow and neither of her foes was used to fighting afoot. One fell, floundering gracelessly under the weight of his armor, and she leaped over him, slamming her body into the second knight and driving her dagger through the eye-slit of his helm as his body struck the wall of the mews.

She was trying to yank her weapon free when the knight who had fallen dragged her from her feet. She fell backward, hearing a ringing of metal as her helm struck the stones, and the enemy knight knelt on her chest. For a frozen instant it seemed he could not figure out what to do next. Likely he had never faced such a situation in his life, fighting on foot and without his sword—Vieliessar realized she was lying on his blade. Then he grabbed her shoulders and began simply to batter her against the paving stones. Dazed, disoriented, she raised her sword, but it scraped harmlessly across his back; she did not have the angle for a strike.

Madness, to think she might die here, wrestling some unknown knight, but she would not use the Light to kill.

Then suddenly he was gone, lifted away. She scrabbled backward, clutching her sword, and saw Ambrant Lightbrother, his arm about the armored neck of the knight, looking stunned at what he had done.

He must have been on the wall with Ablenariel. . . .

"Go. Go," she gasped, clawing her way to her feet, and Ambrant hesitated a moment longer, then shoved the knight forward, turned, and ran. The armored figure staggered, hands flailing. His sword lay on the stones, and the Code of Battle said a swordless knight was no lawful prey.

Vieliessar didn't care. She had never cared, she had known from the first moments she had studied it that the Code was a toy that turned war into a pointless game. Now she felt sick with fury, filled with a rage so vast she could barely breathe. She had followed the Code when she had come against Laeldor, and Laeldor had slain Lord Luthilion, and though he had died as he would have wished to, that was somehow the blackest joke of all. She raised her sword and beat the nameless, faceless knight of Laeldor back, and back, and back again, as he raised empty hands to defend himself and cried out in surrender. He retreated until he fell backward over the body of the other knight she had slain, and then she stood over him, striking at his neck again and again, until the metal of his helm shifted and sheared, until dark blood spurted up and flowed out upon the stones.

Then she turned and ran.

Her sabatons slipped and clattered as she raced up the stairs, for the steps were steep and narrow and her armored boots were not meant for walking upon stone. She reached the broad outer wall upon which the sentries walked and stood for a moment, gazing around herself. The walkway was empty. Outside the castel, most of her army sat unmoving. There was no one outside the castel for them to fight, and no space for them to enter.

Then she saw movement. Ablenariel and Gemmaire crossed the ramparts above the gatehouse, moving in Vieliessar's direction. *They must have tried to go down the stairs on the far side and found them blocked.* Six guardsmen clustered around Laeldor's lord and lady. A castel's guards were its watchmen and last defenders, but it so was unimaginably rare for a castel to be taken that it was unlikely they'd ever done battle face-to-face. Vieliessar ran forward, her sword in her hand. Ladyholder Gemmaire saw her first.

It seemed to Vieliessar that the defenders and the lord and lady in their charge moved as slowly as if they were executing the figures of an elaborate dance. Two of the guardsmen came toward her, pikes leveled. She flattened herself against the battlements as they reached her, and as they hesitated, she grabbed the pike of the outermost one and used it to fling him from the ramparts. The other guardsman clung to the battlements as he thrust his pike at her. She trapped the shaft of the heavy, clumsy weapon against the wall and struck low with her sword. The guardsmen wore chain mail and heavy boots, but no armor upon their legs. The guardsman's face contorted in a soundless scream as he fell.

She felt rather than heard the first click of an arrow against her armor. Four guardsmen remained; the two at the front held bows in their hands. But they carried the horseman's bow, not the walking bow. It would have taken both skill and luck to put an arrow through one of the eye-slits of her helm, and the shafts did not have power enough to penetrate her armor. They continued to nock and release as she approached, but just as she reached them, they threw down their weapons.

Go. She gestured broadly—speech was impossible in the din of battle.

They edged backward, but were trapped between their enemy and their lord. Ladyholder Gemmaire was clutching her husband's surcoat. *He should have faced me,* Vieliessar thought. *He should have been willing to face me.* Everyone held their places for a moment. Then Vieliessar took a step forward.

Ablenariel threw down his sword.

It bounced against the stone and fell with its hilt overhanging the edge of the walk. Ladyholder Gemmaire snatched for it, but too late. The blade overbalanced and fell.

The guardsmen slid past Vieliessar, their bodies pressed tightly against the battlements. Their lord had surrendered. All they wished to do was flee. Vieliessar gestured for Lord Ablenariel to remove his helmet, and when he had, she stepped forward and took it from him. Ladyholder Gemmaire flew at her, fingers curved into claws. Vieliessar struck her, backhanded. The spikes across the knuckles of her gauntlet ripped skin and Gemmaire staggered; Ablenariel grabbed her before she could fall.

CHAPTER ELEVEN

WAR MAGIC

The world itself must bow to the will of the Lightborn. If we choose, we
can drain the life from every leaf and flower, take the beasts of the fields,
the birds of the air, the fishes of Great Sea Ocean itself. For the good of
the Land Itself, we pledge we will never draw so much power from the
land that it sickens and dies, nor will we draw power from the shedding
of blood, nor from death, nor from any breathing thing.

—*Mosirinde Astromancer, The Covenant of the Light*

Ablenariel and his Lady walked ahead of Vieliessar across the inner close. Fighting was still going on, but here, its sounds were muted.

"You will die, Ablenariel," Vieliessar said, "but I wish to show you to Araphant's meisne before you do. If you had surrendered, you might have saved your life."

"Laeldor does not surrender!" Ladyholder Gemmaire said. "Laeldor will fight until the last *komen* is dead!"

"Then Laeldor shall be erased," Vieliessar answered. *As Farcarinon was.*

She led them into the keep. Its chambers and corridors were filled with trampled bodies, shattered furniture, and horse dung. Ladyholder Gemmaire wailed at the sight, as if the condition of the keep was still a thing that could matter to her. As Vieliessar led her prisoners through the Great Hall, Thoromarth overtook her, holding a prisoner by the hair.

"Well met!" he said, as cheerfully as if the two of them did not stand in the midst of an abattoir. "Here is Ablenariel's heir, Prince Avirnesse. We'll have the rest of them soon enough."

"Curse you!" Avirnesse howled, seeing his parents. "Why could you not fight! *Why could you not fight!*"

He was still struggling and shouting as Thoromarth dragged him away.

Vieliessar's warhorns sounded the victory, and the long, slow process of searching the castel began. Some of Laeldor's Household knights had been taken prisoner; most had been slain. Some had been in the castel stables when Laeldor's defenses were breached, and when the outer court cleared, they chose to ride out and die in battle. Prince Avirnesse's older siblings and their households had used the concealed passageway to make their escape. But Nadalforo had discovered the horses waiting at the exit from the tunnel, and took Ablenariel's children and the rest prisoner when they arrived to claim them.

Vieliessar learned these things piece by piece as the day unfolded, as messengers reached her and her captains made their reports. *I must be grateful the casualties were no greater than they are,* she told herself. A keep was not a battlefield, and for every lawful target presented to Vieliessar's knights, there were a hundred that were not. Servants, craftworkers, Lightborn, the noble companions of the Lord and Lady of the keep—none of them wore armor or carried a sword. Most had not been injured, and those who were had escaped with minor injuries.

And my Lightborn are here to Heal them, and to Heal the Laeldor knights who have given their parole, and if we wished, we might all fight again tomorrow as if this battle had never taken place, she thought bitterly.

Tonight there would be a banquet, and she would play her part in the time-honored ritual, taking formal possession of the castel and the domain of the War Prince she had defeated in battle. She would give, if not justice, judgment, and celebrate her victory, such as it was. Every Lightborn here, whether hers or Laeldor's, knew the Light had been used to breach the castel's defenses.

Soon enough I shall learn whether today has been victory or defeat.

She stood upon the ramparts of the castel, watching the last glimmerings of sunset kindle in the sky. For now, this keep was Oronviel's.

Hers.

"My lord."

She turned at the quiet greeting. Ambrant stood at the top of the steps. The ruddy evening light turned the green of his robes to a dull no-color. She gestured to him to approach. "Did they send you to find me?" she asked.

"I sent myself," he answered. "I would speak with you, but I do not know who my words may reach: the War Prince of Oronviel, or Vielies-sar Lightsister."

She closed her eyes a moment in weariness. "Both. Neither. Either. Say what you will, Ambrant. I swear that you will take no harm from your words."

"It was you who breached these walls," he said. Though his words were an accusation, there was no anger in his voice. "Some thought Cele harth Lightbrother had set the spell, for he lies now near to death, and there are those who thought it might have been his Great Spell."

"I am sorry that he has taken such hurt. And I wish with all my heart Luthilion yet lived. But I will not evade nor set aside the purpose on which you have come to have speech of me. Yes, Ambrant. It was I who used the Light upon the field of battle, to gain advantage in war."

Ambrant looked down at his hands, holding them out before him as if they were bloodstained. "I fought today, Lord Vieliessar. I used no Light, but . . . I fought."

"You saved my life," she answered. She did not know if that was true. But it was true enough.

Ambrant shook his head as if the act of thinking pained him. "It is forbidden. What I have done. What you have done. I . . . If it were right, if it were permitted, would I not have cast spells to save my Idronadan, who fell upon the field of battle? I let her die, when I might have turned the blade that took her life."

Vieliessar crossed the space between them in two steps and took his hands in hers. "*You* did not let her die!" she said fiercely. "The Code of Battle, which sets the Hundred Houses to fight as if it is a game—*that* let her die! Hear me, Ambrant. Hear well. I will set into your hands a secret with which you can destroy me, if that is your wish."

He looked up, and his eyes were wild and staring.

"*The Song of Amrethion*—Amrethion's Curse. You know it. All who train at the Sanctuary know it. It speaks of a Child of the Prophecy. I am the one Amrethion foretold," she said. "I."

His hands tightened in hers. His mouth worked, but he could not force himself to speak.

Quickly—as if this were a thing she had told many times, instead of only once to one other—she told him of Celelioniel's decipherment of the Prophecy, her trust in Hamphuliadiel, and Hamphuliadiel's betrayal.

"So I must become High King, or Amrethion Aradruiniel's warning will be for nothing. Against the peril of which he warns, all must fight—*komen,* Lightborn, and commons alike. But I do not violate the Covenant. I never will. Not even to save my life."

She would have withdrawn her hands then, but Ambrant was clutching them tightly. "But this, if, if what you have said—what you promised. . . . Peace and justice, an end to Houses High and Low, to Lords and to Landbond—is it only so they will fight for you, so *we* will fight for you, when the day of the Prophecy comes?" He was stammering and the touch of skin upon skin opened his mind to hers without her willing it.

She saw a storm of images, a lifetime stretching back centuries before her birth, the injustice, petty cruelty, and lies Ambrant had been powerless against. He had faith in her—she was stunned and awed, humbled at the passionate intensity of his belief—and he had known, without truly knowing, that she was not merely War Prince and Serenthon's daughter. He had seen her, and he had *hoped.*

"No. I have not lied. I promise justice always, and an end to High House and Low. I promise an end to war between House and House. But when the Darkness comes, we must fight or die. If we win, then—I promise you, Ambrant—peace forever. If we do not, that, too, is peace of a sort."

His breath caught upon a ragged sob, and now she could slip her hands free and take him in her arms. She could feel him shaking.

"I do not know, I do not know," he muttered to himself as if in delirium. "How can you make such vows? How can I believe?"

She could not ask for his trust, when she had violated it so utterly. She did not know how to comfort him, for no one had comforted her since she was a small child. Any whom she'd dared to love, or even trust, had been taken from her—by death, by betrayal, or simply by the destiny she could not avert. When she trusted now it was as if she gave up hostages upon a battlefield: it was done because she must, because it was the path to victory, not out of love or kindness.

"My father wished to be High King," she said at last. "He scattered promises like seed at sowing time. To his favorites he offered power, and vengeance upon their enemies. And those enemies were afraid of what he might do, and even those who were neither enemy nor friend feared to have a High King who would let his favorites do as they wished. I am not my father. From the day I am crowned, I shall have no favorites. My justice will fall evenly upon the necks of those who are now great lords and upon the necks of those who are now Landbond. And my justice will fall like the rain that wears away the stone, and in the end there will remain only my people." She took a deep breath and stepped back. "Speak to the other Lightborn and say that any who wish to leave me may do so, and I will not take vengeance upon any they may leave behind. But say to those who wish to stay that we must set the old ways aside, for this is not a time of peace."

She didn't wait for his answer, but stepped past him and walked back along the rampart.

L ord Luthilion's body had already been laid upon its funeral pyre. The heads of all the castel guardsmen would be burned with him, their bodies buried so that they might never ride with the Starry Hunt. With Lord Luthilion's death, Araphant passed to Vieliessar. Vieliessar confirmed each of lords of Araphant who had come to fight for Oronviel in their lands and their rank, and took their oaths of fealty.

Aradreleg Lightsister was the only Lightborn present in the Hall. It was she who set the spell of Heart-Seeing upon Oronviel's new lords, but her eyes were dark and quiet upon Vieliessar when she thought herself unwatched.

It was customary to bring the prisoners in halfway through the victory banquet and make their fate an entertainment for the victors. Vieliessar refused to do that. There would be a banquet in Laeldor's Great Hall tonight, but she would give her judgments before it.

Lord Ablenariel, Ladyholder Gemmaire, and their children were led into the Great Hall in chains. "You have lost," Vieliessar said to War Prince Ablenariel. "Your lands are mine and your life is forfeit. Do you choose the Challenge Circle or the executioner's sword?"

Ablenariel did not answer. The chains clinked with his trembling, and he seemed both old and ill, though he had looked hale enough when she had taken him prisoner.

"Come, my lord. Silence will gain you nothing. You must choose, or I shall choose for you," Vieliessar said, as gently as she could.

"I had thought to withstand a siege and so save my honor," Ablenariel answered, his voice weary.

"Be silent!" Ladyholder Gemmaire cried. "If you must die, do not shame us in your death!"

Her words seemed to have some effect, though undoubtedly not the effect she had hoped for. Ablenariel pulled himself upright and faced Vieliessar squarely.

"You have wondered, perhaps, why I did not meet you on the field, when you sent an envoy to challenge me," he said. "You have wondered why I did not send your envoy back to you to offer parley."

Vieliessar nodded slowly. No answer he could make would change his fate, for she could not trust him, and she could not hold Araphant if she pardoned him. But she would not deny him his last words.

"I could not," he said, and now anger lent strength to his voice. "I could not! I summoned my levy knights—my lords—my great meisne— and *they did not come!*"

There was a long moment of silence, and then someone in the hall laughed.

"Silence!" Vieliessar shouted. "Is betrayal a cause for laughter?"

"But they took your side, Lord Vieliessar!" The hall was dark, for the Lightborn had not come to fill it with Silverlight, and she could not see who spoke.

"Each swordblade has two edges," she said. "If the nobles of Laeldor have taken my side, then I shall be pleased to accept their fealty. But in doing so, they have betrayed their sworn lord, and that is a sad thing." She returned her attention to Ablenariel. "My lord, how will you die?" she asked again.

"I would die at your hands, Lord Vieliessar," Lord Ablenariel said. "It is how I should have died." He knelt stiffly, made awkward by the weight of the chain that bound his hands, and gazed up at her.

"A sword," Vieliessar said, getting to her feet.

It took an awkward time to bring one, for no one in the Great Hall had come armed to the victory feast, and when Avedana arrived at last, the sword the arming page carried was not Vieliessar's. The quillons were wrought of gold and ornamented with moonstones, white sapphires, and diamonds as clear and bright as winter moonlight. The pommel stone was made of two half-spheres of clear crystal, and between them was laid a thin leaf of moonsilver cut into the shape of a rearing Unicorn, its detail as elaborate and delicate as lace. But it was the hilt itself that was the true marvel, for it was a soft, iridescent white, as if it were made of shell-nacre. It had a twisted spiral to its shape to provide a firm grip for the hand that held it, but it seemed, when she took it, that it was no carving of stone or shell or ivory, but a thing placed upon the sword hilt nearly as it had grown.

It was Ablenariel's sword. Vieliessar knew this the moment she saw it.

"I shall carry this blade always," Vieliessar told him, taking it up. "In memory of loyalty—and betrayal."

Lord Ablenariel bowed his head, saying nothing. And she struck.

"Alas, you have spoiled your gown," Ladyholder Gemmaire said into the silence that followed. "But perhaps you do not care for fine things."

"I know that you do not," Vieliessar answered, handing the sword back to Avedana, "for you have spoiled something finer than any jewels you own." She did not step back, but forward, and her long skirts trailed through the spreading pool of blood. "Tell me, Lady-Abeyant Gemmaire, do you swear fealty to me?" she asked, her voice soft and cold.

"My husband is dead. I demand to be returned to my father's house," Gemmaire said. Her eyes flickered from side to side as she sought allies, and for the first time, there was fear in her voice.

"Your father's house lies in Caerthalien, does it not?" Vieliessar asked. She knew it did. Everyone here knew it did. The pedigrees and marriage-alliances of the War Princes were as well known as the bloodlines of a favored horse or hound.

Servants had come to roll Lord Ablenariel's body into a cloth to carry it out and to sprinkle sand over the blood on the floor. Vieliessar stepped past them and resumed her chair.

"My father is Lord Mordrogen, brother to Lord Bolecthindial," Lady-Abeyant Gemmaire answered.

"Then I see no reason to deprive Caerthalien of your presence. Lord Rithdeliel, assist Aradreleg to remove the lady's chains. You may go."

Rithdeliel stepped forward, a thousand questions on his face, but he held his tongue as Aradreleg reached out to touch the shackles. Lady Gemmaire shook the manacles from her wrists, lifted her chin, and turned away from Vieliessar, moving toward the archway that led into the keep. Vieliessar raised her hand, and Rithdeliel stepped forward to take the Lady's arm, halting her.

"You said I could go to Caerthalien!" Gemmaire said, turning back to face Vieliessar.

"So I did," Vieliessar said. "Lord Rithdeliel will conduct you to the horselines and have a palfrey saddled for you, and I shall provide you a warm cloak, for the night is cool."

"I have cloaks and palfreys of my own!" Ladyholder Gemmaire said. "What of my servants, my jewels, my clothes, my—"

"Everything that was yours is now mine," Vieliessar said. "I give you your life. And a horse. And a cloak. It is only a few days' ride to the border. Ask for hospitality along your way, and you may receive it. I shall order a safe-conduct sealed for you, so all whom you meet know you ride free by my will. I am sure you would find it inconvenient to be taken prisoner and returned here."

Gemmaire looked around again seeking someone who would take her part. At last she stepped away from Rithdeliel, shaking her skirts out as if the touch of his hand had soiled her, and began to walk toward the outer doors. There was a moment of even more profound silence, as if everyone there awaited some defiant words from her, but none came.

"Now, Prince Avirnesse, will you swear fealty to me? Or will you die?" Vieliessar asked, turning to the next prisoner.

I always find a few executions sets a tone for a banquet," Thoromarth said, pouring wine into two goblets.

"I am surprised you have managed to stay awake through any of mine, in that case," Vieliessar answered tartly.

Executions were something any castel's servants knew how to deal with. Some were bringing out tables even while other were clearing the bodies away, and soon after that the first dishes were carried in, just as if Laeldor Keep hadn't fallen that day.

"Ah, my lord, in your case it's never been the executions as much as the possibility of being executed by your many enemies that lent spice to your banquets," Thoromarth said blandly. "Here. Drink. We won today, you know. Drink. Or everyone watching will think we have lost and that they're to be dead by morning."

Vieliessar sipped her wine. She'd never managed to get used to the taste—wine was either thin and sour or thick and over-sweet. *You won't be dead by morning. But I might be,* she thought grimly. It had not escaped her notice that Aradreleg had vanished once there was no more need for her Magery. Lightborn were often absent from victory banquets, performing Healings, but most of Oronviel had not even drawn sword today. There was not so much work for the Lightborn that they could not have been here, if they had chosen to be. Aradreleg certainly. Ambrant, perhaps—*Komen* Mathoriel was his mother, one of Vieliessar's commanders, and Mathoriel was here.

Ambrant, if the Lightborn gather to speak of what I have done here this day, be my voice, and say to them all I have said to you. For what I have said must be. I can see no way to avoid it—no komen *leaves his sharpest sword in the armory.*

But there was nothing Vieliessar could do now to change what would be. And thinking of swords only made her think of Lord Ablenariel's sword, and of his death. So she drank wine, and did her best to present an untroubled face to her commanders, as if this had truly been a day of triumph and joy.

⊰⊱

Caerthalien ran and left behind / Bread and meat and silk and wine / Horses, hawks, and huntsmen bold / Chains of silver and chains of gold / Swords of price and armor bright / Left behind there in the night / Caerthalien ran and left behind . . .

It was late, and the wine had gone around many times, but as much of the rowdiness from those present in the hall came as much from relief at finding themselves still alive as from wine. "Not bad," Gunedwaen said, gesturing toward the Storysinger. "Almost accurate, too. For a change."

"The comic songs usually have more truth to them than the everlasting praise-singing," Rithdeliel said judiciously. "They'll have to work to turn the conquest of Laeldor into something high and heroic, you know."

As the Storysinger went on, the list of things Caerthalien left behind as it ran from Oronviel's knights became more and more outrageous and unlikely. A bake-oven. Three hundred live chickens. A bedstead with a feather mattress and blankets. *Left behind, left behind, left behind . . .*

"As long as they're singing this nonsense, at least we don't have to hear 'The Conquest of Oronviel' again," Princess Nothrediel said. "I like a song where you know what's going on. You can't tell who you're supposed to cheer for in that one." She wrinkled her nose.

"You're supposed to appreciate their artistry," her brother pointed out, throwing a piece of bread at her. "They can't exactly say Father is the blackest monster ever whelped and that Lord Vlellessar did us all a favor by conquering us. Since she didn't execute him, it would be rude."

"I appreciate the depth of feeling possessed by both my children," Thoromarth said. "It occurs to me that our beloved lord and prince executed the wrong members of my family."

"*I* swore fealty," Prince Monbrauel said loftily. "And so did my annoying sister, here."

"Oh, who cares who rules Oronviel, since it wouldn't have been me," Princess Nothrediel said. "We're going to conquer Mangiralas next! Think of all the horses we can take as spoils of victory!" She leaned across her father and her brother. "When we take Mangiralas, you'll let Father and me advise you on the horses, won't you, Lord Vieliessar? Because I know Aranviorch Mangiralas will try to hide all the best bloodstock, and he knows a thousand ways to make a beast look better than it is—or worse!"

But Vieliessar wasn't listening. She was staring across the hall, into the dimness, with an intent expression on her face. She saw the reflection of the blue-white nimbus on the wall a moment before the cloud of Silverlight drifted through the doorway. If Laeldor's proper High Table had been here, she might have been able to see who came, but without it her angle of vision—even if she were to stand—was too low.

She waited.

A pool of silence seemed to grow outward from all those touched by the Silverlight, but even such a pool was not enough to quiet the cacophony

of the hall. She knew someone was talking to her, trying to get her attention, but the words were meaningless. She only had eyes for the slow procession of the Lightborn.

At last the procession drew level with the high table. Now that Vieliessar could see who had come, her hands gripped each other beneath the
fine white cloth and polished wood of the banquet table. Celeharth. It
was Celeharth Lightbrother who came.

He did not have the strength to walk unaided. Ambrant supported
him on one side, and on the other, a Lightborn Vieliessar did not recognize.

The hall fell silent by degrees. First Edyenias Storysinger stopped, so
the singers stopped, and then those talking among themselves slowly fell
silent, as if silence were the ripples from a stone dropped into a pond of
still water.

"A chair," Vieliessar said, and though she did not raise her voice, Nothrediel and Monbrauel rose to their feet, stepping back to the wall, and
Thoromarth moved aside to leave two empty places beside her. Vieliessar
stood as well, waiting, as with agonizing slowness the two Lightborn carried Celeharth to her. She had been one of the greatest Healers the Sanctuary had known in a thousand years, yet Vieliessar knew even she could not
Heal Celeharth Lightbrother of that which ailed him.

Three things the Light cannot Heal: age, death, and fate.

At last those with him lowered Celeharth carefully into the chair beside her. His head lolled back against the high back of the chair and his
legs splayed out as if he was a child's doll, made of rags.

"You should have summoned me," Vieliessar said, taking his hand.
"I would have come." His hand was icy in hers.

She did not expect an answer. She was not certain what she expected.
But Celeharth drew a deep breath and lifted his head. "There are things . . .
which must be done in the sight of all." There were pauses between each
word, as if they were heavy stones he must roll into hearing, and she
could hear the rattle of his breath in his throat between each. "I saw . . .
You broke . . . the seals and locks."

"Yes," Vieliessar said. She dared not look away from his face. She felt as if her gaze was the only thing that gave him the power to go on.

"Celelioniel." The name seemed to take much of his strength. For a moment Vieliessar thought he would stop breathing. Each breath he took seemed to take all the life he had left. "Did you think . . . she was . . . the first? She was . . . my student."

Celelioniel had been full of years when she was Astromancer. Celeharth was older still. Old enough to have been Celelioniel's first teacher. Old enough to have set her feet upon the road that led to the unriddling of Amrethlon Aradruiniel's Curse.

Celeharth's voice was harsh now, a terrible thing to hear, such a whisper as the dead might make if they were given voice. "Promise . . . The Covenant . . ."

"I will always honor and keep the Covenant," she said. She spoke forcefully, not for the ears of any others here, but because she had the sense that Celeharth was going farther from her with every moment and so she must call out loudly so her voice might reach him.

"The rest does not matter," he said. For a moment the sudden strength in his voice made her hope he would recover, that exacting her promise could Heal him where the Light could not. But then his eyes closed and his hand did not tighten on hers. Celeharth still breathed, but soon he would walk the Vale of Celenthodiel.

"I told him," Ambrant said, his voice shaking. "I said to him all as you said it to me, Lord Vieliessar, I swear it! But he said he must come himself—"

"There are things which must be done in the sight of all," she said, echoing Celeharth's words. "Come. We will take him to the War Prince's chambers here."

"No," the second Lightbrother said. "He would wish to die in his master's pavilion. We will carry him there."

Ambrant gathered the frail body into his arms as easily as he might lift a child. He and the other Lightbrother walked smoothly away, taking Celeharth to Luthilion's pavilion.

Vieliessar turned back toward the hall. *The servants are about to bring out the last courses,* she thought despairingly. *And what will I say afterward?*

Suddenly Gunedwaen slammed his cup down on the table hard enough to make plates and eating-knives jump. "You! Edyenias! Give us *The Conquest of Oronviel!*" he shouted, in a voice that had been trained to project across the din of a battlefield. "You have not sung that this evening!"

Edyenias Storysinger stared at him for one stunned moment, then began to play.

⚒

After the banquet had drawn to its end, Vieliessar made her way through the camp to the Healing Tents. She would not intrude upon any of the Lightborn in their own pavilions, for she was still War Prince of Oronviel and they could not refuse to allow her entrance. But any might come to the Healing Tents to see how the wounded fared.

The place where those tents were set, in the center of the camp, was unnaturally spacious, for when camp had been set a day ago, they had expected the usual number of wounded. The tents that had not been filled by the end of the battle had been taken down again by the efficient camp servants, for anything they could pack before the camp prepared to move meant less work for them later. Each tent was lit from within by Silverlight, for they glowed in the dimness like the paper lanterns of the kite-flying festival. She lifted the flap of the door and stepped inside.

The wounded lay in cloth slings suspended on poles laid between two trestles, the same mechanism of cloth and poles the workers used to carry the dead from the field. If any in the Healing Tents died, their beds became transport to their funeral pyre. It was not possible, Vieliessar had learned, to immediately and completely Heal all the injured a great battle might produce. The attempt would drain the life from the land—if one were lucky. If one were not, the attempt would drain the life from the living, setting the Lightborn who had done it on an inexorable spiral to madness and death. For that reason, the injured were Healed in degrees—save for those who must be Healed entirely lest they die, or the great lords, who were unwilling to endure pain a moment longer than they must.

She had visited a Healing Tent for the first time in the aftermath of Caerthalien's raid. Before that day she had seen injury and death, and had even dealt death, but the sheer magnitude of injury that had met her eyes had stunned her. Tens upon hundreds of bodies, all living, cut and crushed and broken in every way a battle could devise. *It is no wonder the Lightborn support my cause, if I promise to put an end to this*, she had thought then. Now she wasn't sure if even that promise was enough.

There were six Lightborn in the tent, all persons she knew. They moved among the wounded, pausing to inspect a bandage here, gauge the progress of a Healing there. Servants moved among the beds as well, and offered water or medicine or changed a bandage at the direction of one of the Lightborn. Isilla Lightsister was the first to acknowledge Vieliessar's presence. She finished her work at one bedside, paused to speak to her assistant, then walked across the tent.

"Lord Vieliessar?" she said, her voice low.

"I would . . ." Suddenly it was an effort to shape the question. *I have grown haughty and over-proud in these last moonturns, if I cannot speak to a sister of the Light as an equal!* she told herself contemptuously. "I would not take you from your work. But I would also know if I yet have Lightborn to command."

"Ah," Isilla said. "I do not think we should speak here. Leuse will finish my work. We await Dinias Lightbrother, so we may draw on the farther Flower Forests."

Vieliessar nodded and stepped from the tent. She did not say anything further. She had asked her question. Let Isilla answer it in her own time. When Isilla came to join her, they walked in silence for several minutes before Isilla ventured to speak.

"We had thought, my lord, that you had set aside your Light to rule Oronviel, as did Ternas Lightbrother of Celebros when he became War Prince. Aradreleg had said this was so," Isilla said.

Vieliessar could feel Isilla's fear at speaking to a War Prince so boldly, her confusion at not being certain whether she was speaking to one who held the rank and power of a lord of the Hundred Houses, or to a sister of the Light.

"It was what I meant you to believe," Vieliessar answered. "I had also meant to come to you with my arguments of necessity, to speak to you and hear your thoughts, before doing what I did today."

"Yet you would still have done it," Isilla said, a questioning note beneath what seemed to be a flat statement.

"I cannot know now," Vieliessar answered. "Perhaps. I cannot know what you would have said."

"Ambrant Lightbrother says you will not void Mosirinde's Covenant. Celeharth Lightbrother had the same words of you before all in the Great Hall. It may be that you hope you would not, and then a day would come where you saw no path to victory but that."

"Where is the victory in madness and death?" Vieliessar answered. "Or in ruling over a desert? If the princes swear to hold their domain's welfare as dear as they hold their lives, shall a High King hold the whole of the land less dear?"

"And see what care our prince has of her people, who give their bodies to be broken in war," Isilla said bitterly. "You take from the people, and you will take from the land. Kill me if you wish for speaking so. It is nothing to me. I have no family left."

"I am sorry for that," Vieliessar said quietly. "I have no family either. And I would do . . . better . . . than has been done before."

"All say the High King will give justice," Isilla said. "And will end Lord and Landbond, High House and Low, and bring peace. But you are not High King yet."

"Nor will I be without the Lightborn beside me," Vieliessar said. "I cannot become High King by saying I am. I cannot cause the Hundred Houses to acknowledge my claim and submit to my rule except by war. I cannot do all I have said I will do as High King until I am High King."

"Easy enough to say you will do it then, when you have no more need of our aid to help you to your throne," Isilla said.

"I cannot show you the future until it comes. I must ask you to believe that what I say, I will do. I have begun it in Oronviel. The Lightborn are not kept from their homes. They are free to use their Magery as they choose. My knights respect each steading and Farmhold, taking nothing save what is freely offered. Yet I cannot say to Aramenthiali, to Caerthalien, to Daroldan: *do this*. I am not High King."

"You fled the Sanctuary," Isilla said, after a pause.

"I could not become High King from the Sanctuary," Vieliessar answered dryly, and Isilla was startled into laughter. She sobered quickly.

"You ask us to ride to war. I have no skill with a sword, nor am I interested in gaining such." Isilla hesitated, then continued, "the Covenant can be hard to keep."

"Then help one another to keep it," Vieliessar answered. "Help *me* to keep it. I do not think I shall be tempted, but I cannot know. What I will ask of you is more than you have done. But I will not ask you to impoverish the land, to take your power from the living, to do anything which— were I to die in the next moment would leave the land or the Lightborn less than they were."

"We are less than we were for knowing you, I think," Isilla said, sounding disgruntled. "What, then, would you ask?"

"That I cannot say. I can only say the sort of thing I *might* ask. Spells to give fair weather for battle. Seeking and Finding to locate my enemies. Should my foe attempt to force me to besiege him, as Laeldor did, I require the siege broken. A thousand things I cannot now name, for who can know how a battle will run before it is fought?"

"Were we to Overshadow your enemies, you might be High King tomorrow, for they would all swear fealty at once," Isilla said.

Vieliessar had wondered what Isilla Lightsister's Keystone Gift was. Now she knew. "And will you Overshadow every lord and prince of every domain for all the years of their lives? For that is what it would require. I might have Overshadowed any of the princes who now ride in my meisne whenever I chose. I might have Overshadowed Lord Ablenariel. And I did not, for an oath forced by spellcraft does not bind."

"You would have the War Princes give up their power willingly!" Isilla said scornfully.

"You have seen that some will do so," Vieliessar answered. "Others I must conquer and slay." She only heard her own glib words after she had uttered them, and suddenly it was too much. She remembered being a child on her way to the Sanctuary of the Star, promising herself that someday—*someday*—she would return to Caerthalien and slaughter everyone within the Great Keep. She remembered being a Lightsister of the Sanctuary, a healer, a scholar, remembered fighting Death as if Lord Death were her dearest enemy. And now Death had become nothing more than a tool. "And so I end as I began, in asking: are my Lightborn yet mine to command?"

"Perhaps," Isilla said, and in her voice Vieliessar heard wonder that she might speak to a War Prince so. Trust that such boldness would not bring her harm. And—perhaps—the beginnings of hope. "I do not speak for all. It is no easy thing to set aside a lifetime's teaching."

"It is not," Vieliessar agreed. "Yet I must have one answer before this day ends. I must know if I may send a Lightborn as my envoy to Mangiralas, for I wish Aranviorch to surrender to me."

"I do not speak for all," Isilla repeated. "But I will ask." She bowed, hesitated as if she might ask leave to go, then turned away without asking.

And were I not prepared to receive such an answer, better I had not asked such a question, Vieliessar told herself.

⁂

"What?" Vieliessar looked up. The table within her pavilion was covered with maps of Mangiralas, marked over in charcoal with lines of march, the sites of watchtowers and great keeps. Mangiralas was a land of hills and valleys in which it would be easy to hide an army.

Mangiralas's Great Keep stood at the top of a hill, so an army fighting beneath the shadow of its walls would be at a great disadvantage and an army fighting on the flat ground beyond would be in range of archers. If Mangiralas thought to use them.

"My lord," Virry said, bowing sharply. She had been born a Farmholder and was now a commander of archers. "The commons gather beyond the edge of our encampment. They wish to see you. No more than that, but they wish to be able to say they have seen the High King with their own eyes."

"I am not yet High King," Vieliessar answered. "But tell them I shall come as soon as I may."

"My lord," Virry said, with another sharp bow, then turned and walked from the pavilion. Vieliessar heard Thoromarth snort in amusement at the breach of protocol any War Prince would have slain her for.

"They'd better be satisfied with a look. You can't take them with you," Rithdeliel said, waving a hand as if dismissing the entire problem.

"Can I not?" Vieliessar answered mildly.

Rithdeliel frowned. "You'd never be able to feed them. Send them to Caerthalien. Or Aramenthiali, if you prefer. Let them go forth and carry word of the High King's greatness."

"Stop it," Vieliessar said, without heat.

"I'm serious," Rithdeliel said, though he didn't look serious. He was smiling, as if this were a great joke. "Don't you know this is planting season?"

"I'm surprised you do," she answered. She gave up on the map and sat down, certain she wouldn't be left to study it in peace until Rithdeliel had said what he wanted to.

"Of course I know," he said reprovingly. "When you've planned as many campaigns as I have based on whose lands I had to avoid lest I disturb their fields and had them run shrieking to my lord about how I was attempting to destroy them, you'd know too. If your army of commons can convince their fellows to flock to your standard, there won't be anyone left to get the crop into the ground."

"It could work," Gunedwaen said.

Yes, she thought, looking around the pavilion. *It could work. It would not merely strip my conquered domains of the laborers who allow the princes to make war, but* all *the lands.*

"They'll be killed," Vieliessar said. "Bolecthindial and Manderechiel will send their meisnes to turn them back, and kill them if they do not."

"If they kill them, the planting *still* won't get done," Rithdeliel said unsympathetically. "And this winter, there will be starvation. More than usual, that is."

"Because the lords won't open their granaries, or suspend the teinds and tithes," Vieliessar said in disgust. Her own storehouses—those of Laeldor, Araphant, Ivrithir, and Oronviel—could feed her army for a handful of years. Or feed all the folk of those lands through one winter. Perhaps. *If my war continues more than a full wheel of the seasons, I have lost,* she reminded herself. She had already sent forth knights-herald to summon Laeldor's absent lords to the keep, sending each messenger with a grand-taille of warriors in case her new vassals thought to rebel. To muster all of Laeldor's knight levies would require a moonturn or more, and she did not have the time; she would take fealty of her new lords and hope for the best. She knew everyone was waiting to hear whom she would leave in charge of Laeldor Great Keep; she must make time to speak with her senior commanders to tell them what she intended.

When Vieliessar is High King there will be a Code of Peace. One justice for all, be they highborn or low, and all voices heard.

When Vieliessar is High King, domain will not war with domain, for all domains will be one.

When Vieliessar is High King, lords will not steal from vassals, from craftworkers, from Landbonds—

When Vieliessar is High King . . .

She would send the commons throughout the west to preach rebellion. She did not like it. But it would work.

"I shall ask this of them," she said reluctantly. "But now it is time to share with you another thing that is in my mind."

Quickly she explained. To conquer a domain did not strengthen the force she could bring to the field, for to hold what she had taken, she must leave a garrison force and a castellan. Should an enemy attack lands she held, she must retreat to defend them, or lose not only land, but reputation.

"Lord Rithdeliel has already said I should send the commons across the West to spread the word that I shall welcome them all to my banner, and his word is a good one. Now I say I shall do more: I shall strip my domains of every living thing. Let there be nothing for the War Princes to seize upon but empty keeps and deserted farms. Atholfol Ivrithir, I charge you to support me in this, and strip Ivrithir as I shall strip Oronviel."

The meeting exploded into loud argument, as all those in the room began talking at once, arguing vehemently against Vieliessar's plan.

"And put them all *where?*" Thoromarth demanded, winning out over the others through sheer insistence on being heard. "You're talking about four domains—five, if you take Mangiralas!"

"I *have* been paying attention," Vieliessar said dryly. "I shall send them east."

"East!" Rithdeliel burst out. "You don't hold any lands east of Oronviel!"

"But I shall," Vieliessar said. "And I tell you now: I shall strip each domain I take of all it holds and weld my folk into one great army. Every domain I can take and strip before the Mystral passes close for winter weakens the Twelve."

"Winter's going to come no matter what Lord Vieliessar has conquered," Dirwan said logically. "And I'd hate to try to get a flock of sheep over the Mystrals in winter, true enough."

"And eleven of the Twelve are west of the Mystrals," Gunedwaen said, a feral smile on his face as he began to understand the whole of what she intended.

"The Uradabhur is rich, wealthy, and fertile," Diorthiel said. He now commanded all the Araphant meisne. "If you are there and the Twelve are not, I believe much of the region will quickly fall to you."

"It is madness," Prince Culence of Laeldor said. "But Laeldor follows your command, Lord Vieliessar, and gladly."

Vieliessar inclined her head, acknowledging his loyalty. "Many Landbond and Farmfolk crossed the Mystrals to reach Oronviel. If my army were closer, I think even more of them would join me."

"It's ridiculous," Rithdeliel said flatly, "but . . . it could work. If you're on their doorstep with an army and their commons are running off to join it—well, the lords don't have to know the commons are useless in a fight."

"They'll remember the Windsward Rebellion," Nadalforo said. "The Twelve stripped the Uradabhur bare as their armies passed through. They won't want to face that again."

Gunedwaen, Rithdeliel, Thoromarth, and even Dirwan were staring at her in disbelief, but Nadalforo was nodding.

"You will make of yourself a landless joke!" Thoromarth burst out.

"How so, when all this land is mine?" Vieliessar answered. "I do not care who shall ride over it for a handful of moonturns making a brave noise of dominion. It is mine, and it will be mine."

"It's going to be a cold winter," Gunedwaen muttered. "With no domain to return to."

"You and I, Gunedwaen, have both spent colder winters than we'll spend in warm tents with stoves to heat them. Did you think I meant to go back to some Great Keep and sit by the fire when Harvest Moon or Rade Moon came? I cannot. I fight until I win," Vieliessar answered. It was time she let them know this part of her plan, for if she waited until Harvest to tell them they were not to retreat somewhere to rest through the cold moons, they would be angry, feeling tricked. But everyone here was still so disturbed about the idea of carrying all the folk of her conquered lands with them that this new and outrageous statement passed almost unnoticed.

"Followed by an ever-growing army of Landbond who will be missing their pigs and their mud," Thoromarth grumbled. "And which can hardly defend itself if attacked."

"The War Princes will not attack an army of commons," Vieliessar said. "They will take my abandoned domains—and thereby lose a portion of their armies guarding them against one another—and will think only of reclaiming the servants and workers needed to make the land fruitful. Let it be done. And let word be carried across all land I now hold and all I shall take—a domain, a kingdom, is not earth and stone, but people."

⬦

Despite the thousand calls upon her time, Vieliessar visited Luthilion Araphant's pavilion, where Celeharth Lightbrother lay dying in the War Prince's own bed. That he was dying was something no one could doubt. He had not awakened from the swoon he had fallen into in the Great Hall. Lightborn of Laeldor and Oronviel came and went, as did the lords of Araphant, seeming stunned by the death—and the dying—of the two who had been Araphant since the time of their greatfathers. Vieliessar sat at Celeharth's bedside for as long as she could manage, but could never decide what she felt. Was it good fortune that Celeharth would not long outlive his friend and his lord? Was it bad fortune because his death could be twisted into a dagger for her back? Or was it merely unlucky that she should lose the good counsel of a Lightborn who had lived long and seen much? It was almost a relief when, as she returned to Luthilion's pavilion just at dusk, she was met in the doorway by *Komen* Diorthiel, who told her Celeharth Lightbrother was gone. She could see that a body yet remained in the chamber, with a Lightborn beside it, but it seemed to her that body was made tiny by death, as if the greater part of Celeharth had been summoned away.

"I would see him honored in death as highly as the prince he served," she said, and something in Diorthiel's face eased at the words.

"It shall be done, Lord Vieliessar," he answered. "To Celeharth Lightbrother, all honor."

⬦

That evening, Vieliessar once again dined in Laeldor's Great Hall among her commanders, and her thoughts were unsettled, for no Lightborn had come to the feast, even Aradreleg. But she was on display, and she knew it, and so forced herself to behave as if this were any ordinary meal. It was not, for there was a constant churning of bodies moving in and out at the back of the Great Hall. She had sent a message to Virry, saying that the commons might come to the Great Hall in the evening, providing they made no disturbance. She suspected Virry of arranging the matter so that each was only permitted a short time within the Hall, but for the Landbond to see their prince's Great Keep was a liberty of which few of them had ever dreamed.

Tomorrow the first third of her army would depart for Mangiralas. Whether Lightborn rode with them or not.

The first course of the meal had just been served to the High Table and servants were still moving through the hall when she realized someone was approaching her from behind.

"I am here, Lord Vieliessar." Aradreleg spoke softly from behind the chair. "I am sorry for my lateness. It was not possible to enter through the main gates."

"Will you sit?" Vieliessar said. "I shall have a chair brought." Aradreleg's words might be simple truth, or they might be a convenient lie. There was no way to tell. The noise of so many minds would be deafening if Vieliessar tried to listen for one mind alone. But she thought Aradreleg seemed surprised to be asked.

"If it pleases you, then I will sit," she answered.

I shall be sad to lose your friendship if you withdraw it, Vieliessar thought as Aradreleg settled herself beside her. There were few to whom she could speak her mind and she valued Aradreleg's bravery and wry humor. In her first days as War Prince of Oronviel, Aradreleg's acceptance of her rule had given Vieliessar hope that she could find consent among the people of the Fortunate Lands to the things she must do.

"We send Celeharth to the Vale of Celenthodiel tonight," Aradreleg said, leaning over to speak softly in Vieliessar's ear. "Will you come?"

The Lightless went forth on their last journey by dawn's light, for they had no Light within them to show them their road. But the Lightborn walked the road to Celenthodiel by night, so that the Light of its flowers and leaves would show them the path.

"I will be honored," Vieliessar answered.

By the time the last course had been set out, there was no table that did not have two or three Lightborn present.

⁂

The pyre had been built down at the bottom of the orchard, upon the ashes of Lord Luthilion's. Vieliessar walked there with Aradreleg and the rest of the Lightborn who had been in the banquet hall. Other Lightborn were already there, in a ragged circle around the pyre. Vieliessar took her place among them. The blue gown she had worn to the banquet shone in the moonlight while the green of the Lightborn's robes blended with the darkness. None of those present paid any more attention to her than if she wore Lightborn Green as well.

Celeharth's body lay upon a green silk cloth spread over a pyre of aromatic woods and fragrant resins. A funeral pyre might be made of anything that would burn, but great lords surrounded themselves in death, as in life, with rare perfumes and costly essences, and she had given the order for Celeharth's going-forth to be conducted with all honor. His name would survive nowhere but in the rolls at the Sanctuary of the Star, for he had left behind him—so he had told her once—no Line to remember him. But in the moment of his death, he would be splendid, for the night air brought the scent of applewood and spicebark, the deep sweet notes of amber and the sharp green odor of pine resin.

They stood quietly in the darkness until the last Lightborn arrived. Araphant and Ivrithir, Oronviel and Laeldor, all were present.

"We come to celebrate the leave-taking of one of Pelashia's children." Pharadas Lightsister was the most senior of Araphant's surviving Lightborn. "Celeharth of Araphant, you have served long in the Cold World. Go now to the Warm World, where it is always summer, and go with joy."

Vieliessar knew to close her eyes against what came, and—greatly daring—added her own power to it. A flash brighter than the noonday sun, a wash of furnace heat. . . .

Then nothing remained behind but night's blackness and a small drifting of fine white ash. In that instant of intense spell-kindled fire, the pyre and the body upon it had been consumed utterly. The going-forth of one of the Lightborn was swift.

"You said you needed an answer before the day ended," Isilla said, walking over to Vieliessar. "The day is not yet run."

"Nor will I presume I have my answer until you give it," Vieliessar answered.

"Just as you like," Isilla said easily. "Who will you wish to send to Mangiralas? Ambrant? He has skill."

"It is my place to say to the War Prince who has skill as an envoy, not yours," Aradreleg said sharply. "But she is right," she added reluctantly. Aradreleg glanced at Isilla, and an unspoken message owing nothing to the Light passed between the two women.

"It is in my mind to let Ambrant rest a while yet," Vieliessar said, "for his adventure here in Laeldor was . . . taxing."

"Then if you will not send Ambrant Lightbrother, Lord Vieliessar, I would say to you Isilla Lightsister is no bad choice," Aradreleg said. "She is clever enough—if overbold in her speech and manner."

"Says the gentle craftworker's daughter," Isilla jeered.

"Have you yet washed the mud out of your hair, Landbond brat?" Aradreleg instantly responded. A moment later she looked toward Vieliessar with wide, horrified eyes, and Vieliessar knew that for an instant Aradreleg had forgotten who—*what*—she was.

Vieliessar laughed—it *was* funny—and Aradreleg's expression eased. But if she laughed, the moment held much sadness, too, for it showed her more sharply than gowns and jewels and the deference of great lords what a vast gulf there now was between her and those she had once thought of as her peers. Somewhere, in the back of her thoughts, had been the hope that when her great work was done she could simply walk from the High King's palace and be merely Vieliessar once more.

And now she knew that day would never come.

"I shall go and compose fair and clever words for you to take to War Prince Aranviorch, and perhaps, if they are fair enough, or clever enough, we shall not have to fight at all," she said.

⋇

A fortnight after Laeldor fell by Magery, Vieliessar set forth with the last of her army.

Much had changed.

Iardalaith had come to the Sanctuary the year after she did. He had already been in training to become a knight when his Light was discovered. Now she learned he was a cousin to Damulothir Daroldan, for he had come to her in Laeldor both as Daroldan's Envoy and to pledge his own person to her cause. He discovered immediately that she meant to use Lightborn Magery upon the field, and to her great surprise, came to her with a proposal.

He would train her Lightborn to fight. She agreed to allow it.

Roughly a third of those Lightborn who followed Vieliessar, Iardalaith said, had the combination of temperament and talent to become what he named Warhunt Mages. She didn't know the criteria he meant to use in choosing his people, nor did she know, then or ever, if he asked anyone who refused. She left the organization of the Warhunt entirely to Iardalaith.

By the time they reached Mangiralas, the Warhunt had begun to train. Instead of robes, they wore tunic, trews, and boots of Lightborn green. On the field, they would wear chain mail and cervelière cap. Iardalaith mounted them on Thoromarth's swift, cherry-black racers so they could move speedily across the battle.

Some of those who followed Iardalaith were surprising: she hadn't expected Rondithiel Lightbrother to join the Warhunt, but moonturns ago he had left the Sanctuary of the Star and sought her out. She did not know—had never sought to discover—his reasons, but whatever they had been, he had chosen to aid her in her fight.

But if Rondithiel's membership in the Warhunt was a thing unexpected, still more was that of the three from Caerthalien: Bramandrin Lightsister, Pantaradet Lightsister, and Jorganroch Lightbrother, for Caerthalien had the most cause of any of the Twelve to hold itself insulted by her actions. But Iardalaith's Lightborn had quickly abandoned identification with this House or that, becoming merely Pelashia's Children again, as they had all been in the Sanctuary. In the cool twilight, when camp had been set for the day, she watched them drilling upon the field, their spells flickering like summer lightning.

And in the back of her mind was this thought: if the Lightborn could learn new ways and set aside old loyalties, the rest of her people could as well.

⁂

Isilla returned to Vieliessar when the army was halfway across Ivrithir to say War Prince Aranviorch rejected her terms, but offered others: a thousand horses, and a hundred of them to be chosen by her or by her envoy, to defer the battle for two years.

"The horse fair is next year," Rithdeliel said. "He couldn't fight then, anyway."

Vieliessar sat at the table in her pavilion, her senior commanders around her. They had eaten while discussing Aranviorch's offer, and now the maps were out.

"He thinks we'll be somebody else's problem by then," Thoromarth said.

"Normally he'd be right," Rithdeliel said.

"Still, a thousand Mangiralas horses," Thoromarth said.

"When we've won, we'll take all, not some," Vieliessar said. "Tomorrow I send Isilla to reject his offer and call upon him to fight or to surrender. But I wish to know what is in his mind."

"You need Lightborn for that, not warriors," Nadalforo said. "I can guess at his strategy, though. Mangiralas is a Less House, but a wealthy one. They go to war rarely—they have what they want, and what everyone else wants, too."

"Horses," Princess Nothrediel said.

Nadalforo inclined her head. "And they have the Summer Truce, to which War Princes come and where tongues wag freely. Aranviorch probably knows more about what's going on among the Hundred Houses—your pardon, my lord, the Ninety-and-Nine—than anyone else."

"No," Vieliessar said slowly. "The Astromancer knows at least as much. The commonfolk from every domain come to the Sanctuary. I grant you, children know little of the treaties and alliances their War Princes may enact, but they know if it has been a good year or a bad."

"On their *farms*," Rithdeliel said, with heavy emphasis.

"The farms tithe," Vieliessar said. "And the nobles come to the Sanctuary for Healing, and they, too, speak unguardedly."

"We aren't fighting the Sanctuary," Gunedwaen said.

"Not today," Vieliessar agreed. "So. Aranviorch knows much. And of his knowledge, he wishes to delay battle, thinking I shall not be here in two years' time. I refuse. What next?"

"If he meant to surrender on your terms, he would just have accepted them and been done," Rithdeliel said. "You're already nearly on his border. He doesn't have time to send for help. And Mangiralas isn't client of any of the High Houses anyway."

"And no one attacks them," Nadalforo said, "because of the horses. No one wants to risk offending its War Prince and being shut out of the Horse Fair."

"Since we're going to attack, where will they meet us?" Vieliessar asked.

"Here," Nadalforo said, pointing to an area on the map. "The Plains of Naralkhimar, where the Fair is held. Flat, good for fighting, and a sennight from the keep. He'll want to keep the fighting as far from there as possible."

"Defeat him there and push him back toward his keep. The closer he gets to it, the more likely he is to surrender," Rithdeliel said.

"A good plan," Vieliessar said.

❧

I t isn't what you plan to do, is it?" Nadalforo said. She'd lingered after the others had left. "Sit on the Plains and let him hammer you while he waits for reinforcements?"

"As a matter of fact, it isn't," Vieliessar said. "While he's fighting my army on the Plains, I'm going to take his keep and his horses. And then we'll see if he's willing to be reasonable."

"If you can perform such a miracle, he'd be a fool not to be," Nadalforo said.

"I shall require your help," Vieliessar said, and Nadalforo smiled.

❧

T hree sennights later, Heir-Princess Maerengiel and Ladyholder Faurilduin, who was also Aranviorch's Chief Warlord, met Vieliessar's army on the Plains of Naralkhimar. *Mangiralas must be very confident of the victory,* Vieliessar thought, seeing the Heir-Princess's banner, for only two children had been born of Aranviorch's and Faurilduin's long marriage: twins, a boy and a girl. The girl, younger by a score of heartbeats, was heir.

Virry and her archers stood unseen between the destriers awaiting the charge of the enemy knights. When the horns rang out and the drums thundered, the knights of Oronviel did not move.

The enemy charged anyway. Their center was mounted on black horses, all as alike as grains of wheat, and their coats were dark as shadows in the dawn light.

Let them stand, let them stand, Vieliessar thought, her thoughts almost a prayer, for stillness in the face of an enemy's charge went against every instinct of the *komen. And let my infantry survive as well,* she added, for there was no place for them to stand save in the ranks of mounted knights, and no direction for them to retreat but between the galloping destriers when her own line moved.

Closer came the enemy, and closer, and the ground shook with the pounding of hooves. Then, just as Vieliessar began to fear that Virry had left it too late, she heard a shrill whistle and the archers stepped forward, moving as one. Moving with quiet precision, they nocked arrows, loosed them, drew more arrows from their quivers, nocked, aimed, and loosed again.

The first rank of Mangiralas's charge dissolved into chaos. Horses fell, dead or wounded, flinging knights from the saddle with as much force as if the animals had hit an invisible wall. The banner of the Heir-Princess fell to the ground.

The riders in the ranks immediately behind the lead knights collided with the downed animals. More horses fell, more knights were unhorsed. Some riders tried to jump the tangle of bodies and a few made it. Most did not. Virry and her archers turned their attention to the knights. Anyone afoot became an immediate target. Through an eye-slit, above the armored collet, through the narrow flexible plates of armor which protected the midsection, under the arm—anywhere the armor was weak, an arrow from the walking bow could pierce it to wound or kill.

The forward momentum of Mangiralas had been halted. Now Vieliessar gave the signal and Bethaerian blew her horn. The call was taken up by other knights-herald throughout Vieliessar's army, and Virry's infantry used those few precious seconds to begin their escape.

Then the army charged.

The Oronviel cavalry split immediately, galloping around the tangled mass of dead and wounded. If everything went perfectly, Oronviel would attack from behind before Mangiralas recovered from the shock of its disrupted charge.

But even as Vieliessar's knights galloped forward, the Mangiralas forces were retreating and reforming with fluid grace.

It was the beginning of a long day of fighting. Vieliessar's forces suffered brutal casualties, for the Mangiralas *komen* were brilliant riders, and fought with the fury of those who had suddenly discovered war was a costly and terrible event. Destrier and knight moved as one creature, and each taille seemed to know the thoughts of all its members without need for warhorn or signal call. Vieliessar had advantage in numbers, which was all that kept her casualties from being heavier than they were, for exhausted companies of her knights could leave the field for a candlemark or two of rest. But when Mangiralas sounded the retreat a candlemark before sunset, she was glad enough to signal the nearest knight-herald to echo it.

That was not Bethaerian. She had not seen the captain of her guard for a long time. Her banner was now carried by Janondiel.

She took reports from her captains as Avedana helped her out of her armor. How many dead, how many wounded, how many horses killed, how many knights could fight again tomorrow. She'd barely pulled off the last piece of her armor when one of the sentries came to tell her Mangiralas had sent a messenger. She dropped into a chair, barefoot, filthy, still in her aketon and mail shirt.

"By the Light, I hope they come to offer Mangiralas's surrender," she groaned to Aradreleg. "Let the messenger of Mangiralas enter," she said.

The messenger who entered wore, as she expected, the green robe of a Lightborn.

"I am Camaibien Lightbrother," he said. "I come from Faurilduin Warlord, who is wife to the War Prince of Mangiralas."

"Greetings to you, Lightbrother," Vieliessar said. "I am sorry you see us in such disarray, but the battle is but recently over, as you know. Tea? Cider? No? Then I would hear your words at once."

"Ladyholder Faurilduin demands you withdraw from Mangiralas at once, that you deliver to her to do with as she chooses those who unlawfully slew our knights with arrows as if they were beasts of the forest, that you pay to Mangiralas such teind as War Prince Aranviorch shall choose to assess, and that you acknowledge you have offered battle in bad faith, outside the Code of Battle."

"No," Vieliessar said.

There was a moment of silence. Camaibien Lightbrother looked very much as if he wanted to ask her if she actually meant that, but restrained himself. "Have you any further message for Lady Faurilduin?" he asked at last, his voice crisp with anger.

"Say to her that Mangiralas is still welcome to surrender, on the terms I have previously offered. And tell her if she has slain any prisoners she holds, I shall kill her whether she surrenders or not," Vieliessar said.

"I . . . shall give her your words, Lord Vieliessar," Camaibien said tonelessly.

She waved her hand, giving him leave to go.

Komen Bethaerian was not found among the living, or the wounded, or among the dead on the field, nor did Mangiralas send a further message to say it surrendered.

⎯✣⎯

On the second day of fighting, Vieliessar stationed Virry's archers at the *deosil* edge of the field, among several companies of knights positioned as if they were a relief force. This time the infantry had palfreys waiting behind the companies of knights, for the archers were far from the camp. When the call to charge was given, the knights of Mangiralas moved forward at a sedate—even cautious—walk.

When the archers began firing on their flank, Vieliessar and her knights charged Mangiralas at a full gallop. They struck for the *tuathal* side of the ranks of horsemen, out of range of the archers. Mangiralas's center tried to take advantage of that, thinking they could strike Oronviel's midsection while it was unprepared for battle, but the rear ranks of the Oronviel cavalry weren't just blindly charging after the knights ahead of them. At the signal, they wheeled and struck the center of Mangiralas's line head-on. And as soon as the archers were away and safe, the "reserve" companies took the field, butchering their way through Mangiralas's *deosil* flank.

That evening, Mangiralas fought all the way to dusk. They did not send an envoy.

"We can't keep doing this," Aradreleg said that night, when Avedana had finished removing Vieliessar's armor. "We can't!"

"How many wounded?" Vieliessar asked, wincing as she felt her ribs. They'd been bruised yesterday and she'd been hit in the same place today. She was only lucky her armor had held.

"Too many," Aradreleg said grimly. "Here, let me—"

"I'm fine," Vieliessar said.

"If you've learned to Heal yourself, I'm Queen of the Starry Hunt," Aradreleg snapped.

"You're exhausted," Vieliessar protested, but let Aradreleg have her way. She had to fight again tomorrow. "How many of our wounded have died?"

"None—so far," Aradreleg said. "But everyone injured, stays injured. We don't have enough Lightborn for anything else."

"It will be over soon, one way or the other," Vieliessar said wearily.

"You're right about that," Aradreleg said. "Because in another day or two, you'll be outnumbered."

⊰≍⊱

On the third day, when the call to charge was given, the two lines of knights faced each other and nobody moved. Then someone in the Oronviel lines laughed and Mangiralas charged. Their line was ragged, and their knights startled at shadows, jerking at their destrier's reins so the animals danced sideways, but this time no archers attacked them.

Today Mangiralas devoted all its energy to the banner of Oronviel and the War Prince in silver armor who fought beneath it. Three times in the first candlemarks of fighting Vieliessar was unhorsed as her destrier was slain beneath her—she lost Sorodiarn, Grillet, and another whose name she never learned. Each time a horse fell beneath her, one of her guard gave up a mount so she might ride. Each time, Vieliessar could see Ladyholder Faurilduin only a few yards distant, fighting desperately to reach her and end her life before she could gain the saddle again.

Near midday, when the fighting was at its heaviest, Vieliessar heard a flurry of signal calls. Mangiralas, calling for a new attack. *They've figured it out,* she thought, already too exhausted for anything but determination. Any prisoners they'd taken—and she must hope Mangiralas held prisoners, for both Princess Nothrediel and Prince Monbrauel were missing—could have given up the bit of information that would have let Faurilduin learn that Oronviel's camp held many wounded, and few Lightborn to tend them.

But Vieliessar had known her secret would eventually be guessed, and so today she had held back two hundred horse and all her infantry and kept them close beside her camp.

She hoped they would be enough.

The press of the fighting was so heavy no messenger could reach her to tell her what had happened. When Mangiralas next signaled, she was so dazed with fatigue that at first all she could think was that she'd failed, that Mangiralas was signaling for a parley-halt to discuss the terms of her surrender. But as the call repeated over and over again, she finally made sense of it.

They're retreating.

We've won.

As they rode back to the camp, she saw the bodies of those who died defending the camp—and attacking it.

Horses—some dead, some panting pitifully as they lay dying from an archer's arrow. Knights dead of sword cuts, or crushed beneath a horse, or battered to death by a destrier's hooves.

And among them, bodies that were not clad in bright armor.

"Ah . . . no," Vieliessar said, sighing. The infantry were to have retreated once they'd taken their toll of Mangiralas's knights. But some had not. They'd stayed, continuing to loose their deadly arrows at the enemy as the moments in which they could escape trickled away. Then, even when their arrows were gone, they had not run, for Vieliessar saw none clad in the chain mail and surcoat of infantry who had died with their back to the enemy.

"All honor to them," Orannet said quietly.

"All honor," Vieliessar echoed.

When she reached it, she saw that her camp was untouched.

CHAPTER TWELVE

AN EMPIRE BOUGHT WITH MAGIC

Houses rise from Low to High, fall from High to Low, flee into the East,
or are born from ambition and the fires of war. And whether a thing of
scant centuries or able to boast a founding lost in the shadows of the fall
of Celephriandullias-Tildorangelor, every one is the whole. If all the
Hundred Houses save one were to vanish like mist in morning sun,
nothing would be lost, so long as one House survived.

—*A History of the Hundred Houses*

"Y ou've looked better," Nadalforo said, walking into Vieliessar's pavilion.

"I've been on the field for three days," Vieliessar answered. "They killed my horse. Three times," she clarified. She was so tired she was light-headed.

Nadalforo picked up the pitcher on the table and sniffed at it to check its contents, then poured Vieliessar a cup of watered beer. "Drink this," she said. "It must have been some horse, but never mind. You have thousands to choose from now. You could even ride Aranviorch into battle, but I don't advise it."

Vieliessar started to giggle with relief and exhaustion, then covered her mouth with her hand to stop herself. "You got him? Them? All of them?" she asked. Beer was better than water when one had been laboring long and hard in the hot sun, but even diluted, it made her giddy.

"We got Aranviorch out of his keep—not that hard, once you're inside they think you belong there—and your Lightborn got everything

with hooves within fifty miles of the keep. Aranviorch is here somewhere. The horses are heading for Ivrithir. I hope you trust Atholfol."

"Yes. We won."

"Don't sound so surprised, your lords will think you didn't intend
to," Nadalforo advised. "Now I'm going to bed. The only time I've been
out of the saddle in the last ten days was when we were breaking into the
keep."

"Go," Vieliessar said. "And Nadalforo . . . thank you."

"I am your sworn vassal," Nadalforo said, bowing.

⟐

It had been an outrageous gamble, but the only true way of winning
not merely a battle, but a war. Aranviorch wished to fight far from his
Great Keep to protect his herds, for they were the wealth and power of
Mangiralas. It didn't matter how many of his nobles Vieliessar slew or
captured if she did not have the War Prince himself. And he could easily
gain allies against her if he used his herds to bargain with.

So Vieliessar had conceived a double trap. She'd sent nearly all
her Lightborn to bespell—and steal—every single animal Aranviorch
owned. And she'd sent her former mercenaries to take his keep and
bring him to her. Doing that had left her with barely enough Lightborn to keep those seriously wounded in battle from dying—and not
enough to Heal the less badly injured so they could fight again the
next day.

But I have Mangiralas's Lightborn now, she thought. *And I have Mangiralas.*

Victory left her—as she thought it always would—mourning those
who had died so she could gain it. She could not say the cost was too
high. But it saddened her. She sent Harwing Lightbrother to the Mangiralas camp to summon Ladyholder Faurilduin to make her formal surrender. Harwing had never done envoy work before, and he was so
nervous that Aradreleg finally wrote out for him what he must say. He
regarded the sheet of vellum owlishly before nodding and saying he

would say it off just as it was written. He walked into the center pole of the pavilion as he was leaving, and then simply fled.

"Will your Storysingers include that, when they make their songs of this day?" Aradreleg asked, trying hard not to laugh.

"I don't think they'd believe it," Vieliessar said gravely. "Oh, and now I must go and see War Prince Aranviorch." She leaned back in her chair and closed her eyes.

"No," Aradreleg corrected. "First you will bathe—you smell like a wet horse—and then you will eat, and then I will find Brinnie and see if *she* knows the location of the chest with your gowns and second-best jewels. Then you will dress, and *then* you will have War Prince Aranviorch brought to you."

⊶⊷

"W here is my son?" Aranviorch demanded the moment he was brought into Vieliessar's pavilion. "Prince Gatriadde—where is he?"

"Why do you think I have him?" Vieliessar answered, just as bluntly.

"Because he was taken from the keep when I was. I want him brought here at once!"

"Ah." That answered one question that had been puzzling her— why Mangiralas had left the field in the middle of the battle, without her needing to demand a parley-halt to tell them she held the War Prince. Nadalforo must have taken Gatriadde as well as Aranviorch in order to have as a messenger someone whose word Ladyholder Faurilduin—or those in her camp—would believe. "Perhaps his mother will bring him, for I have sent for her. But you and I have unfinished business, Lord Aranviorch. I mean to have Mangiralas and your oath. Give them to me."

"And if I do not?" Aranviorch said.

"Then you will die, and your wife will die, and your son will die, and I shall go to your keep and take it a second time, and slay all who will not swear to me. And if your army wishes to go to war with me, then it must do so afoot, for I have taken from you all the horses which are your great wealth, and they are mine already."

"Why?" Aranviorch roared. "Mangiralas has done nothing to you!"

"Mangiralas did not surrender when I required it," Vieliessar answered bleakly.

Ladyholder Faurilduin and Prince Gatriadde arrived within the candlemark, accompanied by Harwing Lightbrother and Camaibien Lightbrother. Vieliessar was shocked and saddened by how young the prince—now the Heir-Prince, as he must know—was, and remembered again that he and Princess Maerengiel had been of one birth.

"So you have won," Ladyholder Faurilduin said bleakly, looking from Vieliessar to Aranviorch.

"I have," Vieliessar said. "And now I take fealty of your husband. But not of you. Not yet. Did Camaibien give my words to you?"

"As you said them," Lady Faurilduin said, her voice unyielding. "You did not abide by the Code of Battle!" she said accusingly.

"And yet, your knights who rode to my lines in surrender were returned to you." Those who could still ride had been sent back to Mangiralas on palfreys after the end of each day's battle. Those who were too badly wounded to ride had been carried onto the field on litters and left for Mangiralas to retrieve.

"You would have held them to ransom if you'd possessed Lightborn enough to Heal them," Lady Faurilduin said accusingly.

"War is not a game," Vieliessar said sharply. "Nor will I treat it as a game. When I have searched your camp and satisfied myself, then will I take your oath, if you will give it."

"Never," Lady Faurilduin said flatly.

"Faurilduin!" Aranviorch cried.

"Husband, you must do what is best for our lands. But Maerengiel has gone to ride with the Silver Hooves—slain by the cowardly weapons Lord Vieliessar sees fit to bring to the field of honor—and I will not live in a world forged upon the anvil of her devising."

"Do not—!" Aranviorch said, and his plea was to Vieliessar, not to his wife.

"She may die with honor," Vieliessar said, "but if she will not swear to me, she will die. And I will not take her oath until I know any of my people she took prisoner are well, for I swore to her that if she caused the deaths of any who lay helpless in her hands, she would die."

"Then . . . Gatriadde, Mangiralas is yours now. Guard her well," Aranviorch said.

"Father!" Prince Gatriadde said, horrified.

"I know you did not look for this," Aranviorch said with dignity, "but we cannot choose our fates. Only the Silver Hooves may do that."

"Is that your last word to me?" Vieliessar asked. Aranviorch inclined his head. Faurilduin ignored her as if she hadn't spoken. "Then let a Circle be made for Aranviorch's death. Gatriadde, will you renounce your claim to the Unicorn Throne and swear yourself to be my loyal vassal?"

"I—I—I wasn't supposed to be War Prince!" Gatriadde said. "It was Maeren! How can you— You *can't*, Lord Vieliessar the Horse Fair is next year, and—"

"Be silent, Gatri," Lady Faurilduin said quietly. "Your father, your sister, and I are dead and Mangiralas is yours. You are of good stock. Trust in your breeding." She turned away as if Gatriadde no longer existed.

Vieliessar watched Prince Gatriadde as her guards led Lord Aranviorch and Lady Faurilduin to the place they would await their executions, knowing as she did that she had her answer: Faurilduin had let prisoners in her hands die. The prince took a deep breath. "You must tell me Oronviel's terms, Lord Vieliessar," he said with painful dignity. "I did not expect to be War Prince."

She repeated what she had said before—vassalage and renunciation of his claim upon the Throne. She did not detail the law to which Mangiralas would now be bound, for Gatriadde would be oathbound to do all she asked of him, and she did not think he could remember her words from one moment to the next just now.

"But the horses?" he said desperately. "You won't hurt them, or—or take them away, or—"

"The horses of Mangiralas will be in your care," she said, holding up her hand. She meant to strip Mangiralas of all it held, but not to destroy it.

"Yes. All right. All right. I'll swear. I'll do whatever you ask. But I don't—I don't—"

Patiently, Vieliessar took Gatriadde through the phrases of the oath, then had Aradreleg set the spell so he could swear. She had to prompt him several times, and when it was over, he burst into tears.

"There, young lord, hush," Camaibien said, going to him and taking the new War Prince in his arms. "It's done and you'll take no more hurt of it. The Silver Hooves have chosen to give Mangiralas into Oronviel's care, and we must trust in Them, for do They not ride horses more glorious than any we can dream of breeding? Just so. As horse and rider promise to keep one another safe, so shall Mangiralas and Oronviel keep one another now."

"Yes, I—yes. That is so," Gatriadde said. "I may keep him, can't I?" he said in sudden fear, turning to Vieliessar.

"If it is his wish to remain with you, I will not take him from you," Vieliessar said, speaking gently, as to a child. Gatriadde was barely more than a boy, and even if he were to have become War Prince, it should not have been for many centuries. "But I shall need him to return to your camp now and bring to me the Lightborn of Mangiralas, for I have need of them."

"I'll go with him," Gatriadde said. "I should. I'm War Prince now."

"Yes," Vieliessar said. "If you please, go with Lord Gunedwaen to our horselines, and you may choose palfreys to bear you."

Gatriadde nodded jerkily. Gunedwaen stepped to the door of the tent and gestured for the new War Prince to precede him. Camaibien moved to follow, but Vieliessar rose to her feet, gesturing to him to approach her.

"If you take two candlemarks to return my prisoners and bring your Lightborn to me, his parents will be dead by the time he returns," she said quietly. "He need only see their bodies on the pyre."

"If you had showed such honor in war as you do in victory, my young lord would not be forced to a task so far beyond his skill," Camaibien said sorrowfully.

"I will not leave your young lord undefended," Vieliessar answered. "My word to you."

⚜

There was rejoicing in the camp the evening of the victory, for not only had Vieliessar won, but Princess Nothrediel and Prince Monbrauel were among those prisoners returned by Mangiralas. If the war had continued many more days, Thoromarth would have lost two more of his children, for while Lady Faurilduin had not executed any of the prisoners she had taken, neither had she allowed their injuries to be Healed by Lightborn, and about a third of those she had captured had died.

Bethaerian was among the dead.

I should not care more for her life because she was known to me.

Vieliessar left her victory feast early, for she felt an uneasiness in her mind which she would not impart to her commanders. She passed her sentries and walked out among the pyres. Here the War Prince of Mangiralas and his lady. There, the Heir-Princess of Mangiralas. Bethaerian. Virry. Janondiel. She might count until the sun rose and not number all her dead.

"It is not a light thing if you were not raised to it."

Vieliessar glanced back. Nadalforo had followed her from the camp and now stood watching her.

"It should not be a light thing even so," Vieliessar answered, and Nadalforo shrugged.

"It is war," she said. "In war, some die."

"Why do we fight?" Vieliessar asked. Impulse, but also the question that had burned in her even before she ever accepted her destiny.

Nadalforo laughed, a short bark of laughter that held no mirth. "For land, for power, for advantage, for vengeance. *You* fight to become High King, but I do not know why."

"To end this," Vieliessar answered. "And because the day will come when we can no longer quarrel among ourselves."

Vieliessar turned away, gazing out over the battlefield—the encampment of the dead. *I am lonely,* she realized in surprise. It had been years—decades—since she had been a servant in the Sanctuary, spending happy evenings in the Servants' Hall or in the Common Room with friends. She had lost them one by one. She rubbed her hand over her face.

"Victory rides with the clever," Nadalforo replied. "So far you have been clever enough."

I have been lucky, Vieliessar thought, turning back to gaze out over the pyres. "The Silver Hooves grant—" she began. She did not finish the sentence. Nadalforo had gone.

※

It was a moonturn and a half after the defeat of Mangiralas, but Vieliessar and her people had not stood idle. All across the West, rebellion had spread like wildfire, causing more folk to flock to her banner. Places had needed to be found for all, and this time the newcomers were not only the commonfolk of the Less Houses of the West, but their Lords *Komen* and great nobles as well. Where she could, Vieliessar had sent troops to support the Less Houses as they fought the High, but she hoped to avoid becoming embroiled in a drawn-out campaign in the west—and one with a score of commanders, all with different goals.

Nor had Vieliessar herself been idle, for there were other Western Houses whose fealty she must gain though they would never join her in battle. So she had gone to take promises of Amrolion and Daroldan, traveling to the Western Shore to do so.

Now it was time for the next step in her plan. She had always meant to take the Unicorn Throne with as little fighting as possible. Now she meant to cement her victory with retreat.

"We shall take Ullilion next," Vieliessar said, indicating it on the map. "Then I shall divide the army."

"Divide it?" Rithdeliel said. "Is that wise?"

"It is necessary," Vieliessar answered. "One third shall go to Thorom-arth, one third to Atholfol, and the third part to you, Rithdeliel. Thorom-arth, you must ride against Tunimbronor, Vorogalast, and Sierdalant. These Less Houses are disputed between Aramenthiali and Vondaimieriel."

"And neither one will appreciate me riding in to snatch them from their grasp," Thoromarth said. "You should take Aramenthiali first, then those Less Houses."

"If I had an army as great as Aramenthiali's, I would do so gladly," Vieliessar answered tartly. "But I do not. Yet you may not face as much opposition as you think. Vondaimieriel did not declare for Serenthon during his attempt to gain the High Kingship, but neither did she oppose him. And Finfemeras Vondaimieriel was similarly evasive when I sent to him at Midwinter."

"Vondaimieriel's got her back to the Mystrals," Thoromarth pointed out. "Finfemeras is cautious. Vondaimieriel can't afford to lose territory in war. She has no place to go."

"There will be fighting all through that region," Gunedwaen said. "Aramenthiali battles Vondaimieriel this season. Vorogalast and Si-erdalant are in clientage to Aramenthiali; Tunimbronor to Vondaim ieriel. I don't suppose I need to mention that Caerthalien attacks Ullilion as well?"

"Then my task will be easier, for Ullilion will be embattled by two foes," she said.

There was a moment of silence, then Thoromarth spoke. "It is not that I am not grateful to be given an army and a hopeless task," he said, "but you speak of three elements to your army, and yet you claim none of them for yourself. Where will you be?"

"I shall buy us time," Vieliessar answered.

But time could only be bought with information, and so after the meeting had drawn to a close, Vieliessar dismissed her commanders and retreated to the inner chamber of her pavilion to gain it.

One of the things that had bemused—and amused—Vieliessar once she became War Prince of Oronviel was her discovery of the portable spellkits (so called by the Lightless) the Lightborn used. It was true that to cast any of the spells she had learned within the Sanctuary, all that was needed was the power of a Flower Forest and a Mage's own Light, but it was also true that many spells required a particular stillness or a period of cleansing meditation. Nearly all Lightborn meditated regularly, both to still their thoughts, and to take the opportunity to touch the Light without needing to use it.

In the Sanctuary, the elements necessary to ease a Lightborn's path were available in every practice room and sleeping chamber. Outside the Sanctuary, Lightborn might be called to follow their masters on progress, on campaign, or simply to move from manor to manor. To be certain they had with them all they needed, they had evolved the custom of storing their favored items in a special case, which they brought with them wherever they went or were sent.

The one she now used had been Celeharth's.

Made of ivory, it was covered in pebbled, iridescent, red-gold leather: gryphon skin. The hide had worn away at the corners of the box through centuries of handling, and the ivory, yellowed with age, showed through.

The hinges and the clasps were simple things, for any of the Lightborn could Seal a container so utterly it could not be opened by the Lightless, but they were beautifully wrought, of fine gold, in the fashion of feathers. The interior of the box was padded and had been shaped to hold its contents immobile: one fat and two narrow storage canisters, a small cordial bottle, a brazier, a teapot, and a teacup.

The pot and cup were of unadorned shin'zuruf—their beauty came from their exquisite shape and delicacy. The cordial bottle was much the same as any that might have been found within the Sanctuary, but made of white amber instead of the traditional crystal. It did not hold medicine but rather a flower cordial that could be mixed with water. The narrow canisters were of gold, their surfaces elaborately etched with the form of a dragon. One held charcoal disks, the other, Light-incense. The last was the traditional cherry-bark tea canister; this still held tea that Celeharth had blended with his own hands.

The tiny brazier was very old—older, Vieliessar thought, than Celeharth—and carved of cinnabar in the form of a coiling dragon holding a golden bowl in its claws. None of the histories she'd read mentioned dragons as living creatures—but then everything she'd read said unicorns didn't exist, either, and she'd seen one. She wondered if dragons—assuming there were dragons—looked anything like the carving.

She made her preparations with quick efficiency, lighting the charcoal, measuring the tea, pouring water over it from the iron kettle. Once it had brewed, she sipped it slowly, relishing its subtle flavors as she willed her spirit to stillness. When the cup was empty, she spilled tiny grains of golden incense onto the burning charcoal and inhaled the familiar fragrant smoke.

She was ready.

Since the night she had sent him eastward to be her voice to the War Princes of the Grand Windsward, she had done her best to remain in touch with Thurion. There were more reasons than self-interest for her actions: the Lightborn of the Windsward Houses were certainly receiving news from the Houses that held them in clientage, and Thurion must be able to set her facts against his own.

Thurion? Thurion, are you there?

Every Lightborn experienced Farspeech differently. Hers showed her the place she 'Spoke to as if she stood there in flesh.

For a long moment there was no answer, no sense of another place forming its image behind her eyes, and the worry that Thurion might be lost or dead was almost enough to break her concentration.

Then: "Vielle? Oh, thank the Light! It has been so long since we have 'Spoken, and I have heard so many tales of you . . ."

She opened her inward eyes and an image slowly came into focus. He sat in a chamber that was clearly the accommodation of an honored guest—she could tell by the tapestries on the walls, the furnishings, the carpets upon the floors. But the windows were nothing more than narrow slits, instead of the ones she knew from the Great Keeps of Caerthalien, Oronviel, and Laeldor: wide open ones hung with shutters of fragrant

wood or filled with designs in colored glass. It was clear from the open-
ings in the walls that the walls were much thicker than they should be in
any chamber meant to house anything but a prisoner. Thurion was an
honored guest somewhere in the Grand Windsward, then, for the thick
walls were meant to keep out more than the wind and its winter chill.

"I have been much occupied these last sennights, I fear," she answered. "I took Mangiralas as I said I would. War Prince Gatriadde has
sworn fealty to me."

"Gatriadde?" Thurion's mental voice blurted, "but—"

"All the rest of the Line Direct are dead," she answered, knowing
Thurion could feel the sorrow in her thoughts. "But after Mangiralas, I
forged treaties with Amrolion and Daroldan while my army fought elsewhere. I hold much of the West. But what of you? When I last heard, you
had reached Encherelimier to place your petition before Celelioniel's
own House."

"And so I did," Thurion answered; Vieliessar felt the exasperation in
his voice. "It is hard to travel here—they set their castels far from the
Flower Forests to preserve themselves from attack, so I could not go in
person, but I Spoke to many, even Hallorad. And you may see what has
come of my careful work!

"The Grand Windsward is at war. Some of the Twenty see only a second chance to free themselves from the High Houses, but some look
farther than that—Vielle, you do not know what it is like to live here.
There is never a time when one may know himself to be safe! I do not
think there is a single boundary stone anywhere here, for it would be
death to set them and the Beastlings would only remove them."

"It is much like the Western Shore," she answered softly. "There are no
villages there, only great keeps of stone where all shelter, from lord to
Landbond. From Damulothir's own Great Keep I watched Beastlings
pluck fisherfolk from the shore as you might pluck berries from the bush."

"So you *have* seen what it is like to live constantly embattled," Thurion said. "Give the Twenty an honorable reason to come across the
Feinolons once and for all, and who would not? But for now, I may tell

you that Penenjil and six more will fight beneath your banner. Antan-
aduk, Rutharban, Cazagamba, and Narazan say they will give their answer next War Season. Hallorad stands neutral, as always, but Dalwath
Hallorad says Hallorad will sue for terms once you have won. The others
support either Bethros or Haldil, or else pretend to in order to make
their own bid to become Lord of the Grand Windsward when the rest are
weakened by battle."

"Seven is better than I dared to hope," she said. The sense of his
words caught up to her abruptly. "You said they will fight for me, Thurion. But I need them to renounce their claims to the Unicorn Throne."

"They have promised to do so if you win against the Twelve." Thurion's response was troubled.

Vieliessar gave an exasperated sigh. Promises were easily broken, and
if she did not hold the fealty of a domain's War Prince, its knights could
leave the field for any of a score of "honorable" reasons. It was still more
than she'd thought she'd get.

"When can they join me?" she asked.

"The caravans leave for the Sanctuary each spring as soon as Nantir
woriel Pass opens," Thurion said. "It is a long way from the Grand Windsward to the west."

Vieliessar made a faint sound of exasperation, but Thurion was right.
The tribute caravans took moonturns to cross the Feinolon Peaks, the
desert of the Arzhana, the Bazrahil Range, and the Mystrals on their
way west. When the High Houses had gone east to break the Windsward Rebellion, they had made up their arrays mainly from levies upon
their clientage Houses in the Uradabhur rather than move the whole of
their own meisnes eastward.

She sighed in acceptance. "They will come when they will come." As
much as she might rail against the indecisiveness of the Windsward
Houses, she would not herself choose a course that would force her army
to overwinter in a hostile place. *If I had any choice about it,* she thought
wryly. "But you may say to them that to join me, they need not go so far as
Vondaimieriel," she went on. "Soon I come east—I shall cross the Mystrals

just before the Dragon's Gate closes, and take the Uradabhur over the winter. It will be spring before the Alliance can follow me—if it dares to. Let my allies join me there, when it pleases them to do so."

There was a long moment of silence, and Vieliessar had a dim sense of her own pavilion around her, the incense smoke blending with the ever-present scent of horse and dust. That faded as Thurion spoke again

"You can't possibly . . ." he said in disbelief. "Vielle . . . even with just the folk of Oronviel, it would take sennights for you to get everyone through the Dragon's Gate. And now you have . . ."

"Twenty domains," Vieliessar said. "Their folk, their cattle, their *komen*. Twenty." And five more she might yet prize loose from the Alliance, if she were quick and clever. She might make of herself and them such a High House as Jer-a-kaliel had never seen . . .

And it would be extinguished within her lifetime.

"That . . . I cannot imagine so many folk in one place," Thurion said in awe. "You can never move them east in secret. Once the Alliance sees what you mean to do, they will stop you. They'll stop you before you take the pass—Vondamieriel has only to send to Jaeglenhend, and—"

"And she will not," Vieliessar answered simply. "For she will not think to. My enemies will be elsewhere, waiting for me."

"You have a plan," Thurion said slowly, and the dread in his voice made her smile. "Vielle, what do you mean to do?"

"Wait and see," she answered. "Wait and see. . . ."

⊰⧓⊱

As early as Rain Moon, the Old Alliance had agreed Vieliessar was a danger, but they were already committed to their summer's wars and saw no reason to change those plans—until Vieliessar took Laeldor and announced her Lightborn would renounce Mosirinde's Covenant. A moonturn later, she rode to victory against Mangiralas and word came that she had executed all but one of its ruling House.

After that, disaster followed disaster.

The Windsward Houses proclaimed their independence from the West for the second time in a scant half-century.

The Houses of the Arzhana recalled their levy knights.

The Houses of the Uradabhur fell silent, refusing to answer demands for information, for troops, for supplies.

In the west, a score of Less Houses—among them Ullilion—declared for the High King. The Twelve could neither outwait them nor attack each of them in turn, for with their declarations, their War Princes summoned their teind-levies home: craftworkers and Landbond and even, sometimes, Lightborn and knights. The commons didn't matter—most of them were running off anyway—but the loss of troops and Lightborn dealt the Twelve a crippling blow.

And so Caerthalien rode against Ullilion not for its own enrichment, but in aid of Cirandeiron, for Cirandeiron was attempting to hold Less House Brabamant, and, unable to extend itself further when Ullilion also declared for Lord Vieliessar, had called upon Caerthalien for aid.

And Caerthalien gave it.

Unthinkable even in the days of the Old Alliance. But if the Less Houses of the West succeeded in joining forces with Vieliessar, she would at last have what she'd sought from the very beginning: an army large enough to take the field against all four of the greatest High Houses—and win.

We should have killed her, Runacarendalur thought bitterly. *We should have bribed the Astromancer to kill her. What does she know of war, of ruling, of caring for the lands on which you were born so you may pass them on in sacred trust to your own child?*

Nothing.

The shame of knowing this *creature* was his destined Bondmate was worse than knowing he would never rule Caerthalien. With his own death, he could end her life instantly. A blade in the night silence of his chambers. A moment's deliberate inattention on the battlefield. He should have—he knew that now. But by the time she'd taken Laeldor, it was too late. The rot of her preachings had spread like summer wildfire and suddenly the High Houses were fighting for their very survival.

Caerthalien was fighting.

"Skill makes up for strength. As it is in a komen, *so it is in a House. The High Houses are strong, so they need not be clever. The Less Houses are weak. They can afford no imprudence—in battle or in alliance."*

Elrinonion Swordmaster had said those words to Runacarendalur long ago: then they had puzzled him, but during this terrible War Season, he'd had their truth proved to him over and over. Lengiathion Warlord approved no tactics that had not been used by his greatfathers. Caution and superior numbers did not win battles, but Lengiathion's strategy at least prevented the losing of them.

Against War Prince Vieliessar these tactics would be a disaster.

None of his siblings possessed Runacarendalur's skill in warfare. His House needed him. Runacarendalur of Caerthalien would serve his House to the last beat of his heart. Whether it wanted that service or not.

⊰◻⊱

F all back!" Runacarendalur shouted. He stared wildly around himself. His meisne was scattered and Helecanth was nowhere in sight. "Fall back!" he bawled again, striving to make himself heard over the roar of battle. Ullilion had regrouped and Caerthalien couldn't stand additional losses.

Hating his own necessity, Runacarendalur struck at the destrier of his enemy rather than at the rider. His sword bit into the side of the animal's neck. Blood sprayed and Runacarendalur urged Gwaenor forward. He could feel the stallion laboring for breath, just as he was, for the air was thick with smoke. Ullilion's Lightborn had called Lightning down against Caerthalien's army early in the day. If Ivrulion had not already ordered the Caerthalien Lightborn onto the battle lines, their losses would have been unimaginable. Shield had protected them, but it could not protect the grass and the trees, and the summer was a dry one.

His fury at being forced to fight this unclean battle gave strength to

Runacarendalur's aching muscles, and his opponent could not defend himself while trying to control his wounded destrier. Runacarendalur bludgeoned him until he fell from the saddle and Gwaenor battered his armored body into ruin.

For a blessed moment no one was attacking him. Runacarendalur tried to orient himself, but they'd had to abandon the war banners because Ullilion's Lightborn had been using them as targets. He wasn't sure where he was on the field or whose meisnes were beside him. The wind shifted and smoke poured directly over the Caerthalien line. Runacarendalur tried to shout again and choked instead. His ribs ached from blows taken and from the coughing spasms brought on by smoke.

Suddenly—as welcome as a dipper of cool water—came the mellow call of a Caerthalien warhorn. The smoke skirled and thinned and Helecanth appeared. Her white destrier was grey with smoke, and her surcoat was charred in a dozen places and filthy with blood. But she led a dozen knights of Caerthalien. When she saw Runacarendalur she gestured, using handsign because even if she could be heard, her voice was undoubtedly as raw as his. *What orders?*

Retreat, Runacarendalur signaled.

Quickly they gathered the scattered line of Caerthalien knights for an orderly retreat. They'd been the *deosil* wing of the army. Prince Gimragiel had the center, though Runacar had argued long and loud against that, for 'Ragi was quick to anger and reckless on the field once he lost his temper. The plan of battle the senior commanders had settled among them the night before had survived barely halfway into the first charge across the battlefield. Now Runacarendalur didn't know where Caerthalien's center was or if either of his brothers yet lived.

His plan was to retreat to his own lines, collect his reserve force, and try to locate the rest of the army. It would have worked if he'd actually known where his own lines were. Instead, he led the company directly into a force of Ullilion knights.

⁕

It wasn't your fault," Ivrulion said.

"Tell that to Father, I'm sure he'll believe you," Runacarendalur snarled.

The pavilion smelled of wet cloth, wet leather, and grease. The rain made everything worse. Ullilion's Lightborn had worked the weather to douse the last of the fires and wash the smoke from the air. *And spoil their harvest. If anyone cares about that,* Runacarendalur thought furiously.

He'd barely managed to fight free of the Ullilion knights they'd run into. The wind had freshened and sight-lines had cleared, so he and his knights had headed for the tree line. From there, he'd managed to orient himself and lead his force back to their own lines. By then the day's fighting was nearly over. Just as well, since most of his surviving knights were injured.

"Ullilion's Lightborn cast Confusion on the center of the field. It is a minor spell of Overshadowing, bound to an object. We must give thanks their Lightborn are as incompetent at warcraft as ours are—as many of their own knights were bespelled as ours," Ivrulion said. As he spoke, he carefully sponged the blood away from the cut on his brother's thigh. If there were a piece of metal or leather left in the injury after it was Healed, wound-rot could set in.

"Oh, stop that!" Runacarendalur snapped irritably, swatting at Ivrulion. He tried to get to his feet but sank back onto the chest with a hiss of pain. The wash water was infused with AllHeal and Night's Daughter, but they only dulled the pain a little. The gash was the worst of his injuries; the locking-pins holding his right cuisse in place had been sheared through by a previous blow and he was lucky the second strike hadn't cut through the bone.

"I can certainly take my Magery elsewhere," Ivrulion said. "But if this isn't seen to, you won't be fit to fight for the rest of the season."

Suddenly there was the sound of a scream, loud enough to be heard over the drumming of the rain. Runacarendalur again tried to struggle to his feet.

"Sit still," Ivrulion said. "It's nothing. Dom is torturing the prisoners for information."

"It makes more work for our Lightborn," Runacarendalur said uneasily. He'd watched adherence to the Code of Battle slip a little more each War Season since the end of the Long Peace, but he'd never been comfortable with it. He'd made an oath to the Starry Hunt to uphold the Code on the day his father gave him his sword and spurs, and the Silver Hooves spurned oathbreakers.

"No, it doesn't," Ivrulion said. "We can't afford to waste Healing on the enemy and we can't let Ullilion ransom them. I've told him he's wasting his time questioning them about 'Ragi, but you know how stubborn he is."

Runacarendalur sighed. "'Ragi still hasn't come back?"

"No. He might be on the field, but nobody's going to find him in this rain. We'll search again in the morning."

"Wine," Runacarendalur said, and Serogon jumped to his feet to bring the pitcher. "It's freezing in here," he muttered after drinking. "Take some for yourself," he said to the body servant. "At least it's something."

"When my evening's duties are finished, Prince Runacarendalur," Serogon answered.

"No one listens to me," Runacarendalur complained.

"That's because you have a foul temper when you're injured," Ivrulion said. "At least you started that gash bleeding strongly enough that I think it's clean. Now hold still and shut up."

Ivrulion placed both hands flat against Runacarendalur's skin and closed his eyes. There was the familiar flash of panic Runacarendalur always felt at being Healed, the moment of heat that seemed to start at his bones and radiate outward, and then it was done. There was fresh blood still on his skin, but the skin itself was whole and unbroken once more. He leaned over to pluck the cloth from the basin and wipe the skin clean to see.

"You always do that," Ivrulion said. "Don't you think I know what I'm doing?"

"Of course," Runacarendalur said. He yawned. The other thing he hated about Healings was the flat feeling of exhaustion that followed. "It's just that—" He yawned again.

"Get some sleep," Ivrulion said.

"Soon," Runacarendalur promised. He stood, cautiously testing his leg. It was always strange to expect pain that didn't come. "I need to see Lengiathion first." He snapped his fingers, and Serogon hurried over, carrying boots and a robe.

"He won't have answers for you," Ivrulion said.

"Then at least I can make his life as miserable as everyone else's," Runacarendalur answered.

What should have been a long summer twilight was dark with out-of-season rain instead. Globes of Silverlight made the pavilions glow like colored lanterns and more pale azure globes hung in the air above the streets of the camp, but they seemed to give less light than usual. It didn't matter. Runacarendalur could find his way among the tents blind-folded.

He reached his destination and ducked under the pavilion's awning, tossing his dripping cloak to a waiting servant. Inside it was as damp as every other place in camp, but Lord Lengiathion had managed to arrange for braziers, so at least his pavilion was warm. The senior commanders were all gathered here: Rolason, Gambrinian, Livarre, Meralastant, even Elrinionion. Caerthalien had sent her finest to this battle.

"Has there been any word?" Runacarendalur asked, walking over to the nearest brazier.

"No." Lengiathion shook his head. "The servants are out on the field, of course, but—"

"It's dark and it's wet," Runacarendalur finished wearily.

There was another scream, fainter with distance.

"I told him it's useless," Elrinionion said. "We could barely mark our own companies on the field today, and after the first charge, no one carried banners. Why does Prince Domcariel think Ullilion's *komen* will know where Prince Gimragiel lies?"

"Because he wants them to," Runacarendalur said. "If we aren't wait-ing for anyone but Dom, I will not delay our meal longer. Ivrulion will be some time yet in the Healing tents."

They seated themselves and the servants brought in the first course. The talk ran much as it would in the evening after any battle, save that tonight it turned upon the Magery used by Ullilion.

"If everyone is going to start throwing thunderbolts at each other, why take the field at all? Just stay home and have your Lightborn reduce your enemy's keep to slag," Lord Livarre said irritably.

"I say the Lightborn should keep the beer from spoiling and make my *komen* ready to fight each day and leave the rest to us. They don't under-stand war. Why should they? Your brother is an exception of course, Prince Runacarendalur," Lord Rolason said, nodding in Runacarendalur's direction.

"If they're going to throw thunderbolts at us, we need to throw thun-derbolts at them," Lord Lengiathion said. "Will you speak to your brother, Prince Runacarendalur?"

"I can speak to him," Runacarendalur said. "But he'll tell you what he told me: we need to think carefully before we overturn ancient customs. Do we really wish to do things just because Lord Vieliessar does them? And we cannot expect the Lightborn to fight all day and then Heal all night. They are stretched thin as it is."

"You must decide whether you wish to slay your enemy by Magery or have *komen* on the field," Ivrulion Light-Prince said, stepping into the pavilion. "My Lightborn cannot do both."

He walked over to the table and sat down beside Runacar. His hair and robes were as dry as if he hadn't walked across the camp in a rain-storm and Runacarendalur spared a moment for wistful envy. There were a few spells of Magery he wouldn't mind being able to cast.

"Yet Vieliessar Oathbreaker's Lightborn seem to have no difficulty doing so," Lengiathion said. "Oronviel took Laeldor by Magery—and Mangiralas too."

"And many *komen* died in Mangiralas who might have lived had she not," Runacarendalur said with a sigh. "My lords, this wrangling gains us nothing. What of tomorrow's battle?"

"I shall send for the maps once we have eaten," Lengiathion said. "Let us see if we can manage not to get the rest of our *komen* killed. The purpose of war is to inconvenience the enemy, not ourselves."

"*The purpose of war is to win.*" Runacarendalur heard the ghostly whisper in his mind and could not say where the thought had come from.

But he was afraid that he knew.

⊰⊱

Gwaenor shifted nervously beneath him, obviously wondering why they were standing here, rank upon rank in such silence, without horns or drums or the clash of steel. It was late in Fire Moon, a time of hot breathless days and a sky the color of hammered silver. Runacarendalur could look to his left and see the yellow and blue of Aramenthiali, to the right and see the blue and silver of Cirandeiron: two thousand knights, the honored nobility of the High Houses. The lords and ladies of every court west of the Mystrals had come to Farcarinon to see the infamous Vieliessar brought low. In the front rank the War Princes themselves waited, armed and armored, each with their Warlord beside them. A few yards beyond the first rank of silent, waiting horsemen the grass was covered with an enormous white carpet woven with a design of pine boughs in threads of gold and silver, signaling that this was a meeting in truce. Above this was a canopy of white linen as sheer as silk, held up by four poles of ashwood thickly covered in pure gold. The carpet sparkled like winter snow in moonlight, for the canopy did nothing to block the sun.

Beyond the canopy was a wide, shallow brook. The Toharthay was the division they'd agreed on; the far side was Vieliessar's sovereign territory, the near side was theirs. Runacarendalur remembered fighting across the Meadows of Aralhathumindrion years earlier. Then it had been a broad, pleasant meadow edged with mature forest. Now the forest had been cut back until only the Flower Forest remained, to accommodate the pavilions of all who gathered here. They stretched on for miles, a joyous fair. Children flew kites and nobles flew hawks; there had been great feasts held every night and contests of skill each day for the past fortnight. If not for the fact that the thousands gathered here had scared away any game worth hunting, it would have been idyllic—war without pain and loss.

She will come soon, Runacarendalur told himself. The day, the candlemark, every detail of this meeting had been worked out in advance, during a moonturn of arguing with intermediaries. There had not even been an exchange of hostages; if Vieliessar did not come to parley, the Alliance's armies would attack.

So she will die, and I will die with her, for we are bound together and our hearts beat as one. Surely it is some curse placed upon Caerthalien that I should be so bound to this enemy. At least her death will buy a time of peace in which Domcariel can learn how to rule.

Prince Gatriadde had come to Cirandeiron sennights ago, begging for the chance to take revenge upon the monster who had slain his sister and parents and stolen his domain. He knew every secret place where Vieliessar's army lodged, and Camaibien Lightbrother, who had accompanied him, had drawn detailed maps.

The few scouts the High Houses had dared to send into Mangiralas confirmed Prince Gatriadde's story, so the Alliance had sent an envoy to Vieliessar, offering her and everyone in her army a full pardon in exchange for surrender, saying the disposition of her forces was known and War Season was drawing to a close.

And instead of seeking honorable battle, the Child of the Prophecy, the "destined High King" wept like a child and begged to be allowed to surrender. Now all that remained was the parley, under flags of a truce the Alliance meant to break.

Finally there was the distant sound of a horn. Vieliessar and her escort were approaching. They rode from the trees at the far edge of Aralhathumindrion: Vieliessar and two tailles of knights. She carried the parley banner on a slender ashwood rod, the enormous rectangle of white silk floating on the summer breeze. Each side would carry such a banner: the parley truce was in effect so long as both were held high.

Vieliessar's helmet was crowned with a wreath of pine boughs and there was another garland of them about her destrier's neck. She had changed her armor—instead of the familiar silver, she and all her knights wore green armor and were mounted on white destriers, and Runacarendalur saw, with a sensation of incredulity, that she and her *komen* wore the silver and green of Farcarinon. That was bad enough, but instead of Farcarinon's silver wolf, she claimed the Unicorn as her badge.

Wait, he thought in sudden alarm. *That isn't her.*

He could not say how he knew, but he was certain. *Does she think she can meet under a truce-flag without letting us see her face?*

Even if Runacarendalur wanted to give warning, he could not. The protocol for a Parley of Surrender was rigid and exact, its form unchanged for thousands of years. A shout of warning, an unexpected movement from any of the attendants on either side would be considered an attack. If the Alliance did not abide by the protocols Vieliessar would still be dead . . . but they would never regain the Houses of the East.

And so he could only watch helplessly as the False Vieliessar and her escort rode at a slow walk toward the Toharthay. At the edge of the stream they stopped and the woman raised her visor, exposing her face for all to see.

She looked like Vieliessar. Runacarendalur leaned forward in disbelief. *It is not her!* he insisted to himself.

The massed knights-herald of the Alliance sounded a set of signals. *Truce—the foe is in sight—the foe awaits—the parley begins.* The knight at the False Vieliessar's side raised his visor and put his own warhorn to his lips, sounding an identical set of calls.

A Lightborn Runacarendalur did not know came from the Alliance side to test for spellcraft. The False Vieliessar had brought a Lightborn as well. Both indicated there was no Magery being used here. Runacarendalur ground his teeth in frustration. How could the man not *see*?

As the two Lightborn retreated, the first rank of riders set their horses walking slowly forward.

Bolecthindial Caerthalien, Manderechiel Aramenthiali, Girelrian Cirandeiron, Clacheu Denegathaiel, Chardararg Lalmilgethior, Ferorthaniel Sarmiorion . . . every High House War Prince in the West was in the group riding slowly toward the canopy and the carpet. Each was accompanied by their Warlord, and Caerthalien had supplied the knight-herald, so the numbers on both sides were identical.

And to think, I was proud when Father won the right to carry the truce banner by arguing that Vieliessar would expect Caerthalien— where she was fostered—to take control of the parley. Now he wondered if Domcariel would be War Prince of Caerthalien by sunset . . . or if *he* would be.

Kerothay was a young stallion, temperamental and excitable. It was pure vanity for Lord Bolecthindial to keep a destrier when he no longer rode to war, but today his hot-blooded mount served his purposes well. Caerthalien's War Prince was cueing Kerothay to fidget and the bay stallion was playing up magnificently—dancing skittishly, twisting his neck to snap at the animals walking at either side. When the truce banner Bolecthindial carried fluttered, Kerothay sprang sideways.

Bolecthindial dropped the banner, as anyone might.

The knights-herald of both sides sounded a warning call. *A banner of parley is down.*

Kerothay bounded into the stream, apparently out of control. Lord Lengiathion's mount followed instantly, and a heartbeat later, the other War Princes gave chase. Most of the waiting lords *komen* knew nothing of the secret plans woven around this parley, but the Heirs, the Sword-masters, and a few others did.

The party on the far bank scattered as the Alliance horses charged them. As they exploded into movement, the shimmering white banner the False Vieliessar carried burst into flame. The knights-herald of the Alliance sounded their horns again. *A banner of parley is down.* And then: *Attack.*

The woman who had pretended to be Vieliessar slammed down her visor. In that instant, the glamourie on her and her escort vanished. Their horses were no longer white, nor were they destriers—Runacarendalur recognized the long-legged, deep-chested bodies of animals built for speed and endurance. The twenty-five members of the False Vieliessar's party turned and galloped for the trees.

Runacarendalur took a scant moment to shout a few words to Hele-canth even as he spurred Gwaenor forward. *We can catch them—they'll never reach the trees in time to hide themselves!* But before he reached the stream, the sky went from heat-burnished silver to black. Thunder-crack and lighting-flash came almost together and despite himself Runacaren-dalur flinched, but the enemy Lightborn had called a storm, not a light-ning strike. Icy autumn rain sheeted down out of the sky, destroying visibility and making the grass as slippery as ice.

But the *komen* knew the terrain and destriers were trained to run blind if they must, guided by the hands, knees, and voices of their riders. The charging knights barely slowed as they crossed the stream. The tight column spread until the line of knights extended the full width of the meadow. Around and behind him Runacarendalur could hear shouts of glee—if the War Princes wanted to claim victory without battle, their *komen* wanted to fight.

He'd seen an opening ahead, and was just about to spur Gwaenor through it, when Runacarendalur heard screams of agony, close enough and loud enough to slice through the thunder of hooves and the hiss of the rain. He couldn't rein in without being instantly trampled, but he slowed as much as he could, though Gwaenor fought him. There was another flash of lightning—it seemed to make the raindrops hang un-moving in mid-air—and he saw horses down, too many to count.

Trying to jump the downed animals was madness. Anything else was certain death.

With hands and heels he gathered Gwaenor up, and the destrier soared over the obstacles in front of him, then jumped again, quickly, to clear a body in armor lying nearly at his feet. Some of the knights thrown from the saddle were getting up. Others lay motionless, sprawled on the grass. They were tangled, *komen* and horses both, in uprooted stakes and thin coils of painted rope. *Tripwires. They strung tripwires. They knew we'd break the parley truce!* Knowing Vieliessar had expected betrayal infuriated him. If she'd known it wasn't going to be a true parley, why agree to it at all?

The rain was slacking off. He wondered if the enemy thought nobody would be willing to follow them into the trees.

I'll follow wherever you go. Lead me to Vieliessar and I'll kill her myself.

Nadalforo and the Lightborn galloped for the trees. It had taken a dozen Mages to cast and hold the glamourie that gave her the seeming of Lord Vieliessar, more to give the horses they rode the seeming of destriers. The bespellings would have been discovered had Isilla Lightsister not Overshadowed the Lightbrother who would have revealed the truth.

The storm started right on time. Strung low ahead were a staggered series of trip-lines—and if their pursuers continued the chase after running into them, the woods were filled with beast-pits that held sharpened stakes at the bottom. And if there were some still foolish enough to pursue after that, there were more traps waiting. There was only one safe way across the meadow and through the woods, and you needed Magesight to find it. Nadalforo was no Mage, but the helm she wore was bespelled, and through its eye-slits the markers she needed to see glowed with blue fire.

The moment they burst out of the trees, a hand-picked cadre from her old Stonehorse Free Company rode from cover to join them. First Sword Faranglis was leading Nadalforo's destrier; she vaulted from the back of the palfrey and flung herself into the destrier's saddle. Faranglis handed her a sword, which she slipped into the empty scabbard she'd been wearing.

"What news?" he asked.

"Some of them will be right behind us," she said.

"Torch the forest," Faranglis said. "Lightborn can make anything burn."

"Tangisen. Your Keystone Spell is Fire. Do it," Isilla Lightsister said.

The Lightbrother turned back toward the stand of woods and seemed to simply look at it. Nadalforo was about to tell him it was taking too much time, when every tree in the wood—and every leaf upon the ground, every twig, every bush, every burnable thing—suddenly burst into flame. The wave of heat rolled over them with the force of a blow. The palfreys shifted nervously.

"There were people in there," Tangisen said quietly.

"And now they're dead people. Come on," Nadalforo said.

They crossed Farcarinon's derelict fields, moving south at a steady, ground-covering pace. The plan called for them to ride until they struck the southern Sanctuary road and then head east. If Prince Gatriadde and Camaibien Lightbrother had managed to escape in the chaos, they'd head for that road as well. If they hadn't, they'd be with the Alliance army that marched on Mangiralas. They'd escape then and find their way east. Or they'd die.

They'd ridden until the burning woodland was far behind them and the last of the Mage-called storm clouds had drifted away, when Nadalforo saw a flicker of brightness through the trees ahead and reigned in. "We may have trouble," she said quietly.

A moment later, the enemy came into view. Green surcoats with three gold stars. Caerthalien. Some of the Caerthalien destriers wore caparisons, indicating they and their riders had been part of the honor guard. Most didn't.

"I make it three hundred horse," Faranglis said quietly.

"That we can see," Nadalforo said. "Caerthalien musters twenty times that."

She glanced at the twenty-four Lightborn with her. Some looked worried. Some looked terrified. All of them had shed every part of their armor they could safely remove while riding, but they were still wearing too much of it to look like anything but knights. "Go there," she said, pointing toward the right. "If anyone comes near you, surrender at once and say you're Lightborn. It might save you."

"I want to fight," Isilla Lightsister said stubbornly.

"And we don't have time to teach you just now," Nadalforo snapped. "So unless you plan to strike them all dead with Magery—*go*."

"So we fight?" Faranglis asked, sounding pleased.

"Unless you think asking them very nicely to go away will work," Nadalforo said. "How shall we do this?"

"Knights like to charge. I say we make them chase us. We'll get a good idea of how many they are and maybe draw them away from their reinforcements," Faranglis said.

Nadalforo's commanders began riding back up the column of the company, passing her orders to the warriors. Nadalforo called up her mental map of Farcarinon. To the right was a stand of trees covering what had once been a manorial estate. The terrain was treacherous for horses, filled with holes, half-buried stones, and jagged bits of wall. It would have to do.

Thank the Hunt Lord Vieliessar sent us to the parley instead of some of her pretty komen. At least we have a chance of getting out alive. . . .

The Caerthalien knight-herald blew her warhorn. The signal to charge.

⌘

We have superior numbers, my lord," Helecanth said in satisfaction.

"And we will use them," Runacarendalur answered.

The parley knights had been joined by a grand-taille of riders in the browned armor of mercenaries. One of the green knights gestured, and the other green-armored knights, along with the Lightborn who had accompanied them, rode to Runacarendalur's left. None of them had their helms on, and he could see their hair was cropped short. They were all Lightborn. Lightborn wearing armor.

That's how they tricked us.

"We will accept no surrender," he said, and Helecanth nodded. They'd need information about Vieliessar's plans, but they could get it from the Lightborn.

The mercenaries formed ranks, preparing for battle. "Sound the charge," Runacarendalur said, lowering his visor.

Helecanth raised the warhorn to her lips and sounded the call.

Caerthalien charged.

There was always a few moments between the clarion and the first clash of weapons that renewed Runacarendalur's joy in battle, his conviction that the Code was a magnificent instrument that evoked all that was great and glorious in the spirits of those who embraced it. The rush of wind over his armor, the thunder of hooves behind him, the speed and power of the animal he rode—all these things conferred a transcendence not even the Lightborn could know. In the moments of the charge, Runacarendalur was one with the *komen* he led—and not merely with them, but with all who had come before them and all who would follow. It was the closest thing to immortality that any being could possess.

Then his line hit the enemy column.

The encircling maneuver he was attempting fell apart instantly. The rear of the enemy column swung to his right, but not to form an opposing line. They were running for the trees; the head of the column faded back before Runacarendalur's assault before turning to follow those who had already fled. They meant to make this a chase, but the enemy still had to fight through the *deosil* side of the Caerthalien line to escape, and Caerthalien did not intend to let them. Wherever either side possessed a momentary advantage of numbers, it used that advantage ruthlessly. It was butcher's work, with nothing of elegance or honor about it. Runacarendalur withdrew his *tuathal* wing rather than have it chase the enemy across the field, and sent it galloping along the back of his line. If it reached the trees first, he could keep the enemy from vanishing into them like so many rats down a rat-hole, and terrain elements blocked their retreat to the north and west. If he could keep them on open ground, superior numbers and superior skill would grant Caerthalien the victory.

With enough time.

※

Nadalforo's company retreated as planned, but even though it was outnumbered and should have waited for reinforcement, Caerthalien's *deosil* line forced the battle and their *tuathal* line simply vanished. *We're being flanked,* Nadalforo thought, but there was nothing she could do about it. They couldn't run, so they had to fight. She hoped the Lightborn would flee—because if they didn't, if they were questioned, all of them knew at least something of Lord Vieliessar's plans.

Her blade rang off the pauldron of the enemy knight before her. She sparred and feinted for a few exchanges to convince her enemy he knew what she'd do, then swung her mount wide and jammed the point of her blade directly into her opponent's groin. Cuisses only went to the top of the thigh, and faulds to the middle of the belly. The raised pommel of the war saddle and the long chain shirt were supposed to protect the unarmored groin and lower belly. They did their job because *komen* were more interested in fighting beautifully than in killing their foes.

Nadalforo gave her blade a twist as she withdrew it and saw the blood of a severed artery spray; if her foe screamed, there was too much noise to hear, but he dropped his sword and thrashed. His destrier, taking the shift in position for a command, reared, and the knight fell from the saddle. Nadalforo was already turning to find other prey.

She heard the shrill notes of one of her company's signal whistles calling: *disengage—retreat—go right.* It could only be hope, not possibility, for Prince Runacarendalur was out for revenge. He wouldn't retreat unless his defeat was certain, and that meant she'd have to manage to kill most of his attack force.

When she heard warhorns ring out—*the foe is in sight—attack—attack*—she knew reinforcements had arrived. The best her meisne could hope for was to die fighting. *I've never thought the souls of dead warriors go to ride with the Starry Hunt forever, but soon I'll know.*

But when the reinforcements reached the battleground, they weren't Caerthalien's. The newly arriving knights wore green surcoats, but the device on them was a silver Unicorn, not three gold stars. Green surcoat fought green surcoat, and the blazon of the silver Unicorn was every-where.

Once again Nadalforo heard the signal whistles calling for disen-gagement and retreat, and this time she was able to ride free of the melee.

"I thought we were going to die fighting for free!" Faranglis shouted when she reached him. He was already moving toward the road, bran-dishing his sword in a signal: *close up and follow.*

"Not today," Nadalforo answered. Now it was Caerthalien that was outnumbered, but it would take Lord Vieliessar's knights time to slay them all, and time was the one thing they didn't have.

They reached the road. Prince Gatriadde's russet surcoat stood out among browned mail and green armor. Nadalforo was glad he'd man-aged to escape; his role in this had been vital and he'd endured danger and sacrifice to carry it out. She gave the order to form up for another at-tack on Caerthalien—she had no intention of letting Household knights fight Stonehorse's battles—and as she did, she heard someone sound the call for retreat. She couldn't tell which side was calling for disengagement.

Suddenly the Caerthalien destriers turned and bolted, running as fast as they could. Any animals without riders fled as well, quickly pass-ing the others. The moment Caerthalien took flight, Lord Vieliessar's knights galloped toward the road, leaving behind them a field covered with the dead.

The Lightborn had found a way to fight after all.

Nadalforo spurred her destrier toward the relief force's commander. "Making the enemy's horses bolt seems like a convenient way to win a battle," she said when she reached him.

"It only wins the battle," Thoromarth answered. "It doesn't win the war. "

"I don't object to winning a battle," Nadalforo answered. "Especially since it means I'll live to see the rest of the war."

Thoromarth laughed harshly. "I never knew a sellsword to be such an optimist."

⊰⧮⊱

One moment Caerthalien was in the middle of a battle Runacarendalur was convinced they could win. The next moment, Gwaenor— and every other Caerthalien destrier—bolted.

Nothing the prince did slowed Gwaenor's headlong flight. The stallion was insensible to the command of bit and spur. Runacarendalur concentrated on keeping his seat. If he fell from Gwaenor's saddle he'd be trampled by the destriers running behind them. Riderless animals galloped past the knights, and it was a small comfort to know the riderless animals would trip any hidden traps or be the ones to break a leg in a hidden burrow. Gwaenor's neck was covered with foam and bloody foam flew from his jaws. Runacarendalur only hoped the spell set on them was not meant to make the animals run themselves to death.

It had taken them two candlemarks to reach the Sanctuary road. Now they covered the same distance in a fraction of that time. As they neared Aralhathumindrion, the air stank of smoke and roasting meat. They'd seen a column of smoke as they'd left the encampment, but hadn't known what burned.

Now they saw.

There was nothing left of the forest but charred ground and a few charred stubs of trees. Smoke still curled up from the ash and embers of the woodland. The riderless destriers reached the burned area first and ran straight onward. Ash swirled up in a choking cloud around them, mingling with the smoke. But they swerved to avoid the now-exposed open pits, which made Runacarendalur hope the bespelling had lifted. If the horses were no longer bolting in a blind panic, perhaps they would answer to their riders' commands.

"Turn them!" he shouted to the rider at his side. He bawled the command over and over, until it was heard and passed back through the ranks. Simply bringing the horses to a stop wouldn't be enough, even if they could. The others behind would run over them, or past them, and maybe spook them into bolting again.

Gwaenor strained against the rein. Runacarendalur feared he would not be able to make the destrier turn, until from the ranks behind him, a warhorn sounded: *wheel* deosil—*form column—wheel* deosil—*all knights.*

And Gwaenor turned, obedient to a signal he'd had heard every day of his life since foalhood.

By the time they were heading back the way they'd come, Gwaenor had slowed to a canter, then to a trot. Other destriers, still moving at a gallop, passed him, but the whole force had turned in response to the warhorn. At last, the animals were all standing. Winded, blown, exhausted, overheated—but alive.

INTERLUDE THREE

SORCERY AND STRATEGY

In the changeable world of Form and Time the Light had hidden the only weapon which could slay the eternal beautiful children of *He Who Is*. Only the arrogance of the Light had disclosed its secret, for had it not shared that secret with the Elvenkind, the Endarkened would have remained ignorant of it . . .

Until too late.

Virulan threw himself into preparations for the coming war as never before. In the World Without Sun, he made a nursery of horror, taking the races of the Bright World captive and there, twisting them to create the legions of his army. From the Fauns, he created the dwerro. From the fairies, he made goblins. Under his fell twistings, Hippogriffs became Serpentmarae, wolves became Coldwarg. From every living thing with which the Light had filled the Bright World, Virulan made a creature of the Darkness.

He let his monsters breed.

He withdrew his Endarkened from the lands of the Elflings, sending them across the Great Waters to hunt. Even there, he ordered them to work in secret. There would be no gathering of Brightworld clans against him, no warning for the Children of the Light of their fate.

And he himself hunted the Unicorn.

The creature was clever. All was as Uralesse had said: no matter what ordinary concealments of their form and nature the Endarkened used, the Unicorn could sense their presence. Finding where it laired was difficult. Capturing it seemed impossible. But Virulan was patient and clever. He considered the matter carefully, then set his artisans to craft nets.

Miles of nets.

This time, when the creature was spotted, the sky above Shadow Mountain turned black with the flight of the Endarkened. It was a risk to enter the Bright World so openly, but Virulan was determined to solve this riddle. He did not fear the power of the Unicorn, but one must always use the proper attack against the enemy. It was such attention to detail which elevated destruction to the realm of art.

As before, the Unicorn turned and bolted into the Flower Forest at the first sight of the Endarkened, but this time Virulan was prepared. He drove a horde of the Lesser Endarkened after it, knowing the creature would believe it could outrun its pursuers. When it exited the forest on the far side, the Endarkened were waiting. The Unicorn saw the net, but even as it turned to run along it, seeking its end, the Endarkened were drawing the net closed. The Lesser Endarkened swarmed out of the forest, encircling the net from without, holding it firm to the ground.

Inside the circle of netting, the Unicorn stood at bay. Its silver-white coat was fluffed out, making it appear soft and harmless. But there was nothing harmless-looking about the long, spiraling horn, which glowed red.

Virulan landed in the center of the circle, with Uralesse beside him. Virulan had a faint suspicion that being here was not a really good idea. If something unexpected happened, it might give his fellow Endarkened the absurd notion that their King did not know everything that transpired both in the Bright World and the World Without Sun. But from the moment the plan to trap the elusive creature with nets was made—and Virulan was now no longer entirely sure whose idea it had been—Uralesse had seemed to take it for granted that Virulan would of course desire the honor of the capture, or the kill, for himself. It had become impossible to say otherwise without seeming over-cautious, without according Uralesse too much honor.

"What use is your swiftness against our cleverness, Horned One?" Virulan said, drawing himself up to his full, imposing height.

The Unicorn's nostrils flared as at a very bad smell. "What use are your nets against an enemy you can't touch?" it answered. "As for 'clever-ness' . . . well, that's debatable."

"I shall rip that horn from your head and skewer you with it!" Viru-lan roared, lunging for it.

"Oh, please do," the Unicorn answered. It reared up, raising its head high so that Virulan's taloned fingers missed their target and buried themselves in the Unicorn's downy throat.

Pain! Virulan had often dealt suffering to others, but never had he felt such an unholy agony as he experienced at touching the Unicorn's body. The pain was so great, and so unexpected, that he could do nothing to conceal it. He roared with agony and sprang backward.

The Unicorn . . . snickered.

"Foolish Virulan!" it said, its sides heaving with its laughter. "I am purity incarnate! The touch of my horn can turn the most virulent poi-son into sweet water—shall we see what it will do to a creature whose very thoughts are poison?" It reared again, brandishing its horn menac-ingly.

Virulan took a slow step backward. He was not foolish enough to order any of his minions to attack. If they tried and failed, such failure would kindle the ember of rebellion in their treacherous hearts. If they tried and succeeded . . .

It would be not an ember, but a flame.

He smiled.

"Then I shall not touch it—or you. But you will die here this day. And any obstacle you might present to my plans will thus be ended." He spread his wings and bounded into the sky. "Bind it in the nets!" he cried. "We shall see who is the greater!"

The Endarkened hurried to obey, and in moments the Unicorn was buried beneath several hundredweight of bronze nets. When it lay crushed against the ground Virulan stepped onto the pile of nets that covered it, being careful not to let his feet touch its body—and not to let the others see his care

"Where is your laughter now, Unicorn?" he said cruelly.

"Still here," the Unicorn answered, though it was gasping for breath. "You see . . . I am not . . . the only one . . . of my kind. They watch . . . even now. So I must say . . . King of Shadows . . . that the last laugh is . . . mine."

Virulan gazed around himself in horror, but he saw nothing. "Bring stones!" he screamed. "Heavy stones! Crush the life from this witless talking beast!"

The Endarkened hurried to obey and soon there was nothing to see but a mound of stones and the twisted links of the ruined net.

The creature was dead, but even the scent of its blood did not comfort Virulan.

"So you see, Uralesse, it is a simple matter to slay these creatures," he said grandly. "I shall expect you to be more efficient about it next time."

He held Uralesse's gaze with his own. If this had been some concealed ploy of Uralesses's to discredit him, it had failed. If it were not, let Uralesse be humbled by this new task his King had set him. If he succeeded, the hateful Unicorns would be scoured from the world. If he failed, then any threat he might have hoped to present would be ended as well.

"Of course, my king. All will be as you say."

As he watched Uralesse attempt to pretend he was delighted at this new honor, much of Virulan's good humor was restored. Let Uralesse plot. Let them all plot. Virulan was still the master of Shadow Mountain and all that dwelt within it.

And the time of war—and his ultimate triumph—came nearer with each Brightworld day.

CHAPTER THIRTEEN

A PARLIAMENT OF GHOSTS

*The first was Prince Cirandeiron, who rode a white horse and had armor
of gleaming silver. His destrier's armor was silver, too, and there were
diamonds set in his shoes. The second was Queen Telthorelandor, who
rode a golden horse and had armor of brightest gold. Her destrier's armor
was golden, too, and he was shod in cairngorms and purest gold. The
third was Aramenthiali, with a grey horse and jade armor, and every
stitch of his harness was studded with emeralds and green stones. Each
was more beautiful than the next, but Queen Pelashia was the most
beautiful of all, and her horse was shod with diamonds, and her armor
was of crystal, and the sword she bore was brighter than the moon and
the sun . . .*

— *The Courtship of Amrethion and Pelashia*

Candlemarks had passed since Runacarendalur and the other
Caerthalien knights had led their exhausted destriers back
across Aralhathumindrion and placed them in the care of
Horsemaster Filioniel. Today should have been a day of triumph, even
though Runacarendalur wouldn't have been here to see it: Vieliessar
dead, the Alliance preparing to march on Mangiralas and smash her
army, every encampment bright with torches and lanterns, fragrant with
the scent of victory feasts and joyous with songs of celebration.

Instead, the long summer twilight saw a gathering of the lords and
high nobles of the High Houses. Such an assemblage was too large for
any single pavilion to host it, even if the War Princes could have agreed
on who that host should be. Instead, they, their consorts, and their heirs
met beneath an enormous canopy in the meadow, set, ironically, where

the parley carpet had been laid that morning. *Komen* stood guard at the edges of the meadow so that the lords' speech could not be overheard or interrupted.

"What happened?" Lord Bolecthindial demanded.

"Magery," Ivrulion Light-Prince answered superfluously. "I believe it is possible to Ward our destriers so what happened today cannot happen again, but that will take time. And it will take more time if you want every beast in the army Warded as well."

"Do you think they'll do it again?" Gimragiel asked.

"Since it worked so well the first time, yes." Ivrulion didn't have to add the obvious: that Vieliessar's Lightborn not only had more incentive to use Magery on the field, they'd almost certainly had more practice.

"Has anyone seen little Prince Gatriadde lately?" Lord Girelrian asked archly, gazing ostentatiously about herself. "Didn't he ride with you, my dear Prince Runacarendalur?"

"Dead, I suppose," Runacarendalur said, shrugging. "The carts we sent to retrieve our fallen and wounded should be back soon." *If there are any wounded,* he added mentally. The mercenaries had fought like cornered weasels and neither side had offered quarter.

"I only ask," Lord Girelrian continued, "because I could not fail to notice Camaibien Lightbrother is also missing. Unless you believe he, too, was killed in the fighting?"

"You believe this was a trap from the very beginning," Lord Ivaloriel said calmly.

"Well of course it was a trap—only we were supposed to be the ones who set it!" Ladyholder Dormorothon snapped. "Prince Gatriadde told us the truth. I heard his thoughts myself. And so did you, Prince Ivrulion."

Ivrulion bowed, acknowledging the truth of her words. "Prince Gatriadde wished vengeance. The information he provided was in accordance with the thoughts of his heart. The maps Camaibien Lightbrother drew were accurate. "

"But you never set a spell of Heart-Seeing on either of them," Consort-Prince Irindandirion said. "So you don't actually know."

"*No one* set a spell of Heart-Seeing on Gatriadde Mangiralas," Runacarendalur said, locking his gaze with Irindandirion's. "Everyone agreed that True Speech was sufficient. If Gatriadde was not who he seemed, none of us is more to blame than any other."

Runacarendalur held Irindandirion's eyes in blatant challenge. Lord Girelrian was the War Prince of Cirandeiron; Irindandirion was only her Consort-Prince. It did not make Runacarendalur's tacit challenge any less a violation of protocol, and it meant Consort-Prince Irindandirion was more likely to accept: if Runacarendalur won, he gained nothing but Irindandirion's personal possessions, not Cirandeiron itself.

"An important point we would all do well to remember," Ladyholder Edheleorn said, her light voice breaking the tension of the moment. "Prince Runacarendalur is to be commended for bringing it to our attention."

"I still find it hard to understand what the upstart gains," War Prince Clacheu Denegathaiel said. "She approached us asking to surrender. Why these sennights of games if she never meant to negotiate in good faith?"

"It bought her time," War Prince Ferorthaniel Sarmiorion said. Sarmiorion was one of two High Houses east of the Mystrals. "She took Mangiralas. The Less Houses of the West went mad. We heard rumors of treaties with the Houses of the Western Shore, though we could not confirm that. Then . . . nothing. Until Gatriadde arrives, offering to give us her army. And suddenly she begs to parley."

"But what has she done with this time?" Lady Girelrian asked. "She cannot expect us to leave her in peace to winter in Mangiralas."

"I'm not finished," Ferorthaniel said. "Her treaty with Ivrithir required them to assign their claim to the Unicorn Throne to her, as did her treaty with Laeldor. We can assume her treaties with Amrolion and Daroldan are similar. She's counting on us not attacking the Western Shore, and she's right, for it would be madness to weaken our only defenders against the Beastlings. Araphant she holds absolutely, as she does Oronviel. Ullilion has declared for her, and as for the rest of the Western Less Houses . . .

"Either they have declared for her or are simply in rebellion. We do not know, and if we do not, *she* does not. But their rebellion caused us to form this unprecedented alliance, and once she got word of our alliance, she knew she couldn't risk being attacked by our conjoined force. That's why she offered a surrender."

"Which was a ruse. But what does a moonturn or two of delay gain her?" Lord Clacheu said. "It isn't as if we'll forget about her."

Ferorthaniel smiled. "No. But you've forgotten one thing Sarmiorion never can. In three moonturns, the passes over the Mystrals become difficult. In two more, impassable. I'll wager anything you like she's taken her army east, whether you've seen it move or not. She'll winter in the Uradabhur, and I don't think she'll sit quiet when the end of War Season comes. I think she'll fight through the winter. By spring, she'll probably hold the thirty Houses of the Uradabhur in vassalage.

"If you can't keep your client domains loyal when you're camped on their doorstep, what success will you have when she is there and you're on the other side of the mountains, waiting for spring thaw?"

"How kind of you to warn us in advance you're planning to betray us," Ladyholder Glorthiachiel snapped.

"If you think that, you are truly mad," Ferorthaniel said. "Do you think I came west for my health? Even a lion cannot stand against a pack of wolves. Sarmiorion is the only High House in the Uradabhur, and the Uradabhur will fall by spring. Mark me when I say it."

"So do we all surrender now?" Runacarendalur asked angrily. "Bend the knee and bow the neck to a madwoman of an erased House who thinks she's the fulfillment of a prophecy that no one's ever been able to make sense of? And what happens to us—to everything—when we crown her High King?"

"It is not my intention to permit Serenthon's daughter to claim the prize we denied to Serenthon," Lord Bolecthindial growled.

"Then choose," Ferorthaniel said inexorably. "Follow her across the Mystrals now, knowing you must fight through the winter—and know you will have the west to reconquer next springtide—or let her take the

Uradabhur while you make sure of the west, and know she will meet you next War Season with an unstoppable army at her back."

"Aramenthiali rides east at once," Lord Manderechiel said, getting to his feet.

"As does Caerthalien," Lord Bolecthindial said, answering the unspoken challenge. He too rose to his feet.

"—Vondaimieriel—"

"—Cirandeiron—"

"—Telthorelandor—"

"—Denegathaiel—"

"—Lalmilgethior—"

"—Rolumienion—"

In moments all the High Houses present had pledged themselves to war.

❈

From the moment she had conceived the plan, she had known it was more dangerous than any of her commanders could imagine. Caerthalien would be there. Caerthalien's Heir-Prince would be there. Runacarendalur might be slain, and his death would mean hers as well. Caerthalien's Heir-Prince knew of the Bond as surely as she did, and could slay her with a blade to his own throat. The Caerthalien lords were cold and proud, and their hatred for Farcarinon endured a century after its erasure. Did they hold such a weapon as the life of her Bondmate in their hands, they would not abstain from its wielding.

And yet he had. It was the greatest, strangest gift she had ever taken from the hands of a sworn foe. How long could she count upon such forbearance? What was its source?

She did not know.

Nor could she know, until the day she held Heir-Prince Runacarendalur of Caerthalien in bondage. If that day came.

If it does not . . .

Then she would have failed. And Darkness would take them all.

But today, I fight.

In another few sennights it would be a full Wheel of the Year since she had challenged Thoromarth for possession of Oronviel and taken her first step upon the road to the High Kingship. It was nearly two years since the Rain Moon when she had walked from the Sanctuary of the Star for the last time. In all those moonturns she had imagined both defeat and victory. But her imagined path to victory had been nothing like this.

She had meant to gather up a handful of Less Houses—as she had done. She had meant to call mercenary and outlaw to her banner—as she had done. She had meant to lift the heavy yoke of custom from the necks of Farmhold and Landbond and teach them the ways of war—as she had done. She had meant to shatter custom and bring Pelashia's Children to the battlefield—and now the Warhunt rode with her. But never in hope or in madness had she thought that War Princes unconquered would rally to her banner, freely pledging to support her as High King.

Yet beneath her hand she held twenty-five of the Houses of the West in vassalage: their princes, their *komen,* their folk. It was as if her vow to make herself High King had been spark to tinder that had waited long for the kiss of flame. As if Amrethion's Prophecy did not shape only her to its needs, but the folk of all the land.

She would take the Uradabhur as well.

The false parley had bought her the time to move the whole of her force east through the Dragon's Gate. They mustered now in Ceoprent-rei, the northernmost of three linked mountain valleys bordered on both sides by the peaks of the Mystrals. The mountain valley was the last place of true shelter and true safety her army would know, for when they reached the land beyond, they must fight.

Come spring, the Alliance of the High Houses would follow her over the Mystrals, baying for blood. The armies would slaughter each other without mercy or quarter, for the false parley had been a double-edged blade: it had bought her the time to move her army eastward . . . and it had bound the Houses of the Grand Alliance to one another with blood and vengeance.

The Trueborn Houses number twenty in the Grand Windsward, six in the Arzhana, thirty in the Uradabhur, forty-two from the Mystrals to Great Sea Ocean. Seventy-eight War Princes must yet decide I should be High King. If I gain the Uradabhur as I hope, that leaves forty-eight.

The meisne the Twelve could bring to the field was as great as all she might hope to bring to face them, for she knew she could not count on the Houses of the Windsward to ride to her aid, whether they supported her or not. The distance was too great. They would starve before they crossed the Arzhana, and even if they did not, High House Nantirworiel held the only pass which led into the Uradabhur, and it would never let an enemy army pass.

The Twelve would never declare for her without being defeated. And if she meant to defeat them, she must find something greater than swords and *komen*.

Magery is the answer. But I am already using Magery. Perhaps if I hadn't, the War Princes would not have formed their Alliance.

The maps beneath her hands were covered with marks drawn from the whisperings of ghosts. In the past moonturn she'd combed her borrowed memories for landmarks and events of the distant past, hoping they would form some pattern she could understand. Here Lady Indinathiel lost a third of her army. There Lord Githonel set fire to the enemy's croplands. She'd marked the forest in which Lady Parmanaya was lost, the plain on which Lord Tengolin lost the battle because of his feud with Nelpanar, the encampment where Lord Noremallin's army mutinied. The marks all led across the Feinolons, the Bazrahils, the Mystrals. Her ancestors had ridden west, fleeing the fall of Celephriandullias-Tildorangelor. Amrethion High King had died. Pelashia Great Queen had died. And Amrethion's lords had hunted their children, and their children's children, and they had fled west. . . .

"I have had speech of Isilla," Aradreleg said. "Will you hear, my lord?"

"In a moment," Vieliessar said, staring at the map. She finally looked up to see Aradreleg standing before the map-table, looking both worried and impatient. "I plan our victory, and it preoccupies me," Vieliessar said, forcing herself to sound cheerful and conciliating. "If you would rather I did not . . ."

Aradreleg did not answer her smile. "My lord, there is that which you must know. Isilla Farspoke me to say the scouts Lord Thoromarth sent have returned to him."

Vieliessar glanced toward the doorway of the pavilion. It was dark outside now, and the pavilion was lit by balls of Silverlight she must have conjured up herself. On the edge of the map-table stood a platter of food, untouched. She wondered who had brought it. Rithdeliel, she suspected.

"If it is ill news, it is best given at once," she said gently, though Aradreleg's thoughts already gave her a sense of it. The words that followed were Thoromarth's, and in the sharp brief sentences, Vieliessar heard despair.

Though it was already Harvest Moon, the Alliance was not retreating to winter quarters. They followed hot on the heels of Nadalforo and Thoromarth's force. A sennight behind them at best.

I had thought to have more time! Vieliessar thought in anguish. With the Alliance following her now instead of next spring, the Houses of the Uradabhur might be terrified into adhering to their traditional loyalties. If she must conquer Less House Jaeglenhend by force of arms before she turned to face the Alliance, she would have only scant days to do so—but she must have Jaeglenhend's loyalty before she could turn against the Alliance, for no army had ever gained victory while fighting enemies both before and behind.

And I do not wish to face them in battle at all!

"How long until Lord Thoromarth's force reaches Ceoprentrei?" Vieliessar asked, her voice even.

"Two days, perhaps three," Rithdeliel said. His voice was sharp with worry. "My lord, what orders?"

"Why, what orders do you imagine?" Vieliessar answered, making her voice light. "We prepare the army to march—and fight."

⊰✦⊱

As was customary at the start of a campaign, tonight Vieliessar would hold a feast for her senior commanders that would begin with a sacrifice to the Silver Hooves. She gathered from the herds of Mangiralas a dozen flawless colts and the feasting began with their sacrifice.

She was obscurely glad that Gatriadde Mangiralas was not there to see.

The company was by now too large to gather within any single pavilion, for her army numbered in the tens of thousands. She cleared the meadow her skirmishers had used for drilling and her Lightborn restored the turf. Then over all she caused to be set an enormous canopy, its fabrics joined and doubled by Magery until a veil of green and silver stood between the gathered company and the unwavering stars. From her seat at the High Table Vieliessar looked out over the assembly and knew that if she died tomorrow, she would still have accomplished enough to make her name a legend. War Princes of Houses that had fought one another since the Fall of Celephriandullias-Tildorangelor sat in amity— *true* amity—beside sellswords, beside Landbonds raised up to be Captains of Archers, beside Lightborn who took the field wearing chain shirts beneath their Green Robes. In this moment, the High King's pledge was redeemed in an instant out of time, for here there was neither High House nor Low, Lord nor Landbond. There were only her people.

Tomorrow they would march down through the Dragon's Gate into the Uradabhur, and there they would fight, though she did not yet presume to say whom their enemy might be. And they would fight on until her cause was claimed by victory or by defeat, and upon the anvil of that forging they would craft either the sword with which to face the Darkness when it came . . .

. . . or the pyre of their utter destruction.

❦

What do I need to do to become High King?" Vieliessar asked. The banquet was over and it was yet a few candlemarks until dawn.

Over the course of the feast she had turned aside the questions Thoromarth, among others, had asked; they naturally wanted to know her plans, in case those plans were something they might want to argue her out of. But Gunedwaen had asked no questions, and on impulse she had invited him to accompany her on the walk back to her pavilion.

"To win is usually considered a good first step to becoming Commander, War Prince, or High King," Gunedwaen answered as they reached Vieliessar's pavilion. Gunedwaen stepped forward and lifted the tent flap for Vieliessar to enter, bowing as he did so, though not without a generous measure of irony. Vieliessar stepped forward and Gunedwaen followed her inside.

There was no one else of whom Vieliessar would have asked a question such as this, especially on the eve of battle, but Vieliessar trusted Gunedwaen. Not as someone whose fealty she held—for the oath had been in some sense extorted, and oaths had been broken before—and not as a useful ally whose self-interest would keep him from rebellion, for Farcarinon's Swordmaster was uncompromisingly loyal.

No. Though he would reject the very concept, she trusted him as her equal.

Those who held Vieliessar's respect were few. She loved sparingly and despairingly and valued many fearlessly. She could see too clearly why the men and women who fought for her did so. For vengeance. For self-interest, and she did not despise that, for clear-eyed self-interest was precious to her. Uncounted more followed her for the simple fact that their lives with her were better than the lives they'd left, and that saddened her even while she esteemed it as the precious gift it was, for many who had joined her would die before her final victory was achieved.

But Gunedwaen followed her for love. He did not value the future she meant to summon, nor did he believe in the Prophecy she steered by. Yet he would follow her until the day Aradhwain Bride of Battles placed her cold kiss upon his lips and sent him to ride forever with the Starry Hunt.

The pavilion was empty; no doubt her servants had gone to one of the many celebrations being held tonight. But the stove had been kindled and a kettle of water stood steaming gently atop it; spell-lanterns radiated dim light. Vieliessar conjured enough Silverlight to brighten the outer room and saw a tea service arranged on a tray waiting on a table. She shook loose tea into the pot and filled it from the kettle.

Gunedwaen raised her eyebrows. "Despite all our teachings, you still have the habits of a Sanctuary Mage," he said.

"Am I to wait for you to serve me? You have served me well enough in these past moonturns, I think." The tea had finished steeping so she poured for both of them. Steam curled from the delicate cups. "So you say, I must win. And how will I know when I've won?"

Gunedwaen cocked his head, studying her. "People might stop trying to kill you," he offered. "Or not. But the simple answer to your question is one you already know: have all the War Princes proclaim you High King."

"A more difficult task than it sounds. I had hoped," she said, offering up the word with unaccustomed diffidence for she well knew Gunedwaen believed that if one must hope, one had lost, "to gain the Uradabhur before facing the Alliance."

"Whereupon they would concede and anoint you High King," Gunedwaen said. "But that is not your road to victory. It never has been."

Vieliessar gazed at him in puzzlement and after a pause Gunedwaen continued. "I have been a Swordmaster since before your father's birth. Wondertales are my stock-in-trade. Truth matters little. It is what people believe that ends battles or begins them.

"At least half the people out there follow you because you're the Child of the Prophecy, Amrethion Aradruiniel's chosen successor." He waved his hand in the direction of the rest of the camp. "They expect your life and your war to be a wondertale. They want you to be as amazing and unknowable as Great Queen Pelashia Celenthodiel. If you give them what they want of you, they will love you and they will follow you. As will your foes—if you can convince them."

"I am not a—" Vieliessar began hotly.

"Spirit? Great Power? Ancient hero reborn?" Gunedwaen asked. "Do you really think it matters? They want a good story. Give them that, and even the Twelve will bow their necks."

Vieliessar bit back the angry words she longed to say. From the moment she'd begun to realize the sheer scope of the power surrounding her—and influencing her—she'd been uneasy with it. Even if she wasn't manipulating people's minds deliberately, she knew it was happening. The fact that Gunedwaen dismissed it so lightly made it worse. When did what she did to save her people become more terrible than what she was trying to save them from?

She shook her head stubbornly. There were no clear-cut choices.

"You mean to destroy the life we've all led for thousands of years, cast down the War Princes, change everything anyone has ever known, bring 'justice' to the commons, and turn every soul of the Fortunate Lands into a great army to fight an enemy so terrible Amrethion Aradruiniel refused to name it. You cannot do that as a mere War Prince, or even as High King. You must become more than that."

Gunedwaen gazed into the distance. "Serenthon tried. His enemies feared him, and that fear was the greatest weapon in his arsenal. You don't want to be feared, and you're right. Fear is a good weapon on a battlefield, a bad one in a Great Hall. But you must become a legend. A dream all can dream together. A dream they can share and follow. If you do not, your army will lose all hope and be destroyed with its first great defeat. Now it's late, and I've said far too much. With your permission, my lord, I will withdraw."

"Of course," she answered.

Gunedwaen got to his feet and walked to the door of the pavilion. His expression was thoughtful, but she would not gaze into his thoughts. "Rest you well, Vieliessar High King," he said, turning back to regard her.

"And you," Vieliessar said. *As if I could, after that.*

Amrethion High King, what hradan *have you set upon me?*

Her untouched tea had gone cold by the time she rose from the table and sought her bed.

⫘

ong before dawn, the army began to move. First to depart were the
scouts and foragers, not just the commonfolk on shaggy ponies
whose sole task was to warn of the presence of enemy forces in the Mystrals, who had been on patrol since the army had arrived in Ceoprentrei,
but *komen* ready to fight.

Once the scouts were away, the army followed. It was odd to see so
many in the same colors. The infantry and former mercenaries wore tab-
ards, the *komen* wore surcoats, and all were green with a rearing silver
Unicorn upon them. Her device. Her colors. The mark of the armies of
the High King.

Once all had been set in motion, Vieliessar took her personal guard
and rode up to the top of the pass. It was chill and dark, still a full candlemark before dawn. The Dragon's Gate had been worked and shaped
long ago by Lightborn: the pass was broad and open, and she could see
down into the hills on the western side below, where the army of the Alliance gathered.

The earth was a mirror of the sky, dotted with thousands of points of
light. The large ones were cookfires and watchfires. The small ones were
the torches set at the boundaries of the Alliance's camp and in front of
many of the tents. Here and there she could see balls of Silverlight glowing with a moon-blue radiance. She wondered if Prince Runacarendalur
was down there somewhere.

Of course he would be. He was Caerthalien's most able General.

Realizing where her mind had strayed, she shoved the thought aside
irritably. She wouldn't think about him at all save for the Magery that
had made him a knife at her throat. *If we were not Soulbonded, I would
slay him with a light heart. He is all that is corrupt and shameful in the
Hundred Houses.*

"There are a lot of them," *Komen* Mathoriel said quietly.

"Yes," Vieliessar answered. Her personal guard had suffered heavy
losses in Mangiralas, and because of that *Komen* Orannet—a hedge

knight of Oronviel—had become its head, but protocol demanded Vieliessar have a *komen* of higher rank to head her guard, and she valued *Komen* Mathoriel's steadiness. She'd taken care to fill the rest of the places with *komen* of other Houses than Oronviel, for she was no longer War Prince of Oronviel, but High King.

"We will prevail," Mathoriel said firmly.

Vieliessar wasn't certain whether it was tact or optimism that prompted Mathoriel's remark, but it made good hearing.

⊰⊱

W*hat do I need to do to become High King?"* Her words returned to haunt her through the long days of descent through the Mystrals. She stood upon the threshold of a battle she might well lose. Yet it was a battle that must be fought whether she wished to or not, for she had begun her quest to become High King not for power or ambition, but in fear and dread. *The Song of Amrethion* prophesied a terrible Darkness that would ride across the land during the years of her life, and if the Hundred Houses were not united against it, the *alfaljodthi* would be erased from the world. All she had done, all she would do, was meant to prepare her folk and her kin against that day. It was that battle to come she must think of, and not the battles she must fight to reach it. Lose them, and she lost all. But win them . . .

Every war began, so Arilcarion War-Maker had written in *Of the Sword Road*, with its own hero tale, as if it were a great lord who had lived a long life and now had a storysong crafted to be sung over its funeral pyre. And any prince who clung to that storysong after a campaign began would drink to drowning of the cup of defeat and loss, for no mortal prince could force the world to follow their whim as if they wore the cloak of the Starry Huntsman.

She would not have the Hundred Houses' strength to call on if she obliterated it. To imagine a victory that did not begin with the destruction of all the War Princes and their meisnes was madness, but madness or not, it was the only road to victory—*true* victory.

Gunedwaen says I must become a legend, a dream. I do not think I can. We are no longer a people of dreams or trust. Bolecthindial, Girelain, Manderecheriel will never accept my bare word. Oh, if only I could show the War Princes of the Alliance what I have seen in my visions! Surely then they would understand. . . .

Could she?

Not her vision of the city, but the city itself?

Find Celephriandullias-Tidorangelor. Take Celephriandullias-Tildorangelor. Fill its lands with the thousands upon thousands who had followed her out of the West . . .

And the War Princes would rail in vain against a victory already accomplished, for she would *have* the Unicorn Throne.

Oh, it would be only the object and not the vast empire it symbolized, but that would not matter. If she held it, the envoys of the War Princes would come to her there, to seek treaties or negotiate wars. Amrethion's city would become her greatest weapon. The commons of every domain would seek out Celephriandullias-Tildorangelor to become her subjects. Without the farmers and farmworkers, the craftworkers, the servants, those who *worked*, the War Princes' vast armies would collapse. They would be forced to surrender or starve.

There were a thousand reasons not to do it.

To reach Celephriandullias-Tildorangelor—to *find* Celephriandullias-Tildorangelor—she would have to lead her army through the lands of War Princes who owed fealty to War Princes of the Alliance. The lessons she had learned during War Season were clear: fear would cause them to support their ancient masters. She might hope for more, but the best she could expect was that they would merely ride to join her enemy instead of marshaling their forces immediately against her.

Or she might win.

But first she must find her destination.

When Celephriandullias-Tildorangelor fell, the Uradabhur was a primeval wilderness. The maps she had were the best available, but they were limited. Nothing beyond the borders of the domains was shown. Why should it be? Who could possibly need to know about it? All she had to aid her were the ghost-whispers of ancient memories. *Amrethion's lords hunted Pelashia's children, and their children's children, and they had fled west . . .*

If she chose that course, it meant gambling her army on a chance out of legend and prophecy, instead of waging a conventional war she might actually win. And winning, lose—for all of them.

She had as little choice as she ever had.

Only let the day come when the magic of the Prophecy has done all Amrethion set it to do, when I can say I do nothing but by my own wish—and say, too, on that day: it is well.

⤝⦿⤞

"W e will be received by a committee of welcome," Rithdeliel said, gesturing toward the valley ahead.

The day was warm and bright, and a candlemark or two would see them out of the pass and within Jaeglenhend's true borders. Nilkaran Jaeglenhend had come with all his army to meet them. His encampment was set upon a hilltop and his pavilion—striped in Jaeglenhend azure and white—was easily visible even from here. Her scouts had been reporting back for days that Nilkaran had gathered what was probably the whole of his army to meet her.

"*Welcome* does not disturb me," Vieliessar commented dryly.

"They're a few miles off, and Kenyman Scout saw no evidence they mean to attack. Today, at least," Rithdeliel answered.

"Just as well." Her whole force outnumbered Nilkaran's at least ten to one—but her whole force would not be down the mountain for some days yet. "So let us make camp."

"And give him a 'mark or two to brood before you do what you always do," Rithdeliel said.

"'What I always do'?" Vieliessar asked, turning to gaze at him. "And that would be . . . ?"

Rithdeliel smiled. "Why, send an envoy to ask, most politely, that he surrender his armies and his lands and pledge fealty to you, of course."

His comment startled her into laughter, for it was true. But she sobered quickly. Though it had worked often enough to gain her an army, there was an army following her that would not be so easily subdued.

※

There was a valley located only a few miles from the trailhead; Rithdeliel's forces were soon joined there by Thoromarth and his warriors and then by Iardalaith and the Warhunt Mages. Vieliessar's camp expanded slowly and inexorably. Lord Nilkaran's scouts were obviously keeping as close a watch on it as she was on his. But he managed to do one thing to surprise her: he sent an emissary to her before she sent one to him.

Moraigre Lightbrother looked too young to be wearing the Green Robe, but he was obviously used to this work, for he displayed no sign of nervousness at being intercepted by pickets and conducted to Vicliessar's pavilion. It had been the first structure set: orders must be given, decisions must be made, and her scarlet pavilion made a logical focal point for the engineers who must lay out the roads of the camp. Many campaigns ago she had resigned herself to going inside and staying there, no matter her inclinations. It was a waste of everyone's time and energy to constantly have to seek her out. *At least my commanders have the luxury of going where they wish and doing what needs doing,* she thought rebelliously. Moraigre Lightbrother's arrival was a welcome distraction.

"To Lord Vieliessar, War Prince of Oronviel, Lord Nilkaran, War Prince of Jaeglenhend, sends greetings," Moraigre began, when the first formalities were over and he was ready to deliver his message.

"Lord Vieliessar is not Prince of Oronviel," Aradreleg corrected calmly. "Lord Vieliessar is High King of all the land."

"I, well, I have the message as it was given to me," Moraigre said, smiling engagingly. "If its form does not please, I shall inform my lord."

Vieliessar smiled in return. "Let us proceed to the message itself, if you would. What does Lord Nilkaran want?"

There was a pause as Moraigre skipped mentally over several long speeches of flattery, though Vieliessar's True Speech let her hear them as a low mutter in his mind. She had long since given up feeling shame over her near-constant use of it to eavesdrop on all around her.

"He greets you, and wishes you well, and is prepared to offer your army safe conduct to the eastern border of his domain. Escorted by his army, of course," the young Lightborn finished.

Aradreleg was too well schooled to laugh, and *Komen* Mathoriel was too well bred to. Vieliessar sat quietly, her face as smooth as new cream, delaying only to give Moraigre the impression she was considering his master's words. The proposal Nilkaran made was both audacious and clever, for it did not force him to declare for her, nor did it shut the door to such a declaration in future. But if she accepted it, she would be left with an enemy at her back, and *her* enemies would receive haven.

"Your lord's desire to avoid unnecessary battle does him credit," she began simply. "And he knows as well as I that a great army pursues me closely, and when we meet, we must fight."

She felt Moraigre relax, thinking she was going to accept Nilkaran's offer.

"Yet this is an offer I must decline," she continued. "I must and will have Jaeglenhend. I require Lord Nilkaran to swear fealty to me, to place all of Jaeglenhend beneath my rule, to deliver to me for my use all those of his meisne, and to provide me with such provisions and other materials as I may require."

"I . . ." Moraigre was too experienced to show the full extent of his dismay, but he was obviously at a loss for words. Foremost in his mind was concern—not outright fear, but not far from it—at Nilkaran's reaction when he delivered her message.

"It is only to be understood that Nilkaran Jaeglenhend will find my answer disappointing. And he will have many questions. I shall send a messenger of my own with you upon your return, so that he may have answers to all the questions he may wish to ask," she said. *At least those I intend to answer.* She turned to the nearest servant. "Go and bring to me

Iardalaith Lightbrother, if you please. I must send him to speak with Lord Nilkaran, and I have much to say to him before he goes."

⊰⊱

She sent four Lightborn back with Moraigre: Iardalaith, Rondithiel, whose gravitas should be enough to reassure the Lightborn of Jaeglenhend that she kept the Covenant, Harwing, who was an expert spy, and Isilla, whose Keystone Gift was Overshadowing. All were members of the Warhunt, able and willing to fight if they must.

They did not return to Vieliessar's camp until late that night. Iardalaith said they had been forced to sneak from the Jaeglenhend camp under Cloakspell and steal their own horses back. Lord Nilkaran had not mistreated them in any fashion, but he had asked them to remain until he had an answer to send back with them.

"Had we done so, we would have grown old in his company," Harwing Lightbrother said mockingly.

"He means to fight. I am almost certain of it," Isilla said, and Rondithiel nodded in agreement.

Vieliessar glanced around the pavilion. Much of her army was still in the mountains, so not all her Senior Commanders were present, but Thoromarth, Rithdeliel, Atholfol Ivrithir, and Diorthiel of Araphant had been summoned to hear the report of the Lightborn.

"It will be tomorrow, then," Rithdeliel said. "You're here, and most of your army isn't. Tomorrow his knights will still outnumber yours."

Thoromarth nodded in agreement. "Nilkaran knows how close behind us our enemy is," he said. "Expect him to attack you tomorrow, Lord Vieliessar, but don't expect him to stand and fight. He'll want to delay you until the Alliance can deal with you."

"Set his camp afire tonight and he'll surrender at dawn," Atholfol said cheerfully.

"I need to take his army, not kill it," Vieliessar said. "And under other circumstances, I might hold back the use of Magery on the field because I know it will make Nilkaran and his *komen* fight as if they're rats about to be drowned. But we do not have such a luxury. We must win quickly, and that means Magery."

"The Warhunt stands ready," Iardalaith said.

"If we do not carry the day we may at least have the joy of watching Nilkaran try to decide whether he will throw Jaeglenhend's storehouses open to the Alliance when it comes," Diorthiel said with a faint smile. "I do not think he has realized he must declare for you or for them."

"He's that much of an idiot," Isilla said bluntly. "And a monster as well. He sends knights to patrol the countryside for those commons who wish to join you. When his knights catch anyone, they strike off their hands and feet and leave them to bleed to death."

"I wish him joy of finding Farmfolk to reap his harvests instead of leaving them to spoil in the field," Harwing Lightbrother said with an edged smile. Vieliessar did not miss the startled glance that passed between Thoromarth and Atholfol. Her lords had been as shocked as her enemies to discover the depth of contempt their commonborn subjects felt for them.

"I will be glad to offer them my protection," Vieliessar said. "And enrich my army at the expense of Nilkaran's domain."

"He'll realize that he's caught between wolf and lion soon, though perhaps not soon enough," Iardalaith said. "Though I have some ideas on how the Warhunt may hasten his reflections."

"I will hear them in a moment. But . . . can you Overshadow Nilkaran, Isilla?" Vieliessar asked. It was a blunter question than she really wanted to ask; Atholfol and the others disliked reminders of the power some of the Lightborn could wield. But Lord Nilkaran was the sort of prince who guarded his power jealously and ruled by rank and fear. He would not have a strong council of advisors around him, nor would he surround himself with Lords *Komen* strong enough to challenge any decree he made. Remove him and no one else would truly be prepared to take and hold power.

"No," Isilla answered instantly. "I could arrange to get close enough to him to try, but he stinks of Warding." She rubbed her arms through the fabric of her tunic, as if her skin itched. "No spell of control or illusion will touch him, I suspect."

"Of course, there's still lightning," Harwing said cheerfully. "Not that striking him dead would be especially useful," he added hastily.

"Better, perhaps, to convince him by persuasive argument that Lord Vieliessar's cause is just and worthy of support," Rithdeliel said silkily.

"Yes," Iardalaith agreed. "And while you are doing that, I shall take my Warhunt to his castel. We can strip the Wardings from its stones—and the spell's effects will be visible at once, even to the Lightless."

Vieliessar concealed her pleasure; it would not do for her Lords *Komen* to become jealous of the Warhunt Mages and their leader. But Iardalaith's instincts for what would most efficiently destroy an enemy's will to fight were sound: the Wards that rendered a castel invulnerable were the casting of years, even decades, the work of hundreds of Lightborn. If the Warhunt Dispelled the Wards of Lord Nilkaran's Great Keep, Nilkaran's Lightborn could not recast them. This would not be the same spell she had cast at Laeldor—Rot had turned every scrap of metal and wood to dust almost instantly. But now she wanted to display her power, not terrify her enemies into fighting without the hope of victory.

"Let it be done, and I thank you, Iardalaith, for that was well thought of," Vieliessar said, leaning back in her chair to stretch her tired muscles. This would be a night of planning and no sleep. "Now. Have we decent maps of Jaeglenhend? Someone get them, and we will decide where the rest of us are to make this persuasive argument."

She had been War Prince for fourteen moonturns.

Having consulted both the maps and the scouts, she chose a rolling expanse of land a mile to the west of Nilkaran's camp for the battle. The army was impossible to move undetected. There was the jingle of bit and spur and mail, the rattle of plate, the creaking of carts—and the bright glow of the Silverlight the Lightborn cast to light the army's way. Incredibly, despite all of that, they'd encountered no Jaeglenhender scouts or guards. War Prince Nilkaran was either supremely confident or supremely stupid. At last they reached the place Vieliessar had chosen, and her force settled itself in loose array and prepared to wait for dawn.

"What are they *doing* over there?" Vieliessar demanded irritably, glaring at Nilkaran's camp in the distance.

"Sleeping," Thoromarth said simply. "Why not? Nilkaran doesn't expect to find you waiting in his courtyard when he awakes. He expects to send an envoy with the declaration of his intentions while his army drinks its morning ale. Then he'll march, expecting you to fling yourself onto the field without studying the lay of it, so he can cut your force to thread and string with half his meisne while he smashes your camp with the other half."

"I grieve at the thought of how disappointing he must find me," Vieliessar answered sardonically.

"I could go to Lord Nilkaran's camp to tell him we demand he meet us in battle," Ambrant Lightbrother said.

His mother snorted. "I don't have so many children that I wish to lose one. Give it another half-mark," she said, regarding the sky with a measuring look. "Then we can let him know we're here."

"Perhaps he'll invite us to breakfast," Thoromarth said dourly.

"If I'd ever waited to be invited over your borders, you old bandit, Oronviel would've smothered under its herds of sheep long before Lord Vieliessar came," Atholfol said.

"If the two of you want to shout a little louder, we won't need warhorns to let Nilkaran know we're here," Vieliessar said tartly, and both princes laughed.

Autumn was a season of dawn-mist and frost. Even as the sky lightened, the world remained colorless. The destriers were saddled and brought onto the line. The stamp of their hooves and clink of their bridles was muffled by the mist. When the sky had brightened enough that sparks of fire could be seen beneath the lacquered surfaces of armor, Vieliessar signaled the knights-herald. As one, their raised their warhorns, and the mellow handful of rising notes that were the summons and challenge to the enemy rang out. *Come and fight—Come and fight—Come and fight—*

As the echoing sound died away, Vieliessar urged her destrier forward at a slow walk. "Come," she said. "I do not mean to give Nilkaran a spacious battlefield to work with."

⹊⹋

At the end of the day's fighting, Vieliessar could claim no victory. Nilkaran had put just enough knights into the field to keep her occupied, while keeping back the majority of his force to defend his camp. Somewhat to her surprise, he did not send a meisne against her camp, but it was frustrating that when she called for a fighting retreat at midday, she wasn't even able to entice the enemy to follow her, despite retreating encumbered by carts filled with her wounded. By mid-afternoon she'd retreated far enough that Nilkaran's *komen* had given up all pretense of offering battle and had ridden back to his retreating supply train. She called a halt and sent a messenger to her camp, with orders to move as far east as they could before sunset.

"Is that wise?" Rithdeliel asked quietly.

"Dendinirchiel's element should have reached the camp this morning," Vieliessar answered. "And Kalides Brabamant and Brethrod Cirdeval were right behind her. We can't let the Alliance catch us in these foothills."

"I would have said otherwise," Rithdeliel commented. "It's good terrain for an ambush."

"It's good terrain to isolate portions of your enemy's force and hold them while you bring up enough horse to slaughter them," Vieliessar countered. "I think that must be what they intend. The nobles who follow me are inconvenient; their lands have undoubtedly been promised away. Slaughter the *komen* and the princes and the Alliance will believe it can reclaim the commons."

Rithdeliel sighed, wordlessly acknowledging the truth of her argument. "Onward, then," he said.

The next day she discovered Nilkaran had fled, leaving his army in the care of Warlord Handeloriel while he rode south-east with a handful of grand-tailles. Vieliessar knew Nilkaran didn't trust Handeloriel any more than Nilkaran trusted anyone, but he must have given him very explicit orders, for Warlord Handeloriel circled constantly through the eastern Tamabeth Hills. No matter what she did, Vieliessar couldn't force him to a stand. When she attempted to break off, to see if laying siege to Nilkaran's vulnerable Great Keep would gain her the battle she sought, Handeloriel immediately moved to harry her vulnerable baggage train.

And then she ran out of time.

Three days after her first battle with Nilkaran, the armies of the Alliance invaded Jaeglenhend in force. Only the fact that her army had continued moving east saved it from being destroyed immediately. A little thought led Vieliessar to the realization that it was likely that the Alliance had asked its Lightborn to widen the path through the Mystrals so that their army and its baggage train had room to maneuver.

Even the most conservative Lightborn could be pressured into doing that much. And I know whose mind crafted such a clever plan.

Vieliessar called for retreat, knowing two War Princes could not agree with each other, let alone twelve, and knowing that the longer she kept the Alliance in the field, the greater the possibility they would begin to fight among themselves. As she fell back, she expected the Alliance's *komen* to charge and engage, using their traditional tactics: gallop madly into the enemy for the joy of the charge, then fight a series of single combats governed by antique rules of honor.

But the Alliance *komen* did not charge in force. The Alliance commander held back a portion of his troops and, under the cover of the charge, used it to cut Vieliessar off from her vulnerable baggage-train. When he'd done that, he continued to allow her superiority on the field as he drove her wagons and herds back toward the Alliance lines.

At the same time, the Alliance Lightborn struck.

The bright day dimmed rapidly as clouds boiled up over the crown of the Mystrals. The air was chokingly thick with Magery as Vieliessar's Warhunt Mages vied with the Alliance Lightborn—a battle of Magery waged side by side with one of flesh and steel. She had to admit it was an elegant tactical compromise. Most of the Lightborn with the Alliance would refuse to use Magery on the battlefield. But they would see working the weather as only a small compromise with Mosirinde's Covenant.

In time her Lightborn might have prevailed, but most of the Warhunt was still on its way back from Jaeglenhend Great Keep and the storm had a momentum of its own. It was all her remaining Lightborn could do to keep the Lightning drawn from its clouds from hitting Vieliessar's army.

Soon the rising wind was filled with snow. The battlefield became shrouded in white as the out-of-season blizzard strengthened. The sound of the warhorns and signal whistles was muted and garbled by the snow and the wind, making it impossible to pass orders reliably. Visibility was so poor that no one could see the banners carried by the knights-herald.

The storm stripped away every advantage Vieliessar possessed. The snow distempered the archer's bowstrings so they could not loose their arrows; her infantry slipped and skidded on the icy ground. Vieliessar was forced to abandon pursuit of her baggage train and deploy her knights to guard her infantry's retreat, for the enemy, identifying her weakest point, eschewed combat with their fellow *komen* to attack the infantry instead.

The infantry's horses had been lost with the baggage train. The Warhunt could not Call them back, for the whole of the Alliance army stood between the beasts and their summoners. The injured died where they fell, or clung grimly to their saddlebows and rode after the fleeing infantry.

Even then, Vieliessar might have stolen the meat of victory from defeat's cookfire. But Lord Nilkaran had rejoined his army and led it against her defenseless wounded and fleeing foot soldiers. All she could do was retreat, retreat, retreat as she tried to keep her army intact.

She'd never been so grateful for sunset and an end to the day's fighting. She spent the night trying to find the scattered elements of her army. Near dawn, Vieliessar made the only choice she could. South of Jaeglenhend, the Uradabhur became league upon league of primal wilderness.

Nilkaran would still have a declared border, for a border was necessary for the setting of Wards, but he would either have stripped the border towers of their defenders entirely, or left them with so few that the members of the Warhunt still with the army could easily overpower them. The order went to all warriors she could reach, by Lightborn or by Lightless messenger: *retreat on a south-southeast salient. Do not regroup. Do not engage the enemy.*

The border keeps would provide food, shelter, and defense. The forest beyond would return the advantage to Vieliessar, for the Alliance *komen* could not use cavalry in forests so dense a rider could barely pass through them.

If they could reach it.

But if the first day of the battle had been bad, the next was worse. The Alliance had brought its pavilions and supplies up to its battle lines and were able to attack again as soon as there was light enough to see.

Her *komen*'s destriers were cold and hungry, making them irritable and difficult to control. Her army was dazed and groggy from a night without shelter. The blizzard had been raging for nearly a full day and the snowdrifts were deep. Today the horses of both armies floundered ponderously through the drifts, and it was as if the *komen* fought in slow motion through the still-falling snow.

But they fought.

Vieliessar had long-since abandoned the idea of fighting to a victory; all she hoped for now was to retreat with her army. Iardalaith's force had rejoined her during the night, but every spell they tried—*she* tried—against the attacking knights or their mounts simply didn't work. Their Lightborn must have been Warding everything that breathed for sennight upon sennight to have Warded so many thousand *komen* and horses. The only spell that was of any effect was Shield, and to ask her Lightborn to hold it along the entire line of skirmish, for candlemarks, was to ask them to doom the land.

Y ou have to use Dispell!" she shouted to Iardalaith over the clamor of the battle.

She'd ridden back through her lines to give Firthorn a brief respite from the fighting. Most of the Warhunt was gathered at the rear; being willing to fight was not the same as being able to defend oneself on a battlefield.

"Do you think I haven't thought of that?" Iardalaith snapped. "Even if we could, we'd be helpless afterward!"

"Which do you like better—helpless or dead?" Vieliessar demanded. The only thing saving them so far was that the Alliance *komen* couldn't charge their lines at speed. Vieliessar had only been able to find about a third of her army before the day's fighting had begun; the force she commanded was outnumbered two to one.

"You can be both if you have to retreat and we're too drained to protect you!"

"*Think of something.*" She wasn't certain he could hear her. Just as well. She spurred Firthorn away before she was tempted to repeat herself more loudly.

A candlemark later, near midday, the storm finally broke and the clouds rolled back, but Vieliessar could feel the Weather Magery in the air like a dull ache behind her eyes; there would be another storm by sunset. As the temperature rose, the surface of the snow became veiled in mist. Pools of water lay in the hollows of the drifts, flaring like burning silver in the sunlight. When the temperature dropped again, the water-sodden snow would freeze into solid ice. In winter, palfreys and mules wore studded shoes to keep them from slipping on frozen ground. The destriers would have no such protection. There had already been several casualties on both sides as warhorses had slipped in the churned mud of the battlefield and gone down hard enough to break a leg.

The Alliance had remounts available—some of them Vieliessar's, taken as spoils of war.

In the distance, she could see the pavilions of the enemy. For a moment she dared to hope: what Lightborn could see, they could affect, and

Fire was the first spell every Postulant learned. But even Tangisen Light-brother, who swore he could kindle a stone into flame, could not set the enemy's tents alight.

She could feel failure and defeat prowling around the edges of the battle like wolves starved by winter's cold. She didn't think she'd done anything to tempt the Silver Hooves to punish her pride, but They could see into her heart, and oh, there had been a bottomless wellspring of hubris there. Child of the Prophecy. Amrethion's Chosen. Uncrowned High King. She was being punished for every arrogant thought she'd ever had. Her meisne could not hold the enemy off until dark—each candlemark saw their losses multiply as exhausted warriors made fatal mistakes. They might survive another night in the open, but they would not be able to fight at the end of it. The Alliance could defeat her without even needing to engage: her *komen* would freeze to death.

Then—inexplicably—she caught the scent of smoke upon the air and heard the distant clamor of horns—*retreat, retreat*. The Alliance began to disengage.

She turned and looked: their camp was burning.

CHAPTER FOURTEEN

TO FLY BEFORE THE STORM

It is one thing to die for the High King's cause, a second thing to know you died turning a Flower Forest to dust, and a third thing to know even that wasn't enough.

—Iardalaith Warhuntsman, *Of the Beginning of War*

"We didn't do it," Iardalaith said. "I wish we had. But . . . no."

The exhausted army moved in sluggish retreat. Vieliessar didn't know how long this respite would last, but they must use it while they could. A mile to the west, six thousand of the enemy—all wearing Caerthalien colors—sat motionless watching their flight, the only Alliance warriors still on the field. *Someone panicked,* Vieliessar thought with as much satisfaction as she could summon under the circumstances. She'd gathered her commanders to her and now rode with them on the *tuathal* side. This might be her only chance to give them orders and hear their reports. Too many who had gone into battle two days before were missing now. Gunedwaen, she hoped, was with some other element of her scattered troops, but she did not know.

"There's more than one way to set something on fire," Nadalforo pointed out, answering Iardalaith. "You can use a torch, for example. People do."

"But why would they set fire to their own pavilions?" Prince Frochoriel asked, sounding dazed.

"They didn't," Nadalforo said. "At least, I'm willing to make that wild leap of imagination. The Alliance might not be outnumbered by Lord Vieliessar's commonfolk, but it's a near thing. And I'll prophesy further and say none of those commonfolk wish to be returned to slavery."

"You seem to be remarkably conversant with the mentality of farmers and Landbond," Rithdeliel said irritably. His shield arm was bound against his side by pieces of his surcoat; the arm had been broken in the morning's fighting, and there was neither time nor power to Heal it now.

"Yes," Nadalforo answered blandly. "Aren't I?"

"By whatever cause, their camp is burning. But it only buys us a little time," Vieliessar said sharply. "Even their commanders quarreling among themselves won't save us. There's another storm coming. We can't go on like this."

"If you have any suggestions, I'll be more than happy to entertain them," Rithdeliel answered, exhausted exasperation shading into anger.

You won't like it. Vieliessar bit back the words. Rithdeliel would like anything that promised a chance of victory. No *komen* wanted to die in battle as much as they wanted to live to fight the next one, and if Rithdeliel were taken alive, Bolecthindial would make an example of him. Rithdeliel had betrayed his sworn master, and it didn't matter that Thoromarth had forgiven the treason. Bolecthindial would not.

"They want all of us," she said, glancing around to include all the commanders with her and, by extension, the army. "But they want me most of all. If I make it look as if I'm abandoning you, they'll think it's more important to capture me than to continue fighting you. At least I can draw off enough of their force to give you a better chance."

"You *hope* they want to capture you," Rithdeliel said, without a ghost of irony.

"They do," Vieliessar said with grim certainty. "You can't torture a corpse."

"At last you see reason," Iardalaith said. "Of *course* they want to torture you to death. They'll make a Festival Fair of it."

Iardalaith's observation gained him nothing more than a weary smirk from Rithdeliel. "You flee, they follow," Rithdeliel said. "Well enough. Why don't they slaughter all of us while they're at it? It's hardly as if they don't have enough *komen* to do both."

"They're fighting among themselves. You know they are," Vieliessar said. She could not believe the commander whose brilliant tactics had nearly destroyed her would have been such an idiot as to break off the battle when the Alliance was so close to victory just because there was a fire in camp. Inspiration became certainty as she spoke. "When the Alliance retreated, Caerthalien remained on the field. It looks like Caerthalien's been directing the battle so far. I think their *komen* will follow me."

"And that will set the fox among the doves," Thoromarth said with grim satisfaction. "Who holds you prisoner holds all your lands as well."

Nadulforo made a noise of pure exasperation. "Arilcarlon War-Maker is long dead, fool! You know the rest of the Alliance won't meekly hand the West to Caerthalien!"

"You know that and so do I," Thoromarth said equitably. "And I promise you, it won't stop Aramenthiali from turning on Caerthalien."

"So if Caerthalien follows Vieliessar, Aramenthiali will follow Caerthalien?" Iardalaith asked, sounding faintly disbelieving.

"Of course," Atholfol said, sounding surprised he was asking. "If they can fight free of Cirandeiron, of course."

"Not that it matters," Rithdeliel said. "They'll easily overtake us."

"No," Iardalaith said, "they won't. Leave that to the Warhunt."

"Nor do you accompany us," Vieliessar said to Rithdeliel. "I ride with Stonehorse and a grand-taille of the Warhunt, no more. It must appear to any who watch that you have abandoned me—or I you—in defeat."

"Yes," Rithdeliel said thoughtfully, nodding. "You ride south?"

"Where else, when I flee for my life?" Vieliessar said mockingly. "I shall lead them a merry chase through the southern wilderness, and we shall try the impregnability of Lord Nilkaran's border towers."

"Then your army rides north," Rithdeliel answered decisively. "We're only a half-day's ride from Nilkaran's manorial estates. We'll loot them as we ride. We should reach the Great Keep no later than tomorrow's sunset. It should be easy enough to take with Nilkaran's army elsewhere. I hope you won't object if, in your absence, we devote ourselves to slaughtering our enemies?"

"I'm having a hard time now remembering why I wanted to keep them alive," Vieliessar answered sourly. She knew that for all Rithdeliel's light words, taking Jaeglenhend Great Keep would be no easy task.

"The place may be Dispelled, but it's still solid enough to invest while we parley for our lives." Thoromarth sounded almost cheerful. "And if the army besieges us, we have a chance to get our possessions back. I lost a good pair of boots with that supply train."

"Done," Vieliessar said. It wasn't the best possible plan, but it was the best one they could come up with under these circumstances.

"We're still in sight of Caerthalien," Nadalforo said. "My lord, I think this will make a better show if you ride forth with only a few knights and let Stonehorse chase after you."

"Let it be so," Vieliessar said.

"I go with you, and a grand-taille of the Warhunt," Iardalaith said. "Be sure we'll outrun them. This is the Magery we've been preparing all this day against the candlemark of your retreat. I shall set it upon us once we are away. Isilla and the rest will do the same for the army."

"Then let us begin," Rithdeliel said. "It is Harvest Moon, and I have been longing to see a good Festival play."

⊷⧗⊶

The army came to a slow, swirling stop as the plan was passed in whispers. Prompted by Nadalforo, Vieliessar, Rithdeliel, and several others conducted a shouted argument filled with threats and recriminations: Vieliessar was certain they could be heard on the Western Shore, and surely by the Caerthalien meisne.

Then she spurred poor Firthorn away from the army. Diorthiel of Araphant and a ragged handful of knights followed. There was more shouting behind her. Vieliessar's shoulder blades itched. One single thunderbolt Called upon them from this cloudless sky and the ruse would be truth. *Lords of Night, Lords of War, let this work. Manafaeren Sword-Giver, Aradhwain Bride of Battles, I am the sword in Your hands. Star-Crowned, Silver-Hooved, I beg You for this victory.*

Iardalaith and his chosen rode after her, shouting for her to wait.

"You must assume they see everything," Nadalforo had said, and so Vieliessar made as if to stop and let Diorthiel urge her on, crying to Iardalaith to hurry.

Now a flurry of horns sounded from her army as Rithdeliel and the others called them to order.

"Is it working?" Iardalaith hissed into her ear as he reached her.

"I don't know," Vieliessar answered tightly. "Is it?"

"Caerthalien is sending messengers back to camp," Diorthiel announced, looking off into the distance. "If I were them, I wouldn't wait for orders."

"If we don't wait for Stonehorse to get here, they won't be within the compass of our spell," Iardalaith said.

"Just to pass the time—before we face odds of ten to one and *die*—what spell is this that can save us from being taken?" Diorthiel asked.

"You've heard of battle cordial, haven't you?" Iardalaith said, with a small, exultant smile.

Vieliessar had compounded battle cordial many times in her days at the Sanctuary. It made the fires of the body burn star-bright and star-hot, giving its user fantastic strength and endurance—but its use killed, for if the body burned itself out, even the most skilled Healer could not repair the damage.

Iardalaith could now do with Magery what Vieliessar only knew how to do with herbs.

"If there is such a spell, I should know it," she said, piqued. It was a ridiculous thing to be annoyed at, under the circumstances, but . . . every new spell, every variation on an established spell, was brought to the Sanctuary to be taught to the Postulants, for there was no other way to transmit the knowledge of the spells than by passing them from Lightborn to Lightborn.

"If you lived on the Western Shore, you would know how needful such a spell is," Iardalaith said. "We had no wish to bring knowledge of Quicken to the Sanctuary only to have it declared Forbidden."

Vieliessar nodded. "Forbidden" spells could not be taught, and an untaught spell would be lost within a generation.

"I hate to interrupt this collegium," Nadalforo said sourly, as her destrier pulled abreast of them, "but Caerthalien is moving off its mark."

"Now," Iardalaith said, raising his hand.

Vieliessar felt the warm wind of the spell pass over her as if her body were bare of armor. Beneath her, she felt Firthorn's muscles quiver with new vitality.

False vitality.

Their mounts would run themselves to death.

They had no choice.

She dug her spurs into his flanks and Firthorn leapt forward.

⊰⊱

Y ou are fools," Runacarendalur said, his voice flat with anger. "I had them. *I had them.* Are you mewling infants to panic at a few scattered coals? Your idiocy has cost us the day."

"Leash your hound, Caerthalien, or I will do it for you," Manderechiel Aramenthiali said, waving a languid hand. "I do not explain my decisions to children."

Runacarendalur drew breath to reply. Then Bolecthindial cleared his throat, and, acknowledging his father's command, Runacarendalur flung himself into the nearest empty chair instead. He'd told them the commons who'd flocked to Vieliessar's banner were devious and untrustworthy. Why should anyone expect anything other than more treachery and rebellion once they were captured? But his words had been ignored. *And so they have set fire to half the tents in camp!* They were small fires, easily put out. *It did not require the whole of the army to do it,* he thought sullenly.

"You must not be so harsh, my lord husband," Ladyholder Dormorothon of Aramenthiali said, her tone and her words perfectly calculated to incite Lord Manderechiel further. "I am certain the young prince means well. He is only concerned, as a good son must be, over

the welfare of his domain. How will Caerthalien prosper without workers to till the soil?"

"And that touches upon a matter that concerns all of us," Ivaloriel
Telthorelandor said. "We had resigned ourselves to a winter campaign,
but that was before we had the good fortune to reclaim so much of our
stolen property. The passes have not yet closed. It would be sensible to
send the Landbonds back into the West. It will save us the burden of
feeding them."

"*Sensible?*" Runacarendalur demanded in disbelief. "They are *in rebellion*! Do you think they will just tamely return to their hovels and
behave themselves?"

"But their cause is lost, Prince Runacar," Ladyholder Edheleorn of
Telthorelandor said mildly. "They will have no choice."

"And of course we must send people with them to make certain they
settle into their accustomed ways," Lord Ivaloriel added. "We would need
to do so in any event, for they must have escort through the Dragon's Gate."

"Ah, here it comes," Lord Bolecthindial said bitterly. "Just who—my
lord of Telthorelandor—is to look after these spoils of war? And where
are they to be resettled? Do we draw lots for them?"

"Obviously they must be returned to the lands they came from," Lord
Clacheu of Denegathaiel said.

"There speaks the weasel in the buttery!" Ladyholder Glorthiachiel
cried with deadly sarcasm. "Next you will say that Denegathaiel has suffered the greatest losses and should receive the greatest portion!"

"And why not?" Lord Clacheu demanded. "Or are we next to hear
that since Caerthalien now holds all of Brabamant's lands, she should
receive Brabamant's chattels as well? Perhaps you would like to add Ivrithir
and Oronviel to that tally? Laeldor? Araphant? Perhaps all we have taken
rightfully belongs to Caerthalien?"

It was as if someone had dropped a torch in a pan of hot oil, Runacarendalur thought uncharitably. In the space of an indrawn breath, everyone in the pavilion was shouting, demanding the spoils of war be
distributed immediately—and in their favor.

Fools. They believe that a single victory gives them the whole of the war. Heartsick and furious, Runacarendalur rose to his feet and walked out into the camp.

"I see your moderate words and wise counsel did not have the effect you hoped," Ivrulion said, stepping from the door of his own pavilion as Runacar began to pass it by.

Runacarendalur paused and regarded his brother in something like despair. *Gimragiel dead in Ullilion, Thorogalas dead on the Meadows of Aralhathumindrion, Domcariel dead in Mangiralas, and I will not survive Vieliessar's execution. Is Caerthalien to be held by Ciliphirilir after Lord Bolecthindial's death? She would surrender it for a box of sweetmeats and a new jeweled comb! If only 'Rulion were not Lightborn. . . .*

But if Ivrulion had not been Called, Runacarendalur would never have been born.

"What did you expect?" he demanded savagely. "We have barely held this alliance together as it is! It's a sad day when it is victory that destroys us and not defeat!"

His brother merely shook his head. "It is but a few candlemarks until the next storm strikes. They have no food, shelter, or supplies—what can they do but die?"

"She will find something!" Runacarendalur snarled. "I know not what, but she always does! She—"

"Come," Ivrulion said, "take a cup of wine with me." He took Runacarendalur's arm and compelled him into his pavilion.

The interior was dim, lit only by the afternoon sun shining through the green silk. Runcarendalur followed his brother through the second curtain and into an inner chamber, then dropped gratefully into a chair, holding out his hand for the cup of warmed and sweetened wine Ivrulion's servant brought to him.

"You always did have a terrible temper when you weren't winning," Ivrulion commented, accepting his own cup and seating himself close by. "Go and kill some of the prisoners if it will make you feel better. We've won. You know we have. We won the moment you took her supply train. Once Vieliessar is dead, we will declare her followers wolfsheads and leave the Less Houses here to hunt them at their leisure."

"You make it sound simple," Runacarendalur muttered.

"I don't know why you insist on it being difficult," Ivrulion answered. "Your tactics worked. She's finished."

"I couldn't have done it without your Wardings," Runacarendalur said, his mood slowly beginning to lighten.

"And for that we have our enemy to thank," Ivrulion answered. "If she had not taken her Lightborn onto the battlefield, I doubt I could have persuaded the War Princes to permit me to give orders to their Lightborn."

Runacarendalur tossed back the rest of his wine and held out his cup for more. He frowned. "In just a handful of moonturns she's turned the West into ghostlands. Do you suppose, 'Rulion, that she's been what this so-called Prophecy was warning us about all along? "

Ivrulion chuckled softly. "We shall make a scholar of you yet, Rune. If it is not true, we shall certainly say it is." He paused for a moment in thought. "Almost I could wish to take her alive. To know how she   "

"You cannot go in there!" From beyond the outer curtain, Runacarendalur heard the voice of Mardioruin Lightbrother, his brother's personal Lightborn.

"I can and I will—if Prince Runacarendalur is there! My lord prince! Are you here?" Helecanth shouted.

Runacarendalur flung his cup to the carpet and sprang to his feet just as Helecanth pushed through the curtain. Her face was bruised from the recent fighting; her eyes sparkled with urgency. Behind her was Lengiathion Warlord.

Runacarendalur had left Lengiathion in charge of the Caerthalien knights on the field.

"What—" he said, but Lengiathion didn't wait for him to ask.

"Lord Vieliessar has quarreled with her army. She flees south with a few hundred Lightborn and mercenaries. Her army—"

But Runacarendalur was no longer listening. "My armor!" he shouted. "Get me my armor!"

❧

The chill soft wind whipped across Vieliessar's face as Firthorn galloped, as fresh as if he had come scant moments before from the horselines. Behind her thundered her tiny army. Were they tempting enough to lure the hawk from the falconer's glove? She must hope. If they were— If Rithdeliel could flee unopposed— If he could take Jaeglenhend Great Keep—

"Ah, here they come!" Nadalforo cried, raising her voice so Vieliessar could hear.

Vieliessar risked a look back. Caerthalien's knights galloped in pursuit. They outnumbered Vieliessar's meisne as much as ten to one, but her people had several miles head start. There was little chance they'd be overtaken. Jaeglenhend's border was a half-day's ride from where they'd been fighting, but they would probably reach it before sunset.

The day darkened as the afternoon storm clouds swept over the Mystrals. And for once in recent days, something went as she hoped. She heard the distant clarion of warhorns as more knights rode from the Alliance encampment to join the chase—not because more of them were needed to capture her, but because none of the War Princes wished her to fall prisoner to any other. *If I were willing to give up my life to do it, I could destroy the entire Alliance army right here,* she thought gaily.

But she must survive. And so she must find another way.

❧

Mile after mile fell away beneath the destriers' tireless hooves. Their pursuers turned back, for the storm their Lightborn had conjured to finish destroying Vieliessar's army had fallen upon them instead. Vieliessar and her escort simply outran it. Her body ached with the battering of sitting to the gallop for so long; she knew the others must be weary as well. Her mouth was dry and her throat ached with thirst; it had been two days—more—since she'd eaten anything or drunk more than a little melted snow.

Dusk deepened and the horses ran on, exhausted yet tireless.

"There!"

Nadalforo's shout drew Vieliessar's attention. So far eastward its shape was hidden in the tree line stood one of the border towers. She nodded, signifying she had heard, and the whole column began to turn in that direction. With luck, the tower stood deserted.

But Vieliessar's luck seemed to have fled with the day. Nilkaran might have drawn heavily from the border keeps but he hadn't stripped them entirely. They were within a mile of the tower when its main gate opened and six tailles of knights rode toward her, each carrying a torch. Vieliessar's meisne outnumbered them, but Nilkaran's people and their mounts were fresh.

Vieliessar drew her sword and shouted her battle cry. Then there was no more time for thought. The enemy flung their torches to the ground, making a circle of fire in which to fight, and battle was joined.

In its first moments, Vieliessar lost nearly a dozen people. Their bespelled destriers might have been able to run for another candlemark, even two, but they were unable to follow the complex orders that turned a destrier from a method of transport into a companion in battle. Some tried and fell helpless to the ground, their limbs thrashing spasmodically. Some refused, leaving their riders vulnerable to attack. Some simply swung wide of the Jaeglenhend knights and kept running. She herself might have been dead in the first seconds of the battle had she not seized control of Firthorn's mind. She could feel his pain and terror, his utter exhaustion, and it broke her heart to do what she must, but the stakes were too high. Ruthlessly, she crushed the spark of his will beneath her Magery. She felt him dying by heartbeats as she forced him into battle against the commander of the opposing knights. Firthorn wheeled and spun, snapped and kicked, and at last she drove her blade into her enemy's body.

In the same moment she kicked her feet free of Firthorn's stirrups and seized the pommel of her enemy's saddle, thrusting him from his seat as she flung herself from the back of the dying animal to the back of the living one. Around her, others were doing the same.

The field of battle brightened as the Warhunt conjured globes of Silverlight to illuminate it. In the brief instant's respite before she closed with another foe, Vieliessar saw that most of the Warhunt were on foot, having abandoned their palfreys. She knew they were as exhausted as she—and as cold and starved—and far less used to the rigors of battle. But Iardalaith had chosen his Warhunt Mages well: after a few moments to gather their resources, the Warhunt turned its attention to the enemy. Their destriers froze in place or fled the battlefield to buck their riders from their backs and trample them to death. The enemy knights shouted with spell-fed terror, or flung their swords from them as if they'd become venomous serpents, or simply flung themselves out of their saddles.

The rest of the battle was brief.

Vieliessar ran her hand down her new mount's sweating trembling neck. Vital as her victory had been, it left the taste of ashes in her mouth. There was nothing of fairness or even kindness to it. She'd never been indoctrinated in the Way of the Sword, but to win as she had just done seemed very wrong, as if she'd stolen from someone who trusted her.

And that made no sense: these *komen* did not trust her, and no War Prince would surrender an advantage that would give their House victory over another. *The High King must do more,* she thought with weary exasperation.

"Give them the chance to surrender!" she shouted, as she saw one of the former mercenaries stand upon the chest of an enemy, preparing to put a sword-blade through the eye-slits of the fallen foe's helm. "If you do not, you will answer to me!"

"What ransom will you set, my lord?" Nadalforo rode toward her, her stolen destrier dancing fretfully beneath an unfamiliar rider. Her mouth was set in a hard line of disapproval.

"Fealty. As always," Vieliessar answered steadily.

"We still have to take the tower," Nadalforo reminded her.

"You may kill all who will not swear," Vieliessar said, turning away.

The Warhunt moved across the battlefield, finishing the dying destriers and helping the wounded fighters. At Nadalforo's command, the enemy knights who surrendered were disarmed and gathered together, to be guarded by her warriors until Vieliessar could take their fealty oaths. The rest were being executed without ceremony.

Vieliessar glanced toward the tower. The upper windows were lit. Servants still inside. Probably the tower's commander. They were out of bowshot here unless someone in there had a forester's bow. She sighed with weariness. If the tower's defenders would not surrender willingly, the Warhunt could force them out. And any of the tower's defenders would know its second entrance. Even if that were barred, they could destroy the door and it would be easy enough to repair.

But moments later, when she called upon him to surrender, Lord Karamedheliel gave up Oakstone Tower without further battle.

⛬

To become a Warlord—as he had not once, but twice—one studied every aspect of war. A war was a living thing, like a beast, a tree, a child. In Farcarinon, Rithdeliel had owned a library of scrolls that spoke of war—not just the reality of it, but the theory, for the battles the War Princes fought were mere squabbles, as if a child went from babe to toddler over and over, and never became adult. To see the full scope of war, one must turn to *xaique*. A pretense of war, fought because there were no true wars to study.

As the middle game of *xaique* involved defeat and loss, so did the middle game of war.

To retreat across the Mystrals with her army and all the folk who looked to her had been an audacious move, for it cut Vieliessar's enemy off from its supply lines. Rithdeliel would have welcomed a continuance of the string of victories with which her campaign began, but he knew, as Vieliessar did, that many of those triumphs had been built upon the stones of Vieliessar's boldness and the High Houses' inability to see her as a threat. Now they saw, and that advantage was gone. She had frightened her enemy badly enough that its alliance of War Princes was desperate enough to take counsel from one not yet of their rank. One as audacious as Vieliessar, and as brilliant.

That had cost her, and dearly, but one defeat was not the end of the war. Their supply train was captured, but it was intact, and what was stolen once might be stolen twice. Their army was scattered and suffering, but it, too, might well be intact. And if it was not . . .

Lord Serenthon had fought the High Houses nearly to a stand against odds of a hundred to one. The daughter surpassed the father as the ice-tiger in her glory surpassed the kitten on the hearth. So long as Vieliessar High King lived there was a chance of victory.

It was Rithdeliel's duty to save her army so she could claim it.

It was day when they began their northward march. It was dusk when they reached the first of the manor farms. The destriers grazed their way through the last of the standing grain, reducing the snow-covered fields to stubble and muck. Both horses and riders were agonizingly thirsty, but the riders kept their mounts from taking more than a few mouthfuls of water at the stream. If the beasts foundered, it was as much a loss as if they died. There were miles yet to go.

To all the Jaeglenhend commonfolk who approached the army and begged to be allowed to travel with and serve the High King and her army, Rithdeliel made certain the same word was given: the army rode to take Jaeglenhend Great Keep, and all who wished to serve the High King were welcome.

They will know we are coming, Rithdeliel thought to himself. *But who will know? Who has Nilkaran left to defend his keep—and who remained after Iardalaith Lightbrother brought the Warhunt here?*

"They'll devour everything we've stolen down to dry bones," Thoromarth said.

"They'll steal the countryside bare as well," Rithdeliel replied. "Drive our stolen livestock, incite their kin to flight and mutiny, and give us warning of any foe."

"Ah, well, that's all right," Thoromarth said with a grunt. "For a moment I was worried you hadn't thought this through."

Rithdeliel used the halt to pass orders among the commanders. Many of his orders were not orders, precisely: the army's warriors were commanded by nearly two tailles of War Princes, and most of them were here. But he could *suggest*, and he was the High King's Warlord. And so, when they rode on, the army scattered, becoming a broad and rambling line of forage barely less destructive than a raging fire. The commonfolk followed, driving the living wealth of the manor farms before them: horses, cattle, sheep, goats. With dawn, the army left the last farm behind and gathered itself together again. Half a day's ride in the distance, silhouetted against the grey morning sky, stood the towers of Jaeglenhend Great Keep.

At noon they were seen by the tower watch—which told Rithdeliel the tower watch was not as he would have had it—and there was a distant thunder of drums and baying of horns. Two marks past noon, the battered, weary, and truncated army of Vieliessar High King arrived at Jaeglenhend Great Keep on their exhausted and footsore destriers. They had no bright banners. Their armor was filthy and their surcoats were ragged, and more than half their number still bore some unhealed injury.

None of that mattered. What mattered was that they stood before the gates of Jaeglenhend Great Keep and their knights-herald put their war horns to their lips and called to Jaeglenhend's defenders to come and die. The sound of the horns died away into silence, and then the silence lengthened. When it began to seem that they would all simply go on staring at each other forever, Rithdeliel growled and pulled his helm free of its armored collar.

"Do you intend to surrender or not?" he shouted up to the battlements. They were crowded with folk—and if Jaeglenhend had archers upon the walls, its attackers had Lightborn standing ready to cast Shield at the first sight of an arrow in flight. "Don't make me wait all day!"

There was a whispered conversation that he could not make out because of the distance, then some shifting and scuffling. At last a young woman—a girl, really, if she'd flown her kite in the Flower Moon Festival more than two years hence, it would be a wonder—pushed forward.

"Why should we not wait?" she called. "We are here and you are there! And my father will come back and kill you all!"

Rithdeliel turned to the Lightsister beside him. "Is there anyone here who has gone as envoy to Jaeglenhend? Who is she?"

"I will ask," she said, and slipped from her saddle to move on foot through the motionless ranks.

"Indeed we are here," Rithdeliel answered with an assumption of cheer. "And here we remain. Your orchards will feed us well—and give us excellent firewood to roast your sheep and cattle!"

The girl on the battlements opened her mouth to respond, but the man standing beside her—he had the look of someone who'd been Captain of Guards since before Nilkaran's greatsire was whelped—leaned toward her and began speaking urgently in her ear, sending dark looks in Rithdeliel's direction.

"She is Princess Telucalmo of Jaeglenhend," a breathless voice announced at Rithdeliel's knee. He glanced down; the Lightsister had returned, bringing another Lightborn with her. "I am Taraulard Lightbrother. I was born here."

"Did you serve at court?" Rithdeliel asked quickly, for the Green Robes saw everything. But the Lightbrother shook his head.

"My lord held a manor in the Tamabeth Hills. He—I—and his household rode to join the High King last spring."

"Is she Nilkaran's heir? How old is she?" Rithdeliel demanded.

"No. His heir is Heir-Prince Surieniel. He is six. Princess Telucalmo is ten years older," Taraulard Lightbrother said quickly. "She is betrothed into Vondaimieriel. She was to have gone to them this Harvest."

That explained why Princess Telucalmo was here instead of serving as Nilkaran's squire, or riding in his taille. Finfemeras would consider it a personal insult if Nilkaran got the bride of one of his sons slaughtered before the wedding. And because Nilkaran had ridden out thinking it would be a simple matter of ordering the High King to leave his lands, the highest-ranking lord within his great keep was a prince too young to leave the nursery and the lord who commanded it was a princess who had never fought a battle.

"Princess Telucalmo!" Rithdeliel called up to the battlements. "Come forward! Unless you are too frightened to face me!"

The taunt worked. He'd been certain it would. She pulled away from the man beside her and leaned over the battlements so far he thought she might fall.

"I'm not afraid of anything!" she shouted. "My father—"

"Isn't coming," Rithdeliel answered, and a great noise rose as everyone began talking at once. He waited for it to stop, then said, "He is with the army that came from the west. We are here. How many days' provisioning have you there in the castel, Princess of Jaeglenhend?"

Princess Telucalmo didn't answer him. Rithdeliel didn't think she knew. It would have been amazing if she had. He knew such things because it was a Warlord's business to know them. Harvesttide—the end of War Season—was the time when larders were barest. And the castellan had to know that most of their spell-preserved stores were rotting, though Rithdeliel didn't know if the Court did.

The question was asked for show, and it did its work. Soon enough the battlements were cleared of spectators and only the castel guards were left. "I do not recognize your livery," one of them called down. "Is that what bandits and oathbreakers wear in the west?"

"Perhaps you can tell me that—if you make it across the Mystrals alive!" Rithdeliel called back. "I will take your surrender, but only if it is made without a fight."

"As the princess says—we are in here!" the guardsman answered, grinning.

Half of any battle was waiting. Rithdeliel had never much cared for it. He sent most of the army back to the village. The craftworkers had left their livestock behind, and the herds driven up from the manorial estates had followed close behind the army. Soon the savory scent of roasting meat filled the air. Someone brought him a piece of meat wrapped in a piece of bread, and water for his destrier. Someone on the wall—he couldn't see who—loosed a few arrows. They struck nothingness and fell harmlessly to earth.

It was late afternoon, and the shadows were stretching long, when Rithdeliel finally saw and heard what he'd been waiting for: galloping horses and the flash of armor, the drumming of hooves. The group must have fled through a siege gate on the far side of the castel. He spurred Varagil toward them, and the double-taille he'd kept mounted and waiting through the long afternoon followed, but the Warhunt was quicker still. Rithdeliel and his meisne had barely rounded the near wall of the castel before two of the horses in the party broke away, turned, and began galloping toward Rithdeliel's forces. One palfrey carried a slender figure in blue-lacquered armor; the next, a woman carrying a small child before her on her saddle. A third figure followed almost at once—the guardsman Rithdeliel had seen speaking to Princess Telucalmo on the battlements.

The rest of the riders could have escaped, but they were guardsmen, leaving the Great Keep in an attempt to get the princess and the Heir-Prince to safety. After a moment's confusion they came galloping toward Rithdeliel and his meisne.

Rithdeliel plucked Heir-Prince Surieniel from his nurse's arms and flung the startled child to the nearest of his *komen*. Surieniel screamed as he was carried away and Rithdeliel closed with Princess Telucalmo.

If she'd been riding a destrier, if she'd been a seasoned knight, it wouldn't have been nearly so easy, but she was still hammering her heels into her palfrey's sides and sawing at the reins, unable to understand why it would not obey her. She saw the danger too late: he dragged her from her saddle and the Warhunt released her palfrey. With no rider to control it, the beast sped away.

Rithdeliel passed Princess Telucalmo to one of his *komen* despite her shrieks and struggles. As the knight galloped away, Rithdeliel drew his sword and spurred Varagil into the castel guardsmen. They should have retreated as soon as they saw their cause was lost, but every disaster the High King had faced in Jaeglenhend had originated in Nilkaran's lords being more terrified of him than they were of death. Outnumbered more than ten to one, palfreys and chain mail against destriers and plate armor, Jaeglenhend's guardsmen fought to the death.

⊰⊱

After the battles, the flight, the privation of the past days, the surrender of Jaeglenhend Great Keep was almost anticlimactic, but here at last Nilkaran had done their work for them. The castel's servants and remaining defenders all knew that having lost the Heir-Prince to the enemy meant their deaths. Opening the castel gates was their only chance for life, so they took it.

The keep was not large enough to house even the portion of Vieliessar's army which had taken it, and its larders were in as much disarray as Rithdeliel had suspected. But it offered shelter, and the surrounding farms had given them supplies, and there was no harm in being crowded if one was warm and fed. He set the craftworkers of the village to replacing the army's lost supplies, and the commons who had followed them from the manor farms to building an earthworks that encompassed the nearer fields and the castel itself. He did not expect it to provide a great deal of defense, but it would break a charge, and it would keep them busy.

Then he set about gathering the army back together.

Lord Vieliessar's army.

The High King's army.

⊰⊱

The Alliance army prepared for march three full candlemarks before dawn. Its enemy's baggage train followed behind its own, and the mingled herds followed both. Vieliessar's Lightborn, in disgrace for their rebellion, were set to ride between her supply train and the herds, where the *komen* who guarded the herdsmen could guard them as well.

It was still snowing.

The Houses of the Alliance took turns supplying the rear guard, and today House Rolumienion had that dubious honor. Since the end of the disastrous Surrender Parley Theodifel of Rolumienion had heard nothing but talk of the High Houses banding together and their lords cherishing each other as kin. And he had never been so grateful to be the eldest child of a minor lord, for the Lords *Komen* and their princely masters had done nothing but feud among themselves, and it had been a rare day, even on the march, when a Challenge Circle was not drawn.

When the herd beasts stampeded—first the goats, then the sheep, then even the cattle and the palfreys—there were many signs made against sorcery, for the herders suspected the rebel Lightborn had been responsible. Theodifel galloped up to the Lightborn and rode beside them. But he could not tell if any of them were working Magery, so he summoned his *komen* and went to give aid to the herders, for the loss of the herds was the loss of food, remounts, and draft animals.

It was noon before the herd beasts were finally collected and calmed and willing to be driven quietly at the rear of the caravan once more. On his return to the tail of the caravan, *Komen* Theodifel saw at once that the Lightborn were no longer there, but his first thought was that they'd taken advantage of the confusion to ride ahead, for who would follow a baggage train if they did not have to? A moment's reflection told him such an easy answer was folly: the loyal Lightborn would not permit the rebels to join them, and if they were simply riding beside the wagons farther up the column . . .

. . . the hoofprints of their palfreys should be visible in the snow. And they were not.

They were gone.

Heir-Prince Runacarendalur of Caerthalien was an excellent knight, a skilled general, a loyal vassal, and a reasonably dutiful son. He was kind to the servants of his household, courteous to his vassal knights, and gracious to the nobility of his father's court. He held his temper when he would rather lose it, he was tactful when he would rather be honest, and he told the truth when he would prefer to lie. He did not mistreat beast or child, he did not create factions, or join them, or permit them to form about him, and he did not—usually—drive Lord Bolecthindial to threaten to lay him in chains and throw him in the nearest dungeon.

"Will you ask Lord Nilkaran to grant you the loan of Jaeglenhend, Father? For if you mean the dungeons of *Caerthalien*, they—"

"*Be silent!*" Lord Bolecthindial roared. "I will not be mocked by my heir!"

They stood facing one another, scant handbreadths between them, in Lord Bolecthindial's pavilion. Lord Bolecthindial's servants, attendants, and guards had all been dismissed, and the door-flaps were laced shut. Their conversation was utterly private.

Fortunately.

"No—you let *Prince Serenthon's* heir do that!" Runacarendalur shouted back.

Bolecthindial struck him with a closed fist. Runacarendalur staggered back, falling to one knee. Blood dripped from his mouth and soaked into the pattern of leaves and flowers in the thick carpet. He stayed down, digging his fingertips into the carpet's pile. It was better to concentrate on the pain than to think of rising up and choking the life from his father.

Of course, his father was armed and he wasn't. So if he did what he so longed to do, he might solve the problems of everyone in camp at a single blow. Not that they'd have any way of knowing it.

Three days ago they'd been on the verge of unconditional victory. Two days ago Runacarendalur had been stopped from delivering the decisive blow to Vieliessar, her army, and her mad ambitions when the Council of War Princes who ruled over the army—a *council!* was there a madder notion between Sword and Star?—had forced him to break off the fighting because the prisoners had set fire to the encampment. Today the Lightborn who'd sworn fealty to Vieliessar had vanished as if they'd dissolved into mist. Because of that, the army had covered so little distance they might as well not have struck the camp at all—and even *that* didn't matter, because that self-same do-nothing Council could not decide whether to pursue Vieliessar or her army, and so pursued neither.

At last he ran his tongue over his split lip and pushed himself to his feet. "Tell me you'll listen. Or I'll go to Manderechiel and see if Aramenthiali will."

"He will feed your liver to his dogs," Lord Bolecthindial said, his words falling like slow and measured blows.

"Perhaps," Runacarendalur said evenly. "Or perhaps he'll pay heed. Aramenthiali is used to groveling. I'm sure Manderechiel isn't nearly as annoyed to be here as you are."

Lord Bolecthindial turned away and walked to a chair. He sat heavily, as if the need to sit were another enemy he wished to slay. Runacarendalur did not follow.

"My son. You are young yet. You do not understand what a labyrinth of promises and lies rulership is." Bolecthindial was most unsettling when he attempted to be conciliatory. He did not do it well. "Caerthalien's future hangs by the most fragile of threads. It is no secret."

Because three of my brothers are dead and the fourth is Lightborn and I shall be dead before the springtide and who is left? Ivrulion could be Regent for Demi-Princess Mindolin, but she is a child, and the daughter of an elder son at that—and both her aunts must take the throne before her. And they are idiots, but neither is such an idiot as not to see that becoming War Prince would allow them to send Mother from the keep so they need not suffer her interference—and she is a serpent, but she's smart.

"Oh, I see your plan at last!" Runacarendalur announced as if struck by sudden inspiration. "You have a bride in mind for me, and we will all sit here until she has presented me with an heir. An interesting strategy, but do you think the rest of the Alliance will endorse it?"

"Yap on," Bolecthindial answered crushingly. "I am used to barking dogs."

"Very well. Since you invite me to, I shall. Every moment we waste— and we have wasted three *interminable* days already—is another moment in which Vieliessar can hide herself and her army can regroup to attack us again. Rithdeliel Warlord rode north—do you think he won't take Jaeglenhend Great Keep when he reaches it?"

"I think we have his supplies, and his servants, and his remounts, and half his army will be dead long before they see the walls of the keep," Bolecthindial said. "Another sennight, and we'll have every *komen* who can still sit a horse at the bounds of our encampment, begging for pardon. As for the keep—all it need do is shut its gates and wait."

Runacarendalur drew a deep breath to keep himself from shouting. Again. They'd seen Vieliessar claim two dozen Less Houses in one War Season. The commons had risen up for her. The Lightborn had abandoned their homes. War Princes had willingly relinquished their domains to her. If the surviving Houses of the West had not banded together—If they had not moved to follow her with incredible speed—If Runacarendalur had not turned her own tactics against her to take her supply train . . .

. . . this so-called Alliance would be fighting for its life right now.

He was certain of it. What he was *not* certain of was that they'd seen Vieliessar fleeing from an army that had turned against her. If that were truly the case, why hadn't its commanders tried to seek pardon? They'd had Lightborn with them. They could have sent envoys.

"And if you're right, what then?" Runacarendalur said wearily. "True, we said we'd execute everyone who pledged to her. And true, perhaps they don't believe it. But the War Princes? When we took Vieliessar's baggage train we executed their entire *households*, and the Lightborn will bear them word of that—or do you, perhaps, think they have simply ridden off to the lost city of Celephriandullias-Tildorangelor? The War Princes won't sue for pardon, and thanks to us, they have no lands to return to. What they *do* have is tailles, and grand-tailles, and entire meisnes that are still loyal to them.

"Did you think we had trouble with outlaws after the Scouring of Farcarinon? This will be a thousand times worse." He walked over to the table beside his father's chair and picked up a cup from the tray. Without asking permission, he poured it full of wine from the pitcher there and walked away again.

Lord Bolecthindial waved Runacarendalur's comments away irritably. "I never thought you such an idealist. A War Prince without lands is just another landless knight. They can't hold the loyalty of nobles they can't reward—you'll find that's true when you come to rule. Their *komen* will desert them, if they haven't already, and come begging for the scraps from our tables. We have their commons. We have their supplies. We have the Mangiralas bloodstock. We can declare them outlaw and let the Uradabhur deal with a pack of outlaws."

"And that might work," Runacarendalur said. *I don't think it will, but it might.* "*If* we have Vieliessar too. They followed her because she claimed to be Amrethion High King's anointed heir. Oh, and because she promised to free the Landbonds and kill all of us, but the important point is, her army *will* become a pack of landless outlaws without her. But while she's alive—or they think she is—they'll fight." He drained his cup.

"They've already deserted her," Bolecthindial said.

"They haven't," Runacarendalur countered. "If her cause were lost, her Lightborn wouldn't have fled. Why should they? Of all who've defied us, *they* don't need to fear punishment. But think whatever you like. I won't convince you, and for the loyalty I bear Caerthalien I won't try to convince anyone else—if you let me go after her."

Bolecthindial got to his feet. "Think carefully, before I forget you are my heir and remember you are my vassal." Bolecthindial's voice was so quiet that it took as much courage as Runacarendalur had ever mustered to meet his eyes calmly. Bolecthindial in a shouting rage could be dealt with. Bolecthindial soft-voiced and unmoving was unpredictable and deadly.

"Lengiathion Warlord, Elrinonion Swordmaster, Lord Mordrogen—I could name a score of your vassals who would speak hard words to you for Caerthalien's safety," Runacarendalur said steadily. "While Vieliessar is free she is a danger. For who she is. For who the people will believe she is. For what their belief will make them do. If you will not hear these

words from your son, Lord Bolecthindial, hear them from your vassal—"
Runacarendalur crossed the space between them in three swift strides
and knelt before his father, head bowed "—and ask yourself: would Serenthon Farcarinon have balked at a ruse upon the battlefield if it would
gain him time to rally his *komen*?"

There was nothing but silence for long moments, but Runacarendalur
did not dare raise his head. He had risked all on this last throw of the
dice. If his father would not listen, he would have to seek out those who
would. After that, he could never return to Caerthalien while his father
lived.

It does not matter, he reminded himself. *I shall never rule Caerthalien. My only gift to her next prince can be the death of that monster who
wishes to destroy everything that is fine and noble in the Fortunate Lands.*

Perhaps Vieliessar was right about the meaning of *The Song of Amrethion.* Perhaps some great doom *was* coming. He didn't know. What he
knew was that if it did come, it couldn't be fought by Landbonds with
reaping hooks. And the war against it couldn't be led by anyone who
thought it could.

"I do not say you are right," Bolecthindial said at last, "but a small
force set to hunt Lord Vieliessar down is no bad notion. Her execution
will serve as a suitable display of strength to the remnants of her army,
when we come upon them." He rested his hand on the crown of Runacarendalur's head for a moment, then withdrew it. "But come! Get up! It
is unseemly for one born to rule to grovel at my feet as if he were—As if
he were of *Aramenthiali* lineage!" Bolecthindial gave a short, sharp bark
of mirth at his own joke. "And summon the servants! You've drunk all
the wine."

The matter wasn't settled so simply, of course. If Bolecthindial set a
search party hunting Vieliessar without the consent of the other War
Princes, he'd be violating the protocols under which they'd all come to
war, and even Caerthalien could not stand against the power of the rest
of the Alliance. The great cloth-of-gold pavilion in which the War Princes
dined each evening was occupied long into the night as they argued;

Runacarendalur occupied himself by deciding who he'd take with him if he were allowed to go at all.

His own guard, of course: Helecanth and his Twelve. Five more tailles beyond that, as he'd need to deal with any fighters Vieliessar had with her. His brother Ivrulion and as many more Lightborn as Bolecthindial would let him have—twenty would be good, forty would be better—to manage her Magery and the Lightborn with her. Supplies and servants. And once he had the bitch in chains, he'd tell Ivrulion the truth about being Bonded to her. He'd have to. Runacarendalur would need someone to help make sure his death when Vieliessar was executed did as little harm to Caerthalien as possible.

Every time Runacarendalur thought about being Bondmate to Vieliessar Farcarinon (Oronviel no longer existed; let the rebel be ruined under the name she'd been born to) he became so furious he could barely see. To have had his fate involuntarily linked to hers was cruelly wrong.

When dawn outshone the glow of the Silverlight, Runacarendalur still did not know what decision had been reached. The War Council had ended its deliberations some candlemarks before, but Bolecthindial had not seen fit to inform him of their decision and Runacarendalur knew better than to try his father's temper by sending a servant to ask.

He was preparing to don his armor for the day when one of his father's servants arrived, summoning him to Lord Bolecthindial's pavilion. Runacarendalur hastily flung on an overrobe and camp boots and hurried to the meeting. It was still a candlemark before dawn, but the air was already appreciably warmer than it had been at this time the previous day, and his boots squelched over muddy ground—a worrisome foretelling for the day's travel.

When he entered the pavilion he found both Lord Bolecthindial and Ladyholder Glorthiachiel seated at the long table in the outer room. Servants were setting out breakfast breads and meats. Ivrulion followed on Runacarendalur's heels a moment later.

"Here we are," Lord Bolecthindial said. "A happy family, all together."

"My commiserations upon the unexpected loss of Princess Angiothiel and Princess Ciliphirilir, in that case," Runacarendalur said dryly, gazing around ostentatiously.

"Still asleep," Ivrulion said. He walked past Runacarendalur to take a seat at the table, gesturing to a servant to pour him a cup of hot cider.

"Well, Runacar, sit down," Glorthiachiel said irritably. "Don't make me gape up at you. Lord Bolecthindial has distressing news."

"You're deaf, you addled viper," her husband said, as Runacarendalur found a chair. "This was his idea. And since apparently Caerthalien is to be held at fault forever for anything Farcarinon's whelp may do—"

"You should have let me bribe someone at the Sanctuary to poison her," Glorthiachiel interrupted.

"—you will be hunting her down," Lord Bolecthindial finished, speaking louder to drown out his wife's words. "I strongly suggest you succeed."

"What *komen* and supplies does the *Alliance* say I am permitted to take? I shall want Lightborn as well. And Ivrulion."

"They offer *me* a free hand in provisioning this expedition," Lord Bolecthindial said with heavy emphasis. "Undoubtedly they hope I will strip Caerthalien utterly of warriors, supplies, and Lightborn. You may take a grand-taille of *komen* and three score Lightborn, no more. And what supplies you will."

It was more than generous, given that Lord Bolecthindial did not think he should go at all. Runacarendalur inclined his head. "I thank you, Father." Quickly he outlined what he wanted.

"So little?" Lord Bolecthindial said, surprised.

"She had only a taille of *komen* with her, and perhaps some mercenaries. If the mercenaries haven't already run off, I'll hire them. For the rest, I want to travel as fast as possible. She already—"

"—has many days start. Yes. My ears are weary of hearing it," Lord Bolecthindial said. "And before you ask—no, you do not have my leave to go. Send a servant to prepare your wagons. Are you some hedge knight who must do everything yourself?"

⟨decorative divider⟩

While the wagons were being loaded, Runacarendalur sent Ivrulion to Jaeglenhend's Chief Huntsman. Ivrulion could be both charming and persuasive, and from Lady Valariel, he obtained her best tracker, a Landbond named Lidwal. It was nearly midday by the time Runacarendalur's sortie party drew clear of the main force, for the morning had been a nightmare of stopping and starting and unsticking wagons mired in mud. His meisne rode fully armed and mounted on their destriers—Runacarendalur wouldn't make the mistake of assuming Jaeglenhend wasn't hostile; if there was anything the War Princes should have learned from this War Season, it was that the commons and the Landbonds were treacherous and untrustworthy. Beyond that, it wouldn't hurt to give the destriers a little exercise before asking them to plod along under saddle while Lidwal searched for Vieliessar's trail. They gave the horses a good gallop, and then reined them to a walk to let the wagons catch up.

"Maybe you'll be fit to speak to now. My Lord," Helecanth said, once the destriers had slowed.

Runacarendalur grinned at the captain of his personal guard. "Maybe I will. And even more so once we've dragged our so-called High King back to her execution!"

Helecanth laughed and set Rochonan dancing simply because she could. The day was bright and the air was cool. *It's a shame we don't go to war in autumn more often,* Runacarendalur thought. *The weather's perfect for it, and the days run short enough that fighting dawn to dusk wouldn't be any hardship.*

"Time to earn your bread," Runacarendalur said to Lidwal. "What lies south of here?"

"How far south?" Lidwal asked. He looked too amused by his own wit for Runacarendalur's taste.

"I am certain Lady Valariel expects you returned to her whole and unharmed," Runacarendalur said, smiling as if he found Lidwal amusing. "But when you think about it, Lady Valariel is only Huntsman to the prince of a minor Less House, while I am Runacarendalur of Caerthalien. You may not care about that. But my brother is Lightborn, and *he* cares very much. I suggest you tell me what I want to know."

Lidwal glanced from Runacarendalur to Ivrulion. Ivrulion smiled, and Runacarendalur thanked the Silver Hooves yet again for the fortune that had given his elder brother to the Light, for if it had not, he knew he would have faced a formidable competitor for their father's throne—had he been born at all. Lidwal swallowed nervously, and Runacarendalur decided he'd judged correctly: a commonborn who knew himself too valuable to kill often became inured to physical punishment. But the hearth tales of the frightful spells the Lightborn could wield had spread even to crofter's huts.

"I beg pardon, Prince Runacarendalur. I meant no harm," Lidwal said humbly. "From here to the border, a few farms, nothing more. Follow this line due west and you might run into a hedge knight's manor or two, but this far east . . . nothing."

"And what lies on the other side of the border?" Runacarendalur asked.

"Nothing. My lord prince, I swear to you by the Huntsman it is true!" Lidwal cried in agitation. "To the south of Jaeglenhend there is forest. Nothing else."

Runacarendalur glanced at Ivrulion. He'd never campaigned in the Uradabhur, and only ridden over it once, during the Bethros Rebellion. If he wasn't going to fight over a territory, he didn't care what was there, and if he was going to fight over it, he had maps.

"Is the forester lying, Mardioruin?" Ivrulion asked.

"It is as he says, Prince Ivrulion," Mardioruin Lightbrother said. "There is nothing on Jaeglenhend's southern border but forest. Some of the domains east of here extend farther south along the foothills of the Bazrahil range, but to take the Southern Pass Route westward one must jog northward at Keindostibaent and then track south again through the Tamabeth Hills."

"Where is the nearest of the border keeps?" Runacarendalur asked next. Even if there were nothing to the south of Jaeglenhend but a lake of fire, there'd be watchtowers. And there was the Southern Pass road. If travelers from the Grand Windsward could use it, so could raiding parties from Keindostibaent.

Lidwal shook his head. "I know not!" he said quickly, when Runacarendalur frowned. "The hunting is poor to the south!"

And if there wasn't decent hunting, there'd be no reason for the servants of the War Prince's Huntsman ever to go there. "We'll go straight south," Runacarendalur decided. "Ride ahead. Look for tracks."

<hr />

Two days later Runacarendalur was beginning to wonder if Vieliessar had some form of Magery unknown to Ivrulion and other Lightborn. Lidwall's painstaking inspection of the ground made their southerly progress a time-consuming thing, but better that than missing the track. But there'd been no sign of riders, and there was no one to ask, for the few border steadings they encountered were deserted and stripped, their fields either hastily harvested or simply set ablaze. *A grand-taille of outlaws and a demi-taille of Lightborn, and not one blade of grass is bent,* Runacarendalur thought in exasperation. Yet they must have come this way. Their mounts had been weary and starving; they did not possess the stamina to have doubled back or headed farther west. . . .

We're running out of time, Runacarendalur thought uneasily, but he knew that wasn't true. They'd already run out of time. It was Rade, and there was already snow in the mountain passes. Even if he found Vieliessar tomorrow and all her army surrendered at once, they were trapped here until spring thaw. Long enough for the Alliance War Princes to turn on each other, for the Less Houses of the Uradabhur to turn on the Alliance, for anything to happen . . .

Each night when they stopped, Ivrulion Farspoke Feliot Lightbrother to report their continued failure and hear news of Caerthalien. Runacarendalur disliked the sensation of being watched over and second-guessed, but it was a relief to hear that Caerthalien had not been set upon by its allies.

Allies! A pack of wild dogs coursing a fat stag, as willing to bring down the lions among them as to take their lawful prey . . .

As if sensing his brother's growing frustration, this morning Ivrulion had suggested a hunting expedition, and a day of hunting and a supper of roast venison did much to improve Runacarendalur's temper. Afterward he wandered idly through the encampment, stopping here and there to exchange a word or two with his *komen,* then walked out past the bounds. His breath fogged on the air, and the stars above were bright. The Starry Road was a band of Silverlight across the heavens: as a child, whenever Caerthalien rode to war, he would slip away from his nurse—and later, his servants—to stand beneath the night sky, imagining he could hear the cries of the Hunt as they carried away those his father and brothers had killed that day. . . .

"A word, brother."

Runacarendalur hadn't heard Ivrulion approach, but a part of him always expected to suddenly find his brother near, for when Ivrulion had returned from the Sanctuary with Lightborn powers of stealth and concealment, he hadn't scrupled to use them to terrify his newest sibling.

"I stand ready to hear," Runacarendalur said, turning and sweeping Ivrulion a mocking bow.

"I think you should come back within the bounds. Anything might be out here," Ivrulion said.

"I wish it were," Runacarendalur muttered.

"Does it occur to you that we can find no sign of them because they are not here to find?" Ivrulion asked. "In three days, much could happen. They are a sennight ahead of us. If they quarreled— If by some mischance Vieliessar Farcarinon was slain—"

"She is not dead!" Runacarendalur said. "I—" *I would know. I, too, would die. . . .*

He bit back the words unsaid, but it was too late. Ivrulion was studying him with new interest.

"Caerthalien stood in the front ranks at the false parley," Ivrulion said.

"I was there," Runacarendalur snapped. "To see Farcarinon once again profane the Code of Battle with trickery and lies."

"Indeed," his brother said. "I watched you that day. It seemed to me you meant to cry warning to our father that all was not as it seemed."

"How should I have known that?" Runacarendalur said uneasily.

Ivrulion did not answer. "Walk with me, brother," he said instead, taking Runacarendalur's arm and leading him away from the encampment

They walked in silence for a time, until the lights of their camp were dimmed by distance. At last Ivrulion stopped.

"You were much changed upon your return from Oronviel," he said.

"We lost," Runacarendalur said shortly.

He was ill at ease with the direction of Ivrulion's seemingly idle words. He would not have stood for such an interrogation from anyone else, even Lord Bolecthindial, but Ivrulion, of all his kin, was no threat to him. Lightborn might betray—Caerthalien had always safeguarded itself by ensuring that they would watch one another, vying for status and privileges—but what greater honors could Ivrulion wish than those he already held? Ivrulion could never inherit Caerthalien. *So Mosirinde Peacemaker and Arilcarion War-Maker intended, when they drew up the Code of Battle and the Lightborn Covenant. If no Lightborn can inherit a domain, or deed any of their gifts and honors to their children, it only makes sense for them to be loyal to those who can.* Before Oronviel, he'd been confident Ivrulion would outlive him and stand ready to guard the next War Prince of Caerthalien as he'd guarded the last.

And so he would, but that War Prince would not be Runacarendalur's child.

"A tragic day," Ivrulion said smoothly. "And yet . . . I feel there is more to your distemper than a loss upon the battlefield. Oronviel's victory that day touches Bolecthindial's honor—yet it is you who would cast off all reason and sense to compass Vieliessar Farcarinon's death."

"I act for the good of Caerthalien!" Runacarendalur said, but even in his own ears, his words rang hollow. *I will not be Bonded to a monster!*

"And yet . . . Is it good to withhold from Caerthalien that which may profit it to know?" Ivrulion asked silkily. "I think you have a secret you wish to confide in me, brother."

There is nothing to tell. He opened his mouth, the words ready on his tongue.

But those were not the words he spoke. Instead, "Vieliessar Farcarinon is my destined Bondmate," he said, and saw Ivrulion smile.

"So I suspected."

"You— How dare you bespell me, as if I were—" Runacarendalur willed himself attack, to draw his sword, to strike down his treacherous brother. Instead, he staggered backward a few clumsy steps.

"Some treacherous vassal, some outlaw, some Landbond rabble?" Ivrulion said lightly. His smile was a cold and predatory thing. "But dear brother, what may we say of one who has held Vieliessar Farcarinon's life in his hands this half-year and forborn to take it?"

"No one would believe it was other than a plot by Caerthalien to . . ." Runacarendalur's ragged words faltered to a stop, but at least this time they were his own. He imagined he could feel the Magery Ivrulion had netted him in like a cold slime upon his skin, taking from him all dignity, all choice . . .

"As my choice was taken!" Ivrulion said, and for once the cold, controlled voice held bright anger. "I was Heir-Prince to Caerthalien! I! You were not even thought of! It was to have been mine! Instead, I am a servant, to scrape and bow, to take orders like the lowest hedge knight, to see my children dispraised, having nothing unless the charity of the next War Prince decrees it! Do you know what my Midwinter Gift was in the year I was Chosen? A sword. I had ridden to war as our father's arming page. In the summer to come, he would have made me *komen*. But I did not ride to war that summer. No. When War Season came that year, I was at the Sanctuary of the Star, scrubbing pots and sweeping floors. I comforted myself with the knowledge that Domcariel was slow and foolish, and I would still rule Caerthalien with him as my puppet. And when at last I was released, I discovered they had bred another heir. You."

"But you were Called. . . ." Runacarendalur faltered, still stunned by Ivrulion's fury. How could 'Rulion have held the dream of Caerthalien so close that none of them had suspected he was rotted through with cheated ambition?

"Called!" Ivrulion spat. "I was never meant to go before Astorion Light-brother in Open Court that night! It should have been Carangil or Feliot, who knew what they should see and what they should not. Helegondolrin-dir Astromancer was as rotted through with dreams and ambitions as both her successors. It was her scheming that set me before Astorion. But I have been patient. And my patience is to be rewarded at last. . . ."

He is mad, Runacarendalur thought in horror, trying desperately to guard his thoughts from Ivrulion's hearing. He would die, and this madthing, this witchborn traitor brother, would be Regent. . . .

"Oh, Rune, sweet brother," Ivrulion said, shaking his head sadly. "Do you think me so simple? Come. Let us see what we may make of this Bond of yours. . . ."

Runacarendalur stood helplessly as Ivrulion advanced upon him. He felt cool hands pressed against his temples.

And then there was only light, and pain.

⊰⊱

For a moment Runacarendalur could not think where he was. He thought hazily of battle, of being struck from Gwaenor's back and carried to the Healing Tents. But his fingers flexed in night-chill grass as, with a groan, he opened his eyes. The sky above him was pale with dawn, and even that small light was enough to send lancing pain through his head. He winced, turning his head to the side.

"What a pity," Ivrulion said.

"That I'm alive?" Runacarendalur asked after a moment, his voice, a hoarse whisper.

"That it didn't work," Ivrulion said reprovingly. "I'd hoped to locate the supposed High King through your Bond. But alas, my poor skills proved inadequate to that task."

"I'll see you dead." With a supreme effort, Runacarendalur rolled onto his stomach. Nausea surged through him but he fought it back as he struggled to rise.

"By the Light, I never before thought you stupid." Ivrulion stepped forward and hauled him to his feet. Runacarendalur balanced on unsteady legs, swaying and gasping. "Do you think I'm going to let you fling yourself at our dear father's feet and confess?"

Runacarendalur shook his head, trying to clear it. Would Bolecthindial believe him? It didn't matter. He had to try.

"You see, dear brother—or you should, since your tactical skills have made you the darling of the Storysingers—one does not throw away a useful weapon. Go to Bolecthindial to confess, and you will find you cannot. Take up your courage to end your life and your Bondmate's, and you will find you cannot." Ivrulion took him by the arm and began to walk him back toward the camp. Runacarendalur staggered and stumbled beside him, helpless to resist.

His strength returned swiftly, though his head ached abominably. After a few paces, Runacarendalur yanked his arm free and took a step backward. His hand closed over the hilt of his sword, and as it did, he vowed to the Silver Hooves that one of them would die here this day. Perhaps both.

He pulled at the sword with all his strength. It did not move.

"Attempt to kill me, and you will find you cannot do that either," Ivrulion said gently. He smiled, and for an instant Runacarendalur saw his brother, his ally, his friend . . .

Then Ivrulion's dark eyes grew hard and cold. His smile did not change.

"Now come. Your *komen* will wonder what has kept you from your bed all night. And I am eager for my breakfast."

CHAPTER FIFTEEN

THE HERO TALE

*Every war begins with its own hero tale, as if it were a great lord who had
lived a long life and now has a story-song crafted to be sung over its
funeral pyre. And any prince who clings to that story-song after a
campaign begins will drink to drowning of the cup of defeat and loss, for
a war is not a warrior, and no mortal prince can force the world to follow
their whim as if they wear the cloak of the Starry Huntsman.*

—Arilcarion War-Maker, *Of the Sword Road*

It took you long enough to get here," Rithdeliel said.

"I thought we should see something of the countryside, since we'd
come all this way," Gunedwaen answered, and Rithdeliel laughed.

It was a full sennight since the disastrous battle in the storm. The great
manor houses they had passed on their way to the keep had been utterly
deserted, as destitute as if they had been sacked, and so Gunedwaen had
dared to hope other parts of the High King's army had escaped the enemy's trap. But he had not truly believed until he saw Lord Rithdeliel riding
toward him on his great grey destrier, two tailles of *komen* behind him.

"Come and see the castel instead, old friend! If we are crowded
there—and we are—we are at least well fed!" He gestured to the knight-
herald beside him. The knight-herald raised his horn and sounded a call,
and Gunedwaen gestured to his own knight-herald.

*That damned rascal's lucky we still have a herald and a warhorn with
us—but that's a Caerthalien-bred Warlord for you: always sure the world
will run as he wishes, and not as it wills . . .* Gunedwaen thought sourly.
Every Swordmaster was a cynic and pessimist; good fortune only made
them suspicious.

As his knight-herald's call echoed Rithdeliel's, the *komen* behind Gunedwaen began to cheer. The sound grew louder as it was taken up by more and more of them, the impulse of it rolling backward through the ordered ranks in their formations, dipping as komen paused for breath, swelling anew as they shouted in loud fierce joy.

But Rithdeliel's boast of triumph was—much as Gunedwaen had suspected—a show for the *komentai'a*. Once he was behind closed doors with Rithdeliel and the majority of the surviving War Princes—sour luck indeed to find so many of them here; if it had been left to Gunedwaen he would have dropped them all into Great Sea Ocean and called it a good day's work—he heard a different tale.

Vieliessar High King was still missing.

"What do you mean you don't know where she is?" Gunedwaen demanded. "It's been more than a sennight since the Alliance proved it could fight—they could have executed her by now!"

"They would have gotten around to mentioning it," Lord Thoromarth said. "If you think Nilkaran Jaeglenhend doesn't know where we are, you're mistaken—Lord Rithdeliel threw his court out of the keep when we took it."

From his seat by the window, Rithdeliel bowed ironically, not getting to his feet. "We kept the Heir-Prince," he said. "And his extremely annoying sister. I believe they're in the dungeons."

"So Nilkaran knows you have his keep and his heir," Gunedwaen said. "And you think—what? He'd ask the Alliance to trade Lord Vieliessar for them?"

"I *think* the Alliance would know where to send its knights-herald to show us her severed head and invite us to surrender," Thoromarth answered caustically. "But they're chasing their tails. Aradreleg Lightsister and the rest of our Green Robes escaped the Alliance and reached us yesterday morning. Aradreleg said the Alliance Lightborn lifted the storm so they could try to track Lord Vieliessar—so of course their wagons are now mired in mud. She's got a plan to get our equipment back, too—if you don't mind a little fighting."

"You've got half the Lightborn of the West here," Gunedwaen said. "Why don't you just . . . ?" He waved his hand wordlessly.

"Apparently Magery isn't that useful unless you want to either strike somebody with a bolt of lightning or freeze them to death in a blizzard," Kalides Brabamant said, sounding irritable. "I've seen Alasneh Lightsister Call my lady's gloves across the castel dozens of times. But several thousand Lightborn cannot do the same for a few carts."

Gunedwaen knew better than most Lightless what the limitations of the Light truly were. Even if the Lightborn could Call the contents of every baggage wagon to them—a thing by no means certain—all the living things would be left behind. "I've never objected to a fight," he said mildly. "What is this plan?"

⊰⊱

For nearly a two sennights since their capture, the surviving commons of the High King's baggage train had followed the enemy army. They had no choice. Any who ran was cut down by *komen* on horseback or dragged back to the encampment to suffer a more lingering death. The escape of the Lightborn had been the only triumph they could claim, and it was little enough to warm shivering, ill-clad bodies or fill stomachs pinched with hunger.

But now the enemy had brought them to Jaeglenhend Great Keep.

Too far! Tunonil thought. *We are still too far distant!* It was almost a league from where the wagons stood to the castel walls—and the protection of the High King's army. If the commonfolk tried to reach it afoot, they would surely be cut down as they ran. Nor could they bring with them the precious sumpter wagons. Those stood unmoving, their wheels spoked, for the Light's Chosen of the High King had been Calling since dawn, and already their flocks of sheep and goats, horses and cattle, had headed the Call. Only the oxen and mules remained behind, shackled to their unmoving wagons, but even that was a victory for the High King, for it was not merely her wagons which must be held immobile, but all of them.

When Tunonil and all the rest had first been captured, the oxherds and muleteers had seized the best of their draft animals for their own wagons and carts, and now those beasts who could be Called were scattered throughout the combined baggage train. So the wagons stood motionless, and the *komen* armed themselves, and the War Princes shouted and argued over what was to be done and how.

The clamor of the war drums could be heard in the distance, and the warhorns sounded. The knights were calling for their destriers to be saddled and their weapons to be brought. Soon the two armies would clash.

At last the army rode forth. Even though these were the warriors of the enemy, sworn foes of the High King, they were a splendid sight to see, for every horse and rider wore bright silk and the armor of the *komen* was as bright as butterfly wings. Behind the warhorses and the wearers of bright armor and silks came a second army of servants. Their palfreys were laden with baskets of food and drink, for the great lords went to war as to a festival, and among the servants rode the Light's Chosen who served the enemy.

"You! Get down from there! This wagon isn't going anywhere, so get to work, you lazy brute!"

The speaker was no great lord, but he carried a whip, and no Landbond's life was held dear by any but themselves. Tunonil climbed down from the wagon bench. The carts were being unloaded and their contents laid upon the ground, and he could see that other prisoners were already carrying baskets, boxes, rugs, and chairs to the place where the servants meant to set their masters' encampment. Even the paddocks and the horselines were being prepared for their masters' return, though there was not now a single horse in the whole of the camp, for most had fled candlemarks ago and the rest had been ridden to war.

The work was hard, though Tunonil was used to hard work and there were many hands to help. But they had all been days with scant food and little water. Burdens he had carried lightly and eagerly in the High King's service were now nearly too heavy to lift. And those servants of the enemy ordered to labor beside them rejoiced in making their tasks harder, pushing and tripping them just to see them fall. Tunonil was only glad matters were no worse, and he was surprised to find—when he returned to the carts for another load—that great barrels of beer and cider and water had been taken down and opened, and they were not stopped from drinking their fill. Cider was sweet indeed to the starved and the thirsty, and if the servants of the enemy jealously claimed all the beer for their own, what did that matter?

In the distance there was a sudden great upswelling of sound, as warriors shouted, drums boomed, and warhorns cried. The ground—even this far away from the charging destriers—trembled.

The battle had begun.

It was on his third return to the carts that Tunonil saw Light's Chosen going among the wagons, with servants behind them. At each wagon they paused, and laid a hand upon the brow of the beasts yoked there. If the Light's Chosen nodded, the servants would unhitch the animal. If they shook their heads, it was left in its traces. At first it seemed their work was random, but as he watched he saw that each one they uncoupled or unyoked moved eagerly toward the Great Keep.

It seemed madness and rebellion, but after a few moments Tunonil understood what was happening. The Light's Chosen meant to drive the carts to the battlefield, to bear away the wounded for Healing as they had always done. For that reason, they separated the High King's beasts from their own to be sure of driving teams that answered to no one but their masters.

By now the lesser servants reeled with drunkenness and beer, singing and shouting gaily to one another, for the kegs of strong ale had been many, intended for twice the number who drank of them, and to be thinned with water besides. Some worked, some idled, some crept off to sleep. It was then that Tunonil saw the shape of what the High King's people must do to win their freedom. No one would trust the High King's people to do the work of preparing pavilion, kitchen, or larder, so once the pavilions had been set, their labor was finished. They could not make their escape unnoticed or unseen. But they could go at a time when no one who saw them would dare to follow. All the lords had ridden forth, and there was no one remaining with the authority to rule over the servants of every House.

In murmured half-sentences, Tunonil passed the plan to as many as he dared, for it was important for them all to remain together. He was soon glad he had done so, for the enemy was not one army, but many. The servants of *this* House treated them as enemies, while the servants of *that* House said that if they would pledge themselves to obedience once more, they would be fed and clothed and nothing would be said of their flight. And the servants of yet another House asked no promise of submission, but said food would be found for the children if they would bring them once the kitchens were ready. To all who spoke, the prisoners returned words that were soft and meaningless, and when the servants of the enemy became occupied with their tasks, the High King's people slipped away.

For the first time, Tunonil could see the battlefield clearly, and when the wind shifted, he could smell the blood.

The fighting had spread out across the field in front of the Great Keep, and eastward as well. There was a great earthwork surrounding the castel—new, for Tunonil could see the raw earth of it—and it divided each army into two forces, fighting on either side of it. Riderless destriers galloped through the battle, and here and there he saw flashes of bright purple light. The castel's battlements were lined with Light's Chosen, and now and again the front wall of the castel flickered with the same light. Tunonil could not tell who was winning.

The refugees did not walk directly toward the Great Keep, for that would be to walk into the battle. But a little distance from the western wall of the Great Keep was a stand of trees, and some of the oxen that had been freed from the wagons could be seen moving toward them with steady deliberation. Tunonil knew both armies would avoid that place— the enemy, because he feared it held the High King's archers; the High King's warriors because it did not. It was there that the High King's people would wait.

If they reached it alive.

"At least no one is calling down storm or lightning," a woman walking beside him said. "It is why the War Princes are not holding back their reserves—see?"

She had to put her mouth close beside his ear to be heard, for the sound of the battle was like the bellowing of an ox and the clanging of a smith's hammer and the roar of a stormwind all commingled and magnified a thousandfold.

"Such knowing is not for mere Landbonds," Tunonil said ungraciously. The woman was not someone he knew, but more than a few of the enemy's servants had seized upon this chance for freedom.

"Fool!" the woman said. "Do you think I was born in silk and silver? I was born a Landbond, just as—"

She broke off as a knight galloped toward them. There was barely a mile between them and the edges of the battle, and as soon as they'd seen the enemy knight he was almost upon them. Many screamed and ran—as if that might save them—but just as the knight drew his sword, the purple light appeared before him. Horse and rider struck it as if they struck a wall, and fell to the ground, both dead. A cheer went up from the people at the sight, and Tunonil's heart filled with joy.

"You see the High King has not forgotten us, even in the heat of battle," he said to the woman beside him. "Can you say such of your great lord?"

"Are you disordered in your wits?" she demanded. "I spit on Aramenthiali! Do you suppose I could return to the encampment and take up my life again? How long before Heart-Seeing was set upon the servants of Lord Manderechiel's tent and it was discovered I lied when I said I had his order from Lord Malanant to prepare the tents?" She spoke loudly enough now that those nearest could hear.

Wide-eyed, Tuonil said, "That was you?" Truly, this was a deed worth remembering, and telling over so that the tale could be passed on forever.

"Think you I acted alone?" the woman of Aramenthiali demanded. She made a sweeping gesture that took in the plodding thousands ahead of them. "I would swear to you that a hundred—a thousand—more—of those here served the High Houses this morning! How think you so many kegs of ale came to be set out? Or you found yourselves excused from your labors so conveniently? Even the Lightborn . . . I do not say they have joined your cause, but tell me, you who know all—from what noble families do the Lightborn come?"

"From none," another woman answered. "All know the Light favors the commons. It is our recompense for lives of labor and hardship."

"And so some of them were willing to say they believed my words, and if the camp were to be set, why should they not prepare to bring the wounded for Healing? Easy enough to bring back fleeing beasts once the battle was won," the woman said.

Another group of knights galloped from the battle, intent on attacking the refugees. The two in the lead galloped into walls of purple light and died, just as the first had, but the ones behind them had enough warning to rein in. Tunonil hoped they would simply return to the battle once they saw their prey was not undefended, but instead they moved forward at a walk. The marchers began to scatter. Tunonil froze where he stood.

Then one attacker began to beat at his arms and chest—Tunonil could see the bright silk of his garments had gone grey with frost—and the silks of another burst into flames, so that his warhorse galloped madly forward to batter itself against another wall of purple.

The remaining knights turned and galloped back toward the battle.

At last—welcome sight!—Tunonil saw the Light's Chosen of the High King riding down the line on horseback, to see if all was well.

"Are you the last? Are more coming? Oh praise to the Light, Tunonil—I did not think you would survive!" Aradreleg Lightsister said as she reached them.

"Takes more than hard work and light feeding to kill a Landbond," Tunonil answered gruffly.

"Are you the last?" Aradreleg repeated, and Tunonil nodded.

"No more. Some may have stayed, but—Mistress High House here says some of their folk are with us."

The woman from Aramenthiali tried to glare at him, but the relief of freedom was too sweet. "My name is Tance," she said. "Not 'Mistress High House.'"

"I'll bring you to the gathering place so you can rest. There's not much there, but there's water . . . and pikes. Lord Rithdeliel said if you managed to escape, you should be ready to fight."

"Is there a bow?" Tance asked. "I was a forester in Lord Malanant's household."

"A forester?" Aradreleg said. "Praise the Light indeed! Your skills are welcome! Come—Tunonil, help her mount; I am needed elsewhere, and she is as well—"

Tance looked stunned at the swift change in her fortunes, but did as Aradreleg said. A moment later, they galloped away.

⌁⌁

It was dusk by the time Tunonil heard the hornsong that signaled the High King's victory and the enemy's retreat. It was much like the end of every battle Tunonil had ever seen. Wounded knights moaned or shouted, wounded horses screamed, dogs howled and barked as they ran among the fallen. Uncounted hundreds of gleaners walked the battle-field, separating living from dead, friend from foe, and shooing away the ravens that had come in the thousands to gorge. Before morning, all that would lie upon the field would be the naked bodies of the enemy dead: their own dead would be brought back and prepared for the fire. Tunonil had learned that the High King was not here—but safe, *safe*, everyone agreed—so he wondered what would become of the enemy knights abandoned here if they could not pledge fealty to her.

He hoped they, too, would lie naked and abandoned on the field in the dawn light.

The end of the battle was only the beginning of the work for those who had not fought, though few grudged the labor now that they were the High King's folk once again. There were horses to saddle, mules to catch and rope together, and oxen to collect and match into their familiar teams, for now the wagons they'd left behind must be brought to their encampment.

Tunonil had asked what was to keep the enemy from destroying their undefended wagons, and Harwing Lightbrother had laughed.

"Why, *we* are, of course! They won't burn them or loot them or even carry them away while Shield is set upon them! We have been watching the wagons all day, as carefully as we watched the battle, and no one has gone near."

Tunonil led his oxen back to the wagons. Even though the last light of day still brightened the sky, globes of wonder-glow had been set shining here. When he reached the carts, Tunonil saw knights, blood-spattered and weary, sitting their destriers in a line between the workers and the camp of the enemy—and beside them, rank upon rank of Light's Chosen. He unblocked the wagon's wheels, set the yoke upon the oxen's necks, then coaxed them into place along the tree and chained the yoke to the shaft.

Once up on the wagon's high seat, Tunonil looked back. Half the pavilions he and his fellows had labored to set were down again, and some were being put back up. He didn't see the enemy army, but he didn't stay to look.

The High King had won. That was all that mattered.

***

To be a War Prince possessed of a Name and a growing legend had its advantages, Vieliessar discovered. Border Lord Karamedheliel, master of Jaeglenhend's Oakstone Tower, did not need to be convinced that her word was good and her dealings fair; nor did Vieliessar, for her part, fear secret rebellion. She did not plan to remain here for long, but neither did she mean to ride forth blindly and unprepared. And so, on the second night after she had taken Oakstone Tower, she retired to her bedchamber—once Karamedheliel's—before the evening meal. It was not the soft bed Vieliessar yearned for as much as for a door that could be spell-locked. She had never dared to do this while on the march.

There were too many calls upon her time, too many urgencies. And while a tent flap could have the same spell set upon it, anyone determined to enter need merely cut the fabric of the pavilion. And she dared not be interrupted while she was Farspeaking.

With all that had happened, it was hard to bring herself to the state of calm her spell required. Even the relief she felt at spell-locking the door of the sleeping chamber did not bring relief, so she wove ward after ward about the room until the walls sang with Magery, taking comfort in the familiar discipline. Silence and Protection and Silence again, until the space began to take on the heavy quiet of one of the meditation chambers in the Sanctuary. She had never realized what a luxury it was to live behind Wards and walls until she left them behind forever.

Her spellkit—once Celeharth's—had been lost with her baggage train. But she had found a way to make do. From a chest in the corner she took a stone teapot and a delicate cup of moon-pale shin'zuruf. She had been surprised but pleased to find these items among Karamedheliel's possessions. Most welcome of all was a tiny brazier, only large enough to hold one charcoal disk. The brazier was very old, carved of white jade with the design of a herd of running unicorns, a golden bowl for the charcoal set in the top. Gazing at it, Vieliessar thought back suddenly to the day she had gone to Earime'kalareinya to sacrifice for victory in battle. Even now, the memory of the Unicorn's radiant beauty, glimpsed and lost, made her heart ache when she thought of it.

Recognizing her mind's attempts to delay her, she opened another box and chose a disk of charcoal, setting it carefully into the brazier's golden bowl. She placed the brazier on top of the chest, then set the charcoal alight with a thought. Iardalaith had given her a wooden canister of tea, and another of incense. Now she shook loose tea into the teapot, then filled it with hot water from the kettle. As she waited for the tea to steep, she opened the incense box and teased out the tiny bone spoon inside, then scooped a small mound of incense crystals onto the charcoal. At once they began to bubble and melt, and soon the sweet, rich scent of incense filled the chamber. When the tea was ready, she poured her cup full. The cool sweetness of the tea mingled with the warm sweetness of the incense, familiar and soothing.

By the time she'd finished two cups of tea, the calm sense of *weight* she'd always somehow associated with complex and delicate Magery had settled over her. She folded the bed's coverlet to serve as a cushion and settled herself upon the thickly carpeted floor.

Thurion? Thurion, are you there?

Since the day she had sent him to the Grand Windsward, Vieliessar had tried to Farspeak him as often as she could. But the Windsward was so far to the east that it might be afternoon there even when night had fallen in the West. And Farspeech only worked when both Lightborn had minds that were still and quiet, awaiting the message. They had missed each other as often as not. The last time she had been able to contact him, she had been in Ceoprentrei.

She could no longer easily recall how many sennights had passed since then.

For long moments she called and received no reply. She was about to give up when:

"Vielle? It has been so long! Are you well?"

She opened her inward eyes and saw what she expected to: the image of a chamber in some Grand Windsward castel.

"We reached the Uradabhur safely enough. Things have not gone well since."

She quickly told him the whole: the battle with Jaeglenhend, the Alliance's pursuit, her defeat in battle, her flight. "I can only hope my people survive, but I fear for those who lie in the Alliance's hands. I hold the fealty of twenty-five Houses, Thurion. Take my army and my life, and the High Houses become rich. They intend to execute all who have sworn fealty to me and divide their domains among themselves."

"And they have every reason to choose that course," Thurion said slowly. "Why should they fear the vengeance of the Silver Hooves when it did not fall upon them for the destruction of Farcarinon? But this could help us. Once word spreads that the High Houses now follow a strategy of conquest and annexation . . ." There was a long pause as Thurion sought for words. "Many will see that choosing your side will allow them to retain their lives, if not their sovereignty. Gain enough Houses, and even this Alliance cannot stand against you."

This disconcertingly insightful analysis of a situation Thurion hadn't even known about a tenth-candlemark before only made Vieliessar miss him more keenly.

"If I yet have more army than the handful that accompanied me in my flight. I shall try to reach Aradreleg next, to see what news she can give me. If she lives," Vieliessar added softly, for Aradreleg had been among those captured, and though no War Prince would execute her, any Lightborn might choose to. "But tell me your news," she urged. "I need your council. And my own situation I know."

She felt him laugh just a little. "My news is much as it was the last time we spoke, save for this: the Silver Swords leave within the sennight. Master Kemmiaret swears he will bring the Silver Swords across the Arzhana before the passes to the Uradabhur close."

"And what does Melchienchiel Penenjil say?" Vieliessar asked.

"She says she will come—this season if she can. But you know she will be more cautious with the rest of her meisne. The southern route isn't wide or gradual enough for supply wagons, and the northern route is held by Nantirworiel. Methothiel Nantirworiel usually doesn't care who uses the pass so long as they pay, but—"

"—but it's different when he's being asked to let an enemy army through," she finished for him. "If the Silver Swords would like to conquer Nantirworiel on their way west, that would be very useful to me."

"I'll mention that to Master Kemmiaret," Thurion answered dryly. "The Houses that have declared for you are all mustering their meisnes. Kerethant and Enerchelimier join Penenjil on the march. I think Artholor and Hallorad also plan to come at once, but they lie east of Penenjil and neither will risk a Windsward crossing or an ascent of the Feinolon Range in bad weather. And if the weather turns early, all of them will stay in the Windsward until spring rather than be forced to winter in the Arzhana."

"And rather than ask their Lightborn to divert the storm—or open the passes," Vieliessar said.

"Yes," Thurion said regretfully. "It is much to ask of them."

Vieliessar sighed in acceptance. "They will come when they will come. At least they are willing to try." As much as she might rail against the indecisiveness of the Windsward Houses, she would not herself have chosen a course that would force her army to overwinter in a hostile place. *As if I had any choice about it,* she thought wryly.

"I would conjure summer myself, if it would get me to you faster," Thurion said. "I've missed you."

"And I, you," she answered, swallowing hard. "I wish you were here now. I could use your wisdom."

"Any aid I can give you from this distance, I give you gladly. You know that," he answered.

"I hope I shall always know enough to value my true friends," she replied impulsively. The grief and longing she heard in her words was so raw it made her wish she hadn't spoken.

"I promise I will always be that," Thurion answered quietly. "But come. Tell me what you need."

She had tried to reach him on impulse, not truly believing she would manage it, and the pleasure in the contact had allowed her to forget the war for a few moments. But now—

"I need to find the Flower Forest of Tildorangelor," she blurted. "And I have no idea where to look!"

There was a long, meditative pause.

"I don't know where it is either, Vielle. But I could find it with enough time—and power," Thurion answered.

"What are you saying?" Vieliessar asked sharply.

"You took the same lessons I did from Rondithiel Lightbrother, and I am sure he has not changed his lectures from one century to another," Thurion said.

"Probably not," Vieliessar said. "And since he is here, I can hear them again any time I wish to."

Thurion laughed. "I would not dare dream of such great fortune! You are truly blessed. But listen. For spells such as Fetch and Send we must know exactly where we are touching with our Magery. But not to use Door," Thurion continued, in the cheerful tones of a patient instructor. "Door is a spell that requires great power, and that is why we are taught to cast it only between Flower Forests. And why did Rondithiel Light-brother say that was?"

"He said it is because within the Light there is only one Flower Forest, which makes no sense at all," Vieliessar said. "But—"

"But it is true, at least in a sense," Thurion said. "The Flower Forests all touch one another in the Light. Have you never reached through a nearer Flower Forest to a more distant one? Oh, no, of course you have not," Thurion said hastily, sounding embarrassed and contrite. "You were not taught to Heal on the battlefield. If you had been, you would know. With enough time, power will flow into the Flower Forest you have tapped from those more distant, but often we cannot wait. So we reach for the distant ones directly. We can, because they all touch."

"But you can only do that within a domain," Vieliessar said slowly. That much she knew to be true.

"Yes," Thurion answered patiently. "The boundaries of domains are bespelled so that one domain cannot drain the power from all the Flower Forests of the land. But that does not mean they are not all linked. If they were not, how could anyone use Door across domain boundaries?"

Vieliessar said nothing. Some of what Thurion spoke of—the philosophy that underlay Magery—made sense to her. Much, she suspected, had been laid down like traps and snares to keep the Lightborn from thinking beyond the rote proscriptions handed down from Mosirinde's time.

"But that has nothing to do with the question you asked," Thurion went on. "You can go from any Flower Forest to any other, and so you can go to Tildorangelor as well."

"With enough time and power," Vieliessar said. *And neither is in great supply. Between us, we and the Alliance have already nearly drained Jaeglenhend's Flower Forests.* It did much to explain why, if the matter was as simple as Thurion said, Amrethion's city had never yet been discovered. First one would have to believe it existed, and then, allow some powerful Lightborn the liberty to spend years seeking it. "I thank you for your counsel, my friend. I will speak with you again as soon as I may."

"The Light go with you," Thurion answered quietly, and the spell was sundered.

It was long before she could steel herself to reach for Aradreleg. *Failure will mean nothing,* she told herself firmly. *Only that she is somewhere from which she may not answer. Not death. Celenthodial Flower Queen— say she still lives!*

To her delight and relief, Aradaleg answered her at once. And when she had finished telling Vieliessar all that had happened in the last sennight, Vieliessar began to hope once more.

Rithdeliel had taken Jaeglenhend Keep.

She still had a chance to win.

At dawn two days later, Vieliessar mounted her destrier at the head of her party. From all Aradreleg had told her, the Alliance was well aware the keep had fallen. Since the Alliance hadn't followed her to Oakstone Tower, Jaeglenhend Keep was its next logical target. Smash her army and they would be free to hunt her down at their leisure.

So they believe. But I am not prey to be hunted.

I am Vieliessar Farcarinon, and I will be High King.

⊰⧉⊱

By the time Runacarendalur and his sortie party crossed into Jaeglenhend's manorial lands, he knew the Alliance was in trouble. Manor house and Farmhold alike were burnt out and stripped bare.

"*A War Prince without lands is just another landless knight. Their ko-men will desert them and come begging for the scraps from our tables. . . .*" Bolecthindial's careless words echoed mockingly in Runacarendalur's memory.

"It looks as if a battle was fought here," Helecanth observed, reining in beside him.

"Not a battle," Runacarendalur answered, hating the note of anguish in his voice. "A retreat."

He'd left Vieliessar's army without supplies and thought to starve it into surrender. The tactic should have worked: Vieliessar's vassal War Princes were the leaders of her army. He'd counted on them to do as the Alliance War Princes would have done in their place: quarrel over precedence, demand terms of surrender, or simply abandon the rebel cause, taking their meisnes with them. He'd expected them to fall into disorder and strife. He'd *counted* on it. But somehow—even without Vieliessar—they'd kept order. And to provision themselves as they rode north, they'd ravaged the countryside with terrifying efficiency.

"You've executed their entire households, and the Lightborn will bear them word of that . . ."

Every Ladyholder or Consort-Prince the Alliance had taken captive, every Heir-Prince or Heir-Princess who hadn't been on the field, every favorite servant . . . the War Princes of the Alliance, certain of victory, had taken revenge on all those in their power. It was little consolation to know the princes wouldn't have listened to him if he'd warned them against it. But he'd been as blind and overconfident as anyone.

"Why couldn't we see it?" he said aloud. "Why couldn't *I* see it?"

"Lord Runacarendalur?" Helecanth said, worried.

"What are you waiting for, Rune?" Ivrulion said, riding up. He looked over the stubble of the fields, the stumps of the orchards, the smoke-blackened shells of the manor house and outbuildings. "If I were Lord Nilkaran, I'd petition Vondaimieriel for a remission of my tithes for the next decade or so."

Runacarendalur bit back the furious words he wished to say. Ivrulion's pretence of being a loyal and devoted servant to Caerthalien's Line Direct galled Runacarendalur like iron chains. On their way here, he'd tested the length of the leash Ivrulion held. So far as he could tell, his will was his own, save in three things.

He could not speak of the Bonding between himself and Vieliessar Farcarinon.

He could not kill Ivrulion.

And he could not kill himself.

He'd tried each of these actions a number of times without success, but did not yet hold himself defeated. Perhaps he could write down what he could not speak of. Perhaps he could order one of his vassals to slay Ivrulion, or tell Bolecthindial some story that would accomplish the same purpose—though even Runacarendalur's imagination faltered at the prospect of spinning a tale that would cause Bolecthindial Caerthalien to execute one of the Lightborn. He might say anything he liked—so long as he did not speak of his Bonding—but to accuse Ivrulion of treachery would do nothing but make him look disordered in his wits.

"They're loyal to her," Runacarendalur said bleakly. The realization came too late.

Ivrulion studied him through narrowed eyes. "They don't have any choice," he said after a moment.

"We didn't give them any," Runacarendalur answered. *As you have given me none, faithless betrayer.*

From the moment he first set foot upon the Sword Road, Runacarendalur had ridden to war thinking of victory, not death. Victory was sweet and good, and death, though glorious, put an end to the joys of war. But now death—*his* death—had become the only possible road to victory.

If he could claim it. For now, he touched his spurs to Gwaenor's flanks and urged the stallion into a trot. *Where are they? Thousands of* komen *can't just vanish.*

When the riders appeared from behind a distant building, all he could make out at first was their green surcoats. He brought Gwaenor to a stop and raised his hand. The sortie party waited tensely, not knowing whether they would be attacking in the next few moments or fleeing from a superior force.

But . . .

"That is young Gothael," Helecanth said suddenly. "I know him."

She glanced toward Runacarendalur. He nodded, and she raised the warhorn to her lips and sounded the Caerthalien rally call. At the sound, the scouts spurred their mounts from a trot to a gallop.

"Prince Runacarendalur, what news?" *Komen* Gothael said, as he brought his palfrey to a halt.

"None," Runacarendalur answered. "We've been four days on the road from the southern border. We've seen neither Landbond nor enemy."

Gothael grimaced. "The enemy is at the Great Keep, my lord. We've just come from there."

"Hilgaril, Prince Runacarendalur," Gothael's companion said, introducing herself. "The army fought there two days. All the Line Direct lives. Princess Angiothiel distinguished herself greatly."

"My sister took the field?" Runacarendalur said in disbelief, unable to stop himself. Angiothiel—unlike her twin—had still been a maiden knight, for she'd never ridden to battle.

"What outcome?" Ivrulion asked sharply.

"The army prepares to fight again, Lord Ivrulion," Hilgaril said.

"We lost," Runacarendalur said flatly.

There was an awkward silence, as neither *komen* wanted to agree with him, whether it was true or not. "Report," Runacarendalur said at last.

Both Gothael and Hilgaril were veteran scouts: their report was brief and to the point. Upon receiving word that Jaeglenhend Great Keep had fallen to the rebels, the army had turned to attack it, and had met the rebel force outside its walls. It had fought two battles there but had not gained the victory. Their losses had been relatively light . . . but neither army had offered a parley truce for the purpose of prisoner exchange or ransom. The army had decamped at dawn and was heading for the eastern border. Scouting parties were flanking the army's line of march to collect wandering destriers, locate any *komen* who might have ridden from the field and been overcome by their wounds, and round up livestock and servants who had been scattered during the battle.

Runacarendalur could fill in the details Gothael and Hilgaril either didn't know or didn't wish to repeat: the War Council had decided it couldn't win while the rebels held the Great Keep, and was hoping to lure them away from it by retreating toward Keindostibaent.

An idiotic plan; they'll only leave when they're ready to.

That the livestock had scattered meant either that Rithdeliel had attacked the Alliance's camp—or that all their servants had simply fled during the battle. Some certainly had, undoubtedly hoping to join the enemy once their masters had left. That was bad enough, but that they had fought without a parley truce was worse. He knew it was unlikely that neither army had taken prisoners and he knew without having to ask that the War Council hadn't thought of keeping the *komen* they'd captured alive as bait.

We are becoming lower than the Beastlings, he thought wildly. *Slaughtering brave warriors without concern for the Code of Battle, just as if Arilcarion War-Maker had never lived.*

Thankfully he'd schooled himself to stoicism by the time the scouts reached the worst of their news, for it was bad indeed. In the course of the fighting, the enemy had managed to retake not only their wagons and supplies, but the captive commons and livestock as well—and when the horses had bolted, they'd taken most of the loose Alliance horses with them.

So all we accomplished in the last fortnight is to harden their resolve— and gift them with some additional horses! He gritted his teeth. The temptation to speak that thought aloud was great.

"And Vieliessar Farcarinon?" he asked.

"They fought in her name, Prince Runacarendalur," Hilgaril said. "But she did not take the field."

That's because she's still somewhere in the southern Barrens, Runacarendalur thought wearily. *We're between her and her army. And not one member of this so-called War Council will believe that if we just cordon Jaeglenhend from the Tamabeths all the way to Sadrunath Dales, either she or her army will have to try something stupid to get past us. No. They think she's going somewhere, and they want to stop her. Don't they see that going somewhere isn't the point?*

"Thank you," he said quietly. "You've been very helpful." Ivrulion looked at him suspiciously; Runacarendalur ignored him. "We ride now to rejoin the army."

And prepare for the next honorless, graceless slaughter.

He no longer cared how Vieliessar had duped her vassal lords into mindless loyalty, nor cared that he'd become no more than his mad brother's puppet. While he lived, he would fight. Vieliessar meant to destroy everything the Hundred Houses had spent a hundred centuries building.

And Runacarendalur meant to stop her.

⋈

Ten days after she left Oakstone Tower, Vieliessar reached Jaeglenhend Keep. She encountered the first pickets three leagues from its walls, and by the time she reached its gates, half the army had turned out to accompany her. They cheered her; *komen* tossing their swords in the air and making their destriers dance and rear, infantry and commons walking at the stirrups of those who had returned. It was as if the day had suddenly become Festival Fair. If this was devotion, Vieliessar wasn't sure who—or what—its object was. All she knew was such fervor made her profoundly uneasy, even though she'd forged it into a tool to serve her ends.

"It's all very well to ask people to die for you when you think you understand why they're doing it, isn't it?" Nadalforo said quietly.

"I've never asked anyone to die for me," Vieliessar answered, keeping her voice equally soft. It was an effort.

"No," Nadalforo agreed. "For your cause. For Amrethion's Prophecy. You'll find they don't care about any of that. They'll die for you, not for a dream."

But that is all I am, Nadalforo. A dream.

It was the next afternoon before she could gather her commanders together in a formal meeting to hear what had happened in her absence and to give new orders, for the day and much of the night had been occupied with celebrations and processions. So many of her folk had wished to see her with their own eyes that she had spent candlemarks simply riding through the whole of the camp.

She'd thought to hold back the reason and the destination, but the army she had returned to was a very different thing from the army she'd left. In the beginning, she'd gathered the lords to her with the promise of freedom from High House oppression and the commons with the promise of justice—but now there was no lord who did not mourn murdered kin or vassal, no commonborn who had not suffered anew at the hands of the enemy. Vieliessar had cast aside the Codes of War that turned war from a tragedy into a sport, but she'd never thought about what would come of it. Once she had been all that held her army together. Now they would have fought even without her.

Without quarter, without mercy, and without regret.

So she told them their destination was a legend-place beyond the bounds of any map, knowing now that they would have followed if she'd told them it was the Huntsman's castel in the winter stars.

It took them a sennight to ready themselves. As soon as they marched away from Jaeglenhend Keep, the Warhunt scattered across the land, bringing the word to every steading, croft, and farmhold: *Nilkaran is dead. The High King leads her army to freedom. Will you come?*

They came.

What the commons could not carry with them, they burned. Those who were not willing to come because the Green Robes asked came because their cousins, their sisters, or their greatsires did.

Vieliessar's army swept eastward.

She angled her line of march enough to the north that the Alliance force was in no position to either attack or block her. By the time they realized she meant to ignore them instead of engaging, she had drawn east of their position and was able to swing south again. The Alliance followed Vieliessar into Keindostibaent, where War Prince Annobeunna Keindostibaent was at war with Vithantael Consort-Prince. Annobeunna and most of her army joined Vieliessar, and in her absence, the Alliance proclaimed Vithantael War Prince of Keindostibaent.

In Keindostibaent, Vieliessar had stolen a few precious candlemarks to attempt to use what Thurion had taught her. But whether or not it was even possible, her Lightborn had already taken too much from the Flower Forests of this land for her Seeking spell to work, rushing to cast needed spells before the Alliance Lightborn crossed the border.

She did not find Celephriandullias-Tildorangelor.

By the beginning of Woods Moon the two armies had settled into a grim, slow chase. The Alliance followed too closely for Vieliessar's force to risk stopping even for a day, but too far behind for them to close and fight.

And every day the gap between the two armies narrowed.

Soon enough we'll have to fight, Vieliessar thought. *With swords once more.*

The two armies already fought a war of provision and resource. Vieliessar's people scoured the countryside for anything they could use. In their wake, the Alliance found empty storehouses, empty granaries, empty barns and sheepfolds. If the Alliance wanted to provision itself, it would have to break off its pursuit, and once it did, no matter how far it ranged, it would discover afresh what she'd known from the first: no one domain held enough of anything to supply either of their armies. What the Alliance would demand would be impossible for any domain to give, and what wasn't freely given, the Alliance would inevitably take. It would leave behind it an enemy instead of a subject Less House, and not gain enough of the thousand things an army must have. And any time the Alliance stopped to forage—or besiege—Vieliessar would gain precious time to widen the distance between them.

It wouldn't be enough to allow her to escape without doing battle.

They crossed from Keindostibaent into Sarmiorion as Woods Moon became Hearth, and once more the needs of Vieliessar's Lightborn lay heavily upon the Flower Forests. Magery could no longer be used for the homely comforts her princes had been used to. The power they could draw from the Flower Forests must be reserved to protect them from the enemy.

The weather had held for sennights—a minor miracle, with all the

Weather Magery the Lightborn of both sides had worked—but now it turned at last, and neither side had the ability to stop it. The snow should have decreased the influx of refugees flocking to Vieliessar's banner, but did not.

Ladyholder Varelotiel had joined her lord while the Alliance force was still in Jaeglenhend, bringing all of Sarmiorion's Lords *Komen* and their whole meisne. Glasswall Free Company rested quietly upon its grant lands as its Ladyholder prepared to march. Captain Natrade told Varelotiel she had no interest in riding to war in winter and since Varelotiel hadn't wanted to take the time required to persuade Glasswall's commander to accept such a contract, she'd ridden west without them.

As soon as she'd left, Glasswall Free Company besieged and sacked Sarmiorion Great Keep before riding west as well. Those they left behind were helpless without their masters to keep order, easy prey for any who chose to set themselves in a position of rule—or those outlaws who saw the chaos in the Uradabhur as an opportunity to enrich themselves. The folk of Sarmiorion rallied to Vieliessar.

Sarmiorion's outcast servants and abandoned laborers approached the Alliance army, begging for food, for shelter, for their War Prince and Ladyholder's protection. They were driven away again and again, but the desperate persisted . . . and the truly desperate tried to steal. In the stillness of the night, screams from the Alliance camp would carry across the space that lay between the two encampments, going on for candlemarks until at last they became too faint to hear. Each night the screams would begin again.

It was worse, somehow, not to hear those screams because of the bespelling of her pavilion's walls. Vieliessar found herself awakening in the night, straining her ears against the silence, knowing she'd hear nothing but the breathing of those sleeping around her. When the weather had turned, every pavilion had become a dormitory, for to sleep out of doors was to court death.

Another sennight would see both armies in Niothramangh. *I would not wish to be Mengracharth Niothramangh,* Vieliessar thought grimly.

He has many choices, none of them good. If he didn't surrender what the Alliance demanded, he'd be named rebel and outlaw. If he gave all, his own people would starve. Let his people starve, and they would join the roving bands from Sarmiorion, Keindostibaent, and Jaeglenhend. Try to save them—and his domain's wealth—and make Niothramangh a target for the Alliance and every outlaw in the Uradabhur.

She was not certain what she herself would do in his place.

When the war is over, she told herself again and again, finding it within her mind even when she was thought she was brooding on other things. *When the war is over . . .*

But of course, when this war was over, another would be poised to begin.

⚜

"I say all we need to do is turn and attack them," Atholfol Ivrithir said stubbornly, getting to his feet to lean across the table.

"That's your answer to everything," Thoromarth said. "It won't necessarily *work.*"

"You're blind as well as imbecile," Atholfol snapped. "The vanguard of their army and the fantail of ours are barely five miles apart now. Let them close the distance further, and they'll attack us in force."

"They'll try, certainly," Rithdeliel said.

Vieliessar's pavilion was so crowded there was no need to kindle the stove for warmth, and at that, only her most senior commanders were present. Each day, after combat practice, cavalry drill, and a meal, she gathered some of her commanders to her, doing her best in each sennight to meet with all the commanders in her army, from the War Princes who had pledged to her to the *komen* who commanded but a single taille of knights. But it was in the council of her senior commanders that the army's decisions were made.

"They'll manage," Gunedwaen said to Rithdeliel. "Atholfol is right: let the distance between us narrow any further and the Alliance will attack in strength. But I'm not certain attacking them is the answer."

"Why not?" Atholfol demanded irritably.

"Line meets line," Gatriadde Mangiralas said. "They'll attack in line because there's less danger of riders being fouled if one of the destriers goes down on the ice. We respond in line for the same reason, and also to block a flanking maneuver. But either we commit twice their numbers—and we don't *have* twice their numbers—or they get around the end of our line and reach the supply wagons." Gatriadde had gained a great deal of self-assurance in the last several moonturns; he no longer looked to anyone for approval before he spoke.

"If I were in charge of the Alliance forces, I'd skip the fight and go straight for the supply train," Nadalforo said. "That nearly finished us last time. They won't make the mistake of keeping the wagons intact again."

"We have Wards on the oxen," Rithdeliel said.

"There are a dozen ways to destroy wagons without involving witch-born. Throw a torch into them. Shoot their drivers. Shoot the teams—or, if you want to start a stampede, throw acid on any of the ox teams. They'll smash half the wagons to kindling before you can kill them," Nadalforo said.

"They'd never," Rithdeliel said. "Arilcarion said—"

"Oh, High House Warlord!" Nadalforo said, laughing. "Do you think it matters what some dead clerk wrote in a moldering scroll?"

Most of the *komen* looked shocked, but a few of those present, mostly the former mercenaries and the infantry captains, were smiling or try-ing to hold back laughter. Vieliessar would not laugh: she knew as well as any how hard it was to set aside the lessons of a lifetime. But there was one truth Arilcarion had not set down in his scrolls: *The purpose of war is to win.*

"I was the first to cast aside the Code of Battle," she said. "It is true the Alliance has followed, but it does so without imagination. It merely does all Arilcarion forbade."

"Like slaughtering helpless prisoners," *Komen* Diorthiel said sourly. "At least it was not the *komen* who committed such an atrocity."

"They are still dead," Dirwan said sharply. He was the captain of the infantry, and his units had suffered the heaviest losses during the battles both in Jaeglenhend and in the West. Any who were captured had been tortured to death.

"The fact remains: *komen* expect to fight other *komen*," Vieliessar said gently. "While you and all you lead understand that victory is not always sheathed in the scabbard of battle, the *komen* of the Alliance will resist performing the tasks of 'mere servants who are not true warriors.'"

This time everyone joined in the laughter, as she meant them to. Even if the Alliance thought to destroy her wagons, she doubted they could persuade their *komen* to attack laborers and oxen instead of their fellow knights.

"Someone will figure out how to get it done sooner or later," Nadalforo said. "We have been lucky thus far that no one there is truly in charge. If I were Runacarendalur of Caerthalien, I'd do whatever I must to gain sole permanent command of their army. I'm sure he's thought of everything we have."

So am I, Vieliessar thought grimly. Each day she survived was a new amazement to her—were their positions reversed, she would have drawn a blade across her own throat moonturns ago. But either her Bond with Prince Runacarendalur was not complete or the destiny that had surrounded her from the moment she set foot on this road protected her. *I care not which is true, so long as one or the other is!*

"We have a few days yet to decide how to face their attack when it comes," Vieliessar said. "And to discover a way to widen the space between us. Iardalaith, find Lightborn to ride with the wagons, if you will. Lord Atholfol, it is a good thought to guard them so. But even if we turn aside any attacks, there is yet another matter we must settle. Soon enough we must turn south."

She had become certain that she could not find the location of Celephriandullias-Tildorangelor from within any of the domains. Thurion had said the search would require power, and the defense spells of the two great armies drained every Flower Forest within their range. But south of the Uradabhur domains were lands claimed by no House. She had charted every landmark her dream-visions had given her. The ghost-lords had ridden north and west in pursuit of Pelashia's children. So she must go south and east.

And surely there was a Flower Forest somewhere in that uncharted wilderness.

If there is not . . .

"You can't take an army into the forest," Thoromarth said simply. Beyond the Southern Pass Road lay forest dense enough to give cover to a sortie party. And forest that dense would be impassable to the supply wagons.

"We shall do so when the time comes," Vieliessar said, with more confidence than she felt. "My lords, find me a way to either move us faster or slow the Alliance. And now I give you all good night."

Her commanders—princes, Lords *Komen,* Lightborn, mercenaries, outlaws, and commonfolk—rose from the table or stepped away from the walls. Slowly the pavilion emptied. Almost before the last had gone, Drochondeur, Master of the Household, bustled in at the head of a small army of servants to prepare the outer chamber of her pavilion for night. Vieliessar retreated to her sleeping chamber to let them work. Little had been settled, but she hadn't expected more. She had an idea of what she might do about the Alliance attacks. The rest must wait on inspiration.

And upon my belief that there is a Flower Forest south of the borders. Or I have led my army halfway across the world to die.

⊰⊱

Vieliessar shifted in the saddle, pulling her heavy cloak more tightly around her. Her new destrier grumbled his displeasure, mumbling at the bit. He was a burly bay stallion with a vicious temper; after the third time he'd tried to bite her, she'd named him "Snapdragon," since no one knew his name. She'd chosen him for his strength and stamina rather than his sweet temper—temperament had never yet gotten a knight through a battle alive.

The day was dark and the air was heavy and wet, smelling of snow. The Lightborn of both armies had lost the power to shift the weather long since. Inevitably, the day would come when they must either allow a blizzard to strike—or drain the Flower Forests of the domain to dust to move it.

But not today, Vieliessar thought. *Not today.*

"Ah. There. At last—I was getting bored," Nadalforo said cheerfully.

Vieliessar looked behind her. Two grand-tailles of knights had moved out from the enemy vanguard.

"Inglethendragir," she said, finally identifying the colors.

House Inglethendragir had risen from Less House to High at the end of the Long Peace. Its device was three silver wolves on a purple field— this acknowledged that its elevation had come by the erasure of Farcarinon. Randragir Inglethendragir had replaced the silver leaves of his previous device with Farcarinon's silver wolves..

"There's a surprise," Nadalforo said. "I would have expected them to send one of the Less Houses. Perhaps no one likes Lord Randragir very much."

"They'll like him less a candlemark from now," Vieliessar said, and Nadalforo laughed.

Nadalforo raised the signal whistle to her lips and blew a complicated pattern of notes. Vieliessar reined Snapdragon to a stop as the former mercenary companies detached themselves from the line of march and formed into two ranks facing the enemy. Inglethendragir's grand-tailles broke away from the vanguard and began to move over the ice, spreading from column into line as they did. When they were in formation, they moved to a trot.

"Are you ready?" Vieliessar asked Terandamil.

"We are," the Master of the Archers replied.

Inglethendragir advanced. Vieliessar's force waited. The belling of her banner on the wind—the High King's banner defiantly displayed— was the only movement. The attackers moved from trot to canter to gallop and still Vieliessar's force waited.

"*Now*," Terandamil said.

In one smooth movement, infantry stepped from behind the second rank of destriers and moved into the open spaces between the first rank. Once they had been favored servants of their domains, huntsmen and foresters. Each carried a forester's bow. Terandamil had not honed their deadly skill, for that was a thing only years could do. But it was Terandamil who had told them they were warriors.

They loosed their arrows, and the shots came so close together that the release of the bowstrings was like a rippling chord of harpsong. Three heartbeats later another volley of arrows sang forth, and three heartbeats later, another. The music of the third volley was drowned out by agonized screaming. The ice had grown bright and slick with blood. At the ends of the enemy line a few wounded destriers thrashed.

Most of the rest were dead.

The enemy center was still intact. Some of the knights tried to rein in and turn back. Their mounts skidded and slipped—some fell, and over all the other sounds, in a freakish heartbeat of silence, there was the sound of a leg bone breaking, loud and sharp. Others galloped on, or tried to turn at the gallop, simply did their best to slow down.

Whatever they did, nothing saved them.

Terandamil's rangers nocked and loosed, nocked and loosed, and the long, heavy arrows flew low over the ice in flights as regular and inexorable as the beats of a war drum. Behind the lines of mercenaries a line of palfreys waited, each with a rider already in its saddle. As the archers ran out of arrows, or when a string or bow snapped, that archer retreated. Each archer moved with calm precision, though the bitter cold numbed bare fingers and made bowstrings brittle. Each arrow struck its target: the destriers—and only the destriers. Warhorses were precious and nearly irreplaceable. The fewer warhorses the Alliance possessed, the fewer *komen* they could send against her. And when Terandamil's archers were done, the Alliance had two grand-tailles less.

When all the destriers were dead or dying, the archers walked away, quietly, without display. It was as much a warning to their noble comrades as it was to their enemy.

The attack was over so swiftly the Alliance commanders had no time to ride to Inglethendragir's aid—or summon their Lightborn to Shield them. A few single knights rode out from the Alliance column and loosed arrows, but the horseman's bow had less range than the forester's bow, so the shafts fell harmlessly to the ground. The destriers of Inglethendragir lay slewed across the blood-smeared ice. Some riders had been thrown, some had jumped clear as their mounts went down, some still lay trapped beneath the dead and dying animals. A few moved with daggers to end the lives of the still-suffering beasts.

"It would be funny if it weren't so sad," Nadalforo said quietly, watching. "Even if you lose, it's the end of the *komentai'a*. Everyone now knows a meisne armed with forester's bows can slaughter a troop of knights any time it chooses to. That won't make them massacre their foresters. They'll all scurry to find and train them. We'll be facing them ourselves if this war goes on long enough."

"It won't," Vieliessar said. *It can't.*

"As I say, Lord Vieliessar, I hope you win," Nadalforo said. She reined her destrier around and trotted after the army.

CHAPTER SIXTEEN

WIND AND DUST

For the road is long and the world is wide
The wind is cold and the way is dark
When again shall I see her, Celephriandullias-Tildorangelor, beloved who
has turned her face from me?"

— Perhael Storysinger, *Perhael's Song*

That night Terandamil's archers celebrated their victory and the rest of the infantry joined them. The *komen* and their lords withdrew to their own precincts and the mood of the encampment was unsettled. Vieliessar made a brief visit to the victory feast, then spent a long, fruitless evening pouring over maps of the Uradabhur before retiring to her sleeping chamber.

Sleep did not come. Her mind was too full of problems. The arming of the commons to fight beside the *komen* had always been the point on which her army could fracture. Only the Light could raise one of the commonfolk to the level of the Lords *Komen*. The lords of the Hundred Houses had been convinced the Light was Pelashia's Gift: rare, valued, mysterious. They had even been able to blind themselves to the fact that the mercenary companies, whose warriors were the equal in skill of any *komen*, had held more former farmers than former knights among their ranks.

It was harder to unsee a forester's skill turned to a tool of war, but everyone knew mastery of the forester's bow was a task of years; not even Lightborn spellcraft could change that. *But the pike can be learned in a few sennights of practice, and the infantry have already proven their worth in battle. They cannot stand against charging warhorses—but even* komen *do not do that unless they must.*

Nadalforo would tell her she was worrying about things that would not matter if she lost. Rithdeliel would tell her this would only last for a brief while, for Vieliessar knew that in his heart, he could not accept the idea that war would never again be a contest of skills that were both art and homage. Gunedwaen . . .

He would tell you victory is as much a battle as war. I only wish Arilcarion had written a scroll about that!

By Snow Moon, storms battered both armies mercilessly, and no matter what the Alliance did, Vieliessar did something unexpected, as if she played *gan* when they played *xaique*. And victory slid further from their grasp each day.

They could have won. While they were still in Jaeglenhend, they could have won—if Vieliessar were dead. Her death would have left her army leaderless. Disheartened. They could have spent the winter picking it to pieces.

After Jaeglenhend, Runacarendalur would have cut his own throat gladly. He could not. He'd tried many times to end the life that would end hers.

He'd gone to Lord Bolecthindial and accused Ivrulion of plotting against Caerthalien. Bolecthindial hadn't taken him seriously enough to even become angry.

He'd tried risking his life on the field, but all he'd managed to do was get Gwaenor killed.

He'd begged Ivrulion, humbling himself before his faithless witch-born brother. Ivrulion had laughed.

He tried to murder Ivrulion in a thousand ways. Poison failed and assassins vanished. Runacarendalur couldn't even seek his own death in a Challenge Circle: Aramenthiali had gotten the War Council to forbid personal challenges. With nothing to occupy them—no entertainment, no comforts, and only the faintest chance of fighting—the *komen* were becoming increasingly restive. It was one thing to use a break in the win-

ter weather to go hunting, another to spend sennight after sennight living in a freezing pavilion and slogging through snow all day.

There wasn't any game to hunt anyway. Vieliessar's army devoured
everything in its path like a raging fire. Even the border steadings the Alliance reached were nothing more than stones and beaten earth. The night
watches had been doubled and doubled again, not because there was any
likelihood of an attack, but because the laborers and servants kept slinking away in the dark.

At least with half the camp on watch, they could be sure the *komen*
weren't going to run off as well.

*Each morning we arise to see nothing ahead but trackless white; each
night there is no fire or Silverlight to be seen but ours. The only way to truly
know she still flees us is to send out a sortie party to catch up to her. But
no! The War Council is as bored as I am! It wishes an entertaining surprise, whenever the* High King *chooses to deliver it!*

And soon, whether she could claim victory or not, the Alliance Army
would be destroyed. Runacarendalur growled low in his throat at the
thought, gaining him a startled look from a Household servant. It was
just dawn, and the encampment was readying itself for another useless
day of following Vieliessar Farcarinon, who seemed to have the ability to
make an army numbering nine thousand tailles vanish like windblown
smoke. If not for the impossibility of provisioning such a force, he
wouldn't put it past her to have laid a trail into the teeth of the first heavy
snow and then have settled somewhere to spend the winter in comfort.
Laughing at them.

At least today the weather was clear. And while no one in command
of this ill-starred expedition would consider permitting another sortie
party after Inglethendragir's disastrous defeat, the War Princes knew
entirely forbidding their *komen* to ride out would cause them to go into
open revolt. Runacarendalur pulled the hood of his stormcloak further
over his head as he reached the Caerthalien horselines. He meant to spend
his day—and his foul temper—schooling his new destrier. Bentrain
would never be the match of his beloved Gwaenor, but he'd been lucky

to replace Gwaenor at all. There were already *komen* in the army without warhorses.

Bentrain stood waiting placidly. Runacarendalur unhooked the destrier's halter and led him to the saddling paddock. With the ease of long practice, he tossed the heavy war saddle onto the stallion's back, buckled the twin girths into place, brought the chestpiece around, buckled the upper strap to the saddle, and ducked under Bentrain's neck to thread the lower strap through the ring on the forward girth.

When he straightened again, he saw Ivrulion leading his own mount into the saddling paddock. The palfrey mare was a grey as pale as ice, and every line of her spoke of speed and fire. It no longer surprised Runacarendalur that Ivrulion had managed to keep one of the best animals in the entire army for his personal use.

"I thought I might ride out with you this morning, dear brother," Ivrulion said dulcetly. An ostler hurried forward with the palfrey's saddle—green leather stamped with the Caerthalien stars in gold—and began saddling the mare.

"You must be feeling unusually brave this morning, *brother*," Runacarendalur replied acidly. He turned his back and worked at making Bentrain accept the double bit.

"Merely desirous of a morning's exercise," Ivrulion replied easily. "It grows tedious to spend my days trudging from nowhere to nowhere."

"Then why don't you tell Lord Bolecthindial so, and we'll all go home?" Runacarendalur snapped. He set his foot in the stirrup and swung into the saddle. Bentrain took his usual side step away, but Runacarendalur was already used to the animal's tricks. He gathered the reins, took the bit away from Bentrain, and trotted him out of the paddock.

Ivrulion caught up to him even before he passed the wagons. They rode in silence for nearly a candlemark, until the sound of horns and whistles behind them indicated the army was finally ready to move.

"Are you planning to turn back, or do you mean to ride all the way to Utheleres this morning?" Ivrulion asked.

"I have work to do with Bentrain," Runacarendalur said curtly. "I can't do it if I'm constantly being overtaken by the army."

"Small chance of that," Ivrulion answered lightly. "We seem to be slower to get under way every morning. I believe it may be the cold," he added guilelessly.

More likely the laziness and rebellion of servants their masters will not punish! With a growl of exasperation, Runacarendalur set spurs to his stallion's sides. There was one thing he and Bentrain could agree on: galloping.

The wind pulled Runacarendalur's stormcloak from his head and shoulders and the air was freezing, but the sensation of freedom was too sweet to ignore. He let the pounding rhythm of iron-shod hooves against iron-hard ground lull him for what seemed all too brief a time, then—reluctantly—reined Bentrain in.

Ivrulion cantered up to them before Bentrain had slowed to a trot. "If he fell and broke a leg, you'd have regretted this," Ivrulion said.

"You'd Heal him," Runacarendalur answered. "You must be good for something."

The remark earned him one of Ivrulion's faint, cool smiles. "I'm good for a great many things. I simply won't do what you want me to."

"*Why not?*" Runacarendalur shouted.

"You die, she dies, what changes?" Ivrulion answered, apparently moved to candor for once. "We don't know where she is. Her lords aren't likely to come begging forgiveness if they lose their precious High King. They'll simply become utterly unpredictable and far more dangerous."

"True now," Runacarendalur snapped. "A moonturn or two ago we could have had them!" *We could have kept the War Princes' households alive until we were sure we'd won, instead of giving two dozen domains every cause to seek vengeance on us forever.*

"Maybe," Ivrulion said. "And you would be dead, Caerthalien would be in disarray—and we would all still be here. If you think retracing our path across three domains in utter anarchy is a safe and simple matter, I do not."

"It would be easier if we *did it now!*" *Before our mounts are starving, before some gaggle of hedge knights goes into revolt, before this so-called Alliance shatters into a million shards.* He ground his teeth to keep the words behind them; if Ivrulion was loyal to anything but himself, it was not to Runacarendalur. *I lost all hope of his loyalty when I told him I'd never live to rule.* The thought was bitter, but far from new.

"You won't argue me to your side now any more than you could before; stop trying," Ivrulion said patronizingly. "Would you feel better if I told you the idiotic 'council' is as little inclined to follow my suggestions as it is to follow yours?"

"And you our father's pet!" Runacarendalur jeered. "I'm shocked, Prince Ivrulion, I truly am."

The horses had slowed to a walk now. Runacarendalur glanced behind him. The army was tiny with distance. *I've probably already covered as much ground as it will all day,* he thought in frustrated anger.

"All I say is—" Ivrulion broke off sharply.

Runacarendalur glanced quickly around, searching for some movement, some enemy. There was nothing. Then—

"What's that?" he asked, gesturing toward the trees.

"A problem," his brother answered grimly.

They spurred their horses forward again.

⸙

I don't believe— How could she—?" Runacarendalur sputtered.

"If by that you mean to ask 'Did Lord Vieliessar's army come this way?' the answer is yes," Ivrulion answered. The undisguised irritation in his voice would have cheered Runacarendalur at any other time.

"How?" he repeated.

"Magic," Ivrulion said shortly.

"Helpful," Runacarendalur answered. "Look at this forest, 'Rulion," he said, so shaken he forgot Ivrulion was his enemy. "Even if every single Landbond she has did nothing but chop at tree trunks morning till night, they couldn't clear the half of this in a moonturn."

They'd ridden to the break in the scrub Ivrulion had spotted. Beyond it, a broad, shining path of undisturbed snow led into what should have been dense forest. The corridor stretched straight as a bowshot until distance narrowed it into invisibility. They turned their horses into it. There must be tree stumps beneath the snow—surely there must!—so Runacarendalur sent Bentrain forward at a cautious walk, but the ground beneath the stallion's hooves seemed smooth.

"Fortunately for her, she has Lightborn with her as well," Ivrulion snarled. He reined his palfrey to a halt and swung down to wade through the snow crust to the edge of the trees, then stopped and began digging. "Here. One of Niothramangh's boundary stones. No wonder she vanished."

"You've been tracking her?" Runacarendalur asked.

Ivrulion gave him a venomous look. "We didn't have to. We could follow her Wards. A fortnight ago they seemed to disappear. The obvious assumption was that they'd decided to hide themselves. Obvious—and wrong."

"Why not do both?" Runacarendalur asked.

"You can't be as stupid as that question makes you sound," Ivrulion said flatly. "Haven't you been listening to anyone these past sennights? Or did you simply think you weren't getting hot baths out of some perversity on the part of the Caerthalien Lightborn? There have never before been so many Lightborn gathered together in such a small area. Between her Lightborn and ours, the Light in Niothramangh is nearly gone. It will be moonturns, even years, before there's enough of it here to draw on again."

"But her Lightborn didn't change their spells," Runacarendalur said. "They simply crossed the bounds."

"I knew you weren't actually stupid," Ivrulion said in tacit agreement. "And once they had . . . You cannot feel it, but I can: there is a Flower Forest here more vast than any in all of Jer-a-kalaliel. Untapped."

"And that gave her Lightborn the power to do . . . what . . . ?"

Ivrulion sighed heavily and walked back to his palfrey. "Transmutation, I suspect. Probably to sand; that's what I'd do, if I had the power of a thousand Lightborn to direct as I chose and a wild Flower Forest to draw on. The tree becomes a heap of sand, her army rides over it, the snow covers it, there's no trace she's been there. Or reverse the spell afterward, and you have a heap of sawdust. They won't lack for charcoal."

"That's . . . disturbing," Runacarendalur said.

"Isn't it?" Ivrulion said, swinging himself into the saddle once more. "Because I have no idea what's in this direction, and no one else does either. What I *do* know is they had an easy passage over ground favorable to their wagons, so whatever's there, she's much closer to it than we are."

"There isn't anything out there," Runacarendalur said, shaking his head. "Everyone knows that."

"'Everyone' isn't a madwoman being directed by an ancient prophecy," Ivrulion answered, turning his mount back the way they'd come. "Come along, dear brother. We must tell Father what she has done."

⫸⫷

"We follow her of course," Gallanillon Teramarise said flatly.

Runacarendalur moved to stand at Lord Bolecthindial's shoulder, from which vantage point he could study the map that covered most of the table. It showed only the Uradabhur, from the Mystrals and the Dragon's Gate in the west to the Bazrahils and the Nantirworiel Pass in the east. A line drawn between the two passes was a line drawn through the center of the valley. South of the Dragon's Gate, the Southern Pass was also marked. But a line drawn due east from the Southern Pass was a line that passed through . . . nothingness.

"Into a trap, as I'm sure you meant to add, my dear Gallanillon," Girelrian Cirandeiron said. She made an ostentatious show of settling herself more comfortably at the circular table. There were nearly forty people gathered in the gigantic War Pavilion, most standing. "Of course, perhaps you meant to say something else?"

"We've followed her this far—what's changed?" Lord Gallanillon demanded belligerently.

"What's *changed* is that there's a Flower Forest beyond that border—as

Ivrulion Lightbrother finally deigned to tell us," Lady-Abeyant Dormoro-thon of Aramenthiali said.

"Do you imply I knew of it earlier?" Ivrulion asked.

"I? I imply nothing," Dormorothon replied artlessly. "I only remark it is a great pity you could not be bothered to send anyone across the bounds before now. But I have long said the training under Helegondol-rindir Astromancer was not all it should be. Celelioniel was her chosen successor, after all."

"Then perhaps I am mistaken in believing Aramenthiali also saw no reason to do so. Or perhaps you did, and did not think it worth mention-ing," Ivrulion answered quickly. "Certainly that is to be expected from Aramenthiali—since the training under Famindesta Astromancer was not all it should have been."

"Insolent Caerthalien whelp!" Dormorothon spat. "I should—"

"This gains us nothing!" Lord Bolecthindial shouted.

"Except to remind us Caerthalien breeds spineless cowards and fools," Consort-Prince Irindandirion of Cirandeiron purred.

"Brave words, when you know you cannot be called to account for them," Runacarendalur snapped.

The whispers and murmurs that had been private asides rose in vol-ume as the War Princes and their consorts began to hurl accusations and demands at one another. Ivaloriel Telthorclandor and Ladyholder Edhe-leorn sat quietly, waiting. Runacarendalur could never look at them without remembering that Ivaloriel and Edheleorn were Bondmates. It always irritated him.

Chardararg Lalmilgethior slammed his goblet down on the table. Dregs of wine spattered over the wood. "I can hear this empty barking any night," he said witheringly into the silence that followed. "My lords, Lord Vieliessar has done what she has done. Now *we* must decide what to do."

But his words only brought another round of recriminations and demands. Teramarise favored pursuit. Cirandeiron thought they'd be riding into a trap. Aramenthiali kept bringing up the fact that the untapped Southern Flower Forest existed, but taking no other position. Inglethendragir and Vondaimieriel wanted to pursue *and* send a sortie party ahead of the army. Sarmiorion wanted to continue east to Utheleres and go south *then.*

Most of them are reluctant to take the army in a direction where there's no possibility of remounts—or laborers, Runacarendalur thought. *All the High Houses have client domains in the Uradabhur—only Telthorelandor does not. They still believe they can look to them for supplies.*

"To follow Lord Vieliessar without knowing her destination would be ill-advised," Lord Ivaloriel said yet again.

"Then why not make it impossible for her to reach it?" Ivrulion said. "It's simple enough." He stepped closer to Ladyholder Glorthiachiel and produced a thin, silvery stick of charcoal. "Here is the Southern Pass. We know she's still north of . . . this line"—he drew a raking line across the map directly east from the Southern Pass—"because she can't have crossed it in a few sennights. She's still in the forest. Burn it."

"That seems—" Finfemeras Vondaimieriel began.

"Completely unacceptable!" Lady-Abeyant Dormorothon said. "There is a Flower Forest to the south of the bounds!"

Something you have reminded us of a dozen times in the last candlemark, Runacarendalur thought.

"You do not know it extends so far south," Ivrulion said. "If she—"

"Nor do I know it does not," Dormorothon interrupted. "Once we follow Lord Vieliessar across the bounds, our Lightborn may draw upon it as they choose. We cannot surrender such an advantage."

"My Lady Mother Dormorothon is right—as always," Sedreret Aramenthiali said grandly. "Aramenthiali does not choose to cast away such an advantage, whatever Caerthalien may wish." He had become War Prince during the fighting in Jaeglenhend, but everyone knew who ruled Aramenthiali in truth.

"It's hardly an *advantage* if Lord Vieliessar has claimed it first," Lord Bolecthindial growled.

"But Lord Bolecthindial, how can she?" Ladyholder-Abeyant Dormorothon asked in tones of dulcet innocence. "One can only claim a Flower Forest by enclosing it within the bounds of one's own domain."

"Then—" Ivrulion began.

"I do not believe there is anything further you can tell us about what Lord Vieliessar has already done, Lightbrother," Lord Sedreret said.

"I see there is not," Ivrulion said, after a moment of silence. "Lord Bolecthindial, have I your leave to withdraw?"

Bolecthindial waved a hand irritably. "Go, go," he said. "Both of you," he added, as Runacarendalur opened his mouth to speak.

⊰⊱

He had to run to catch up to Ivrulion, who was stalking up the North Road of the encampment as if he were the Starry Huntsman himself.

"I think that went well—don't you?" Runacarendalur said. "Are you enjoying being brushed aside while Vieliessar Farcarinon does whatever she pleases? It must be galling to know she has done nothing save by your desire for the last four moonturns . . ."

"Be silent!" Ivrulion snapped.

Runacarendalur laughed. "Make me, dear brother."

Ivrulion turned and glared at him. Runacarendalur smiled wolfishly. This was not an isolated camp on the Southern Pass Road. This was the main road through the Alliance encampment. Any spell Ivrulion cast would be sensed and noted by a dozen Lightborn, and if the spell's target were not a lawful one . . .

Ivrulion snarled under his breath and turned away. Runacarendalur grabbed his arm. "Oh, but you must come and take a cup of wine to celebrate, for inevitably the War Council will choose your plan in the end. And now I'm imagining what Father will do to you when you finally have to tell him why it means my death as well. I'm sure it will be terribly painful."

He wondered how long it would take the fire to sweep over Vieliessar's army. Her Lightborn wouldn't be able to stop it; the Lightborn who'd tried to halt the burning of Araphant had needed to summon rain to quench the flames, and no one could make it rain in winter. A blizzard intense enough to quench the fire would quench the army as well.

They'd die. *She'd* die. And he'd die. It would be worth it to know she was dead before him.

"Imagine what he'll do if I don't have to," Ivrulion answered oracularly. "Oh, very well. I don't know what you think you're accomplishing by playing the gracious host."

"I'm patronizing you, *dear* brother. It's something you should be used to by now," Runacarendalur answered mockingly.

"Should I? And do your chains gall *you*, Heir-Prince Runacarendalur?"

"Perhaps," Runacarendalur answered, still cheerful. "But if they do, I console myself with the knowledge it is not for much longer."

But on the following dawn, when he dragged himself groggily from his bed, it was to discover that the War Council wasn't going to burn the southern forest.

They were going to follow Vieliessar's army into it.

⊰⊱

In Snow Moon Vieliessar's army crossed the southern bounds of Niothramangh and passed into the depths of a forest no *alfaljodthi* had ever seen. Vieliessar rode out ahead of the army every few miles to blaze their path. Those Lightborn who had Transmutation as their keystone spell followed. At their touch, great trees turned to sand and collapsed, to return to their native substance a few moments later. To destroy so much forest merely to make smooth their passage disturbed Vieliessar, for the farther they'd gone, the wider the path they cut, until by midday it was nearly a mile across. But if the decision had been hard, the choice had been simple: hundreds of miles of forest turned to dust—or the lives of everyone who rode with her.

Before she had crossed into Niothramangh, she had told Iardalaith to send Warhunt Mages south, for her tactics would depend on her resources. Iardalaith had gone himself, to come reeling into her pavilion giddy to the point of drunkenness with the bounteous Light of the

Flower Forest he had discovered. It was to the south and west; Iardalaith could not accurately gauge the distance, he said, as it was stronger than any he had ever sensed. He named it *Janglanipaikharain*—star-bright forest. Perhaps it was the same one Lady Parmanaya had vanished into thousands of years before.

With this knowledge, Viliessar had made her plan.

They would cross the border a full sennight before the Alliance. When they turned southward, they would vanish to the senses of their Lightborn hunters, and until they saw the trail her army would inevitably leave behind it, the Alliance would think only that her people had drawn upon the Flower Forests of Niothramangh to hide them. Her own commanders had been so stunned at the thought of leaving the bounded Uradabhur that she knew the tactic would not occur to the Alliance. They would look at the forest and see a thing impassable.

But it was not, by the grace of Janglanipaikharain's seemingly limitless reservoir, a wellspring of power that had not been touched in the whole history of the Hundred Houses.

The first night after they crossed the bounds, Vieliessar wrapped herself in a Cloakspell and walked from the camp.

The air was too cold to hold scent: if it had not been, she would have been able to smell the good fragrance of roast meat, for with the power of Janglanipaikharain to draw upon, the Lightborn had Called herds of deer and flights of birds to their cookfires. Their supplies continued to dwindle, but this night, at least, all had eaten well. What would come tomorrow would depend on what she found before tomorrow's dawn.

Her steps broke through the surface of the snow; here beneath the leafless trees it was deep, but not as deep as it had been in the open land. She walked for miles, reveling in the silence, the solitude, the sense that for a little while she need answer to no necessities but her own. At last, reluctantly, she came to a stop. If she could not find what she sought here, she would find it nowhere.

She laid her gloved hand upon the trunk of a greenneedle tree and felt its sleeping life, and through it, the life of the whole forest: vine, bush, and grass, lichen and moss. The life of the world, which Mosirinde's Covenant protected. And beneath it, beyond it, the hot bright life of Janglanipaikharain, its power hers to draw upon.

Thurion said that all the Flower Forests were One in the Light, and so I might walk from Janglanipaikharain to Tildorangelor in a single step—if I were in Janglanipaikharain.

Well and good. But as much as she needed to go there, she needed to lead her army, her people, there even more. And so she wound Janglanipaikharain's Light about her hands as if it were skeins of silk, and cast her spell.

Find.

In her mind she held her image of Amrethion's study, the delicate desk of golden wood, the wall of windows. The great green sweep of valley from the window Lady Indinathiel had gazed out of. The star-bright perfection of the Unicorn she had once glimpsed.

Find!

The Light was her guardian, her lover, her companion, her tool. It was all of truth and reality she'd possessed since the spring of her twelfth year. Its wisdom had set her on this path, its strength had preserved her, its need drove her onward.

FIND!

Heartbeat upon heartbeat she drew in power and built the spell. It fluttered against her heart like a falcon on the glove, dreaming of prey. Suddenly, so swiftly she could not anticipate it and prepare herself, the power flew from her like the shaft from a forester's bow. In the sky above, she heard silver hooves ring against starlight. The Light roared through her, a depthless, sourceless torrent.

Until at last, its work accomplished, it struck, and held, and drew the last of the spell energy to it. Moonlight on snow became the ringing of bells, the tocsin of silver hooves, the wind that felled not trees, but empires. . . .

There were hands on her shoulders, shaking her to consciousness, raising her from her knees. The snow had melted around her; her boots and trousers were soaked through, her fingers numb within her gloves.

"Vielle! Tell me you live!" The most welcome, most unexpected voice roused her instantly from unconsciousness.

"Thurion!" she cried.

"Did you think you could set such a weaving and I would not hear?" Thurion asked. His smile barely disguised his worry.

She groaned as he raised her to her feet. "Am I a child, to have been so overset by a spell?" she grumbled. She began to shiver, and he laid one hand, palm flat, against her shoulder. She felt his Magery cascade over her, warming her and driving the wetness from her garments.

"What have you done?" he demanded.

"It seems you are always asking me that," she said with a shaky smile. She looked past his shoulder, toward her encampment. She had ordered them to strict discipline, for sound and light would carry across the bounds even if Magery did not. The Findspell she had cast had roused the Lightborn; she could see faint sparks of Silverlight moving about in the distance like the glowbeetles of summer. Soon enough they would find her missing.

"I have set a spell to show me where we now must go," she said, and Thurion's eyes widened with shock—and hope.

"You have found Amrethion's city," he said. "With this . . . it is as great as Tildorangelor herself."

"I hope it is not, for I mean to claim Tildorangelor for my own, and should the Alliance also be able to claim such power the battle will be dreadful indeed," she answered.

"And Amrethion's city. And the Unicorn Throne. You have found them all," Thurion answered as if he had not heard her.

"I have done as I must," she said. She pulled her cloak more tightly about her. "Now come—if the spell has called you, I know it has wakened all my folk."

Gunedwaen and Harwing Lightbrother found them before they had covered even a third of the distance back to the camp.

"It would indeed make good hearing to know for what cause you have stolen into the night to make yourself the target of any sword," Gunedwaen said with heavy irony. He swung down from his palfrey's back and gestured for her to mount.

"*Thurion?*" Harwing said in disbelief.

"I had thought to have quiet and shelter for the casting of my spell," Vieliessar said to Gunedwaen, "but if Thurion was roused by it—"

Only then did it occur to her to marvel at the power of the spell that had brought him here, for the power needed for Door increased with the distance traveled, and he could not have known to draw upon Janglanipaikharain's Light to open it. "Where were you when you came to me?" she asked suddenly, turning to Thurion.

"A guesthouse in Utheleres. I was in meditation, hoping to Farspeak you with the news. . . ."

"Iardalaith 'Spoke with one of our spies among the Alliance Lightborn," Harwing said. "They have heard nothing."

Vieliessar nodded. The boundary Wards had protected her from detection, as she had hoped. But the bond she shared with Thurion was deep and reinforced by their continual use of Farspeech. He had sensed her spell because he was trying to reach her.

They were safe.

"Then we still have the advantage, until they strike our path. Come, Gunedwaen. Ride behind me, and I shall speak to you of the weaving I have done this night."

⚍

Vieliessar gazed around at those whose lives stood like marking stones along the path she had taken to this moment and this place. She commanded a force as large as that of the Twelve; her Lightborn wore armor and fought on the battlefield; her commonfolk bore arms and fought beside *komen*. She had made herself the tool of Amrethion's

Prophecy because if she did not, the Darkness would come and destroy all she knew. And in becoming that tool, she had changed the world.

She did not know if that was better—or worse.

It was still candlemarks before dawn; she had gathered to her not the senior commanders of the High King's army, but those who had stood as friends and guides upon the long road Vieliessar Farcarinon had walked to get here.

Lord Thoromarth of Oronviel, whose faith and generosity humbled her when she thought of them. Thurion Lightbrother, who had broken with the custom of centuries to follow the dictates of his reason, not his heart. Aradreleg Lightsister, who walked a careful path between the old ways and the new. Rondithiel, her first and best teacher. Lord Gunedwaen, who had taught her the Code of Battle and followed her even when she shattered it. Rithdeliel Warlord, born to Caerthalien, who had broken his heart to give Serenthon victory, and who had risen from the embers of betrayal to do more than that for Serenthon's daughter.

Harwing. Iardalaith. Nadalforo. Changed by what she had done just as she had been changed by Amrethion's Prophecy.

Her vassals, all. Just as she was vassal to the land itself.

"I have this night discovered the path to our destination," she said.

"A destination is always a useful thing," Rithdeliel said calmly. "I hope there are stores of grain there. And wine."

"Of these matters I know not," Vieliessar said, "but I know our victory lies within Celephriandullias-Tildorangelor, and there I will lead us."

"Grand words fit for a wondertale," Thoromarth grumbled. "But say if you will, Vieliessar High King, where it is you would bid us have your army go?"

"South," Vieliessar answered. "South, and south again, until we reach the end of the world."

And its beginning.

Thurion's presence was a gift. The news he brought was fresh: Penen-jil and Enerchelimier had managed to reach Oblivion Gate in time to pass through to the Arzhana; Melchienchiel Penenjil had sent the Silver Swords on ahead, with Thurion to guide them. He had expected trouble in the Nantirworiel Pass, for if Methothiel Nantirworiel had not taken the field, he had certainly chosen his allegiance. But if Methothiel was for the Alliance, his meisne was not—since his father's time, Foxhaven Free Company had been sword and shield to Nantirworiel. Thurion did not know their fate, or Methothiel's. All he knew was that the pass had been clear of snow—and utterly deserted.

But welcome as Thurion's presence was, he remained only three days before bidding her farewell.

"I do not wish to be away from Master Kemmiaret overlong," he said. "And besides, I am needed to lead the Silver Swords to your side. Utheleres is as yet untroubled by battle, and we can find provision and shelter all the way to Lurathonion Flower Forest. Once we cross the southern border, I shall come to you again, to be certain we do not lose our way."

"For that I am grateful," Vieliessar said. "And for Penenjil's grace in making such a journey in winter."

"As to that, I think Penenjil has been privy to more of Celelioniel's learning than any of us know," Thurion answered. "I could wish . . . they knew the whole of it."

"I do not think even Amrethion Aradruiniel knew the whole," Vieliessar answered. "Go with the Light, my friend."

"And you, my king," Thurion answered gravely.

⚜

South and south again.

It was odd to look upon a place and have no name to call it by, for every stone and forest and meadow within the Fortunate Lands had a name. For a sennight her people made a game of it, vying with one another to coin the most outlandish and ornate name. *Enemy's Doom. Ice-*

trees Forest. Smoketree Reach. But at last they settled on a simple one: *Janubaghir. Southern forest.*

Celephriandullias-Tildorangelor was the first thing in Vieliessar's thoughts each dawn, the last thing she saw behind closed eyelids at night. It drew her like a needle to the lodestone, and her army followed where she led. As Snow Moon drew to a close, she and every Lightborn in her force felt the Alliance cross the Niothramangh bounds to follow them.

The Alliance Lightborn drew instantly upon the bounty of Janglanipaikharain and moved immediately to the attack—and Vieliessar's Lightborn to the defense—but whatever their calls upon its Light, that Light still seemed inexhaustible. All along the line of march, storms quarreled and fought through the sky as the Alliance sent storms to harry them and the Warhunt sent them away again. Limitless Light had the same effect as none: the two armies fled and followed and little else was changed.

As Cold Moon gave way to Ice Moon, Vieliessar's force reached the southern border of Janubaghir. The stars and the sun told them they were far to the south of lands any of them knew; Lord Gatriadde thought they might even be south of Mangiralas's southern border, and Mangiralas extended furthest into the south of any of the domains of the West. In the far distance, the Bazrahil Range was visible, and before it, a plain that stretched on as far as the eye could see.

Someone named the southern plain *Ifjalasairaet*—wind and dust.

The land was flat as a tabletop. The Alliance army was a bare fortnight behind them when they reached the southern plain, and Magery swirled about both armies, its tides thick enough to choke any who could perceive the Light. The war had become a war of Lightborn, as each side attempted to discover a way to use Janglanipaikharain's power to gain advantage over the other—and if they could not, to exhaust its Light so that this became a war of *komen* and destrier once more.

Never had anyone witnessed—or performed—such a profligacy of spellcraft. Vieliessar's army had come to Ifjalasairaet a thing of rags and patches, privation and rationing. Now each suit of armor, every pavilion and rope, had been Restored until it might have come that instant from the hands of the craftworkers. Every injury, no matter how slight, was made whole. Wells were sunk into the earth each time the army stopped, striking deep until they overflowed with cold pure water, enough for all who thirsted to drink their fill. Transmutation turned water to cider, to beer, to milk, to wine. Spells of multiplication, taught against days of dire famine, turned a handful of grain to a wagonload, an apple to an orchard, a scrap of dried beef to a succulent feast for thousands. Faded colors of surcoat and pavilion grew bright, destriers and their riders grew fat. The night watches blazed, not with Silverlight, but with honest warming flame against a plain turned lush and green out of season.

And here, at last, the plan Vieliessar had set in motion in Oronviel's Great Hall bore fruit. Her army was her future empire in miniature: Lightborn, Landbond, and Lord united as one in her name. It was an army of refugees, of renegades, runaways, outlaws, exiles, of all who had cast off the old ways to search for something . . . better. Of War Princes who yearned for peace. Of Lightborn who had embraced the field of battle.

In armies the size of the two which opposed each other here, even ten thousand Lightborn would not make much difference to the outcome of the battle yet to be fought.

But ten thousand Lightborn who were *free* . . .

The Alliance horded the Lightborn spellcraft among its lords, using their Magery to protect themselves from servants they had come to distrust. They expended Janglanipaikharain's power and their Lightborn's strength on attacks that experience had already shown them were futile. And day by day they closed the distance, as if the sight of Vieliessar's army goaded her enemy into doing the impossible.

And still Vieliessar led them south.

They were but a sennight behind her when Vieliessar's force at last reached a barrier it could not pass.

❄

She and a few others rode far ahead of the vanguard, across a plain whose spring-lush grass, withering in the cold, was already dusted with fresh snow. Her army stretched out behind her, mile upon mile, marching within a shimmering haze of Shield: all the folk of every domain she had claimed, whether by force of arms or peaceful surrender, all who had fled to her for sanctuary. She knew what she must find to save them, yet in the clear merciless light of day, Ifjalasairaet's Wall stretched unbroken as far as the eye could see. She reined Snapdragon to a halt and gazed at the cliff face in silence.

"Are you sure this is . . . ?" Iardalaith said beside her, his voice pitched for her alone.

"I am," she answered. "Amrethion's city lies beyond this cliff."

How will we reach it? She could hear Iardalaith's question as if he had spoken it aloud, but she had no answer for him. Her spell had found the city. She had never wondered if there were an entrance to it. *We can hold this ground until Janglanipaikharain is exhausted. Then we must fight. And starve. And die.*

The only road to victory lay through solid rock. An army that could not retreat was helpless.

She bit her lip until the blood flowed bright and bitter in her mouth. She wanted to weep as if she were still a child, to cry out at the unfairness of it. Amrethion had promised her that she was his true heir—she had seen him, walked the halls of his great palace in visions.

Celephriandullias-Tildorangelor—*White Jewel, Fire Forest . . . When shall I see you again?* Lady Indinathiel thought. *Our fellowship is broken, our ancient trust betrayed. All that is left to us is to keep faith. To destroy that which never should have been . . .*

Half in memory, half in dream, Vieliessar looked out across Ifjalasairaet. But it had not been Ifjalasairaet to Lady Indinathiel. It had been Ch'rahwyr-thrawnzah, Border of the World—and she had wept behind her battle mask when she rode out onto it leading her army, for

Kalalielahwyr, Heart of the World, was broken beyond mending, and she'd felt her *hradan* heavy upon her. . . .

Lady Indinathiel's memories were a hundred times a hundred centuries old, and somewhere in that vast gulf of time the pass had closed.

"There is a pass," Vieliessar said, her voice raw with cold and anger. "I shall find it. But for now, let us not make an encampment, but a fortress. Let the camp and the pasturage be set forth at the cliffs themselves—and let it be bounded with walls as high as those of a Great Keep."

Iardalaith gazed at her for a long moment in silence, then turned away to give orders. A few moments later, the signal horns began to call to one another along the line of march: *Halt. Make camp.*

She had led them for so long, both hands filled with miracles, that few in all her meisne doubted she would bring forth more.

"If this is where we are to die, it is as good a place as any other," Gunedwaen said. He had approached her alone, and in such silence that she had not heard him. "Yet if it is, I ask one last boon of you, High King of Jer-a-kalaliel."

She knew she should chide him for speaking of defeat so glibly, but she could not. He, alone of her nobles, had not used Janglanipaikharain's bounty to clothe himself in state. His rags were warm—but still rags. His mount, one of Thoromarth's cherry-black darlings, was muddy and ungroomed. *He masks his true self as a last weapon*, Vieliessar realized.

"Name it," she answered.

"Let Janglanipaikharain become an empty cistern before we fall. Let the army that vanquishes us starve and die beside us."

Why not? she thought. It seemed to her, in that unguarded moment, that her whole life had been nothing but an endless series of questions, each "why" leading her farther along the path that brought her here, to a cliff that held her victory in an immovable grasp. *It will not matter,* she told herself. *Should I fail here, Darkness will claim all, in the end.* For the first time, the thought did not kindle defiance in her heart. What was darkness, but the end of day?

I am weary, she realized in surprise.

"Let it be so," she said softly, bowing her head. "Now leave me, old friend. I wish to be alone."

⧽⧼

The Silver Swords of Penenjil arrived just as the gates were being raised.

Vieliessar stood at the far end of the encampment's main road. Her pavilion stood at one end of it and the entrance to the camp stood at the other. The North Road was the broadest way in any camp, for it was good fortune to give the Starry Hunt a fair path to enter by, just as Arilcarion had decreed. After so long spent overturning the wisdom of centuries, it gave her a tiny thrill of shame to heed it now. But soon it would no longer matter.

It was dusk; it had taken the Lightborn the whole of the day to surround the camp with a rampart of earth and turn that earth to seamless stone. Her craftsmen took care to leave an opening in the wall, which they framed in oak; then they sculpted mud and water into two great doors that the Lightborn turned into solid silver. Upon each panel stood a Unicorn rearing in defiance.

The gates glittered in the last rays of sun, bright panels of new-forged metal, taller than a tall tree. Their surfaces shimmered with Magery that lightened them so that the craftworkers could handle the huge panels as if they weighed no more than a painted screen. When they were sealed into place, she knew, the people would cheer, and then there would be a feast in the twilight, and through it all she would make a show of approval. As if the path to victory was a thing she held in her heart until the moment to unveil it arrived.

There were vast scorched circles on the plain beyond, where Thunderbolts had struck the ground and fire had smoldered for a time, and above them the sky boiled like a cooking pot. In the distance, the sight of it now blocked by the wall, the Alliance army marched toward them, its front rank verdant with Lightborn. The roiling mumble of power was so chaotic it masked the spell Thurion cast until the moment Door— profligate, wasteful, unheard-of to cast so far from a sheltering Flower Forest—opened.

The Silver Swords galloped from nothingness to Ifjalasairaet—a full grand-taille of *komen* and destriers plus one green-robed Lightborn. As Door opened, the power of the spell broke over the plain like a great wave, sweeping all others before it. For a moment the sky was clear, the glowing violet shield of protection vanished, and Vieliessar could feel the drain upon the great reservoir of Janglanipaikharain.

Not enough to empty it, not yet.

Craftworkers scattered as the great silver doors suddenly took on weight and fell with an impact that shook the ground. The Silver Swords galloped through the gap in the wall. Vieliessar snatched at the lines of power, feeling the weavings of others brush her own. Above her, the sky boiled to black again as the Alliance Lightborn recovered from their shock, but the light-nings they cast struck harmlessly against the Warhunt's Shield.

Komen and archers ran toward the North Road from everywhere in the encampment. The road was filled with destriers under saddle— dancing, rearing, ears laid back with terror.

"Where is the High King!" an unfamiliar voice shouted.

"Here!" Vieliessar cried. Thoromarth and Rithdeliel were running toward her, swords drawn. She stepped forward before they could reach her. "Here," she repeated. "I am here."

One of the *komen* urged his fretting mount forward. His surcoat was of grey silk, the emblem on its face a sword in bright silver. He bore not one sword, but two—one such a sword as any *komen* might wear, belted upon his hip, the other so long it must be sheathed against his back. He reached up with grey armored gauntlets to remove his helm. The face revealed was of an *alfaljodthi* much past his middle years: the hair in its elaborate knight's braid had already taken on the silvery sheen of age.

"The Silver Swords of Penenjil are here, High King," Master Kemmi-aret said. "As we swore to the last High King we would be."

As he spoke, Vieliessar felt the chains of prophecy coil around her more tightly than before.

⚜

I could see—feel—what you were doing," Thurion said.

"I suppose every Lightborn from Great Sea Ocean to the Grand Windsward could as well," she answered, and Thurion smiled.

She'd taken a precious moment before the evening banquet—more of a celebration now than before—to hear Thurion's report. Master Kemmiaret had been able to give her little more than an account of time and distance and weather: they had crossed the Nantirworiel Pass without challenge; the unrest across the Uradabhur had as yet touched Utheleres but lightly.

"If I hadn't already known about Janglanipaikharain, I would have been horrified," Thurion said with a smile. "Of course, there's hardly anyone who doesn't—the Alliance Lightborn Farspeak everywhere even if ours don't. And the drain on Janlanipaikharain was constant, if high. Then today . . . I thought the battle had begun. I had to bring the Silver Swords to you while I still could."

To come and die here with us, Vieliessar thought. But what other course did he have? He was Caerthalien-born. No House would give him sanctuary against Bolecthindial's wish. Nor would any of the Twelve trust a Lightborn who would betray his lord so blatantly.

For the first time in sennights, she thought of Hamphuliadiel and the Sanctuary of the Star. Did he still reign there as Prince of Nothing? Who would send Candidates to him in Flower Moon?

Would Flower Moon even come? If it did, would she be here to see it?

"I am glad you came," Vieliessar said. "I would have you beside me when I claim the victory."

⚜

The banquet was long over. Around her, the encampment dozed, behind walls that only needed a handful of sentries to defend them. In

Ice Moon the days were short and the nights long and cold. The solitude was strange and welcome.

Vieliessar, dark-cloaked, walked through the camp to the cliffside. Celephriandullias-Tildorangelor—the Ninth Shrine, the lost city of Amrethion Aradruiniel and Pelashia Celenthodiel—lay upon the far side of the cliff. She could feel it. And it might as well lie on the far shore of Graythunder Glairyrill, for the way to it was barred beyond opening. Transmutation could turn earth to water and wood to stone. It could fuse stone to stone and render the walls of a Great Keep unbreakable—but only when the object so bespelled had bounds. To set Transmutation upon Ifjalasairaet's Wall would be death to all the Lightborn who worked the spell—and if it had taken the power of thousands of Lightborn to forge the path through Janubaghir, how many more would it take to make a path through miles of rock? Even to try would bring death to Jangla-nipaikharain, death to all who worked the spell—and death to the whole of Vieliessar's army afterward, for without her Lightborn to Shield them, the Alliance Lightborn would be able to set Thunderbolt to destroy her encampment, Fear upon her army, and Shield to imprison tailles and grand-tailles of her warriors for Alliance *komen* to slay at their leisure.

She would find another way. She must. On unsteady legs she walked up to the smooth stone face and pressed her hand, palm-flat, against the stone.

Recognition.

As if a faithful hound had waited a lifetime to greet its master once more, Vieliessar felt the shock of force and fire—as if she had come home, as if she laid her hand upon the Tablet of Memory in her own castel and felt there the memories of the generations of her Line. It was soundless sound and lightless light, a great tolling peal of recognition, as if Light called to Light—but strange and ancient, no spell-weaving she knew. For a brief instant the stone seemed as clear as water. Within it she could see the bright silver lines of Magery. Layer upon layer of bespellings, coils and knots and labyrinthine twistings . . .

Her hand slipped from the stone as she sank to her knees, weak and groggy. Powder-fine snow covered her to her waist. The cold of it burned her bare hands.

"What are you— What did you— Are you— *Vielle!*"

Thurion hauled her to her feet. "What have you done—what did you do?" he babbled, and she could see shock and fear upon his face.

"I don't know!" she blurted.

Thurion stepped away from her to touch the stone. The cliff was as smooth and featureless as the wall of a Great Keep, as if it were no natural thing, but something crafted by Magery.

"What did you do?" he demanded again, as if she were some erring Postulant whose spell had gone terribly awry. Behind them, she could sense as much as see globes of Coldfire winking into life across the camp. She must have roused every single Lightborn in it. And probably in the enemy camp as well.

"The pass is here," she stammered. "It's here."

"What did you do?" Thurion repeated. "Vielle, what did you do?"

Beyond that, she could hear the words he did not say.

Vielle, what are you?

⟞⊨⟝

Hush, hush, let her tell it," Isilla Lightsister said. A dozen of the Warhunt had gathered at the Wall, all asking questions. Over Isilla's shoulder Vieliessar could see more hurrying through the camp to join them.

"Beyond this cliff lies Celephriandullias-Tildorangelor. And the Unicorn Throne. Take them—reach them—and we have won." She had answered the same questions a dozen times, but she could not answer the true one: how could she open the pass?

"With blood," Rondithiel Lightbrother said, as if she had spoken aloud. He had been studying the cliff face in silence for some time.

"Blood?" Thurion said, startled. "It is forbidden."

"Do you seek to lesson me in the keeping of Mosirinde's Covenant?"

Rondithiel asked mildly. "I should despair of you, young Thurion. What did Mosirinde say of blood?"

"That blood holds power, and to take power from the blood is to take life," Thurion said. "To gain power from death brings madness."

"This much is true," Rondithiel said. "And yet—"

"It doesn't matter," Vieliessar said quietly. She touched the wall again with her bare fingers, and felt the thrumming of response. Ten thousand years ago, some unknown spellbinder had set this spell here, awaiting her touch. But not Vieliessar Farcarinon's. The touch of the Child of the Prophecy. Amrethion's chosen heir.

When she'd begun her quest, she'd realized she swam amid tides of power linked to Prophecy—power that gained her belief when it should not have come, trust when she had done little to earn it, success beyond luck and skill. It had shaped her to its needs, moonturn upon moonturn. She had been more than mortal flesh. She had been a tool of ancient power, and that power compelled more than her. It had bent the folk of the Fortunate Lands to its need. Princes had set aside their power for her. Commonfolk had risked their lives.

But not for her. For the Prophecy whose instrument she was. And even as she accepted that, she had fought to remain Vieliessar. No longer. To be less than the Prophecy's instrument was to doom all who had placed their lives and their trust in her hands.

She took a deep breath, facing the cliff, and released every shield she had lived behind since long before the Light came to her. Wariness, mistrust, suspicion . . . she released them all into the winter wind. She let go of the masks she wore, concealing her true self from everyone. She unwove and abandoned the shields all Lightborn wrapped themselves in, guarding themselves from the touch of a mind, from an errant Foretelling, from the history borne within the shape and flesh of every thing, living or unliving. . . .

She was the ancient rock and the blood-soaked earth; the wind above, the unmediated hopes and fears of every living creature in her array, the hand that forged the steel, the beasts and trees slain to make saddle and cart and harness. Serenthon's heir, Nataranweiya's child, vanished in that moment, swept away before the need, the insistence, the demand . . .

The Prophecy.

It is so simple.

She did not know who thought the words, or who heard them, or who laughed in joy to see bright metal sparkle as a sword was drawn ringing from its sheath. She did not know who cried out, who grasped the blade with a naked hand, who thrust hand and blade and blood together against the raw unyielding rock.

And then she was herself again, Vieliessar, staring at the Unicorn Sword where it lay upon the grass, its hilt and pommel shattered, its un-housed blade blood-bright.

"*Run,*" Thurion said.

He grabbed Vieliessar's arm and yanked her away from the cliff face. Vieliessar stumbled, then ran with him. Around her she could see the other Lightborn running, shouting warnings to the camp beyond. The ground shook as if at the charge of ten thousand *komen,* a hundred thousand, of all the *komen* who had ever lived. The shaking became a rolling that made them trip and stagger as they ran; the ice beneath Vieliessar's feet cracked, shattered, sprayed up before her. As if a door had opened, she could feel the radiant upwelling of power. Not the familiar and finite power of Janglanipaikharain, but power a thousand times greater—fresh, untapped . . .

She felt the uprush of spellcraft—someone had managed to cast Shield—and stopped. She yanked her arm from Thurion's grasp and turned.

A shimmering wall of Shield stood between them and the cliff face. Mounded against it, halfway up its height, was a hill of sand-fine grey dust. The blood mark she had set upon the stone was gone. And where it had been . . .

Vieliessar ran back until the violet wall of Shield was a cool slickness beneath her hands. Unaccustomed tears prickled at her eyes, and despite everything, she wanted to laugh out loud.

They will all believe I planned this. . . .

Dargariel Dorankalaliel—the Fireheart Gate—was open for the first time since the Fall of Celephrandullias-Tildorangelor.

Its walls were even and straight, just as the cliff itself had been, but not smooth and unmarked. As far along the passage as she could see they were carved with the images of Unicorns, a herd of Unicorns all running toward the plain.

She fell to her knees, laughing in relief, in joy, in homecoming, knowing this was not the end of Amrethion's Prophecy but finally, at last, its beginning. The night was filled with shouting and the sounds of warhorns as her people armed and rallied against an unknown foe. She could hear hoofbeats as the first *komen* rode toward the cliff shouting questions, the babble of voices as the Lightborn answered. Silverlight flared, turning the face of the Shield-wall to a bright mirror, hiding what lay behind.

She got to her feet and turned to face the camp. *Komen* were riding toward her. Behind them, the camp itself was alive with light and movement.

"What have you done?" Thoromarth bellowed as he reached her, his voice a battlefield shout.

I have found the Unicorn Throne.

"I claim this place—it is mine—and yours. All of you—go through it—everyone—" Her tongue tripped and stuttered over a thousand commands. "Clear the rock—set my marker stones—!"

Pelashia's Children had come home at last.

⚜

A sennight ago, the victory song had been in every throat. The Alliance scouts had brought the same word for a fortnight: Vieliessar drove her army directly toward an unbroken cliff wall. She would be trapped against it, unable to retreat, and when they held her at bay, they would drain the Southern Flower Forest—it did not truly matter which army accomplished that—and then the Alliance would drive the rebel's army of losels and rabble down into dust.

Then, astonishingly, instead of preparing for battle, Vieliessar had set a wall twelve cubits high around the whole of her encampment—and to mock them, set such doors in its gate as might grace any High House Great Hall.

"Siege," Bolecthindial growled. "She can't be serious."

"You keep saying that," Runacarendalur said. His smile was bitter. "She has always done exactly what she says she will."

Bolecthindial gazed into the distance. Behind him, the Alliance camp spread over miles of this desolate plain. Shield shimmered above and around them, a constant unwelcome reminder that this was a war of Magery and not of honest skill. In the distance, the last light of day turned the silver gates of Vieliessar's encampment to fire and blood.

"Once the Light fails, we can starve them out," Bolecthindial said.

"If we have, oh . . . ten times their supplies," Runacarendalur answered lightly. "I trust our Lightborn are moved to prepare such bounty? Or does the War Council mean us to die here in the moment of our victory?"

"That is hardly your concern," Bolecthindial said repressively.

"No," Runacarendalur said quietly. "It won't be."

Bolecthindial regarded his son narrowly. Since the retreat from Jaeglenhend Keep, the Heir-Prince had been in a strange humor, by turns rebellious and reckless. *He sees the disaster this war has brought, and what it has cost us,* Bolecthindial thought grimly. Half a year ago the War Princes had made grand promises to one another—of setting aside old grievances, of unifying in the face of a grave threat, of increased wealth and dominion and security for them all. And at first it had seemed an easy thing, a possible thing, to strike down Serenthon's mad whelp and thus secure their safety and prosperity forever.

But disaster had followed disaster. In Jaeglenhend she gained victories where she should have suffered defeats. The Alliance might have turned back then, awaiting a more fortunate moment to smash Vieliessar's ambitions., but the secret the High Houses held silent in their throats was that Windsward Rebellion was too recent, too nearly successful, for them to permit Vieliessar even the illusion of victory.

And so the Alliance had followed Vieliessar beyond the edge of the world.

We were fools, Bolecthindial Caerthalien thought bleakly. *Better to have let her claim the Uradabhur, the Arzhana, the Grand Windsward. Such a "kingdom" would never endure. We could have crossed the Mystrals in spring, taken the Uradabhur back domain by domain, gaining wealth and provisions and sending a vast sea of commonfolk running to their "High King." If she rejected them, her claim of being their savior would vanish. If she claimed them, she would be forced to feed them in their thousands and ten thousands, and thus render herself vulnerable.*

The thoughts were bitter, for they were not his own words Bolecthindial called to mind, but his son's. His Runacarendalur, the flower of the Caerthalien Line—the glorious prince who could have made Caerthalien's long-held dream a reality and claimed the Unicorn Throne for himself. From the time Vieliessar had gained Oronviel, Runacarendalur had warned and pleaded and badgered him, until Bolecthindial had shut his councils from his ears and his son from his sight.

But he'd been right.

"We shall not gain the victory by gazing upon the foe," Bolecthindial said. "I shall take my leave. You are expected, of course, to dine with us."

"Of course," Runacarendalur said. But he did not look away from the distant walls.

⊰⊱

That night, the Alliance War Council debated long into the night. The strategy was clear: drain the Southern Flower Forest so it could not be used, then besiege Vieliessar and take her fortress by traditional means. In the end, the Alliance would triumph. The War Council had even agreed that they would question Vieliessar before executing her, to see if Celelioniel had told the truth about being able to interpret the prophecy contained within *The Song of Amrethion.* Once Vieliessar was dead and her Lightborn reclaimed or executed, the Twelve could set to work discovering the source of this "Darkness" and deciding—if it existed at all—how best to crush it.

Implementation of this simple plan, however, was a matter for endless debate. What spells should they order their Lightborn to cast to achieve this? What stockpiles should they conjure? How would their injured be tended, if only Lightless healing could be offered to them?

The War Pavilion was Shielded by the conjoined spells of a thousand Lightborn. No spell could be worked within it, no listener could eavesdrop upon it, no blade could pierce its fabric, no fire could burn it.

No sound could penetrate its walls.

But even its labyrinth of bespellings was not proof against the shaking of the earth that came in the darkest candlemark of night. Cups fell from tables. Tent pegs worked free of the earth, until the gold fabric hung limply from its wooden framework and the slender shafts creaked alarmingly. It took candlemarks to restore order in the camp, and it was not until dawn that they understood what had happened.

The distant cliff was no longer a seamless unblemished sweep of stone. There was a pass.

⊣⊢

For the next six days, as the army advanced, the Alliance Lightborn attacked the High King's keep. They scoured the ground with winds that ripped the grass from the soil and the soil from the stone beneath. They struck the cliff face with Thunderbolts until the vitrified stone glittered like ice. Waterspouts ripped from underground rivers spun across the gutted land, turning the churned earth to mud. Hyperborean winds turned mud to ice. Fire seared the very air, turning ice to steam, turning steam to blinding blizzards that left the walls of Vieliessar's fortress drifted high with snow.

The fortress itself was untouched, and on the evening of the sixth day, there was no more prairie to cross.

"This is madness!" Sedreret Aramenthiali said, when the War Council had gathered once more. "We have achieved nothing!"

"Oh, I hardly think it is nothing," Consort-Prince Irindandirion of Cirandeiron said, fanning himself languidly. "It is entertaining, after all."

"And useless!" Sedreret snapped. Bolecthindial found himself wishing for his old enemy's return. Manderechiel had been a bloody-minded brigand, but he'd never belabored the obvious.

Dead. Like Jaeglenhend, Mangiralas, Araphant, Ingelthendragir, and half the Houses of the Uradabhur.

"What do you suggest, Lord Sedreret?" Edheleorn Telthorelandor asked. "With a pass through the Southern Wall available to her, we must assume Vieliessar retreats through it. Once she has accomplished that, she has won. Or do you mean you will send Aramenthiali into such a killing box—in the event her walls fall?"

"I am saddened to hear such . . . *prudence* . . . from your lips, Lord Edelhorn," Dormorothon said, the twist of her lips indicating she meant another word entirely. "My son is correct: we have thrown the whole power of our Lightborn against her fortress and done nothing but make a waste of the land. And what shall we do tomorrow? We are within the shadow of her walls. Do we ask her politely to ride forth and give battle?"

"I'm surprised you dare rebuke us, Lightsister, when the failure is yours," Girelain Cirandeiron said silkily. "The walls were raised by Magery. The pass created by Magery. Yet your own spells have been . . . surprisingly ineffective."

"How dare you so insult my lady mother?" Sedreret demanded, rising to his feet. "I demand—"

"Aramenthiali *demands*?" Girelain asked in feigned disbelief, her lips curved in a chill smile. "I did not know you had such a sense of humor, Lord Sedreret."

Bolecthindial rose to his feet. Around him, conversation died.

"Call me," he said heavily, "when you have discovered something that will work."

He turned and strode from the tent.

—✦—

Runacarendalur was waiting for Bolecthindial when he reached his pavilion. He was sprawled in Bolecthindial's favorite chair, a cup of wine in his hand. He did not rise to his feet when his father entered.

"I am in no mood for your whining tonight," Bolecthindial snapped. No servant came forward to take his cloak. The servants had been running off or dying for moonturns now—to the point where the *komen* diced for pavilion servants instead of gold—and even Bolecthindial's household was a shadow of what it had been half a year before.

He dropped the garment on the floor and glared, but Runacarendalur did not move. If it were anyone else, Bolecthindial would have punished such insolence with his sword, but it seemed to him almost as if Runacarendalur had courted death for sennights. He would not oblige him.

"No?" Runacarendalur asked. "Then what of my counsel?"

"What counsel can you offer?"

"Better than your War Council," Runacarendalur said, and despite himself, Bolecthindial laughed sharply.

"I shall have you flogged."

"Do," Runacarendalur invited. "But Heal me afterward, for you will need me to lead your meisne into battle. She will fight—and soon."

"You're insane," Bolecthindial said. "Why should she fight when she has somewhere to run to?"

"Because she means to be High King," Runacarendalur said evenly.

Bolecthindial looked around. He frowned anew at the absence of servants, then walked to the sideboard and selected a cup and a bottle before settling into a chair. "That is hardly fresh news," he said as he filled his cup.

"Perhaps not," Runacarendalur said. "But it is information you have all chosen to disregard. She flees, you follow, nothing changes. She must offer battle and force your surrender. Until the Houses gathered here have pledged fealty to her, she has not won."

"So she will fight," Bolecthindial said in disbelief. "When?"

"As soon as she can," Runacarendalur said, as if it was obvious.

"She's done nothing but run since Jaeglenhend."

"And a costly flight—to us—that proved to be. It is not running, Father, when you are traveling to your chosen battlefield."

Bolecthindial regarded him measuringly. He had seen such despair before, but only in the face of a vanquished enemy. "Go to bed, my son," he said with surprising gentleness. "Tomorrow, we begin our siege."

He was wrong.

INVASION AND INFAMY

Mist rose over the surface of the blood in the obsidian bowl. With the Obsidian Mirror shattered beyond re-creation, Virulan had to find new ways of seeing beyond The World Without Sun. This one combined business and pleasure.

He gazed at the images of blood and slaughter forming within the mist and smiled, baring gleaming fangs. The Elflings were so proud of their armies, of the skill of their warriors. Virulan knew the truth. Skill was meaningless when confronted with power.

The dainty banquet of death was a pretty sight nonetheless.

"They are so confident," he murmured aloud. "Century upon century, they have bred like the vermin they are, refining their arts of war, believing themselves the greatest power in their world. They slaughter brother, sister, their own children. They make war upon those creatures whose lands they have claimed. And they look to a time when they will be victorious over all. But that time will never come."

And best of all, a faint echo of true Darkness had found a home within their hearts. He had watched, gleefully, as fear and ambition caused them to cast aside the rules of chivalry by which they had lived for so long, watched as expediency tempted them to commit greater and greater atrocities. Only the Elfling Mages had stood aside from that rush to infamy.

Until now.

Now, at last, one of the Elfling Mages had followed his brethren down their twisted path. Anger and cheated ambition had gnawed at his soul since childhood, and slowly—oh, so slowly—it had led him to . . . compromise. From the moment Virulan had found the Elfling, drawn by the sweet scent of moral rot, he had watched avidly as Ivrulion of Caer-thalien made bargain after bargain with himself.

At first, the Elfling Mage had acted to further the ambitions of his House, holding himself above the promises he had made to his teachers. He had done what he thought best, never realizing that from the moment he placed his will above that of his masters, all was lost.

Always, Ivrulion chose the logical, the expedient, the efficient over oaths and honor. Virulan was charmed. No Brightworlder could ever hope to equal the majesty of the least of the Endarkened. They were too cowardly, too weak. But the spark of Darkness Virulan saw in Ivrulion grew in unexpected ways. Sometimes the Elfling lied to himself about his motives. Sometimes he saw them clearly and rejected anything that might curb his desire.

Ambition was the link between the Endarkened and the Brightworlders, the one thing that could cause Virulan to name those evanescent bags of meat his distant kin. Ambition led them to war. Ambition led them to treachery. Ambition led them to betrayal.

Ambition led them into the Dark.

Virulan could not know where this would ultimately lead. He could know Ivrulion's intentions, it was true—they were so clear that only his blind, foolish, Brightworld kin could remain in ignorance—but he could not see What Would Be. Still, he could watch as, sennight by sennight and moonturn by moonturn, Ivrulion expanded the catalogue of things his ambition found acceptable.

He could watch as Ivrulion led his people to war.

It was delicately done, the work of a lifetime of idle remarks and casual observances. His colleagues and his masters drank his poison as if it were sweet milk, certain of his loyalty and his honor. Certain of the presence of all the things he had abandoned so long ago. Soon every death among the Hundred Houses could be laid at his doorstep.

Soon the end would come.

Soon it would be time for the Light to dim, and then gutter out entirely.

The images faded away.

Send me a sign, Elfling, Virulan breathed over the cooling blood. *Send me a sign that the day has come for the Endarkened to ride to war.*

To war, and to triumph.

CHAPTER SEVENTEEN

THE FALL OF
THE HUNDRED HOUSES

It is said the High King gained her throne through seven great battles:
Oronviel, Aralhathumindrion, Jaeglenhend, Niothramangh, Cirdeval,
the Barrens, and the Shieldwall Plain. Oronviel was a Challenge Circle,
Aralhathumindrion only a skirmish, and the Barrens was not a battle at
all. But Storysingers shape history as cabinetmakers shape wood, and it is
left for Loremasters to decide the truth.

—Thurion Lightbrother, *Vieliessar's Tale*

It was nearly dawn. The fortress the Warhunt's Magery had made
echoed with emptiness; its tents and pavilions, herds and flocks, wagons and all who would not take the field this day, were gone. The last
of the wagons labored through the pass; the sound of hooves on stone,
the creak and thump of wagons, was loud in the night silence.

For nearly a sennight, her folk had passed through Dargariel Dorankalaliel into the Vale of Celenthodiel. Reports had trickled back of a vast,
lush, deserted domain ringed by mountains, of a deserted Great Keep
atop a spire of rock, of Flower Forests too vast to map.

Vieliessar had not yet seen it. It would be hers—if she could win the
day.

She had thought that claiming the Unicorn Throne would be enough
to gain her the victory, and it would—but only if she could show her enemies what she held. The pass stretched for miles. The Alliance would
not follow her through it—Arilcarion taught that such a tactic was sui-
cide, and the Alliance Warlords would heed that ancient counsel.

And so she'd planned this battle, the words Princess Mieuroth of

Gerchiliael had spoken moonturns ago echoing through her mind: *My lords, we are not alone in this! There are many who would choose to join your cause—but how can it be, when each knows any they abandon will be cruelly punished?*

Today those lords and those princes would have their chance. All they need do was throw down their swords and ride to her lines. Let enough of the Alliance army pledge to her, and the victory was hers.

The only way to get them to do that was to offer her enemy a show of battle.

Her commanders had tried to argue her out of taking the field in her own person, but she'd never considered agreeing. Perhaps there was wisdom in their words, but how could she ask her foot knights to stand against charging destriers, ask the Lightborn to believe she would never lead them to flout Mosirinde's wisdom, if she did not trust in being Child of the Prophecy as her armor and shield?

She'd never had any other choice. She had never forgotten her vigil in the Shrine of the Star

"You have come to end Us . . . for you are Farcarinon. Death in life. Life in death. You will be known when We are forgotten " The Starry Huntsman had spoken, and within that vision had come another: a cold and darkling plain, a balefire burning star-pale with magic, a creature neither *alfaljodthi* nor Beastling standing tall and proud beside a *komen* in whose veins her own blood coursed. *"The Land calls you. The People call you. I call you.* He Who Is *would return to the world, and so we summon you."*

"And will you spill your own blood to save the land?"

I will. The question had not been asked of her, but every day she had answered it. *I will. I will.*

"I will," she whispered aloud.

"I still think you're an idiot," Thoromarth said quietly. "My liege."

"Think what you like; it's too late to change my mind," she said. "Are you ready?" she called.

"We are, my lord," Iardalaith answered.

"Then let us begin."

There was a flare of brightness as the Warhunt cast Shield just within the fortress walls. The walls ran for a league in each direction. Twelve cubits high, three cubits thick.

The Warhunt turned them to water.

The spell that had made them was powerful. The one to unmake them was more powerful still. It seemed to Vieliessar that she could hear Janglanipaikharain cry out in protest, and she knew the Flower Forest did not have much more to give. For an instant, the dark stone stood solid. Then suddenly it was clear, a crystalline battlement glittering in the light of Shield.

Then it fell, water crashing and spreading across the gutted frozen surface of Ifjalasairaet, a great wave that rolled outward toward the enemy. It spread and slowed, until the whole expanse between Vieliessar's army and the Alliance camp sparkled like a vast mirror.

"Drop the Shield," she said, more calmly than she felt. "Sound the call to battle."

⚔

Caerthalien held the enemy center. Both Rithdeliel and Gunedwaen thought a few of the War Princes would ride with their meisnes today, but not the Houses of the Old Alliance. So it was Prince Runacarendalur of Caerthalien who sat beneath Caerthalien's war banner. Irony indeed if hers was the sword that killed him. Perhaps the power of Amrethion's Prophecy would save her life when he fell.

The enemy line was twice the length of her own. The Alliance meant its *komen* to sweep around her, encircling her force and driving her *tuathal* and *deosil* wings over her archers and infantry. Her strategy required them to do the opposite—she needed to trap the whole of the Alliance force within her own, pulling them away from their reserve units. That was one reason among many she'd chosen to give up the momentary advantage of meeting them in the charge.

She took a deep breath as the signal to attack was sounded. Vieliessar felt the maddening itch of Light wash over her skin as the enemy Light-born fought to strike at them and the Warhunt opposed them. It was as much a test of strength as anything else, for Janglanipaikharain was still a reservoir of Light, not Sealed to either side, and so superiority in the duel of Lightborn would come from tactics, not raw power. *No commander can ride two horses at once,* Rithdeliel had told her over and over when he moved from training her as a knight to training her as a general of armies to come. She banished the Lightborn from her mind. She must trust Iardalaith to do all she would do herself—and more.

The enemy moved forward at a walk for a few moments, opening out the lines of close-packed destriers. Then a second signal came; the enemy moved to the trot, and the ground began to shake with the hammer of steel-shod hooves. She counted heartbeats as the first ranks moved to the gallop, pulling those behind with them as fluidly as if they were pearls on the same strand.

Now that the Alliance *komen* were committed Vieliessar's pikes and archers began to walk forward as unhesitatingly as if they did not walk into Death's embrace. The archers began loosing arrows as soon as the enemy was in range, and horses and riders began to fall. The enemy line shifted, folded, re-formed into column. Then the flying column of Alliance *komen* struck her pikes. A full third of her infantry went down under the force of the impact.

She hated the thought of riding over her own wounded. She had no choice. She flourished her sword and urged Snapdragon forward. On her *tuathal* hand, Rithdeliel's force spurred their mounts forward, the wolf-howl of Farcarinon bursting from every throat. The wild ululation made her hackles rise and she found herself echoing a war cry that had not been heard since the day Serenthon Farcarinon fell in battle.

Battle was joined.

Her sword seemed weightless in her hands. She feinted at a neck then struck at a shoulder.

"To make armor flexible, it must also be weak. Here are the places to strike an armored knight."

The breastplate could not be easily pierced. Backplates were lighter and covered only the upper back, for the Code of Battle forbade an attack from behind. Belly was protected by thin bands of metal. The underside of the upper arm was protected only by chain. The inner elbow was un-armored. The arm from elbow to wrist was shielded by a light vambrace, the hand and fingers by a studded leather glove.

The destriers rarely wore armor.

An Aramenthiali warhorse reared to attack. Her sword bit deep into its throat. As it fell, its rider's head went back. She struck at the exposed jaw. Blood gushed. Snapdragon spun away.

She shifted her weight in the saddle without thought—heel here, knee there, sit back, sit forward—and Snapdragon turned and whirled and lunged in a deadly dance, striking what she could not reach, adding his force to her blows, shielding her from danger.

"Your destrier is your most important weapon on the field. Learn what he can teach you, and teach him well."

Caerthalien gold-and-green, Aramenthiali blue-and-gold, mixed with green-and-silver as the enemy column plunged deep into her line. Now the archers would retreat. Now the waiting wings would ride to flank. The events of the first moments of battle—what should be, for she could not see what was—ticked through her mind like the drops of water that had measured out her days in the Sanctuary of the Star. An enemy struck at her arm; she dropped her shoulder and the blade rang off her gorget and bounced away.

Turn and strike. Strike and live.

She had not ridden to battle with a standard-bearer beside her, but her green helm was banded in moonsilver, a coronet of Vilya blossoms inlaid into the lacquer. Symbol of rule, dominion, kingship. It drew the enemy to her as if she had bespelled them.

Nadalforo forced her mount forward on Vieliessar's *tuathal* side, caught a descending blow on her bracer, then struck across her saddle in a spearing motion. Her blade slid between the plates of belly armor, thrusting the knight from his saddle. Her mount lunged forward. Vieliessar spurred Snapdragon through the sudden opening.

She had never seen, never fought, a battle as Arilcarion would have them fought—a thing of lines of retreat, negotiated abeyances, battlefields with unassailable bounds and safe places to rest an exhausted mount or change to a fresh one. The summer wars of the Hundred Houses were hedged about by a thousand rules. This was no summer war. It was a battle fought without quarter, without surrender. Any warrior who rode alone from the press of battle was hunted and slain like a deer in the spring.

The sun climbed higher in the sky. The field shifted as the ground became clogged with dead. Tailles and grand-tailles fought free of the carnage only to regroup and attack again. The screams of the wounded and dying blended with the hammering of sword on sword, sword on armor, the blurt of warhorns relaying unheeded signals, the skirl of signal whistles, a hundred shouted battle cries. Her body ached with the battering of sound, her flesh was numb beneath the shocks of a thousand blows. There were no landmarks here except for the cliff, and she could not raise her eyes from the battle to see if it was behind her, before her, to her left or right. There was only the enemy, and surcoats ripped away or stained with blood. She fought toward each half-glimpsed battle standard.

"*To slay a battle captain is to slay twelve* komen; *a taille looks to its captain for direction.*"

She did not see Caerthalien's banners.

Her sword arm ached. Snapdragon's neck was covered with foam. Riderless destriers plunged wildly through the melee seeking escape, or stood over their fallen riders until they too were slain. The moments of the battle unfolded in a thousand disjointed images. Here a warrior dragging an enemy from his destrier's back and throwing himself into the vacant saddle as his own dying mount went to its knees. There—impossibly—one of her infantry still fighting, covered in blood, a blacksmith's sledge in each hand. A Lightborn on a palfrey, armored only with a violet shimmer of Shield, her hands filled with hunting spears. A *komen* fighting afoot, standing in a ring of dead.

The air sizzled and crackled with Magery. She saw a string of sunbright flashes and knew someone had Called Thunderbolt. She didn't know which side or where it struck. Her mouth tasted of blood and metal. Her throat ached with thirst. The Alliance Lightborn lashed the frozen, hoof-churned, bloodstained plain with flame, raised winds to send grassfires toward her forces, called down the lightning. The War-hunt turned the wind, wrestled each Thunderbolt away from its intended target, summoned brief sharp blizzards to quench the fires. And with every spell cast and diverted Janglanipaikharain was drained further.

Through it all, *komen* fought *komen* with steel and steel-shod destrier. Grimly. Desperately. Soon they fought as often to capture a riderless destrier, for a moment in which they could stop to snatch precious mouthfuls of ice or clean snow for themselves and their animals, as for a victory. There were no charges of line against line any longer: Alliance *komen* and High King's *komen* moved at a slow walk to take a new position, counting as precious the time it took for their opponent to gather their force and move to engage. They had been fighting since daybreak without rest, without water, and it was near to midday. The fighting had become a thing of slow and measured re-formations and brief vicious clashes.

Then the Alliance called for an abeyance.

Vieliessar heard the call in disbelief, but quickly passed the signal to honor it. It would give her force the chance to regroup and perhaps to retrieve some of her wounded. She still had most of a grand-taille with her, slowly forming up in a classic square. Barely a bowshot's-length away, a group of the enemy were—equally slowly—retreating to their own lines. Across the field, she could see the Alliance War Princes watching. They'd begun the day with a mounted escort. The *komen* remained, but they'd given up their destriers to those on the field.

"I thought you'd like to know we're winning."

Gunedwaen rode up to her. One of his pauldrons had been sheared away; he'd lost his helmet and replaced it with a sellsword's cervelière. He handed her a waterskin and she gulped its contents eagerly.

"Winning?" she asked, her voice a rusty croak. "What news?"

"The messengers say Celenthodiel is orderly. Your archers guard its entrance. Lord Annobeunna has placed arming pages along the length of the pass to assist the wounded who reach it. And the others."

The tone of his words made her glance toward him. "Others?" she asked sharply.

"You said their *komen* would surrender if we helped them do so. You're right. They are."

"You can't know that," she said. She meant it for a question, but she was too tired. The words came out sounding like an accusation.

But Gunedwaen smiled. "I can. When I see a dozen swords lying on the ground with no bodies near them, I know it's because their owners threw them down to surrender."

You cannot imagine they follow the Code of Battle upon this battle field! she thought indignantly.

Gunedwaen pointed and Vieliessar turned to look. Riding in the direction of the pass were eighteen knights. They were fresh and unfazed, their warhorses and their armor pristine and unsullied, and all wore blue and gold surcoats blazoned with the black horse of Aramenthiali. One even carried a standard with the Aramenthiali bannerette upon it and some personal pennion below.

Her *komen* should have turned to engage, but they didn't. The Aramenthiali *komen* moved past them, behind them, toward Dargariel Dorankalaliel.

Their hands were empty.

And yet they do, she thought in disbelief. *They disarm themselves upon a field where both armies fight without quarter, trusting in my honor. The honor of the High King.*

"We're going to win," she said.

"If we don't all die first," Gunedwaen said cheerfully.

⋇

They'd all known this battle would be a costly one, for Vieliessar Far-carinon could bring to this honorless field of slaughter an array nearly equal to their own by forcing the *komen* of the High Houses to face criminals, mercenaries, Landbonds. She had already shattered Mo-sirinde's Covenant and brought the Lightborn into battle. She'd rejected Arilcarion's wisdom to fight without decency and without honor, forcing them to do the same. Bolecthindial watched the battle begin, saw the flower of Caerthalien—yes, and Aramenthiali as well—destroyed by Vieliessar's archers and pike-wielders. But then he had seen *komen* clash with *komen* as was right and good, offering up their lives to the Lord of the Night Wind, He Who held the destiny of all the Hundred Houses in His hands, He Who gave the gift of eternity to those who died in His service. Bolecthindial had believed in victory then.

He believed until he saw *komen* wearing the colors of Teramarise, Vondaimieriel, Rolumienion, Jovadigalas—of every House of the West—throw down their swords and ride to join the enemy.

We should never have attacked simply because she offered battle. We ought to have known better. Should and would and ought—did not Lord Toncienor, Swordmaster to my mother, tell me "should" and "would" and "ought" were three great armies who always fought on the enemy side?

It had taken him most of the morning to get the rest of the War Princes to agree to call for abeyance. That Vieliessar had chosen to honor it did not make Bolecthindial feel any better.

⋇

"It is rather difficult to fight a battle if your army has deserted," Edhe-leorn Telthorelandor drawled.

Fewer than half the War Princes of the Alliance array were gathered in the golden Council tent. Those who had ridden out this morning might now lie dead or wounded, their Houses in disarray, their Lines shattered. A disturbing number of others had simply refused to come.

Sedreret snarled at Telthorelandor's choice of words. "My *komen* do not desert! The witchborn sow has bespelled them!"

Edheleorn raised an eyebrow at that, for all knew that Ladyholder-Abeyant Dormorothon was Lightborn, and waved the protest away with a languid hand. "It does not matter what words you use. The truth remains: they do not fight for us."

"This is unacceptable!" Ferorthaniel Sarmiorion roared. "I name them traitors and cowards! Are you all so spineless and weak that no *komen* will follow you?"

"Fine words from Sarmiorion indeed! Where is the largesse your vassal domains should have bestowed upon us?" Sedreret Aramenthiali said. "Is Sarmiorion so spineless and weak that her vassals will not obey her?"

Ferorthaniel howled with outrage and sprang to his feet. Dormorothon rose fluidly from her seat beside her son, standing straight-backed and furious.

"This does not solve our problem," Edheleorn said. His voice was quiet, but it stopped the War Princes more effectively than if he had deafened them with a shout.

"Perhaps—in your vast wisdom—you will now counsel us on how to keep our meisnes in the field?" Bolecthindial said heavily. It was only by the grace of Aradhwain and Manafaeren that Runacarendalur's name was not numbered among the catalogue of the missing and the dead. He had stormed from the field at the head of a ragged handful of *komen*, too furious at the abeyance to even acknowledge Bolecthindial's presence as he rode past him.

"Perhaps we should not," Edheleorn answered.

"I offer Telthorelandor my condolences on his sudden impairment," Girelrian Cirandeiron said. "It must be dreadful to face a life of darkness after being renowned so long for your clear sight—or am I mistaken? Perhaps you actually are aware of the pass through the cliff after all?"

"You cannot insult me, Girelrian," Edheleorn said. "One can only be insulted by one's equals. Abandon your foolishness and state your point."

"It should be obvious even to you, dear Edheleorn. Farcarinon retreats through the pass her Lightborn have made. Already her supply train has preceded her, for it is nowhere to be seen. Let this day come to an inconclusive close, let her follow her army, and how many of our people will join them?"

"If they try—and we stop them—we diminish our army by our own actions. If we fight on with those of true and proven loyalty, we shall have no choice but to do battle by sending our army into Lord Vieliessar's pass." Edheleorn spread his hands wide. "We might as well cut their throats ourselves."

⁂

The blade trembled in the air. Mage-forged and spellbound, sharp as winter's first frost, it had been his father's first gift to him. His hands shook. Every muscle strained.

He could not force it against his throat.

With a cry of despair, Runacarendalur dropped the weapon to the carpet and flung himself into a chair. The pavilion was empty. There was no one here to bring him a cup of hot wine, help him off with his filthy and blood-clotted armor, or draw a bath.

Our arming pages and squires joined us on the field. If our servants have not fled outright, they hide, awaiting the outcome of the day.

And all he could see when he closed his eyes was a moonsilver crown of Vilya against a green helm. "*Beloved*," Runacarendalur snarled in rage.

"Do you say so, dear brother? Rejoice. You may join her at last."

Ivrulion shimmered into existence, a thin cloak of grey fabric pooling at his feet. Its surface shifted as if it were made of smoke, and Ivrulion's hands vanished into its folds.

"Monster!" Runacarendalur screamed. He flung himself at his brother's throat, only to crash to the carpet, trembling, as every muscle betrayed him.

"Such drama," Ivrulion said coolly. "When I am here to grant you what every noble scion of the Hundred Houses should value more than life. Victory."

"It isn't me you want to be talking to, then," Runacarendalur growled through gritted teeth.

"No," Ivrulion agreed. "But I think you should be present, all the same."

What treachery is this?" Mindingener Jovadigalas demanded as Ivrulion and Runacarendalur entered the Council tent. The guards who should have stopped them stood frozen. Bespelled. "Do you seek to set yourself above us all, Bolecthindial?"

"My father is as witlessly conventional as the rest of you," Ivrulion said, sounding bored. "He would never presume to set himself above you without first placing a sword at your throats. No. I have come to see whether you wish to win—or to become Farcarinon's lapdogs."

"To win, of course," Sedreret Aramenthiali said. He strove for a patronizing tone and failed. "I wonder why you did not come forward earlier, if you hold the secret of victory."

"Because he—" Runacarendalur struggled to speak the truth— Vieliessar, the Bonding, Ivrulion's betrayal—and found himself forced once more to silence.

"Because my aid comes at a price," Ivrulion said, ignoring him. "You would not have been willing to pay it while you could see any other path to victory."

"If you have come to mock this council, remember you have sworn your fealty oath to me," Bolecthindial said. The half-threat was a thing of reflex; if Runacarendalur was Bolecthindial's son in thought and action, Ivrulion was Glorthiachiel's. Glorthiachiel had always thought about what might be before facing what was; her clever mind had brought Bolecthindial and Caerthalien many victories, but she had also guarded against dangers that had never come to be.

"I did so swear," Ivrulion agreed smoothly. "Now you must choose: hold me to those oaths and covenants—or claim the victory." He smiled coldly. "You cannot force me to give you what you seek."

"Oh, stop your posturing, Lightbrother," Girelrian Cirandeiron said crushingly. "Tell us your plan and name your price. We shall enjoy the joke, I promise you. Then you may leave, and we shall return to matters no mere Lightborn can comprehend."

"How is it that you have held my father's respect these many years?" Ivrulion asked, as if he truly wanted to know. "Lord Bolecthindial is not known for idiocy."

"I thank you for that, Ivrulion," Bolecthindial said, speaking before Lord Girelrian could respond. "Speak. If you can give us the victory, you will not find me ungenerous."

Ivrulion met Bolecthindial's gaze for just a moment, and Bolecthindial felt a pang of unease. Ivrulion's eyes were cold, and it had been many years since Bolecthindial had seen such hatred displayed so openly. "I will give you the victory, and you will make me your heir. I will be War Prince of Caerthalien upon your death. My children will become my heirs in turn. Ronadaniel will become Heir-Princess Ronadaniel. Huthiel will become Prince Huthiel."

"Ridiculous—and impossible!" Chardararg Lalmilgethior said.

"And what of Prince Runacarendalur?" Runacarendalur said savagely, for these were words he could speak.

"Prince Runacarendalur will not survive the day." To hear the words said so openly, so coldly, was enough to silence even the War Council. "My request is neither ridiculous nor impossible—if you all agree to it," Ivrulion added. "If I fight on the field, why should I be barred from rule? Either way, my lords, choose. I cannot give you victory if you have already lost."

"No," Bolecthindial said flatly. "You dare speak of mur—"

"And Aramenthiali says yes," Sedreret replied. "Must we vote upon this as if we are commoners?"

"I do not *vote*," Lord Edheleorn said crushingly. "But before I agree to set Prince Runacarendalur aside—he yet lives, my dear Ivrulion—and accept a Lightborn as Caerthalien's future War Prince, I wish to know how you mean to accomplish what all our meisnes together have not."

"And I do not!" Bolecthindial roared, overturning his chair as he rounded on Ivrulion. "Shall I listen to you plot the death of my heir and say nothing? I—"

"I plot nothing," Ivrulion said. "I speak only truth. Prince Runacarendalur will not survive this day. Nor will his death come at my hand."

⌗

This was his intent all along. From the moment Ivrulion had compelled him to break into the War Council, Runacarendalur had felt nothing but horror. Ivrulion had planned this from the moment he had learned of the Soulbond. He'd seen a chance to gain Caerthalien for himself—not as Ternas of Celebros had done, through regency, but as War Prince in fact.

No matter the cost.

Bolecthindial turned to him, silently demanding answers. And all Runacarendalur could do was cover his face with his hand and turn away.

"Meet my price, and I shall give you an army that will not desert and will not retreat, Lord Edheleorn," Ivrulion said calmly. "It will slay Vieliessar Farcarinon and every soul who has sworn fealty to her. You will have the victory. And undoubtedly you will hope for Lord Bolecthindial to enjoy many long and happy years."

"How do we know you will not take this army and make yourself High King?" Lord Sedreret demanded.

"It is your army, my lords, not mine. I do not want the High Kingship. All I want is my birthright. Caerthalien."

Suddenly, sharp in Runacarendalur's memory, was a Midwinter Feast he had never seen, but of which he had been told many times. Ivrulion had stood, had spoken the words that had led them to this day.

"Test me, Astorion," Ivrulion had said, laughing. "I leaped the fire this springtide—you must Call the Light in me as well!"

Would any of the rest have happened—Nataranweiya's marriage, Serenthon's plan, Farcarinon's erasure, Vieliessar and her tangled path to rule—if Ivrulion had never gone to the Sanctuary of the Star?

"It does not matter, Father," Runacarendalur said softly, putting a hand on his father's arm. "Come. I must prepare to ride out once more."

"You have no need to flee, Caerthalien," Lord Girelrian said. "I believe we are all agreed. Prince Ivrulion will be acknowledged by all of us as Heir-Prince—if he gives us the victory."

With such a majority, the rest of the War Princes would have no choice but to agree as well.

Even Caerthalien.

"Then swear it, and I shall begin," Ivrulion said.

Bolecthindial turned away in silence and walked from the tent, Runacarendalur beside him.

⁂

He paid little attention to Runacarendalur as he walked toward the Caerthalien precinct. No War Prince could ever love the rivals who might at any moment destroy lands, family, children—every hostage to the future Time had scattered in their paths like poisoned sweets. But Bolecthindial Caerthalien had long ago learned that hate was a toy for children. The War Princes were beyond both love and hate . . . at least the ones who survived.

Twice in a lifetime is twice too many to look upon my fellow princes and call them "ally." Of all my peers and rivals, the one I came close to calling "friend" was Serenthon Farcarinon, and yet I betrayed him without a thought. I lost no sleep over it.

But even as he'd marshaled their allies to betray Serenthon, Bolecthindial had never hated him as in the last several moonturns he had come to loathe his fellow War Princes. And now they had forced upon him the ultimate insult. *But there is time yet to set that right. Let Ivrulion gloat over Caerthalien while he may. If only one of my sons is to survive this day, it will not be him.*

Bolecthindial had been fond of all his children. Vieliessar had taken most of them. He would trade the life of one of the survivors for the life of the other—for Caerthalien.

It had all—always—been for Caerthalien.

As they reached the door of the pavilion, Bolecthindial heard the horns echoing through the camp, signaling the end of the abeyance. He turned to Runacarendalur.

"There is one last duty I must ask of you, as liege if not as father."

"Father, do not think—I swear to you, what he has done does not—"

"Nor will it," Bolecthindial said. "And so I charge you—survive this day. Do not rashly seek your death. What is made can be unmade. You will know that when you are War Prince."

For a moment it seemed Runacarendalur would refuse him. Then he grasped Bolecthindial's gloved and jeweled hand in his bloody gauntlets, and raised it to his lips.

"I swear to you, there is no other prince among the Hundred Houses I would ever have followed as gladly as I have always followed you, Father," he said.

⚒

Their breath smoked on the chill air as they walked out onto the deserted battlefield. The air swirled with power, low and hot and forbidden, for it was the power spilled forth by the dead along with their blood. To Lightborn senses, it hung over the battlefield like a dark fog. The Sanctuary taught Mosirinde's Covenant even before it taught Magery: *do this, do not do that.* Years ago, Ivrulion had realized those proscriptions were the marker stones leading to power unfettered by the shackles of convention, power undreamed-of.

"I do not understand what we're doing, Father," Huthiel said.

"We are gaining victory for Caerthalien and the Twelve," Ivrulion answered.

"If I am to help Caerthalien to victory I must do it by the sword, and yet you refused to let me fight today—it was humiliating to see my *komen* led out onto the field by Uncle Rune!" Huthiel protested. "They must all think me a coward."

"Soon they will not," Ivrulion said, stopping. "If you had been a prince, as you were meant to be, you would have learned that it is the duty of the elder to sacrifice themselves so that the younger may flourish and rule, for only in that way can the House itself flourish and command."

"I was raised among princes," Huthiel said stiffly. "But—"

"Know that you are truly a prince of Caerthalien, Huthiel," Ivrulion said. He drew his son close and kissed him upon the forehead. "Now I will teach you there are more paths to victory than can be gained by the sword."

He stepped away from Huthiel and closed his eyes. The blood-drenched earth had frozen; it was black and glittering, like dark glass. He raised his arms, feeling a thrill bordering on ecstasy as he swept up that forbidden power and began to shape it.

Rise.

Janglanipaikharain had been drained of nearly all it could safely give. Now Ivrulion took the rest. Hundreds of miles to the west, the ever-living trees became a ghost forest. Fruit and flower and leaf, dead and withered, fell from lifeless branches, moss and vine turned brown and crisped away into dust. The soil in which Janglanipaikharain had once bloomed and flourished became lifeless sand.

Rise!

The power swept across the battlefield, shaped by Ivrulion's will and resonating to his desire. All around him, lifeless flesh stirred to answer the call.

RISE!

For a moment the bespelling trembled on the knife edge of failure. Then Ivrulion turned swiftly and drew the knife he'd held concealed in his hand swiftly across Huthiel's—*Prince* Huthiel's—throat. Huthiel's body fell to the ground. Wisps of steam rose from the fresh-spilled blood. The dead face still wore an expression of surprise.

Let this sacrifice seal the spell.

The power of Huthiel's death coursed through Ivrulion's veins like fire and wine, the gateway to power even he had only dimly imagined. Now he could feel the living heartbeat of the world—and with all his mind and will, Ivrulion plunged the dagger of his spell into it. Life and death were one. Ivrulion threw back his head and howled his triumph.

I name this place Ishtilaikh! *Ruin!*

Then the power crested like a great wave and rolled back toward him, feeding on death as it came. Ivrulion screamed as he saw the danger, but it was too late. Power filled him, transformed him, enflamed him with a ravenous hunger that must be fed on death—a hunger that could never be satisfied, never be slaked. The ice beneath his feet became fog. The grass became dust. The soil became lifeless sand. Ivrulion was no longer *alfaljodthi*, Trueborn, Pelashia's Child. He was Darkness. He was Hunger. He was Death.

And the dead answered his call. Huthiel stirred, rose, then staggered across the battlefield to where a sword lay abandoned and clutched its hilt in still-cooling fingers. Destriers lunged to their feet, dragged themselves inexorably from pitfalls. For mile upon mile across the sprawling battlefield, dead flesh, blank-eyed and shambling, rose and began to move southward toward the pass, driven and animated by the will of that which had once been Ivrulion of Caerthalien.

⊰◲⊱

The Alliance warhorns sounded, signaling the end of the abeyance. Vieliessar felt a pang of relief. By now the Alliance must have realized that its *komen* were deserting. That was why they'd called for the abeyance; many of those who would have ridden to her under cover of battle would not do so openly. She had been afraid the War Princes would refuse to continue to fight.

Silver Hooves grant I may demand their surrender when night falls!

She could not say whether she hoped for or dreaded the possibility that Runacarendalur might be among those to concede. If he lived . . .

Fool! Even if you gain the victory, you can never acknowledge he is your destined Bondmate! He is Caerthalien, greatest of the Hundred Houses—all would see your words of peace and justice to be a sham if you did!

"My lord! Do you see—" Rithdeliel began.

Vieliessar never heard the end of Rithdeliel Warlord's question, for suddenly a wave of foulness poured through her Shields as if they didn't exist. She dropped her sword and clawed at her armor as bile rose in her throat. Each breath she drew seared throat and lungs. She felt her flesh rot and liquefy. Her ears were filled with gibbering, with the chittering laughter of things that could not exist.

This is not real! This is not real!

Her Shields had saved her life a thousand times in the Sanctuary of the Star. They could not protect her now. She clawed at her helm, trying to shut out the terrible unreal sounds. Shouts of alarm, screams of terror, were transformed into prophecies of destruction, abomination, *loss.*

If I could open my eyes—oh Blessed Pelashia, let me open my eyes! she cried silently. But the darkness invaded her with every breath she took. With all the strength she possessed, Vieliessar tried to claw her way free—back to light, to life, to sanity.

And failed.

❦

W hat's he doing?" Sedreret Aramenthiali demanded. His voice was a conspiratorial whisper despite the fact that Ivrulion and Huthiel were much too distant to hear him.

"A Great Spell," Ladyholder-Abeyant Dormorothon said. Her tone, arch and patronizing, managed to imply that Ivrulion had consulted her for advice and now acted at her direction.

The War Princes were gathered near the place they had stood all day to watch the course of the battle. It had fallen by lot to Bolecthindial to give the signal for the charge—a twisted acknowledgment of their bargain—but when he had seen Ivrulion on the field, he hesitated. *I am tired. I think too much,* Bolecthindial told himself. He wanted to be home, on his own lands, dealing with matters he understood.

The wind began to rise. In the distance, Bolecthindial saw Huthiel fall to his knees. He turned to give an order—Caerthalien to the field, to strike Ivrulion down—when Dormorothon screamed and flung herself from the padded bench where she'd been sitting.

Sedreret was shouting, demanding Healers and servants to attend his mother. Bolecthindial ignored him, his attention fixed on Ivrulion. The army was disordered, confused, its elements jostling one another as this meisne sought to move forward, that to stand.

And on the battlefield, there was movement where there had been stillness.

"Oh, that fool," Edheleorn Cirandeiron said in a flat stunned voice.

It is you who are the fools, Bolecthindial thought numbly. *You did not ask Ivrulion how this miraculous victory he promised was to be achieved.*

"*Mazhnune,*" Consort-Prince Irindandirion said, sounding awed and delighted. "He has raised up an army of *mazhnune* to fight for us."

All across the field, dead things staggered to their feet. Bolecthindial saw Vieliessar's army dissolve into chaos as every animal in it fought to escape. "Sound the retreat," Bolecthindial said.

His knight-herald shook out the pennion banner and raised the warhorn. But before he could signal, Irindandirion snatched the warhorn from his hands and put it to his own lips.

Charge. Charge at the ravaal.

Before the notes had died, the first ranks spurred their destriers forward. The terrified, overexcited animals went from trot, to gallop, to ravaal in heartbeats, pulling the rest of the army after them. As they neared Ivrulion, the destriers began to veer sharply to avoid him, moving directly into the riders beside them. Horses and riders fell in a widening wave. Ivrulion stood transfixed, arms spread wide, in the center of a churning column of dust.

The sky above him was turning black.

Bolecthindial spurred his mount forward. If it had been his Kerothay,

Bolecthindial could have ridden him into the Star-Forge itself, but Kero-thay was dead. This mare shied violently before he had closed half the distance to Ivrulion, and Bolecthindial had to fight her to a stand before he could dismount. When he released the reins, she bolted. Bolecthin-dial drew his sword.

One moment he was running forward, his sword raised. The next, the hilt was forge-hot in his hands and every piece of metal he wore was a live coal burning through leather and cloth and skin. He roared with pain as he fell to hands and knees.

He sucked air and coughed, gagging on the dust. *The grass is gone,* he thought in vague surprise. All that remained was a pale, soft dust, so fine-grained it was slick as oil. He coughed again and blood spattered the backs of his gauntlets. He would not admit fear, but the sight of his own blood galvanized him, and he clawed his way to his feet. He took a step, slipping and staggering as if buffeted by stormwinds. Pain made him gasp and shudder and fall again. Ivrulion seemed farther away than be-fore. The rings on Bolecthindial's fingers had charred through the gloves beneath them, the jeweled clip in his hair had burned through it.

I cannot die before I make right what all of us set wrong out of fear and greed and ambition, Bolecthindial thought vaguely. Those were the tools all of them had used against others all their lives. Double-edged tools, like the swords they gave their sons and daughters while they were still children, before sending them off to war. *We should not be surprised our children become sharpened blades as well. . . .*

Blisters welled up on his skin, and broke, and bled. He gasped for air, but there was nothing but soft dust, stifling him, strangling him. He made one last attempt to get to his feet. But what rose and walked long moments later was no longer Bolecthindial Caerthalien.

⊰⊱

"Fall back!" Rithdeliel shouted, hoping he could be heard. Horses screamed as they were pulled down by *mazhnune* wearing *komen* plate or sellsword chain or the leather of infantry. Strike off head or limbs, and what remained kept fighting. Worst were the *mazhnune* destriers, who trailed their spilled guts across the ice or galloped with broken necks flopping limply. The living destriers feared them more than they feared the *mazhnune alfaljodthi.*

The first ranks of the *komen* were fighting on foot now—even if there had been enough horses, they were impossible to control close to the *mazhnune.* When the *mazhnune* began attacking, they'd scavenged whatever infantry weapons they could find to arm themselves—you couldn't kill something that was already dead, but at least you could hold it in place while your comrades chopped it into enough pieces that it stopped moving. The Lightborn were the easiest, for they'd worn little or no armor. The horses and dogs were hardest—the dogs were small and fast, and while the horses could be stopped by striking off their legs, it was nearly impossible to do that without suffering losses. *We can't afford losses,* Rithdeliel thought bleakly. *Every living thing that dies on Ifjala-sairaet rises again as an enemy.*

The *komen* knelt, one knee raised, each holding a pike or a spear. They might have been waiting to receive the charge of a maddened boar, a bear, a stag—winter was a time for hunting, just as summer was a time for war. Or had been. The seasons had all run together. It was winter, and they stood on a battlefield . . . being hunted. Rithdeliel watched bleakly as the lines of defenders shattered instead of retreating. Only about a third of them were retreating to regroup. The rest had become monsters.

"Rithdeliel! Hurry!" Gatriadde shouted, staggering as he ran past him. Rithdeliel turned and followed. Gatriadde had anchored the *tuathal* center of the outer defense. He couldn't remember now who'd been on the *deosil* edge. Thoromarth? Atholfol? It didn't matter. Whoever had been there had let some *thing* approach too closely, thinking it was still alive.

Thinking it was some comrade.

He reached the next line of defenders. On the battlefield things burned, adding smoke to the dust that filled the air. Desperate for light, the *komen* had set fire to everything that would burn. The burning wreckage gave barely enough light to show the *mazhnune* walking slowly and with terrible patience toward the defenders. Perhaps it was a mercy that it was too dark to let Rithdeliel easily distinguish the surcoats they wore. Soon enough the deathless enemy would reach their lines, and they would fight, and lose, and retreat again. They were dying by fingerswidths. Half the Alliance was fighting at their side now, and half the High King's army had become *mazhnune*.

The sounds of battle were strangely distorted, for only the living cried out. Somewhere in the darkness Rithdeliel could hear the high frantic yelping of a terrified dog; he felt shame at wanting it to go on suffering so the *mazhnune* would not gain another warrior.

Somewhere behind him, Rithdeliel heard *komen* shouting wildly. For a panicked moment he thought the *mazhnune* had broken through. Then he heard hoofbeats and saw a destrier charge across the battlefield at the gallop. Another of the defenders, heart and spirit broken, had been driven mad by the bright torches of the Alliance encampment. The sight of it mocked the defenders with the promise of warmth and light and safety: the *mazhnune* were not attacking them. *Yet,* Rithdeliel thought grimly, but for once thoughts of vengeance did not comfort him.

The deserter managed to force his mount through the first line of *mazhnune* before it threw him. He got to his feet and ran on toward the travesty of sanctuary. Rithdeliel had seen what came next too many times tonight; he pulled his gaze away from the running figure. The horse was galloping wildly around the battlefield, seeking escape but shying away from the clusters of *mazhnune*. Eventually it would exhaust itself or fall into one of the traps and break a leg, but in the end, the outcome would be the same. Nothing left Ifjalasairaet alive.

The lone *komen* was pulled down and the screaming began. For an instant, Rithdeliel permitted himself to close his eyes. Every bone and muscle ached. He had no idea how long he'd been fighting.

War was like *xaique*: a master player chose the desired outcome before the game began. On this *xaique* board there were no good choices left. Vieliessar could seal herself, the commons, and a few thousand of the *komen* into the Vale of Celenthodiel and lose her bid for the Unicorn Throne. She could stand and fight—and die.

There was no third choice. They'd tried over and over to kill Ivrulion. Spells didn't touch him and no warriors could get close. Rithdeliel had even called up one of the rangers to try the forester's bow: Terandamil Master Ranger himself had come. Three tailles of dismounted knights had accompanied Terandamil to keep him alive until he was within range of his target.

Terandamil had loosed a dozen arrows. All had been whipped away by the wind. Terandamil and all but six of the *komen* who had stood with him were now *mazhnune*, and Rithdeliel knew it was useless to keep trying. Every failure armed the enemy further.

In the last moments before the new assault, Rithdeliel walked up and down the line, offering quiet words of encouragement and issuing final orders. He made it to the far end of the line without seeing Thoromarth, but Thoromarth might have taken an element of the line and moved forward. When the *mazhnune* concentrated on the center, the flanks did all they could to regain ground; when the flanks were attacked, the center moved up. They fought endlessly over the same few yards of ground, but the alternative was to lose.

The *mazhnune* were close enough now that faces, surcoats, and armor could be identified. There were groans and muffled curses all along the line as warriors recognized their dead comrades among the ranks of the enemy. Rithdeliel recognized more than one of the attackers, but his rage and despair were too deep for speech.

Thoromarth of Oronviel advanced toward Rithdeliel's position. He wore no helm. The broken shaft of a spear protruded from between the bands of his faulds. The hilt of a dagger glinted in his eye socket.

Rithdeliel tightened his grip on his swordhilt and prepared to fight on.

Vieliessar did not know how long it was before the world righted it-self again. She forced herself to open her eyes. Better to know the worst at once. She was almost surprised she could see.

"Praise Sword and Star—I thought we had lost you," Aradreleg said in a shaken voice.

"Not yet." Vieliessar blinked at the fabric blocking her sight of the sky. An unfamiliar pavilion. "Where . . . ?" she croaked. Her tongue felt thick and her mouth tasted foul.

"We did not wish to place you in one of the Healing Tents, lest the people worry. This tent is mine."

"I am in Celephrandullias-Tildorangelor," Vieliessar said, and Aradreleg nodded.

"I had been seeing to the wounded who came through the pass, making a tally of the Alliance *komen* who surrendered, so we might know if any were of sufficient rank that they must swear to you. Then the sky . . ." Aradreleg swallowed hard. "The sky went black. A candlemark later, Lord Rithdeliel brought you. He said to keep you here, then went back to the fighting."

"Rithdeliel must ever believe himself to be my nurse," Vieliessar said dryly. "Where is my armor?" she asked, for she had been uncased as she lay insensible.

"I—Lord Rithdeliel said . . ." Aradreleg said desperately. Her thoughts swirled, making them difficult to read.

"Send someone for it. And I will need a destrier," Vieliessar said. "And find someone who can tell me what's going on out there."

It was Atholfol of Ivrithir who came, with Dinias Lightbrother beside him. Dinias was hollow-eyed and pale, so weak Atholfol gave him support as he walked, though Atholfol was missing his sword arm from the elbow downward.

"Sit quietly, my lord," Atholfol said as he entered. "For the news is bad and you must hear all of it." He gestured with the bandaged stump. "I am grateful to see you alive, my lord. They say I can be made whole again, but that I will sleep for a sennight afterward. I say this is no time for sleeping." Aradreleg's tent was but a single chamber. Atholfol lowered Dinias to the chamber's only stool and passed Vieliessar a flask. The tea it held was cold and sour, but no chilled cider had ever tasted so sweet.

"I will show myself once I have heard your report," she said. "Then I must return to the fight."

"You must not," Dinias blurted out. "And I don't think you can. None of us can—Lightborn, I mean. Those of us who were on the field . . ."

"Screamed as if poisoned," Atholfol said, "and fell insensible to the ground when they stopped. I had just put Dinias over my destrier's saddle when I took this hurt. And yet I account myself fortunate."

Vieliessar waited in silence, for Atholfol's telling of his tale would shape his thoughts to make them more easily read. When he had finished, she regretted her Gift of True Speech, for it had showed her more than he wished her to know. Two candlemarks ago Atholfol had been on the field, watching the Alliance array gather as the abeyance ended. Dinias had ridden to his side with fresh orders, for much of the Warhunt was acting as messengers. Atholfol's meisne was ordered up the field to support Thoromarth's force. He had given the order for them to regroup and form column when he saw two men—one of them Lightborn—walk out from the Alliance lines.

"I did not mark them, beyond calling them fools, for any cloudwit could see the Alliance was preparing to take the field. Then the bane-storm came, turning day to night, and Dinias fell. I think many—all the Lightborn—were struck down in that moment. I rode to him and slung him over Penstan's saddle . . ."

And one of the dead lying nearby rose to its feet to strike at him.

"The horses went mad," Atholfol said grimly. "Dead were rising up everywhere. I grabbed Penstan's stirrup. He dragged me from the field. I ordered retreat. I do not know if anyone heard me."

"I came to myself in the pass," Dinias said, taking up the telling of what had happened. "I stopped Lord Atholfol's bleeding. Dargariel Dorankalaliel was filled with retreating *komen*. We had no choice but to go all the way to Celenthodiel. After the first wave, they started bringing in the Warhunt. Those they could reach. Everyone wasn't affected equally. It seemed like the stronger you were in the mind magics, the worse it was. But I went back as soon as I could." He shuddered, and swallowed hard. "My Keystone Gift is Transmutation. Some Lightborn talk to horses. I talk to rocks. Even so . . . it was bad. One step past the border stones and you feel *that* all over again. No one's made it even ten paces past the border stones before being overcome. I tried. Isilla too. I can't even sense Janglanipaikharain anymore. Tildorangelor is still safe— for now," he said, wiping his eyes dry with his fingers. "We are help-less."

"*Mazhnune*," Vieliessar said. The misplaced dead. It was something from a nursery tale: Heir-Princess Berendriel of House Notariel fell in battle, and when the Starry Hunt came for her, she refused to go with them. And so Berendriel of Notariel became *mazhnune*, unable to live again or to truly die.

"A counterspell—there must be something—" Vieliessar said.

"It doesn't matter what we try—Dispell, Rot, Storm, Thunderbolt, Overshadowing, Fire—nothing happens. They walk through Shield as if it is not there. Whatever the spell is that has raised the *mazhnune*, it devours all magic. Isilla said we were only feeding it on Tildorangelor's power. . . ."

And without Magery to stop them, only her army lay between the *mazhnune* and the pass. If they broke through that cordon, they would carry the spell of their raising with them, and so destroy the protection of the boundary stones. They would consume Tildorangelor as they'd devoured Janglanipaikharain.

"How far can you retreat from the entrance to the pass?" Vieliessar asked.

"We have not yet had time to map the vale," Aradreleg said. "Many miles."

"That much is good," Vieliessar said. She forced herself to stand, to walk to the door of the tent. The sky above was dark, black clouds glowing green with sullen flares of lightning.

"Bring my armor," she said. "And a horse."

The destrier they brought for her was a stallion whose coat was the pale silver of a swordblade. The ostler who brought him said his name was Winter. She swung herself into his saddle and looked around.

Her people had set up the encampment about a mile from the entrance to the pass. A cloud of Silverlight hung over it, bringing its tents and people into sharp focus. The once open space at the mouth of the pass was clogged with *komen* and destriers—even at this distance, she could see that most of them wore the livery of Alliance Houses.

"Dinias, seek your bed; you have done well this night. Lord Atholfol, if you are the most senior of my commanders, I must ask more service of you this night. Aradreleg, find me those whom I may use to carry messages through the camp."

She set Winter off at a slow walk, wondering if she presided over her own defeat or if victory was still possible. From the moment she'd realized what path was laid out for her by *The Song of Amrethion*, she'd told herself this war was the only way, even while she'd wondered if there was another. Each death suffered in her name made her more determined to avert the next: having begun by believing the war yet to come must be fought by all the Hundred Houses together, she'd still desperately yearned to fight as a lone champion so no others must die. It was a deadly flaw in a General of Armies, a worse one in a High King. If she did not apportion both responsibility and danger to all her subjects, she would leave them unable to act save at her order. Helpless.

And so, even though every fiber of her being urged her to spur him through the pass, to take the field, she knew she must show her people she yet lived. They gathered around her, making Winter fret and sidle, reaching out to touch her, to reassure themselves.

"Vielle!" Thurion pushed through the mob of people. "You live!"

"As do you," she said on a wave of relief. "Walk with me."

With Thurion at her stirrup, it seemed the people did not press as close. She ordered the flocks and herds moved south, away from the encampment, the palfreys and destriers unsaddled and turned loose, the mounts of the enemy *komen* who had given their parole unsaddled and freed as well. The baggage train she had sent through the pass this morning—still intact—would go south until a messenger reached it to tell it to halt.

None of those she asked after—Gunedwaen, Thoromarth, Rithdeliel— could be found. Save for Atholfol, her War Princes were all on the field— or dead. The encampment was a scattered thing of households and families with no clear master. In desperation, she placed Lord Atholfol in charge of it, and gave him orders to move everything he safely could southward, away from the entrance to the pass.

"And you, my lord? Where will you be?" Atholfol asked.

"Where I must be," Vieliessar said.

She turned Winter's head toward Dargariel Dorankalaliel. It was empty now; she did not know whether that was a good sign, or bad.

Thurion caught up with her soon after she had entered it, seated on some destrier he had snatched from its master. They rode in silence. There was nothing to say.

She did not summon Silverlight to guide her through the darkness, for it would mark the entrance for the enemy. Silversight showed her the carven walls as sharp as if by day. But beyond the entrance of the Dargariel Dorankalaliel, everything on the plain was darkness and shadows. She could see her army forming a barrier between the entrance to the pass and what lay beyond it. Those she could see were only the last line of defense; from the sounds, the fighting in the front ranks was heavy.

Vieliessar dismounted, walked forward until she stood just inside the boundary stones. The field was dark, lit only by the eldritch glow of the clouds and the flare of lightning. The clouds above shone with the black-green of a long-dead corpse. They swirled around a disk of unclouded sky, and within it the stars burned blood-red. Jagged violet lightning sketched across the clouds and swirled around the window to the stars. Lightning struck the ground all around the figure who stood in the center of a circle of lifeless dust that swirled as the clouds above swirled, a desert that grew larger with every moment, and though the wind raged across the plain, it did not touch him.

"How in the name of Sword and Star did we come to this day?" she said softly.

"There stands Ivrulion of Caerthalien," Thurion said, pointing toward the distant column of dust and lightnings. "Ask him."

Vieliessar drew a shaky breath. She'd feared the Light, hated the Light, and loved the Light, but no matter how she had changed, the Light had been as constant as sunlight and stars. Thurion had once called it the heartbeat of the world, and told her sensing the Light was like hearing the heartbeat of a loved one. She'd accepted his words, but she only understood Thurion's truth in the moment it became a lie.

This is how it all began, Vieliessar thought, dazed. *Mosirinde's Covenant teaches that blood magic leads to madness and destruction. Celelioniel wanted to know how Mosirinde knew—and unriddled* The Song of Amrethion *instead. I am the Child of the Prophecy, and because of that we are all gathered on this battlefield to reap the terrible harvest of forbidden magic.*

Thurion laughed shakily. "And so we end as we began, on a battlefield from which spellcraft is barred."

"This is not the end, my friend," she said. *I swear to you it is not.* "What I began, I shall end." She swung down from Winter's saddle, tossing his rein to Thurion.

"I beg you, do not go," he said. "The spell still runs."

Vieliessar nodded curtly. "I could ask no one to face such foulness again," she said. "Do not reproach yourself for not doing a thing no one could do."

But I must try.

⚜

He saw her fall.

It did not matter that it was dark, that the air was fouled with smoke and fog, that her surcoat was in rags and her armor besmirched with mud and blood. He would have known her anywhere.

His lord. His liege. His life.

She had lifted him out of disgrace and exile with a tale he did not credit for a cause he did not believe in. But she was Farcarinon, and Gunedwaen Swordmaster would have followed her to the Vale of Celenthodiel if she had asked.

He barked out a shout of hoarse laughter. She had asked. And now they would all die here, her cause unwon.

No.

I failed the father. I shall not fail the daughter.

He handed his mare's reins to the *komen* beside him and swung down from the saddle. He flicked his cervelière from his head, dropped swords and daggers, stripped his armor from his body. "Tell Harwing he is my heir," he said, and began to walk across the broken ground.

All his life he'd known the Green Robes spoke of their Magery as Light, but this light was not the cool radiance of the moon. It the unforgiving blaze of sun, of fire.

He passed the place where Vieliessar lay, still fighting to rise, to go on. He thought he heard her cry out at the sight of him, but he did not stop. To stop would only be to draw attention to her; her safety lay in misdirection, and misdirection was a Swordmaster's greatest skill. He raised his hand to close it about the amulet at his throat. A silver nail within a drop of amber, Mage-crafted, bespelled. Harwing had given it to him, last night as they lay together. *For luck,* he said. *For protection.* He had not asked then what spells it held, and now it was too late.

He would not see Harwing again.

One step, then another. And another. Forward. His heart thundered in his chest as if it were a war drum. Each beat was a stabbing agony behind his eyes. Gunedwaen felt a rush of wetness upon his face as blood burst from his nostrils, rilling steadily over his face with every painful heartbeat.

Only a little farther.

Let the *mazhnune* give their attention to the army instead of a lone man afoot and moving slowly. Let none of the new-risen dead stand between him and his goal. He'd thought for some time it was possible to move across the field unopposed. All it required was skill and nerve.

He had both. He had thought them lost, once. She had restored him. He had pledged himself her sworn vassal.

All he had was hers.

Every step was agony. His vision fogged, his chest burned as if he starved for air. The pain was the pain of beating, freezing, burning. Blood-tinged tears burst from his eyes. There was a brief, lancing agony as his eardrums burst and blood trickled down his neck.

Pain was an old friend. Year by year, Caerthalien had taught him its true meaning. Hunger and cold and the lonely anguish of survival. The pain of maimed limbs that could do nothing. Death was a small thing, for he only went to keep an appointment far too long delayed. Dust filled his eyes, his nose, his mouth, blinding and fine. He staggered against the storm, forcing his eyes to slits.

Not far now.

He could smell burning, as some forgotten bit of metal heated forge hot, but where it burned him, he did not know, for his whole body thrilled with agony. His mouth filled with the metal taste of blood. His progress slowed to a spasming shamble, as if his body had become a *mazhnune*'s dead flesh. He raised clawed and shaking hands to wipe his eyes, to see what lay ahead.

From the center of a widening circle of desolation, Ivrulion gazed upon him with eyes that were black and sightless with blood. His mouth drooled dark ichor in the green-violet light, blood gushed from his nose, dripped from his ears, sketched dark tear-tracks over his face. The wind whipped the blood away; where it struck Gunedwaen, it smoked and burned. Gunedwaen staggered into the whirlwind across scorched and smoking dust. His body shook and trembled, each beat of his heart so violent his chest felt bruised from within. What was this pain in comparison to all he had suffered through the years until Serenthon's daughter recalled him to life?

It does not matter if *I die. It matters* where *I die.*

Not far now.

He could no longer see. Over the howling of the maelstrom he heard the wild silver bells of the Hunt riding across the sky.

I come, Huntsman. I come.

A body beneath his hands. A throat. The touch of Ivrulion's flesh seared his skin as if he grasped forge-hot iron, but he did not feel the fire. He was far away, on a battlefield in autumn, where Farcarinon's silver wolves howled against the sky.

Then there was nothingness.

⊰⊱

There was a bright flash, as if a kindled pyre suddenly fed upon oil. There was a great trembling as all the *mazhnune* fell in the same moment, and suddenly, across the whole expanse of Ifjalasairaet, there was utter silence and stillness. For a heartbeat there was darkness, but as Rithdeliel gazed toward the sky, the clouds began to scud away.

The spell was broken.

With a weary exhalation, he leaned on his swordhilt. Only the silhouettes of horses and riders standing motionless upon the plain let Rithdeliel know he was not the last living thing in all the land. He did not know how long he stood watching the sky above lighten into blue before he heard the first warhorn sound. It was no call he knew, merely a single note, sustained for as long as the knight-herald had breath. But its meaning was plain.

We live.

⊰⊱

He passed the War Princes as they rode toward whatever remained of Vieliessar Farcarinon's army. They paid no attention to him; he was just another filthy, exhausted warrior making his way to camp. They rode without armor or escort, and Runacarendalur knew then that Vieliessar had won. The War Princes were riding to surrender. He did not see his father among them. Perhaps he was dead. Perhaps they'd slain him when they saw what Ivrulion had done.

He should ride after them—ask—claim Caerthalien if Bolecthindial was dead. But what then? He could not bear the thought of kneeling to Vieliessar and offering her Caerthalien's fealty, and his.

He could not bear the thought of taking her as his Bondmate.

The encampment seemed utterly deserted, the sight of his own pavilion like something out of another lifetime. Slowly and stiffly he slipped from Bentrain's back; the destrier stood wearily, head hanging. He looped the animal's reins over the saddle and patted him on the shoulder. "Go find someone to take care of you," he said. "You deserve it."

As if he understood, Bentrain sighed gustily and began walking slowly toward the horselines. Runacarendalur entered his pavilion. It was deserted, but there was food and drink laid out on the table, and a bowl of washing water stood beside Runacarendalur's favorite chair. He wondered who had left it for him.

He poured a tankard full of weak beer and drained it twice before he began the long work of removing his armor. It was sheer bliss to unlace his akton and peel it away from his bruised and sweat-fouled skin. He sopped one of the cloths waiting neatly folded beside the washing bowl, and scrubbed himself as clean as he could.

I am Prince Runacarendalur of Caerthalien, he told himself. *Caerthalien, greatest of the High Houses.*

He shook his head. No longer. There were no more High Houses. Vieliessar had won. And whether she had summoned her victory by fair means or foul, he knew he could not stay to see it. With dragging steps he walked through the curtain into his sleeping chamber. Boots, trousers, tunic, the heavy stormcloak he hadn't worn on the field. It took him a long and aching while to fumble his way into his clothes. He left the tray of his jewels untouched.

When he walked back into the outer chamber, Helecanth was waiting for him. She'd removed her helmet; her face was bruised from the blows she'd taken in battle.

"My lord," she said.

Runacarendalur laughed jaggedly. "Did you not know? We have a High King now, and she means us to be done with lords and vassals."

"You will always be my true lord, Runacarendalur Caerthalien," Helecanth answered.

Even though he'd half suspected it, to hear himself named War Prince of Caerthalien was like a blow to his chest. He shook his head mutely, reaching for his sword. It lay propped against the chair where he'd left it.

Helecanth stepped forward quickly to pick it up, then stepped forward to arm him. He stopped her for just long enough to slip the ornamental buckle with Caerthalien's device from the baldric, then stood quietly as she buckled it into place.

"Where do we ride, my lord?" she asked when she was done.

"No." His tongue and his mind were thick with exhaustion; he struggled to make himself clear. "I go into outlawry. I will not kneel to a High King."

"Then Caerthalien fights beside you," Helecanth said steadily.

"Do you think I mean to take my House into useless rebellion?" Runacarendalur said. "I go because the High King is my destined Bondmate—"

His words stumbled to a stop as he heard what he'd said. *Ivrulion is dead. The* geasa *he set upon me is broken.* Once he'd yearned for this moment, for his freedom. Now it seemed a distant and trivial thing.

"She is my Bondmate," he repeated. "But I reject her, and I reject her kingship. All I ask is that I may never hear the name of Vieliessar High King again." He closed his eyes in weariness. "Stay, Helecanth. They will need you."

"As you have ordered it, I will obey," Helecanth said. "But you will need a good horse. Come."

Numbly Runacarendalur followed as she led him from his pavilion. The weight of the sword upon his hip was the only familiar thing. Helecanth led him to the tiny paddock in the middle of the Caerthalien precinct where horses were held saddled and ready for Caerthalien's great nobles. Helecanth's Rochonan was there, muddy, blood-spattered, and weary—and beside her waited another mare. A pale grey palfrey, fresh and alert. Her saddle leather and her bridle were both deep green, the saddle stamped in gold with the three stars of Caerthalien. *I suppose my brother won't need her now.*

"Thank you," Runacarendalur said. "You have been a good— You have been a good friend to me, Helecanth."

"It has been a privilege to serve you, my lord," Helecanth answered gravely.

Runacarendalur walked over to the mare. She nuzzled at his chest, obviously hoping for treats. He stroked her nose in mute apology, and with a grunt of effort, thrust his foot into her waiting stirrup and swung into the saddle. *She was Ivrulion's, and I do not even remember her name. . . .*

"Fare you well, Lady Helecanth," he said.

"Sword and Star defend you, Lord Runacarendalur," Helecanth answered. She nodded once—as if some question had at last been answered—and turned and walked away.

Nielriel. That is her name. Nielriel.

Runacarendalur pulled the hood of his cloak up to cover as much of his face as he could, and turned Nielriel's head westward. In the distance lay the forest the army had crossed to reach the place of its destruction—trackless, unmapped. It would conceal him. Where he went then, he did not care. There was nothing left for him in the Fortunate Lands, but the forest would be a good place to hide.